The Red Garnet Sky
Hannibal Barca of Carthage

The Red Garnet Sky

Hannibal Barca of Carthage

A Historical Novel

Gordon Zima

SUNSTONE
PRESS

SANTA FE

Sunstone books may be purchased for educational, business, or sales promotional use.
For information please write: Special Markets Department, Sunstone Press,
P.O. Box 2321, Santa Fe, New Mexico 87504-2321.
Cover artwork by Paula Zima
Book design › Vicki Ahl
Body typeface › ITC Benguit Std
Printed on acid-free paper
∞
eBook 978-1-61139-266-1

Library of Congress Cataloging-in-Publication Data

Zima, Gordon.
  The Red Garnet Sky : Hannibal Barca Of Carthage : a novel / by Gordon Zima.
    pages cm
  Includes bibliographical references.
  ISBN 978-0-86534-988-9 (softcover : alk. paper)
  1. Barca, Hamilcar, approximately 270 B.C.-approximately 229 B.C.–Fiction.
  2. Carthage (Extinct city)–Politics and government–Fiction. I. Title.
  PS3626.I4868R43 2014
  813'.6–dc23
                              2014009470

WWW.SUNSTONEPRESS.COM
SUNSTONE PRESS / POST OFFICE BOX 2321 / SANTA FE, NM 87504-2321 /USA
(505) 988-4418 / ORDERS ONLY (800) 243-5644 / FAX (505) 988-1025

To Phyl

Agreat stage, coinciding with a man who can load its dimensions with a soldier, a statesman, a scholar, a husband, a father...all of these men in this one man, is not a commonplace. Alexander measured out in some of these ways. Running a fine comb through history, a few others might come out, in some of these ways. But this man—Hannibal Barca of Carthage— also used true smiles and humor, making this paradigm harder to match until history opens its troves for more inspection.

BOOK ONE

The Oath at Carthage

1

9 years
238 BC—Byrsa Hill at Carthage

C louds were starting to crowd the twilight over the city of Carthage. In them he could see images of horses, birds, towers, walls, faces that were turned away from him and some that looked at him so that he could almost hear their words. His small feet left the rough cobblestones of the street and stepped on the first marble steps of Melkart's temple. He tried to match his father's steps, and he counted fifty of them before his father waved an impatient arm at him and then toward the temple.

He had been here before, but the sunlight had been a bigger piece of his courage. He remembered his strong grip on his father's hand, and once his mother's too. Now the dark shadows started to get frightening as he reached the temple veranda and then walked between the bronze pillars which were signals of the god's presence and then into the sanctuary room where a sacrifice was to be made for his father, General Hamilcar Barca. He could smell the frankincense wafted from the tripods in the sanctuary toward Melkart's nostrils. His stomach tightened, but he was Hamilcar's oldest son, and he walked steadily and stood very straight. This was a moment to make his father proud. Finally, he could see the three priests of Melkart around the altar and he heard the cry of a calf as his father and two of his officers reached the dais. The light from wall torches threw shadows around the room, those of the men swarming around the sacrifice, and then a quick one of the calf just as it made its death throes.

This sacred room had a marvelous decoration of gold and ivory on plates and small pillars, like the chryselephantine miracles that Phideas had made for Athena Parthenos at Athens, and again in his tribute to Zeus at Olympia. But the shadowed animation of the torchlight fought with this beauty and then the calf's death rattle was the only sound in the world.

He stopped about twenty feet from the alter as his father joined the ritual of sacrifice. He saw his father raise a gold goblet to his mouth and drink the calf's warm blood. The goblet was shaped like an eagle's head, with ruby eyes set through the gold so that light could make them like real. As Hamilcar raised the goblet the torches gave him light for the eyes. The boy saw the red of blood, the red of ruby, against the peaceful miracle of Phideas and he wondered which part of Carthage he would serve—the beauty, or the blood. Hell seems close here, but the peaceful miracles of the temple were what claimed him and this helped him meet his father's eyes and his officers' as they turned away from the alter and walked toward him. He'd seen blood and beauty almost fused together—initiation into the Carthage of his time, into his father's ambition which the disk and crescent of their goddess Tanit had shined with gold on land and sea. His name was Hannibal Barca, son of Hamilcar. He was nine years old.

2

9 years
238 BC—Carthage

"Do you want to come with me to Iberia, Hannibal?" This question had meat on it and it came like a spear right at him. "Sometimes I use too many words. My plans need *continuity*. They also need *strength* the Romans haven't seen—and *strategy* they haven't seen. All of this is *scope*. Do you know what *scope* is, Hannibal?"

"We have monkeys and a gorilla at our villa at Hadrumetum. I think that gorilla has more *scope* than those monkeys."

He didn't try any of the other eyes—the high priest Acherbas', the other priests', his father's officers', before he made more of an answer for his father:

"I will try to learn the ways of your plans. I would like to come with you to Iberia."

Hamilcar took his son's hand and led him back to the altar. He placed Hannibal's right hand on the still warm body of the sacrifice. The priests had taken official positions again. The torches made a new part of the shadow play move against the chryselephantine embellishment of the sanctuary, but Hannibal didn't see it. He was still looking at his father, his right hand his only concession to the calf that had given its life to these oaths.

"Do you swear that you will never be a friend to the Romans?" Hamilcar asked.

"I swear this," Hannibal answered, and his father let him remove his hand from the calf. This time, he danced with most of the eyes around him. His father's officers there were Carthalo and Maharbal. The voyage to the eyes included them. Maharbal was one of the greatest cavalry officers of that time. Carthalo was a general pillar of strength for his father on land, and on sea when this was necessary. Perhaps Carthalo's eyes caught him a little longer than Marharbal's, but he and Marharbal were friends, and a shorter moment of eyes was enough for them. Sometimes another officer near his father was his son-in-law, Hasdrubal the Handsome, husband of his sister, Amalkre.

After his father, the officers and two of the priests had left the sanctuary, Hannibal and the high priest, Asherbas, watched the Hamilcar procession walk into the shadows of the great hall, past the bronze pillars, into the darker shades of the temple porch and disappear into the night. Hannibal had just taken a man's oath. There would be no hand holding now for the son of Hamilcar Barca. He walked with Asherbas along the path his father had just taken. When they reached the plaza, the statues and ornaments had the intriguing mysteries of darkness. But Asherbas pointed toward the sky in the direction of the Pillars of Hercules, toward Iberia. Great convolutions of thunder clouds were squeezing a bloody hue from what was left of the sunset. This aggression seemed to increase in the Iberian direction of an oath that was still warm on him.

"That is not a good portent for you, Hannibal." Ascherbas was still looking at the western sky. Close to him, Hannibal could now see the amulets and rings of this priest's office, and the distinctions of his robe from his father's simple tunic. Acherbas was his mother's friend, a sometimes confidant of his father. His voice was familiar, friendly. "It is not propitious for you, now. I think you should grow up a little more before your father's Iberia."

But this was his father's moment. He had touched close to a sanctity of a god, his voice had fused with his father's ambition, close to a memory of Phideas' glory. These were good portents close to his chest, not in the skies at the end of the world.

"I think I will grow up under those clouds, Acherbas." The tall priest saw that there was still good posture in the short white tunic beside him. He saw more portents in a young face still bathed in the remnants of the western sky. And Archerbas also thought about mountains that sometimes come to the core of clouds like these, putting majesty and strength into them.

He had finished his exercises and ablutions for the evening meal. One of the young Greeks of his house, a frequent wrestling and boxing partner, approached, gave him a playful salute and told him that the Lady Barca wanted to see him in her rooms. He dressed himself in a white robe with a geometric design along the hem. It would catch his mother's eye. His sandals were Greek, with an ankle banding of silver-worked leather. He chose the smallest silver chain and turquoise amulet in his collection for his neck and chest. A conference with his mother before a meal that brought all of the resident Barcas together was not unusual. But today there had been happenings: Melkart, a sanctuary, the touch of General Hamilcar, a high priest and him looking at portents in the sky. As he walked through the atrium toward his mother's rooms, he was excited as much by memory as by anticipation of his mother's inspection of his memory.

When he entered her suite, her Nubian attendants, Tiba and Maga, were ministering to her as she reclined on a cushioned couch, fresh from her bath. The Lady Barca, in her middle thirties, reflected the complex heritage of Carthage—Assyrian, Greek, Hebrew, Armenian, Egyptian nuances which created a woman capable of holding her ground against her husband, Hamilcar, who was presently the most powerful man in Carthage after his recent bloodletting in the revolt of the mercenaries. She was wearing only a filmy silk sheath that concealed nothing of a tall, perfectly proportioned woman who could embrace a chase on horseback, or the most aggressive lover, with equal ease.

She motioned her son closer to her when he hesitated about intruding. She had never denied her children—her sons Hannibal, Hasdrubal, Mago, her daughter Amalkre—access to her, and that included a mutual frankness as to revelations of the body under natural circumstances which was not unusual for the time among the Greeks. And this lady had assimilated many of the Greek ways, sometimes to the consternation and—his gods help him—the delight of her husband.

Hannibal came close enough to read the playful eyes of her Nubians, and close enough for her to read his eyes. He kissed the tip of a finger in the hand she held out to him.

"I heard about an oath in Melkart's precincts . You and your father are conspiring to take you away from me—to the Barbarians!" Tiba continued to brush her hair. Maga polished her toenails. They were full featured girls who liked to copy all of the provocative talents of their mistress, including minimals of clothing under natural circumstances. Hannibals's tutoring in concentration was valuable now as he coupled to the lady's eyes and words.

"Father asked me to come to his sacrifice for the Iberian plans." He paused, and he tried to find an easy path to her eyes. They were blue, but he'd never seen a blue that could rove among the shadings she could take into hers. "After the sacrifice was over, Father asked me if I wanted to go to Iberia with him." This question was different when he could feel Melkart's breath than now, when he was in his mother's breath and eyes. But he had serviced the question for his father, and would do it now . "I said I would like to go to Iberia with him. Before I said that, Father told me that he needed continuity for his plans. He talked about strength, strategy...and scope."

"By Tanit—was this a sacrifice, or a university?" Tiba and Maga stopped their ministrations. The lady's pose hadn't changed. Her movements were in her eyes, around, on him. "And *scope*—do you understand that word?"

"I gave Father a definition." He could smile, and she saw some of her husband there.

"The damned Romans have already taken too much from us, this family. Your father has spent most of your life away from us—Sicily, Sardenia, Corsica, even that cursed Iberia that is swarming on us again." She moved her legs enough to let Tiba put silver embossed sandals on her feet. "The power of our family—the power of Carthage—is in our trading, agriculture and livestock... manufacturing. Our family's blood is close to *all* of this. You have seen all of this—you have *felt* all of this. This where your power should be. I don't want you lost in this revenge that will have no end. I think we are clever enough for both Rome and Carthage to live in the same world."

She assumed a better posture for Maga to brush her hair. "This little trick of a peaceful world will take our best men to make it work. Alexandria is your example for what can be done by cooperation guided by clever men and women. A swarm of peoples, with every inheritance under the stars for aggression and greed and power lust, has been kept together to build the greatest city of the world—a living temple to intelligent man. I want you to be a part of *this*." Her eyes strayed for the moment of her last word and when she came back to him he could see new reflections in them. He had some answer for her, so he didn't move toward her.

"I know about these strengths of ours. I think they will never be great again if Roman greed and arrogance swarm over the world."

"Your father has hammered those words into you! By the gods—you are only *nine* years old! You sound like one of the old men in the forum belching their platitudes that have bled our strengths for years." She could modulate her voice between imperious royalty and the softest courses of diminuendo. It had gone toward softness at the last. She knew she had lost him. She knew he was a special gift blended by Hamilcar's antecedents and hers. She would have to take what parts of him the gods would leave after they had played with him.

"I was standing on a veranda last night. I saw red clouds in the skies toward the west—toward that damn Iberia. I didn't like the omen of that. That was before I knew about your oath." Maga was resolute in giving final touches to her lady's hair. She was allowed a short grace of time and then a lady's hand said enough.

"Acherbas and I saw the same clouds, Mother. He didn't like the omen of them either."

"He was fresh from your altar words. What didn't he like about those clouds?"

"He said I should grow up a little before I went toward them."

"My Etruscan friend, Zortibas, respects Asherbas. Both of them have the Etruscan gift of pulling truth from omens. What answer did you give Asherbas?"

"I said I could grow up under them—those clouds."

She held out her hand to him, and he stepped close enough to take it in his right hand. She drew him closer, close enough to interrupt the rouge that Tiba was putting on her lady's lips. These lips brushed his cheek.

Almost her whisper said, "You have some of my dreams swimming inside you."

Hannibal moved his own whisper close to her cheek. "You are the most beautiful woman in the world. I love you." He returned her cheek kiss. And when he noticed Maga and Tiba using their playful eyes on him, he kissed the Lady Barca full on the lips, and then, making no further concession to her, he started to walk away in an aura of his own challenge to the future...as much of an aura as nine years of earthhood, and a son of the Lord and Lady Barca of Carthage could manage.

Hamilcar had built a gymnasium at their villa at Carthage. He had built another one, larger, with more concessions to Spartan and Athenian custom, at their estate at Hadrumetum. At both of these places, the pools were large enough to satisfy athletic tastes in swimming. They also catered to voluptuous relaxation under various degrees of sun and water exposure. The reason for this overt bow to Greek passion for the body part of man was that it didn't exclude females and most particularly the Lady Barca who had been testing Greekness in most of the ways she could find. Her techniques for doing this were usually stronger than the various shades of Hamilcar's famous rebuke.

She was crossing from the swimming pool to the shady panoply of a reclining room in the peristyle. She left her footprints on the mosaics, and when passing over a playful dolphin in a naughty frolic with a mermaid, she smiled and put a toe on the dolphin's head. She was not encumbered by a robe, or towel. Her instant of distraction gave him enough time to creep up behind her and encircle her waist with an arm, saving his other arm for whatever impertinence she might suffer before trying some new wrestling tricks on him. He knew she'd been practicing that morning with one of her Greek trainers.

His surprise, his pressure, caused a little gasp, with a legs and buttocks reaction that tapped only a small part of her potential there. He turned her to face him, and he licked a drop of pool water that had survived on her chin up to that moment. He was wearing a loin cloth. When he turned her, she used her right hand to grab the top of his garment, leaving her left hand free to counter his further program. Her long hair now showed none of Tiba, or Maga's careful work, only a wet sheen of blondness that enticed his hands to it...but he had to be careful now. She had suddenly given her censure more scope than his attentions.

He called her Hippolyta on these occasions, when she gave him enough reflection of an Amazon. Sometimes he called her Asherah, the Canaanite sea goddess, when he had her in the water, or on the waters of Carthage in a sail boat, or the little training boat for rowers she had made him make for her. She called him several names on these occasions, like adon, the Semite word for lord, or Marduk, the chief god of Babylon who had several attributes attractive to an Amazon. Now, she whispered *adon* to his lips. He picked her up and carried her to the reclining sanctuary she had already selected. On the way, a whisper like *Hippolyta* came out from him against her ear, and then he set her down on silk cushions, but for the moment she parried his further moves.

"Hannibal has made an oath for your Iberia." Hamilcar's expedition was days, perhaps hours, away, and she didn't have time for subtler words.

"It was *his* oath."

"Melkart's precincts—you, your officers, the shadows of the priests... these could pull *any* words from him. He doesn't understand that oath—he's too young for it. His future is here at Carthage, building our strengths that can match Rome's in our part of the world." His nuzzle of her neck was partly frustrated by a hand, her strength was always a surprise for him. "This Roman obsession is madness. Last twilight, there were bloody pillars of clouds in your damn Iberian direction. These are bad omens for you—certainly for a boy who barely knows his mind's bent...has seen *nothing* of the barbarian wildernesses."

"You and your Etruscan have been playing at haruspices again. And that oath—the twilight's whispers travel like Mercury around here."

"Asherbas told me of it."

"Sometimes you are too close to that priest."

"You married a daughter of a high priest of Melkart. I claimed intelligent familiarity with priests at Tyre—I claim it here. Their advice has been useful to you here, in Sicily, probably places only the gods know about. As for your particular complaint, Acherbas is a friend of our family. I believe your oath—Hannibal's oath—is tied to that word, *friend*, in a special way." This time she let his nuzzle work.

Holding both her hands for protection, he kissed her. "I've seen every color that Zeus ever put into a cloud. Sometimes redness is a torch lighting to new paths. I deny the evil of your view toward the Pillars." He insisted the closeness of their faces with a finger pressure he was careful to keep tender. When he brought his lips from her neck toward her lips, she cooperated a little, and she heard some breath sucked into her husband..

"You know I can't abide the Roman insults to us. Those Carthaginian strengths of yours will be *nothing* under a Roman yoke. Those strengths will come back to us after that yoke is gone." They both had time to study the intricacy of shadows that draped the marbles and ebony lattices of their privacy. "I am 35 years old—and by the gods I'll be older before we can stuff that yoke into the Roman throat. The boy will be my continuity—he is a *special* presence, I think. You know it, too." He had moved close enough to her to complete his last speech as a soft whisper against her neck.

"His education?..." She left a finger on his cheek after she said this.

"You have been making a Greek of him since he was born. Give him the best Greeks you can find to keep the Greekness coming in him, even that damned Spartan, Sosylos, if you want. But Hannibal will begin to teach the Greeks before he is much older."

"I will never see him again."

"Nonsense! When I have cleared away some of your damned wilderness, you can come to us—or if you don't want to, I'll come to you."

"You mean *we* will come to me."

"*We* will come from time to time. I'll not let you forget that you have a husband—or a son"

"Prove it—now" He had been positioning himself for this very moment of her command.

One of his little conceits was a presumption of great geographical knowledge. He would, in some moments like this, show her how the great Carthaginian explorer, Hanno, had taken his ships along the African west coast. He would use her body as his mapping ground. He would use his hands to show her special features of Hanno's odyssey. He would use his lips to show her where Hanno himself had made special discoveries the farther south he went. And when she was a fully cooperative geographer, they sometimes voyaged together in the mutual strength and curiosity that always emboldens, enlightens, adventure. But she would have no geography now. This man was about to leave her, again, and not even the strongest powers of Asherbas, or Zortibas, could tell when he'd return. She had found his loin cloth again sometime ago and this time when she removed her hand, the cloth came with it, exposing an erection that she had already partly built. When her lips and mouth started to complete this particular construction she heard his moan that was not equipped for love words. His—their—pillar became monumental, and then she rode him in a superior position, putting pressures on him that only a specially endowed equestrienne can achieve. When he tried to assume some authority, she thrust her tongue into his mouth, still working their lower quarters, and she gave him words for both of them. When she finally released him, his plans for other parts of her had been disabled by her aggression. But her now ministrations to this man were comprehensive, inventive...restorative, and she left him province for his authority that really surprised both of them.

He wore a general's paraphernalia...silver embossed cuirass and greaves, Carthaginian colors on his under-tunic, the sword she had given him from Tyre, the dagger he'd had forged and tempered from Phoenician steel on Sicily's Mt. Eryx and then had decorated by a Nubian craftsman with a hand for ivory, silver and leather and red garnet—*the Carthaginian stone* the Romans called it. The silver helmet was in his hand, but she knew that his long black hair was a good stage for it. She had made him trim his beard for this goodbye. Actually the trimming had happened before they began their goodbye several days and nights before.

In public now, she had to call him Hamilcar, favored by Melkart. But privately, she couldn't abide the parochial god obsession of the Carthaginians that had plastered their names around the pillars of their gods like shingles. So, family after family, generation after generation, Hamilcar, Hannibal, Himilco, Hasdrubal, Bomilco were names that cursed historians and mocked the parts of the Carthaginians that were innate genius. The Greeks had better taste here— Epaminondas, Pericles, Alcebiades, Thucydides, Xenophane, Aristophanes, Aeschylus—you could roll these around your mouth and get some fix on the personality of them. Her Hannibal was cursed by one of these Carthaginian shingles. Would anyone ever pull him out of the parade before him, after him? These shingles were an affectation of the military paragons of Carthage, they would swallow him up in that damn wilderness. And she would be too far away to protect him.

They had taken their private goodbye an hour before, Hamilcar and Hannibal from her and the other children in the atrium of their villa. The words were over now, here in the forum below Byrsa Hill where a benediction for Hamilcar's ambition and an oath for Hannibal's promise had been made in Melkart's restless shadows. The Lady Barca was standing alone on the steps of a fountain. She wore a white chiton, girded by a woven gold belt with tiny ruby embellishment. Her usual cloak of Tyrian purple was around her shoulders. Tiba had put her hair into a Greek pile with a strand of Indian pearls keeping the order of it against the freshening breeze that had come up from the Mediterranean to make a final goodbye for Hamilcar. The pearls matched her nearly invisible tears.

He saw her and rode up to her, reining the black stallion to within reach of her hands. She had often matched him, this horse, on her white Persian, along the beaches, and in the flat race lands and arbored hideaways of their villas. She wasn't riding with him today. Hannibal was riding a small Numidian pony, and he came up to them. Before he could speak, one of Hamilcar's Numidian officers rode up and presented Hannibal with a leopard skin belt, Hannibal held it out to his mother, She came close enough to fasten the belt on him. Then she stepped away, under the aura of a full panoplied general and a boy with no martial parts on him but a Numidian leopard belt clasping a white tunic in the Greek fashion.

She raised her hand in salute. Hamilcar, Hannibal, and Hamilcar's officers near to her reciprocated. Hasdrubal *was* handsome in a cuirass only slightly less glorious than his father-in-law's. Her daughter, Amalkre, had taken her own vantage for goodbye on nearby steps, and Hasdrubal's final salute was a model of diplomacy as it bisected the two ladies. And then, the vanguard of the Second Punic War marched toward the Pillars of Hercules.

If Carthage's glory of ships had been intact, Hamilcar's expedition would have sailed to Iberia in a full power of aggression and sustenance. But Carthage had underrated Rome's ability to suck ships and technique and strategy from the Greeks of the Italian peninsula, so now Hamilcar would have to creep on African land toward the Pillars, sheparding a covey of supply ships away from the tentacles of the Roman cruisers.

3

9 years
238 BC—Africa, Iberia

The core of Hamilcar Barca's army for Iberia was made mostly from African sinews: Libyan blends for his heavy foot, Carthaginians for his heavy horse, Numidians for his light horse. The mercenary backbone of Carthaginian armies was not in good repute at this time, and he had left their dead scattered around the precincts of Carthage to prove it. From the carnage of the mercenary revolt, he had salvaged, or recruited, Balearic slingers, Greek foot sprinkled with a few Spartan representatives, and a complement of Iberian foot and horse just decent enough to give him some homegrown color when he stepped on Iberian ground. He had twenty elephants this time, mostly the little African foresters whose Indian, or Indian trained, mahouts could sometimes make them behave. He didn't trust these big ears, but Pyrrhus had sprung them on the Romans at Heraclea and the Roman panic there had been good enough to give them a presence with Hamilcar. They were strangers to Iberia, and a little panic might be useful with some of the tribes in that wilderness. But it was his African sinews of foot and horse that he was going to rub on Hannibal in their march to the Pillars.

From Carthage to the Pillars where he would make his crossing to Iberia would take 20 days with cavalry, 90 days with the mixed bag of assets he was carrying now. One of these assets was still wearing the short Greek tunic and the leopard skin belt. But after ten days under Hamilcar's military discipline, the face, even the body under that tunic, had more of the campaigner in it than his mother's darling. The boy was still riding the Numidian pony, and it hadn't been two days on the trail before envoys from the Numidian cavalry would sidle up to the Hamilcar party and invite Hannibal to a little ride with them. He couldn't keep the boy away from those Numidians forever. These invitations got more precocious, and the boy's stirrings in his saddle more restless. Finally, Hamilcar brought his right arm in a sweep that included both Hannibal and the present swarm of envoys and off they went. And they kept going off on rides that circled the army, pounded through spaces in the army, tested parts of their route—the hilly places, the watery places, the flat places made for cavalry. They picked up Numidian supplements to Hannibal's irregular escort that brought rebukes from Hamilcar's officers for the overly exuberant riding lessons, cavalry lessons, that

Hannibal's father had started. But that Numidian leopard had hopped out of the bag and together with Hannibal would grow teeth for the Roman Wolf.

"Maharbal was angry, Father?" He had come to Hamilcar's tent from a very recent Numidian foray. He was presentable enough for campaign purposes, and for the evening meal he shared with his father. But the hair that African wind had tangled, and eyes still lighted by close conjunction with horses—challenges from riding mates and riding ground—was not a good stage for Hamilcar's anger. By the gods, he had never seen so good a clay for making a cavalryman. Another Roman surprise was making here.

"He was...slightly." The right word didn't come. Maharbal, the premier cavalry leader of the age, had seen much the same images that Hamilcar had made from what stood in front of him now. Both men had grumbled about making the campaign a playground for the boy and the Numidians. But both men knew that these Numidians could be a special fork of lightning in the thunder clouds ahead with the right man to make them laugh, to make some play of war, to coax them into disciplined units of a whole strike of lightning. He couldn't bring Maharbal into this rebuke too much without lying. The boy was still at attention, although that smile kept flicking in and out of proper respect.

"Have you learned...*anything*?" Lord General of the Army Hamilcar asked his son.

"Their turns, the fast turns before you can set yourself—I've never seen anything like it. And the making of abreast formations from files, and back again. I almost took off the shield of that Iberian captain."

"I heard about it. Some said he was laughing too hard to kill you." By Melkart, how could he get back into this conversation with this nine year old centaur in front of him. He shouldn't let his smile cooperate with the boy... perhaps some word here about discipline...no one likes a showoff, et cetera. "You and Maharbal will have some lessons when we get to the other side of the Pillars. You seem to have a little flair for cavalry." By his Lady of Tanit, he had never been famous for understatement, before.

"When will we get there, Father?." Hannibal had received an official nod for relaxation, but he was standing. He had been wearing Iberian cavalry boots since he started his Numidian studies—soft black bull hide that caressed his calves, a little silver stitching that one of the leather men had put on for him. The boy wore no dagger, or knife. Suddenly Hamilcar, for long years a soldier of Carthage in the bloodiest casts of action, was shocked by the thought that it would be a shame when the time came to put steel on the boy's body...in his hands.

"If it was just you and those damned Numidians—about ten days. But the rest of us will have to crawl along the ground. It will be about eighty days for it."

"Why didn't we take ships?"

"We don't *have* any ships...to speak of."

"Why?"

"By the gods! My invitation to you for this trip will curse me, yet! The Romans sank some—*we* sank some. The Romans made seamen out of themselves, with plenty of Greek kisses. We let them. We let them intimidate us. So we crawled back into an empty seashell for a navy."

"We don't have *any* ships, Father?"

"You know we have some." Hamilcar pointed toward the sea where his little supply fleet was trailing him.

"They're turtles. Where are our quinqueremes?"

"Those turtles may keep us alive for a while in the wilderness. They're sprinkled with a few of your precious quinqueremes, lightly."

"Will we ride on a quinquereme, Father?"

"When we get to the Pillars."

"I was told that you are a famous admiral."

"Who said this?"

"Mother, Asherbas, Zortibas, the new Spartan tutor, Sosylos."

"They talk too much. In Sicily, I *had* to become an admiral for a little while to keep the Romans from starving us."

"You must have done more than herd turtles. They said you tweaked the Roman nose on land—*and* the water."

"I used some quinqueremes, a few triremes, to do that. We took our tweak right to the Italian coast, up as far as Cumae. The Roman mouths slavered curses at this—we *loved* it!"

"Do you like being an admiral more than a general?"

"A man can wear two hats. On water, you are at the mercy of more gods. On land, a man can sometimes warp himself to improve his fate. On sea, this is often impossible. On balance, I like the land better." Hamilcar didn't say it, but he had made the boy a mountainous precedent that would be hard to climb.

Hamilcar could have told him that the army was more than light cavalry, more than Numidians who licked the froth that spilled out of battle. But this wasn't necessary. In the days between them and the Pillars, the boy touched every arm of Hamilcar's: the other Africans, the Libyan-Phoenicians who were a movable rock with terrible teeth; the Greek mercenaries who gave him a chance to practice the Greek that Sosylos was hammering into his skull, and who made stories about gods and heroes that made him restless to become a man. He knew some of the officers in his father's Carthaginian guard of cavalry from their visits with his family at Carthage, sometimes at Hadrumetum. Their horses were bigger and stronger than the Numidian's. Sometimes he got to test them when the conversation, and Hamilcar's schedule, were propitious. He showed them that he could make a conservative, stable, disciplined heavy cavalryman when not too many of the Numidians were looking. The Iberian foot and horse gave him the chance to practice their language, to study their laughter and some edges of their anger, their judgment of a man. Their horses were larger than the Numidian's, smaller than the Carthaginian elite's. They were blended from stock that had come into Iberia from Celtic countries of southern and eastern Europe, strains that had drifted across the great land bridges that touched Mesopotamia and the eastern lands toward Persia. They let Hamilcar's son test these horses a little. Some of their polite smiles didn't get all the way across their mouths when he stepped away from privilege and showed them pieces of what they liked in a horseman. When he took on more of their language, he could make more excuses for riding their horses, and he wasn't bashful about brushing their horse—*his* horse—against the bright white tunics of the Iberian foot with their crimson borders, and their swords, the *falcatas* that would make another surprise for the Romans.

One day, Synhalus, the doctor and surgeon who had come with Hamilcar to keep the pieces of his army together, examined Hannibal who had inadvertently complained to one of his father's lieutenants that his butt and legs were tired.

"Does *this* hurt?" Synhalus had long fingers that could probe like steel pieces in places that usually hurt.

"By Zeus—yes!" He was lying on a camp cot in his own tent, he and Synhalus alone in that tent, although his father was aware that an examination was in progress.

A few more probes, and proper responses. Synhalus was a tall Carthaginian who never used extra words. Even around Carthage where there was incentive for flamboyance, he was famous for modesty and for his medicine. And the word, obsequious, never referred to him. He made a last pass with his hands over Hannibal, then he got tall again.

"You will keep off the horses for a few days. Your aches and pains are normal for a young idiot who doesn't know how to say *enough* to a horse."

The very day that Synhalus had rendered his service to Hannibal, Hasdrubal rode up to Hamilcar's tent where Hannibal was reporting, after Synhalus' exam, to his father. They had been sometime companions on this land voyage, and Hasdrubal had been another one to admire certain cavalry proclivities, sometimes in front of Hannibal, most times, not. The guard at Hamilcar's tent saluted him as Hasdrubal strode inward. Hannibal was standing at attention in front of his father's field desk. This day there were no Iberian cavalryman's boots on him.

"Synhalus says that you will live." Hamilcar's voice was soft, a close listener could have made a sigh from it.

"Father..."

"Silence! What did Synhalus say to you?"

"He called me an idiot."

"We *are* making progress here. What else did he say?"

"To stay off the horses."

"For how long?"

"He didn't say."

"Perhaps your butt will tell you—if your head cannot. I expect you to listen to your butt, Hannibal."

Hasdrubal was the only one in the tent with an obvious grin. He raised his hand to claim a place at this conversation among cavalrymen, not his specialty, but he knew that a horse was a good stage for him, he was not called *The Handsome* for nothing. Hamilcar nodded in his direction, his eyes mostly still on the place with a sore butt.

"I have anticipated this emergency. Our craftsmen in the armory at Carthage did a good job on it."

"On *what*?" Hamilcar had now focused on the speaker.

"The chariot. There has never been a better accommodation between a horse and a sore butt than this. Tuthmosis would like it."

"*Pharaoh* Tuthmosis?" Hamilcar's interest had been pricked by his son-in-law. But he could dissemble. His lady had often accused him of this.

"The very same. We have a fine little example of his genius outside: bent wood framing, woven leather siding and front. The spoked wheels are a marvel of delicate strength and beauty. A graceful curved shaft has been yoked to two beauties which are not your Numidian nags, always one jump ahead of the Devil." Hannibal's interest had been pricked by *chariot*, but the words, *two beauties*, put real meat into Hasdrubal's remarks for him. Hamilcar had started outside, Hannibal close after. Hasdrubal's grin, bigger now, brought up the rear.

In front of Hamilcar's tent there was a fine replica of a war chariot that Tuthmosis had indeed used to advantage over a millennium before. The wood portions and exposed framing had been painted white with gold touches a conservative man might admire. The leather sides and front were embossed with the Barca coat of arms, an aggressively curious lion on prowl on a log against a palm tree that marked an Africanscape. Two black horses were in attendance. They were Iberians whose attributes and heritage were already familiar to the prospective charioteer. The driver attendant stood at attention as the Hamilcar party approached. Hannibal was the first to reach the chariot. He had seen some examples of this almost outmoded weapon before, but this little beauty was an original for him, and his father was not entirely innocent of it.

This land voyage between Carthage and The Pillars could tax a man. Hannibal's affinity to horses had been a poor secret among the Barcas, and Hamilcar and Hasdrubal had talked about a suitable platform for a young campaigner when a horse would not be appropriate. This beautiful look at the past was the result. They stood quietly as Hannibal moved around the vehicle admiring Carthaginian craftsmanship and Egyptian design. When he got to the horses' heads, between the heads, the driver close to him, grins spilling all over, his father asked him how his butt would like *this* seat.

"It will like this wonderfully, Father. May I drive it?" He matched looks with the driver and some accord seemed to be hatching already, with Hamilcar's permission.

For the rest of the way to The Pillars, he learned how to handle two horses tied to an ancient treasure. He understood that two men—a warrior and a driver—were needed here, so the regular driver's presence was part of a natural exhilaration that allowed him to play either driver, *or* warrior. When Hamilcar's land armada crossed flat places where the chariot idea had been born, Hannibal and his friend Zanta—the Nubian driver who kept the horses, the chariot, and himself polished backdrops for the touches of gold on his arms, his chest, and the chariot—would cleave into the air on runs that gave the long maned Iberians, and occasional Numidians, a good workout. They alternated playing driver, warrior. Zanta's driver was better than his warrior. This was good because it gave Hannibal's warrior more chance to talk with Hamilcar's men.

His Greek was coming to the point where he and Sosylos could go beyond baby talk for a while, but he was still the moon away from the books, the plays, the heroes that Sosylos, and the Greeks in this army, could talk about. He'd had experience with Libyan dialects at his homes in cosmopolitan Carthage, and he could walk into some of the jokes and some of the bragging and complaints of the Libyans in his father's train. They made art galleries of their hair, each tribe hewing to its own fantasy of trimming and braiding hair with particular ornaments that included ostrich and peacock feathers. They were heavily muscled men, and under a tutor like Hamilcar, they were pitiless aggressors who would be another surprise for Roman arrogance.

He had heard about the Balearic slingers that Carthage had used for very light artillery in many of their armies. Semi-Iberians, he could use some of his new Iberian words on them and, with an interpreter to move things along, he got close enough to handle their weapons: a short version of the falcata slung from a broad leather belt and the fascinating assortment of missiles—shaped flints and marbles and lead pellets they shot from three different slings, depending on the range of their target.

"I hear they are very good at targets," he said on a day when his butt gave him permission to ride a horse, and the horse had taken him to the Balearic contingent.

"*Very* good, Prince Hannibal," Silenus, his young Iberian Greek interpreter, said. The gist of this conversation was getting to one of the Balearics, whose equipment Hannibal had been inspecting. Also, Hannibal had picked up a lead pellet from the slinger's missile bag and he was flipping it, hand to hand, in a provocative way. Silenus found a corn cob nearby and held it up, in a provocative way. The slinger got the message. He took the corn cob, pierced it with a stick and set up the stick in good African sand about twenty paces away. He selected one of his slings, placed a lead pellet in the cup and, with a minimum of preliminaries, he propelled the pellet on its way. Hannibal heard the snap when the pellet struck the cob. And he heard a second snap, when the slinger cut the stick with another pellet shortly thereafter. From the audience attracted by this visit of the young prince—with a good seat for a horse and the big curiosity—another slinger repeated this fete of arms, at a distance of about forty paces against a Greek-style helmet.

"I've heard that the Judean slingers could cut a hair. These men could give them a good go, I think." He was talking to Silenus. He turned to the first slinger, who was still close to him. "What is their longest range?" Silenus put in several words for the slinger. The slinger chose his largest sling, a smooth marble piece for it, and then without going for a target, he whipped his sling into the air toward a strip of white sand that bordered the close Mediterranean. They could all see the pellet splash the sand. It was farther than most bows of the time could shoot the best arrows. The other slinger repeated the action, using his memory of the sand splash as his target. The second splash seemed to satisfy everybody.

"Would you want to be a Roman at *that* distance, Silenus?"

"Not without a good helmet, Prince Hannibal. I would like it better if they were shooting at me with arrows."

"Not if they came from scorpions, or the bigger catapults." Hannibal turned toward his audience, and thanked them for the demonstration. Still looking at them, he continued with Silenus: "These are bees with big stings. They can jump about like bees, swarm like bees." Silenus saw a remarkable sight just then when he looked at Hannibal's face. No nine year old boy, with his mother's love still warm on him, should let his eyes roam over a military contingent like Hamilcar could do.

Elephants were old friends to a boy from Carthage. The little foresters from the forests and grasslands of North Africa made wonderful pets. With a good mahout, and circumstances that didn't frighten or surprise them too much, they had been useful weapons for Carthage in Africa and Sicily. But they would always be pets for Hannibal. And when he called on them as a general, rather than a friend, the image of sending children into a man's world never left him. One of Hamilcar's elephants was named *Surus*—the Syrian. He was the only Indian elephant in Hamilcar's train, and the only Indian elephant Hannibal had ever seen. Taller than the foresters, he was young when Hannibal first saw him. Suta was his Indian mahout and when Hannibal was in an elephant mood, Suta told him stories about elephants in India...and a Greek named Alexander.

The strip of Africa that had held them between Carthage and The Pillars of Hercules alternated fertility with wilderness, the fertility having been the drawing power for the Phoenicians from Tyre. It had made a major agricultural power of Carthage. The spine of mountains that paralleled their track, and separated them from the great oceans of sand to the south, intimated wilderness and a savage barrier to travel. Across the blue straits, whipped by perpetual breath from the western ocean, there was more wilderness and savage barriers. While they waited for the transports to return from Iberia for the troops, Hannibal had plenty of time to study these new views and watch Hamilcar's parade down to the embarkation point for them. Ninety days had moved him closer to his father's men than he had ever been. It was still *Lord Hamilcar* that the breeze, the wind, and the rarity of still air, took as their big burden of communication. But *the young one—the young Prince Hannibal*—was also being picked up now and Greek, Libyan, Punic, Numidian, Iberian sounds were getting woven into a new fabric whose tendrils couldn't stay away from Hamilcar's ears.

"A quinquereme, Father!" Hannibal pointed eastward where one of five quinqueremes that had been sprinkled into the transports was maneuvering.

The transports, Hannibals's turtles, were using sails and oars to get them across the straits. When they went in the direction of Iberia, the carved horse head the Carthaginians put on the sternpost of their freighters, and the fat belly, confirmed what Sosylos had said the Greeks called them: tubs, sometimes horses. But this quinquereme was something else. She was low in the water, her polished black hull propelled by 170 oars, and there was no mast on her this day. She was practicing for the passage to Iberia, and it was Hamilcar's intent that her rowers would give his son a lesson in Carthaginian history in that passage. In a close pass to the embarkation point, Hannibal got a good look at the name device on the sides of her bow. It was the Barca device, the lion and palm tree specialized for long distance viewing in burnished bronze. Her prow post was shaped in an eagle's beak, and this design went into lower bas-relief sculpting that accentuated the eagle's eye, in good conjunction with the name device and the reputation of Hamilcar Barca. Her stern post was carved as a graceful sweep of fanned eagle feathers that bent back over the hull to form the support for the commander's canopy.

Hannibal was standing close to his father when he saw this ship of prey whitening its blue cushion in the straits, power and rhythm in the revelation of its legs. *This* was a ship his father could have used to tweak the Roman nose.

"I have seen two hundred like this in one fleet. " Hannibal didn't need to look at his father to savor that memory. His father had given him a short lesson on disappearance, where there had been a Roman-Greek magician with Carthaginian assistants to whisk away whole fleets.

All of them, the body of Hamilcar's responsibility, were across to Gades in Iberia, the foot, the horse, the elephants. A small boat took him, his principal officers and Hannibal to the quinquereme for the final passage. A gangway was lowered from the deck of the quinquereme to the boat and Hannibal was the first aboard, overriding the captain's salute to his father, propelled by his father's smile. They had come aboard close to the stern. A linen canopy was suspended from rigging attached to the large sternpost. Hamilcar, his officers and the ship's officers, went to its shade. Hannibal ran toward the prow.

The smell of this ship was wonderful: woods from Africa, Sicily, and Asia, the special perfumes of papyrus, hemp, flax and Iberian esparto grass from the ropes and hawsers, pitch from the Rhone valley, Egyptian linen in the sail lockers. When Hannibal got to the end of the deck at the prow, the standard of the Goddess Tanit thrust against the vault of sky—a pole of ebony wood, surmounted by her crescent and disk, also of ebony but plated in gold. Two long red streamers of silk were fixed to the pole below the crescent and they obeyed the impulses of the freshening breeze. From ashore, this standard was overpowered by the ship. Close up, the morning sun cooperated in a revelation of Carthaginian pride that had been to all the waters east of the Pillars, and into the northern and southern infinities of the western ocean beyond the Pillars, paths whose particulars were still locked in secret archives of Carthage and Tyre. Sosylos had told him about some of the great voyages of the Greeks and the Phoenicians and the Carthaginians. His mother had talked about the Carthaginian strengths like this. He was standing on a deck that could be turned toward either war or the peaceful progress that had been in some of her last words to him. The ship had cast off its connections to Africa, and he could feel and hear the oars starting to turn her into the course for Iberia.

"Now we have our *trierarchos*," the captain stated, sweeping his hand in a bow that brought the ship under Hamilcar's sway. Greek was common in Carthage at that time, and in most speech and writing of the military and civilian worlds. The acting captain's concession of the captain's role to Hamilcar was acknowledged by Hamilcar's nod and a smile that didn't look for Hannibal.

"No, No. I like you standing here. Let me and my people be passengers for a little while, we have had a long walk from Carthage. A splendid ship, Captain. I admired your practice maneuvers, I never could get that fancy when I had one under my command."

"I think you got too fancy for Roman tastes. My congratulations for those Italian raids. They were our last good tweak of their big beaks from the sea."

"I like your phrasing. Maybe no more from the sea, but we still have a little room on land. I think I can get a better grip on their big beaks standing on land. " Hamilcar introduced his officers, and the captain his *kybernetes* (navigating officer), his *prorates* (bow officer), his *keleustes* (chief rowing officer). Hamilcar's contingent wore short white tunics unembellished by official or personal decoration. The ship's officers were similarly dressed, except for head bands that presumably identified them at the various distances of the ship. Visible crew members were naked and barefooted.

"And that young one who just made an inspection of my prow?"

Hamilcar had an opportunity now to look where he had last seen Hannibal. "I call him Hannibal. I hope before this voyage is over, you won't have inspiration to use the word, devil, in his case." Hannibal was, in fact, walking back toward the stern, a trip with plenty of interruptions for more inspection. His presence on Hamilcar's cavalcade to Iberia was never a secret, but it had mounted more stature when stories of precocious cavalry antics and curiosity about Hamilcar's military structure started to trickle into the various cadres, some of whom had naval connections.

"Does *this* quinquereme come to your specifications?" Hamilcar asked the youngest of his complement who had just come under the shade of the stern canopy. He was, had to be, a good student of eyes, and the immediate faces around them, so he knew he had just asked a foolish question.

"This is a wonderful treat, Father. You could have taken us by turtles."

"No. You had me prepared for a quinquereme long before we left Carthage. What did you see on the bow?"

"The eagle prow and Tanit's standard." Hannibal was looking toward that standard and its red streamers. "I could feel this ship even before the oars started to move."

"You will feel much more of her when the swells get their fingers into us out in the straits." The captain turned to Hamilcar. "With your permission Lord Hamilcar, it is time to go." A nod and a smile that covered him and Hannibal was enough permission. The captain gave several commands to the navigating and rowing officers. The rowing officer shouted another command down the gangway that led to the rowing decks. In seconds, the ship gave

Hannibal more of the sensation of her crew assimilating with her, becoming one with her: the bow officer on his station like an appendage of the prow eagle, the beat of the mallet down on a rowing deck putting the rowing officer's commands into a starting rhythm for the oars. The captain's authority flowed to the navigating officer in quiet words that were recast by the navigator for the helmsmen manning the tiller oars. She quivered when her oars took their first good bite of the Mediterranean, and then as the beat established momentum toward the open straits of Hercules, Hannibal could feel her through the soles of his feet, heard her responses to the strength of her oarsmen and the protests of the intruded water through her deck and hull voices. They were not more than a long slingshot into the straits when the captain's promise of swells was fulfilled—small, almost imaginary at first, but they had good authority within a few more boat lengths and then this quinquereme gave Hannibal a taste of what Hanno and Pytheas had felt against their faces, legs and feet and then the full stature as they faced unknown worlds.

When the captain was satisfied of their progress, he gave the order to his rowing officer to let the *auletes*, the piper, take the beat from the mallet. The simple tune that flowed up from a rowing deck was authoritative as to the beat and much more in tune with the whited blues of water and the air that bounded them. The sea birds swept them in noisy challenges, and the exhilaration was rampant in anyone standing where Hamilcar and the boy were now standing—the command deck of a quinquereme of Carthage. The sharp prow and lower bronze ram were cleaving their path into the straits where men had come to look for the rest of the world. Spray and wind were not selective on these two faces. They were both exultant with their progress and at this moment Hamilcar's proposition of *continuity* seemed completely justified.

"A dolphin, Father...two, three more!"

They were now escorted by creatures with plenty of connections to the gods. And in their phosphorescent sheens that intersected the waves ahead and around their bow, Hamilcar saw omens that could counter the clouds his lady and Asherbas had conjured over these Pillars that were now a part of him and the boy.

Their course was due north to cut across the Atlantic swells as soon as possible, and then to parallel the Iberian coast to Gades. The captain let the young one with the great curiosity put his hand on a tiller oar to feel the pulse of the ship and the water. And then they went below to the rowing decks, where the piper filled the spaces with sound that leavened the burden of the oars.

Hannibal wanted to go to the lowest rowing level. One man was on each oar here. When he walked a little way along the rowing gangway, he found some smiles that came at him through the severest voluntary discipline that man had ever devised. He diagnosed some Greeks here, and he used some of his words on them that made more smiles, if not more words. On the middle rowing level there were two men on each oar. There were two men on an oar at the top level, which made five rows of men serving the oars on each side of the ship, and this made a quinquereme. A distribution of this power among three decks had served the Carthaginians well in peace and war. Others had tried a two deck distribution—two men, and three men oars. And a single deck nightmare of five men oars had also been tried. But they all made for five rows of men on a side, and they were all called *quinquereme*. When he looked along a gangway and saw the naked muscles of this ship working to the piper's tune, the meaning of the word, *devotion*, was burned into him more than Sosylos' precepts from Sparta had ever done. And he would learn that aristocracy, *command*, were papyrus structures without it, and they worked only when this word *devotion* flowed two ways—*from* him and *toward* him.

After they crossed the straits, the rowers held position while the mainmast was raised and the mainsail hoisted. When the sail was full of a northeasterly breeze, the rowers could rest. The *elaiochreistes*, the 'olive oil anointer', serviced them, and the *hegemon ton ergon*, the 'chief of activities', supervised food and drink distribution to the muscle power Hannibal had seen, closely. For the few complaints after the crossing, the *iatros*, the ship's doctor, made his rounds.

"By Tanit!" Hamilcar was standing slightly forward of amidships and had a good look at the front of the mainsail when it filled out. Against the brilliant white linen, a red lightning stroke was blazoned, and not modestly either. It dashed from the top left to the bottom right of the sail's yardage. Barca was *thunderbolt* in Punic, and the captain of Hamilcar's flagship was a good enough friend to play advertising with him as they approached Gades. The captain was standing at the stern and Hamilcar's oath was swept back to him on the legs of a strong voice and the local aerodynamics. Hannibal was with the captain. His father's voice and posture of surprise were enough to get him running forward.

"It's the Barcas for Gades!" Hannibal cried when he saw what Hamilcar was still looking at. "Have you done this before, Father?"

"Not as loudly as *this*." He waved his arm in a sweep that took in the sail and the captain who was still testing the local sounds and postures. Then he put this arm on his son's shoulder, both of them still filling their eyes with red lightning from a pristine cloud. "...But I could have used it."

"Just in case your messages to Gades didn't wake them up, Lord Hamilcar." The captain had assessed a safe situation for himself and had come forward.

"I could have used your modesty, Captain...some time ago."

"Off Lilybaeum when you ran pigs in under the Roman beaks, off Cumae when you raided their stores, also just under the Roman beaks. But you didn't need to advertise then."

"You presume that I need to now?"

"The stiff-necked magistrates at Gades, those snotty priests swarming around Melkart's precincts...I submit that a little advertising won't hurt."

"Maybe we should put in the oars under the sails—just to make a maximum entry to their damn harbor." Hamilcar was just swimming along with the Captain's joke.

"I have anticipated you, Lord Hamilcar," the captain said. Hannibal was at a party of three wide grins.

Phoenician and Carthaginian roots were deep into Gades. Centuries before the low black beauty with the captain's surrogate insolence swept into the harbor, under a duality of sail and oars that made a fine entrance and a spectacular sweep up to the moorage, these people had used Gades as the focal point for collection and transshipment of copper, iron, silver and gold ores from the accessible parts of Iberia. Some tribute was paid to both Tyre and Carthage. But Gades had managed to cling to the precarious edge between subservience and independence by her management of the restless interface between the potential masters from the east and the natives who had a panoply of precedents from prehistorical ancestors and the various intrusions of the Celts that included suspicion, no aversion to the military arts, artistic proclivities. And coming from all of this there was a core of these natives where laughter, dancing, music, anger, pride, revenge, and loyalty to good leadership, were never far from the surface. A stew like this had made the kinds of Greeks, Spartans and Macedonians who had caused thunder in other places.

They were expecting Hamilcar Barca. The grapevine carried by merchantmen and the odd military vessel that touched their harbor gave them some precursor of him. Their own visitors to Carthage picked up plenty of talk and whispers. When his supply fleet put his baggage and sustenance on the mainland near them, and then came back and did the same for his foot, horse, and elephants, they had another good basis for expecting him. Now, as he advanced along the quay with his officers toward the official delegation of the city magistrates, and the religious presence of Melkart, their basis for expectation was fulfilled.

"Quite a show, the captain made a good entrance," Hamilcar mumbled to Hasdrubal as they strode toward the greetings of Gades.

"He didn't need it. Your name has been dug in for some time, I'll warrant. Have you been here before?"

"I piddled around the east coast a little, years ago—Malaka, Maenaca— just enough to smell the onions and the silver. Some of their women are worth looking at."

"You're talking to your daughter's husband." Hasdrubal shot a quick look at his father-in-law.

"Forgive my shocking breach of your *pristine* image." All of this had been almost *sotto voce* in respect of the imminent collision with a big greeting.

Hasdrubal, Hamilcar, and the other officers were wearing knee length tunics with the geometric design trademark of Carthage along the bottom edge; military style open-toed half boots in a polished black leather that would catch the eyes of the native artisans. Silver and gold personal jewelry was limited to neck chains and rings. The ruby in Hamilcar's ring and the yellow diamond in Hasdrubal's would trap the late daylight of Gades and give the greeters some conundrum about which Carthaginians were coming at them—the sybaritic aristocrats who plumbed every luxury and debauchery, or the merciless butchers who had piled the dead from Egypt to the Pillars. Actually, this was precisely Hamilcar's intention. He was hoping to use Gades as his HQ until he could swing his arms in a bigger arc across Iberia. He had no designs on their autonomy so long as it didn't interfere with his action.

The prosperity of Gades was based on its middleman position for the metal ores that flowed from the interior and had sent sparkles to the various conceits of every corner of the civilized world for centuries. So long as he kept *his* Carthaginian Sybarite in plain view, and didn't stomp on *theirs*, they would cooperate. These postures would be upset if his soldier pissed too much on their little island. But his soldier and his Sybarite had to keep their hands within holding range. This situation would tend to keep eyes at Gades open wide to the various opportunities and consequences he represented.

Both languages, Punic and Greek, flowed when Hamilcar's party came together with the Magistrates and divers city officials in the congregation of greeting. Hamilcar introduced his officers. Hannibal, who had been in the rear of the Hamilcar-Hasdrubal parade, stepped forward when his father brought him into the formalities. Sosylos had gone ahead with the troops. He was in the greeters, and he was close enough to the introductions to smile when his protégé gave his Greek some practice.

Hamilcar carried a goatskin sheath with the gold seal of Carthage that held his letters patent from the Carthaginian Senate. It was his official authority to use Gades as his HQ under the sufferance of the city authorities. It was his official authority to undertake such action as he designed to further Carthaginian interests on the Iberian mainland. It was a masterpiece of brevity, seething with potential, depending on whose hands held it. Hamilcar stepped closer to the

Chief Magistrate. He made a minimal ceremonial bow and then presented the gilded vehicle of his authority. Under the scintillations of Carthaginian rings and gold chains, it seemed to be acceptable from most of the perspectives facing Hamilcar. A conspicuously tacit acceptance.

"We are honored by your *visit*, Lord Hamilcar." The Chief Magistrate out shown Hamilcar in his robe and the scepter of his office. He wore a flat hat with Iberian embroidery work that used some of the native gold in its design. He'd also made Hamilcar admire the way he got in first licks by limiting Hamilcar's presence. "...And the young Lord, too." Hannibal was the brief target of magisterial attention.

"Sir, this is a great honor. We expected a few heads bobbing here and there, but this multitude is overwhelming." Hamilcar pulled in some priestly heads in the sweep of his look over the 'multitude.' "I hope my people have behaved themselves." He, of course, meant his foot, horse and elephant precursors who were safely lodged on the mainland by his orders and the sighs of the magistrates.

"Indeed. We are out of the mainstream of power like that. Most impressive and under *such* control." *And by Melkart's grace, it will stay that way*, was a private addendum. The purpose of Hamilcar's military arm had been the subject of speculation at Gades when only rumors had come from Carthage and the incessant hubbub of the waterfront at Gades. They had heard about Rome. Roman galleys had even swept close to Gades, and Romans had touched the mainland near Saguntum. They had heard about a war with Carthage, and a general who had kept Carthaginian honor intact on Sicily's land and waters. There had been insulting abrogation of the peace treaty by Rome which had sent its shocks as far as Greece and Asia Minor to the east, and Iberia to the west. But how that insult had dug into Hamilcar, had made an oath for the *young lord* under Melkart's auspices, was not part of this magistrate's knowledge. Hence his private prayer to Melkart, of most recent instance, didn't have enough scope, but it got powerful orchestration from a lightning stroke on a big sail that had finally materialized right at his feet.

"I am anticipating a prosperity for all of us," Hamilcar said. "Carthage is pushing at her limits in the homeland. I think this: Iberia will give us all new prospects for orderly growth, in her land, on her waters." For a moment, the magistrate savored Hamilcar's word, *orderly*. It had implications that didn't necessarily involve Rome. So far, the greatest contest of wills in living memory along the axis of Carthage and Rome had barely touched them. Rome's present worries on her doorstep had kept Iberia comfortably peripheral. But *this* Hamilcar had worried them. And he was standing within arm's reach of their comfortable periphery.

The Palace of Magistrates was a modest edifice and grounds by Carthage's standards. After the welcoming banquet, and at the moment when the mutual glorification was about balanced, Hamilcar said that his party needed exercise after the hours of the quinquereme's hospitality.

"Melkart's precinct's are in easy distance for legs?"

"For *your* legs, Lord Hamilcar." The toasts had softened this evening for the magistrate, who was a student of words.

"In that direction, I believe." Hamilcar pointed toward the opposite end of the narrow island that contained Gades.

"About twelve of the Roman miles, Lord Hamilcar."

"By the gods! You give too much to our sea legs. Do you have some horses for an evening ride?"

"Our Iberian nags may not come to your standards, Lord Hamilcar. But we will try. Ten, twelve for your evening ride?"

"We have had some appraisal of your *nags*." Hamilcar turned to Hannibal, who had been an attentive, if sleepy, bystander at the reception banquet. "Do you think we could get to the temple and back if they tried to carry us?"

The young lord's eyes had quickened to opportunity remarkably fast.

"If they are like the ones I rode, Father, you will never worry about getting back—staying on might be a worry." There was that triad of smiles again, involving Hamilcar, Hasdrubal and Hannibal...even the magistrate looked pleased.

Hamilcar, Hasdrubal and Hannibal were the front rank of the riding party dedicated to homage to the Gadesian Melkart. Hamilcar's attendants in the second rank included Carthalo, Marharbal, and Synhalus. Three subalterns brought up the third rank. Hamilcar insisted on an orderly pace, although from time to time he had to let his son prance ahead a few paces. This island did not promise beauty. A composite of rocks, sand, scrub oaks, cypress and pampas grass was the main of it. Across the water, it was the mouth of the Guadalete River which accessed the interior treasures, and the larger mouth of the Baetis north of them, that put the significance into this island.

Hamilcar turned to the rank behind him. "You see, Synhalus, fresh air is *not* poisonous." His doctor had not accepted some evening exercise on a horse with grace, or silence. They had just come to a vantage where pillars against a twilight sky and orderly arrays of cypress signaled a god's precincts. At this auspicious moment, Synhalus didn't feel any burden of reply. This ground didn't give Melkart's homage the elevation advantage he enjoyed at Carthage, but Hamilcar and his friends were not disappointed at this first real revelation of potential of their new land.

The priests had reasonably anticipated Hamilcar's visit this day. His given name was homage to this god. His family name was assimilated to this god. He had been known to sacrifice to this god at Carthage and there were rumors that the young Lord had also been close to Hamilcar at one of these times. A cadre of Melkart's priests stood at the entrance to the temple. Hasdrubal offered some local orientation:

"They say we are confronted by celibates."

Maharbal had to pick this up."Too bad for the locals. They look to be in good shape, taller than some of ours. How do you like the shaved faces?" Hamilcar and the others had not yet dismounted, but they had stopped, at a respectful separation from the priests.

"I hear that the heads are likewise. Maybe that encourages celibacy hereabouts. I don't think it would at Carthage. Maybe those hats would." Hasdrubal had just commented on the conical hats of the priests. Their robes were elaborately full, with splashes of metallic and herbal colors catching bits of the twilight.

Hamilcar's dismount signaled a beginning of homage from Carthage. He led his group toward the priests, stopping about ten paces from them. The whole aspect of this temple from his present vantage was satisfactory. They had found good marble for it—the pillars, the paving of the approaches, the steps to the porch—what he could see of the sanctuary beyond. The two ritual pillars at the entrance to the porch were sheathed in gold and carried embosses that probably glorified some connections with the Phoenician motherland, including exploration. This was a famous port for embarkation into the unknown seas west of here. The priests had lighted more than the housekeeping quota of braziers for this visit. As their smiles opened the temple to Hamilcar, gilded bronze tripods flaming with supplements of frankincense welcomed these Carthaginians who would feel comfortable in these essences of light and aroma.

This temple hewed to venerable Punic design which limited the roof to the god's sanctuary, the place of sacrifice. The main hall was a courtyard, outlined by Corinthian columns on three sides. The sanctuary was the central portion of a three storied structure at the far end of the courtyard. The temple was distinguished by a complete lack of cult images. But in its pure presentation of a god's presence, none of it could insult a Carthaginian who had seen the places of Melkart, and Eshmoun and Tanit on Byrsa Hill. Greek virtuosity in assimilating gods with mythic heroes, and attributes of the natural world, had gradually infused Carthage until the panoply of its religion and its temples would have virtually covered the holy places of Athens, or Pergamum, or Ephesus. And now its cult tributes in gold and ivory and marble rivaled these citadels of Greek devotion. This temple of Gades didn't need supplements. A man could stand in this courtyard and pull his thoughts together without artifices. If he could communicate with a god, this was all he needed.

Hamilcar, followed by his company, walked toward the sanctuary, his path lighted on two sides by flaming braziers, the shadows they made from Hamilcar's procession animating the walls of columns. The priests had flowed out in front of him and were at the entrance to the sanctuary when he arrived, obviously the high priest and three of his acolytes of undistinguished rank. The smiles were still there. But Hamilcar had made no arrangement for sacrifice, or special ministrations short of sacrifice. It was his move.

"We have come to savor some small part of this temple. Your hospitality is a cherished conclusion to a long odyssey."

"*Conclusion* is a difficult word, Lord Hamilcar." The high priest was also a student of words, or he had trapped some nuances from the Chief Magistrate who, in fact, had been close to him at the first reception. "We are honored to afford a step toward your new world." This priest had been listening when Hamilcar put some meat on his letters of patent.

"Of course." Hamilcar's smile was a natural inclination. He had admired the scarcity of the sycophancy so far on this island. "I want to state my objectives again—here, as close to Melkart as I need to be at this time." The priest's smile was a good brother of Hamilcar's as he waited for the statement that would be sufficient for this visit. Hamilcar looked around to include his men, and the boy, in his statement:

"May Melkart grant us his grace of success in the journey ahead of us. May our success be measured by the people of Gades, the people of Iberia, and not be found wanting by them. I swear my devotion to this end and to the eternal glory of Carthage."

The purity of these precincts from artifice gave Hamilcar a possibly useful addendum: "I pledge to dedicate a statue of Hercules, of Etruscan marble, full figure, by the best sculptor of Greece, or Ionia, for the grounds of this temple... placed at the sufferance of Melkart." This marble was in stock at Carthage and Tyre. Getting the right man to it, at either place, was no problem. Getting it to this island, might be, unless the fins of the Roman sharks could be clipped a little.

It was a fine altruism. But just before it, that summation word *Carthage* had left loose ends again. The high priest sighed inconspicuously.

4

15 years
232 BC—Iberia

Hercules was in place at Gadesian Melkart's precincts. Hamilcar had brought an Ionian sculptor to Tyre and a full sized Hercules in a lion's skin loincloth—looking skyward, his hands in a nonviolent supplication for a new task to his measure—had been wrought. The still busy Phoenician and Carthaginian commercial network had devised a non-suspicious itinerary for the statue on board a Tyrian freighter, and one day it had come to the dock at Gades. The priests had admired this collaboration among Etruscans for the marble, Ionia for the sculptor, Tyre for husbanding the marble, Carthage and Tyre for the itinerary, Hamilcar for the initiative and the money that had glued it all together. By their own grapevine, which rivaled the magistrates', the priests knew about the advent of the statue before Hamilcar. One day Hamilcar received an invitation from the high priest to attend an installation.

Hamilcar was standing in twilight again, on Melkart's site, close to part of the oath he had made in front of this sanctuary. The statue pleased him. It posed no prickly cult problems…it was a finely constructed man appealing to the heavens for more challenge. It posed no threat to the local god's priority. So the priests had found a place for its pedestal on the tiled veranda that faced Iberia, and they had oriented Hercules so that his supplication went in the direction of the mainland point the Iberians called Puerto Real, the site of Hamilcar's field HQ.

The Ionian had pulled another miracle from the marble. Hamilcar stepped closer to Hercules. He'd paid for him, so he touched him, his finger savoring a genius of sculpture, his memory savoring his Lady's connections to this Etruscan marble which spanned more than pulling omens from thunderclouds. For an instant, he worked *her* into this smoothness under his finger. The Etruscan living entity had almost vanished under the Roman heel, but there were memories of them in the art and the engineering and the agriculture and the architecture that now had the Roman stamp on them. And when the panic of someone else's conquest gripped the Roman throat, it was the Etruscan haruspices they turned to for churning livers and chicken guts into comfortable auspices. Now he had given part of an Etruscan memory to Gades, and it had circumvented the Romans beautifully—Etruria plus Ionia plus Tyre plus Carthage equaled *this* Hercules.

"It is a fine statue, Lord Hamilcar." The high priest was watching Hamilcar's close inspection. His tall conical hat made a good accent for the twilight around this temple, but the subtleties of his face were obscured by his westward, twilight ward, position from Hamilcar—a situation advantage that sometimes is an incentive for candor from at least one direction.

"It is a fine site, too," Hamilcar said. "The outlook of Herculean endeavor toward my humble diggings on the coast is a particular pleasure. We will take all the help we can get—*from* the skies, or *under* them."

"In six years you have put your name deep into Iberia. You have gone ahead of Hercules. I wonder where he is looking, *now.*" The priest's distance from the statue and Hamilcar was unchanged. Where Hamilcar had gone in the six years had brought new streams of silver into Gades—one third for Gades, one third for Carthage, and one third for Hamilcar. The one for Gades had plenty of trickle into Melkart's purposes as defined largely by this priest.

"I think he is looking *east* a little, *north* a little."

"That would make a *northeast* look, Lord Hamilcar...it could rub against the Bastetani...the Carpetani. If this look decided to get a little bigger...the Celtiberi, too." Hamilcar's face was the more readable one in this chat, but he could make a mask of it under a noonday sun.

"I will try to play the good ambassador."

"I wonder if such a man can be pried away from the good general, Lord Hamilcar."

"I am studying that very point."

In the six years since he and the young one had shared the quinquereme in the straits, Hamilcar had had little time to play the father. The Iberian tribes were not putty. They had made him pay for every mile, every fraction of a mile, that he advanced his standard into the convolutions of plains and hills and mountain spines, and the valuable ores that would weld his empire together in this Iberia. He *had* played the good ambassador. He now had a promising cadre of Iberians enrolled in his graduate school for the light and heavy horse disciplines, and for wedding these arms to his foot contingents where other Iberians were learning to make an army with his Libyans, Carthaginians, Numidians, and Greeks. All of this under the shadows of his officers, Carthalo, Marharbal, Hasdrubal, a dozen more who had held Sicilian ground and waters with him, had been with him when he pulled the mercenaries' vise off the throat of Carthage. The priest had just recited the names of the tribes he had already met. Some of them were soldiers in his training. Some of them worked in his mines and smelters. Some of them in a cooperation of food production under his agricultural specialists. A cornucopia of sustenance for him lay in this land, and for the time when he decided to turn his army toward Rome.

The priest had added the Celtiberi to the finale of his short soliloquy. These people had used the mines of the Baetica as their treasure house for centuries. When Hamilcar pulled these mines under his standard, he offended the central power of Iberia—a mix of Celtic and pre-historic Iberian roots that had made the preeminent culture of Iberia, with martial qualities that could make the best friend, or the worst enemy, for Hamilcar Barca in this land.

Two of their kings, Istolatius and Indortes, had come down on his farthest camps, savaged some of his workers' villages, destroyed mining and smelter installations. He could have taken a decent, diplomatic, retribution from them. But Indortes had left his calling card in the form of a crucified Carthaginian officer, with Indortes' personal mark on the spear thru his chest. This particular officer had shown precious initiative in ameliorating Iberian suspicion and putting a good face on the Carthaginian case. He had been a strong hand on the shaft of Hamilcar's standard as he inched it forward.

Hamilcar personally led the punitive task force that focused on Istolatius and Indortes. Istolatius managed to escape with the remnant of his cavalry, Indortes was not so lucky.

He spit his defiance in Hamilcar's face. His curses pranced around the prediction that the gods would grind Hamilcar into the dust the way Hamilcar ground the ore he had stolen from the Celtiberi people. He gave no inch to Hamilcar. He gave Hamilcar no place where mercy could have settled. Carthaginian torturers had set fearful precedents of every scheme devised in the terror colleges of Mesopotamia, Asia and Africa to prolong and enrich the agony before death. Hamilcar gave Indortes to them without reservation.

The priest knew this story. Hamilcar's torture virtuosi had burned one of his crucial bridges while they were extinguishing Indortes. He knew that the Celtiberi cast a long shadow across Hamilcar's ambitions. He had virtually called out Indortes' name to Hamilcar as he stood near his Hercules. Hamilcar had seen Indortes' eyes torn out under a burning sun. The heady froth of the successes of those years, bubbling up from a bloody and vengeful brew, had made him undervalue Celtiberi memory.

The boy's curiosity about his father's military structure had not waned. His focus was still on the light and heavy cavalry, but he had looked around at the aspects of the foot soldiers enough to recognize some of the whole of it— cavalry *and* foot; mutual exploitation of power and the manipulations of power that made surprise and penetration, division, flanking, envelopment. Pieces of all this were coming to him from Marharbal, Carthalo, Hasdrubal, and their officers and men who allowed him to come close enough for questions and close observation.

Hamilcar and Marharbal put him through some cavalry drills when he had grown enough to grip a horse better, although he had demonstrated this grip for several years before they conceded a place. In the drills with mixes of foot and horse, Marharbal now had an observer on horse who could put much more scope into his questions. The Numidian cavalry was still playful with him, but they had to give him places in their formations when he made challenges they couldn't resist.

He saw Hamilcar's foot and horse after a campaign, a raid. Some of this observation was part of his father's curriculum—sheens of sweat on men and horses, enough touches of blood here and there, with insults and brags that had enough laughter to show that a good action had been done. Some of this observation was accidental—massive smears of blood on men and horses, woven with wounds accordingly, and there was no laughter in either the eyes or the mouths. He talked about his father's curriculum, not the accidental parts, but it was all part of his curriculum.

Sosylos, the Spartan, put another curriculum on him, and Silenus, the Iberian Greek, was threatening to do it, too. Silenus interacted between Hannibal and the Iberians. He had also become an instructor in the Iberian culture, and this faculty had moved him underneath the panoply of instruction that had hovered over the young prince since Carthage. Silenus was well built. His Greek face had been tempered by several generations of Iberian assimilation. He could laugh quickly. He could pull myths and facts into a conversation. Frailties and virtues of the gods, and their ladies, could come in when non-official conversation needing bolstering. He and Sosylos had included physical development in their ministrations to their charge. Silenus usually got into the boxing and wrestling, while Sosylos participated in the less sudden exercises for muscle enhancement and coordination.

"By the gods, Silenus, you're impertinent."

"A biographer needs to be, Prince Hannibal. Your thoughts, impressions, likes and dislikes are meat for my project."

"I didn't authorize it. Sosylos laughed about it."

"Sosylos is dedicated to stuffing you with the Greek world—I am dedicated to seeing what you make of it."

"How far will you take it? I have nothing for such a project that could fill a papyrus any larger than a wheat stalk."

"Ah, that's for the gods to decide. I can't wait until you are a finished project, until all the dice have been cast in your life. I will put it down as it comes, and hope."

"That the laughter from Olympia doesn't blast you into the Mediterranean!"

"You could have made a better insult—into Hades, into the cesspools of the Styx before I got to Hades. I'll have to remind Sosylos to touch up your insults—a *real* Greek must be a virtuoso there...it is his barrier to an incestuous coupling of egos when more than one Greek stands under the same tree."

"What will you call this monument to imagination which wastes good papyrus—or parchment, if you should happen to be prosperous at the end of it?"

"I haven't cast that die yet...but *Exploits of Hannibal* has been nibbling at my mind."

"*That* will leave a great void for your pages to fall into."

"I have some basis for worry about getting my hands on *enough* papyrus— or parchment. Your sword play is showing some promise, for example."

The sword play had come under other tutors. Shortly after his father had made a HQ between Gades and the temple on the island, he had found a Greek and an Iberian among his foot cadres who knew how to beat some foot and hand dexterity into the lad while coupled to a sword and a big wooden buckler. This education moved with just the portion of bruises that kept education ahead of discouragement. At first the swords were wooden, weighted along the blade with enough lead plugs to give them a realistic heft. With the Greek tutor, the equal weapons had a symmetry along the blade and through the guard and hilt, a heritage of the hoplites. It was a thrusting weapon, and even with the wood, it had balance and it could show the way to parry and feint and thrust. With the Iberian tutor, the first swords had the graceful curvatures of the blade, and along the guard returning to the edge of the blade, that was the hallmark of the falcata, the Iberian evolution that had borrowed from the Greek kopis and the Indian strategies for getting slashing power into a blade. This sword put thrusting and slashing into the close-up province of the foot without compromising its radius of action, and the Romans would go to school on this one after it put new dimensions in the piles of their dead. The Iberian showed Hannibal some facets of the parry and thrust and slash potential of this weapon that thumped his buckler and the exercise padding on his head and body.

Under the auspices of the Greek, and the Iberian, the young prince was developing slipperiness in his legs and arms, in the conjunction of these with his torso and the semi-blades that finally put some mutuality into the thumps. He was now as tall as most men of his time, though fifteen, and he would grow more. Sosylos and Silenus' disciplines, the horses, the work with spears and javelins that came with Spartan tutors, the sword work, some archery with Asian compound bows, put efficient muscle on him. Even the Balearic slingers got to exercise his eye and arm. It was Hamilcar's purpose he was serving, the general, not the father. Although much of what he had been doing would have fit on the normal stage of an Athenian aristocrat and his son, Hamilcar was usually not on *this* stage. The tutors were his surrogate in weaponry. Hamilcar was making a warrior for his continuity.

But Hamilcar found occasional interstices of relaxation between his expeditions, and the punitive raids that were relative to the expeditions. "By Ba'al, I wouldn't want to be on the other side of that sword from you—wood, or not." He had come on the conclusion of a pass of arms between his son and the Greek. The Greek saluted Hamilcar, and retired for some needed rest, walking away with the thought that when they went to steel, this young one would bear *close* attention.

Hannibal removed his padded helmet and walked toward his father. They were now almost of a height. When Hamilcar put out his right hand, the handclasp was like that of two men. Hamilcar had let his beard cover the lower half of his face again. His hair was still black, curls distributed about the beard and head that could make a good prop for a rogue, a commander in his various poses and realities of anger, pride, laughter, or a king fit for Carthaginians, or Iberians, where perhaps a touch more of the actor was needed. He had several new scars on his face. His eyes—even when they looked at the boy now—couldn't let go of his scenes in this Iberia where relaxation and pleasure for his man, his father, had been thin instants against the time of his general. Formal fighting, where your dispositions could be set up against the enemy's under some grace of time, were rare here. These Iberians took every advantage of their own ground to keep formalities to a minimum. It was creep, and sneak, and hell for leather riding and running with horse and foot that defied the rules of formations—theirs, his. And when it came to man on man, horse to horse, he had never seen better—not the Romans on Sicily's land and water, or the mercenaries around Carthage who had his own stamp on them. If he could manage to put these people into an army with his Africans, under the discipline of his Greeks and Carthaginians, the Italian fields could look like Carthaginian festival grounds.

Hamilcar was hiding something behind his back. Hannibal had noticed this before the right hands got together, but when he was close to his father his eyes were on his father's face.

"You have been working with poor counterfeits...*this* is what the falcata is about."

Hamilcar's left hand came around and he handed the hilt of the working sword of his Iberian foot to his son, a flash of sun on the polished blade. As Hannibal's right hand gripped the leather rings of the hilt, his left hand traced the silver embossed guard that swept over his fingers back toward the edge of the blade. This sword had the carbuncle, the red garnet of Carthage, in its pommel, held by a lattice of silver embossed steel. It was Hamilcar's personal weapon. The leather rings of the hilt were dark with sweat, earned by military exercise that had not been counterfeit.

Hannibal took a fencing pose and moved the sword with wrist and arm impulses that were becoming authoritative. The balance of it, the continuity of it with his hand and arm, was a revelation after the wood. He tested the edge of the blade with his left thumb. It was like a razor, and when he looked up at his father, words were really redundant. He flashed the blade in the sunlight several times and then he handed the sword back to his father—the red garnet foremost and collaborating with the sun for both of them. His face was radiant with pleasure.

"It took a long time to bring that steel to you." Hamilcar put the sword on his head and pulled down on both ends enough to flex the ends more than half a hand's breadth away from the horizontal. When he released his force, the blade recovered. " I could do this a hundred times and the result would be the same—you'll have to take my word, I'm too tired to play smithy for you." He put his free hand on his son's shoulder as they walked toward the Barca compound where food was waiting. "The Sumerians and the Hittites learned how to pull carbon and shit from their iron...and then how to put some of the carbon back. The Iberians have taken this kind of iron and learned how to forge and temper it. They have done clever things with the charcoal fires and their quenching baths to put hardness along the edge without brittleness in the blade."

"Where do they get the iron, Father?"

"First, across the land bridges from Asia Minor, into the Celts. Some of these ingots finally got down into Iberia. But they've learned how to make their own iron from some of the best ore in the world. They've learned tricks from India and China, the Persians, the Babylonians, the Assyrians, the Egyptians... the Phoenicians."

"I'm glad you finally got *us* into this steel, Father."

"You will learn that the more of the world you can sweep into your heart and mind and eyes—the better for you." He held the sword up for general inspection again. "This sword is proof of this view. I think it will help us make an army that can play in Italy."

Following his father into Iberia—on a horse—was the best of his exercises. Hamilcar was making an inspection of one of his mining sites near where the Baetis river was born in the mountains the Iberians called the Sierra de Segura. The town called Castulo was near his mines. Hamilcar's column was exclusively cavalry this time, twelve of his Carthaginian Sacred Band heavy horse, twelve of his Iberian horse. The Carthaginians gave him a showy breath of the gods; the Iberians were proof of his affiliation with this country. His son rode with the Iberians. His solid white tunic, girded with the Numidian leopard skin belt, blended well with the red bordered tunics of the Iberians. He was the only horseman who was unarmed, and unhelmeted. But this was intended to be a show of Hamilcar's diplomatic side, so such a rider was no anomaly among the easy shouts and laughs that flowed along with the other parts of Hamilcar's design. When they drew near Castulo, Hamilcar turned and beckoned Hannibal forward, to his side. This way, they went into Castulo.

When Hamilcar and Hannibal rode through the gate of the village chief's villa, Hamilcar caught her in the corner of his eye, but his son met her look fully. She wore a long skirt, with the Iberian flare for bold colors. Her blouse was brilliant white. Hamilcar's son's survey was enough to pick up the silver in her earrings, and her necklace. Her black hair, lustrous in the sunlight, was evidently used to independence and it was long enough for her to pull a lock of it over her shoulder as she watched Hamilcar's cavalcade go by, the young rider on Hamilcar's left the center of her focus. When Hamilcar paid his respects to the chief and his staff, this girl was in the atrium where her father had placed his greeting to Hamilcar. She stood against a tiled wall of a fountain, a perfect fusion with what Hannibal could see of her villa.

"You honor my little house, Lord Hamilcar." The chief's bow was less effusive than a Carthaginian's might have been under the same honor. It accorded with bows Hamilcar had seen from Greeks who kept an honorable past in close touch with their present man.

"Your cooperation has been one of my sources of smiles—a reservoir that has had less in it than I might have liked." Indeed, he had played his diplomat well in the first contacts with this chief and his people...foresight that had blended Greek and Iberian skills and muscle into his local mining and smelting projects, here mostly silver. This chief had used a Delphic heritage of accommodation to Fortune and had so far kept mostly Hamilcar's smooth edges—the diplomat's—next to his people. This Hamilcar's reputation had gone into many channels, including the Roman, and the Greek which had branches in every port of the Mediterranean. The Greek stronghold of Massilia in southern Gaul, and their colonies along the Iberian east coast, were feeders of this reputation that informed this chief. If Hamilcar's juggernaught was rolling toward Italy, best to find some paths for it that saved his flowers and vegetables.

While his father and the chief chatted about their affairs, Hannibal's communication with the girl was handicapped by language and separation— about twenty paces. Hamilcar's peripheral vision was excellent. This was a crucial prerequisite for a general and a diplomat, also a father. It picked up some of Hannibal's dilemma. Therefore, he put a question to the chief about his family, turning his torso enough so that the question intruded some of the axis between his son and the girl.

"Two sons and a daughter. The sons are some of your foremen at the mines, and they'd better be working now. The daughter has shown an impudent curiosity and is standing close to you." He proved this by using his torso like Hamilcar had done and then beckoned to the girl to approach the conference. She was tall for her age, like another young one in the room, and she walked toward her father with an athlete's grace and a priestess' assurance—none of this being missed by either of the Barcas.

"This is Inanna for you, Lord Hamilcar." Her bow was a perfect complement of her father's. She had a presence which both Hamilcar and Hannibal had to relate to Lady Barca, and there were other parts of her in that direction, too.

"I must include Castulo in my itinerary more often." Hamilcar's Greek was excellent; he used it more than Punic since he had come to this ground on the other side of the Pillars. He also knew how to present himself to a lady.

"We must make our hospitality encourage that plan, Lord Hamilcar." She hadn't looked at Hannibal during her approach, or now while she was performing for her father. Hamilcar recognized the classic mold in her speech. He knew about her Delphic antecedents. And for a moment his imagination was equal to the task of assimilating her with Apollo's sanctuary.

"My son, Hannibal." What Hamilcar needed to bring his son into this conversation was mostly redundant. Hannibal's bow had been practiced in various privacies at Carthage, usually just before a meeting with the Lady Barca, therefore, it had unexpected panache and authority. He didn't say anything, but her eyes had made a couple with his again, and she pulled a small smile out of him.

"I have heard of Prince Hannibal." She was back to Hamilcar again, but she'd left unfinished business with her acknowledgment, which Hamilcar picked up.

"Perhaps the horses have carried his name. He is threatening to unseat some of my cavalry officers already. Do you like horses, Inanna?" There, he had given a bone for his son to carry.

"I love them. Father has given me a white mare that he swears has Parthian blood."

"That mare *has* come a long way." Hamilcar turned to his son, forcing an issue. "We still have some talk left. Perhaps you two can find a horse to look at for a while." His regimen for his son the past six years had been for a soldier, a continuity. The father part of him had been a damn faint presence, but it had just intervened. The chief's own perceptions of a young axis which needed a little serving had kept abreast of Hamilcar's.

She sensed his reticence was nothing more than finding words to put between them. So she used her Greek slowly, and made a path to him with words and gestures, the complexions of her face. Sosylos, and his predecessors, had put enough Greek into him so that he was soon comfortable with her communication, and he got enough of himself into it to make her smiles a bigger part of this viewing of a horse.

"*Inanna*...it doesn't sound Greek," he said, after they had admired her mare, Diana, for some time. His father had told him that Castulo had been founded by Greeks, so he had expected an avalanche of Greek, but not in such an interesting form.

"It isn't. Father happened to get caught up in some Sumerian poetry—and *she* popped out."

"What kind of poetry?"

"Love poetry."

"She, Inanna, was *in* the poem?"

"Very much." She might have been a synthesis of Greek and Iberian blending, but when he looked at her, particularly when her soft words were also in the moment, he could build the classic Greekness on her he'd seen on marbled goddesses. Some of them were playful, like she was, some of them promised plenty of capacity for that mind *and* body game the Greeks had made into a philosophy of life. His mother had this, this girl seemed to have it. By his father's Hercules, they had barely met! He would probably never see her again. But as they walked back toward her father's villa, their words were now enough to carry the thoughts without the hands and faces. She had pulled him to that level, and Sosylos would have to dig deeper into his dictionary now.

"Is it a long ride from Gades to *here*?"

"For your Diana, and my black Iberian, it wouldn't be long."

"Haven't you named him?"

"You Greeks have the words. When you see him...you may have a name for him."

"I will ask my father if we have excuses to go to Gades."

"I will ask my father to make some, if necessary."

"How long will you be here, Iberia, Hannibal?"

"I don't know. I've heard my father call me his *continuity*...that could mean forever." He let some silence come along with them. He admired her stride, and for the first time he noticed she wore riding boots, thin marvels where an Iberian craftsman had fused simple elegance to efficiency. "...But I don't think so." She turned to him, the question didn't need her words.

"My father is using Iberia as a step to Italy. Everything he—we—do here has that mark on it. That makes your question too complicated for me."

That night after her father's banquet for Hamilcar, she played the aulos for them, a kind of oboe whose clear tones seemed a perfect companion to the Greek and Iberian amalgam she and her father had achieved in their home... rounded intersections of walls to walls, walls to ceiling. It had the floor plan of a Grecian villa, but this softness of intersections was there, even fireplaces were bound into it. And the tiles of Iberia in the walls against white stucco and in the floors against parqueted oak and marble complemented the vases, the wall and window hangings, the sculpture and painting that had the Greek mark on them, or the Greek bow to other civilization.

When Hannibal and his father left for Gades early the next morning, Inanna was standing near the gate, her goodbye mostly for the young rider alongside Hamilcar. Hannibal's curriculum had broadened some very recently. He was proud of his initiative, but Hamilcar had played a father's card in this game, too.

The trireme that swept into Gades harbor carried an unmarked white linen sail. Her hull was also white. The gold leaf on her prow and stern posts was not warlike, and the long silk streamers, red and blue, fixed to the head of her mainmast, were definitely not warlike. This display, with accents which only an unimpeded sun and whited blue water can make, was capped by a virtuoso exhibit of oar power as she maneuvered for docking. This boat was for someone who found pleasure in fast things like horses, boats like this, and dolphins. It would probably please a lady of this kind. Hamilcar saw her standing on the bow deck, wrapped in a long cloak, colored by the purple of Tyre. She wore no hat, and her long blond hair flowed in the breeze. Three others were standing near her, all in white cloaks...his sons Mago and Hasdrubal, his daughter, Amalkre. He hadn't seen this lady, nor the other part of his family with her, for the six years since he had left them in the forum at Carthage.

He met her halfway down the gangway, an impetuosity with some hazard potential if any passion was involved. The gangway of a trireme was not a lovers' playground.

When she recovered from his kiss, she pushed him away enough to look at him, and then she helped both of them get to the dock with some of a general's decorum. On solid footing, he gathered his sons and daughter into another embrace, words from all sides trying to bridge the years.

"My vow to Ba'al, Lady—you are a treat for me!"

"Your bear is back again," she said, putting a fond finger to the beard near his chin, and then letting it rove around the part near his cheeks. She had admired the curls of it when he had *gone bear* at another time, but now most of her addendum was for their private time.

"Who is that tall person who seems to intrude our gathering?" The Lady Barca was looking at a tall person who wore a white tunic and the leopard skin belt she had clasped around his waist six years before. The person's smile was impudent. It had played around the faces of his two brothers and his sister, but now it was back again on her. The face was tanner, leaner, with some marks she hadn't seen before...around the chin, a line near his left ear, perhaps one close to the corner of his mouth. She couldn't find the boy in his eyes. Even when he came to her and they were close as a kiss, he had mostly a man's eyes.

"It's your son who went to Iberia, Mother." This came softly against her cheek.

"You're as tall as I." Her look swept over him, the tunic no camouflage of the supplely muscled frame a cavalryman could use.

"Not near so beautiful."

"You've worked on your compliments." The lady made a slight adjustment of her torso toward her husband. "He has...*local* targets for his practice...the compliments?"

"One has recently tested him. I don't know if he was found wanting—I didn't ask her."

"Then this *continuity* business...it hasn't been *all* blood and gore?" She could put complexions in her eyes you couldn't keep up with. This question was up for grabs between her husband and Hannibal. Hannibal took it.

"Father lets me off the hook once in a while." How long he had been *on* the hook before the Inanna surcease was a thought that just skewered both of the males.

Then Hannibal piled into Mago and Hasdrubal, and took Amalkre into a hug.

"Too much for sea legs, Hannibal," Amalkre said. "You *have* grown." This was murmured into his shoulder and it was the mixed appreciation of a sister and a woman. Her husband, Hasdrubal, was on an inspection tour, but he had known she was coming. They were going to try to rekindle their marriage on this Iberian ground.

The Roman patrols were not bothering this part of the world. The Cisalpine Gauls were threatening to shake off Roman encroachment in northern Italy, and there were challenges to Roman presence along the eastern Adriatic. So the trip from Carthage to Gades had been at the captain's discretion, and he had taken the historic option of northwest toward the Balearic Islands and then west to the Pillars of Hercules and Gades. The weather had cooperated with them and the dolphins had accompanied them. The ladies had fed the sea birds, remembered their Greek poems and Homer's odysseys, and the peaceful cast over everything had given the boys plenty of time with the officers and crew.

Hamilcar's villa at Gades was a greater concession to a military man than an aesthete. Hasdrubal, Amalkre's husband, tended more to the latter man, and he was responsible for letting some representatives of Iberian comfort and artistry creep into Hamilcar's place. Amalkre was quick to claim her quarters and a long soak in a hot tub. Hannibal and his brothers, swarming with memories and new reports, had gone to their wing.

For a bear, with, he said, no female entanglement for six years, he was a reluctant model of restraint. The lady had shed her cloak. Under it she wore a white linen tunic with a blue silk sash, sensible simplicity for the sea transit she had thoroughly enjoyed. She had the flush of a sea adventuress to compound the rest of her and she was sorely straining her husband's resolve of only gentle aggression after the six years.

She walked around his bedroom suite, the modest overtures to luxury she found here not promising excitement for the rest of his villa. This lady was mistress of a large Carthaginian palace and country estates which would have comforted an Alexandrian or Athenian aristocrat.

"Charming...and a sea view, too." She had paused by one of the large doors that opened to his private veranda.

"The bay of Gades. For the sea...you'll have to come closer to the bed, to the windows, on the other side of the bed." He was down to his loincloth, barefooted, and in excellent shape to guide her to the next part of his itinerary. He waited for her decision—more studied casual inspection, or compliance with probably not a one-sided will for conjunction. The lady walked toward the windows which, as he had said, were in the direction of the large bed. At a place where the bed and a good vantage for window viewing were about equidistant, he intersected her walk.

"*Hippolyta*." He breathed this name against her throat, bending her against the bed to make this part of her more accessible. She pushed him away and stood up. There were two authors to this play now. The sash of her tunic had come off, and then her tunic under his hands. She was down to a sheath, a filmy white masterpiece her dressmakers had coaxed from silk that had come from China to India to Carthage to find her. This delightful obstacle also came off under his hands and then she grabbed his loincloth and, with a yank, made two naked bodies in his bedroom.

"The sea..." She made only this little concession to his itinerary, before she grabbed the pieces of his bear that were closest. Their recent separation had made his sometimes voyager on her body a stranger now, and she pulled his face against her breasts, using the best pieces of his bear she could find. With this invitation, his lips brought her nipples to full standing and as he worked lower on her, to the wonderful silky V of her, he heard her voice change from the simply aristocratic to the temple-ensconced Mesopotamian aristocrat in the full throes of obligation to making sex a paean of democracy. He didn't have the initiative for long. An Amazon was wrapping her legs around him and had worked up a very useful pillar for him that she still caressed manually and orally, just before she showed him new ways to think of the word, *cooperation*. She had the advantage of a recent invigorating sea voyage. He had the disadvantage of recent rigorous campaigning. He was, therefore, the lower body on the bed, legs and arms fully splayed in surrender, when the Lady Barca finally said, *enough*.

"That *is* a good view of the sea." She was now wrapped in an Iberian shawl which his housekeepers had managed to plant in his room. It was woven from Egyptian cotton, and she had to admire the colors and the design of Iberia in it. Her hair was appropriately tousled for the afterwards mode of an Amazon. The soft light dressed it, but he had never been so close to *real* Hippolyta when he looked at this lady, who had forsworn the attentions of Tiba and Maga for some time, who had been his co-captain of discovery. He was still horizontal on their arena, watching a renewed inspection.

"How is your *continuity* coming?" Hannibal's appearance had shocked her when he suddenly materialized at the gangway of her trireme, the maturation... height, muscular progress, a handsomeness like a Hellenistic prince...but she saw the marks on his face, his first steps toward the warrior in his eyes. At Carthage, she had shared her blue eyes with him. They had enjoyed playing the game of *finding* with their eyes. He'd found images in her eyes. After he had told her about them, she did this with him. They had pulled in every god and goddess they could think of, the embellishments about equally shared. Their eyes had been one of their precious playgrounds. But she would have some trouble with that game now. He had a man's eyes. And when they came close enough for the greeting kiss, he couldn't hide the part of them that had seen the blood spilled for his father.

"You've seen him. He's almost a cavalryman."

"Nothing more?"

"I have forced *nothing* on him. You know how he has been with horses. They are a natural extension of him. I would like to use this for my purposes, but it will be *his* decision." Hamilcar didn't tell her that he almost dreaded handing killing steel to this boy. It would have uncovered too much of him... he couldn't afford to do this, not with *her*, not with his officers and men, nor Hannibal. He had declared his purposes before the senate at Carthage. He couldn't afford to release any more of himself in front of them. He was still a young, youngish, man, but he didn't have the strength anymore to squander part of him on sentiment.

"There is a girl?"

"I took him on a diplomatic inspection."

"Only the smile of your diplomat foremost."

"Precisely. We went to Castulo...about four day's ride. I have silver mines, smelters near there. Castulo was founded by Greeks from Delphi."

"She is a *Delphic* Greek!" This from a famous champion of Greek assimilation.

"She is. She is also Iberian. She is a beauty. She is intelligent. She has a sense of humor. She didn't kiss my ass. I like her father. He has been a pillar of my strength in his country. Some of this effect has diffused to other parts. He is indispensable." Hamilcar took a long breath even though he had almost recovered from his lady's ministrations.

"When *is* the wedding?" She had turned enough from the window to let a puckish smile flow to him.

"I hope they can get together from time to time. She is also a nut about horses. The *three* of you would be formidable."

"She sounds *absolutely* delightful."

"How long can you stay with me?" He was off the bed now, walking toward her. She threw off the shawl so that there would be two naked bodies in that room again.. This didn't stop him.

"Until you order me away." She touched a curl of his beard, one near the left side of his mouth that had been particularly impudent very recently, and then she wound her arm around his neck.

"A month of us in this wilderness and you will be ready for your trireme."

"I wish it were *our* trireme." She kissed him. "We should have our *real* voyages, to some of your outrageous places." He had been a warrior for Carthage all his adult life. She knew that his imagination, at times abetted by hers, would be their sailing place...but she would never tell him this.

"I will try to bring the girl here. I don't want to take you there."

"I thought your standard was well placed between here and there."

"This damn Iberia is like the Delphic girl's temple to Apollo...a wonderful aspect in the whole, but when you try to get close to the Pythia, the heart of it, she's swarming with guardians. If you get past the guardians, the mists and vapors keep you at bay, you never see her face. I can't trust a face I can't see. Here, there's more than *one* face to worry about."

"You took Hannibal."

"He is not the attraction for trouble that you would be."

"I probably can take some compliment from that." She lifted her chin.

"The capture of my most precious possession by people with the bargaining power of the Devil is not acceptable to me now—or ever." He kissed her.

"That *is* a compliment. How long will *you* stay here?"

"I intend to move my center farther east, and north along the coast. If we can consolidate our power, make an army with these Iberians, we can play in Italy for a little while, then home to Carthage, forever." He had looked away from her just after *Iberians*. She had looked away from him just before *forever*.

"Then you have just promised me a visit by this Delphian. How did our son take to her? His father seems to have been well taken."

"Horses were the first rope that pulled them together."

"The others?"

"She let him practice his Greek. Your Sosylos has done a good job with him, but he will have to speed it up, now...get him into Homer, Sapho...the comedies."

"*Sapho*? Good God what other ropes were there?" Her tendency to revert to monotheism when excited was not revolutionary. This creed had permeated the Mediterranean world for centuries before her. Some of the gods affecting her world had been paraded for social, recreational, erotic purposes for years. Thoughtful people knew it, and some were changing their affiliations.

"I told you she has a sense of humor. Apparently he picked up on it as soon as she let him into the conversation."

"Beautiful you say?"

"As interesting a synthesis of Greek and Iberian as I've seen here."

"We can explore that reminiscence later—in six years, you must have *piled* them up."

"I suspect she has been well trained in her classic antecedents, powerful allure to a lad whose mother has been Hellenizing him since he could walk."

"Did you hear him mouthing any of it—her *classic* roots?"

"He mentioned Homer several times...Plato and Aristotle...Aristophanes I think."

"How long *were* you up there—this *Castulo*?"

"One day—actually an afternoon, night and morning."

"God...I *must* study her notes. What do they call her?"

"Inanna."

"That's not Greek."

"She told Hannibal her father had pulled it from a Sumerian love poem... in a literary sense, she's very similar to you...my interpretations of you."

"I don't think the Phoenicians got as far as the Sumerians."

"They got *everywhere*."

Hannibal had never been bashful around the opposite sex. This lady, her daughter, her handmaidens, the other females inside her radius of action, had put no unreasonable barriers in front of him...a natural frankness of Greeks. So his presentation of himself—in fun, or seriousness, was not much handicapped by female presence. This Inanna could bring some balance to her husband's continuity program which had hurried up the man, her son, who had shocked her at the quay.

A number of people cooperated with the Lady Barca in the respect of Inanna's prospective visit. Hamilcar's letter to her father had been delivered by a relay of horsemen in less than a day. The last part of the relay consisted of an escort of six Iberian cavalrymen for Inanna should she decide to visit Gades. The decision had Hannibal's father's obvious approval. It would take no Archimedes to deduce that Inanna's father had colluded in this decision. It would take no inspiration from Sapho's sighs to nudge Inanna toward a favorable decision. And after her father had made her entourage, a carriage of Greek design for her and one for her baggage, her father's offer of a chaperone declined by her, the cavalrymen started her to Gades. The people of the Olcades and Carpentani near Castulo, the Oretani, the people of Corduba and Hispalis along the Baetis river, the Turdetani in the land as she approached the coast...all of them knew about her. Her way was easier than Hamilcar's might have been. She was *of* this country.

Hamilcar's signal system announced her arrival at the coast. He sent an Iberian copy of a lembos for her crossing to Gades. This was a 16 oar version of the ship the Illyrians had used for successful piracy along the Adriatic, a swift little devil that could wet an appetite for speed and impetuousness on the water. The Iberian sailors had put some extravagant streamers on her stern post, and someone had found flowers to wrap around the neck of the eagle head on her prow. The rowers put her into the quay at Gades with a flourish that brought shouts from Hamilcar's brood on the land—Hannibal, Mago, Hasdrubal—and an uninhibited wave from his Lady, who had discouraged a stuffy formal reception of Inanna at their villa. After the gangway had been lowered, Hannibal showed his famous non-bashfulness around beautiful women by running toward the lady who had appeared at the top of the gangway. Stunning in a black cloak from an Iberian loom around her, two thin white silk bands trying to impose some order on a Greek style coiffure of long black hair. She extended her hand. Hannibal escorted her to the land.

"The excuses *have* come together," he said.

"Well...it *was* sudden." Her look at him was partly frustrated by the prospect of another reception—obviously some of his family who were holding back, thank Zeus for it. This was all coming at her too fast. But she *did* see another tunic on him, a woven sash with Carthaginian geometry in red, blue and yellow, a thin silver chain necklace. As they stepped on land, she noticed his sandals. They took some liberties with Greek tradition, but she liked them: full ankle bands of red leather imprinted with stripes which carried the colors of his tunic. The tall lady, blond, must be his mother. Her mother had had a bearing like this—thank Zeus for the smile. She looked close to a queen. Who are those boys with smiles like Hannibal's? How would she cope here? Lord General Hamilcar and her father had almost *pushed* her into that carriage. Of those two conspirators, only Hamilcar was here. He was standing back from the closest group of the family, but she noticed him. This was what he wanted so the smile she could see on him was no surprise, comforting, and no surprise.

The tall blond lady wore the cloak of Tyrian purple of her own voyage. As Hannibal's escort stopped in front of her, Innana made a slight bow, her eyes, however, meeting Lord Hamilcar's lady's, who made a sudden bridge:

"No room for your horse, Inanna? I so wanted to see her." She held out her right hand. When Inanna's right hand clasped it, it was capped by the lady's other hand.

"You'll have to come to Castulo, Lady Barca." Inanna's eyes were chestnut brown, the lady's blue, and here was a good dance between them. In several years, Inanna would be close to the lady's height. When the hand clasp persisted, and it insisted her progress toward a carriage, Inanna looked at Hannibal, then the other boys who were grinning like the apes who—she had heard—scrambled about the nearby Pillars of Hercules. Hamilcar was not denied his greeting. As his lady and Inanna brought their smiles toward him, he made a slight bow, stepping aside to give a clear passage to the carriage.

"I have said I admire your father's efficiency and cooperation. You have just put more debt on me, Innana." There was no general in his apparel this day. Hamilcar wore his white tunic with the Carthaginian borders around the hem and sleeves. A gold chain on his neck winked at her, and an expert had pulled a handsome man from the black curls on his head and beard. A general's eyes did the best they could to greet this beautiful guest.

"My father sends his greeting to Lord Hamilcar. He was impressed by your escort."

"But were *you* impressed?"

"It was overwhelming. I felt like a princess...going through Corduba...and Hispalis."

"They didn't throw stones?" Hamilcar's question was shocking if you didn't notice his smile.

"Pomegranates, someone tossed me a pomegranate, and there were some flowers, red anemones."

Hannibal had to get in here, and Sosylos would have been proud. "Ah... that pomegranate. Someone tried to assimilate you with Aphrodite." There was some blush on his target, but she put it together with a smile.

"And the red anemones, Innana. These are Adonis' signs. You *must* be careful with all these portents crowding you." The Lady Barca had released her hand, but the eyes and the smiles of these two wouldn't let go of each other.

As her land escort went toward the Barca carriages, introductions to Hannibal's brothers, Mago and Hasdrubal, were done. Younger than Hannibal, all of the boys had Hamilcar's black hair, with curls imminent. His brothers were shorter than he, but the faces, frames and muscles looked to service all the imaginative deviltry she suspected was in Hannibal's bag. Near the carriage, another woman stepped toward Innana. About Innana's height, she also wore a cloak against the vigorous wind of the straits. It was white.

"Black and white we are, Innana. Welcome to Gades...welcome to Barcaland. I am Amalkre, Hannibal's sister, his sometimes conscience, although my power there has waned lately." Her Greek was excellent, a synthesis of Ionian and Alexandrian strains that tutors and travelers had brought to her. She had once thought about being a priestess of Tanit. Slim, graceful, a face that could challenge, beguile, chastise, work every attribute of a priestess. But she had read too much, mostly in the Greek, and Tanit's aura no longer appealed to her. She had never seen the children sacrifices, but the rumors had been persistent and this parochial aberration was enough to divert a mind now sensitized to a world view. Innana wore no jewelry. Amalkre wore pendant earrings where tiny gold cages held Indian rubies. The collar of her coat was opened enough to show a woven gold throat choker. Her eyes and lips were subtle advertisements of the age's best cosmetics in an expert's hands. Her hair was black like Innana's, Greek styled, tiny gold embossed tortoise shell combs instead of silk ribbons.

Amalkre offered her right hand to Innana. It was the Delphic Greek lady's second handshake since leaving the ship...the first, a near queen who seemed to have strong affinities with the outdoor world, including horses. The second, a sophisticate who could probably debate Hellenistic philosophy and religion with her, and diagnose the male psyches which cluttered the world—in, or out, of the temples.

"I told your father that I am overwhelmed—you aren't helping me in that, Amalkre."

"She has a tendency to monopolize, Innana. Keep away from her aura," this from Hannibal. He was overpowered by two smiles, some soft laughter with it, but he managed to take the lead in Inanna's final steps toward the carriage.

At the banquet that night for Inanna at Hamilcar's villa, the young ones, Hannibal, Mago, Hasdrubal, and Inanna found plenty of common ground after Inanna had let some of *her* Amazon come out—horses, archery, swimming, some of her scholar, some of her imp touched with a Grecian and Iberian amalgam of beauty and poise that had all of them scrambling for words for her.

And there was a short time for Inanna with Amalkre after the banquet, in a tiled veranda where there was a soft caress of sea breeze and sea sounds for them. Inanna wore a red silk cape over a white, pleated, cotton tunic. She wore her mother's pearl necklace, with small gold loops at her ears. Amalkre wore a pale yellow silk chiton, over thin white linen. With a collar of woven silk which used Tyrian purple with red and yellow in an intricate geometric design, a head band of finely woven gold centered by a tiny triumvirate of emerald-ruby-emerald, she was close to her priestess that night.

"Who is your god for war, Inanna?" Amalkre had broken a long silence. The two ladies were standing close together.

"I haven't called on one, but there is Kronos, or Saturn—if I need one."

"In Babylon they had Ninurtu...maybe he's closest to the Barcas."

"This is too beautiful a night for such a god."

"Not for Barcas." Inanna *had* to confront Amalkre's then hard eyes, and what she saw made her cloak useful against the extra chill. "Barca women must be brides of the war god. Their men are bound to this god—not to any woman—and these bonds will tear their men away one day."

Amalkre looked away, even the sea sound and the breeze sweeping tiles and leaves and fronds made a shocking silence for Inanna.

Amalkre finally turned to Hannibal's new friend, and she had made a small smile along the way. "Forgive me. I have blundered into your night with ravings, and I didn't need your Pythia's bay leaves to do it." She touched Inanna's hand. "Father has accused Mother of too much use of her Etruscan sage, the haruspex, too much wallowing in his omens. I'm famous for blundering into privacies without even an omen to stand by me."

"The wars finally came to an end for my father. He has made a good life for us and he is less than your Barcas...why?" Inanna tried to frame the question that could make a bridge to Amalkre, over her apology—a bridge between *good life* and the Barcas.

"*Rome* is why...she is swarming around the Barcas. I am eighteen years old, Inanna. I cannot remember when my father ever had Rome out of his head."

"This is *Iberia*, Amalkre!"

"This is a *steppingstone*." Amalkre tried to make a smile again, but she had no material. Earlier that evening, the travesty that *her* war god had made of her marriage had surfaced. Hasdrubal had been away on an expedition since her arrival. He had been hers for only one year since their marriage. She had let some of this spill on Innana—inexcusable in the venue of joyful acquainting of the last hours. Amalkre tried her apology again. Inanna's smile was a denial of intrusion neither of them believed.

In the week her father had allowed her for the visit, Inanna and Hannibal used two white Iberians to explore the horse trails of Gades' island. One day they got as far as the precincts of Melkart.

"It is wonderful...his smoothness...and he looks *interested* in Iberia." Inanna was on the veranda of the temple, touching Hercules.

"Father pulled some strings to get him here. The marble came from a vault at Tyre, a sculptor from Ionia, and then a clever sea route from Tyre to here to get around the Romans."

"Amalkre mentioned the Romans." Since that night, Amalkre's inadvertence had been fuel for thought. But Inanna was young, her father and mother had given her enough perspective to override some perturbations...and she liked this boy who made her think of Hellenistic princes. So—*who* were the Romans?

"How did she...mention them?"

"She warned me about the god of war. Apparently he puts his nose into Barca affairs too much, and the Romans are always with him." Enough, she would let this be her answer.

"Amalkre's imagination is famous. If it gets together with my mother's omens some amazing fantasies can come from *that* conjunction that Sosylos and Silenus couldn't think their way out of. Do you like Amalkre?"

"Very much. She looks and acts Greek, too...but..."

"Give it to me...I have reservations about her, too."

"There is a specialness...she *listens* to the air. She would have had a place at Delphi...I would take her prophecies seriously."

"Did she give you one?"

"She said that Barca women must be good at sharing."

He moved close to her. Only when he had helped her with her saddle had they touched, and it was fingers. She had made a very good entrance with his father and mother, and Mago, Hasdrubal, Amalkre. She could provoke parts of him that even his friends Sosylos and Silenus hadn't reached. She was beautiful as his mother and Amalkre were beautiful, but she had uniqueness he hadn't seen or felt before. "That is a broad compliment...did she say *she* qualified under it?"

"She put her man—men—into it." She flipped her fingers.

"She's qualified to do that...she's married to Hasdrubal."

"Hasdrubal! How many of them *are* there?"

"That name, like mine and Father's, is perpetual—it sticks to every family tree in Carthage. What *about* her men?"

"We must be getting back to your father's house. It's late...I'm hungry." He stepped between her and her impatient Iberian.

"You haven't answered my question."

"She will have to do it—it's too much for an empty stomach." She pushed him in the belly. He managed to catch the offending hand and pull her to him. He had never kissed a woman, other than his mother, on the lips. He corrected that omission in full view of Hercules, who probably wouldn't have rebuked him.

Innana had returned home. Hasdrubal had come back to Gades and Amalkre had joined him at his villa near Gades. It was Hamilcar and his lady's turn to make the pilgrimage to Melkart. It was close to the time for them to put another separation between them—as far as Iberia to Carthage, as far as the Roman obsession to Carthage.

"Hannibal and Inanna made a good precedent. This *is* a good ride." She had just tethered her horse near the temple. She wore trousers like a Celt cavalryman's and a long sleeved cotton blouse. All white, with a red silk sash. Her hat was an Iberian straw design and her rakish shaping of it, its leather band worked with red and silver threads, and her long blond hair which was completely independent again, completed his Amazon for that day.

"What did you think of her?" Hamilcar had opted for some of the costume of an Iberian cavalryman—short white tunic with crimson borders on a V neck, the sleeves and hem. They both wore Iberian cavalry boots—trim, calf-high, tan leather of a softness that Iberians could produce.

"I predicted her...remember?"

"You said something like *absolutely delightful* in a rare weak moment."

"I take *nothing* back. I'm afraid I have competition for my boy...*and* his thoughts."

"She came close to conquering the other boys, too. Amalkre..."

"I saw them together several times. I hope our daughter didn't put on too much of her priestess act. She can be overpowering if you let her do all the talking." The lady had seen more than just a conjunction of Amalkre and Inanna. She had seen a sudden change of mood strike Amalkre and then flow into Inanna. Amalkre's prescience was a complement of the lady's sensitivity to omens. In propitious moments together, they *did* make strange worlds that could defeat Sosylos, or Silenus, and when their creations spilled out of their privacies they had frustrated, even angered her husband. This day, with the exhilaration of the ride, moments of limited passion with her companion rider, the culmination at the temple where a piece of Hamilcar was now installed... these parts of it had held down a premonition of tragedy that had become an almost excruciating privacy for her. It seemed to swirl around Hamilcar, but there were other faces in it. The gods, *God* help her, she had seen pieces of faces that she could make into Amalkre, Hasdrubal...Mago, *her* Hasdrubal, *her* Hannibal. No Omens had started this. Premonition, a prerequisite for good haruspex work according to Zortibas, had done this to her. It had started before her trip to Gades...in truth, when Hamilcar and Hannibal left her in the forum at Carthage six years before. This premonition had sucked sustenance from her ever since that time.

Hamilcar walked close to her. As Lord General of Carthage, prescience was a prerequisite. Not the grotesques, or erotica, or aesthetic aberrations—but it had served him, saved his life a hundred times, and had given him a step for approaching his lady on occasions *just* like this.

"Your wonderful trireme is starting to look good again?" This was the softest approach he could make to her mood, to the reality of his empire in Iberia that was pressing him to continue his action. During her visit, he had played the husband for her as when they were newlyweds. She had combined her bride with her Amazon for him with breathtaking virtuosity. He had played the father even before she came, a much deferred concession to the nonmilitary parts of the boy whom he had selected for continuity. And making Inanna's presence here at Gades had been a continuation of the father, a precious surcease from a regimen of conquest and preparation that had filled the shadows of his own dreams...he had closets of his mind he wouldn't open for *anyone*.

He needed all of his actor in front of her now. They kissed. There was a mutual resolve in it against foreboding, against the realities of their life. So it was a long kiss, renewing *all* of the pressures of passion, and they tried to pack their memories with it.

5

18 years
229 BC—Iberia

A meteor striking the mantle of the earth over Gades and burning out on a trajectory toward Rome would have left an earth trace very like Hamilcar's when he moved toward his new HQ at Akra Leuke—the White Headland, on the Iberian east coast, southwest of the Balearic Islands. He had his own precedence along this route. His forays up the Baetis valley, even somewhat beyond Castulo, which was now a mark on their maps that his son Hannibal could touch blindfolded, had shown the Tartessi and the Bastetani who he was and what he could be when someone got between him and his plans. These people were well disposed to cooperate in Hamilcar's drive toward the new point for his standard at Akra Leuke.

Phoenician precedence along his route was older than Hamilcar's. Explorers, entrepreneurs and settlers had left seeds and some paving stones in front of his army that had sprouted in the old Tyrian colonies of Malaka, Sexi, Abdera, and when he matched looks with these people it was Phoenician to Phoenician, or it was Phoenician to a good memory of Phoenicians. This fact helped to temper the famous Hamilcar anger. The high priest at Gades had to admire this temperance.

Akra Leuke had fine views of the Mediterranean. And in right moments of wind and clouds and sunlight, and moonlight, well focused thoughts could go east-southeast from there to Carthage quite easily. It had a splendid vantage for beauty and memory. When Hamilcar built his villa there, he put a tiled veranda in a place where there was maximum vantage for memory—which happened to coincide with the one for beauty.

It was after the day's last meal. It was a propitious time for close memories and further memories because this veranda was caressed by sea breezes as soft as an evening in any part of the year could make them. Two young men stood on it, facing east-southeast, toward Carthage. From a distance, their clothes signaled assimilation with the country behind them—white tunics, red-bordered on the neck, sleeves and hem, sandals of Iberian leather with inimitable compromises between utility and artistry. Closer, the faces showed amalgams of African shading with what shades Iberian wind, sun, dust, heat, sweat, a little blood, fear, exhilaration and discovery could bring to a man. Hannibal was several inches taller than Mago. He had two years' advantage of age, and six years' advantage of Hamilcar's school for continuity. Mago had stayed when Lady Barca returned to Carthage three years before. Their other brother, Hasdrubal, had returned to Carthage as his mother's escort and their father's surrogate in matters of platonic comfort, and family affairs needing a male presence.

Both of these boys on Hamilcar's veranda had their father's black curly hair. Hannibal had been advised by a person of Delphic antecedents to hew to the Hellenistic prince mode. An African sculptor at Gades had even done a bust of him that was to be put into bronze. The sculptor had seen the same Greek prince in him that Inanna had seen. So Hannibal used the silk, or linen, headbands with some hair trimming that could be called *princely discreet.* Mago had been impressed by Iberian gypsies. They were great with horses, knives, wrestling, women, songs, and passion that could streak across every emotion invented by man in the time it took to bring a drink to the lips—and put it down. They liked to use silk, or cotton, headbands, and if they exploded with color so much the better. They were broader than Hannibal's *princely* one, so that meant the hair needed more length and curl to balance them. Mago was wearing a dark purple band this night that was a compromise between gypsy and decorum. Hannibal's was white silk, and it caught the declining twilight better than Mago's.

"How far?" Mago was still looking east-southeast. His target didn't need specification. Hannibal had done his share of looking in that direction from various vantages of Akra Leuke, including this veranda.

"Depends on how you want to go."

"Let's sail from here—go direct, let the Roman patrols try to catch us."

"Then, a quinquereme with good rowers, friendly winds and currents... maybe four day's time.

"Let's sail from here to the closest good place in Africa for horses. Let's take a horse relay from there."

"I'll give you Cartenna as your ship target. With the same ship and crew, about a day. For your horse relay, I'll give you some Numidian devils and let's give them a day and a half. For your second choice then, maybe two days and a half." Hannibal's look had paralleled Mago's during his calculation. Both of them had seen a lady their father sometimes assimilated with the Amazons, and behind *her* was a white fairyland city that climbed up to a glory on Byrsa Hill.

"By Zeus, you've thought about it, too...those numbers didn't jump out of thin air."

"I've done other ways—want to hear?"

"You're practicing frustration now, big brother. Speaking of frustration, what are your latest calculations about the fair Inanna?" Mago put in the right look to Hannibal, the twilight compounding the gypsy imp under that dark purple headband. He had to wait for the frustrated swain to turn away from Carthage, and he got a long, pure, dose of the soft sea sound that still caressed them.

"Father said that the Romans are sending a delegation to inspect him."

"What does Inanna have to do with *that?*"

"He said he will take them to some of his mines."

"Ah, Castulo! We will be part of the inspection party, big brother."

"Inanna doesn't need *that* much inspection. You have your own targets." Indeed. In the sparse interstices of Hamilcar's regimen for them, Mago had identified a number of attractive targets among Iberian females of various social and age strata. His gypsy affinity had been no handicap there.

Their flux of communication with the Mediterranean was uninterrupted for several minutes while the subject of lovers slipped away.

"I've heard Carthalo and Marharbal talk about the Celtiberi. Is Father worried about them?"

"My approach to the inside of his head is no better than yours, Mago. We are close to their territory here. I know that Father has unfinished business with them. There was trouble with two of their chiefs who attacked his mines and killed a favorite officer."

"Did Father bury that trouble?"

"It takes two shovels working on that, theirs and his. I think only his shovel got the work." Indortes' fate had not been a well tended secret, and Hannibal had heard enough of it to sensitize his ears to the word *Celtiberi* ever since. That word had picked up stature the closer they got to Akra Leuke. He had also been privy to some of the ways others, Carthalo and Marharbal for instance, rolled that word in their mouths. Mago obviously was at some disadvantage here, and he wanted to keep it that way. Their father had shown them his soldier side and his diplomat side since the Indortes time. They were standing on a triumph of his diplomacy. And they would move into the Celtiberi country on the backs of more of these triumphs, leaving the bad memories far behind.

The advance to Akra Leuke had more meaning than this Celtiberi prophecy. Greek colonists along the Catalonian coast, in Saguntum, Emporion, Barcino, Cypsela, Rhodus, and then along the southern coast of Gaul to the citadel of Greekdom at Massalia, had conjured portents that fit *their* case when Hamilcar left Gades and put his standard into Akra Leuke. Greek and Carthaginian argument over entrepreneurial prerogatives throughout the seas under their sway—Mediterranean, Tyrrhenian, Ligurian, Ionian, Adriatic, Aegian, Black, even Atlantic—had been a persistent fount of action and reaction for centuries, and when there was no obvious ground for common cause against the savages outside their world, this argument had kept passions in practice.

In the instance of the Carthaginian incursion orchestrated by Hamilcar, the Massalians were delegated as spokesmen for the Greeks to the Romans. Any Greek colonial with an ear to the breezes that fluxed around the Mediterranean, and a memory that could put Rome and Carthage on the opposing poles of the same axis, had basis for worry that *this* Carthaginian posed more than an entrepreneurial threat. The Romans were still preoccupied with Celts in northern Italy, and the Illyrians along the east coast of the Adriatic. But the First Punic War was still a delicious taste for mouths in the Roman forum and the name *Hamilcar* raised by these Greeks put more flavor into their protest because he had been a particularly thorny obstacle to this Roman victory. A Roman delegation to Hamilcar was in order. Carthage seemed to be well patted down, but a look at what these Greeks were shouting about was in order. Notice of the mission was sent and properly acknowledged by diplomat Hamilcar.

Hamilcar had a dock at his villa. It could accommodate two quinqueremes and the miscellany of smaller craft that served his purposes for personal and family travel, and such tentacles of diplomacy, trade and supply, intelligence, and visitation as he directed to this private point of his new base. The Roman mission had been so oriented by explicit directions.

The Romans used a trireme to make the visit. As it warped up to his dock, Hamilcar watched from the uppermost stage of the terraces that connected the villa with the quay. They hadn't been seafaring until the exigencies of the First Punic War made them drag a navy out of the Greek ship building and ship management and ship fighting talent that was lodged in the Greek and Spartan enclaves on the coasts of southern Italy. Even then, a shipwrecked Carthaginian quinquereme gave them a bonanza of fine points of craftsmanship that had enhanced the 'miracle' of the Roman metamorphosis to sea lords. Their oar work wasn't bad, he thought, but he'd seen better on his own decks, and the ship itself lacked subtleties of pride and challenge that were still hallmarks of Carthage. He saw three white togas descend the gangway and approach the first stage of his terraces. Their walk would take them over flagstone, and then up four terraces that were progressive revelations of Iberian talent in putting terrazzo artistry into broad sweeps of cement. On a projection of the topmost terrace which commanded a view of eastern Iberian waters, and the sea lanes to Carthage, Hamilcar had placed Tanit's standard. For this day's visit, the gold-sheathed disk and crescent device bore two silk streamers, red, long enough to play with the breeze that accompanied the Romans up the walk. Hamilcar's greeting stance was close enough to this proclamation of Tanit to give these visitors a conjunction of Iberia and Carthage that they could stick up their ass, and take back to Rome if extraction was inconvenient before they left.

One of the togas had a purple stripe, the other two were unmarked. Before his visitors reached his level, Hamilcar had seen the calceus, or Roman boot, under each toga—red for the purpled gentleman, brown natural for the plain gentlemen. And as they accomplished the last elevation, he was close enough to see gold rings of the equites, knights, on the right hands of the plains, and none to grace purple's hand. Apart from the stripe, purple was coy about patrician embellishment. This adornment, all in all, showed at least one patrician, probably at least one aspirant patrician. He might get to use his Greek, and caress more than one syllable in a word, in the imminent conversation among fellow diplomats. Purple was frankly the oldest of the Romans, and his eyes, if not his mouth, would be the best target for fashioning the conversation. Hamilcar was unattended at this moment. He was the focus of this visit and he would tolerate no dilution of this focus in the interest of putting a proper presence in the Roman face.

The Romans had stopped about twenty paces from their host. The process of shortening this distance was the first diplomatic chore. Give them enough leisure to let the Roman breaths catch up with the air at this level; give it enough leisure to bring them under more of the Iberian substance that wrapped *this* Hamilcar. This last was the tricky part. They knew he was a soldier—with a long memory—and ass kissing was not his forte. His diplomat was a new man. Use him to shadow his soldier for a while, to imply a comfortable retirement home for his soldier in the Iberian wilderness, away from degenerate Carthage where dangerous ambition could find sustenance. But let the soldier side peek out enough to keep Roman expectations comfortable with this Carthaginian-Iberian in front of them. Hamilcar wore a white tunic with Carthaginian geometric designs worked into the hem and sleeves. But his feet were sheathed in Iberian sandals, and he wore a belt whose leather's qualities and subtle ornamentation in silver picked up these attributes of his sandals. He could sense the enigma of him impressing these Romans, and this made his welcoming smile better for his purposes.

"Pardon my elevation advantage, gentlemen...a slight incident involving a horse made my right leg temporarily unworthy of a *lower* greeting." Hamilcar was true to his statement, he let them erase all of the distance. And they had a good look at Tanit's standard on their way.

"No pardon is needed, Lord Hamilcar. As you would be quick to assert, Roman sea legs are notoriously fickle...we welcome the advent of our proper legs." The unambiguous patrician's insistence of the Roman land presence was well done. With the Carthaginian navy almost a memory, land presence was crucial to containing ambition that might be lurking around these premises. Hamilcar had started speaking in Greek, and the Romans continued in Greek of almost equal quality. The smile on one of the equites suggested the presence of a translator who might not be needed. The patrician introduced himself, his aides, names only, and admitted that Greek was not universal by one of the equites. Hamilcar said that he would see that this man was as well communicated as the others. Then he motioned the Romans toward the villa, formed a couple with the patrician, and began his progress as a host along a flagstone path that his gardeners had garnished with noteworthy examples of Iberian flowers, shrubs and trees. The season, the time of day, and their conjunction with the insistent breeze, brought in a strong aroma of orange and lemon, lime.

"This is no *wilderness*, Lord Hamilcar...a paradise of surprise." The floral touches were enough for the patrician's compliment, but the burgeoning amenities of Hamilcar's villa promised as much as one could find around the seaside playground of any Roman aristocrat from Capreae to Baiae.

"You can appreciate why I'm bound to it, now." Hamilcar didn't bother to test the Roman's face. His point of serious commitment to Iberia seemed to be coming along well.

"What would a famous warrior find *here* for occupation?" In passing, the patrician gestured to a particularly interesting cluster of ferns and flowers that was not indigenous to Rome. His question was a crux point, and it pointed at Hamilcar sooner than he had expected, but the Roman reputation for aggressive curiosity was on the passport of this purpled gentleman.

"He would labor in his silver vineyards, Gaius Publius...to send indemnity to the Romans. You will remember we are under a heavy burden...first 3200 talents of silver...then you kissed us with another 1200 talents...4400 talents over *ten* years." Their walk had been uninterrupted by this summation of Carthaginian ignominy, other floral distractions target enough for the Roman eyes.

They had reached the first outcropping of the villa, a handsomely flag stoned terrace that seemed to wrap all sides. Where they entered it, a ebony wood structure supported both tiled roof areas and open lattices incorporating wisteria and grapes. Large clay pots were a malleable feast of citrus and pomegranate, figs and even dates which the Iberians had succeeded in miniaturizing. Hamilcar led his party through this other paradise surprise for the patrician, toward the reception wing. His answer to the Roman's *occupation* question walked along with the party without reaction until just before they entered the senior structure.

"That is a heavy burden for *one* man, Lord Hamilcar."

"I have tried to make it as pleasant as possible. You have already complimented some of my efforts in that direction." Their walk was now along a teakwood floor that had given Libyan-Phoenician parquet specialists scope for design and realization. The walls were white plaster, some teak or ebony paneled. Pottery and woven hangings, furniture, and occasional rugs where international skills were confirmed in patterns and textures of wool, silk and cotton, attested that Hamilcar's heavy burden was being sustained under conditions of exquisite pleasure and workmanship.

"When you *actually* go toward this burden, where do you go, Lord Hamilcar?"

"We will see some of the mines. Fortunately, with respect to your indemnity, silver is our best product here. We have a little gold, some iron. But it is silver that keeps our noses to your grindstone."

"Again, your devotion to what some of us hold to be unreasonable indemnity will not go unrecorded in Rome." The two equites had been as busy as the patrician filling their eyes with Hamilcar's delicacies. But it was Gaius Publius who was still Hamilcar's target for conversation. Their sporadic eye contact, and eye to face brushes from both directions, had trickled nuances which fed the actor in both men. Silenus had told Hannibal that it takes one actor to know another. Hamilcar had stapled this wisdom into *his* journal long before, and had exercised it under field conditions.

"I am counting on that, Gaius Publius." Hamilcar had not lied about his effort on behalf of the indemnity. Before moving from Gades, the one third share of the silver he had been sending to Carthage had made big inroads on the indemnity. At Akra Leuke, he had reduced friendly tribute to Gades by half and increased Carthage's share proportionately. The Carthaginian Senate's smiles about him had widened since the advance to Akra Leuke, but he could use Roman smiles to cushion his Iberian sojourn. The silver trail—Iberia to Carthage to Rome—was the best possible venue for the smiles, and he would goose these Romans with a dose of silver to send their good report on its way. Silver would also tend to keep Gaius Publius' actor a discreet, reasonable, man.

This was the second time they had seen each other since Inanna's visit to Gades. Akra Leuke is closer to Castulo than Gades, and Hamilcar's connections to the Castulo area—mining and smelting supplies, people and people's supply traffic, bullion transport—were complex enough to accommodate a young swain's occasional visit. It had been six months since their last meeting. Inanna and Hannibal were the same age, but she had gone into dazzling womanhood quicker than he had shed all of his boy, although she was impressed by his progress in *that* direction.

"Is the Roman visit going well, Hannibal?" They were standing on the prominence of rock that gave them a wonderful perspective of the hinterland where the Baetis River was born. Inanna was wearing a white long sleeved cotton blouse of a loose weave that the Iberians had designed to cope with their heat and cold. Her skirt, hand woven of silk and cotton, dark reds and black, was long enough to let it swirl around her black Iberian boots, short enough to give her legs some play in front of a horseman who was already sensitized to the artistic efficiency of certain Iberian products. The cluster of thin silver wires forming the loops for her earrings gave him a tiny flash of sun to compound his image of her.

"Father seems to have everything in hand. He introduced me to them: a patrician and two knights." He wore a white tunic with no colors. A silk scarf tied around his waist put in the color for him, it was purple, and it had come from Mago's inventory of *basic Gypsy—conservative*, under Mago's advice for this visit. His sandals were simple Iberian walkers. He had stepped away from the cavalryman image for this lady, but his *Hellenistic prince* was intact from the neck up. He took her hand and started them along a path that promised some shade in an oak grove after a few hundred paces. A cluster of red blossoms was only ten paces for them.

"Anemones!" Inanna knelt and favored them with some touches and two sniffs. She wore her hair unconstrained this day, and the lustrous black fountain of it spilled over her neck as she bent to appreciate nature's jewels. Once, on the previous visit, when the silk bands that held her hair in the Greek mode had come undone (Hannibal denied responsibility), letting it out like it was now, he was ready to call her some name that would couple beauty, wildness, wisdom, and propensity to horses, something from the pantheon of goddesses, or the Amazons. But his father had preempted the Amazons, and he only got as far as Diana with the other, before she preempted *him*. "I have name enough, now, Hannibal. *Inanna* can cover *all* of your possible situations. I saw a book of father's love poems. I'm afraid he has linked me with a Sumerian love goddess of *very* precocious reputation." So Inanna it was then and Inanna it was now.

He plucked a blossom and put it over her right ear, tucking the hair to give the flower a chance. She didn't need lip rouge. Her lip color, cheeks, all of her he could see was perfect assimilation with this wonderful country that was his father's treasure house. They had kissed in Melkart's precinct's on Gades— only once, and it had surprised her: first for just the occurrence on such short acquaintance and second, for his virtuosity. He'd had practice under a lady of

Carthage's tutelage, but he didn't tell her. They had kissed during his previous visit to Castulo. They had just brought their horses into what she called her corral. They had slipped off their saddles like eels, and their coming together was inadvertent, but they took advantage of it and whether he kissed her—or the other way around—was irrelevant to the action. She had upgraded *her* virtuosity since Melkart, considerably. After the anemone, he moved closer to her. She had toyed with several perfumes before meeting him this day, and settled on only a suggestion of a dab of rose water under her chin, and underneath the ear where he had placed the flower. There was a vestige left for him. Because, before her lips, he had followed her perfume trail from her ear to just below her chin.

"What does this Roman visit mean, Hannibal?" The lady's retreat from an ambitious love goddess was remarkable.

"Your Greek friends between here and Massilia asked them to check up on father."

"Why? My father has said that Hamilcar has made a great success of his Iberian mission."

"The face of *success* depends on who is looking at it. Greeks and Phoenicians, Carthaginians—Romans, are specially good at warping a face to fit their purposes."

"What is their purpose now, for the face your father gives them?"

"Intervention."

"These Romans in my father's house are only the second ones I've ever seen. I don't think *my Greek friends*, as you call them, want them crawling around Iberia...or Gaul."

"Father's reputation has fanned out ahead of him, with many distortions. They are afraid of him. They make the mistake of thinking they would rather cuddle under Rome, than Carthage. Speaking of *faces*, father has said that the closet where the Romans hide theirs would scare *any* Greek who ever labored in tragedy."

"Has your Sosylos showed you any Greek masks—the tragic ones?"

"We've done some plays—Aeschylus, Sophocles...one of Euripides. He has some masks, but we've mostly played comedy with them."

"Your Roman ones would *have* to be scary to exceed the good Greek ones."

"Father has said that the Romans will put a new perspective into tragedy—terror."

He took her hand and moved them toward the grove of oaks. She had made him carry what she called a *bota*, a small skin bag containing some of her father's red wine. When they got to the oaks, and found a bed of moss on the north side of a grandfather tree, they sat down and he made her drink the stream from the bota under his direction. It wasn't a bad moment for him, only a drop missed her lips and he caught it with his lips before it soiled her blouse. She reciprocated the service and didn't make any drops on him. But this was no excuse for abstinence. This kiss was their longest, and they excursioned into new pressures.

"Father told me that Hamilcar's villa at Akra Leuke is beautiful. When will I get to see it?"

"We must be careful in our itineraries now...people are getting suspicious."

"Of *what*?"

He kissed her again. "They think we like each other. They think we will use *any* ploy for our objectives."

"What *are* these objectives, Hannibal Barca?"

"You said that Hasdrubal and Amalkre visited you." He could be an eel in ways that didn't have anything to do with a horse.

"Amalkre is *so* beautiful...and she has almost made me an expert on the Barca family."

"By Zeus!—she wags her tongue too much sometimes."

"She told me that Hasdrubal—*her* Hasdrubal—has more politician then warrior in him."

"He helped father in Carthage when the Hanno faction wanted to kiss the Roman's ass forever."

"Father has mentioned this information. They have not been friends of the Barcas?"

"They are sometimes called the *Peace Party*. They are mostly interested in servicing the landed aristocrats who like the status-quo with Rome. It brings them enough gold without getting into sticky matters—like the *real* future of Carthage. Their perspective doesn't reach further than their gold hoards." He tipped the bota to himself, and then she demanded equal treatment.

"And Amalkre's Hasdrubal?"

"He helped to build the People's Party at Carthage. There have always been concessions to the people in our constitution—he helped to put some heft into their voice. He talked about a Carthage that could be prosperous for *everybody*. Father heard him. They met, and their perspectives seemed to swim together. It was the people's voice that got loud enough to put father on the path to Iberia...with a big push from Hasdrubal." He leaned close enough to set the stage for another kiss. "Amalkre's Hasdrubal, as you called him, helped put me *here*."

"Amalkre said that he can see an empire here in Iberia that might fill out the Barca perspective." Her finger touched the cleft in his chin, moved to the little scar near the corner of his mouth—a souvenir of a riposte that lacked expertise by a hair's thickness. There was a small scar on his neck below an earlobe, another on his chest just below his throat. They had already talked about these before—he could be quite dramatic about them, she could be quite solicitous about them. No words now. His eyes were her target for a moment, the lips and forehead, then the eyes again. The warrior was replacing the boy, but the warrior was beginning to crowd the graceful prerogatives of his Hellenistic prince.

"Iberian empire is not inconsistent with the Barca perspective—oh one who talks to Amalkre." Two could do the finger touching of another's face.

"I can see Prince Hannibal prancing around such an empire...hardly ever mentioning the Romans."

"Is this your Pythian's whisper from Apollo's sanctuary?"

Amalkre had been more explicit in her last conversation with Inanna. She had coupled the statement about Hasdrubal's local political bent with Hamilcar's ambition to play in Roman fields—not a well guarded secret in the Barca councils. These two tendencies were not necessarily mutually supportive of the Iberian continuity Inanna had just put in front of Hannibal. The association of the anemones, of their very recent pleasure, with the blood of Adonis was another aspect of their last moments she would not bring in front of him.

"These are *my* whispers, Hannibal Barca." Then it was her lips that she wanted to put to his full attention.

They started the walk back to her father's villa. They talked about the few adventures that Hamilcar and her father had managed to send their way. They talked about trails that would be good for riders—here, and at Akra Leuke. And there was time between the talk that Inanna used to think about Amalkre playing priestess again—putting material for omens, premonitions in front of her. She knew Amalkre had turned much of this back on herself and that another voice, other ears, were needed to calm her in what must be a wilderness for this Carthaginian princess. Inanna also used the silence to put Hannibal into an Iberian empire where she wouldn't have to share him with the damned Roman specter that seemed to enlarge itself the closer she got to him.

Hannibal reflected quietly on what Inanna had just told him about Hasdrubal, on what he already knew about Hasdrubal—the dichotomy that might be building between his father's ambition for Carthage and Hasdrubal's cast for Iberia that could divert crucial energy and treasure from a desperate game. This girl beside him was also a treasure, and he thought about the conflict between her and this *continuity* business that was pushing him deeper into its mold. His mother had survived a situation like it—she had accommodated it. She and Hamilcar had made a great love out of it, more precious by the fugitive, elusive parts of it. He and Inanna could do this, with the gods', God's, grace on them.

When they entered her father's gate, the Roman inspection party was standing near the veranda that introduced the front of the villa. Hamilcar and her father were blended with three white togas and such of their officers and foremen who continued to serve the inspection. Hamilcar saw them and swept his arm from them to him, an invitation from the Lord General of Iberia which vectored the way for their next steps.

"My son and his riding companion could tell you about more of our secrets near Castulo, Gaius Publius."

"Your own expedition for us in that direction has been most satisfactory, Lord Hamilcar...and this just an *example* of your mining ventures in Iberia" Not a question, an audible note to himself which got Hamilcar's tacit, smiling confirmation.

The Romans got a good look at indigenous beauty when Inanna came closer. The flush of exercise on a classic Greek face that the Romans had seen on Roman copies of Greek marbles, topping frankly Iberian paraphernalia of dress and ornament, gave Gaius Publius another stimulating piece for the enigma that Hamilcar had started. The equites were also not bashful in looking at her beauty. Now Inanna had three more smiles to cope with—Roman.

"Her name?—this riding companion to Prince Hannibal"

"Inanna, Gaius Publius." Inanna's father made the introduction.

The Roman patrician bowed slightly to her. "What a great pleasure, Lady Inanna. Your father has told on some of your Greek secrets...Delphi is one of them, I believe. Have you exercised your oracle here...in Castulo?"

"Your honor is unjustified, sir. Such oracle as I have is for the goats, maybe occasional chickens. Father would *never* tolerate more pretension." Her smile was a masterpiece of mystery that Gaius Publius would remember when he got back to Rome.

"Sometimes we labor over the Sibylline books. Your interpretations could be *most* illuminating." He wouldn't let her off his hook. He had been poking around mines and smelters all day. She was just the invigoration he needed. One day, this Roman and others would dig into these books in panic and they wouldn't like the illumination this friend of Hannibal might have put on them.

"Thank you, sir. But those are even *farther* away from me than the Pythia at Delphi." She turned toward her riding and walking companion who had been a close listener of this exchange between his lady and the Roman patrician who obviously, among his attributes, had an appreciation of beauty and intelligence. "Perhaps Prince Hannibal could make a prediction for you. The coupling between the Etruscans and Carthaginians is famous. There *has* to be some oracle in him." The Roman had started this, she had not backed away. She was very close to a disturbing precociousness, but the smiles around her— Hamilcar's, her father's, the two equites', the purpled Roman gentleman's, and Hannibal's, denied this impudence.

"Prince Hannibal..." The patrician, turning, made the barest perceptible bow to his target.

"I will say that we will meet again, Gaius Publius—perhaps in Rome." Hannibal had picked up Inanna's challenge with aplomb. What the Roman saw in his eyes gave him more meat for the Barca enigma he had been stumbling into ever since he touched land at Akra Leuke.

"I have filled out my honors for this day." The Roman's smile spread around the congregation and it was a fine ending for the day when Hamilcar and the Roman mission patted each other's head.

The Chief of the Oretani Celtiberi had sent Hamilcar an invitation for a parley about setting up mutually satisfactory spheres of influence. An advantage of flat land near where the west to east bound Jucar River was joined by the Cabriel tributary, flowing in from the northwest, had been suggested as a meeting site. The country between Akra Leuke and this site gave few avenues for leisurely travel. A determined native force would have a paradise of ambush opportunities along any conceivable route for Hamilcar as he approached, and then entered, the Jucar valley. This chief, Ambon, was known by Hamilcar's staff to be a spokesman for the network of Celtiberi that dominated the great plateau of central Iberia. In this region, there had been a fusion of prehistoric Iberians with Celts who had drifted into Gaul from the Celtic founts in northern and eastern Europe and then southward into Iberia from Gaul.

Hamilcar had met some of these people before and after the Indortes affair. There had been tenders of conciliation from various levels of their hierarchy which seemed to bow to the inevitability of Carthage in Iberia. Some of these seemed to acknowledge provocation which excused the treatment of Indortes. There had not been much explicitness here. But Inanna's father had given Hamilcar a new Iberian word—*Eldorado*. As applied to this land, this word meant the *golden place*, and the country of the Celtiberi was this to Hamilcar. There were mineral and agricultural bounties there that could complete the foundation for the Iberian steppingstone. Its people were intelligent, artistic— resourceful and brave, according to Hamilcar's own observations and his intelligence network. He had seen enough of their men to know that an infusion of them into his army could be crucial to the strength for his play in Italian fields. So *Eldorado* made the offer of cooperation more explicit for Hamilcar than it really was, and this word also lighted the optimism which invited Hannibal and Mago into his escort.

Hannibal had made impressive progress under his regimen. By the gods, he was close to a cavalry leader now. Mago looked to be Hannibal's studious acolyte and he would soon blend into Hamilcar's strength in the way according to his talents. This expedition would give the boys an example of showing *presence* to the other real power in Iberia. It would be an example of confrontation that would help justify what he was making of them. He hoped that it would do these things under a panoply of unforced mutual respect with the Celtiberi that could make almost a pageant for them—with an inspirational panorama of Eldorado in the background. Conjunctions like this could mark a memory forever—they could nudge a man toward particular destiny.

Hamilcar had ordered a 90-horse escort: 60 Numidian light, 30 Carthaginian heavy, baggage for four days, accoutrements for men and horses to show a presence of Carthage. To accommodate the rough country, the escort was structured in ranks of three: ten of the Numidian advance guard, five of the first contingent of heavy horse, then Hamilcar and his staff, five of the second heavy contingent, ten of the Numidian rear guard. A short baggage train trailed the rear guard. Baggage was usually under closer protection, but Hamilcar didn't want to perturb the beautiful symmetry of his column. Hannibal and Mago rode two ranks behind their father, just in front of the second heavy horse. Hannibal rode the right position of his rank and Mago the left. A Carthaginian heavy cavalryman carrying the standard of Tanit for the column rode between Hannibal and Mago. The standard pole was ebony wood, and the disk and crescent blazed with gold plate.

The Numidians wore tan tunics, braided red rope belts and white cloaks. These men, who were almost centaurs, were barefooted and they controlled their horses by leg pressure and a rein of braided red leather around the neck. Their advance guard was equipped with leopard skin saddle blankets, and their rear guard with lion skins. Small round shields of bull hide, a bronze emboss at the center and a bronze rim, were slung over their shoulders. They were armed with two light javelins and a dagger that hung from a clip in their belt. They had never worn helmets, but Hamilcar had ordered a uniform style for their long braided hair which made plenty of show in lieu of helmets. This spectacular consistency was not usual for his wildly exuberant light cavalry with a penchant for individuality, but Hamilcar had designed a presence into this token force and they were part of it.

The heavy horse was an elite group drawn from Carthaginian aristocrats. Their standard uniform needed no coaching from Hamilcar to make his presence. They wore Greek style helmets, muscular cuirasses over red tunics, and greaves—all armor of polished steel. The white horsehair plumes on their helmets made a good statement between the glistening black heads of the two Numidian formations. Each heavy cavalryman carried a round, bronze sheathed shield and was armed with a long spear and the falcata.

Hamilcar wore the same clothing and armor that had paraded in front of his lady in the forum at Carthage—silver embossed cuirass and greaves, silver mounted helmet, the white under-tunic with Carthaginian decoration. His Sicilian dagger, and the sword from Tyre his lady had given him, completed the outward commander. His sons wore the Iberian heavy cavalryman's white tunic with scarlet ribbing, bronze helmet with cheek guards and bronze breastplate. They each carried a small round bronze plated shield slung over the shoulder. They wore the falcata, but carried no spear. Hannibal and Mago were here by a father's invitation that had been colored more by pageant than menace... although only the gods could know what Hamilcar had put into the private closets of his head about this trip. Every man here of his staff, every Carthaginian cavalryman, carried more than the trappings of pageant into this confrontation with the Celtiberi. Their memories might have been longer than Hamilcar's, but they doubted it. They knew about the *continuity* that rode with them now—and they shared the commander's supplication to Melkart that it *would* be pageant, ceremony, for the education of these young ones. Hamilcar had ordered a token force. The boys, therefore, rode inside a token protective aura.

When this column got into motion, the disciplined power of horses and men fed sound directly to the ears inside it, and the sound was replicated from passing faces of the land with different voices. No exercise, chasing phantom enemies across familiar fields, could ever be like this. Although talk in the ranks was discouraged, Hannibal couldn't help himself. He and Mago rode matched black Iberians, a good contrast with the grays of the Carthaginians. He glanced at the flash of Tanit's standard alongside him, let his look sweep over to Mago.

"Ho Mago!"

"Ho Hannibal!" Mago wasn't diverted from his forward look. The sweep of the column was almost overpowering—the sound, the sights—all of this focused on a shadowy objective their father had called pageant, ceremony. Mago wore the fighting falcata for the first time. Hannibal had complimented him on his progress with the exercise weapons. They had even done some passes together and not all of it had been laughter. Mago had only carried the spear in field work to train his body to balance a weapon under the twists and shocks of cavalry horsemanship. This part of his skill was not so far along, and he didn't envy the Carthaginans' spears.

Hamilcar's silvered armor flashed in front of them in interstices of the column. He had never been in formation with his sons. He had watched their practices, sometimes openly, often from private vantages where a general and a father could come closer together. Hasdrubal was not in this column. He had insisted on a backup column from another direction, but Hamilcar would not let caution intrude upon the pageant, so Hasdrubal was cooling his heels at Akra Leuke. Both Hannibal and Mago were truly sorry about this. Of all their father's men, Hasdrubal was the one to make a pageant to please *any* god.

Their first camp was going to be in an oak grove near a sandy sweep of the Jucar, about two hours ride after they entered the Jucar valley. Hamilcar had ordered colorful tents, striped red and blue, with broad awnings to accommodate the laughter and story telling after the evening meal. When the column entered the valley, Jucar's breath swept them—a compound salutation made partly in its source mountains west of them, and partly in its Mediterranean end to the east of them. Then the sound of the Jucar and the convolutions of the land directing its course started to enfold the column. The veterans in the column savored the invigoration of the air, but the trail the land was giving them was more conducive to alertness than invigoration.

Two hours away from the first camp, from the pageant tents, a Numidian in the front rank of the vanguard spotted a sign of Celtiberi—a quick movement of white against a landscape that had an advantage of height on the column. A strong sun had also put in a flash of steel large enough to be trapped by the animal eyes of the Numidian. He raised his arm in conventional warning and then pointed to his discovery, ahead and to the left of the column. This stopped the column without Hamilcar's order. The shock of the stop rippled through the column in good order, including Hannibal and Mago's rank, which upheld the standard of horsemanship. They couldn't see what had stopped the column. They saw one of their father's officers ride ahead to the vanguard and talk with the Numidian who had raised his arm. This was still a day away from the meeting place. Surely Celtiberi hospitality didn't come out *this* far. The column had stopped in a defile made by the steeply sloped land on its left and a low ridge of rocks it had picked up between the trail and the river.

The sign could mean anything, but Hamilcar didn't want to analyze it from his present disadvantage. He ordered the column forward at a progressive speed and they were at the gallop when they passed below the sign place. The defile narrowed and then they came out of it where the land made a broad sweep to the Jucar on their right, the last hundred yards of it mostly sand and gravel. To their left, the land sloped upwards to a large saddle area between two oak studded hills. This saddle was carpeted with short grasses and wild grain. It was a perfect vantage for hospitality, or cavalry.

In the flux of his reconnoiter as they flowed into the vastly new situation, Hamilcar—by the gods it is *true*—spotted a cluster of red anemones on the hillside below the saddle. *His lady would have smiled here—she would have brought in the Adonis' blood thing again. She had used the word **adon** with him—the last time at Gades, not so far from here.* The Celtiberi were in cavalry only this day. There must have been a thousand of them—the backside of that damn saddle could hide another thousand. They were in informal array. They were in motley dress. Some showed white tunics, but it was a generally motley crowd, showing spears and swords—good horses, mostly blacks and browns. If their leader *was* Ambon, his horse was foremost, flanked by a standard bearer on his left and a lieutenant on his right who seemed to be pointing to various details of Hamilcar's accoutrements and situation.

Hamilcar ordered a stop, and a left face which brought the full files of the column to a fronting of the welcoming party. Mago was now in front of Tanit's standard, Hannibal directly behind it. The nearly vertical sun brought the gold of the disk and crescent into a fine conjunction with the Celtiberi. It was a perfect target for Ambon's lieutenant's own reconnoiter. Hamilcar's silvered armor near it was also a natural focus which seemed to draw Ambon's attention, although subtleties of observation had to be impossible at their distance.

Hamilcar saw that the host looking down on them had none of the graces of hospitality. He was a day's ride from the designated rendezvous, was standing with a token, peaceful force on a ground that gave Ambon every advantage. He had made a schoolboy's mistake in putting optimism over reality. He had, therefore, put his sons in terrible jeopardy. Without turning away from the Celtiberi, he gave an order which flowed right and left to his officers:

"Do not turn away from them. I am going to make two columns, separated where I am now. I will lead the forward column toward the river. Pass the order for the rear column to form a screen around my sons—the heavy horse closest, the Numidians to be front and rear guards. They will do this as soon as I turn to the river. Tell them...tell them to take my sons home by the route we came. I think we are looking at Ambon's full force now...they should be able to brush off anything he has planted along the back trail. Give these orders—*now*. When we are ready—tell me to raise my hand. When my hand comes down, we will separate. I apologize to you for my stupidity. I have been *honored* by your comradeship. The gods grace Carthage! The gods grace every man in this column!" These words were meant for a rostrum, or some vantage of a field that gave decent odds to the speaker. They were spoken in normal voice, but the silence that had been cast by the Celtiberi over the column let the words flow forward and backward for astonishing distances. Hannibal and Mago heard them. And even before the formal orders rippled up and down the column by surrogate voices they were ready to be implemented by veterans who could pull Hamilcar's thoughts from wisps of the air and make execution of them.

"You may raise your hand, Lord Hamilcar." His officer made no whisper. It was a full voice. It accepted no apology for stupidity. It was assimilation with the best commander Carthage had ever put into a field.

Hamilcar raised his hand and shouted, "Forward column—follow me!" Then he whipped his column toward the river. It had gone from rank to file formation in the way he liked and the Celtiberi were treated to a classic cavalry maneuver that had some points of precision and timing Alexander would have envied. The silvered armor left no mystery for Ambon. It was leading the column headed for the Jucar. It was Hamilcar he wanted. And by a shout and a sweep of his arm he sent his cavalry after Hamilcar. Before the front rank of Celtiberi were halfway to Hamilcar's column, the rear column had done Hamilcar's orders and Hannibal and Mago were encased in Carthaginian heavy horse, with lion Numidians in the van and rear. This column had come to a well formed gallop before Hamilcar reached the sands of the Jucar. When it got to the defile where the Numidian had spotted Ambon's treachery, Hannibal turned to the officer near him.

"I must see...*my father*." Before an answer, he broke formation and somehow found a trail for his horse to the top of the little spine of rock that paralleled the Jucar. Mago followed him. From the top, they saw that Hamilcar's column was trying to negotiate a crossing. His leopard Numidians were trying to screen him by an action on the beach and the Carthaginian heavy horse was spread around him in the water, engaging Celtiberi from every quarter. They saw Numidians cut down. They saw Numidian lances work on Celtiberi throats. They saw a desperate tightening around a center of action that had to be their father. A point of silver flashed under a swarm of swords and spears. The overwhelming echelons of Celtiberi cut into the Carthaginian horse until only two of them were at the center, where some silver still sparked inside a storm of steel. Then there were no more Carthaginians, or Numidians. They had spread Celtiberi dead around them on the beach and in the water, and they had been soldiers for Hamilcar. Where the center had been, where Hamilcar had been, a redness was spreading around dead and living men and horses, and then the Jucar started to take it to the Mediterranean where Carthage could look at it.

"Father...*Father*..." It was a scream in their throats, but neither Hannibal, nor Mago could make a sound of it.

"Your father wants you to go now...Lord Hannibal." The officer had come up the rocks to them and had been in the silence that choked the voices. His hand was on Hannibal's shoulder. This officer had been with Hamilcar in Sicily on Mt. Eryx where Hamilcar's forces had been the last Carthaginian bastion against the Italian Wolves, and on the quinqueremes when Hamilcar had played admiral and pulled his gauntlet along the Italian coast from Ostia to Cumae. This officer had told Hamilcar that leaving Tanit's standard on a promontory of the Roman naval base at Ostia would make a good statement—and Hamilcar had let him do the honors with a disk and crescent that they could still see a Roman mile at sea. This Carthaginian had just made another step along Hamilcar's way—it was *Lord* Hannibal, now, and when the gods were ready for him, it would be *Lord General* Hannibal. And he had just put Hamilcar into the *present* tense for his boys—this was the closest coupling he could make between them and the continuity plan that was Hamilcar's poorest secret.

The ride back to Akra Leuke was not silent only because of the speech between the horses, their equipment, and the faces of the land which now used mostly whispers and expected no answers from the riders. Hannibal and Mago were in separate mobiles of pain, where memories, expectations, plans—*unmitigated* shock, churned the faces, the scenes, in front of them in juxtapositions of time which had no logic except almost paralyzing grief. A pageant had disappeared in front of them like a lightning stroke—majesty and blackness interchanged in an eye's blink.

Their connections with their father were different. Hannibal had shown precocity that stepped ahead of his years when frogs and sand castles should have been on the boundaries of his scope. And this precocity had provoked attention from a father whose success had depended on reading potential signs in associates who might hold his life on their spear points one day. The oldest son—this reading of potential—made easy steps to the continuity that Hamilcar had confessed to his lady, and his officer had just confirmed in front of Hannibal. Mago had accepted Hannibal's specialness with the natural grace of an artist trying to fit his talent into some facet of a scene that was in front of him, or other scenes in the niches of his memory. His own precocity could pull laughs, tears, anger, frustration from his father, his brothers and his sister—and his mother who was always the best at reconciling the whole pile of him, for her own use if not on behalf of the rest of the family. Mago would make a useful man for the Barcas. He would ascend to just below Hannibal, be his surrogate when laughter, inspiration, extemporaneous plans and courage were needed from another source.

The remnant of Hamilcar's column that came into Akra Leuke carried the first information of Hamilcar's fate. The lion-skinned Numidian guard was still in pristine pageant condition, but they rode to their compound with an absence of smiles and playful gestures that stuck the first arrows into the chests of the onlookers. The leopard-skinned contingent of the Numidians was now scattered over the hillside above the Jucar, on the sands leading to the Jucar, in the water which moved Numidians, Carthaginians and Celtiberi on an irregular itinerary to the Mediterranean. The Carthaginian heavy cavalry was never lavish with emotion, but the faces of *their* remnant were warped into masks a blind man's fingers could translate. Hannibal and Mago's faces were undistinguished by any accent which could relieve the depression carried by the column Hamilcar had devised for his boys' lives.

Hasdrubal was waiting on the steps of Hamilcar's formal HQ, a compound of single story adobe buildings which connected to his villa via a path his Iberian gardeners were determined to make a surcease for him going to—or away from—his soldier. The Numidians had dismissed themselves, a not shocking breach of formality under the circumstances. Hannibal and Mago were still in formation with the heavy cavalry when the order was given to present to Hasdrubal. They had been in the same file, and now they were side by side in the middle rank facing Hasdrubal. The commander of this vestige of a pageant saluted Hasdrubal, who had prepared himself some time ago to receive the shock of what was left of Hamilcar's token escort.

"I have the...I must report the death of Lord Hamilcar." The officer had made a masterpiece of his face for dispassionate reporting...but he couldn't say any more on his own.

"What happened?" Hasdrubal's look swept to Hannibal and Mago after he had presented the question. By Ba'al's breath—there were no boy soldiers here. *All* eyes were front and center.

"Near high sun, before our first camp, we were confronted by a large force of Celtiberi—all cavalry. They had picked their spot well...we had no chance to escape."

"*You* did."

"Lord Hamilcar gave his life to make that possible. Two columns were made on his command...one for himself...the other for Lord Hannibal and Prince Mago. Lord Hamilcar ordered *our* column to retreat by the way we had come. He would take his column toward the river. On his command we executed his orders...his plan to divert Ambon away from...his sons...was successful."

"Ambon—*he* commanded this treachery?"

"We believe it was he. There was a royal standard beside him."

"I will carve that name into my chest so I can poultice it with his agony. What happened next?" He didn't look at Hannibal or Mago—he *knew* they would still be front and center.

"The retreat of our column was without incident. We stopped at a vantage a little later where we could look back at Lord Hamilcar's column."

"At this time you confirmed the...the death of Lord Hamilcar?"

"We confirmed that his troops were justifying every part that he had put into them. We confirmed a conjunction in the middle of the river that will be perpetual honor for Hamilcar Barca—and Carthage."

"Where were Lord Hannibal and Prince Mago at this time?"

"Beside me...they had preceded me to this...vantage."

"They had broken formation?"

"They had followed their duty, Hasdrubal. At that time, *they* were my commanders."

"To your knowledge, is Ambon still alive?"

"I have no reason to doubt it, Hasdrubal."

"Indortes started this. Ambon will finish it—by Ba'al, I swear this."

"It would be my *greatest* joy to savor the full majesty of this vengeance with you, Hasdrubal—*every* particular second of it."

"Then ration your joys carefully for a little while...I want a *hungry* receiver of them when we meet Ambon again. You may dismiss your company, Captain. I hereby acknowledge receipt of Lord Hamilcar's last message."

They were standing on the veranda which commanded the wonderful view of the sea. Here your thoughts could flow to Carthage, to other parts of dreams. Hamilcar had received the Roman nose-poke mission here. It was twilight of the day that had closed Hamilcar's eyes under the Jucar. No great imagination was needed to find whispers in the northerly breeze that had Hamilcar's accents in them.

Amalkre had left her priestess in her rooms. She wore the simplest white chiton, a braided black silk cord around her waist, no earrings, no headband. She looked like Hamilcar's young daughter waiting for his ship, but her eyes were not appropriate for joy. They still bore the ravages of wild grief that had been made by the young girl, the priestess, the mature woman fluxing in and out of her—*all* of their voices prompting her face, her body motions, during circuits of her rooms that had frightened her handmaidens away. Hannibal and Mago had finally found her and taken her to the veranda. The last Barcas in Iberia managed to make a pool of their grief which seemed to quiet all of them, although no one had tried any words for a long time.

"You are returning to Carthage?" Amalkre looked at Hannibal. Her voice could have been plucked from stages used by Euripides' words.

"Hasdrubal is commander now. He told me that he needed diplomats more than soldiers...that Carthage is where I could put this *extra value* into me." Hannibal's face had been turned away from her and Mago, so the little caress of two words was all the cynicism they got from him. When he turned toward them, he said, "I wanted to be with the punitive expedition against Ambon." His eyes at that moment were the ones that had confronted Hasdrubal, and there had been the first strong tension between them over this Ambon business before he had conceded to the authority that the army, the Senate at Carthage, had confirmed and his father had designed.

"I saw Sosylos talking with you. What did he say?" Mago needed all the comfort he could get, and he guessed that Sosylos might have trickled enough into Hannibal's ears for all of them. He saw the back of his brother's head for a long time, and there was all the silence the Mediterranean breaths would allow.

"He told me that Hamilcar's *continuity* needed service from many sides—apparently, Father had agreed with Hasdrubal." Still no face of him for either Mago or Amalkre.

"About *what*?"

"About *me*! About the damned diplomacy—we're going to kill Romans with *diplomacy* little brother."

"May I put on Zortibas' funny hat, *big* brother? You always admired his prescience—Mother, too."

"Do it."

Mago let his Gypsy imp in long enough to make the motion of putting on the tall conical hat with the Zodiacal signs that the Etruscan, Zortibas, sometimes affected under an ecstasy of his powers. He pulled out the first smiles to be seen on Amalkre and Hannibal in a long time. Hat in place, he said, "An army can find new arms and legs with diplomacy—and it can shrivel into dust without it." No counterfeit Zortibas voice, it was pure Mago. And the simple majesty of the pronouncement shocked Hannibal and Amalkre, and surprised Mago. The shared moments on the flagstones of this outlook had quickened all of them to truthful whispers. The ones that had just been put into Mago's mouth had justified Hannibal's departure. Further along, they could be useful for an epitaph.

"What would be good to say to her, Sosylos?"

"By the gods, Hannibal, I am not your whimpering scribe...looking for an idiot's bouquet to a lady...besides, I don't know her."

"You have seen her...you have heard her voice."

"You presume too much—you compliment my eavesdropping too much."

"You haven't answered my question." The young swain was posed, quill in hand, over a parchment that was destined for Castulo. Pupil and tutor were ensconced on soft chairs on a portico of Hamilcar's villa. Lilac and citrus aromas were conducive to passionate effusions.

"You *do* have a problem of dealing with strong beauty...and she appears to have a mind and a tongue to service it—if my eavesdropping was as good as you seem to think."

"It was. Well?"

"Tell her you have to leave her for a while, that she should be coming with you, but the gods have denied you this pleasure. Tell her that you are leaving to become something of a diplomat, and that if you succeed in this, you will be a much more formidable lover...able to fend off *all* her protests."

"That is not *too* strong?"

"By my gods again, Hannibal...all of those poems—and plays—*have* been wasted on you. She can handle this. She will probably send you a reply that will show you nooks and crannies of a *classical* Greek that will curl your hair—not that it needs more curls."

"How shall I start it?...Dear Inanna...Dearest Inanna...My beloved Inanna... Inanna."

"I like the last. It is simple. It is economical. It paves the way for an ascent into passion that gives you all the latitude you need. If you start *too* fast, you'll be breathless when you should be eloquent and inventive—you will disappoint her. Don't turn her letters into a tutoring for *you*."

A letter was done. After the consultation it had to be a collaborative affair, and from the vocal parts that seemed to be true precursors of the written parts, Sosylos considered it time well spent.

Mago watched the quinquereme take Hannibal toward Carthage. Amalkre had uncovered some of her thoughts for him, later for Hannibal, about her Hasdrubal's ambition—about an Iberian empire that would be glory enough for any man, men, without a Roman addendum. She enlarged on just Hamilcar's ambition, questioned the justification for the Barca presence *here—now*. She had warned Inanna about the sacrifices of Barca women to the war god. Hasdrubal's bent away from Rome might be surcease from the continual blooding on that altar, and such ambition could be served from the powerful—and civilized— vantage of Carthage. Iberia was accessible from there. Powerful ligaments serving *all* the parts of peaceful ambition could be strung between Iberia and Carthage. Hasdrubal was already a people's hero at Carthage. This was a step toward his ambition that he didn't have *here*—Hamilcar's blood spilling down the Jucar was proof of this, and this scene was now a true part of the clouds of omens that had filled her with the faces of her family even before the expedition to the Jucar. But in her private moments with Hannibal a few hours before his quinquereme, it had been mostly memories of Carthage for their talk—spoken and unspoken: the lady who had played Amazon and Carthaginian queen for them, a handsome Lord General who had played the full father for them, a princess girl who had played priestess pretensions around the heads of her brothers and made them her acolytes when she could stop them laughing. The omens hadn't intruded her Hannibal goodbye, but play acting had been in their repertoire before. During their final kiss she tried to pack him into her memory, just like another lady and another kiss—under Gadesian Melkart's aura.

During *their* goodbye, Hannibal had told Mago to be a good student in Hasdrubal's school. "We will play in the Italian fields together, little brother," he said just before the belly slap that put an end to the goodbye. As Hannibal's quinquereme became smaller on the path to Carthage, Mago *had* to put Hannibal into Amalkre's revelations, extrapolations, about her husband. Hannibal's *we* had made room for him—Mago, on a broader stage, also room for a Hasdrubal—brother, or brother-in-law? When the quinquereme went over the horizon, Mago knew that it was Hannibal who had already answered that question for their father.

6

23 years
224 BC—Carthage

The column of matched grays, Cyrenians, spirited devils to match the Carthaginians riding them, threaded through a rocky pass that tested the consistency of the three file formation. When it got to the edge of the plain where the bay of Tunis could be seen, and the great wall that Carthage had laid across the isthmus on the horizon, formation and speed were easier. But the leader on the right file, and his second in command on the left file, kept everything in order.

"Not bad for a bunch of foppish dilettantes, eh Hannibal?" Hasdrubal, the left file leader, didn't turn toward his subject, whose smile might be too hard to analyze anyway.

"I object for the whole damn column, Hasdrubal—Hannibal's opinion, or not." This had rumbled toward the front rank from a rearward horseman. They were all of an age, 18 to 24, from the first families of Carthage, too young to go with Hamilcar, to young to die with Hamilcar. This class favored the cavalry because they had easy access to good horses. They had estates where they could chase each other. They could bring up a wind on a horse that made a great stage for shouting their bragging, and for sheltering miscellaneous transgressions.

Hannibal recognized the objection. "I *also* say not bad for a bunch of dilettantes," he said, putting in the right name. He swung the column toward the blue target of the Bay of Tunis and then he settled it in a conservative canter toward Carthage.

"For the gods' sake, Hannibal, can't we have some *faster* fun? We'll be through the damn gates in a moment."

Hannibal didn't recognize this voice, but he tossed an answer into the air and let it take its chances. "We will show some discipline. We don't dress like a cavalry—but we'll act like it. Incidentally..." this time he turned his head enough to give his voice to the whole column of 30 riders, "you people are starting to *look* like cavalry. I liked your formations back on the Bagradus. You could probably scare some Romans, if not the Numidians. That's progress." Their uniform was a white tunic, black and red braided leather belt, Carthaginian style heavy cavalry black boots, floppy, broad-brimmed white linen hat with black leather chin strap. Some had stuck a white ostrich tail feather into their hat band. Because of the hats, somebody had called them Hannibal's Mushrooms, but the hats *were* his idea and the clothing people at the armory had put his sketch into a reality that pleased him and the other Mushrooms. These hats had a way of popping up in non-cavalry ways around the precincts of Carthage where young bloods wanted to impress the opposite sex of various hierarchies. Hannibal himself didn't exploit the hat for this purpose, but his brother Hasdrubal and most of the others could play the unofficial cavalier to the hilt under the right provocation. Hannibal's name was getting into conversation around Carthage as much as Hamilcar's. Being one of his men—Mushrooms, or not—put extra swagger into a man that was an appreciating asset.

This troop of his peers was part of Hannibal's military time since he had returned to Carthage. On the field trips, they would practice formations he had learned in Iberia from Maharbal, the Numidians and the Iberians. They would study battle sites—where the Spartan Xanthippus had defeated Regulus' Romans at Tunes, where Hamilcar had trapped the mercenaries near Utica and then the denouement in the defile near the bay of Tunis where he had ended the bloody insurrection. Maharbal had put *cavalry terrain* sensitivity into him, had quickened him to land and infantry dispositions that could put the right kind of cavalry into a terrific advantage over troops handicapped by habit, sterile practice, and command arrogance not responsive to opportunity or innovation. At the right conjunctions of terrain and memory, his Mushrooms had to scramble to keep up with his stream of consciousness instruction, but he was making cavalrymen out of them. They had no weapons yet, but without what he was giving them, weapons could be only collectibles for the grave details.

The other part of his military time at Carthage was spent in the great armory workshops inside the system of walls around Carthage that made Roman claims to precedence in massive military architecture and innovative construction totally false. The battles with the Greeks in Sicily, with the Romans in the First Punic War, and Carthaginian panoramic inquisitiveness, had filled their archives with samples of the evolution of weapons and armor. A man looking to analyze and critique this evolution could find an unparalleled museum and laboratory in the Carthaginian armories. Hannibal, alone, and later with Hasdrubal, worked with Carthaginian men and officers. Most of these men were Hamilcar's veterans, the nucleus of strength he had left for Carthage. There was talk, argument, cajoling, testing, until they had discarded the archaic from the new promise that gave guidelines a commander and his armorers could use for another day. Celtic and Iberian weapons were also represented. Against targets for a broadsword, Hannibal proved that the Roman laughter about Celtic swords withering on good Roman helmets and shields was outdated. The European

Celts had obtained ingots of high quality iron from Asia Minor and their iron wizards of La Tène had learned how to copy this iron, and further to make steel of it. It was forged and tempered until it became a sword blade that could cleave Roman armor. He already knew about the Iberian falcata and the straight cut and thrust sword of the Celtiberians. Some halls under the Carthaginian battlements rang with the sound of steel on steel, the laughter and cries of fencing, the diagnosis of contests between men with weapons that usually had either Hannibal or Hasdrubal mixed up in it, often both at the same time.

Sosylos had come to Carthage with Hannibal. He still played the tutor, but he was also usually at the place where some of Hannibal's thoughts on weapons and tactics were put on parchment, or papyrus. The word *pretentious* never occurred to him. *Precocious*—he had almost used this word up on his charge, this Hannibal Barca who had obeyed the other Hasdrubal's order to put more diplomat into himself, but not leaving any of his soldier behind. Silenus had remained in Iberia as Hasdrubal's liaison with the Iberian Greeks. He had not forgotten his Hannibal Chronicle. Silenus had charged Sosylos with keeping good notes on Hannibal, and Sosylos was now trying to keep his Greek hyperbolical tendencies in line with his laconic Spartan when it came to reporting on this shade of Hamilcar who rode his Mushrooms into exhausting lessons, beat ideas and weapons on Hamilcar's veterans—when he wasn't studying diplomacy in the public buildings, forums, and streets of Carthage.

Sosylos' responsibility to Hannibal Barca, levied by the Lady Barca with Lord Hamilcar's grudging concession, also had Inanna parts. There was a moment between the diplomat and the soldier that came on a veranda of the Barca palace at Carthage with a Mediterranean vantage, at the time of day when sunset-colored clouds and whispers of a western breeze could turn a susceptible man's head toward Iberia.

"She says that she will be a withered old hag before you see her again." Sosylos had just finished reading Inanna's latest letter to Hannibal, who had handed it to him without comment, and he had already acquired the westward look even as the letter settled into Sosylos' hand. Sosylos was not given to recapitulation until completing his reading, but a crucial point had arrived early in the reading. He looked at Hannibal. Hannibal's face was not accessible, directed as it was toward Inanna. Sosylos dug into the letter again:

"She threatens to hide in a wine amphora on one of the big freighters and come to Carthage." This slid along with Sosylos' reading.

"She would be a *drunken* old hag if she did that—of no possible use to me when she got here." The Hannibal head was still westward bound, but he *had* been listening.

"The big distance between you puts extra facility into your words, Prince Hannibal, also it seems to help your bravery—I wouldn't want to use those words in front of her."

"Do you like the sketch she put in of herself?"

"It shows more of the Pythia than I remember...possibly in a late stage of the smoke from the bay leaves. The hair shows some wildness and the eyes and mouth in accord with all of this. This is a woman who will not suffer your procrastinations much longer, my prince."

Hannibal gave up the outward far away orientation and sat on the marble bench alongside Sosylos. "I cannot take responsibility for this procrastination. She *knows* the constraints on me."

"In your last letter, did you tell her that your diplomat was coming along?"

"I said that I have made a fool of myself in the forum, on at least two streets leading to the citadel on Byrsa Hill, in the Hall of the Council, and almost in the Hall of the People's Assembly."

"That style doesn't fit with the innovative, passion-drenched swain that I've tried to make for you. No wonder this letter lacks her standards in wit, humor, and innuendos tending to Aphrodite." Sosylos put the disappointing letter on the marble bench.

"I will strive toward your swain next time, Sosylos. Did you have her other letters bound?"

"You asked for soft goatskin binding, well sewn to withstand *frequent* perusal. I have had this done. The letters made two volumes...we are ready to start a third."

"I wonder what she has done with *mine?*"

"Didn't she say, about three letters ago, that they made excellent archery targets?"

"She didn't say what her arrows did with them."

"I remember something about them doing *very* well when she could put your face on the target. As I said, you are dealing with a classic Greek here—maybe some Spartan infusion we haven't known about, or she has not confessed."

"She's too playful for a Spartan."

"Do you remember our talk about Tyrtaeus and Alcman?"

"Your Spartan poets...I remember. They tugged at different parts of your precious historical image."

"Go on, we're making progress here."

"It was Alcman who jerked *my* images around. He got his inspiration from a lyrical, artistic...*sensuous* Carthage. Perfumed acolytes of Terpsichore are hard to balance against the *invincible* hoplites you've been pushing into my face."

"I tell you...*both* of these are in the truth of Sparta. And I rest my case that the fair Inanna may very well be a present consummation of them. Spartan antecedents have a nasty way of trickling into Greek strains, even those shadowed by the Pythian Apollo at Delphi."

Hannibal stood up, walked to a balustrade, and picked up his Carthage-Iberia axis again. "So, where do we stand on this? She has been using me for her archery target. She has threatened to pack herself into an amphora so she can surprise me on the quay—here! I am confused."

"You are besieged by a classic Greek woman. Your mother seems to appreciate her. I suggest you resign yourself to your very good fate and devote more time to diplomatic work...you will need *that* part of your considerable talent with her."

The consecration to the people's will and voice in the forum of Carthage lacked the expanse of Athens', or Rome's. It was crowded between the military and commercial harbors and the Byrsa Hill. The long, narrow central plaza was broken by fountains and pillars celebrating Carthaginian history, a cavalcade that invariably had the sea, seamen and ships put into the bas-reliefs and fuller carvings to this memory. Taking *largeness* in the respect of architectural scope, quality and artistic presence of construction, the weight of the words sounding inside their walls, the *larger* buildings were on the Byrsa side of the plaza. The Hall of the Council was here, also the Chamber of the Sufets and the offices of the pentarchies.. When officially occupied, the essential government of Carthage was in these buildings—the Council of one hundred and four senators for the decisions on politics, economics, military operations; the sufets for legal decisions affecting citizens and various amalgams of citizens with foreigners; the pentarchies (five men squads) for the hands-on implementation of Council and sufet decisions affecting greater Carthage and her protectorates.

Temples and colonnaded plazas crowned Byrsa Hill. Some of these structures spilled over the crest toward the forum on terraces where a Carthaginian variety of beautiful plants, flowers and trees in both formal and luxuriantly rampant designs, accentuated the structural continuations and eventually came around to the roofs of some of the buildings in the forum. The Hall of the Council building had some of the qualifications for an acropolis. The portico of Corinthian columns along its full length was done in Athenian Pentelic marble. This building was one of the beneficiaries of the crowning from Byrsa Hill, and some of its Corinthian capitals were garlanded with bougainvillea. The interior walls were either marble, or Egyptian syenite, a gray rock with feldspar scintillations, depending on the designers' caprices in playing sunlight, or lamplight, or torch-light to aesthetic advantage. All doors, light fixtures and braziers were gleaming bronze. The principal interior decoration was terrazzo, done with shaped glass and marble pieces in a matrix of Carthaginian invention. Mythical story episodes, mostly sea-bound, with appropriate water creatures and human intruders, were the subjects of terrazzo art that had no precedence in Greece, or Rome. This was displayed in sections for occasional relief of the predominant marble on the floors and walls. The building comprised offices for senators and staff, a central chamber for the full panel of senators, a smaller one for a special nucleus of thirty five senators, an inner committee of the Council to which supreme decisions in all Carthaginian matters, except law, had a tendency to gravitate. In both of these audience chambers, the only sitting provision was for the senators, an array of marble benches whose accommodation to the human behind encouraged short speeches and shorter entreaties. The benches had a generous elevation advantage over the supplicants' arena. Long, narrow windows in both audience chambers were covered by Phoenician-Carthaginian triumphs in flat glass manufacture, presumably an inducement for illuminated proceedings.

Although the Carthaginian constitution had bowed explicitly to the people, and had drawn admiration from Plato that surprised both him *and* Carthage, the people's voice in Carthage had been mostly loosely woven whispers, rarely a concerted, sustained, majority that could penetrate the Council, or the sufets' sanctuaries. The pentarchies who came to real grips with administrative details were closest to the people, by necessity, and sometimes the whispers lingered longer with them to some effect.

The Hall of the Assembly of the People was, therefore, not on the Byrsa side of the forum. Building-length steps led to a portico whose columns bore Egyptian date-palm capitals. The columns were plastered and painted pink veined green to simulate Sicilian marble. The bulk of the building was made of pink sandstone from the quarries at Cap Bon. The interior was an unpretentious, scaled down copy of the principal auditorium of the Council. Stadium style seats faced a plain arena where a walking speaker, or a small, less active congregation could be accommodated. It was situated directly across the forum plaza from the Hall of the Council, without the intervening grace of a fountain, or the inspiration of an inscribed pillar. A citizen stepping into a high noon from its shadowed portico would face the intimidations of North African sunlight and the presence of the Council Chamber simultaneously. A packet of dreams could come undone quickly here.

Hannibal was standing in the plaza, between the People's Assembly and the Council buildings. He was facing in the direction of Byrsa Hill, the strongest sector of the Greek, Mesopotamian, Egyptian, Phoenician, Carthaginian synthesis swarming around him.

What did the Carthaginians think would happen to this dream of marble and bronze, the magics of their botanicals, if the Roman boots tramped into here? The Italian Wolves had virtually no art of their own. They had copied the Etruscans, the Greeks, the Easterners, the Celts, *everyone* who could show them what do with stone and marble and gold, ivory, bronze...all of the ligaments between the artist, the artisan, the architect and the creation. They had made a politics, a diplomacy, of destruction and then the metamorphosis to the Roman form from the useful ruins. His father had seen this disgusting vision for this forum, for Carthage entire. He had died on *his* mission to prevent it.

Sosylos, Silenus, his mother, Zortibas, Acherbas, and now Inanna, had put him into this forum perspective as a thoughtful man with Greek sensibilities. His father had put him into it as a thoughtful man with a soldier's, and a soldier administrator's, sensitivities. The words he had just listened to in the Council chamber still stuck to his ears. He had come as an implicitly invited monitor of its proceedings, a Carthaginian aristocrat as a son of Hamilcar Barca, therefore a qualified monitor, and participant in any conversation the senators deigned to make in the public parts of their precincts:

"The *Iberian Colony* of the late lamented Hamilcar Barca seems to have put on even more pretension lately."

"What are the *latest* whispers in the western winds from that place?"

"Hasdrubal has had coinage made with his image...and there appears to be assimilation with Melkart there."

"There are some precedents for this...on the verge of imperial ambition, I think."

"The esteemed senator perhaps is recalling Alexander of Macedon."

"Hasdrubal has read his Greek history...perhaps some of it—near to Alexander—has stuck to his ambition."

"Speaking of Hasdrubal's coinage: we understand that over one half of the silver from the Baetis mines is now spilling into his vaults at Carthago Nova."

"Carthago Nova—New Carthage! If we are looking for pretension this is all we need. Have the implications of this *New Carthage* been explored?...I've been away to Alexandria."

"Hasdrubal took some steps backward from Hamilcar's HQ at Akre Leuke and put a new jewel into our crown—his New Carthage!"

"I wonder if *backward* is useable here. We hear that he has consolidated his positions with the Iberian tribes, building on, enlarging, Hamilcar's scope at the time of his...accident. Also your *our* has some ambiguity sticking to it—does it have as much Carthage as Hasdrubal in it?"

"From the glimpses I've had of the administrative traffic between

Hasdrubal and Carthage, I would have to conclude that *independence* is a word he has trouble keeping out of his head, mouth, and off his quill."

"I've borne more than a glimpse of this traffic, also some second-handed interceptions of his traffic with the Africans around the Straits...and some southward along the African Atlantic coast—I could make a tempting morsel of *empire* out of all of this."

"My friend confuses *morsel* with *monument*, or perhaps *major monument*—which is what the Iberian Peninsula plus the African tendencies would make."

"Monument to Carthage...to Hamilcar...to Hasdrubal? One wonders about the dedication here."

"There are rumors that, when he planned his palace at Carthago Nova, he consulted with Eastern experts so that Babylon and Nineveh would be *more* than faded memory in his part of Iberia. Have you seen it, Prince Hannibal?"

Hannibal's clothing and position on the marble tiles of the auditors' arena were not conspicuous. But he had been noticed, and now he had been officially recognized. The senator's question jerked him out of his private reveries centered on aspects of Iberia that hadn't been in the stream of consciousness conversation that had just pointed at him.

"No, sir, I haven't seen it. It was built after father's...after I returned to Carthage."

"And an unambiguous ornament to us you have been since that time...a veritable reincarnation of Hamilcar...a *young* Hamilcar."

"My father left many footprints around Carthage. I've stepped on the *edge* of a few of them—nothing more." Hannibal bent his diplomat's head.

"We would like to hear some of Prince Hannibal's perception of his brother-in-law, Hasdrubal. Despite the five years he has honored us here, in Carthage, away from the *direct* visions of greatness, he must have some observations."

This statement came from the elder Hanno, Hamilcar's principal rival for military authority before the Mercenary Revolt, and still the chief spokesman for the aristocratic oligarchy, the basis of the Peace Party in Carthage, whose major tenet was opposition to any form of revenge against Rome for the military and economic disasters of the First Punic War. Although they paraded this philosophy in the guise *of let well enough alone*, actually the status quo they had orchestrated with the Romans had improved their aristocratic status in all the important respects.

Before this Council, Hanno had tried to have Hamilcar tried for treason, accusing him of causing the Mercenary Revolt by his military policies in Sicily. About this time, Hamilcar and Hasdrubal—*Amalkre's* Hasdrubal—came together, and Hasdrubal's politicking on behalf of the people paid off in a rare instance of public outcry against Hanno's patently false charges. Hamilcar's genius had, in fact, saved Carthage from a bloodbath the mercenaries could have made *inside* her walls. Hanno was discredited, but not acted against in the usual Carthaginian sense of a crescendo of agony prior to crucifixion. Hanno managed to retain his status as senator and gadfly of Hamilcar's Iberian campaign and continued to nurture his own ambitions.

When Hamilcar was killed, Hasdrubal became Hanno's logical focus. His present attention to Hamilcar's son and heir apparent had been delivered from a rear, off-center, position of the senators' benches. Some vocality, with a nice shading of diffidence, was the way he liked it. He had a son, his namesake, who was taking notes. Hannibal hadn't changed his position on the marble arena under this new limelight cast by Hanno. The address of his head that he'd used to answer the first Hasdrubal question was good enough for Hanno's, so he put his answer into a beam that was well received by Hanno, but made him only a peripheral target.

"My lord Hanno's compliment to my memory, my place on the Iberian hierarchy...and my access to General Hasdrubal's head is unreasonably gracious. I remember Hasdrubal as my father's friend, and my friend. My last sight of him was when he took a punitive expedition against Ambon."

"This retribution was successful, I recall" This was the first senator again, a better target than Hanno for Hannibals' voice.

"My father's body was not recovered. Ambon's *was*."

"You have your father's gift for succinctness, Prince Hannibal. Ambon is the Celtiberian chief responsible for Hamilcar's death?"

"He *was*."

"He is not Hasdrubal's prisoner, now?" The Council's information lines between Carthage and Iberia were good. But it didn't know enough about Hannibal's.

"For an hour, or so, he was. Then—in front of his own headquarters— Hasdrubal made him pay for his treachery to my father."

"By his own hand?"

"I believe that Ambon received the full ministrations of our executioners...a *virtuoso* performance played before the remnants of Ambon's forces."

"This tells us about Hasdrubal's capacity for vengeance. What can you tell us about his capacity for *emperor*?" This was Hanno.

"I believe everything he has done in Iberia has been consistent with my father's plans. The silver, the part that stayed in Iberia, has been mentioned. It has gone to build our strength there...recruiting and training of Iberians, and now Celtiberians, the production and refinement of weapons. The diplomacy will expand the scope of this to the entire of our Iberia."

"That *our* word again. How do you use it, Prince Hannibal?"

"*Carthage* is how I use it. That is how my father used it—it is how Hasdrubal uses it."

"You have shown us a glimpse of a formidable army being stirred from the pieces your father took to Iberia, from what he found there and from what Hasdrubal has found there."

"I believe my father left for Iberia with the Council's cachet as a *military* man—*not* a farmer, or trader. I repeat my belief, Lord Hanno, that Hasdrubal's progress has been consistent with my father's mission. If he has put an imperial cast on his house and headquarters, then I believe it is in *this* service—imperial Carthage, *not* imperial Hasdrubal."

"Five years away is not good for a *present* perspective. You have been listening to us today, Prince Hannibal. We wondered about another word... *independence* that seems to be sticking to your friend, General Hasdrubal... and then that word...*imperial* seems to come right along with it. You see how little things like this can get us excited?" This was another senator.

"There has to be as much administrator, as general, in Hasdrubal, now. I think his tendencies to independence are to expedite the administrator. My father told me about some of his problems in Sicily, and his solutions. Iberia is farther from Carthage than Sicily. I think Hasdrubal is *still* looking at my father's plans...and experience."

These, *his*, were the last words he remembered from the Council meeting of that day—they trailed him into the forum plaza, into the sheen of an African sun that could boil the bullshit from words and put a man's face close to Reality's. He had been in the arena of the full Council many times since his father's death, as a spectator and listener, then an occasional speaker when a comment was tipped his way. When the questions started coming to him—about his obvious interest in military affairs, the Mushrooms that he had whipped into the best cavalry around Carthage, the weapons survey and testing and practice and some evolution that he was doing in the bowels of the armories inside the walls—then *his* diplomat got more practice. He had pulled his foot out of his mouth a few times, made some answers that Sosylos approved, and, on balance, had gradually put together a packet for a diplomat—grace under provocation, some facility in turning a question toward his competence, toward better stages for his opinions. Sosylos had made Inanna a proving ground for this new part of him.

Today, they had tried to put Hasdrubal in his face. They reveled in the silver stream that came to them from Iberia, but they worried about the dedication of any empire centered there. Hamilcar's Roman obsession—how to balance this empire against the vestiges of this obsession: what did he know about this, suspect about this? He and Mago had kept a line of communication open that wasn't in today's stream of consciousness from the senators' benches. Mago had dug deeper into the diagnosis of Hasdrubal's regime than anyone did today and his recent letters diluted some of the compliment of Hasdrubal that he had just rolled in front of the Council. But in the last years Hasdrubal had been closer to his father than any man. If he had to shave the compliments, the Hall of the Council that usually contained the Hannos would be the *last* place he would do it.

The word, Romans, hadn't come up from either the benches or the arena today. It was on the tip of Peace Party man Hanno's tongue. It was in the mouth of every other senator, and it may have been close to birth at some of the mouths near him in the arena. But if *one* word could be put on Hamilcar's purpose in Iberia—on the deathly frustration on the Jucar that intruded the final image of his lady—it was Romans, *Romans*. And this word *would* be sounded here another day, with, or without, Hannibal Barca standing in front of it.

She had taken a sudden detour from the regular trail and now she was ahead of him, a wonderful maturity of a woman, clad like a Celt cavalryman, a blend with her white stallion that *any* cavalryman would have liked. She had left her hair long to keep Tiba and Maga in practice, and because the years had put nothing in it that offended eyes, or a finger's caress by the women and men of her life. It was unfettered today—it was the streamer of her challenge to her soldier son who had just put his Cyrenian gray into high gear to catch her. Then they rode almost boot to boot to the top of a hill that overlooked much of the Barca estate at Hadrumetum—and eastward of them, beyond sight but never memory, the Maltese Islands rode in the Mediterranean's blue panorama, and northerly a little, Sicily. Landside, the ranges of grapevines and olive trees climbed from the sea in terraces and then took the conformation of the hills and flatland in a sweep of the agricultural power that was a bulwark of the Barca family and part of Carthage's crown.

She got down from her horse, a graceful dismount that close coupled her to Hamilcar's *Hippolyta*, and also put her close to the soldier who called her, mother. Celtic checkered cavalryman's trousers clustered over black riding boots near the ankle, a black belt of Iberian leather segments linked and clasped by Iberian silver, a long sleeved white cotton shirt, and then a loose leather chin strap around her throat held the hat she wasn't wearing against her back. When she was an arm's reach from Hannibal, she put the hat on her head, gave quick tugs in two places that put *her* logo on the hat. Then, head back, the murmurs of the Mediterranean memories on her face, part of the Phoenician, Greek,

Etruscan enigma of beauty, impishness and intellect of her in front of him, she said,

"Is *this* enough cavalryman for you?" Her hands were on her hips, her boots stood apart in an active stance.

He pretended a commander's survey of the recruit, toe of boot to top of hat. It was a model of his Mushroom hat, sized for her by his guess, and a lucky fit, made by one of the craftsman in the armory. He didn't wear his today, but he was in the Mushroom uniform otherwise. He didn't say anything, but he stepped toward her and put a kiss on her lips before he got back, quickly, to his pose. "Much too beautiful for a cavalryman, they would all follow you to hell—and where would I be, then?"

"I doubt this is dispassionate inspection. I hope you don't interview *all* your recruits this way." She took his arm and they led their horses to where a kind of gazebo had been made for hikers, or riders, to tarry, made of pine wood with still enough freshness to put the right perfume into their air. A view of Barca agriculture was still there as they stood in the shade of the gazebo.

"You have made a paradise here." Hannibal's look had just swept from the Sicilian direction to the mosaic of vines and trees below them. Sometimes with *her* Hasdrubal in company, they had walked and ridden over all of the Barca estates in the five years of his visit: Hadrumetum; the plantation near Thuburbo Majus in the drainage of the Bagradas river where cereal grains— wheat, barley, corn, maize—were grown on the largest scale in Carthage, also flax to feed the spinning and weaving mills for the Carthaginian linen that now was rivaling the best Egyptian; the estate on Cap Bon, near Neapolis, where figs, dates, apples, pomegranates mingled with more grape vines. The Barca wine was made at both the Cap Bon and Hadrumetum sites. The shipping amphorae for it bore the lightning slash of the Barca's, like the sail emblem that had lead Hamilcar into Gades.

"Hamilcar made a paradise here...I've just tried to keep it going." Lady Barca was too modest. She was the core of it and had been since the day the messenger had brought her the news of the death of Hamilcar. It filled her being and crowded out the sorrow of his loss. She had overseers, managers, crew chiefs, clerks, scribes, lawyers, engineers, to help her—and Libyan, Egyptian, Numidian, Sicilian, Greek, Tyrian Phoenician and Carthaginian threads in her workers' tapestry. Some of them were Hamilcar's veterans, a few were Hamilcar's prisoners, most were immigrants to Carthage drawn by the agricultural virtuosity that the Carthaginian, another Mago, had formalized in his treatises on this subject. There were no slaves on the Barca estates, although some had come to them in that status. *Satisfaction in the life, satisfaction in the work* was one of the Lady's tenets and her foremen had reason to know she meant it.

"I need my *own* continuity, Hannibal Barca." She didn't look at him, but she had just put the essence of the remainder of her life into words. Mago was already in Iberia. Hasdrubal was here. Hannibal was here. But *Hamilcar's* continuity was standing next to her, and she had seen a comet blaze across the night from her private veranda at Carthage that she could take into this moment. This young man man next to her was a special gift of the gods, God, and Hamilcar—*like that comet.* He could pull Hasdrubal and Mago into his orbit and there would be no continuity for her to talk about. He was the focus of this thing that now intruded most of her...the dreaming, and now the waking parts of her, so he was the logical focus of her statement of need.

She had seen more of his metamorphosis to the soldier when he returned to Carthage. Several new scars and a cast to the eyes took them further away from the boy and the man she could use for *her* continuity. He was now taller then she, muscles honed to a cavalryman's form. His poise and handsomeness moved him closer to a Greek than a Phoenician. Sosylos, Silenus whom she hadn't met, earlier tutors, his own curiosity and intellect, had also moved him closer to the Greek ideal of *international man* than most of the Carthaginians she could name. She had never heard Hamilcar's misgivings about putting killing steel into his son's hand. But she had come close enough to it with her own thought, and she had just vocalized part of it.

"Father said that he would return from Italy, and be part of the Nova Carthago *here.* I swear to you I will do this"

"Hamilcar died even before Italy, the Romans. You should do your swearing in front of powerful gods, Hannibal—not me."

"You saw Father's Hercules at Melkart's precincts in Gades. He is a good one to swear before, I think. *He* survived some bad missions."

She came close to him, touched his cheek with a finger, let it rove down to the corner of his lips, then the cleft in his chin. Then, for an instant, they touched their lips.

"I *do* have a place here for such a disciple. If you can get close to your father's Hercules again, tell him about *that.* Perhaps he can let you spare some time for me." Her actress had been part of Hamilcar's entrancement. Her actress had just kissed her son.

No word about the sessions, planned and inadvertent, with Acherbas and Zortibas that had put more omens, visions, prophecies into her, a sometimes unleashed phantasmagoria now that Hamilcar's calming had gone forever. When Hannibal came to the palace at Carthage five years before, she had asked him if he had been with his father when he was killed. He said that he had been in Hamilcar's column and that he had been swept away by a protective cocoon when Hamilcar divided his forces to save his their lives—Mago's and his. Did you see *anything*, she'd asked. "I saw father die in the middle of a river, surrounded by dead Celtiberians," he had replied. This was all they had said about the end of Hamilcar, the beginning of a continuity that endangered *hers*, a step closer to the mouth of a vortex that could spin her anywhere.

Hannibal was now 23 years old. He was still a virgin in the sense of probing his full physical satisfaction from a woman, although from the time he lost interest in teething toys, his mother, her friends and servants, had not denied him mostly exterior knowledge of the female form. Taking a kiss sometimes beyond its decorous perimeters had been in this repertoire. Opportunities were not his problem. The raw material for them, for his follow-up decisions, had been in Iberia as a young man, and back in Carthage as a man with impeccable credentials as an aristocrat, a conversationalist with international flavor and the leader of the Mushrooms who themselves spread a powerful aura over eligible and aspirant eligible females of every rank. He was handsome in the way of a Hellenistic prince who had already ventured outside the philosopher's gardens into realities that put a commander's mark on him. A few scars, well placed around such a face, were *no* handicap to such opportunities. It had to be something to do with priority of passions. His view took in a broad spectrum that had settled on no particular priority. He liked women, but until Inanna, special interaction with them had just not occurred—Carthaginian custom strongly to the contrary.

His father had seen some imbalance in the Iberian curriculum, and he had played a father's card with the opportunity of Inanna, several times. The quality of her conjunctions with his son had also relaxed some of his own obsession a little. Before the Jucar River jerked savage memory out of the convenient shadows, Hamilcar had, in fact, been a better balanced man because of Inanna.

In one of her recent letters, Inanna had surmised that Hannibal was now a connoisseur of debauchery, at the least *well* schooled in the chemistry, physics, and the *mechanics* of love. Her arrow had not hit a bull's-eye and Sosylos knew this in the thousand ways of the close tutor, but he had been silent on this subject that had suddenly made a presence.

"By the gods! This is insufferable! She...she takes too much under her wing with this."

"I warned you, my prince. You are dealing with a classic Greek here. They are frank in their appetites, in their appraisal of appetites and in their designs pushing *all* of this forward to their satisfaction. She is clearing the stage she will share with you of hypocrisy."

"You make some...*design*...in this?" Hannibal had plucked the letter from Sosylos and was staring at it, seeing the convolutions of memory of her, the real parts, the parts she had been putting into her letters that might *not* be real.

"Ask her if she is soliciting on her own behalf here...*that* should get a good rise from her, and it may give you valuable guidelines for parts of your education that have been outside my purview."

After this tutorial, there was an exchange of letters between Iberia and Carthage that Sosylos, a privily endowed man again, felt deserved special binding. The crux of it came with two letters: Hannibal's initiative wondering if she was worrying about him not getting into good form for her. And Inanna's quick reply stating the following:

...You impute a lecherous mewing to me, Hannibal Barca. I can tell you that there have been <u>hundreds</u> of times that I could have scratched such itches with <u>dozens</u> of drooling idiots who pass for men here. I have not done so because of a <u>rapidly</u> fading memory of a boy who promised to come back as a man. Do I want a rank, driveling novice crawling all over me in a comedy of clumsy groping if such consummation <u>should</u> be granted by Apollo? I tell you no. I tell you I deserve <u>much</u> better than this—look to <u>all</u> the aspects of your education, Hannibal Barca. Sosylos knows what I'm talking about.

"I don't deserve being planted squarely in the middle of this," Sosylos protested.

"It was *your* advice to test her for hypocrisy. She has pushed it right back on me. She has put the *full* burden of ecstasy on *my* shoulders. Damn her Apollo! Which way do I step now?"

"Am I *still* in tutorial status, my prince?"

"By Ba'al's beard—I'm *stuck* with you."

"Your next step should tend toward the Lady Barca. We are mired here in matters *far* beyond my competence, although Inanna seems to have left you no room for lies, or hypocrisy in the consummation that your mother's compassionate God shall surely give you two."

"We are close to laughter here that could make the trumpets in front of Jericho sound like whispers. My mother *revels* in a good laugh."

"Perhaps a more subtle approach—turning Inanna into a challenge for *Carthaginian* womanhood might do the trick."

"*What* trick?"

"You're getting too far ahead of me, my prince. Let the gods play with this a little while. Do I have your permission to put on Mercury's shoes on your behalf?" Sosylos got a suspicious nod, and a barely audible assent for his pains. He was turning away on the first step of this mission, but he stopped and faced his charge again:

"If I invite your mother into this little problem and should she find it interesting enough to take a step toward it, she would be in a posture of some vulnerability...some delicacy, a target for your own laughter and I can't be responsible for where *that* could lead."

"You expect *gentle* compliance from me? This would tend to reduce that laughter?"

"Within reason, my Prince, within reason. *Gentleness*, at the wrong time, might be an enemy of satisfaction here. We've done enough comedy together... some Aristophanes could be warped very close to what we have here. Play with it, Hannibal—you have *all* the equipment you'll need."

The Lady Barca had appointed Sosylos tutor for Hannibal. He was allowed to work with Hasdrubal and Mago, occasionally, but his focus was Hannibal because of special circumstances put on him by the father. Hamilcar's concern about the balance that had led to Inanna was not exclusive. His lady had preceded him in this even before the Iberian expedition. And when this graduate of most of Hamilcar's curriculum had appeared before her again at Carthage, the question of balance was again put to her by almost the whole of this soldier son in front of her. Sosylos, therefore, had good access to her on tutorial matters and when he mouthed the *balance* word himself—with letters to bolster his point—he had a *very* attentive audience.

"I suggested he approach *you* about this, Lady Barca...my competence falls into a pit of inadequacy here." He was in an anteroom of her apartments at the palace on Byrsa Hill. No Celtic cavalryman here. She was quintessential aristocrat, but this put Sosylos at some advantage because it was more of a *Greek* business that took him to her that evening.

"This is a *very* serious matter, Sosylos." She had used formidable resources of control to sustain her *concerned mother* against what could have easily been a sophisticated woman of the world convulsed by laughter about frustrated passion. She struggled against a smile, using the technique of rereading the pivotal letters to avoid an eye to eye confrontation with a man who most certainly was privy to almost every emotion pulsing in her at that moment.

"Yes, my lady. I...I suggested to Prince Hannibal that, perhaps...this could be cast as a challenge to Carthaginian *womanhood*...implying that this might open the door of acceptable response a little...wider." This brought the eyes—that had skewered even the redoubtable Hamilcar in anger, question, and spectrums of passion that had him hunting for new names for her—up to Sosylos'. She swept Sosylos' face with silent inquiry, her face no clue to how far she might push her agreement with him—*if* she agreed.

"I think I can say that your messenger role has been fulfilled," her eyes, and other parts of her face still held in delightfully precarious equilibrium. This man had studied in Athens and Sparta and Alexandria. He was qualified to appreciate her. Some of this fluxed between them, then Sosylos bowed and left the lady to her private resources of emotion.

Several days after Sosylos had confessed his incompetence to her, the Lady Barca entertained two of her friends—the Lady M, and the Lady S, at a swimming afternoon in her private pool at Carthage. The heavy exercise was over, now the three of them were on linen-sheathed pads, in a shaded portico of the pool. Lady Barca lay against a mound of silk cushions while Tiba attended to her pedicure. Her posture gave her some viewing advantage of her guests, who had abandoned themselves to individual conceptions of relaxation while Maga attended to a massage that had finished with Lady S, and was coming to Lady M. Diaphanous silk robes were worn by Lady Barca and Lady S , but Lady M had anticipated Maga and was naked. These ladies each promoted the powerful physical essence of *woman* with their own particulars of leg, thigh, breast, and back sculpting which complemented two maturely beautiful faces, and a younger beautiful face eager to discover the basis of nuances of laughter which sometimes stepped outside her experience.

The Lady Barca saw two laboratories here for the part of Hannibal's curriculum that Sosylos had just dumped on her. The lady S's—mature, experienced, insistent. The Lady M's—inexperienced, on the threshold of becoming an absolutely delightful practical field exercise for a man who had just graduated from Lady S. The Lady S was newly widowed. The Lady M not yet married. Both had shown extreme interest in the idea of challenge to Carthaginian womanhood that Lady Barca had just relayed to them from the Iberian *wilderness* before the crystal pool started to close over their smiles, and then more details when three shining water-emerged nymphs had a long delicious privacy before Tiba and Maga insisted their attentions.

Tiba and Maga were finally dismissed, but not before they had picked up some threads of the conversation and intimation that put Prince Hannibal into the aura of these ladies in a shocking, absolutely tantalizing, way.

"You suggested *your* guest wing for the...university," the Lady S.

"It would give me more stature as a dispassionate academic," the Lady Barca.

"You—dispassionate? Never!" The Lady S again.

"For me, too, this *dispassionate* approach?" The Lady M's eyes were wide open.

"I doubt it, considering your...finishing position, but then my son's progress will prompt you."

"We will have some chats about...scheduling." Lady Barca's survey of her professors was entirely satisfactory: veteran, and novice here, both with a solid commitment to instruction where the lines between teacher and pupil could become fuzzy from instant to instant.

Several days later, Hannibal was summoned to the room his mother used for her estate office. She was sitting behind a large marble topped table, with gilded bronze trimming. Several scribes and a secretary were busy in an adjoining room which was well screened, visually and vocally, from the lady's command center. As Hannibal entered the room, she was putting finishing touches to a note to her Hadrumetum manager about the grape harvest. She was the Carthaginian aristocrat this morning, with Greek accents of hair, subtle gold touches about her neck and ears. Hannibal came to attention in front of her, and saluted.

"New recruit for your service my lady."

"Charming. Your attendance *is* requested, as a matter of fact." Hannibal had been steeled by Sosylos for this moment and he was ready to play her game—within reason.

"Sosylos has mentioned a...a little business between you and Inanna. I believe you permitted this." His mother glanced up at him.

"I did. He has bowed to greater authority—something I like about him. He knows his limitations, is quick to invoke aid rather than plunge both of us into a useless quagmire."

"It is a quality that I admired long ago, and acted upon...to your benefit I think."

"Yes Mother." *By the gods' beards, keep my face straight, now.*

"I have enlisted two tutors who have agreed to assist on this problem of Inanna's perception. You have met both of them." She brought in Lady S, by name. "She has agreed to a session, or sessions, as needed, of a...fundamental nature. She brought in Lady M, by name. "She has agreed to a session, as many as needed, of practical exercise of what you learned in the prior class. These will be held in my guest wing." She perused one of the papers on her desk. She *had* been piling it on him and casualness was appropriate. After several seconds of respite, she snapped a quick look at him." You will be advised in plenty of time as to *when*. Any questions, Hannibal?" The last few seconds had taxed both of their straight faces, but they'd managed.

"You have taken too much on top of your regular burdens here—I apologize for the necessity of it." His mother had to find more sustenance in her papers at that moment, but then he joined their eyes. "Carthage has been said to be a paragon of debauchery—apparently, I've squandered too much time on other parts of her."

"That will be to Carthage's glory, Hannibal Barca. As for *my* time, I shall dedicate some of it to a very special Iberian lady."

Hannibal went to attention and saluted again, then he left. *By Melkart, she has wrapped compliance around me now.*

The grounds of the Barca palace on Byrsa Hill were mostly contained in terraces that flowed downward toward the inner wall of the city that girded Byrsa on its western side, away from the sea. The gardeners had surrendered enough of the second terrace to make an archery range under Hamilcar's orders, and his lady's specifications. Archery was a good surcease from riding that kept eye and muscle coordination on its toes. And pulling a recurved compound Parthian bow enough to give an arrow a good smack against a target at forty paces was a satisfying release for tension, anger, or frustration, that might have found its way to the bow stand. Putting an arrow on its target, in appropriate company, likewise emotionally occupied, was also one of the best ways Lady Barca had found for putting a light touch on the essential patterns of a crucial conversation.

She had enticed Hannibal to this spot several days after Lady M had decided that her part, the practical field exercise of the *Iberian answer*—as Lady S had put it—was done. *Continuation* had been passed from Lady S to her by the Lady Barca. She had serviced it with talents she knew she had, and with some that *he* had drawn out of her, playing the not so bashful student... and never had that word, *continuation*, been surrendered more reluctantly.

"A good shot, Mother." She could group ten out of twelve arrows into a span of three cubits at this range. Today she had been somewhat disconcerted, although as her son had just claimed, she could rise to an occasion. Hannibal was also competent with the bow, though he counted the sword, spear and javelin practice more relevant to the present military scene. The Parthian bow, in military weights, was a good weapon, but it would need more time to become a dangerous discipline to Western echelons in the hands of significant commanders. Hannibal stepped to the bow stand and eventually released an arrow.

"We've crowded the bull's-eye!" the lady exclaimed, delighted. She waited for his next shot, longer than she expected.

"I have *several* bull's-eyes, Mother...to which *crowding* are you referring?" He was taking plenty of time nocking his arrow, the target his excuse for not looking at her. They had exchanged very few words during, and since, the lessons in another technique—just enough to greet, make sensible dinner conversation, and then mostly early to bed excuses afforded him because of strenuous activity in the armories, or with the Mushrooms, at the least.

It was not the lady's turn to shoot, so he had just placed her on a very inconvenient time point without any archery diversion. But she was not easily intimidated. Anyone who tossed a bait of words in her direction should expect quick action—like a minnow in front of the tuna that cruised the waters around Carthage—and Hannibal expected no less.

"Why, *Inanna*, of course—an absolutely delightful bull's-eye."

He set his arrow, took his stance, pulled and released.

"There you go, Hannibal! *Closer* to the mark this time...and without any of my crowding." It was her turn now, but she had just turned the sharp point of the repartee back on him. She was looking straight at him. She had set her bow on the rack, and was now confronting the student who had just completed one of Cupid's courses, as far away from Mars and Hercules as she could make it. He looked like a man—some of her friends had used the phrase, *a god incarnate*, on him when inhibition had been let loose under her sway as a hostess in this palace, or on the sweeps of the country estates where inhibition had even greater scope. She waited—let him make her believe some of this image of him.

His bow joined hers on the rack. He stepped toward her, and came close enough so that a lip kiss was within his range. She wore her hair long this time, its amalgam of silver and bronze caught in a silk ribbon that let it cascade down her back in a non-braided sheath. She wore an athletic tunic: linen, short sleeved, the hem high enough to show her youthful legs from the knees down, Greek style sandals with ankle straps. She was a perfect *Iberian answer* on a broader stage, herself.

"This...*crowding* business..." he had shortened the distance between their lips even more, his eyes making a very limited survey of the wonderful enigma of her that tested even Sosylos' armor of well being—that *ataraxia* way that he had been trying to hammer into his charge, "...it was impertinent... it was an outrageous extrapolation of authority turning these ladies, however attractive, into your servants in this manner."

"By who?" She had not retreated. She was the Tyrian priestess now defending her substantial perimeters of mind and action. She was making her own very limited survey of him—she had dealt the cards, let him play one, or two, in front of her, now. Her *special curriculum* ladies had not said much to her, afterwards, or needed to. The lady S had reported to her wearing a loose fitting chiton that she confessed gave solace to muscles she hadn't used for *ages*. During her brief report, she inadvertently made slight motions with her legs, and hands , mostly her legs, that signaled a close memory of progressively blatant exercise, particular to a young man who had been a very quick, and insistent, study. The young Lady M's report had less physical embellishment, but her lips and eyes tried to help her define other particular exercises that pulled a woman out of her she hadn't known, who would value further demonstrations... that is, more time to polish her instruction.

"You...*and* Sosylos." Then he grabbed her, and he made a lip kiss on her that shocked her—*was he continuing the seminar on his own? How dare he play Oedipus with me!* He bent her backward, testing her resistance—which was considerable on several fronts. When he released her, he was prepared for hand, arm, or foot response from an expert. She stood still, hands by her sides, her fingers in graceful repose instead of fist-like. Her lips still smarted. She used this effect as an excuse to give him the next word.

"See, Mother...you've made a monster. Your ladies have unleashed the beast that was *just* below my skin." She didn't like his smile. But it refuted his words—and it *was* the man's response she had been looking for. Then, he took her hand and pressed it to his lips, a much softer, more appropriate salute to this lady who had worried on his behalf about *balance*—and *Inanna*—and gone beyond words to his assistance. The smile was still there, but it had shed every shade of tease, it was a complication of what she meant to him, what she had done to him, *for* him...what she would like to expect of him.

Sosylos had said to let the gods play with this a little while... when would they release me, Sosylos? They've tumbled me between two goddesses...this was fun for everyone. But when will they let me go, Sosylos? Hannibal had a new core strength—like it, or not.

The sleek, black-hulled trireme had rounded Cape Gammart and then Cape Carthage, and was now sweeping south toward Carthage, the orange pink and red garnet shades of sunset starting to fill the northern sky behind her. Just north of the rocky cothon entrance, a massive fort bristled with terraced emplacements for catapults for defense of Carthage's mercantile and military ligaments to the sea. Approaching the harbor entrance, the trireme's officers could see the large iron chain links, looped around a capstan that could be used to block the harbor. The channel to the first, mercantile, harbor was seventy feet wide, and it gave a good stage for the trireme's rowers. The rowing officer commanded a beat that took the vessel toward the mercantile lagoon at a smarter pace than necessary. Inside the first harbor, after exchanging lamp code signals with the naval harbor master, the ship approached the channel to the circular naval harbor also with more panache than was absolutely necessary. As it swept into the naval harbor, a shouted command from a shore officer assigned a docking shed to the visitor.

This vessel bore most of the hallmarks of a Carthaginian, but it had some blazes on the bow and stern, and Lord General Hasdrubal of Iberia's standard at the masthead. The black of the hull was unique due to a durable, smooth finish put on it by Iberian Greek craftsmen. Coupled to an expert set of rowers, this ship had no match for speed on the Mediterranean, or the seas touching it. A few officers who had seen some of the glory of Carthage on the sea were standing about the quays at that moment. And this ship had just pushed a big piece of fresh sea air into the cobwebs of the cothon for everyone who saw it. Torches were lighted on either side of the assigned shed, oars were shipped and final maneuvers made to slip her into port like a massive eel.

The naval harbor master couldn't resist personally greeting *this* crew:

"By Ba'al's breath, you Iberians haven't forgotten what a Carthaginian is all about."

The captain gripped his hand and smiled—it was all the answer needed. Torchlight played on a sea-swept face, and flickered on the red eagle's head blaze on the chest of his black cloak—Hasdrubals' mark. Hasdrubal's mark also on his eyes and mouth, a blaze which had just brought pride into this harbor, a commodity in short supply lately for Carthage.

"Messages for the Barcas...for Prince Hannibal...for Lady Barca," he said.

"Carriage, or horse, Captain?"

"I know the way—a horse will do for me. My crew is hungry, thirsty. That damn beat east before the headlands at Hippo Diarrhytus was tougher than usual."

"We will take care of them, Captain, you can be sure. Good messaging with the Barcas."

"It *won't* be." His eyes and the harbor master's locked in the fusion of torchlight and twilight, and then Hasdrubal's messenger strode toward a horse, and a palace on Byrsa Hill.

Under command of the perpetual sea breezes on Byrsa's top, oil lamps in bronze receptacles around the main gate of the Barca palace flicked a greeting to the captain. He twice pounded the bronze fist holding the lightning bolt against the heavy oak door. Street traffic in this quarter was always sparse and well mannered. His sound made an exclamation point in the night for this reason, and because it was late for visitors. A peep port was opened behind a heavy iron grill and a gruff voice challenged the disturbance. Hasdrubal's mark on a naval captain moved him through the palace hierarchy without the usual jockeying for authority and peek inside the messenger's head. The only words had been the captain's: "My messages are for the Lady Barca and Prince Hannibal." When he reached the intersection of two hallways in the living quarter's wing, the major domo requested that the captain wait.

She was wearing a heavy silk robe over a night dress, hair and face composed for an early bed. Tiba wanted to accompany her, but she came alone, every talent of her haruspex, her seer, credentials straining toward the lone figure of the captain standing in her hall, too little light to give her much preparation for the part of the message on his face. She stopped a few feet from him, waiting:

"My Lady Barca...the Lord General Hasdrubal bids me give you a very sad message..." She had received such a man five years before. But it had been under the bright sun and green panoplies of Hadrumetum which made it a little better for her. He had told her about Hamilcar's death. She clenched the fingers of both hands, but was straight tall in front of this shadowed man. A moan of Mediterranean breath slipping through a nearby lattice bolstered her premonitions. She raised her chin, and gave the barest nod of command to him to uncover his sadness.

"The Lady Amalkre...has died...five days ago in Carthago Nova."

"How...did she die?" The words were easy—collection of her breath for them was not.

"A fever...with complications of breathing. Synhalus did everything he could for her."

"Ah...an old friend. Give him my greeting...my thanks." She had turned slightly away from him, bringing a shadow to her privacy, to her eyes. *Amalkre... my dear, you slipped away much too soon...now you'll have a big advantage on me with your direct connections to the mysteries we played.* She turned back to the man before her.

"I thank you, Captain."

"There is more, my lady...for Prince Hannibal. Hasdrubal has ordered him back to Iberia." She flinched this time, but her camouflage was still good. The captain fought an unseemly impulse to take her in his arms for some softening of the harsh presence he had brought to her. *"Officially...*I should tell him myself...but if you..."

"When...for him?"

"The tides and winds, and Hasdrubal, suggest dawn in two days, my lady, at the cothon."

"He will be ready, Captain." She intuited some of his feeling, and the gentle service he did to her offered hand could have been *Hamilcar's*.

She was the messenger, now. Any basis for reluctance, pit of the stomach dismay at Fate's timetable, couldn't delay her. Hasdrubal's black ship in the cothon would be no secret by early morning, and its significance would be in the thoughts and conversations that wouldn't exclude her sons. She had accepted the captain's hand, and part of his responsibility. But the night could still grant her some buffer of memories—of rationalization of the two blows just dealt her. Sosylos—*he* was the link to them when she planned a peaceful progress for her sons, and even to Hamilcar, a sometimes reluctant Grekophile...but these men had talked and listened to each other, so Sosylos was also a link to Hamilcar and she needed Hamilcar's strength now, through Sosylos. Tiba had joined her. She sent Tiba to find Sosylos. She paced along the balustrade of her private terrace, waiting for him, trying to fend the maelstrom of images that was climaxing now—a derivative of the times when she opened her thoughts to Acherbas, Zortibas and *Amalkre.* She invoked her single God, but her focus was poor...and she knew it was a very late prayer.

"My lady..." Sosylos knew he had to touch her, her grief was palpable from the distance of his first sight of her, and their past communions could justify a touch. His soft voice was first, and then he grasped both her hands that had settled on the balustrade. She didn't turn away from a look into the night that gave her a few precursor stars, some coupling of the Mediterranean with a feeble moon—amenities for her eyes if she wanted them.

"Amalkre...is *dead*." Her voice quality was appropriate, but it was a stranger to Sosylos.

"I *know*, my lady." It was almost a whisper.

"Hasdrubal has ordered Hannibal back to Iberia." Then, she turned to him, his touch gratefully accepted, appreciated. "I promised to pack him off at dawn in two days."

"You *knew* it was to be, my lady...the gods have swept him up into their grounds."

"Does it *have* to be tragedy, my Greek friend...this *sweeping up*?" She had wept tears before he came to her. Their tracks were almost gone, and he found some small pieces of a smile on her, now.

"I have hammered your son with *dozens* of cases where gods and men have *refuted* tragedy in their communions...comedy, two-way philosophizing over the gamut of experience are also possibilities." She seemed receptive to him. He pushed it a little further: "I hear that his gamut has been...enlarged lately, under expert tutelage. I'm, jealous—*only* of the quality of the instruction, of course." Her smile was not subtle now. He had heard Hamilcar use the name *Hippolyta* with her—it could be used for her...for this moment.

"He will be carrying baggage from *all* of us, Sosylos. But I have Hasdrubal left for the target of an old woman's contentment."

Sosylos should have left it at that. He had helped her back from the darkness at the balustrade, it had been enough. But the aphorism, *forewarned is forearmed*, was too seductive.

"Hasdrubal and Hannibal are close, my lady. I think Hannibal may take a passenger on his comet."

"Has he *said* this?" She was calling on her actress now. Sosylos' words about this pairing of two of her boys would be only confirmation of her own knowledge. *Mago was already in Iberia. My God—they are all gone on that damn comet!*

"I have seen them together these years at Carthage. They have blended in the Mushrooms, a natural commander and lieutenant, and the armory sessions—you can hardly separate the enthusiasms."

She whirled to him. "You have not left me *any* comfort, Sosylos." That was not true. His touch of her hand, moments before, had pulled her back from a path some had found irreversible...and then the momentary scintillations of the *special tutoring* had been on his initiative.

"I will be going with him, perhaps *them*, my lady. Silenus is committed to a chronicle on him...he wants my notes."

"Surely, not *everything*, Sosylos." Hippolyta was partly back again, prancing up.

"I say let the Lady Inanna decide *that*." Sosylos *had* to kiss her hand—she *had* to let him.

In two days, by dawn at the cothon, there were two Barca men ready for the lustrous black ship. As it slipped out of the entrance channel into the sea, Hannibal and Hasdrubal looked toward Byrsa Hill and the lady who had helped them make a good goodbye. The man standing near to them was likewise focused, and he had been her lieutenant for a little while.

7

26 years
221 BC—Iberia

The Meseta is the bare chest of Iberia. This muscled plateau pushes against the northern mountains, the Pyrenees, the Portugal escarpments to the west and the Sierra Morena and Sierra Nevada to the south. It touches most of the great Iberian watercourses. There were people who crossed this land, used it, could be enticed to use it, by men who paid them the courtesy of visions that included them in prideful ways. Some of these visions needed the sweep this land gives for a man on a horse, the scope it gives to every conceivable conjunction of men on horses. It is a country where cavalry can be born, practiced, whetted to an edge peculiar to a commander's whimsy, or visions, or any obsessions with perfect couplings between foot and horse that make an army he could take anywhere into his plan of the world.

Two Carthaginian officers were on a vantage that gave them basis for critiquing a cavalry exercise, sitting their horses, on a promontory of rock overlooking the classroom that was a small piece of the Meseta, with flats and gullies and undulations where surprises could be made with a good formation and quick embarrassment with a bad one.

"Hannibal's Lusitani are promising...maybe too damn playful, but better that than scarecrows sitting plow horses." Maharbal spoke to Carthalo who was on his right. They watched a tight column of horse, three files of twenty five, climb out of a gully, angle toward a crest, and then disappear into an undulation. These were ambush maneuvers and their leader snaked the column in and out of visibility with a relish that Maharbal and Carthalo could taste from their considerable distance.

"I would use more than your compliment on him." Carthalo was trying to fix the elusive unit leader ahead of the right file. "I'm afraid Hamilcar has spawned a cavalryman for us. Be damned! He goes into these people—the Carpetani, the Turdetani, these Lusitani and he smells a cavalryman at a hundred paces and draws him in. Hamilcar did some of this, but he was not a cavalry maniac—this one *is*."

Maharbal also found the fixing of the position of Hannibal Barca in that terrain a chore at that distance. But he continued to fill his eyes with a cavalry that seemed to use the land as a friend like none he had ever seen. "If the Celts drew enough Roman blood along the Po and on the doorstep of Rome to fertilize bumper flower crops, then we may be looking at a Carthaginian botanical paradise that will cover *all* Italy. This cavalry maniac may be the key to Hamilcar's treasure chest. You and I are supposed to be cavalrymen. He has shown both of us a marriage of foot and horse that could make the worst surprise the Italian Wolf ever had."

"Would Hamilcar's treasure chest be sitting in the Roman forum?"

"It's there, Carthalo. Also the delicious Po valley...Etruria, Campania, Apulia—wherever we would like to plant the disk and crescent."

The column had just reappeared and was coming toward them. Hannibal had them down to a gracious canter, a delicate little step they could parade under the eyes of two of the greatest cavalry commanders of the western world. "I hear he's poked around some in the Celtiberi country. Now *there's* a sleeping tiger that we could harness to Hamilcar's chariot."

"Apparently he's made some of them talk more about cavalry than the bloody memories between us. You just used Hamilcar's name again. For me, I'm going to settle Hamilcar into splendid memory and start to use *Hannibal* in my words more. We've had doubts about Hasdrubal the Handsome. I don't think I still have many about Hannibal the Cavalryman. I think I'm susceptible to his seduction."

"To sin, or glory?"

"Glory of course. But you are older. Is it true they are mutually exclusive, Maharbal?"

"Hannibal seems to have less tendency to mix these rewards than Alexander. If we follow this young one, I think we will see parts of heaven and hell that even Hamilcar is now denied—and he led a damn full life I can tell you."

"Sin and glory wise?"

"Absolutely. He was a full man."

"I've seen the Lady Barca...he was also an endowed man."

"I think her aura spreads to the very cavalryman who is close to enveloping us—this has to be counted among *his* endowments."

The man who had usurped the unit leader's prerogative for some needed exercise had just waved the unit leader back to his command, and ridden up to his observers. He was wearing the Iberian cavalry white tunic with red trimming, Carthaginian heavy cavalry boots, no hat or helmet. His face had put on a few creases the Lady Barca hadn't seen, and the African-Iberian patina of it was now close to the equilibrium that the Meseta and the rest of his Iberia could bring to it. His mount was a black Iberian, with minimum embellishment.

"By Ba'al Hannibal, you're shaming all of us. You don't come to that snaking around for another year yet. These are supposed to be raw recruits, floundering around in the *oulamoi*, the *rhombos*, and the *embolos* configurations!" Maharbal had just reeled off the classic cavalry formations of the square, the rhombus, and the delta-shaped wedge, that the Greeks, the Thessalians, and the Macedonians via the Scythians, respectively, had brought to various battlegrounds. "And no Mushrooms today?" Most of Hannibal's Mushrooms were distributed as unit leaders among the cavalry forces in Iberia. Maharbal had just recognized another achievement that had impressed him and Carthalo as cavalry professionals.

Hannibal saluted Maharbal and Carthalo, formally, and with a grin. He put his horse to the left of Maharbal, which made a rank of Hannibal, Maharbal, and Carthalo that confused the local formal hierarchy of the cavalry, but not the actual one. Lord General Hasdrubal had appointed Hannibal Chief of Cavalry upon his return from Carthage. Maharbal was Hannibal's deputy commander of heavy cavalry, Carthalo his deputy for light cavalry, which included the effervescent Numidian jewels in the Carthaginian crown. Hannibal had taken command by Hasdrubal's command. But his concession to the greater experience and knowledge of Maharbal and Carthalo—who had served under Hamilcar—was a continuing exercise of his new diplomacy that both Sosylos and Silenus admired, and these deputies, in natural course, were forming crucial ligaments for the present and future Hannibal Barca.

"I've planted the Mushrooms here and there, Maharbal. I hope they will make a good harvest for you and Carthalo."

"I'm still thinking about that hat—making it official for *all* of us."

Hannibal had presented Mushroom hats to both his deputies. Carthalo was particularly sensitive to the extracurricular intrigue of it, upholding the cavalryman's *balance* that Hamilcar would've understood. Maharbal had put his hat on privately and snapped the brim into a few provocative postures, but he was not the public cavalier of Carthalo, so he hadn't endorsed it yet.

Hannibal waved his unit leader toward further exercise that took the column away from that observation post. "Your oulamoi, rhombos...and embolos are fun, Maharbal. We put six ilai in and out of all of them the other day near the Tagus."

"*Ilai?* We're using Macedonian now for *squadron?* "

"Blame Sosylos and Silenus—and every damn historian who can get close to me. They *will* shove me up Alexander's ass so I can savor the fullness of him." Hannibal watched the column disappear into one of the Meseta undulations that he had just caressed himself. "I think we can find formations that will chew up that parade ground posturing. It might scare cavalry...but it's the foot that the Romans want to put in front of us, and that's where I want to go—into their foot, after I've chewed their horse."

"You scare *me*, Hannibal, if that's consolation." Carthalo's imagination was equal to the burden of putting this cavalry maniac close to his Numidians—a wedding of mutual attraction that could sweep terror across the Roman foot and horse before the nuptials were hardly consummated. His Numidians were the finest light cavalry in the world. There were whispers of some in Asia who could match them, but he knew they could chew up any substance he could see from any vantage he could reach. He was a commander himself...enough of one to know a greater one.

"Do you like what you've seen of the Celtiberi, Hannibal?"

From the first time that Maharbal and Carthalo used *Prince* on him, Hannibal had insisted on his name without that, or any, title. There were several Hasdrubals about—his brother, the Lord General, and a young cavalry officer who would bear watching, but no other living Hannibal who could confuse a conversation in his zone of action.

The Celtiberi had been a carefully circumscribed topic of official speech since some of them had died in the red froth with Hamilcar on the Jucar. But now they were a major fact of the nearby Carthaginian horizon. Hannibal had made overtures to them, slanted to a cavalry presence and potential that could be a major bolster to his expeditionary force. And a complement of their cavalry would encourage a contribution of their massive foot presence. The Celtiberi were the best of the Iberian military resources, and the largest. Maharbal's question to Hamilcar's son who had been close to Hamilcar on that Jucar day was, therefore, appropriate in the present context.

"If we can bring them into our cause it will take Italy out of dreams and into a better perspective. Their riders, discipline, equipment, are the best I've seen among the natives. I like their horses. They are bred from European and Asian strains that have already made some of the best cavalry. They have developed scale armor for horse and rider that we would do well to study. We have already felt the quality of their swords and spears. If the Romans still laugh about Celtic equipment, I think we can make them *die* laughing. Yes, I like what I've seen of the Celtiberi, Maharbal. They have offered us a token squadron to test compatibility."

"Under *our* command?"

"Ambon's shadow isn't as long as I'd feared, Carthalo. Some of them know about Hamilcar's better parts. They have evidently watched our foot and horse playgrounds. You and Maharbal have been a good advertisement for us— their scouts are better than we knew."

"Hamilcar pulled various natives to us. Your reach has been longer than his, Hannibal. We will have to put them into *our* uniform or the curse of the rag-tag mercenary gypsy band will dog us all the way to Italy. I want the Romans to see a consistent terror—I want the last thing they see to be a *consistent* terror." Sudden far horizons were not strangers to Maharbal's eyes.

"Carthalo has dressed his Numidians a little closer to your mold, Maharbal. If *they* can accept this, then so go the Lusitani, the Carpetani, the Erdetani, the Turdetani...the Celtiberi." Cavalry Commander Hannibal raised his arms and made their spread wider with each recitation of a people. He finished the *Celtiberi* with a laugh, eyes that flashed across the great Meseta proving ground before they settled back on Marharbal and Carthalo. Carthage was not famous for its citizen armies. She had made a usually useful art of the mercenary recourse, and was now equipped with a commander who, from virtual outsiders, could fashion as much devotion as any Greek's who'd ever served Athens, or Sparta. Hannibal would make an army for Carthage that would need new adjectives beyond *mercenary*.

The little foray into the hinterland had lasted four days longer than Hannibal's prediction. It was late when he slipped into the pool at his apartments at the palace at Carthago Nova. He could still feel the horse working under him, every muscle of him thankful for the cool kiss of water that took away some souvenirs of days in the saddle. He was striking out toward the far edge, toward an array of bronze sculptures that depicted the transition from a mermaid to a full bodied nymph, full size, and there were four transitions that brought a finny and scaled torso to the shape that was classic woman in every particular. The ultimate statue showed the lady full standing, surveying conquest material, one of her hands on her hips, the other touching a strand of long hair that draped part of her left breast. He thought about *his* lady as he stroked the water toward this fantasy of her. During one of the last times when his head was not in position to see the statue, the scenery had changed. When he came to the surface, and looked again, there were two ultimates for his pleasure. The new one, copied the bronze's pose in the main, but it was ivory colored in the twilight, slightly taller than the bronze, and there was a mane of ebony hair that spilled around the right shoulder, and a strand of it supported against the left breast by her hand. It was a brazen imitation of the original, particularly in the way it taunted the original by open lips that somehow had trapped moisture, and eyes which invited torchlight into her pose. He came to the pool's edge. The mermaid progression was several paces beyond the edge. She held her pose while he pulled himself out of the water, and strode to her. He stopped within touching distance. He would show her that his resistance had been improved by these Meseta outings.

"I didn't want to wake you." He studied her eyes. Her lips gave no signal. She could be enigma personified, as Sosylos could attest. He waited. She uncurled from her imitation enough to put one hand behind his head. Then she pulled that head, and moved herself so she could put their lips together. He put one hand around her left breast, the other behind her and then he made their conjunction closer, their lips still locked. When she had enough kiss, she got position and leverage to push him into the pool, and she came along because their legs were entangled.

Finally, against the side of the pool he had come to one summation, and just brought her to her second of present instance. Her recovery of an almost full voice was remarkable.

"Did you get to the Celtiberi, Hannibal Barca?" She used his full name at her pleasure—in her letters, in various moments of their time together. She had extracted some intimate words from Sumerian texts of her father, and she used these also at her pleasure, and usually denied him full translation. She played a finger against his lips, and around a face that formed more of the commander every day. There was a tiny new scar, but she only questioned it by a little hesitation of the finger.

"It was satisfactory. I think we've tapped a new vein of horse and foot. They are still suspicious, but they really made the first overtures, so that's progress." His flick from man to commander could also be remarkable.

He kissed her. She helped him blend their eyes in a way that was inimitable to her. He could save speech in this way more than with anyone he had known. His mother was powerful in this respect, Amalkre, too. But Inanna was an evolution of the mysteries that had come through Delphi and neither the Lady Barca, nor Amalkre, had come that way. Some of the speech they just saved would have been about his Celtiberi excitement. She had met Hamilcar. She had heard some of his ambition from his own lips, from his family. She knew that this man who had enveloped her with love since his return from Carthage was Hamilcar reincarnate. He was probably *more* than Hamilcar, and for this she would measure joy by the minutes, hours—but certainly not the years. Amalkre had warned her about the Barca women. She had letters from Lady Barca which were maternal casts of a son's adoration, but they were also warnings, explicit or not, that counted *years* with Hannibal Barca as too precious substance for practical thought.

Three years before, when Hannibal returned to Iberia by Hasdrubal's order, he went to Castulo as soon as he had satisfied official amenities. In his letters, Mago had told him about trouble in the mining districts, so the wings on his feet were pulsed by both love and concern.

He came unannounced, his pull to Inanna was stronger, therefore swifter, than any precursor he could send to her. He was wearing his Mushroom uniform, largely because of the hat which he thought would give her a frivolous first look at him, rather than the sterner image he now could summon easily. The servant announced him to her father, who now was spending more time as the villa master, than at the mines, for various reasons that were part of what pulled Hannibal toward him. Her father came close enough to him to wave him toward the side of the villa where his rarest botanicals were supervised by his daughter, who happened to be there at the moment.

She was wearing a white smock, ankle strapped Greek sandals, a large, floppy straw hat of Iberian mold. As he took a minimum path toward her, the sun put a tiny reflection of silver from her throat band in his eyes. She looked up while he was still too far away to logically signal himself by various courtesies. But these two weren't logic bound and she saw him, and then she started to run toward him, their doubled approach making a collision much sooner than he could manage on his own.

They had kissed many times before. This one set a record for duration, comprehensive attention to lips, the area around lips, ears, under the eyes, the eyes themselves, necks, and he was tending toward her breasts when she finally pushed him away, managing a laugh between heavy breaths. Her hat had fallen to the ground, his had survived her. She touched his big brim, and the chin strap, her eyes dancing between the hat and the elusive target of his eyes which tried to comprehend her. No words had been said—perhaps *Hannibal Barca* and *Inanna* could have been made from some of the convolution of lip sounds that tried to compress five years into that moment.

After she insisted on better amenities to her father, they were standing on a veranda of the villa that overlooked a tributary of the Baetis. Her father had conceded them quick privacy toward relief of a tension that was palpable to him even when he watched her writing one of her famous letters.

"You're larger...also maybe handsomer. And you've got a new scar."

"That you *know* of." For a moment he moved closer to facilitate her inspection, then he backed away, trying to make a serious face.

"I think you should come to Carthago Nova."

"You are proposing."

"I am close to it. But I think you should come to Carthago Nova, *now*."

"You are complimenting me with a mistress status."

"What you do before we are married will be entirely at your own discretion." They had stayed close enough together so that a kiss inclination—either side—could be handled quickly. But then she demonstrated that such inclination, for two like them, can perch on a razor's edge.

"You think that your devastating attraction is a monument of temptation for me that will make a mockery—an inconvenience—of marriage?" She'd stepped outside kissing range, a lambent twilight in her eyes part of her response.

"You could never allow a mockery of our marriage. It would be my greatest honor, no matter what the gods had done to *us* before it...or what the gods do to *me* after it." Maybe Sosylos, even Silenus, could take some credit for that declaration. But she knew that it was mostly Hannibal Barca. It was enough to bring her back within range, and they used it.

"What reason could I give Father for coming to Carthago Nova?" She was close enough to his ear that her whisper was like thunder to him.

"Tell him that your imminent husband is worried about the troubles in the mining districts. Tell him that, though he is a bulwark in his own district, this other man of your life would be happier if you were closer to the authority." The word *authority* had some ambiguity sticking to it, but he smiled with it, and she accepted it.

"Where would I live there? I have no connections there—no friends. It is far away from Father."

"I would propose an apartment in the palace for you. You will have the best possible connections. You already have friends scattered between here and Carthage. Your father will sigh in relief when the last of the fierce letters has flown from his nest. You will have no more need of them since you can bedevil me directly."

"I have other correspondents."

"So my mother told me. You two have the world to talk about—she will keep you in books and gossip and mystical speculations that will feed your bedevilment of me."

"You fear this bedevilment is a persistent thing, Hannibal Barca?"

"I'm counting on it. My *frequent* invocations for protection will keep me closer to the gods, thus you will make me a more prominent target for their favors and therefore, mercy."

She could have moved that *mercy* word around between them, but it had ambiguity sticking to it, too, not all of it playful.

They didn't mention Amalkre. She and Inanna had become close friends. Her grave was at Melkart's grove at Gades. They would go there together.

That day, he insisted on paying another amenity to her father before he returned to Carthago Nova. They approached him in his study. He had Greek, Sumerian and Egyptian books and scrolls scattered around him. He watched them close their distance. He was ready for anything. She had made him ready for anything.

"Sir...I want to marry your daughter."

"I cannot pretend terrible shock—you'll agree?"

"What is your opinion of this?"

"I was close to your father. Do you want my opinion of your father's opinion—about this?"

"I consider it indispensable."

"You and Inanna owe Hamilcar a debt of introduction and implementation."

"I am well aware that I must add this to the mountain I already owe my father."

"Hamilcar, privately, told me he hoped that two sparks would join to a reasonably steady flame."

"I think I understand this symbolism." Hannibal had studiously avoided looking toward one of the sparks in this triad of confession and revelation.

"I think it is a reasonable extrapolation of a reasonably steady flame to marriage."

"My father held a high opinion of you...I am only beginning to savor its basis."

"I concur in Hamilcar's opinion—in this Inanna instance. This is my permission. That gives you *two* fathers' permission. Inanna's mother is not accessible to mortals. She would have liked your mother, therefore, I will count your mother's opinion as double toward this permission. What *is* her opinion?"

"My mother has supported this marriage on several occasions...several bases." At that moment, Hannibal's ears came closer to a flush than ever before, they were dangerously susceptible to interpretation by an even casual observer, which Inanna was not. She chose to defer her comment on his ears.

"Then we have a quadruple permission here. It needs only one more." Inanna's father turned to her, an attention that had been conspicuous by its absence so far.

"I will accept Hannibal Barca's proposal, Father. It is a superior state to others that have come to mind...recently." Her father was enough for her eyes.

"I would kiss your daughter, sir, to...consummate this agreement, but I risk over zealousness today." Hannibal reached for Inanna's hand, and did it service, under her gaze that had imperial quality, tempered with Delphic prescience.

The palace Hasdrubal had built at Carthago Nova had certain measures that were superior to Hamilcar's villa at Akra Leuke. His private apartments had greater scope for self indulgence. There were two audience chambers, instead of Hamilcar's modest office, where congregations of about a hundred, or ten, respectively, could be coped with without bringing Hasdrubal too close to public intimacy and the claustrophobia of unpleasant discussion which seemed to have a rising incidence with him. For pleasanter occasions outside the privilege of his private apartments, he had a large dining hall and a reception room for exercising other social graces he might need in Iberia. The connecting halls were longer, wider. His verandas were wider, more enveloping, and they were distributed among three levels on the terrain he had selected overlooking the Mediterranean. If he had nudged the design toward Babylon as a senator had claimed, then he had been subtle about it. Such a critic would have to roam the verandas and their gardened perimeters to find the botanical extravagance that Babylon might have been...the conjunctions of floor, wall, and free standing art with botanicals that Babylon might have been. Some of this flowed into the interiors, and Hasdrubal had given Iberian artisans and gardeners, some Greeks and Easterners of similar bents, almost free rein in finding something they could brag about. Amalkre had been alive during the planning and building, and her mark was there in the mix, the presences, of art and botanicals and architecture where a mind fit for either calm repose, or unfettered mystery, could find sustenance. Her mother would like this place. Hannibal liked it—the senators be damned. In the brief time he had been back in Iberia, there was still plenty of it for him to discover.

He had requested an audience with Lord General Hasdrubal shortly after returning from Castulo. Walking along the hallway toward the smaller audience chamber, he was Hasdrubals' officer. The short white tunic hemmed with Carthaginian geometricals in black red and gold, his short cloak of patterned white wool bearing Hasdrubal's red eagle blaze near the heart zone, epaulets in woven silver and gold identified his cavalry affiliation. His black dress boots bore a sheen that owed more to the initiative of a man-servant than his vanity. A dagger hung on his belt, a cavalryman's weapon. The handle was circles of leather interspersed with silver and ivory rings. The pommel was spherical sections of bronze and silver, with a red garnet at the focus. The blade was Phoenician steel, polished like a mirror—it had been Hamilcar's dagger, a miracle of recovery near his last battlefield. On more social occasions, he would wear some gold...a ring, some small chain around his neck. But this visit was difficult to place, so he was conservative.

Before he got to the small audience chamber, Hasdrubal met him in the hall. The long tap of boots against his parquet and marble floors had made a look at *this* burgeoning presence irresistible. He'd heard about Hannibal's defense of him in the Council. He'd heard about the Mushrooms, and its officers this young one had brought to Iberia. He was trying to keep a precarious balance between empire and service to the Barca dream—but this young one could push him along that dream faster than he might like. The nonaggression treaty he'd signed with the Romans two years before had quieted them, particularly it had quieted the nervous old ladies of the Greeks of Emporiae who had run to the Romans—again, when it looked like the Carthaginian juggernaught was reemerging and pointing toward them. The Romans had plenty to occupy them with the Celts in the Po valley, so this treaty had given him some cushion for consolidating Iberia in his fashion. Perhaps he'd brought this young one back too soon. And Hasdrubal had come along with him, another one who could push him toward that Barca dream too fast. By Ba'al, now he had all three of Hamilcar's precocious pups on his doorstep, with Mago already here.

If he heard Hamilcar's whispers as he watched Cavalry Commander Hannibal close with him, the smile he couldn't avoid pushed them away for a moment. There had been undeniable coupling between these two...here, at Carthage, and when he collaborated with Hamilcar in producing the chariot to give respite to a horseman whose heart was stronger than his butt and legs on that long trek across North Africa.

"By the gods, Hannibal, your footfall has an ominous presence in this place." Their hand clasp came with that. Hannibal was slightly taller than this Hasdrubal now. Both of them wore their hair in various designs of the classic Greek mold: Hasdrubal's now grey streaked, Hannibal's raven black, both naturally curled. The faces were two versions of the Hellenistic manliness that subsumed intellectual and sensual potential.

"You do me no favor by *that* compliment, Lord Hasdrubal—if I thought I had intruded your prerogatives, or..."

"*Ominous* is not as good as *awesome* here. That's my word, Hannibal, *awesome*...it gives you more scope under my smiles than *ominous*."

"I like it better, sir, but I will continue to study your smiles...carefully." He followed Hasdrubal into an ante room and then into a private alcove where soft couches and cool drinks, iced by snow from the Sierra Nevada, were waiting. He remained standing after Hasdrubal had found a couch. Hasdrubal waived him toward another couch.

"This audience has military implications?"

"I hope not—but some husbands would nod against me here."

"My amatory consultation is not worth your effort these days, Hannibal. Your brother, Mago, is getting a reputation in this respect—*he* might be your man."

"Not in this case, sir. I want to marry Inanna."

"She's a beauty. She has a mind, wit, and all the things that a woman ever needs to keep a man on edge Get her my boy, she may tend to calm some of that aura that I'm inclined to see pulsating behind you."

Hasdrubal had followed his own advice. Amalkre was hardly cold in her tomb at Melkart's grove at Gades before he took a Celtiberian princess to his bed as wife. Within the perimeters of it accessible to Amalkre's family, it had been a good as possible marriage between an ambitious politician and soldier and a woman who tried to balance conjugal duties with a mind and imagination which could course outside Hasdrubal's purview, to his amusement, his profit, sometimes his anger. Amalkre had never been discussed since Hannibal's return beyond Hasdrubal's quiet statement that he had made a tomb for her on a site that probably would have pleased her.

"Then this is your permission?" In some respects this was still an official visit. Formal coupling between Carthaginian officers and natives needed official approval, not so high as Hasdrubal, but approval. The smiles, grins, were threatening the formality here.

"It is. What would she like for the ceremony? We will have it here."

"She will not take her vow before either Apollo, or Dionysus. She tells me that these gods are too frivolous. She has mentioned Asclepius."

"I believe my statuary here doesn't include him."

"Eshmun's temple is the largest and richest in Carthage. Some of the Greeks in Carthage and Tyre have assimilated him to Asclepius."

"That's close enough for our purposes. By Eshmun's' balls, they'll send us a decent replica of him for our wedding—or their silver river may have some holes in it." Hasdrubal's *our* just put the strongest possible official endorsement on Inanna and Hannibal.

Letters were sent to Carthage about the wedding, at least two of which went to the Lady Barca. Before the wedding, within a moon's cycle, a large box arrived at Carthago Nova via a swift packet ship. A week later, a statue of the neo-Asclepius—about half size, but bronze, well worked, in a pose that would give a supplicant both inspiration and courage—also arrived on Hasdrubal's private dock.

Inanna came to Carthago Nova two weeks before the wedding. Hasdrubal had an apartment prepared for her whose separation from Hannibal's could be called discreet, or frustrating, depending on the point of view. One evening she was walking in the garden that adjoined her apartment. She was wearing a long chiton, with a red cloak. Her hair was caught up in a classic mold of Greece, with some constraint by a white silk band that picked up a little of the Carthaginian geometricals on the hem of her gown. Tiny gold pendant earrings, without gems, were her jewelry.

There was a movement near one of the paths of the garden, and then Hasdrubal's wife, Medina, a princess of the Tagus Celtiberi, materialized. Medina was no concession to Greece. She wore a white, bottom flounced, Iberian skirt, girded by braided black leather with a silver clasp. A black shawl of intricate embroidery was draped over her white silk blouse and unconstrained long black hair overlay the intrigues of the shawl. Her jewelry was multiple silver hoop earrings, and a woven silver throat band centered with a ruby. Medina's face had the tight sculpture and prominent nose of the Iberian, a stage where beauty, frivolity, and the passions given to this kind of woman could play havoc with a man, or another woman not similarly armored. She stopped about five paces from Inanna. They had never met. Medina had changed places with Amalkre fast enough to pulse some of the tapestries on the walls of the private apartments. She and Hannibal, and his brothers, exchanged amenities, but there had been no woman-to-woman axis for her to test herself, her position in a household, or the empire where the Barca name and presence were almost ubiquitous.

"Our garden is honored by a fusion of Greece and Carthage, tonight. You are a perfect accessory for it, Inanna."

Inanna held her ground, and sent a smile toward Medina that had no subterfuge. "May I say that your *Iberian* presence rounds out the accessories for it, wonderfully?" If Medina had put any challenge into her word *accessory*, Inanna had just turned it around, and made another smile, also without subterfuge, come from Medina. They continued the slow walk around the garden that Amalkre had started. The rich botanicals were enough to carry the conversation, but there were some short diversions that pulled Medina and Inanna closer together:

"Hannibal will be Hasdrubal's strong right arm, Inanna."

"I fear that Hamilcar's shade may be pushing both of them too fast. Do you hear his whispers, Medina—*Hamilcar's*?"

"Carthage has put monitors—Hasdrubal calls them spies, into Iberia. The whispers are getting much more complicated. I hope we can become close friends, Inanna. I hear you have Delphic antecedents, so I'm counting on your calming perspectives."

"The Pythias put out as much fear as joy. I may not be equal to your task, Medina." Inanna came close to Hasdrubal's wife, kissed her, and as she stepped away," But I will try to work on your calming—if you promise to work on *mine*."

Neo Asclepius had been installed in a bower of Medina's choice. His aura was bolstered by a fusion of colorful botanicals, red, white, yellow, lavender, that her husband had to say was Babylonian—*shamefully* Babylonian, with a playful eye to the Carthaginian representatives who would attend the nuptials. When the moment of ceremony arrived, Inanna's father and Hannibal were standing in front of the bower, about twenty feet in front of Asclepius. Hasdrubal, Medina, and the wedding guests were arrayed behind the principals. Inanna entered the bower by a side path. Two Iberian maidens attended her, carrying bouquets of the tiny blue flowers Inanna had used in the chaplet under her veil. Her gown comprised several layers of silk; the inner layer was white with a vertical striping of silver threads, fitted to her so that it sculpted her body from knees to breasts. The outer layer was also white, styled like a chiton, sheer enough to give a stage to the inner, silvered, mould of her. Her veil was yellow, also silk, and sheer enough to dispute its intent. She wore short heeled slippers, saffron colored. This subtle revelation of Inanna was enough to perturb the breath pattern of her husband imminent, but it was the hem of her veil, and the broader hem of her chiton which put her father's breath into this effect and magnified it for Hannibal. Indian thread artisans acknowledging their Chinese basis with gold and silver thread and other colors of their palette, had put memories of Sumeria, Armenia, Persia and Egypt into the hems. The Lady Barca had also supported this particular culmination of her son's bride. When Inanna stopped in front of the bower, she made a slight obeisance to Asclepius, and then turned toward Hannibal and her father. The ambient light collaborated perfectly with the amorous goddess that her father had started and she had never bothered to deny—especially in front of Hannibal.

Her father and Hannibal stepped toward her, and then they separated, her father on her right, Hannibal her left. The guests, witnesses, also moved closer to this crux of the wedding.

"I give this woman for the procreation of legitimate children."

"I accept," Hannibal said.

"And one talent dowry."

"I am content," Inanna's husband concluded. The dowry was a term in the equation of marriage. But he was standing close to a wife that all of the Barca's treasure couldn't buy. He sneaked a peek at her, but she had anticipated him and met his eyes.

The wedding banquet filled the palace dining hall. Sosylos, Silenus, managed to pay their respects without more than ceremonial comment. But in Sosylos' case, there was a moment of the eyes between him and his academic charge that was an inadvertent masterpiece of private encyclopedia. Inanna had been momentarily diverted by another joke of Medina's which accompanied ribald recitation from guests and entertainers alike. And her veil still obeyed custom and was in place, so any surveillance of her husband had to be imperfect. Yet why did the color of Hannibal's ears from another time manage to intrude that instant of Sosylos?

They were escorted right to the door of their apartments, pummeled with confetti and bits of quince, and sweetmeats, and the wails of flutes. Inanna actually managed to nibble a bit of quince in deference to her fertility obligation, and her husband had the fun of wiping her chin under her veil which was still resolutely in place. His brothers Mago and Hasdrubal had been close attendants to them in the ribald panoply that insisted in covering them after the bower formalities, during the banquet, and along the procession which took a very roundabout path to the newlyweds' apartments. Just before Hannibal scooped Inanna into his arms and stepped across his threshold, Medina came close to Inanna, raised her veil enough for a lip kiss, and whispered something that gave Inanna and Hannibal basis for laughter, and some apprehension, respectively.

The Lady Barca's gift had provided for the apparel Inanna could wear in the interval between her wedding gown and the nuptial bed. More silk, but unadorned sheerness, of various colors for her own designs of beguilement. But she never got to them. Her husband carried her directly to the bedroom where they would lay together for the first time. A monumental frustration was about to end. She had waited for him. He had enrolled in a special university for her.

He removed her slippers first, then the chiton, the veil still in place. The silvered sheath of her was still at full advantage because he had kept her standing, walking around her during his ministrations, reveling in the perfection of her, her knowing surveillance of *him* bringing her eyes and lips into the full panorama of her for him. Before he started to remove her inner sheath, he had to inspect the full mould of her, partly by finger touches, partly by lip touches when his resolve of the casual, nearly surfeited, aristocrat had slipped down another notch because of *her*. He slipped the sheath off her shoulders and started it downward, the revelation of her breasts momentarily halting the kiss he inserted under her veil. When she was all undone, except for the veil, he laid her on the bed against a mound of pillows while he prepared himself for her. She had seen him nearly naked on several of their swimming episodes. She had not seen this full maturity of him, and when he moved toward her in the full regalia of a smitten groom, she was not inclined, or able, to bring up any diversion of speech from her extensive repertoire. Her chaplet was at a crazy angle on her head, but it fitted this moment of her even though all she could provide for it was a vision of her for him.

When the veil came off, there was no ceremony. It was pulled by him— maybe her—in the throes of mutual revelation that he had started by his lips and hands and had now come to the part where gasps, little cries, more tries for breath in the interstices of the sounds which came from both of them, held sway. He was insistent, tender. He led her to where she led him, and then the wonderful cycle started again but without repetition, only a discovery that fed on discovery. When the amenities of the bed were a shambles, they had to rest. This wisdom came to him first, then it trickled to her, though when she rested she was on her knees, their eyes close enough for her to suck secrets from him that his mouth might deny.

"Should I say *virtuosic?*" It wasn't a whisper, she had found voice enough for a solid inquiry.

"It might betray a lack of sophistication if you did." He had enough energy for a quick kiss, though *his* voice was close to a whisper.

"Ah...but to recognize it is no shame on me. I bask in it. I *revel* in your university."

"Where did you get *that* word?" Sosylos—damn his eyes—made an instant's intrusion.

"It was a word, *naturally* beckoned forth in the face of virtuosity. A man—like you—would have had suffered diversion from a relentless soldier's program to achieve it." She leaned back against a pillow which accidentally still partially fulfilled its destiny. In her speculation she played her eyes around various parts of her arena, which was mostly him. He moved to restore some of her closeness.

"*You* are my university."

"Perhaps." Why did his ears suddenly intrude—again? Not the *present* ones—the ones that had taken a definite blush when he laid his mother's permission for the marriage in front of her father...the *bases* of her permission.

Ah! She had committed too much to her letters. Sosylos was his tutor. In this office, he was privy to most of Hannibal. Sosylos could read. He could teach. He could advise. Her husband was insisting on more of his rights at that moment...she started to comply, but she was still capable of speech:

"I think my correspondence with your mother has just put on more scope." This didn't deter him...it might have even enlarged his immediate program for her.

Much later, she put on one of the bedroom silks from Carthage...it was pale yellow, the miraculous delicacy of it mocked modesty, and she found a way to drape it around her head, then down her body, so that with touching her fingers to the various symmetries of the silk, and slight body movements, she was the animation of any goddess he could think of at that moment. They went to a private veranda under stars and moonlight. At the balustrade, Mediterranean whispers enough speech for them, she found that kissing a closely conjoined naked husband, while sheathed in silk that was almost nakedness, was delightful and likely to be habitual. Hannibal stepped away enough to make a speech to her:

He looked up, located Polaris, and pointing to the star, he said, "Firm thou art; I see thee, the firm one. Firm be thou with me, O thriving one!" He turned to Inanna. "To me Brihaspati has given thee. Obtaining offspring through me, thy husband...live with me a hundred autumns." The moon-bolstered axis of their eyes completed that recitation in silence. She had to come closer to him, but not so much as to hamper an observation, with a question.

"That was...Greek...Greek like. I...*adore* you." It was almost a whisper, a perfect prelude to further proof of her confession, then, "Who is Brihaspati?"

"Don't know. Your father said something about the old Hindus...he must be one of their gods—obviously a benevolent one."

"My *father*?" He had made many discoveries in her eyes in the past hours. He had just found another wonder of surprise in them.

"I asked him for a poem...*something* I could say to you that would touch the country of that tantalizing Sumerian nymph who's been bedeviling me. His immediate Sumerian notes were elusive on this subject, but his Hindu were not...he told me this was the best he could do on short notice."

"The Hindus and the Sumerians *obviously* shared many sensitivities. I am content," she said, paraphrasing the formal almost-husband of hours ago. This was a diminuendo that ended in a whisper, and it *was* the prelude he had been waiting for.

The coastal plains near Carthago Nova were not the harsh presence of the Meseta, where any conceivable terrain for horse and foot practice could be encountered, studied and worked from every angle a commander could imagine. These gave flatness, where large horse formations could be developed and honed, and integrated into attack strategies with foot contingents for various enemy dispositions. There were three Carthaginian officers watching a horse and foot exercise this day, horses perched on a promontory of rock overlooking the field where a thousand horse and three thousand foot had been maneuvering for several hours. A cloudless sky put a deep blue into the Mediterranean backdrop in front of them.

"You like to play games with straight lines, big brother," Mago said to the Commander of Cavalry, who was watching the foot form an advancing convexity, with cavalry on the right and left wings. Horns were signaling, and the response to them wasn't bad, but they had a long way to go. They knew about the Roman horns—the lituus, the buccina, the tuba, and the cornu. The last war with them that had spilled over Sicily and North Africa had given them good examples of the ways the Romans used them—the sounds peculiar to the them, the patterns of use of the sounds. The Carthaginians were developing new horns, and new signals which could cut through battle hysteria to a man's consciousness, keep him close to *his* plan, closer to *his* life.

"Do you remember your naval history, little brother?"

"I'm a *Carthaginian*. By Tanit's tits, big brother—I've had it stuffed into me."

"So, there was another Hamilcar who had some business on the waters off Cape Ecnomus. He liked to play with straight lines, too."

"Sicily. The Romans beat the hell out of us in that battle. Where's your brag here, Hannibal?"

"Hamilcar pulled the Roman fleet toward his center by advancing it toward them, and then when he had them huffing toward it, he pulled it back and had them set up for a nice slaughter with his wings."

"The slaughter was the other way around—not a good memory for us."

"His line officers had no balls—or brains. He handed them a slaughter on a silver platter and they pushed it away. "

The horns had just sent an array of signals over the field. Hannibal watched the center of the advancing convexity of the foot start a pull back maneuver that could suck an over zealous adversary into deepening wings. It needed plenty of polish, but these troops—Iberians, some Africans, Balearics, were beginning to understand his lectures about pulling an enemy into your advantages, using his habits and the cooperation of the cavalry that Hannibal was bringer closer to the foot operations with every practice.

"Your Mushroom planting is coming along, Hannibal." Brother Hasdrubal's attention had been on the cavalry phase of the exercise that was concluding in front of them. He mentioned several unit commanders who had once been in the column that he and Hannibal had led along the Bay of Tunis, and through the gates of Carthage.

"When they have five, ten thousand horse around them, and a hundred thousand foot swarming around *that*, they will be coming into their own."

"By Melkart's resonant member, you do have *big* plans brother." Looking at the field in front of him, it was hard for Hasdrubal to put another hundred thousand into it. It would take an imagination comfortable in hell's fire to do that.

Riding back to Carthago Nova, Hannibal, Mago and Hasdrubal had kept silent, letting the horses make the noise until their summaries of the day came to various ends, at various times.

"The Celtiberians have a knack for cavalry. " Hasdrubal turned to his companions.

"*And* the foot," Mago added. "That's a stream that could put big muscle into the expedition. Can we keep them coming toward us as allies? " Hannibal was the logical focus of that question, but the horses put down a lot of hoof beats before he answered. Mago had to interpret that silence. "He's tired, Hasdrubal...it will come."

"This...*tired*...is it the commander that does it—or the bridegroom?"

"No bridegroom here, Hasdrubal. I've been able to call the fair Inanna, sister, for *three years*."

"I'd have bet on your marriage shortly afterwards, little brother...she is inspiration for it." Hasdrubal reached out and managed to pat Mago's horse.

"Hannibal has stolen the only woman who could tie me into blessed matrimony."

That did it. Hannibal replied to Mago's question that now had whiskers. "...If Hasdrubal can keep his damned Secret Police off the Celtiberian's backs."

Hannibal had come close to argument with his chief on this subject several times. Hasdrubal the Handsome always used the argument that he had to let the Council and the sufets—the personification of Carthage—poke their noses into Iberia to keep them calm. That meant political, economic, and military advisors from the Council. It also meant the Secret Police, a venerable backdoor arm of the Council whose total presence had waxed and waned, depending on the content of paranoia in the men who came to the head of Carthage.

At the moment, the Council liked to keep this big eye in Iberia. *Per se*, this was not Hannibal's problem. It was the back-up to these nosey squads that bothered him—the torture, the quick incarceration and execution. And the hostages from noble Iberian families, even their wives and children in some cases, to enforce good behavior. *Good behavior* was bloated with ambiguity, and the muddled objectives of a Council far removed from a scene that hundreds of conscientious Carthaginians were trying to make profitable for Carthage, and prideful for the natives according to various measures that included mining, manufacturing, ship building, farming, as well as the service of some Barca dreams that might not coincide with Carthage's.

Hannibal didn't add anything to his answer. His feelings about the Secret Police had been well aired in front of his brothers and Inanna, Medina, and the other Hasdrubal. His native recruitment strategies were increasingly hampered by this souvenir from Carthage that was diametrically opposed to his personal and official styles.

He had hurried to Castulo three years before because the Secret Police had made a suspicious hell hole out of mining and smelting centers that had been running smoothly under Hamilcar. Inanna's father, hence Inanna, had been threatened by them when he objected to the threats to his workers. When Hannibal declared his feelings for Inanna in front of Hasdrubal, he also cast a small Barca gauntlet that resulted in Hasdrubal's first significant direct opposition to the Council, a relaxation of the surveillance in the crucial mining and smelting areas. Any appeal to the preservation, even brightening, of their silver river from the Iberian springs was the best way to put opposition in front of the Council. Hasdrubal used this technique and had had no problems from this particular bit of recalcitrance.

His real problem, like Hamilcar's, was buried in a perspective that looked ahead more than sideways and behind. He had expedited some of his own policies in Iberia by allowing the Carthage interference. One of his penalties for this concession was that many of the footprints of the Secret Police were necessarily outside his purview. When a young prince of the Tagus Celtiberi had objected to the wife of a neighboring kinsman being taken as hostage, under the *good behavior* policy that Hasdrubal had not leashed sufficiently, he went too deep into Carthaginian territory with his complaint and was taken by the Secret Police. While appeals for mercy trickled toward Carthago Nova, he was tortured to death by a sub-authority that had had a miserable autonomy in nearly all of Carthaginian Iberia under Hasdrubal the Too Farsighted.

The rest of the ride toward Carthago Nova was again mostly left to the horses' hoof beats. The tendencies of the other Hasdrubal to kingship, emperor, were a sometimes joke among these Barcas. He had had coinage made with an assimilation of himself to Melkart. He had worn a gold crown in some meetings with native authorities. But he had kept the Romans quiet by a non-aggression treaty, and he had been diplomat enough, and kingly enough, to bring tribes under his sway that were gradually confining Roman sympathizers to a few coastal cities.

Hasdrubal the Handsome was an intelligence, an illusion, an ambition working in a complex country and situation. No one *knew* him, probably himself included. Hannibal had confessed this belief to his brothers and Inanna. He was thinking about it now as the escarpment that held the palace and Inanna came into view. Hamilcar had not bothered to look back enough. Such a look was forced on him one day on the Jucar. *By the grace of Melkart who shares the silver shine on your coins—look over your shoulder more often, Hasdrubal!*

Rain squalls spawned by an Atlantic storm battered the palace. A full moon and the howling pulses of wind, made animated shadows of inanimate subjects. Sophocles, Euripides could have put words on a background like this to fit their premonitions and the following action. The palace guard had been relaxed to a cluster of three men at the gate, and when a black cat ran, or was thrown, in front of their guard post, they came to noisy life, threw pebbles at it, stared after it with curses and laughs, and then retreated to their shelter as the terrified animal ducked into a farther corner of the night. Another more sinister piece of blackness had just flowed past the guards, but toward the palace— larger than a cat, athletic leg strokes moving swiftly from the guarded perimeter toward a residential interior mostly committed to sleep.

"I have heard more than rumors, Hasdrubal. My maids...people in the markets, are talking about this Carthaginian presence that is *no* diplomacy. It is spreading blood and terror over innocent people." Medina wore a peignoir of white cotton. The Egyptians had put silk into it and it presented her body to a close observer almost without reservation. Her maidservant had brushed her hair. It spilled down her back and into black strands over her shoulder which she stroked with a finger. No jewelry. She took her look away from her husband long enough to remove her sandals...her last concession to the world outside Hasdrubal's bed. He was standing near the bed, watching this progressive revelation of her that had not gone stale three years after she had replaced Amalkre.

"I can't be everywhere, every time." He moved toward her. He was naked, and he wasn't interested in conversation. She was standing full, her statement unsatisfied, his present requirement overriding it. She didn't move to accommodate him. But her breasts moved with quick demands of breath in a passion of concern he wouldn't understand in that moment of tender lover, or officer—whomever he would choose. He had left a gold arm band in place, and she eyed this ornament that had been an unpleasant accessory of other couplings that had also had less than mutual resolve.

He had changed from the impetuous, no dissembling, officer with playful fantasies that seemed to cope with her reasonable and unreasonable Iberian passion. The scope of their earlier married whispers had changed... the confessions of his day that brought the hero, the fool or wise man of him to her...the spoken tokens of love that prompted her to exceed him in these soft declarations, had diminished, they had almost gone. There had been no children in those more than three years. Now, she didn't think she wanted his child. She had just posed a serious state of his affairs and he had dismissed it with a triviality. These Carthaginians were trying to make a conquest here with all the solid attributes of empire—but it could be a gory wash away if they didn't put their savagery far behind their management and diplomacy. This man in front of her had not decided where to put these good attributes—or himself— and she was beginning to think he *couldn't.*

The shadows thrown against the complication of verandas, passages, walls, floors, hallways surrounding the inner apartments were not all imitations of animation. The blackness that had slipped past the outer guards had worked itself closer to the nucleus, by trial and error. A single guard, blocking a corridor leading to a bronze door that bore Hasdrubal's red eagle's head against a gold plate, would reveal the nucleus.

"I don't like these complaints intruding our bedroom." He stepped closer to her.

"This seems to be the only place where you listen to me, anymore."

Another step put him within touch of her shoulder. He used the closeness and ignored her slight flinch. These Iberians wore their passion on all parts of them—it was a matter of sorting it out for your purposes. He pulled her toward him and kissed her, moving his hands around her buttocks and an accessible breast. He stopped a kiss that was only his, and tried to find better accommodation in her eyes.

"What you've just worried about is *my* responsibility and not a fit province for you." She saw an instant of her first Hasdrubal as he made a small smile and continued to search her eyes. "I pray for your better Iberia, Medina. I have good men on my side...I will have more—I think this is a realistic prayer."

"Where do you say this prayer, Hasdrubal, where your gods *and* mine can hear them?—this is an important communion."

He picked her up and carried her to the bed, his lips working her lips, her neck. Her peignoir was no barrier, although he let it be a delicious intermediary for a few moments as his hands and lips worked a larger territory of her after she was on the bed. She heard him say that he could handle only one communion at a time. Then she gave up that stage to him.

Wind noises covered the blackness that had found a central corridor, a glimpse of a lone guard. A vase crashed to the floor from the muscle of the wind. The guard ran toward the noise, opening Hasdrubal's nucleus.

Medina was no longer the unnaked one in that room, and this category entitled her to a limbo where frustration, anger, lustful recapitulation were put together and made her a party to the nonsensical stream-of-consciousness conversation he had started without her.

The blackness got through the eagled door, and found the bedroom after separating the wind sounds from the almost rhythmic sounds that had both carrying power and easy identification. Neither occupant of the bed saw the intruder, who played the voyeur before his assassin's role. He stepped closer to the bed, pulling a sword and a dagger from underneath the black cloak that had blended him into that night. His head was also uncovered. It was Celtiberian, shaded more to the Celt than the Iberian. A gold neck chain and small gold earrings put a noble stamp on him. He was young, probably not more than twenty five. As he weighed his weapons in practiced motion, his face was an interesting amalgam of the appreciative student and the obsessive revenger, a tragedy of purposes that had fulfilled the stages he'd crossed that night.

"Your memory of your people's blood is too short, my lady." His voice timbre, his language, skewered into Medina's enforced reverie. She screamed when she saw the intruder, and this pulled Hasdrubal up to *his* surface. He saw the sword and dagger, expertly poised. He didn't move.

"I am an ambassador of the Tagus Celtiberi." The Celt named the noble who had received the beastly ministrations of the Carthaginian torturers a few weeks before. The weapons were steady on their target and Hasdrubal knew that death had come into the room.

"I am sorry about your chief—it was not done under my order." He had engaged the young one's eyes, but this parley would be a short one, and no words could change it. But he was a man, a husband, a sometime soldier—so he had to make a move. He pushed Medina away from the Celt, and tried to swing his legs into a fighting stance. Medina screamed again as the sword and then the dagger found Hasdrubal's chest and neck, respectively. His blood spurted on her, on the bed clothes, and marked the Celt as he looked at Medina, hesitated a moment, and then ran from the room, her screams accompanying him. Medina, painted with Hasdrubal's blood, ran from the apartments into the hall, toward Inanna and Hannibal, her choked hysteria trailing across appropriate stages. The Celt was stopped before he left the palace. To what promised to be his detriment, he was taken alive, virtually unscathed.

Inanna gripped Medina with both arms to keep her from falling, Hasdrubal's blood now shared between them. Hannibal didn't need an explanation; he rushed to Hasdrubal's apartments, leaving Inanna to cope with a night that had fulfilled its qualifications.

"He's dead...he's dead." Medina's hysterical effusion was barely decipherable, but Inanna's face was close to Medina's, her lips trying to contact, to calm, an elusive target. Inanna maneuvered them to a couch, Medina's hair falling around both of them, clotted blood its only decoration. No questions, but Medina wouldn't let it go at that. Inanna's ministrations had recovered some of a voice that had used only screams for its best effort the past seconds.

"I could feel the premonition—like the knife that finally came. He wouldn't worry about it. He said...he said he had good men around him who would help him take care of my...worries. By your Zeus, Inanna, he could look ahead— but not enough *around* him. Death was coming toward him...he could have defended himself weeks ago—but not *tonight*." Memory of instants ago twisted her face and took her shaking voice into another deep place.

"Hannibal has said some of this." Inanna had not yet taken the implication of what Medina had laid in front of them. She was still bound with Medina's life.

"He had changed. He had pulled away from me...I could have done more...I started to wallow in my own tears...I should have thought more about *him*...I should have *done* more for him. Inanna—I am a *princess* of the tribe that *killed* him!" Medina's face, close to Inanna's at that crux of misery, was a perfect conclusion for the stages she had shared that night. Inanna was silent, her Greekness fusing with Medina.

When Hannibal returned to his apartments, Inanna had placed Medina in the hands of her maidservants, with instructions for a carefully attended bath, massage, and a drug helpful toward relaxation and the deep sleep that was her best refuge. Inanna had not yet shed the night robe that had Hasdrubal's marks. But this was a match for Hannibal's own robe which had souvenirs of his close attention to Hasdrubal's remnant. When he entered the ante-room to their bedroom, Inanna happened to be there. She had been trying to settle her own inclinations to flee, of this way, or that way—to Hannibal, or Medina, or just into the night to let the rain try its cleansing against the misery that clung to her. When they faced each other, an observer would have had hard pickings between the two of them if he looked for calm resolution of the rest of that night. Hannibal's eyes picked hers up, roved beyond her to a room that had been *their* arena only an hour ago—superior in mutuality to a now bloody other one close in space and time—and then to the portico where the vestiges of a declining storm could be seen and better heard. His eyes and face were more suited to the portico. When he spoke to her, he faced that direction before he faced her:

"Three of Hasdrubal's officers came to the room while I was there." He hadn't turned to her yet. "They called me...Lord General Hannibal." The finishing diminuendo ended in her direction...a tightening of the lips that wasn't a smile, his eyes sharing what was left of shocked surprise with her. The implications had just struck Inanna. A hand covered her mouth, her eyes were wide enough to receive more of him, but he only looked at her, a twenty-six year old soldier who had just received as much of Hamilcar's shade as anyone would ever get. He came close enough to touch her robe, on a spot of Hasdrubal.

"You came close to hell tonight—I swear that I will not put you in that way again."

"You did *nothing* in that way. You had premonitions about Hasdrubal and you were not alone there. Heimarmene closed his book on Hasdrubal tonight—there was *nothing* you could have done about it."

"I don't put so much on your Fate—your *Heimarmene*—as you. I had more than premonitions. I had knowledge of Hasdrubal's trouble that killed him. I could have moved in that direction to help him."

"Medina said almost those words as I wiped blood from her face. You two put too much on yourselves. If you could be all places, at all times, you could perhaps interfere with Heimarmene—but you can't." She touched a spot of blood that his fingers had moved from his robe to his chin. He had just revealed that her god had looked in his direction. The implications were starting to swarm on her. She didn't say anything. He gave her the opening:

"I am Hamilcar, now." This time the lip tightening came closer to a smile, but it was a cavalryman's smile...a sometimes enigma where a saber's edge can determine which way the corner of a man's mouth will turn given an accident of opportunity. She took the enormity of his declaration, also the tentativeness of it.

"You will have good people on your side. I am paraphrasing some more of what Medina told me." But she didn't couple the words to death like Medina had done.

"You...and you...and *you*—that's three of them." He finally got around to a kiss.

"And Mago, Hasdrubal, my correspondent who is a Carthaginian lady of note, Sosylos, Silenus to record you for posterity, Maharbal, Carthalo...so *many* of them."

"Are you finished? If you gave Medina a bath, you can give me one."

"Not quite...there's another *one*. You will soon have the opportunity to show your merits as a father." That took him away from her lips for a moment, his eyes surprised, shocked, delighted, a much different casting than for his Hamilcar announcement.

"A boy, or girl?"

"Even Pythia in the throes of her thickest bay and laurel smoke couldn't tell you that. You will have to be patient." He had finally made a smile on her that could have gone to laughter at another time, but his interrupted kiss stopped all of that.

8

28 years
219 BC—Iberia

T he column had the body and sound that three thousand horse, ten thousand foot, twenty elephants, and a baggage and booty train appropriate to it and a successful campaign in rich country, could bring to it. It had the sheen of deep sweat, fatigue concession—fatigue resistance—that only successful work against good adversaries can also bring. They had swept deep into the Vaccieni territory, taken the strongholds of Salmantica and Abula, and were now trailing Carthaginian presence southeast through the part of the Meseta that crouches between the Tagus and Durius watercourses. This expedition was close to putting significant Iberia into the Carthaginian camp, a cap which had taken almost two years from Hasdrubal's death to put on.

"Praising Ba'al's balls, Hannibal, you've nudged us damn close to the Roman limits that the Handsome One put on us." Maharbal rode on Lord General Hannibal's left. Carthalo was on his right. Mago and Hasdrubal were in cavalry units behind them, and so were his Mushrooms.

This army was coming together. They had blooded against good men, well armed and horsed. Faces—actions with the faces—swarmed him and he was taken away from Marharbal's statement for some moments of recapitulation. By whatever panoply of gods you wanted to scratch, this army *was* coming together. He could feel it in the horse separately, the foot separately and most of all, he could feel it in the conjunctions of horse and foot they had made under serious action. This column was not fleshed out yet with the full talent he would bring into it, but it was palpably a worthy receptacle for his Africans, and his plans beyond the Africans.

"The Romans should have studied this land more. They left us a big gate in their fence where the Jucar decides to take a little northern stroll." The elements and the land hadn't put any more color into Hannibal's face, he had reached that equilibrium long before. His hair was a little longer, less sculptured, his general body honed to a near equilibrium of bone and muscle. His inventory of scars had given Inanna progressively more field for discovery, and she would now have even more. He wore a dust soaked red cloak over a cavalryman's tunic that was a compromise between the Carthaginian and the Iberian in style and field decoration. His Greek-style helmet, muscled cuirass, and greaves were plain steel. At the insistence of his staff, his helmet was distinguished by a plume of red-dyed horse hair. No other helmet in this army was so marked. He wore a sword, the Iberian falcata Hamilcar had awarded a promising swordsman, a round shield with the Barca blaze of a lion against an Africanscape. Hamilcar's jeweled dagger hung from his belt. His eyes, his face in the near vicinity of his eyes, were where time had put most of its mark. Inanna had tried to find the playful boy in them, had tried to coax red ears back on him again after she had made a close sounding of his eyes...but she had given up on this, contented now to draw a smile from him that she could still escalate into the passionate exercise that was a goal—boy, or no boy.

"Another time around that Roman gate, Hannibal, and you'll have all their kissers pushed up against the Mediterranean...maybe the old ladies of Emporium and Massilia *have* something to worry about." Carthalo's Numidians had seen action on this expedition, and what Carthalo had seen of it had put him even closer to the plans of this young commander who had to be called *cavalryman* before he was called, *soldier*. When he turned in his saddle to put his words on a better line to Hannibal, he saw something that kept the words coming:

"A scouting detail is putting hell to their horses to get to you, Hannibal."

The three lead officers turned toward the rear of the column. A secondary dust column pointing their way confirmed Carthalo. Hannibal raised his arm for stop.

"Lord Hannibal, we are favored by a good-bye from some Iberians." The scout had reined close to his commander, the way Hannibal liked it.

"Who?"

"They were spread out, but we spotted a few standards...we think we saw Vaccieni, Celtiberi...maybe Carpetani."

"How many?"

The scout turned to the others in his detachment, who came closer. "We didn't see the full array..."

"You can make a good guess, man—what did the hair on your neck tell you?"

"A big bunch of foot—maybe fifteen thousand. Five, eight hundred horse."

"How far behind us?"

"If we stop at the Tagus, they'll be nipping at us in four hours."

"By your Ba'al's balls, Maharbal, we've got somebody to give us a push through that Roman gate—the wrong way." That was all the conversation before Hannibal signaled the column to double time toward the Tagus.

Hannibal had ordered a defensive formation along the right, near, bank of the Tagus: elephants and slingers in frontal array, his foot behind them, his cavalry divided between his flanks, the baggage train closest to the river. The scout had given him a good guess. Four and a half hours after he was in place, the first signs of the good-bye party appeared, about a half mile from the Carthaginian position. This separation was preserved while the newcomers fully assembled by a process that was not conducive to envy. Carthalo addressed Hannibal—he mumbled to Hannibal, while drawing a practiced eye along the Iberian frontage, "Closer to twenty thousand foot...maybe a thousand horse."

"We left some loose ends, Hannibal." Maharbal's voice was better modulated, but it also paid respect to the size of the goodbye delegation and its constitution. They had just left battlegrounds that complimented the probable people in front of them.

Hannibal was studying the movement of horses around an array of standards that suggested a command center:

"They haven't decided which part of us they want to bite," he said. He watched the Iberian confusion for several more minutes. Then he rode closer to Maharbal and Carthalo, his deputy commanders.

"I would like to stand like Hercules in front of them until dark. Then we'll make fires."

"For us—or them—Hannibal?"

"For *them*, Carthalo. While they're wondering what delicacies are crossing our lips, we'll cross their damn river and look for a better place for their reception."

Hannibal got his column across the Tagus under a very good subterfuge of contented camping. His scouts soon reported that the Tagus made a nice U-bend within an hour's march. Centered on the convex side of that bend, now on the left cheek of the Tagus, he put his force into an array similar to the first, but with the crucial difference of a ford between him and the Iberians. He had invited them to a natural approach to the cooling hospitality of the Tagus that would give him almost automatic flanking position where he could suck their foot into his horse and elephants, before his foot returned their goodbye kisses.

The early morning consternation of the Iberians was fueled by the disappearance of a juicy morsel and its reappearance at an advantage of the Tagus that Hannibal had discovered and they had forgotten.

The Iberians threw parties of foot into the ford where they were met with arrows and slugs from slingers, and then by elephants and horses who crushed them. When the Iberians put their entire foot into the action, Hannibal pulled his elephants and horse away and uncovered his heavy foot. A disciplined advance of foot into the center of the Iberians, bolstered by his reformed horse on the flanks, worked a slaughter. He captured two chiefs of the Vaccieni, two of the Carpetani, and one of the Celtiberi, but he left more of his credentials floating down the Tagus like rafts of driftwood and scattered along its banks for a mile. He kept apart from contact in this action, although the sight of its bloody foam recalled a memory of foam like this, with Hamilcar in it, that almost pulled his sword into this river. Mago and Hasdrubal had not been so detached and they, particularly Mago, had made bloody substance of memory.

It had been a six week expedition, mostly planned action, with a surprise addendum that put a bigger conclusion into it than he could have imagined. He wanted to surprise her, so he slipped past his palace guards with a wink and a pursed finger to his lips. He did this again when he started to encounter household staff, and they let him go to his privacy of privacies, presumably unannounced, to make a presentable man from his miserably grimy campaigner. When he emerged, he was in a fresh, unadorned tunic, sandals, and a bit of gold chain around the neck. His manservant had tried to make a few passes at his hair, and finally succeeded in the closest approach to the Hellenistic prince he could make at that time, given an impatient client, and slippage away from this mode that Iberia had forced on this five year husband, two year father and Commander-in-Chief.

He walked to their apartments by a roundabout way that had sometimes actually surprised her, although her surprise could be acting that Thespis would've enjoyed. He was turning into a corridor that culminated in their bedroom wing, when a two year old Amazon rushed into it from the other end, followed very shortly by her mother—both of them unbashful about their screams and laughter which were rapidly converging on him. And both of them wore identically styled simple tunics, unadorned like his, ready for the roughhouse that was inevitable. Inanna let the young one be first with him, and he swept her into his arms with a terrible growl that didn't affect the laughter and little screams that came mostly from near his arms.

"Kyniska," he breathed into the long hair that was gathered in back by a small loop of braided gold...like her mother's hair, except Hannibal nuzzled a blond at the moment. She could say *daddy*, and she did. He whirled her about several times, and then without letting go of her, he somehow got Inanna into his clutches, and Inanna admired the dexterity that could achieve a solid kiss under these conditions.

"You could have warned me." Inanna had escaped, and was trying to find some severe demeanor, although her hand testing a curl underneath his silk headband was inconsistent with this. "And you've left your soldier at the door... no breathless anticipation of me that would have brought him right into me only a few months ago." He set his daughter on her feet, put one hand on Inanna's hand, still on his head, and the other around her waist.

"I stunk from horse and from everything between here and Salmantica—not fit for my two ladies." His kiss now had better purchase of her and it was a good precursor to more comprehensive affection that they would both put into another part of that roughhouse. "And as to that surprise—your scouts have a place with my army *anytime*."

"I had a warm bath prepared."

"May I intrude?" He had butt and leg muscles that could spend the rest of their life in a warm bath.

"It was for *you*...you great bear—you might have scratched her cheek with all that enthusiasm." It would take a few days, with his good razors, to regain his home face. That offended cheek was now in a grin that alternated between her mother and daddy. Her hands were also shared between them. Her name...*Kyniska*...had been born in a quick conference between Inanna and Sosylos, when Hannibal 's joy at a daughter had not seemed enough for either of them. In this conference, Inanna had prompted Sosylos with a tidbit:

"Spartan women have been models of independence for the Greek worlds. They have been property owners, businesswomen, they have..."

"Been horsewomen, chariot drivers...veritable Amazons." Sosylos had let that word loose before its implication for the immediate Barca clan had bowed to him. Inanna was obviously riding along with his historical backup. Big eyed, she stepped closer to Sosylos:

"Do you have a name for this *chariot driver*?"

Sosylos' memory accommodated them. "*Kyniska*, daughter of King Agesilaus—she was the first to win in the four horse chariots at Olympia."

"What did she look like?"

"I have no idea my lady. But a princess, an athlete, every facility catering to her whims—the natural aptitudes of the Spartan women that had breathtaking precedence with Helen. These things should let you say she was as beautiful as you want her to be."

"We will call our daughter, *Kyniska*, Sosylos."

"You will *suggest* that name to Lord Hannibal, Lady Inanna and giving it your strong endorsement...respectfully strong."

Inanna's smile, consonant eyes, capped that impromptu crisis. "You will, of course...corroborate, if absolutely necessary?" For the barest moment, she was caught on a tiny prick of reality that Sosylos knew was no handicap to either of them.

Sosylos', "Of course, my lady," was absolutely redundant.

Hannibal had been mightily solicitous of Inanna's recovery, comfort, and he had held their still unnamed daughter and walked with her in various places where he could nuzzle and coo her without too close surveillance. After such a private sojourn in one of their gardens, as he handed her back to a reclining Inanna, Inanna whispered, "Kyniska thanks you," when their daughter's cheek was close to hers again.

"What did you call her?"

"*Kyniska.*"

"What kind of a name is that?"

"Spartan." That pulled his attention closer to her.

"By whose authority is this *Spartan* attribution?" As if he didn't know.

"Sosylos'...she was a daughter of King Agesilaus, a horsewoman."

After *horsewoman*, he was on his knees in front of her, looking at their daughter. Inanna put in the crux credential at that moment: "She was the first woman to win at the four horse chariots at Olympia—driver, or sponsor, we're not sure—but it's the spirit that counts."

"What did she look like?" It was a natural question for a man, bolstered by ligaments of husband and father.

"Sosylos says that, given her situation, precedents, and prerogatives, we can attribute as much beauty to her as we please—without fear of dissension."

And *Kyniska* it was. As the long blond hair crowned her...and her shape and structure moved her quickly from crawling to stumbling walking to near equilibrium running, to nearly exuberantly confident running...he saw the Amazon in her that neither Inanna, nor Sosylos had broached in front of him—but that was another absolutely redundant thing.

They were now close to the warm bath. An attendant for Kyniska appeared, swept Kyniska into her arms and took her to some morning commitment. Inanna and her husband kept moving toward the bath.

He had moaned, and sunk into the warm caress that wasn't hers, up to his eyes, then over the top of his head. When he came up, her lips were close to the little fountain on his lips. His cooperation pulled both of them under, and she had to use some interesting leg entanglement and finger pressure locations to extricate herself and bring both of them to air again.

"Your ecstasy is *not* flattering," she said, rebuking his almost orgasmic communion with the warm water. But she understood the priorities of a man—a soldier like him, who had shed no stitch of Hamilcar's mantle since the terrible night of the shrieking shadows.

He came close to her, moved his hands against her breasts and then let one of them stray farther south on its own itinerary. Its impudence pulled a gasp from her, precursor as it was to his erection which was unambiguously flattering. As he moved her around the bath, she worked her legs around his legs, his back, and all the time her lips were fused to his when she wasn't rediscovering the territories of his face, ears, neck. His ears had done their duty. They had confirmed one of his best compliments to her, another Amazon's compliment to her, so they were now on no special agenda, only part of a regular one which was in progress.

Her head lay back against the smoothly contoured tiled edge of the bath, while his still water-bound attentions to her throat and her lower latitudes reached another culmination that had to be his last if her endurance had any say. Attributable laughter, a shouted rebuke, were suddenly projected into their tiled and marbled sanctuary, whose replication put the sound into barely earthbound consciousnesses. A naked Kyniska was upon them, followed shortly by her attendant whose grabs were continuing to be fruitless.

"I am sorry, my lady, my lord—she can..."

But Inanna and Hannibal never got to hear another version of what *she can*, because Kyniska had jumped into the bath, her flying nakedness giving her mother incentive for a scream and her father a shout, both responses degenerating into laughter that left the attendant at an embarrassing vantage. With Kyniska safely draped between her and Lord General Hannibal, Inanna reassured the attendant. "...All right, we'll bring her back."

Kyniska couldn't swim yet, but this was no handicap. She was a screaming, laughing ball that went between her mother and father, mostly on the surface. But Hannibal liked to take her under the surface where they could look at each other in the water world and see mermaids and monsters, respectively. Inanna couldn't keep *her* mermaid out of this other dimension of the roughhouse, so there were three-faced apparitions where the eyes swam very close together in play with bubbles and sounds, and fingers and swarming hair. When they exploded to the surface in concession to their mortal forms, it was Kyniska who was first to want to do it again.

"Take her, my husband is exhausted." Inanna handed her protesting daughter to Kyniska's handmaiden.

"Is my *exhaustion* a tribute to you, or Kyniska?" He had pulled her toward the center of the bath where his body was the logical locus for her fingers and toes needing repose or a target. She chose fingers, around his neck, simultaneous with lower latitude exploration which tended to confirm her charge to the handmaiden.

"This great battle on the Tagus..."

"I'm scarcely home...no official words yet...now you're talking about my itinerary." He had resources for a kiss. It was a wet one, and it slipped off her lips down to the tip of a breast. Her scouts *were* good. The Delphic Pythia would have been a sham without *hers*, so there was precedence here. "It was unexpected. It put us closer to all of Iberia." She gave him a pause. "It was confirmation." He took their eyes out of lock with the last word. It needed explanation. She prompted him.

"Of part of my army...of the power I can make of it."

She didn't need any addendum to this about Italian fields. On the night when he and Medina had brought some of Hasdrubal's blood into their bedroom, he had told her that *now, he was Hamilcar*. This claim had never wavered. It seemed far away when their daughter made mermaids and monsters with them. But her invocations to Asclepius denied this—almost unseen in their wedding bower, before that bower, and then afterwards at the various pauses Hannibal gave her. This god, this compassionate god, he *had* to give them moments like this to counterbalance the voids without him that Amalkre and Lady Barca had promised would come.

That night, their bed showed ungentle continuation of the questions and answers. But she had finally conceded legitimate fatigue to him and while he sprawled he seemed to dream. When she came close to his lips, their movement with slight sound gave her less than the quick movements of his lidded eyes which seemed inconsistent with earned repose...and she was grateful for his exclusion of her there. She put more questions to him, some statements about love and her commitment to *them*...all of it was unilateral, softest whispers, her passion making no concession to a nonreactive target. Then she slept.

Mago, Myrcan, Barmocar...Amarcar, Sulan, were his attendants under the auspices of the Senate and the sufets. They had been assigned as his consultants and auditors on economic, political, diplomatic and military matters that conceivably affected the whole body of Carthage. Most of them had been with Hasdrubal; most of them had been tolerated by him, and this attitude had fed the suspicion which had confronted Hannibal in the Senate chamber. He had pulled these men closer to himself as Lord General Hannibal. Without Carthage, without its endorsement of men, materials, ships, a policy of progress, he could become less than a mercenary, or a miracle of self sufficiency. At this time, he tended to shy away from miracles. The victorious campaign he had just completed, capped by an unexpected gift of culminating victory over the most powerful tribes, needed discussion with his consultants. Maharbal, Carthalo... his deputy commanders, Adherbal, his chief of engineers, would sit close to him when this meeting of friends occurred. Sosylos and Silenus had been variously close to him during his progress from boy to commander. They would attend him now, close to the arm of official Carthage.

Hannibal's smallest audience hall could put his people, and his auditors and consultants, advisors, into a cozy conjunction that fostered soft speech, the eye contact that could lead such speech to confidences, jokes, and the other peripherals to substantive agreement that actually accomplish it. Hasdrubal had put a throne-like chair for himself in his largest hall and a pretentious central chair in the smaller one which Hannibal had rejected for a chair like those provided for his conferees who did not stand entirely.

Hannibal was about to conclude his summary of the Iberian progress of Carthaginian empire. On a large papyrus sheet attached to a wall, he had put charcoal pencil marks that summarized the status of tribal allegiance following the Tagus victory.

"The Celtiberi, Carpetani and Vaccieni have decided they like to kiss us more than they like to fight us."

"The Celtiberi are our biggest asset?"

"I think their foot and horse contingents—now and future—will be an important muscle for us. They also have connections with Celts in Gaul and Italy that have interesting potential for us."

"I have heard rumors about inquiries we are making to some of these faraway Celts." The *we* the Carthaginian delegate had just used was an interesting affiliation with Hannibal that was slippery enough to give him an in, or an out, depending on Fate's caprices respecting Hannibal.

"I must let you peek into my dispatch case more often, Barmocar. We *have* sent inquiries to Celts who favor one side of the Alps, or the other."

"These were pleasantries about flora and fauna, and the gods who cavort with them." Barmocar, the senior Council representative, let his voice fall between a question and a statement, a practiced artifice of his trade.

"Only so far as these things would affect an army passing their way." This was a statement which could alarm a pacifist, or a disciple of Hanno, the Peace Party man, who cherished his perilous equilibrium with Rome. No one in that room suffered from the delusion that he was in the presence of a pacifist when he looked at Hannibal Barca at a time when the word, *Rome*, was nearby. Hannibal's word, *army* had no shocking power. "And to fill out your surmise, Barmocar, I must confess that inquiries have crept into the Po valley, even to the economic citadels of Campania. As you know, these places are Italian appendages of our Roman friends." Inanna would have appreciated the acting it took to make a sweet mouth when her husband cuddled the words, *Roman* and *friends* together.

"These peripatetic inquiries would *still* be related to flora and fauna, and cavorting gods, Lord Hannibal?" Barmocar could smile, and he did.

"If it pleases you, Barmocar, I could cast them in your light...if you keep it broad enough to cover an army, or an entrepreneur or trader or a banker—even a colonizer."

"These are precursors of a conqueror, an enlightened one. May I ask about your time frame here, Lord Hannibal...how excited do you want us to be?" If Hannibal had made the addition of Rome itself to the itinerary of his inquiries he would have put almost immediate excitement into that room, but for a while this could be his secret and Maharbal's and Carthalo's, and Adherbal's.

"I think we have come to a pass here, *Iberia*, that will put some wings on that time frame, Barmocar." Hannibal had been standing for some time, most of the others had used various public and private excuses for doing the same. His smile was comprehensive, taking in his own staff, and the delegates from Carthage. "Why I think I can hear wings *now.*" The drama was reinforced by a slight inclination of his head toward an opened window that had assured fresh air for this meeting, but the movement was redundant. But all they needed were his eyes, which seemed to see various wings that could start an army moving.

Myrcan, a Senate representative who kept a close ear to the vibrations Hannibal's cavalry put into the earth, was also interested in the word *inquiries* that had been slipping around that conference room. "How do you define *inquiries* Lord Hannibal?" Like the others of his delegation, he wore a short white tunic with Carthaginian geometric designs on the sleeve and bottom hems. Various personal jewelry affectations of these men included rings, arm and wrist bands, necklaces with and without pendants. Solid gold was dominant, the red garnet, sapphire and ruby were their favorite gem stones. Myrcan had chosen a gold neck chain and a ruby on gold ring this day. As he put his question, the dynamics of his hand, and the ambient light, favored his ring for the moment of Hannibal's attention. Aristocrat to aristocrat, was the coupling here, an aid to communication.

"Why, these are questions, statements to grease the answers, silences to let an answer mature, silences to listen to your head when there are no questions."

"You could put a lot into such...inquiries, Lord Hannibal. Words like *spy*, or *agent*, could fall into them easily, I think."

"Our friend, Barmocar, has complimented us with the phrase, *enlightened conqueror*, Myrcan. This is premature, but we will husband these gracious words for future use. This attitude, I think, gives your *inquiries* word a lot of scope—we won't deny this."

"What does this word tell you about the Po valley, Lord Hannibal?" Mago, a delegate who had strategic pretensions, and promising attributes therein, had put this query.

"It tells us that the Celts, the residents and those flowing around and across the Alps, are bringing living space ambition, and other very interesting credentials, to someone looking to confront a far ranging wolf."

"These other credentials?"

"Foot and horse actual and potential talent and weight that could be honed to the standards to which we aspire, and will need."

"We have heard that the Celts are a big bluster, swinging swords that melt on Roman armor."

"We hope the Romans continue to believe this—they may be choking on their own blood when they are disabused of this."

"About the inquiries that have enjoyed the southern exposures and Elysian fields of Campania...what do *they* tell, Lord Hannibal?"

"The Italic Confederation, that is the body and promise of Rome, is threatening the economic autonomy and prosperity of Campania with Capua its focus and citadel. It is also making these egregious overtures to Tarentum and the other Hellenistic cities and communities of southern Italy. Our inquiries suggest that success in northern Italy could prompt large-scale defection from the Confederation, and disabuse inclinations in that direction. A man given to visions might enjoy the spectacle of wolves being crowded into a progressively smaller pen, if he toys with the fruits of these inquiries enough." Hannibal wore a civilian tunic, Iberian sandals. His dress and jewelry ostentation was conservative. A close observer could see that, in the whole of him, he subsumed bits of Carthage, Iberia and Greece. If this observer lingered on his face, the charge of *visionary* could reasonably be laid on him. Myrcan picked up this word.

"Take us back to the wings of your timetable, Lord Hannibal. If your visionary should start to move toward his visions, I wonder what would trigger this—given of course, propitious omens covering the rest of the enterprise."

Hannibal used the walking spaces among his guests and came close to Myrcan, the strategist and questioner:

"The town of Saguntum is a Roman protectorate. It has both pro-Roman and pro-independence adherents. I think a case could be made for liberation of Saguntum from the Roman yoke. I think this would qualify for your *trigger,* Myrcan."

"You would provoke war with our Roman friends?" By the treaty of Lutatius Catulus, a reasonable conclusion to the First Punic War had been drawn which left room for reasonable friendship. Although the execrable Roman reaction to Hamilcar's subsequent expedition to Sardinia, allowable under the treaty, had warped the possibilities of friendship, they had not vanished and were, in fact, exploited on a daily basis by Carthaginian aristocrats under the aegis of their Peace Party. So, Myrcan's question had parts of truth and irony hovering around his *friends* word. For the Carthaginian guests, its net effect was a light silence, almost intruded by snickers. For the Carthaginian hosts, there was a deadly silence, which reached back to Hamilcar.

"In the Council, I claimed that Hasdrubal was continuing in my father's direction. In your presence—the Council's surrogate—I claim that I have been Hasdrubal's continuity, and that we are close to fruition of my father's ambition to tweak the Roman nose on its own ground. Iberian silver and gold, with fair diversion to Carthage, has paid for the means to do this. Outlays from my personal fortune have also paid for these means. Hamilcar's culminating ambition has been cut in stone at Carthage for a long time. The senators have looked at it, stared at it, cussed it, kissed it—but it is *still* there. It is as good a standard for Carthage as we will ever have, hereafter." His last *we* put him above Hasdrubal, who had borne some confusion about loyalties. It also put him above Hamilcar if, in his last days, Hamilcar's recapitulations of Carthaginian ingratitude had been too frequent, too strong.

"An attack on Saguntum is prerequisite for this...continuation of Hamilcar?" This crux question put Barmocar at room center, Hannibal close to him.

"The pro-independence Saguntines have been badly treated by the Romans. As Iberians, they have as much right to our protection as the pro-Roman faction has from Rome's. I think this policy will be supported by the Iberian tribes we have taken into our Alliance—now comprising virtually Iberia entire. A stand at Saguntum will weld this Alliance closer together. It will promote the fusion of our purposes and their capacities which is absolutely indispensable to our expedition."

"It will put the official stamp of war on your enterprise, Lord Hannibal."

"In the eyes of the world this is *also* indispensable."

"Do the Iberians enjoy some precedence of us in this Saguntum ploy?"

"No. I intend to call a congress of the Alliance and tell them what I have just told you. I will propose myself as the Alliance Commander-in-Chief."

"*Actually* you have achieved this eminence...officially..."

"I have not. The formalities are important here. They are impressed by them, by trappings of authority and..."

"Divine intervention. Your coinage assimilating yourself with Hercules was a notable step in that direction, Lord Hannibal."

"Hasdrubal led the way there. He came close to Iberian empire which could have been his glory."

"And Carthage's?"

"I prefer to think so, Barmocar."

Mago, with strategist pretensions and credentials, had not got far away from Saguntum. "Saguntum is a fortified town, I think." He had turned to Adherbal, Hannibal's Chief of Engineers.

"It has a strong, tight fortification that is situated on a difficult rocky base."

"Then, this will be no token assault." Mago spent a moment of his eyes on Hannibal before returning to Adherbal.

"We think that a sympathetic approach to their problem will lesson the difficulties.

We will appeal to reason, arbitration, the advantages of Iberian union away from the razor's edge of Roman benevolence."

"This presumes a pro-independence majority. You are dealing with many Greeks here. You may meet a classical Greek resistance if they turn up too many bad omens in their chicken guts after your approach to reason."

"Mago, we invite you to our strategy sessions." Hannibal had just virtually invited Carthage to the same sessions, where a nearly unanimous nod could spread the glory, or blame, over a broad front.

Three weeks after Hannibal had defined *Roman Trigger* for his Carthaginian guests, he convened the congress of Iberian princes at his palace. This time, he used Hasdrubal's largest audience hall, and he sat for a while on Hasdrubal's throne while he let the Iberians make various summaries of the situation between Iberia and Carthage. He heard some of Hasdrubal's, and then some of *his* souvenirs sweep the room: the intimidations and violations of the Secret Police, Hannibal's own expeditions which had touched most of significant Iberia with his mark, and the Carthaginian ambitions which posed poorly defined incentives and penalties to the natives.

Hannibal made his recapitulation of each point. The Secret police, and a skewed memory which put too much scope and autonomy on them, had brought the assassin to Hasdrubal's bedroom. Hamilcar had also paid for a convenient memory. Hannibal put both of these cases before them. He justified his program of expeditions, and he told them that his memory was better than Hasdrubal's, or his father's.

"I ask for your conference whenever—wherever, I have incurred your anger. I suggest that reasonable men will take that course. We will, therefore, take that course."

He frankly stated his Iberian objectives. His military bent was too well emblazoned from Gades to the farthest corner he had touched to be coy about it now. With Iberian foot and horse, Iberian armament, Iberian temperament, Iberian courage and resourcefulness, he would make the finest army in the world. A king of the Ilergetes, a tribe that stood close to a logical path to Rome, asked him what he would do with such an army.

"Why we will adventure, a little beyond Iberia. Do you think that *Lugoves* would frown on this?" He had just put the sun god of Celtic Iberia into the conference, using their own language. "I think that he would envy every step we would make with such companions, every opportunity we could seize with them. I ask to be your Commander-in-Chief for this adventure."

Redundant, or not, this petition filled Hasdrubal's big hall with more sound of boisterous harmony than it had ever held.

Then he moved to the trigger. He reviewed some history of Saguntum: the tentacles of Rome that now lay over this fair city of Iberia; the attempts of the pro-independence faction to throw off these tentacles; the savage Roman reprisal, which put the pro-Roman faction at intolerable odds with all Iberia; the precedents which would not permit Carthage to suffer this abuse by a notorious interloper of countries, nations...human decency. This was the trigger, but he didn't identify it. He put Saguntum in front of them as the first cap they would wear in the great adventure. He didn't broach the cornucopia that lay open to them in Italy. He would save this until the day, the hour, he made actual steps toward Italy with his companions. He had stood away from Hasdrubal's throne when he asked for his mantle of command. He had walked down into them when he answered the Ilergetes question. He was a focus of them, their annulus around him, when he put Saguntum in front of them. If the enthusiasm was perturbed by this specific of plans, it was palpably in his favor.

He walked from the room, unattended at his request. A man who identified himself by dress and ornamentation, a noble of the Gaulish Celts, stood near the doorway that would release the Commander from the physical Congress that had just anointed him. A close approach was naturally inevitable.

"I am Auros, of the Volcae."

"I am Hannibal, of the Carthaginians." Hannibal admired the well fitted long trousers, polished cavalry boots, silk shirt, wool vest and short cloak of the man almost as much as his good Greek that had opened their conversation. His cloak was pinned by a silver brooch that put a ruby-eyed snake's head into classic Celt clasp design in a virtuosic way. A gold arm band flashed outside the cloak, and a pendant, held by a gold chain, completed his jewelry. The pendant consisted of a coral colored enameled field interspersed by a filigree of gold wire that made a sylvan scene with a stag and hound contending. The economy of wire presenting the art here was also a virtuosic challenge of the Celt jewelers. The Volcae chieftain wore a dagger from a belt hanger, the belt clasped in silver by the double voluted 'S' of the classic Celt.

They were of a height, so the eye axis was comfortable, the mutual compliments on a minimal path. Hannibal wore Hamilcar's dagger, he admired the Celt's.

"May I see your weapon?"

The Celt obliged, the dagger's horse head pommel settling on Hannibal's hand. "Shall we reciprocate?" Bowing slightly to the Celt's counter-question,

Hannibal handed the gem-centered pommel of his dagger to the Celt underneath two warriors' smiles.

The Celt's dagger was a miniature of a saber: shape and symmetry very like the kopis, the sword that had filled the hands of the Greek hoplites, a graceful messenger of death that might have come from Etruscan sources, and Thracian and Eastern, also. Its steel was polished like Hannibal's, its edge was also razor like. The horse head pommel was bronze, and its handle was leather rings interspersed with silver and agate rings. Hannibal balanced it, held it so that more light could come from the blade.

"I don't think this, or its big brother, would wilt on Roman armor, Auros."

"Its ancestors cleaved Roman heads aplenty. This steel is *better*."

"The falcata is obviously in your debt. With your steel in it, I think we will play some good music for the Roman Wolves."

"I liked your speech, Hannibal. I have talked to some of your emissaries in my country. You will have a good path through us. I cannot answer for some of the others—the Medulli or the Centrones, for example."

"When I pray to *my* gods...I wonder if I also pray to *yours*, Auros."

"You are suggesting some communion of prayer to our mutual benefit, Hannibal?"

"I think that my fate is closely bound with yours, Auros. I think some practice of this kind of prayer would be in order, now."

"Your speech seemed to give an imminent itinerary. This suggests little time to practice the prayer you are calling *ours*." And then, as they exchanged blades, Auros said, "Did I just have the honor of Hamilcar's weapon?" The stories about the Barcas had had a wide audience.

Hannibal nodded, acknowledging a compliment, and then he turned it toward some philosophy. "My father...my wife's father...my wife, they have all looked eastward from time to time. Your blade has flowed from there. I think some other parts of Celtic power derive from there."

"You are tying this *mutual prayer* to the East, Lord Hannibal?"

"I am looking in that direction—some far looks , some not so far, for my strength. I cannot take all of it from Iberia and Carthage."

"Some of my people...my relatives, are in that direction from you. Then, if you keep flying in that direction, there are Greeks...and so on to the restless memories of Alexander."

The study of complexity in smiles could have found a university in Hannibal's and Auros'.

"You are anticipating me, Auros. Accordingly, my staff is always open to you. I have heard about your holy men, the Druids...I will be able to use them."

"I think you will find them, they will find *you,* if you keep looking eastward. But they will be harder to crowd into your mutual prayer than I."

"Then you *will* say this kind of prayer for us?"

"I will try to find some basis for it, Hannibal. Do you Carthaginians have a game called *follow the leader*?" Hannibal's unadorned gold chain necklace was no strong statement against the Celt's, but it was abetted by the sunlight in that moment in a way that pulled a Celtic smile to it.

"We tend to be cautious about such games, but I have played it. I think we may be starting it again…may I borrow your word, *imminent*?" Auros' answering smile was subtler, but it would still fit into this game.

Mago and Hasdrubal had taken the evening meal with Hannibal, Inanna and Kyniska. Some vestige of the Congress had pulled Hannibal away, but his orders to his brothers to not spoil Kyniska any more, lingered, if not obeyed.

"It is much too soon to put her on a horse, Mago."

"Inanna, you were precocious in this respect."

"How do you know this?" She was white and pale yellow in silk and thin linen. She wore a lapis necklace that had come recently from Carthage to her. Kyniska was not the only spoiled one under this roof. A tortoise shell comb set with tiny rubies tried to give some order to a then rambunctious Greek-mode coiffure that bolstered Mago's claim of precocity.

"Your father's ear is not monopolized by Hannibal. We have *our* talks."

"I will have no secrets left." Kyniska used this moment to jump on a reclining Hasdrubal who then made a good horse for a while. This left Inanna and Mago somewhat private and somewhat close. The Congress, and the meeting with the permanent Carthaginian delegation, had spilled into the evening a little before Hannibal left. Inanna's Delphic prescience wouldn't let it rest there. Her husband had been animated, talkative, playful in his husband and father modes, but he had been exasperatingly uncommunicative. Mago tried to correct this as soon as Kyniska and Hasdrubal galloped by them.

"Hannibal is close to throwing his dice in front of the Romans," he said, taking her hand. He had once confessed to Hannibal and Hasdrubal that this lady had been the only inspiration he had found for wedded bliss. She had heard about this. She might have been slightly closer to Mago than Hasdrubal because of it, but she kept the safe perimeters for everyone, and Mago really had no advantage except for her hand she had just let him take.

"I have heard the name, Saguntum…and much more of it recently. Do these tie together, Mago?"

"Hannibal and Myrcan, the sufets' man, called Saguntum *the trigger*. I think it will do for this."

"For what?" Mago's swim in her eyes could be only by invitation, and she had just offered it.

"For finally pointing Hannibal's juggernaught toward the Romans."

"That word has awesome connotations if you are a Hindu. What does it mean if you are Carthaginian?"

Mago released her hand and walked toward a portico that reflected a twilighted Mediterranean presence. She followed him, another question still touching Mago's back.

"I think it will mean much the same thing, if you count pouring devotion into it; if you make it terrible from the Roman side of it. They have never seen one like Hannibal. Alexander never saw one like him, Inanna." She could see his eyes when he said that. Hannibal would need men who could hang on to a juggernaught through hell fire if his course was that way. This young soldier-brother's eyes put him into that privilege.

Hasdrubal brought his rider close to Inanna near the portico, then he and Mago left, each shooting his variation of the military salute to her.

"We will also have to be good soldiers, Kyniska." Her daughter now had possession of her Mago hand. She was growing fast—like silphium, the plant that promised many kinds of marvels and poured gold into North Africa's Cyrene. Inanna picked her up and their paralleled faces looked at the sea. Kyniska promised marvels, and she would pour her gold into Hannibal and Inanna. *Please...Asclepius...or Carthaginian Eshmun if it please you...let her be a part of us...let him be a part of us for a longer time.* Inanna's tear intruded Kyniska's delighted communion. When she turned to her mother, Inanna had made her actress face again—so quickly, as Hannibal could attest.

There had been surrogate Roman ears in Hannibal's Congress. They had never been famous for reconnaissance, or espionage, but on presumptive major stages they could put in an ear, or two. In the case of Saguntum, there were Iberian Greek ears aplenty which sat on one side, or another, of intervention in Saguntine affairs by the Carthaginian, Hannibal. Taking about 1100 miles by land from Nova Carthago to Rome, or about 850 miles by sea and a little land, the courier's arrival at Carthago Nova, 12 days after the Congress, indicated efficient Greek to Roman transfer of information and a short Roman conference about it. The courier was a Massilian Greek, a representative of the Andorran and Massilian colonies whose nervousness had been stirred by Hamilcar, and kept moving by Hasdrubal and Hannibal. His message was that Lord Hannibal would be visited by a Roman embassy within a week. He had just handed Hannibal the end of a chain: Carthaginian Iberian activity-Greek nervousness-Greek complaining to Rome-Roman delegation to Carthaginian Iberia. A chain with links like this had come to Hamilcar, then Hasdrubal. But this chain was warmer than the others. It had passed close to Saguntum and Hannibal...but the Romans didn't understand this heat source yet.

The Roman quinquereme had slipped into a privileged dock of the cothon at Carthago Nova. Its official passengers had been conveyed to the palace by litters. They were attended by an aide-de-camp to the main hall of the palace that culminated in the audience halls, in this case the smallest one because both the size of the imminent conference, and its probable subject, would work better under enclosure of some intimacy. These courtesies, and this conclusion, were Hannibal's.

He wore civilian clothes—a short tunic with minimal Carthaginian decoration and Iberian sandals with embossed red leather around the ankle. His gold chain necklace also tended to move away from the military man. He had been away from campaigning for several months, so his good home razor, barber, and Inanna's close surveillance, had put some of the Hellenistic prince back on him.

The Roman embassy had four members. All of them wore togas, two of which were purpled. The two plain ones were supplemented by the gold rings of the equites. The calceus boot was worn by all: red for the aristocrats, brown for the knights. The senior member had been to Iberia before. He had met Hamilcar and Hannibal, and Inanna. He was Gaius Publius, and it had been ten years.

The footfalls echoing in that hall were still the fascination that had pulled Hasdrubal out to meet Hannibal, bearing the petition of a prospective bridegroom. Hannibal anticipated *his* visitors some twenty paces before the audience hall. He waited for his aide's introduction, then he approached Gaius Publius.

"Your honor to my father has finally spread to me, Gaius Publius...I am indebted to both of you." Hannibal had a slight height advantage of all the Romans. Publius had the best perspective of him, now and past, and the metamorphosis from father's son to probably absolute commander perturbed his breathing pattern during Hannibal's compliment. Specifics about this change, even rumors, estimations and speculations, had prepared him a little for this Hannibal. But the actual presence of him put all of this into movement that was disconcerting, justifying his prior warning to the rest of his embassy that they would be careful of Roman bluster in front of this particular Carthaginian.

"I remember a young man telling me we would meet again, Lord Hannibal." Gaius Publius introduced his staff, sweeping a smile over everyone that was a complication of emotions Inanna would have admired, and studied. Publius was now a senator. The other purpled toga held Justis Flavius, a quaestor, on the threshold of senator. Hannibal heard the names Marcus and Albinius used in connection with the two equites.

Hannibal gestured toward their audience chamber, and started everyone toward it. "Rome and Carthage have been moving along under the peace accord of Lutatius Catulus...perhaps Rome better than Carthage. That our paths should cross again was almost inevitable I think. You honor my prescience too much, Gaius."

When they entered the chamber, Hannibal gestured again, bringing comfortable chairs and couches into his hospitality. He chose a chair that could be a natural focus of this company. Gaius thought about his host's gentle recapitulation. Hamilcar had been enraged by that treaty, even more by Rome's arrogant abrogation of Carthaginian rights to Sardenia adventure. He was sitting within six feet of Hamilcar's replacement...his reincarnation, some had said his metamorphosis to a new level of obsession with redressing the outrages of the First Punic War. *Prescience* wasn't the right word here. Now those images of rumors and facts were swarming on him again, but he could still turn that senatorial smile on everyone.

"We hear that you are dissatisfied with the status quo at some Roman protectorates... Saguntum comes to mind." Gaius Publius didn't want to use such an early broach of the mission's purpose, but *inevitable* was a word that had been used here already and it was useful now.

Hannibal's centrality in that room was suddenly better defined by the postures of Justis Flavius, and the two knights, with Gaius Publius the reluctant head of the Roman arrow. They had to wait a few moments while they watched an interesting progression of slight surprise to slight amusement to some alignments of the pedagogue on Hannibal's face.

"Carthage has ample precedence for interest in oppression. We think Saguntum is a present, massive monument to this practice. It is, therefore, becoming anathema to us." He let his face make a small smile, but the Romans stayed with his eyes where the tricks were fewer.

"Perhaps Lord Hannibal would favor *us* with specifics." The imperial *we* and *us* from Hannibal's side pricked his guests, particularly Flavius and the equites.

"Your brutal suppression of a petition for independence is specifics enough—there was no conference but what you could bring with whips, swords and finally the axe." The quaestor, Justis Flavius, had made the question Hannibal had just answered, so he continued to look at Flavius, an early thirties man who would parade his consummate credentials for the Senate whenever he could. "Your Saguntine friends have studied your methods well and are applying them to their neighbors, the Turboletae—close friends of ours. Usurpation of territorial and trading prerogatives are other specifics I can put on your plate, Quaestor."

"Some of your specifics may be overstated, Lord Hannibal. A few recalcitrants being punished would hardly make a ripple in Carthage. Your precedents are more comprehensive than you claim—brutality and uncommon virtuosity with the torture are also within them, I think."

"Your historical byway is not germane to this chat, Justis Flavius. I am Hannibal Barca. I will answer to history, but my answer will begin *here*, not in the warped Roman archives for Carthage." He moved his foot along a line of the tiled floor, making a baseline for the chat that was fairly unambiguous. He looked at the knights, a small smile still useful. He was devising special receptions, just for them.

"You are proposing an attack on Saguntum?" Flavius was upstaging Publius, but he *was* moving the chat along.

"We will explore viable options for handling our dissatisfaction with Saguntum."

"If your option should happen to be attack, this would be intolerable insult for *us*, Lord Hannibal." Flavius had achieved the crux of the embassy. Flushed, he turned to Gaius Publius for confirmation. The Roman problems with Campania in southern Italy, the Celts in northern Italy, and Illyria along the northern Adriatic coast, were unresolved enough to inspire more roundness in Roman reaction to an attack on Saguntum than the sharp point Flavius had just pointed at Hannibal. Flavius, therefore, didn't get any bolster from Publius, whose eyes had never left Hannibal's.

"Then we will explore our viable options for *that*, when it comes, Justis Flavius." Publius' wince was small and private, but he was grateful that Hannibal's diplomat was larger than Flavius'. Hannibal had, in fact, just given them some grace of response that Flavius seemed determined to obliterate.

"I believe you are a father, Lord Hannibal." Gaius Publius' statement was the terminus to the business of the chat. He was determined to protect Hannibal's grace period against further histrionics. Remembering Hamilcar's son on a sunny veranda of Castulo ten years before, a smile came easily, and Hannibal appreciated the presence of a second diplomat in the room.

"She is Kyniska. She is an Amazon, and she has stolen my heart and won't give it back."

"That *is* intolerable—what do you propose to do about *that*?"

"Why, there are riding lessons, archery, gymnastics, and philosophy... mathematics."

"How *old* did you say she is?"

"She has a little more than two years—but she doesn't live in calendars."

"We hope your schedule will give Kyniska plenty of her father, Lord Hannibal." Gaius Publius' smile spread to his embassy. It was a dismissal. It was an end to formalities that had come close to irreversible arrogance. It was an invocation to reasonable gods that had already been made by Inanna and the Lady Barca, but would have very few Roman echoes.

And then just before Hannibal took leave of him, near the litters that would start a chain moving back to Rome, Gaius Publius said, "I still credit your prescience, Lord Hannibal...I think we will meet once more—in, or near Rome, as you said." The eyes, and the following silence would have been enough for them, but they inspired Publius to a little more. "...I wonder which end of your sword will be presented then?"

"I'll choose the pommel end, Gaius Publius. We are both students of fine craftsmanship." The youngish one had left him another good out, so Gaius Publius used it without further eloquence.

Following Gaius Publius' return to Rome, another Roman embassy got to the Carthaginan Senate, also in very good time. It was one senator, two quaestors, and a scribe who presumably guaranteed accurate reporting of the proceedings to the Roman counterpart of the faces opposing him on the senators' benches. The scribe's official ear also was a stage that could tempt an actor to unreasonable extensions of himself.

"Your interference in Iberia has jumped the bounds of our generous tolerance, as subscribed by both of us in the treaty of Lutatius Catulus." The Roman senator had just summarized the rumors of Hannibal's intentions toward the Roman protectorate, Saguntum.

"It will also violate the treaty of Hasdrubal with us which limited Carthaginian aggrandizement to south of the Jucar river." Saguntum was, in fact, some forty miles north of that river which had carried a lot of Hamilcar's blood to the sea. The word, *aggrandizement*, put in another increment of sharpness to this chat among allies. It moved the senators closer to the edge of their benches. This Roman was doing a good job of bringing the blood in this hall to a satisfying stewing point. Hannibal's adventures in Iberia had also been bringing up the blood around general Carthage to a point it hadn't been since Hamilcar's glory days, and some of the eons before him when it was Queen Carthage...it was Mother Carthage...it was imperial Carthage, guardian of the western sea and the worlds of the Atlantic infinity.

"Hasdrubal's treaty was never ratified by us. It was his private business with Rome, and we recognize no limitation contained therein." That statement could have kept international lawyers busy for months. If Hasdrubal *had* operated under a private license, then the river of Iberian silver and gold he sent to Carthage had endowed him with a tacit approval for his activities equivalent to a gold plated patent of authority from its Senate.

"We wallow in *ancient* history. Our basis for interpreting General Hannibal's intentions are sound. We demand his recall from Iberia and the abrogation of his authority that now stands him as an arrogant affront to Roman autonomy."

"We think you husband your word, *arrogant*, too closely, Senator. Give a little to yourself." Various Carthaginian senators were picking up the answer to the Roman.

Hanno, the head of the Peace Party, was some distance from this conversation, both physically and conceptually. He had sniped at Hadrusbal, and then when there was no Hasdrubal, he had transferred his affections to Hannibal, a moving target that radiated provocation for the comfortable status quo that hung on a placated Rome.

"I agree with the proposal to recall Hannibal...for conference. We are not sufficiently in tune with his ambition. This could leave us with unacceptable options if he decides to play at Alexander." Hanno had some basis for his remark. Hannibal's admiration of Alexander was no state secret of Carthage.

"Saguntum must assume the blame for any reprisal against her cruelty to the independence faction and her burgeoning arrogant interference in the affairs of the Turboletae—her neighbor, and our ally. If Hannibal should choose to support such reprisal, he would be following Carthaginian precedence in such matters." A general statement, and it could have come from the general voice of that assembly—Hanno had been pushed aside to allow room for a rare effusion of pride of Carthage within the Council.

"This is your last word?" A gauntlet, and one hand of the generality picked it up:

"I think we can make a better one, Senator. Let's say that any adjustment of the unpleasant situation at Saguntum will be regarded as a *parochial* affair— certainly not worthy to challenge the alliance that Carthage has enjoyed with Rome for a longer time than has Saguntum." This was another out that Gaius Publius could add to Hannibal's. The scribe had been too busy to be colored by the flush on his senator's face, now speechless, so *this* out traveled intact back to Rome on an official archive, as a last word.

9

28 years
219 BC—Saguntum

Hannibal's overtures to the magistrates of Saguntum were designed to encourage conference. His envoys were abruptly dismissed with the advice that no amount of conference could abolish the ignominy of slavery under Carthage. This attitude left him with two options: resignation and destructive embarrassment, or attack.

His Chief of Engineers, Adherbal, had given him the available details of Saguntum's ability to resist his inevitable option: the town was a virtual fortress situated on a rocky ridge far enough from the ocean to eliminate naval action that Alexander had found to be his salvation in his long siege of Tyre. The western side of this ridge afforded some advantage in slope for siege engines, although the complete annulus of solid rock around the town was a depressing stage for siege operations. The slope advantage of the western side was countered by the thickest walls, and the highest tower of the town.

Hannibal made the first conventional move in attacking this city by putting the ditches and palisades of circumvallation around the city on its closest earthy perimeter. Various artillery of siege had been in preparation in Iberia for weeks, and the armories of Carthage had started to send more of the same including the most recent designs of arrow, stone and dart throwers. There was wood enough in Iberia to make the towers and covered sheds for the battering rams and sappers if the bluster of preparation, and a few missiles lobbed over and against the walls, failed to impress the inhabitants.

He had ridden around the town, solely and in the company of Maharbal, Carthalo, Adherbal, Mago, Hasdrubal...any of his commanders who could turn bits and pieces of Saguntum around in his perspective as besieger. These rides had defined his target better, but the only exhilaration he could pull out of them was linked to the novelty of his first siege, a massive tweak of the Roman nose that would probably inaugurate the Barca parade into Italy under sanctification of formal war by Rome and Carthage.

This was no ground for exercising and refining his foot and horse or for perfecting the conjunctions and dispositions of them that would bring the Barca lightning down on civilized fields for significant battle. You kept Saguntines off the walls and tried to sneak your people over the walls by ladders or gangplanks from towers. Or you tried to put your people against their people *on* the walls, in an acrobatic exercise where no soldier should ever have to confront so many kinds of death. And if you couldn't go *over* the walls, then you punched a hole *in* the walls, or you mined the walls and made part of them fall over. You stuffed your men into these holes and breaches and hoped they could push against the defenders enough to make a panic and then a surrender. The unknowns were in what your spies hadn't told you about the defensive architecture, the anticipations that had been made for siege and—what no one could tell you—the quality of the defenders. There were Greeks inside Saguntum and this fact could suggest some answers to these questions.

A siege could make tigers from shopkeepers and housewives who could stir as much hell into a defense as any soldier. All you could do was to keep pushing your men into this possible hell until you ran out of defenders by dint of starvation, or disease, or the quicker deaths—or *you* ran out of resources, which here was not a conceivable event. A prescient man, particularly one standing in front of his first siege with whispers of hell and glory—hell *or* glory—swarming him, could do a lot of anticipating himself.

Three weeks of stones, arrows and darts from his artillery, the best of the time, had not impressed the Saguntines toward capitulation. They had even returned some of the missile shower in their own fashion. Hannibal had ridden with cavalry details too close to the walls on several occasions, to show himself, to show personal commitment to the next stage of this affair after they had rejected talk about it...possibly even to show them that talk was *still* an option. The Saguntines had anticipated the last of his rides and hidden a sortie party of one hundred spearmen behind a rock abutment that Hannibal had used as his personal showplace. Maharbal was with him this time, and an escort of fifty horse.

"You are getting too close, Hannibal. Their scorpions could put an arrow this far—and the bastards have decided to get playful with us." Maharbal had barely finished this good advice when two Saguntine scorpions, double arrow throwers, whistled their shafts in front of them. This distraction gave the spearmen an opening. While Hannibal's detail was making a quick course adjustment, the front rank of spearmen appeared over the rock and launched in his direction. He was very good at deflecting missiles and swords with his shield and sword, in moving the horse-couple of him into an impossible target. But the avalanche of spears had focused him, and no defense can be always perfect. One of the spears hit his left thigh. He succeeded in removing it, but he was incapacitated and Maharbal and two other riders kept him upright and his horse under control while they rode away from the ambush. The balance of the Carthaginian detail, there was a Mushroom in them, swept past the spearmen and launched a javelin response that put the blood account back on their side, but the sight of a wounded Hannibal was not compensated by this.

She waited until all of the attendants had gone from his bedroom and then she knelt beside him, listening to the breath of heavy sleep that Synhalus' drugs had induced. When she first saw him—when they brought him in after hours of careful transport by fast ship and then a litter carriage to the palace—she had to put a hand over her mouth to stifle a cry that the marks and color of pain on his face had made. Before the expedition he hadn't told her much about Saguntum, in a way that told her more than he'd intended. Mago, with asides from Hasdrubal, had defined Saguntum as a devil of a town, crouched on a throne of rock, and radiating Greek sneers. Hannibal *had* said that, if it came to siege, it would be good practice for him and his men. That first look at him had filled out his silence in a terrible way. Saguntum, that damned *Saguntum*, had brushed him with the death wings. Asclepius...*Asclepius*...what are they doing to him? Kyniska wanted to see her daddy. She couldn't let her see him now. She kissed his cheek, and then his closed eyes. He mumbled something... but she didn't want to know the words.

Synhalus had told her that the wound was deep, but fortunate in respect of bone and crucial ligaments, that he would need several weeks of rest before he could think of walking about. She'd mentioned the hot pool. Synhalus said that this would be fine as soon as the bandages could come off. She'd mentioned him sleeping apart from her and wouldn't it be better if she were close to him. Synhalus said that this would be fine after her husband had come along a little more. Before Synhalus left her on his last official visit, he'd kissed her hand, and told her that his patient's best medicine, her medicine, was still a little while away. She kissed her husband's lips and wiped his forehead with a bit of linen. Synhalus wasn't there now. She could lie beside him for a moment...just a moment. One of his arms was uncovered, the one closest to her after she lay down. She put his hand on her breast. It was covered by her nightgown...she uncovered that breast and replaced his hand, looking at him all the time. Kyniska could fit in between them now, but Kyniska would have to wait her turn with Hannibal Barca.

While Hannibal was out of action, his engineer, Adherbal, put up several towers with battering rams. The stone slope around the towers posed massive problems for his people, but using rawhide-covered sheds to protect his crews, they put winches next to the walls and worked the rams into position. The stone and arrow shooters on the towers kept the Saguntines away from the top of the wall. When they pounded a hole in the wall, the foot poured into it, and had their first man-to-man with the defenders. No maneuvering room here, it was a spear of men against a replenishing wall of men and the desperation was spread on both sides of the action. When the Carthaginians had made a little progress beyond the local ruin of the wall, the Saguntines brought up falericas. This device comprised an iron pot containing burning pitch fortified with sulfur, an iron pipe attached to the burning pot, a bellows attached to the pipe to drive the acrid smoke and burning fragments out of a spigot attached to the pot. They forced the withdrawal of the attackers with this chemical weapon, and Synhalus had burned and choked men added to the nightmare of cut, slashed, and holed men to show for that day's work.

This particular horror of siege was not over when Hannibal returned. Over the protests of his officers, he had gone into the breach, and gone far enough beyond the wall to get within range of heavy rocks that were thrown from an inner redoubt. By the grace of his gods' mercy, certainly that of Inanna's merciful one, Asclepius, such a stone crashed within brushing distance of him and he was escorted from that particular hell by two lieutenants who dared to confront his obstinacy.

Hannibal ordered a larger tower, modeled after the one Demetrius Poliorcetes, the besieger of cities, had used against Salamis in Cyprus. After Adherbal succeeded in bringing this monster against the wall, Hannibal had sheds placed along a hundred paces of the wall's length. He then commenced mining this section of the wall, with his massive tower providing background music of two battering rams working its section of the wall, its heavy stone and bolt throwers keeping the Saguntines awake to listen to his music. After two weeks of his sappers' work with pickaxes, the temporary wooden trusses were burned away and a large section of the outer wall collapsed. Marharbal—and every officer who could get close to Hannibal—declared that this rush of foot into the breech would be without him, and he finally listened to them. The first waves of his men got into two streets of the city and found both of them blocked by temporary walls, with missiles raining into their front and on top of them. The section of the city affected by this massive breach was also protected by an inner labyrinth of walls and passages that made another piece of hell. After three attacks through this breach, Hannibal ordered a stop.

The Saguntines had suffered. But a peace conference was further away now than it had been when he had sent only his embassy into the city. And he had suffered—personally, and his men. He walked with Synhalus every day and night through the sick bays, and talked with his wounded, complimenting their courage, talking about the road ahead that would lead to better fields than what was in, and around, Saguntum. Then a kind of surcease was ordered on him. The Tagus Celtiberians had killed two of his officers detailed to them for military training and a strategically important section of his Iberian allies was threatening to come undone over this incident.

"You are my spearhead here now, Maharbal—show me some progress when I get back."

"Too bad we couldn't put most of them into *our* side, Hannibal...we've uncovered a beast here that could give us dragon claws when we make a closer greeting for our Roman friends."

"I've been remiss here. It was my responsibility to make them allies instead of the fanatical patriots we've got."

"I dispute you there, Hannibal. You've made a courage here that every man of yours will take as far as you want us to go." Hannibal had made his claim of error while turning his horse toward the Tagus battleground. Maharbal had to shout his rejoinder at him, and because of that, part of a private talk spilled into some of the other men and made smiles there.

Maharbal moved the towers and sapper's sheds along the wall to make another breech into what looked like a more vulnerable part of Saguntum. It was a good guess, assisted by famine and disease ravages that had killed a quarter of the population. When his new section of the wall collapsed, his foot moved into the city without the inner wall obstacles that had set them up for the burning kiss of the falericas. The Saguntines who were still mobile ran into the citadel, their last bastion of defense. Hannibal's expedition to the Tagus rebellion returned just when Maharbal was considering his assault on the citadel. The expedition had been a wonderful invigoration of soldiering compared to the static hell pit that was still Saguntum.

"I want to make one more peace proposal to them before you pull down their last roof. You've made me look like a general again, Maharbal."

"It's been all pushing blood and guts against their stones, Hannibal. This is no ground for you, and your compliments are not for me." Maharbal waved his arm toward battalions of the men who had dented and penetrated Saguntum and were now close to the conclusion of it.

Hannibal himself called to the people behind the defense remnant of the citadel. He carried his shield, and this was backed up by a dozen more ready to make a protection for him.

"You have shown your courage beyond any measure. I would be proud to count you as ally. Send your embassy to me—I would like to talk, instead of fight, anymore." There was a long silence for an answer, and then an arrow clanged against one shield of the wall around him. This was the Saguntine final answer, and he told Maharbal to go ahead with *his*.

Adherbal brought two towers through the latest breech and winched them up to the citadel. This was flat ground now, a geographic nod toward Hannibal's side that, with only the skeleton of a defense left, made the last few hours of Saguntum a terror of desperate alternatives for the natives, a revenge for frustrated assault and the memories of a hellish variety of death and maiming for the attackers.

"It is over, Hannibal." Maharbal and Hannibal were standing outside the ruins of Saguntum. Black clouds from the last fires in the citadel put an accent on Maharbal's statement.

"How many are alive?" Hannibal's eyes swept a wide perspective of his first siege. Present vision, memory of two near passes of the death wings over him, put a bile in his mouth that made the word, *victory*, impossible. This Saguntum had taken two thousand of his best men beyond recall. It had put some new facets of him on stage—the improvisations for problems of siege that even Alexander's overblown genius and understated luck at Tyre hadn't confronted. And troop loyalty and sacrifice that had put some of Maharbal's compliment on this stage. Maharbal had told him that this was not *his* ground. One day he would turn that wisdom back on his Chief of Cavalry when the portals of Rome itself seemed to beckon.

"I think there are none...possibly a few children escaped their parents."

"What devils have helped us here?—parents against *children*, Maharbal?"

"The dead have been piled by our hand, and by suicide, their own ways of assisting deaths. Saguntum has set no precedent here—it is almost an axiom of siege against a prosperous city, or an acropolis, filled with a certain kind of people."

"By all that the gods mean to me—there'll be no more of this under *my* hand."

Hannibal sent the massive booty obtained from Saguntum to Carthage. It arrived three weeks before the Roman embassy. The booty was accepted, and thereby did the Saguntum affair get merged into official Carthaginian policy.

"We demand the immediate recall of Hannibal and his officers to Carthage...and his transfer to Roman jurisdiction for trial. We demand the immediate evacuation of all Carthaginian presence at Saguntum and restoration of the Roman protectorate status quo." The senator, Fabius Buteo, of the gens Fabia, had spoken. He wore the purpled toga, red calceus shoes, and the general imperium of the Roman senator. He was backed at a discreet separation by three quaestors, two knights, and a scribe.

The full array of Carthaginian senators faced him in the Council chamber. The two sufets, Bomilcar and Imilco, sat in the focal section immediately in front of the Romans. They usually avoided general Council sessions, but a Roman of the gens Fabia was too good to miss. And the thundercloud blown toward Rome by young Hannibal Barca made their presence irresistible.

"You overblow your credentials, Fabius Buteo. We have stated our position on the Saguntum affair before, quite unambiguously, to your predecessor embassy. The treaty of Hasdrubal is not binding on us in Iberia. It was not binding on General Hannibal when he went to the assistance of our allies, the Turboletae, and the independence faction at Saguntum." The sufet, Bomilcar, had spoken. His son, Hanno, was on Hannibal's staff. This fact put extra sheen on his words. He hadn't had the chance to look into a Roman senator's eyes for years. In the right light, under special scintillations of Roman humiliation, this was a heady prescription for summary and positioning.

"This is your last word?" For the moment, Fabius Buteo confined his actor to only these words, a slightly raised chin giving them some spraying scope.

"*Our* senators have recommended that Rome take this Saguntum affair in a parochial light. It is not of sufficient importance to override the peaceful compact we have both enjoyed since your Lutatius Catulus wrote a sparkling finis to our first unfortunate military conjunction." Imilco couldn't let Bomilcar hog this stage. Furthermore, his sense of irony, and the point he could make of it with his spoken words, were almost unique on the Carthaginian side of this chat. But he had just reoffered the *out* that had been made before in this room before another Roman, and Fabius Buteo rejected it.

He thrust his right hand inside his toga. "I have either peace, or war, here. Which will you take?" He'd put his direct question to the side-by side sufets, then, posturing now, he put it silently to the assembly of senators. These Romans had been tutored in drama by the Greeks and Etruscans and evidently they remembered some of it.

"Why...then—we'll take *war*, Fabius Buteo." Bomilcar's answer swam along well with the Greek and Etruscan precedents already in this hall. It was quickly overborne by the Carthaginian chorus around him that made *war* a bigger word.

The ship was a Carthaginian modification of a lembos, single-banked, forty oars, adaptable to either square or lateen rigging so she could run with most of the moods of the Mediterranean wind. She was black-hulled and smooth finished like Hasdrubal's eel that had slipped in and out of Carthage taking substance for the Lady Barca's tears both ways. She, and her sister ships that Hannibal used for packet service, could outrun and outmaneuver any ship on the Mediterranean. This ship had an extra large stern awning for special passengers, with suitable amenities for personal service.

As she swept around Cap Gata bearing westward toward Gades, the captain ordered both oars and sails to give her the special presence that signaled Lord Hannibal aboard. And the rowers put their backs into a special service because there *was* Lord Hannibal, the Lady Inanna, and a very precocious package of curiosity and vivacity named Kyniska, aboard. Also Kyniska's nannies, because only one wasn't enough. Hannibal and Inanna stood under the stern awning. The natural breeze compounded by the ship's motion ruffled their close-coupled cloaks and swept a tendril of Inanna's long black hair toward her husband, who promptly captured it with a finger of the hand that wasn't clasped to her waist.

"We could sail around Africa on this," she whispered. "...There are all kinds of mysteries and wonders down there." The Lady Barca had whispered almost the same words to Hamilcar.

"How do you know this?" He'd moved close to her ear and with appropriate voice put his question during the most intimate conjunction they could make under the circumstances.

"Your great navigator, Hanno, is no mystery to us. He left a very precocious trail for his followers." She was watching a nanny trying to corral Kyniska's latest circuit of the ship, but she was aware of his soft approach. He had told her that they would be going to Gades to pay homage to Amalkre, to see his statue of Alexander and Hamilcar's Hercules again...to be together for a little while away from his soldier's ground.

He had told her a little about Saguntum. Others had told her more. It had been an exercise in courage and determination that spread its victory over all of his army. He had paid one price she knew about, several others she didn't, although her Delphic-wrought imagination was equal to this task. The almost total death of the Saguntines was hard to reconcile with him. Mago, then Maharbal, had told her about the peace and truce overtures that nearly killed him. They put the options he'd had as Commander of the Army in front of her, then some of the conclusion was easier to accept. The terrible part of Saguntum for her, the part that brought Amalkre and Lady Barca into it, was that she knew it was his gateway to killing fields that stretched into the horizons of the Romans and only the gods knew where else. They had picked him up as their latest curiosity, to see how close a mortal man could get to them. His idol, Alexander, had come close, in many judgments, but then crazed debauchery, possibly assassination by a frustrated constituency, had been the end of *that* glory path.

Kyniska was running toward them, easily evading the nanny who didn't quite know how much laughter to put into her rebukes. Kyniska...she would be a part of him that would stay after he had marched from Carthago Nova with his army—the ninety thousand foot, twelve thousand horse, and forty elephant thunder of it that Mago and Hasdrubal had put into words for her. Kyniska had reached them. She grabbed at the mass of cloaks between her parents and let them decide who was going to throw her into the air. It turned out she got air born by both her mother and father, and then she got cuddled where three faces could be swept by the same wonderful breath of this ship. Her blond hair resembled the Lady Barca's and some tendrils of it mingled with her mother's lustrous blackness so that now Hannibal had two insinuations of his ladies across some of his face, and no free hand to defend himself. Kyniska's delighted giggles were enough vocals for that moment. The captain was loath to disturb that scene, but there was a decision to be made.

"Lord Hannibal...Lady Inanna...forgive my intrusion."

"Nonsense, Captain, we are passengers on *your* ship." Kyniska had managed to work herself to the outside of her daddy, so Hannibal had spoken from an interior position, bracketed by his ladies. This particular captain would trail this commander over several Olympian battles. But this image—Hannibal grinning between the resident beauties of his house—would keep strongest in his memory.

"We could turn into Malaka for some respite from the sea, before the run to Gades."

"I think we *would* enjoy some land legs for a little while, Captain." Inanna's words and smile were as good as Hannibal's nod for the captain's order.

After they had captured Kyniska again, dined alfresco under palms, and made a sedate walking tour of a part of the Malaka port, the captain made an exit from that venerable outpost of Carthage that outshone his entrance. As they sailed toward the westward Pillars, and Gades, Kyniska noticed the lightning stroke emblazoned on the sail, and she was closest to her mother when she did.

"It is your Daddy's mark."

"*Thunder?*" Kyniska looked at the sail, and then her daddy, when she made her second question.

"Very *big* thunder." Inanna had answered almost in whisper, and she looked only at the sail.

Hannibal had been back to Gades many times since he had ridden with Hamilcar to Melkart's precinct's for the first time. His father had pledged and accomplished a Hercules for the temple. He, now in the commander's role, had pledged and accomplished an Alexander for the same place. And when he returned from Carthage after Amalkre had gone, he had stood in front of her tomb and they had talked together for a little while.

Hasdrubal had maintained a small villa between the city and Melkart's temple at the southern end of the island. Their first day was spent there as a family with Kyniska. They took carriage rides. They put Kyniska on horses in front of her mother, then her father. They chased each other along the trails on the land side and then they chased sea birds on the sea side. After putting a toe into the Mediterranean, Inanna declared it too cold for swimming. So their swimming was done in the villa pool, where Hasdrubal's Iberian artisans had put down broad sweeps of shining tiles that had sea fantasies worked into them and gave Kyniska a ground where she could run, and get down on her belly to trace the designs, and ask questions about what she saw.

They swam naked in the pool together. A father played dolphin with his daughter, she riding his back, he swimming fast as he could until another dolphin called Inanna plucked her off and made away with her to a swimming lesson that Kyniska wouldn't confine to the shallows. Afterwards, they lay on soft towels on the tile and pointed to shapes the clouds had made for them. It was precious time. And when she saw a favorite cloud image dissolve in an assault by dark vapors with no artistry, Inanna had another measure of transient preciousness...but it was private. She moved closer to her husband and Kyniska, so that they finished the best part of that day by making a triptych— she, Kyniska, Hannibal, piled together...apprehension, delighted exhaustion, grateful surcease, and not a word spoken, even when an attendant covered most of them with linen and reminded them of the evening meal.

The second evening was for Inanna and Hannibal. She rode a white mare, he a black stallion, and before they got to Melkart's precincts she had proved that her mare was as fast as his stallion. Their horses were Iberians, which meant infusions from Persia and where the Sumerians had been, even from the steppes of far Asia where wild men and horses were almost one piece with the wind. He made them stop at the edge of the temple grounds. A temple acolyte secured their horses, and then they walked toward Amalkre, passing first Hamilcar's Hercules, and then Hannibal's Alexander. Both life sized, Hercules looked toward the Iberian mainland, Alexander toward the sea.

"You've put a scroll in his hand." Inanna walked close to Alexander, her first inspection, although she'd had invitations to him before.

"He has nothing to prove as a soldier. I wanted to nudge him a little toward the statesman."

"Do you think he likes that?" She touched Alexander's robe that was not for a soldier. He was on a pedestal so his face was too far away from her fingers.

"If he is working with the gods now, then he must be working like a statesman because what he put together as a soldier has almost vanished. I wanted to give him some of that *continuity* in that statue." Inanna was about to use that word—the Lady Barca had used it in front of this man—but asking about Inanna's continuity now would not relax any of the burden that Heimarmene had put on him. She would play the stateswoman herself. A weeping, hair pulling, self-serving harpy was not what he needed now. *Asclepius...please keep me strong in front of him...and after he is gone.*

Hasdrubal had put Amalkre on a point of land between the temple and the sea. The sarcophagus was white marble from an Etruscan quarry. The sculptor had placed a gracefully proportioned casket sheath above a pedestal which had a full-length maiden at each corner, heads slightly lowered in accordance with their burden, but each of them looked outward, toward new mysteries, and there were four versions of a small smile. An arbor of cypress led from the temple to her, leaving her view of the sea unobstructed. Flowers, in season, were around her pedestal.

Inanna had been here before. As they walked toward this vestige of Amalkre, Hannibal took her hand and both of them heard the sound of Amalkre's voice:

For Hannibal it could have been remembered in her outrageous interpretation of dreams, various perceptions of omens, portends, that usually had him mixed up in them. Just before returning to Carthage, his last sight of her, she had been filled with this, and she had found little in this to cheer him, so her words he remembered *now* was when she told him that they would all come together at Carthage again after he had become a great commander. She had used her actress on him, and Lady Barca had tutored her well in this indispensable Barca discipline.

For Inanna, the Amalkre voice that spoke to her now was a soft insistence that anyone contemplating closeness with her brother, in this instance Hannibal, would be advised to savor the minutes and hours...days with him, and not to look to the *years.* But Inanna had said something to Amalkre at that time that illumined part of her specialness even then...that the gods were still trying to decide what to do with him—and don't interfere with this process; it wasn't *necessarily* bad.

Inanna and Hannibal both wore pendants, silver bas-reliefs set in oval frames of woven gold wire, hung on fine gold chains. He had brought them out of his baggage the night before, after Kyniska had succumbed to as much activity as her parents could give her.

Inanna's carving was a replica of his face that had been used on the coins where he had assimilated himself to Hercules and Melkart, but with some personalizing for her sake that brought him closer to the young man in bronze that the Greek in Volubilis had made for the Temple at Gades. She had seen this bronze, admired it, and he had remembered.

His carving was a replica of the statue he'd had made of her that presented her as an Iberian princess, arrayed for festival fun and games. One day he had returned to the palace when she was entertaining a delegation of noble ladies from the Carpetani. They had promised her dancing in their festival costumes. Hannibal had heard flute and timpani music and laughter and was stopped short at the sight of his wife practicing a dance step under expert instruction. She wore an elaborate headdress, a bejeweled cap supporting large cylindrical sections over her ears that were intricately carved in radial and circumferential patterns. They had put a three-stranded necklace on her, hung with pendants that had invocation and magic and whimsy with Celtic precedence of five hundred years in them. Her movements, the progressions of her face, hands, general body, would have fitted Amalkre's conceptions of artistic ecstasy driven by breaths of various visions—which in this case would have accorded with normal Celtic conception. Hannibal never intruded this occasion...but he had remembered it.

Years before, on an evening at Carthago Nova, after they had tested each other's endurance and ingenuity in the lists of passion, he said, " Such a face, coupled to imminent motherhood, shall be given to posterity."

"How would you do me?" His statement had been playfully delivered... she was still equipped to retaliate in kind. Her question was murmured just after her kiss of his chin.

"I remember an Iberian woman—looking very like you—who was shameless in her evocation of the decadent Celts." He had to confess that he'd spied on her nearly private festival.

"What do you remember about her?" Her finger touched his lower lip, and then one of the ears that had once told on him and a university.

"That I would capture her...with your motherhood face...for my private treasures."

"You said...*posterity.*"

"That will come *after* me." Then his lips stopped her words.

The Greek he'd brought from Tyre for the sculpture was given the dress and ornamentation props courtesy of the Carpetani ladies. The subject lady was reasonably accommodating in her posing...although there had been interruptions from the Lord Hannibal for this and that of the pose that sometimes had everyone laughing. The Greek did a test work in sandstone, a waist-high version of the lady that seemed to put both the consecrations of imminent motherhood and the erotic implications of temple festival into one piece. Hannibal and Inanna accepted it, with mostly private qualifications and estimations. Hannibal ordered a marble of the work, and placed the sandstone version in his study where, in the meantime of the marble accomplishment, she would never be far away. The Greek put a living quality into the marble that was beyond the sandstone. Hannibal gave the commission of the pendants to him, and also the Alexander that was going to Melkart at Gades.

His pendant showed mostly the face of her statue—virtually classical Greek, with a contemplative cast that could take her presence *anywhere* she chose to grace the world. But there was enough of the headdress exuberance to tell on this part of her, too. She liked the pendant he would wear. When he'd put it on last night, and she saw it against his chest, she came close to him so he could savor copy and reality close together.

Commenting, again, on his pendant for her, she said, "The Greek has taken away some of your godliness...I could like *this* man." She said this in front of Amalkre's memory, and some of Amalkre's words, her whispers, were in Inanna's spoken words.

"I'm glad he pleases you." Hannibal stepped close enough to kiss her, no sacrilege in front of Amalkre because, together, these women had talked, laughed, whispered, and conjured images about this man. "I'm glad he is able to be close to you...as much as you want him." He turned away from her, looking past Amalkre's attendants to the sea. She knew that the crux of their visit to Gades was close. He had made the silence, so let him break it...she didn't trust her voice.

"When the weather turns propitious for expedition...I will leave for Italy."

"When?" One word wasn't hard to do, but its breath burned her mouth, so it came as a whisper.

"Probably—near the end of May." This gave them a few weeks. Amalkre's insistent voice wouldn't let her play the mewling wife, nor would her Greekness, which had been admired by the Spartan, Sosylos. Damn Sosylos—he had set *impossible* standards for her!

"How will you go?" They had walked away from Amalkre toward the sea. A little perfume from Amalkre's flowers had entered the moment of that question, making it easier.

"I will take the main column into Catalonia, leave some garrisons to protect my back...then into Gaul." He came close to her. "I will have a Celtic princess for company." They kissed. She separated them, but left their eyes very close together.

"Is this Celtic person qualified to...uphold *me*?"

"I think she is your *personification*—thoughtful, studious, curious, playful, uninhibited, wanton...beautiful." He kissed the end of her nose.

"By your Ba'al's own pendant, I thought you were leaving me a boring old hag—you saved yourself, just in time."

That night, their tired Iberians put to bed, Inanna set out to prove every attribute of her that her husband had recited near to the vestige of one who would have certainly approved such a performance. It needed some books, which she had. It needed some poetry, which she would recite. It needed some papyrus paper and at least one pen for explaining and questioning geography, this was equipment of the villa. It needed some sheer silk sheaths in beguiling colors, which she had. It posed the question of when to bring the silk into all of this business. She solved this question. And when she told Hannibal that she could go with him, that Celtic woman were famous for their independence and strength and support of their men, that she could help rally such women to his cause in Gaul, and then in the Po valley where more of his precious Celts were, Hannibal could give only one answer to this *thoughtful, studious, curious, playful, uninhibited, wanton...beautiful* woman:

"My army can have only *one* commander."

BOOK TWO

Italian Fields

10

29 years
November 218 BC—The Po Valley

The light inside the large tent was served by oil lamps because Hannibal had lingered overlong among his foot and horse before joining the congregation he had ordered to attend him there. The composition of the faces of his officers, his attendants Sosylos and Silenus, and the Carthaginian representatives to his expedition, was nearly identical to his conference at Carthago Nova when he had defined the word *trigger*, more particularly the phrase, *Roman trigger*. The new faces belonged to two Celt chieftains of the Insubres and Boii tribes, respectively, and Synhalus, his Chief Surgeon. No one sat on the camp stools. When Hannibal entered the tent, he already had a mobile audience to react to him. The lamplight abetted the fugitive complexions that put edges of each man's privacies of exhilaration or dismay or anxiety... or fear, on involuntary stages where a word might be redundant, or a real, or false, reflection.

"My apologies, gentlemen—I had to wander again among the miracles of recuperation you have wrought."

Inanna would have been shocked. The words had come from a stranger's face, a metamorphosis worked by man and nature over the six months they had been separated. But he was alive. He had lost twenty thousand of his best troops. He had cursed his Alps transit decision a thousand times. He had used every prayer he had, every invocation Sosylos and Silenus had, to every god, relevant or not, that he had ever whispered to or laughed at. The ice and rocks and boulders and topography, some of it contended by hairy fanatics who wanted to make a test against him, made impossible trails and death traps for man and beast. Then his engineers, and all of his men, made them actual trails and monuments to courage. And finally they had the miracle of the vista of the Po, and a descent into its valley that was a continuing revelation of relative softness and mostly private gratitude to the unknown panoply of the gods who had listened to him, his men.

Hannibal had started to move into his congregation, shooting general and private recognitions with eyes and a few words, when another man entered the tent. His officer's cloak, and what peek of his uniform it allowed, showed him to be a sparkling clean man. His face, the eyes particularly, was charged with exhilaration, the seduction of new challenge—nothing of him marked by the Alps transit which had put stages in that tent that no one in it, Hannibal included, could say were under his control as a man—or an actor.

"By what gods we have left! Bostar!" Hannibal rushed to his aide-de-camp, and clamped an arm lock around his shoulders. Bostar was quickly surrounded by other greetings, and Inanna's shock could have just had a twin. The quick flash of Hannibal's face, the others, revealed a sudden nightmare to the newcomer. He had left for the temple of Zeus Ammon at the Siwah oasis in the Libyan Desert shortly before Hannibal had crossed the Rhone. His orders were to seek the temper of the oracle about the Italian expedition. He had heard that Hannibal had eluded the elder Scipio in southern Gaul and had disappeared into the geography of the Alpine massifs. Nothing more until the messenger had reached Carthago Nova and told that Hannibal had emerged near Turin and was consolidating his position before proceeding south. *Consolidating his position!* These were near scarecrows—or must have been, taking a few weeks recuperation away from them. He forced himself to meet Hannibal's eyes. He saw the smile that was inimitable Hannibal. He was locked against a great commander and actor, so this part of the conjunction was not surprising—but a man would have to be Phidias to pull the Hellenistic prince out of that face, away from constructions in the eyes that only touches of hell and desperation could put in them. When Bostar finally put a good laugh together, Hannibal uncoupled and let him sweep around the others, a panorama that gave no surcease to a shock that had tested every measure of insouciance and playfulness that Hannibal's association had put into him.

"Gentlemen, a breath of Alexander has just come in." An exuberant Hannibal's smile was rampant now. Alexander had, indeed, sought the same parcels of encouragement, inspiration, aggrandizement, from Zeus Ammon at Siwah. In his case, his campaign had reached a peak where he could now talk with gods, hopefully on an even basis and the priests of Ammon had had some difficulty in differentiating the light that came from their visitor and from Zeus Ammon's virtual presence that swarmed around them. Hannibal had just handed another stage to Bostar. The young officer pulled himself up to his Siwah persona, a facile transition from shock that Inanna herself had also accomplished in the near vicinity of Hannibal.

"The priests were impressed by our ambition, the scope of our enterprise, Hannibal."

He swept his audience again, intercepting Hannibal several times before settling back on this logical focus. Bostar had stood in the middle of Hannibal's host when it left Carthago Nova for Italy. The memory of it was his principal baggage for Siwah, and the incentive for his barely concealed insolence when he entered Zeus Ammon's precincts as Hannibal's surrogate suppliant. The faces in this tent bespoke some alteration in Hannibal's significance. What he had seen of the army outside had fostered the premonition that the faces inside the tent had realized. But Hannibal had just offered him a stage for inspiration. Hannibal had talked to him from such a stage. So he would play the man now— when inspiration was like the continuity of a heart's blood for the men in this tent and outside it.

"I was privileged to have the high priest serve the offices for the oracle, Hannibal." Bostar waited for any comment from his audience; nothing came but palpable expectation. "He seemed well advised on our expedition. He mentioned some numbers for our foot and horse...even elephants, which were damn close."

"Our cloak of secrecy around the Mediterranean playground is like a net, Bostar." The smile on Hannibal had simmered down, but there was enough of it left to chastise a young officer for moments of shock and dejection in the aura of Hamilcar Barca's son.

"He asked about the scope of our expedition. I told him that it was reinstatement of the significance of Carthage. He said that he had heard about such scope from a man called Hamilcar Barca. I said that this was the very same scope—promulgated now by *Hannibal* Barca."

"And at this point he raised his hands to shield his eyes from my aura which must have projected from you like sun beams."

"He smiled—I don't think I ever saw more dimensions in a smile."

"I must find this priest when I have more time—I can use *all* of his dimensions." If Hannibal gave a slight prompting for a young officer to channel his exuberance it was a masterpiece of subtlety.

"The priest asked me what I sought from the oracle of Ammon. I said that Lord Hannibal had asked me to petition for an opinion on his prospects for Italy."

"You asked for an encyclopedia from a busy man. Evidently he didn't have you ushered away—you show no signs of frustration."

"He said that some prospects looked very good for the Romans."

"I may have you ushered out myself—but then you don't look like a man facing my notorious rebuke, either."

"I started to object, he raised his hand, telling me that I needed more patience. Then he said that Roman prospects were hinged on complacent adversaries who saw sucking the Roman tits as their principal destiny. He said that the Greek, Agelaos of Naupactus, had been talking about *clouds in the west* that should encourage the Greeks to mend their squabbles and put up a united front to destiny, like they had done for the Persian host. I asked the priest what these clouds had to do with my petition on Italy. He said that probably they hovered over part of the Roman arrogance and that—like the weather—it could go one way, or the other, for this arrogance, depending on the resolution of the ones looking at it."

Bostar's virtual soliloquy had pulled his audience closer to him, including some of its frustration. "By the Egyptian balls of your damn Zeus Ammon, Bostar!—did you ever get to the oracle?" Maharbal's was now one of the close faces.

"The priest formalized my question about Italy on a papyrus sheet and disappeared through the portals to the sanctuary. He came back sooner than I expected."

"Well?" This time the face of Myrcan, one of the Senate's representatives to Hannibal, pushed closest to Bostar.

"He said that the oracle had corroborated the clouds—it had even made them *red*, and had said that they would soon make a cover over *all* of Italy like the Romans had never seen before and it could suck the life out of them." His audience shouted, slapped him on the back, laughed, put the slapping all around.

It was an ambiguous oracle. A Greek had seen dark clouds shaped like Romans marching toward him. An oracle of Zeus Ammon had found it expedient to make those clouds red, and to shape them like Hannibal, marching *toward* the Romans. But at a juncture where every healthy, battle-tested, man and horse was like a ruby, they needed Bostar's recitation of Zeus Ammon's oracle like they needed their next breaths.

He had come down into the valley of the Po with twenty thousand foot, six thousand horse, seven elephants, a baggage train—the remnant of thirty-eight thousand foot and eight-thousand horse, thirty-seven elephants, and a much larger baggage train that had crossed the Rhone six weeks before. What he had left was the heart of his army, a nucleus for growth in the days, the weeks, whatever time the gods who had listened to him through the Alps would give him before the Roman juggernaught started to roll in his direction.

Most of the particulars of Roman strength were no surprise for a staff that had Hamilcar's notes to read. Before Hamilcar, three hundred years of military and trade intercourse, both allied and contentious, had left few secrets of the Roman military face. And after Hamilcar, months before his expedition, Hannibal had put down his own gossamers (Inanna's word) of intelligence that had spread into some corners of the Roman center of gravity. He had not confessed all of this to the delegates from Carthage who had decided to ride his whirlwind into Italy.

If they brought their full standing army against him, a trained and disciplined corps comparable to the best in the Mediterranean world, it would be about thirty-two thousand Roman foot, thirty thousand allied foot, nearly four thousand Roman and allied horse. If they brought up their first reserve force, it would mean twenty thousand more Roman foot, thirty thousand more allied foot, and almost as many horse again, would be put into the field to join his game with their standing army. And if overconfidence started to besiege Hannibal, or his staff, the Romans could bolster these numbers with militias from the Italian colonies loyal to Rome—an addendum that could conceivably bring several hundred thousand more foot and horse, of various qualities, to the pull ropes of the Roman bells throughout Italy.

Leukon, a chieftain of the Boii, had moved close to the nucleus of Bostar's inspiration, and, therefore, close to the man who suffered no title but Hannibal. Like the other Celt inside the tent, Thyresius, a chieftain of the Insubres, he wore a cloak over part of the virtual Celt cavalry uniform: checkered trousers leather-bound at the ankle over soft boots, a corselet of fine-linked chain mail, a silver-linked belt clasped, in Leukon's case, with a red enameled buckle—in Thyresius' case, with a plain silver intricacy of the double voluted S Hannibal had seen on Auros of the Volcae, west of the Rhone, a lifetime before this night. These men had come directly from action against the Romans near Bresica, where their tribes had ambushed a small Roman army under the Praetor, Manlius, hence the chain mail was not affectation. Their cloaks were black, hand woven wool, and there was embroidery around the hems in gold and silver that tended this part of them toward affectation. But they were kindred spirits, suffused with Roman contention, and this put all the parts of them, including blue eyes, and long blond hair and mustaches, into the right perspective for that tent.

"We would be privileged to be some of the pillars of your Italian temple, Hannibal."

"Leukon, you have not anticipated me. I have seen this temple in enough detail to make a model of it now—Celtic pillars are indispensable to it."

In sessions with his senior officers, pre and post Alps, Hannibal had put more detail into this Italian temple. His expeditionary army had been the first pillars he placed into a construct that had been building in him almost since the day Hamilcar had started to talk to him about a continuity. His second pillars would be the Celts that he could pull out of the Po valley and the vast reservoir of them in Gaul. Under leadership that could balance discipline and strategy with fearless battle exuberance that had no match in the world, his Celtic arm could be indispensable, as he had just told Leukon. But he had given Leukon only a playful compliment relative to his presentation of the Celts in private sessions, where Maharbal, Carthalo...Mago, Hasdrubal, and the others qualified to look at the uninhibited Hannibal saw a panorama that went far beyond the measures of Hamilcar's obsession. His third selection of pillars was the Celt-Iberian army under his brother Hasdrubal that he expected would be ready for Italy when *he* was ready for it. The remaining manpower potentials of Carthage and her African allies, particularly the Libyan-Phoenicians and the Numidians, were his fourth consignment of pillars, and it would be reality so long as strong voices at Carthage carried his name to the Senate, and his Italian mission took first service of Carthage's ships and men. His last consignment for the Italian edifice with his inscription was what he could pull out of the potential of the Greeks, or the Macedonians, for Phillip V of Macedon was becoming a seductive ally for a man who would tickle the Romans from both ends of an east-west axis.

Maharbal had asked him about the phasing of these pillars—the interplay among them that empowered each of them for all. The site of this question had been on the Italian side of the Alps, at a time when Hannibal had found his quiet voice again for the gods. He told Maharbal that Heimarmene would dictate the answer to that question. Inanna used this name for this god of fate, and everyone within Hannibal's voice knew it, and thanked her for her presence alongside this man, at this time.

"Your people and the Insubres are moving the Romans about even now, Leukon—already we are comrades in arms."

"We hear that the consul Tiberius Sempronius has left Sicily, and is hurrying to pat us down at Brescia, Hannibal."

"We hear much the same, Leukon. Also, the other consul Publius Scipio is hurrying to put you in a squeezers. I had the pleasure of a brief encounter with him before coming here."

The Carthaginians in that tent were well apprised of the movements of both Scipio and Sempronius, but they were relieved to find that the Celt intelligence extended somewhat beyond what they could see from the top of a horse. Again, Hannibal had not put the full form of a statement in front of Leukon. Both Scipio and Sempronius now knew that he had come into Italy— that he had taken Turin and left a bloody message for the Celts to choose between him and Rome, that he was nestled at this time among friendly Celts and this bower was likely to expand under the heat of mutual affection.

One of the threads of his gossamer had reported that the Romans had been shocked at his appearance in Italy, and that both consuls were focusing on him and the Celt uprising in the Po. Scipio was now near Mutina to assist the praetor, Manlius. Sempronius was approaching this vicinity under forced march to assist Scipio. The 'pat' Leukon anticipated from the consuls had more scope than he knew, but he improved his compliment for Hannibal:

"The trials of putting yourself in this valley, into the shadow of the Roman arrogance and then, scarcely recuperated, your instruction of the Taurini in loyalties...I will repeat myself, Hannibal—we would be privileged to be a pillar of your temple here."

If Roman prescience had put their troops in front of him when he came out of the Alps, it would probably be over now, and his skull on a pole over Turin. But the gods who had listened to him had extended the reach of their mercy and the Romans had not been there.

Favorable impression of the Celts was crucial to his first steps in this valley. He had besieged the town of Turin, the capital of the Taurini, a tribe friendly to Rome. He gave them the option of surrender and alignment with him. When they refused, and told him that the Romans would swat the Carthaginian fly that had blundered into their valley, he took the city and killed most of the men of military age. The soldiers he spared were combined with Celt captives he had taken in the Alps. He made a gladiatorial arena in front of Turin, and told the prisoners that they would fight each other for their lives: to the victors would come a good horse, armor, and the honor of serving Carthage. The scene in that arena, the story of it, made part of the impression he wanted for the other Celts of the Po. His own arrogance in taking the citadel of a Roman ally, when he should have been licking and bandaging his souvenirs of the bloody Alps transit, was a larger part of the impression. Leukon's and Thyresius' presence in the tent, with Roman legionnaires under assault by their troops at Brescia, was proof that he had taken the right steps under an exigency of weakness and Roman-granted opportunity. At Turin, he had taken survival action. And he would defend it in front of Inanna...if he lived to see her again.

Now he had a little time to bolster his corps by what was left in them, what he could give to them, and the armed comradeship the Celts could be induced to give him. The other pillars would not be needed if the Celtic one couldn't be emplaced—soon. Leukon's plea for comradeship was *manna*, and the best commander, and one of the best actors the Celts would ever see, had reduced the triumph of it to a handshake and a smile.

"Your Celtic pillar is forming up, Hannibal." Maharbal was standing in front of the commander's tent. Tanit's disk and crescent, gold plated, set on an ebony wood standard, put some extra particles of lamplight into both sets of eyes in this conversation.

"Leukon and Thyresius might bring some useful foot and horse to us...I pray that we will have time to use them."

"What gods are we praying to this evening, Hannibal?"

"I don't know which ones answered us in the Alps. We put a lot of invocations into the air…many of our men and animals still need assistance. I'll go with Inanna's Asclepius tonight—I could use him myself."

"What particular prayer do you have in mind for Asclepius, for your *Celtic* pillar?"

"Quantity, quality, susceptibility to discipline and instruction, and all of this in a timely package before Scipio and Sempronius catch their breath."

"When do you plan to kick out what breath they may have sucked up already?"

"Carthalo's Numidian patrols have spotted some of Scipio's people near Stradella and Clastidium. I would like to move him further east, toward Placentia and Cremona. The Ticinus and Trebbia rivers do some interesting twisting around in that country. I think we can find a good playground over there."

"Are you inviting our new Celtic friends to play with us there?"

"If Myrcan's numbers for Scipio and Sempronius are not too much understated, I think we will find the Celt susceptibility to us will be enhanced after we've left our calling card with Scipio again. I'll not press them—let's play the reluctant brides for a little while."

"Scipio's horse roughed up our Numidians on that first occasion, as I recall."

"Those Numidians were a bunch of children on a lark when they were surprised. This time they will have you and Carthalo to put better steel up their ass—and they will have some strategy to go along with that insertion. I'm counting on Scipio's good memory of horses' asses running away from him—it will be called, *opportunity*, I think."

"Thyresius told me that he has a visiting Druid. Your friend Auros of the Volcae told you that a Druid would probably find you, Hannibal."

"By Ba'al's withered pendant, Maharbal, you can remember the words…I'll have to be more careful around you."

"You have been giving all of us perspective on the Celts. Perhaps this Druid can refresh the amphorae you've been pouring from on our behalf, Hannibal."

"I think you just told me to get some more education, Maharbal."

"With all deference, I think these Druids have a reputation that should meld wonderfully with the mysteries you've deigned to reveal to us from time to time. And you've put the Celts into prominence for your Italian temple—I don't see how you can gracefully avoid this Druid, considering all of this precedence."

Maharbal was a friend, a virtual confidant of Amalkre, Inanna, and the Lady Barca, from whence came much of the substance of the mysteries he'd just mentioned. He had brushed words with these ladies of Hannibal, playfully, the lightest touch of their inimitable perfume on theirs, a prescription for recuperation from the brutal persistence of a cavalry commander's responsibilities. To top these credentials, Maharbal had been one of Hamilcar's strong arms. He was one of the great cavalry commanders, an indispensable ligament of Hannibal's strength. Hannibal was, therefore, not disposed to object to either Maharbal's choice of words, or his prompting to meet a Druid.

Carthalo and Maharbal had insisted on an escort of twenty Numidians, although the direction of Hannibal's quest was away from the latest sightings of Scipio's people, and its location in the Insubres country was close enough to Hannibal's camp to almost guarantee safety for him both ways. Hannibal and two other riders were in the van of the party of horsemen. He and the two of his right and left carried shields and swords. They wore helmets, but no additional body armor. The Numidians carried their standard shields, lances, and daggers. This particular group rode on leopard skins, an elite designation which justified Hannibal's confidence in dispensing with cumbersome body armor. If he ever needed people to close on him for his protection, he would take these over any he had ever seen, or heard about.

"How is this Druid called, Hannibal?" Silenus was the man on his left.

"Thyresius called him Cathbad, some Celtic name from God knows where...probably deep in Gaul." Hannibal's tendency to go to the monotheistic oath was increasing, and its Lady Barca implication had almost disappeared.

"We are not to have the privilege of attending your meeting?"

"You are *not*, Sosylos." Sosylos was the man on his right. "These Druids are said to be a touchy lot—I wouldn't want you to bear any responsibility for a poor meeting." Hannibal's credentials for peeking into a Druid's head were not so great, either, but Sosylos was nothing if not discreet.

Thyresius' directions had been explicit enough. *Go to such and such a hill configuration. Bear left at the base of the largest hill to a creek. Cross the creek and follow it upstream to an oak grove. Dismount, and follow the path into the grove to a large oak holding a mistletoe wreath. The Druid will instruct from there.*

They rode without talking until they splashed across the creek, and then only some exclamations of pleasure for a little cold dousing after a dusty passage.

With Sosylos' and Silenus' good respects on his back, Hannibal dismounted and walked into the oak grove, its burgeoning cool shade, autumn spectrums of light and shade—and the prospects of a Druid—putting the first solid relaxation into him he'd had in weeks. Sosylos had murmured about a letter to Inanna several times. He would attend to it. She and Kyniska must be wondering about him. The damn rumors always were hard to deal with. A red squirrel darted in front of him, and then a large jay squawked at him before wheeling off to an oak sanctuary. *Hannibal* didn't mean much here. Kyniska would have been delighted and Inanna would have already been yards in front of him. The large oak with the mistletoe blaze suddenly loomed in front of him. He walked past the Druid's sign into a space where there had been footsteps before, random patterns suggesting an arena, or unseated amphitheatre. Here the natural canopy had suddenly suffused the light with a soft mystery. Inanna's Delphic antecedents were a perfect credential for this place of fugitive light and shadow that could hide a Druid.

Hannibal stopped at the focal point of the space. He removed his helmet, and wiped his face with a bit of silk that hung around the neck of his riding tunic. *Let the Celt make the next step, this shade is too good to leave. Maybe he had denied Sosylos and Silenus some earned pleasure—but it was too late now.* He had just done a quick pass at his neck with the silk when the immediate population increased by one.

"By Teutates! I've finally come close to Hamilcar Barca." The voice was soft, like the space around it, perfectly modulated and, therefore, projected.

Before he looked toward it, Hannibal could make no decent guess at what age person to expect. If a man took care of himself, was able to protect *his* values, a voice could go to the grave like the young shadow of an old man. He had a good vector on the voice and turned toward it. Against a natural background that put browns, grays, blacks, and gold randomly, he saw a tall patch that had some of these colors, but ordered in patterns he'd heard other Celts call *plaids*. But the interface here was subtle, and if the other hadn't spoken, he could have been a piece of this forest for Hannibal. From about ten paces, Hannibal could now see more of the long cloak, gold threaded along the front and bottom hems, the Druid's hands clasped in the front, a gold ring the only evident jewelry. The posture was rod-straight and Hannibal had no height advantage here. But it was from the neck up that the words had come, and it was this region that fixed Hannibal's eyes now that the Druid had materialized. The unmustached face gave a frank stage for venerability. Hannibal's guess lay somewhere between 70 and 90. He had never seen a tonsured priest of the Celts, and here was one...the white hair shaved across the crown of his head from ear to ear, leaving a diadem several inches high that was a perfect accessory for blue eyes that could match any temper the Lady Barca could put into hers.

"That is the best compliment you could have given me—Cathbad, I believe?" Hannibal walked toward the Druid. He stopped short of the distance of a hand clasp, testing the local formality. The Druid completed the distance himself and surprised Hannibal by his strong grip. Before he spoke again, the Druid nodded, still uncoupled from the other eyes:

"This is a quick sanctuary, my local *nemeton*, Hannibal. Thyresius did what he could to accommodate a nosy priest at a busy time." He motioned toward a path behind him. Following, Hannibal passed canopied structures that could have been altars and approached a round shelter with a beamed conical roof, shingled with reed plaits. The Druid strode through the open door and obviously intended the same for his visitor. The exterior light coming through the door and a partial window annulus in the roof structure was still strong enough to show bundles of reeds for seating, and several low tables, one of which held two silver cups and a bowl of fruit. Two ceramic pitchers near this table were promising. A man could sleep on the large pile of sheepskins and under blankets near it that were on the periphery of the single room. The woodwork here and in the appendages they had passed, even for *quick* structures, was skillful and efficient and didn't surprise Hannibal. Cathbad had addressed him in Greek, closer to the classical mold than Auros'...again Inanna would have smiled in these precincts. This also was no surprise. The Greek-Celt couplings were strong, complex, and even the scholars had been arguing about precedence here and there. Reed bundles tended to center a patch of the floor covered by white sand, a bundle in the middle of it. Cathbad motioned toward this bundle.

"My temporary throne, Hannibal—I invite you to one of the inferior positions." Hannibal had been looking at Cathbad, so the smile that came with these words put Hannibal on one of the other bundles without any troublesome hierarchy. Before he sat down himself, Cathbad walked to the table that held the cups:

"I have beer, or spring water."

"I've had your beer in Iberia, it's habit forming." A good enough answer for Cathbad who brought two cups of beer to the conversation.

"Thyresius offered me a servant, but I've got out of the habit of one." Cathbad assumed his throne and tipping his cup toward his guest, took some of his beer.

As the cool beer slid down his throat, Hannibal privately reinforced his Iberian confession about it.

"I've got two Greeks waiting for me outside your nemeton—don't put too much guilt on me with your hospitality." He held the silver sheath for his beer toward the light and admired the stag and hound emboss on its side as he talked.

"Sosylos and Silenus are good connections for you, Hannibal." This facile identification was still no surprise. All of this meeting so far had said that

Thyresius' introduction to this Druid had been well planned and researched.

"They have put history, art, drama and Greek into me. I don't know what use I can make of that with the Romans." Cathbad admired Hannibal's accent. Sosylos, the Spartan, had been a good tutor. He wondered how Silenus fit into this man. The Celt threads of intelligence had been well worked into Iberia, even Carthage. Hannibal *would* have been surprised at what this Druid knew about him.

"Then you know that we have been comrades-in-arms for a long time. You will find some of our marks in Rome, and along the way there." A hundred and seventy-four years before, on the Allia river banks, Cathbad's kin had slaughtered a Roman army and gone south to sack their capital. In varying degrees of intensity, success and failure, they had bedeviled the Romans ever since. "Have you heard of Brennus?"

"Which Brennus?—the one on the Allia river, or the one who took a parade of your people through Macedon and into Greece? I think these namesakes were roughly a hundred years apart."

"By Teutates! I like your Sosylos, maybe your Silenus!"

"You have invoked this god twice—who is he?"

"One of our war gods, the one with particular association to thunder and lightning."

"You *are* working this kinship business with me. My father had lightning blazed on his sails."

"Also some of his amphorae, Hannibal. I've tasted his wine. I like it. I would like to see that blaze spread over a bigger part of the world."

"We are still talking about wine?—and how in the dreams of Ba'al did you know about the Barca amphorae?"

"Hamilcar used many Celts in Iberia, Sicily, Africa. Those who perpetrated the African revolt are our shame, but there are too many proud memories around Hamilcar to let that stick in our throat. The Barca amphorae, and the lady who keeps them filled now, are no mysteries." This sudden interjection of part of his private values into a space near a nemeton of a Druid, by a Druid, on the brink of the Roman fields, was a surprise Hannibal's actor's face could barely control.

"I will need your people to move that blaze you just complimented into Italy." This Druid had made his connection with him, most of the amenities were over. Hannibal's last words had been soft as the ripple of residual autumn in the oaks around him, but they were chiseled clearly enough for this Celt.

Cathbad picked up a loose reed and started to draw on the white sand page in front of them. He put in the outline of what could be the Iberian Peninsula, merging it with southern Gaul. And then he moved the reed in a quick delineation of Gaul, giving some details Hannibal had never seen...bringing in the ocean boundaries to the west and north, even the big islands of the north that Greeks and some Carthaginians had made familiar ground long before him. Then Cathbad went to the north and northeast and added the lands of the Belgae and the Germani to his map. He lingered over his last marks:

"The Belgae and the Germani are here and they could be the steel that will put your blaze into all of Italy—if you can get to them. Oh, your friends the Insubres, the Boii and what's left of the Senones, will help you, but these others might be the *keystone* for your Italian temple. I know about some of your Roman numbers—you will need almost as much reservoir for *your* work, Hannibal Barca. We have put *our* blaze into Italy—right into the Roman heart. But, with a few exceptions, we have wasted thousands of good men under commanders whose only quality was impetuosity and a death wish that benefited nobody but the Romans. A certain kind of commander comes only once in centuries. We have not been favored by such men, perhaps Brennus came closest. Incidentally, he took fifteen thousand horse through Macedon and Greece. The quality of his cavalry should interest you, Hannibal. Advanced for its time, our generation of it, under that commander I mentioned, could be irresistible—coupled to what I hear about your Numidian, Iberian and Carthaginian horse."

"Your compliments are flowing too fast for me, Cathbad. And you mentioned an Italian temple. This fantasy popped out from Leukon yesterday. It's traveled far since then." Perhaps, but Maharbal, Carthalo, and some others of his right hand had heard him build something very like a temple when Leukon wasn't around, but Cathbad's ears were. "I've heard of Brennus' cavalry. That *trimakisia* concept, two mounted servants for each cavalryman is interesting. It suggests some cluttering—it also suggests a pride and focus that could tie your word, *irresistible*, into a Celtic horse contingent."

"Ah, my bow to Sosylos again for your Brennus memories. And your new friend, Leukon, has the reputation of bringing his inspirations in line with others—he might be a useful ambassador for some purposes I've just mentioned."

"To those northern climes that might freeze a delicate Carthaginian?"

"Hamilcar Barca and Hannibal Barca are names that have not succumbed to those climes. The Romans have been our adversaries for generations. Anyone who has inspired, or threatens further contention with the Roman juggernaught, is very interesting to us. His name tends to flow around our parts—including the northern ones." When Cathbad used his word, *threatens*, it came from an old Celt, who had walked and talked and listened in most of the citadels of the Celts, who had analyzed and rejected and burnished values and ambitions in these places, and who had just spent this word on possibly a unique match for it. Cathbad stood, and replenished the beer cups. Then he started to pace the room, mostly where a still seated Hannibal could see him.

"Your lesson to the Taurini has also walked around a lot of our places already."

"That was survival, Cathbad—but the price of that message might have been too high."

"We have bloodied ourselves uselessly against the Romans too many times. The incentives of the Italian fields are not so bright anymore—this lodestone that has drawn some of our best people southward is close to exhaustion. That certain commander, with the right ambassadors, might make some rejuvenation that could send the chicken guts from Roman auspices flying over every stone in the Roman forum...I consider your Taurini lesson part of that rejuvenation."

"I've heard that you have auspicious powers that could clarify this optimism."

"Probably overstated. I have lingered over some consecrated ground, the templum, trying to pick auspices out of bird flights. I've stared into lightning and listened to thunder replications from every natural mirror you could think of. I've stared at various presentations of various guts myself in the service of auspices. My successes shall remain ambiguous for your benefit, Hannibal."

"What is this business of *shape lifting?*"

"Assumption of desired forms and shapes. I tried to make a tree for you, remember?"

"Your voice saved me. And the art of illusion, more of your magic?"

"The pinnacle of this art is probably the *airbe druad,* laying an invisible, impenetrable, hedge around an army."

"By your Teutates! You and I could conquer the world with *this* jewel of your crown!"

Cathbad's smile walked with him, also his cup of beer. Hannibal stood up, walked to the Druid, and touched their cups, the stag and the hound on his silver performing as well as antiques could do in that light, promising more with some promotion and burnishing.

"My thanks for your wonderful hospitality, Cathbad. I'll try to reciprocate someplace between here and Rome. I wonder if we can mingle your Teutates' lightning with the Barca blaze?"

"I won't make any illusion for you now, Hannibal Barca—let me use a crutch for my answer: Heimarmene will decide our next conjunctions, but perhaps we can nudge him a little."

As they walked out the door, Hannibal didn't bother to ask how Cathbad got a little part of Inanna into their talk. This man was modest about his credentials, but you could take what you wanted from his eyes and face, and this made an Inanna question impertinent, even redundant.

"Your knowledge of the consuls Publius Scipio and Sempronius Longus is probably better than mine. Do you know the names Fabius Maximus, Claudius Marcellus and Gaius Flaminius?" They had reached the glade where a Druid had almost hidden from Hannibal.

"The Fabii were a strong voice in our first war with Rome. The memories of it rankled my father and pushed me toward *this* war. Quintus Fabius Maximus will be a man to watch. He has strong connections with the Hanno faction in Carthage, possibly the biggest worry I left behind there. I will study this man as we move toward him. Claudius Marcellus is an aristocrat of Fabius' circle. He's also the best Roman general we will look at for a while. Four years ago he postured in front of your people at Clastidium, over the body of your king, Viridomarus. Marcellus also merits our close attention. Gaius Flaminius is a refreshing personality. He abhors the pretensions of the Senate, ignores much of its direction. He likes to build roads and circuses. He has pushed Roman colonization here in the Po into the throats of your people. He is a self-styled people's champion. If we put up a large enough mirror for him to preen his glory, I think we can suck him with us and make him follow *our* itinerary. This is the most interesting part about Gaius Flaminius, I think."

They had reached the large oak with the mistletoe blaze. Cathbad stopped them. "If I had your years, Hannibal Barca, I would be obsessed right now with opportunity—for you, for us, for our conjunctions."

"A lot of you has spilled over on me, Cathbad. I'll carry some of this exhilaration for you."

The Druid put his right hand on Hannibal's shoulder. "What we have left here in the Po Valley, along Picenum, and in Umbria, will help you—foot and horse, and our craziness that I think you can tame for your purposes. But some of you will have to go to the Belgae and the Germani for the final part of the arm that will kill the Hydra-headed Roman infestation that is choking Italy, and the other parts of the world it can get to. It sucks on other civilization. It kills what it can't make into its image. It stifles the nutrients and the cross-fertilization that makes the miracles—it makes old men into farting fools, spouting beer breath."

"At the least, I would like some more of your beer, and for my friends." Hannibal nodded toward his waiting company, Sosylos and Silenus standing a few paces in front of the Numidian escort. They had come on this little ride with Hannibal for a closer look at this Druid.

"I will send you a few barrels." When Hannibal waved Cathbad toward the audience, the Druid didn't move. "A little mystery here is good, Hannibal. From this distance...with a little distraction...I could make a good illusion." Cathbad suddenly pointed to the sky and cried the Celt word for raven—twice. When Hannibal and the audience turned back to where Cathbad had stood, there was only air in that space, and provocative whispering from the oak grove.

Scipio had had some time to digest Hannibal's baptism of Turin, and the overtures of the Insubres and Boii. The Romans thought they had patted the Celts of the Po into military insignificance, but the Hannibal presence could change that comfort which had given the consul, Publius Cornelius Scipio, and his brother, Gnaeus Cornelius Scipio, the opportunity to look to political and economic wealth in Sardenia, Corsica and particularly in an Iberia without Hannibal. This man had suddenly perturbed this empire vision. The Roman presence around Placentia, Cremona and Mutina had been temporarily reasserted by reinforcements, Celt confusion, and the news that both consuls, Scipio and Sempronius, were bringing their standards to the Roman troubles in the Po valley which now included Hannibal Barca, the Carthaginian.

When Scipio arrived at Mutina, he took command of all Roman forces in the area. He was now on the right bank of the Po, Hannibal on the left. Scipio felt that he could block further Celt friendship to Hannibal by moving to Hannibal's side of the Po. He crossed the river between Placentia and where the Ticinus River joins the Po from the north and took a position near the mouth of the Ticinus. This ground was favorable to cavalry. But *cavalry* had not yet burned into the Roman consciousness. Hannibal 's present horse was six thousand plus any Celt addition, Scipio's horse was less than a third of this. The Ticinus offered many fords for cavalry, another factor that a man who had put horse and foot into a mutual ecstasy of power could exploit.

"Scipio has thrown a bridge across the Ticinus after crossing the Po." Carthalo repeated his scouts' observation to Hannibal. Hannibal and his staff were on horseback about twenty miles from Scipio. When he moved toward Scipio, he had considered various ploys for putting the Roman on better ground for cavalry. The news that Scipio had left a good position at Placentia and was moving toward this kind of ground was his incentive to ford the Ticinus near Lake Maggiore and move south toward Scipio on the east side of this river. Carthalo's message was shortly expanded by another scout's report:

"The Roman has heard about us on this side of their little river. Now he doesn't want to use his pretty bridge—he wants to come see us on *this* side."

"By Cathbad's Teutates' Celtic balls, Carthalo, Scipio must have read the pages we have written for his actors—he's coming right into our ground!" Hannibal wheeled his horse to the direction of his army, and his staff tried to follow.

11

29 years
November 218 BC—Ticinus River

Three Carthaginian officers had taken an escort of fifty Numidian horse for a little morning ride southerly along the Ticinus river. They were in a locality, in a moment of autumn, where the complexion of their air was tempered by both the great spine of the Alps behind them and beginnings of the Apennines in front of them. And the Po valley put its own essences of quiescent fields and arbors into that morning. Scipio was moving northerly along the same river, on the same bank, in roughly the same conjunction with the air temperers, presumably enjoying the same invigoration.

"He knows we're coming. We know he's coming. I think we will have our first real handshake with the Romans soon, Hannibal." Maharbal didn't need to turn to the man between him and Carthalo, all of their orientations were fixed southerly. Then, a moment like all three had had on the Tagus a year before, happened again, some of its words almost echoes of the other time: "A scouting detail is putting more hell to their horses to get to you, Hannibal."

Carthalo had made the announcement again, by sheer accident his eyes had made this particular out of the panorama they had all been looking at. If Hannibal remembered the Tagus connection with that moment, he ignored it. Maharbal's previous statement held sway here and the small dust cloud accompanying the Numidian outriders was Maharbal's exclamation point.

"We are about to get some details, gentlemen: how Scipio is dressed, how he has catered our reception, what he expects of us...almost indispensable handshake material."

His Numidian captain came close and parallel to the stopped rank of commanders, Hannibal's style, then he rode along it and back again, placing his report before all of them.

"The Roman has put only his velites into his foot. He has about two thousand Roman and Allied horse and about a hundred Celt horse with them." The velites were the lightly armed skirmishers used to get the enemy's attention and promote his confusion before the ministrations of the hastati and the principes, the legionnaire backbone of the Roman, and the triarii, also legionnaires, but with older backbones.

"Scipio has taken us too lightly, I think. But I like the meal of his horse he is giving us. His velites will leave us hungry."

"We will put mostly horse against this welcoming party, Hannibal?"

"You and Carthalo have been bragging about your Numidians, Maharbal. I think a good stage, just for horses, is ahead of us. How far do you say, Captain?"

"About ten miles, Lord Hannibal."

"The ground between us?"

"I *like* it." Coming from a cavalryman, this was Hannibal's answer.

Synhalus and his crew of veterinarians had worked miracles with their wine baths, salves and medications on the horses. The Insubres had brought some of their medicine to Synhalus and he'd learned new tricks, using mistletoe, selago, and verbena, for helping the man on top of the horse return to good spirit. All of Hannibal's horse needed exercise. Scipio had thrown dice blazed mostly with horse. It was only courteous to play the offered game.

"Greet Scipio with our full horse, Maharbal. Let the Numidians play with your Iberians and Carthaginans for a little while."

When about two miles separated them, there was perturbation of dust that said the sights and sounds would be coming. At one mile, Scipio's double line was evident, no structure yet.

"Put us in one line, Maharbal. I want to show him some width that will kiss his flanks."

Maharbal placed the Numidians on the flanks, the Iberian and Carthaginian heavy horse in the center. Now all of Hannibal was properly constituted to shake the hand Scipio had offered.

The Roman's structure was now clear—his velites and Celtic horse were in the front rank, his Roman and Allied horse about fifty paces behind, in parallel rank. Scipio had them down to a slow advance when Hannibal was in view.

Hannibal, Maharbal, Carthalo and another cavalry officer, Hasdrubal, rode in a parallel rank in front of Hannibal's corps. The sound of six thousand horse behind them was about to be penetrated by the sound of roughly two thousand horse ahead of them, aided by what the velites could put into the air by clanging shields and shouting.

Hannibal raised his hand. His command contingent stopped. He turned his horse to face them.

"Gentlemen, we are about to graduate from Iberia and enter another classroom. I am proud to have your company here. Let's take our apple to this classroom and see if we can find a teacher." Then he put his gray Cyrenian into a trajectory toward his army and again his company tried to follow him, the only red-plumed helmet in his army an elusive focus.

Before he reached a battle command position, Maharbal had a few words with Carthalo. "I want ten of your best Numidians, the leopard skins, to watch him. This is his first big step into Hamilcar's dream. He will try to take too much to himself, ignore his dangers. I don't want it to end here. We will have to educate him a little on how much of himself he can give to us at any time. Tanit and Ba'al for you, Carthalo! For him! For us!"

Carthalo's Numidians formed up five and five, right and left of Hannibal as he moved his corps toward Scipio. He rode about thirty paces in front of his line. The escort had been accomplished with aplomb, conviction, and Hannibal smiled about it but was careful to keep his face turned to Scipio. The velites were getting their shouts and clangs to him now, and Hannibal could see the red cloaks of tribunes dispersed among the foot and horse. Between the lines of the velites and the Roman horse, he could see a command group which contained more red cloaks and one rider distinguished by a gilded helmet and cuirass, the helmet red-plumed...a consul or legate's paraphernalia.

He had thought about where to put himself in this battle. On the Tagus expedition, at the unexpected aftermath which was almost his Iberian zenith, he had kept behind the front rank—but close enough to let his people know he was there, their principal conductor. A few times before the Tagus finale, near to Salmantica, he had broken this rule of almost surrogate command and gone to his sword when a local situation needed bolstering, or so he thought. But, afterwards, Carthalo and Maharbal had told him that his moments of fun with the blade took away his moments of command. There had been some blood smears on all the faces of this little chat so no one could find any insolence in it, and Hannibal had remembered it. And on one of these occasions of his blade, before this chat, a Carthaginian heavy infantryman, almost within the arc of his commander's blade, called out a warning to him, "let *us* do the fighting." Alexander had shown such rashness on many occasions and on many occasions his memory had come very close to abbreviation because of it. Sosylos had reminded Hannibal of this after he'd heard from Carthalo and Maharbal.

When the velite introduction to Scipio's line was about a five hundred paces away, Hannibal ordered the signal man within range of his voice to sound the charge, and horns which had been specialized to cut through Roman bluster and static put this command over all his corps. Hannibal led the charge for a hundred paces and then he and his Numidians flowed back behind the line of heavy cavalry as it came to full charge. He came back far enough to get perspective on his Numidian wings. They were holding their sectors smartly, and as the sound of his six thousand horse started to mingle with the Roman sounds, he cried his father's name...but *Inanna* and *Hippolyta* also intruded this auspicious moment of a young continuity.

He had equipped his heavy horse with mailed chest and forehead armor. The light spears, hastae, of the velites started to rattle against his heavy formations but they were ineffective. Against advancing foot, the velites could schedule their attacks, gauge distance for launching their missiles, and husband their missiles for best effect. But against a charging wall of armored heavy horse all of this confidence disappeared, and Scipio's velites fell like wheat before a mower. Hannibal rode back and forth, over almost a half mile of line as his heavy horse smashed Scipio's foot and speared into the Roman heavy horse formations. No signals were needed at this time. He had ordered charge. In obedience, his line had broken the Roman front line, including its Celt cavalry appendage, and now it was continuing his order into the Roman and Allied horse. No man could describe the sound of such battle...no man's ears could understand it. It was progressive cataclysm that spilled agony and exaltation and every component of men and beasts over where it traveled—the ones in its van partly its conductors, the ones in its wake, trying to fix themselves in heaven or hell.

Hannibal and Carthalo's orbits on this field intersected for a moment, Hannibal's Numidians permitting this.

"Turn the Numidians into his flanks as fast as they can go."

"They're ahead of you, Hannibal. They're chewing up what's left of the velites who retreated through their horse."

"When they eat enough velites, they can take a bite of Scipio's heavy horse, some of which has dismounted." And the Numidians were ahead of Hannibal there, too. Many Roman heavy cavalrymen had become foot and the Carthaginian heavy horse was demonstrating, as it had in Sicily against the Romans an age before, that it was death come on horseback for such men. Hannibal's Numidian wings had piled into the rear of the Roman heavy horse and were collaborating with the frontal attack of the Iberian and Carthaginian heavy horse in a slaughter.

Hannibal rode back toward the center of his center, although a geometrician would have gone crazy here with the symmetries that were fugitive and powerful and suddenly asymmetries—all of it bathed in the *sound.* He saw flashes of red cloaks, then a sheen of gilded armor that jerked back and forth before it fell to the ground, a focus of Roman desperation inside a ring of aggression. He was diverted by some other action, but later he was told that Scipio had been rescued by his son, Publius Cornelius. How old?, he had asked. About seventeen we think, he was told. Is Scipio hurt? He was very close to death inside us...young Publius pulled a miracle out of that field, they answered. It seems young Publius had hitched his star to miracles early on.

"It is complete disorder with what's left of them now—shall we chase them, Hannibal?" Maharbal's orbit had finally intersected Hannibal's.

"No, I am content. Scipio has our calling card now, and while he recuperates he can read it. We will get ready to make it bigger for him and Sempronius when he catches up."

"The Celt scouts tell us that Sempronius is breathing hard someplace between Ariminum and the Trebbia."

"He is bringing a nice piece of pie to join Scipo's. I think we'll have something *very* tasty to bite into in a few days, Maharbal." Hannibal's helmet and cuirass had blood marks. Whether from splashes around him, or from his own sword, he didn't tell, and Maharbal didn't ask, although his order about the leopard skinned Numidian shield around Hannibal had been accomplished, and its message had been received by Hannibal without any baggage of questions and answers.

"I would value your impression of us, today, Hannibal."

"I congratulate you and Carthalo for what you've done with the Numidians. If there is a better light horse in *this* world, I don't know about it. I congratulate you for your heavy horse. You have taken our tattered victory standard from Sicily and planted it squarely in the Roman face on his own ground. They never saw horse like ours—on the fields ahead of us they never will have seen a conjunction of horse and foot like ours." Hannibal rode close enough to his chief of cavalry to put his right hand on Maharbal's shoulder. "You are Hamilcar's best gift to me. I invoke Inanna's Hiemarmene long enough to say I would like to stand in the Roman forum with you when we look down on a Roman salute."

"I accept this honor. I amend it only in the respect of the salute—a long deferred kiss on our ass would be my vision of it."

The morning of the battle, both Sosylos and Silenus had come to Hannibal arrayed as heavy cavalrymen. He had permitted this license several times before in Iberia, providing certain guidelines for his mentors that limited their devotion in impending action to peripheral observation. On the morning of Ticinus, Hannibal had been preoccupied more than usual when his Greek shadows materialized in the command tent.

"Where do you think you're going?" He was getting better at putting his official face toward them, especially with staff officers swarming him under urgencies of battle.

"We're ready for you to define *that* particular, Hannibal." Both the speaker, Sosylos, and Silenus were at some semblance of attention. Hannibal shot several looks at them while fending off various urgencies.

"You will follow the heavy cavalry, close enough to keep some Roman from picking two ripe plums, but far enough away to keep a heavy cavalryman from using you as squires. Do you remember your *Brennus* lesson, Sosylos?" By Ba'al, here he was turning on the teacher:

"Perfectly, Lord Hannibal." Sosylos used that title sparingly, inserting it, along with a proper face, at just the right instant of his temperamental charge. Inanna had been mixed up in several of these instants. "I suggest you are alluding to the famous *trimakisia*...the two squires for each cavalryman."

"I am, and there will be none of that here—see that you two don't get in the way."

He could have added, *and see that you don't get hurt.* But that would have spoiled everything, and as he turned away toward another urgency, both Sosylos and Silenus knew this.

The first half of expedition was the military part...the planning and the fighting. The second half was the sustenance of men and animals to keep the first half going. The Insubres had been a gift of the gods when the Carthaginian army staggered out of the Alps and needed sustenance and recuperation. Hannibal was sensitive to the outlays the Celts were making for him, and he had sent scouts out as much for forage and victual purposes, as for military intelligence, to relieve this burden on prospective allies. Clastidium was in his region. It was a Roman supply depot, and it was a tempting target: he was between it and Scipio and Sempronius, and it was a strategically placed asset for the games he expected to play with the consuls near Placentia and Cremona. While his cavalry rested from their Ticinus exercise, his Iberian and African foot was preparing to break their fast from fighting, and his patrols were supplementing Celt information about the Roman movements and disposition, he rode to Clastidium with Carthalo and Mago and an escort of a hundred Numidians. Single scouts had reported no Roman presence in the neighborhood.

"You've sucked them to the east, Hannibal, worrying about you, and they left this plum in our lap." They could sense Clastidium close to them, and no Romans yet, as the scouts reported.

"Let's tip-toe up that hill and peek over...maybe there *is* a plum waiting for us named Clastidium." Hannibal defined the path to their first observation point. The party reined short of the crest of an elevation overlooking the fortress.

Clastidium was a compact aggregation of brick and wooden buildings, surrounded by a wall that would tend to discourage a Celt foraging party. The gate was closed, but nothing evident on the walls. It was not a spectacle promoting fear from either attack, or defense, perspectives. They circumnavigated Clastidium, keeping a distance which seemed to be more discretion than was necessary, but occasionally swinging in to advertise their circuit. They returned to their first vantage, this time forming along the crest unbashfully. The officers' body armor, which Hannibal had ordered well polished for this ride, used a propitious sun angle for more advertisement. Two of the crests on the Officers' helmets were black, one was red and by various gossamers' news this was now known from Iberia to beyond Athens as Hannibal's mark when immersed in his own forces. His presence before Clastidum was now fairly unambiguous. The Numidians in clean white tunics, bearing polished shields and weapons, matched black horses, set up in a line abreast behind Hannibal. Mago had insisted on carrying Tanit's disk and crescent for this party, and he moved his standard up front, holding it so that its gold sheathing made another good mirror for Clastidium. They waited for at least five minutes, no sound from them or Clastidium—just two ravens that made a close pass at Hannibal with comments. Then the gate started to open.

"Shall we charge, or escape, Hannibal" The answer to Carthalo's sardonic question hinged on the structure of the resolution behind that moving gate.

"Give them a few seconds to explain themselves—if this is their assault, it's the sleepiest one I ever saw."

The single paneled gate opened wide and a man walked out, unescorted, apparently unarmed and unarmored. He wore a white tunic and sandals. There were no people behind him.

"Here comes a priest looking for a congregation." Hannibal watched the approach for a few more seconds and then turned to Mago. "Move the standard close to him and tell him we would like to arrange a little picnic for some men and horses."

"This is a *Roman* depot, Hannibal. This is like setting up an alms entreaty for Carthage next to their senate building."

"I'd like our greetings to match the strangeness of their reception."

Mago shot a quick look at his brother and then rode down the hill to put Hannibal's proposal to the Clastidium reception. He stopped about twenty paces short of it and planted Tanit's standard. Then he dismounted and stood alongside the standard, still no sound from the fortress in front of him.

"I am Dasius, commander of Clastidum." The first speaker had now also stopped, leaving about ten paces of separation. He had used good Greek, because he was Greek.

"I am Mago, of the Carthaginians." Mago's inspiration for good Greek may not have been as big as Hannibal's, but he had been prodded into it by military necessities, and by a Greek lady of Hannibal's acquaintance and inspiration.

Dasius raised his right arm in salute, not vintage Roman but respectful enough for an officer in mufti. Mago moved his right hand on a quick trip to his heart zone.

"As Lord Hannibal's present voice, I'm to ask if you could arrange a picnic for some men and horses."

Dasius looked past Mago to the party on the hill. The Numidians had moved into double lines abreast behind Hannibal and Carthalo, making a more compact target for the sun and a stronger image for Dasius. "I could cater such a party easily. If it contains Lord Hannibal, perhaps I would need a little longer to accommodate such an honor." Dasius and Mago had come close enough now so that the stages of both faces could carry more of the chat. Because of Celt and Roman shouts and whispers, a crescendo that had started near the Rhone and come to a climax at Turin, Dasius had to acknowledge the fact of Hannibal in the Po valley, even if a famous presence had not suddenly come within a breath of Clastidium.

"The scope of your hospitality is as great as its surprise, Dasius. I will convey it to Lord Hannibal. What would you say, however, if the party I had in mind contained a large part of an army...foot, horse, elephants...for example?"

Dasius motioned toward Hannibal's hill. "...That is the van of a *larger* honor?" That it might also be an *imminent* honor, put some edge on the softness that Dasius had been promoting.

Mago had to laugh, a reaction that went at least as far as Hannibal.

"If this is a precursor to battle, Carthalo, then Mago has just put new definition into anxiety and terror."

"Perhaps he's talking to a comic they've sent out to laugh us to death. Mago is quick to pull a laugh out of words, quick to send it crawling toward us. He's the best possible first audience for them...for such a purpose."

"I'll wait a bit before I cover my ears, Carthalo—do what you want about yourself and the Numidians."

In answering Dasius' question, Mago tried to promote Dasius's softness with just a tincture of menace. The situation at Clastidium was still a mystery, just compounded by its commander, but a tincture seemed better than a dose, so he said, "The van is where Hannibal is, Dasius...sometimes this can make a long neck on an army."

"Even some miles long...in some cases, Mago?"

"Exactly. How shall I convey your answer to Hannibal?" Mago had just put extra breath into Dasius.

"I would like the honor of making that answer myself, Mago." The images on the hill were irresistible to Dasius, and he turned toward them while answering.

Mago saluted Dasius again, returned to his horse, mounted and rode back to the hill, leaving Tanit's standard in front of Clastidium and Dasius.

"He is named Dasius. He says he is the commander of Clastidium...he wants to speak to Hannibal."

"Then let's go down to him." Hannibal led the way to just behind his standard. He dismounted while Mago, Carthalo and the Numidians made a formation ten paces behind him. Hannibal walked to within four arms' distance of Dasius. Dasius made it two arms.

"I am Hannibal Barca."

"I am Dasius, commander of Clastidium. Your emissary, Mago, has requested sustenance."

"*Sustenance* has some desperation clinging to it, Dasius. At this time—in this beautiful Italian autumn—I prefer *supplies*, that word has some grace of time embracing it."

"Mago mentioned an army in this connection."

"Mago has a refreshing and sometimes valuable tendency to dramatics. But I will let the word *army* stay in this conversation." Hannibal found Dasius to be a pleasant target for words...well groomed, Greek styled hair, Greek fastidiousness in his dress, classic Greek in his speech. This was no Roman... nor, by a little more intuition, was it a Roman trick. But Hannibal was perfectly sensitive to the open gate, and its background. There was nothing there that tended to discourage this chat—in fact, the strangeness of it almost compelled continuation.

Dasius was sensitive to Hannibal's dilemma. Within reasonable limits, the Carthaginian in front of him was said to be compassionate. In Dasius' opinion, it was his move now:

"I am from Brindisi. By accidents of chance that would bore you, I trickled into the command of this little pile behind me. I am a Greek, however, and I have decided that my loyalty will go to someone who can keep the Roman Wolf away from Magna Graecia—from my vantage now this looks like you, Lord Hannibal." Punic agents had probed the discontent of the Roman allies of Southern Italy since before Hamilcar. The Roman intrusion of the economic spheres of Campania, Apulia, Brutium and Lucania had bred resentment and outrage that could yield sustenance to the right commander attuned to these signals. Hannibal knew about much of this, he had put it into his plans. The man here, in front of a Roman depot crammed with a harvest that could put a sheen on his men and animals for weeks, was unexpected bounty. But it needed further definition, so he waited for more of Dasius.

"I am surrendering Clastidum to you. If I had a Greek uniform I would have worn it. I am wearing my costume of a Greek civilian—and as a Greek civilian I make this surrender."

"I presume you speak for the contingent—inside?"

"There *is* no contingent except for a few Celts who work for the depot. Scipio sucked all of the Romans out of here when he went by a few weeks ago."

"We have just shaken hands with a few of them, I think."

"The Ticinus River. My congratulations, Lord Hannibal."

"Zeus, Mercury, Apollo are still useful gods for you, I think. Which one should I use when I swear surprise at your quick intelligence of us?" This Greek commander, whom Scipio had left behind in his dust, knew about an action that seemed only hours old.

"Take Mercury—I hope he can continue to make quick delivery of good tidings about Romans."

Hannibal turned toward his escort. Carthalo and Mago had been close enough to savor this conversation, and the Numidian captain of the horse knew enough Greek to add his smile to this substitution of a peaceful cornucopia for a nasty little fight. Hannibal motioned Mago and Carthalo forward. They dismounted and he introduced Carthalo.

"Gentlemen, Commander Dasius has rendered us the compliment of peaceful surrender of his charge. Scipio left him in a vacuum which we will be happy to fill." He turned back to Dasius. "You and your people inside will need our protection and support."

"I would be honored to serve you in some way, Lord Hannibal, beyond this moment. My Celts would appreciate access to their people."

"My purse, of this moment, holds two hundred gold pieces. Distribute this to your people as you will, Dasius. As for *your* bounty for us, I will send wagons when we have inventoried it." Carthalo carried the gold as a contingency of this ride. He went to his horse, returned with a leather pouch and handed it to Dasius. The Carthaginians then mounted their horses. Hannibal rode close to Dasius:

"I have two Greeks on my staff now...a Spartan and an Iberian. I would like another one who is familiar with part of our itinerary. I consider *you* as part of your bounty, Dasius—I will hold you to your word." Hannibal waited until Dasius' smile was fully developed, then he wheeled his formation away from Clastidium, toward Publius Scipio and Tiberius Sempronius.

12

29 years
December 218 BC—Trebbia River

"We've got a bigger piece of pie to bite into—Sempronius has huffed and puffed his way from Ariminum and joined Scipio west of the Trebbia, about seven miles from Placentia." Mago had just come back from a scout and he was putting charcoal lines on a papyrus sheet in front of Hannibal.

"And Scipio?"

"Is nursing his wounds and the Celts tell me he is content to let Sempronius prove his audacity against you."

"With the help of Scipio's people, of course."

"We will be looking at about thirty-six thousand Roman and Allied foot, flavored with about four thousand horse, both Roman and Allied." Mago looked up at Hannibal and then swept across the other close faces: Maharbal, Carthalo, and a few of their deputies. They were in a tent near Cambio on the Po. It was after the dinner hour and oil lamps had started to compound the restless complexions facing Mago. Mago's information had come from personal observation and interviews with Celts who had trailed Sempronius and Scipio over much of the span of the Po valley.

"What is the country on the side of the Trebbia across from our Roman hosts?"

"You will like it, Hannibal, and the horses will like it. It has a meandering watercourse about a mile from the Trebbia, heavily overgrown." The last part of Mago's answer was like an afterthought, but it put a private exclamation point into Hannibal.

"*How* heavily?"

"You and I could play a good game of hide and seek there."

With the Roman hoard at Clastidium safely tucked away in their train, supplies and men streaming into them from the Celts, a rehabilitated corps and the Ticinus overture played out to Hannibal's tune—they were ready to move in force toward their Roman hosts. Hannibal crossed the Po at Cambio and proceeded down its right bank toward Placentia. Thyresius had brought three thousand foot and two thousand horse to him from the Insubres. Leukon had brought six thousand foot and three thousand horse from the Boii. These were fighters, not honed to his style yet, but they would bring the muscle he needed against the two consular armies. He could hear—and feel—twenty-nine thousand foot and eleven thousand horse behind him now and he still had a few elephants for old time's sake. Not what he had when he crossed the Rhone a lifetime ago, but he had proved that the teeth he had left could take a big bite of the Roman ass and Heimarmene would have to decide how it went with some new teeth, some more ass.

On his way southeastward along the Po, he passed through country of the Anares, a Celt tribe which the Romans still counted as friends. He sent Marharbal out with two thousand foot and a thousand horse to pillage a few villages, and set some fires—just a little general hell to let the Anares know he was there. The plumes from Maharbal's fires were a twenty mile advertisement that was picked up by some of Sempronius' scouts. Sempronius sent out his own horse. Maharbal had orders to play with any Romans who came out to greet him, and then to run back to Hannibal's shelter like a scared rabbit at a time deemed propitious by Maharbal.

"By the gods' balls, Hannibal, I don't like running—but we put a lot of confidence into Sempronius today. It may be useful later." Hannibal's Chief of Cavalry had just thundered back into camp with his Numidians, who were virtuosi at pillaging and putting big black plumes into the sky.

"Sempronius would like to make his mark before Scipio recovers, and before new consuls are chosen for next year. I think we can tease him into our game. He's now an impatient man, my friend, so let's court his famous audacity."

Sempronius and Scipio were now encamped close to each other west of the Trebbia, about nine miles southwest of Placentia. Hannibal came along the Po and planted himself about five miles southeast of Placentia, between the consuls and the Boii country. Boii were now part of his foot. In particular, he had made them the center of his foot line and this maneuver did the double duty of enraging the consuls by his intimidation of their principal Po stronghold at Placentia, and complimenting the Boii by the prestigious line assignment and placing his shield between the consuls and the Boii homeland.

The evening of his first Trebbia camp, Hannibal took a ride with Mago, westward, toward the Trebbia and the Roman position.

"And there's your hide and seek place." Hannibal had already been convinced that his horse would like the ground east of the Trebbia—his side. Now he was looking at the meandering watercourse Mago had also identified. "I agree, little brother, we *could* have fun here." They rode about a mile along the brush covered channel that roughly paralleled the Trebbia, about two miles to their west. "But you will have to play this game yourself."

"You will be taking the spa waters near Placentia?" Mago's gypsy was still close to his surface.

"I will be trying to move the Romans around this beautiful field so you can make a little surprise for them"

"How large a surprise am I going to make, Lord Hannibal?" Mago had a hundred ways of applying that title to his brother.

"I think a thousand horse and a thousand foot, good people, will make what I want for Sempronius."

"I will have my crew ready for you bright and early on the morning you greet Sempronius...and extend condolences to Scipio."

"We will move our camp closer to the Trebbia...about three miles from our friends, tomorrow. On the next day, we will greet and condole."

"So I have tonight, tomorrow, and tomorrow night to contemplate and prepare."

Mago had just brought his horse head to head with Hannibal's, so the eyes were close-coupled.

"Nice try, Mago. You will be in place *tomorrow* night. I suggest you and your people eat well, just before leaving your burrow in the field on the morning I will need you."

"Anything else, Lord Hannibal?" Well, he was putting himself and two thousand men into a forward position in front of the fearsome Roman. He was entitled to press his tease a little.

"I also suggest a hot olive oil rub for you and your people before you crouch in the brush. If the weather today is a harbinger, it will be a hellish day for you."

"The weather spreads over *both* sides of the Trebbia, big brother."

"I am counting on that, *little* brother."

Hannibal had moved his camp, as he promised Mago. Mago was hiding along a half mile of the ambush he'd promised Hannibal. On dawn of battle day it was cold, and snowy. The Trebbia's water was an ice bath.

"Take all your people across the Trebbia and wake Sempronius up. Set fire to some tents if you can, make plenty of noise and kill a few Romans like you really mean business. Then get back here on my flanks, and we'll put our greetings to Sempronius all together on our side of the fair Trebbia."

The Numidian captain nodded and saluted. Carthalo and Maharbal seconded Hannibal by their close presence. Fifteen minutes later, forty-five hundred Numidians splashed across the freezing water of the Trebbia and charged Sempronius' camp. It was still near dawn of a day that had picked up most of the miseries of winter. The Numidians killed the Roman outposts and swept into the perimeter of the Roman camp, putting javelins into tents with unknown effects and into bodies that had started to swarm into that day with various qualifications for battle. When Hannibal's wake-up call turned back toward the Trebbia, Sempronius ran out of his tent into a minor hell of fires, curses, and samples of the Numidians' work with the javelin at long and close quarters.

An enraged Tiberius Sempronius shouted the question, "Who did this?" He was answered. He had chased this swarm of African barbarians back to their camp just two days before. Now he would have to put another lesson on them. He gave one order that called out his full cavalry to battle. Then the heavy flow of his vengeance pulled another order from him that called out his full corps to battle. The consul Sempronius was now on the second page of Hannibal's script for Trebbia, part of which called for Sempronius to ignore Scipio's excellent advice about using caution in front of this particular Carthaginian.

Before the Numidians returned, Hannibal had put his corps into battle formation somewhat north of Mago's ambush, roughly parallel to the Trebbia and about a mile east. He had ordered a hot meal for his men, and then olive oil rubdowns, before committing them. Sempronius' men were now wading a breast-deep Trebbia without the luxuries of breakfast, or oil. Hannibal waited. He probably had a massive advantage of Sempronius right now, but he was on stage here before the Celts of the Po, and probably also some of the Celts of Gaul and beyond that Cathbad had identified as the ultimate pillar for his Italian temple. For *this* stage he preferred the symmetries and more orderly perspectives of a fully arrayed land battle to the feeding of the Trebbia with a progressive massacre that had no grace but victory.

When Sempronius was finally and fully arrayed, his army—literally almost *two* consular armies—occupied a frontage of about a mile. His foot was in the usual three lines of the hastati, the principes, and the triarii, with his horse on the flanks and his velites in front. The foot was arrayed in a checkerboard pattern which left no clear file through the formation. Sempronius placed his Celt foot auxiliaries on the left of his legions. His placements gave him about nine hundred feet of depth.

Hannibal's heavy infantry was in a single line, arrayed in the hoplite phalanx, eight deep. His skirmishers, the light spearmen and the Balearic slingers, were loosely dispersed in front of his line. Because Sempronius had more foot, his line exceeded Hannibal's in length. Hannibal put his horse on extreme wings which matched Sempronius', and placed his elephants in the gaps between his horse and his line of foot. His greeting to Sempronius now appeared frankly and relatively simply presented—except for Mago. Eighty thousand men were ready to play the game of combat on its fundamental board.

His Numidians were returning from their wake-up call. Hannibal screened them, and opened the action by moving his light foot and Balearic slingers toward the Roman velites. These troops quickly beat back the velites, who retreated into the checkerboard of the legions. The Balearic slingers had shown off for him on the way to the Pillars with Hamilcar. Now he could admire them under field conditions against a Roman target, their lead slugs and stone pellets wreaking havoc against lightly armed opposition that would take a weapon evolution of more than two thousand years to equal in respect of the trinity of rapidity of discharge, accuracy and lethal range.

Hannibal ordered both of his cavalry wings forward against the Roman and allied horse. His horse was the great surprise he had brought to Italy, and it smashed into the Roman horse and drove it from the field in a progression of sharp exchange that quickly became a route. Part of his horse followed up this retreat while the remainder cooperated with the light foot in sweeping into the Roman flanks. His elephants drove some distance into the edges of the Roman line before they were turned back. Hannibal then ordered them against the Celts on the Roman left, because their shock value was greater there than against Romans who had been blooded on elephants by Pyrrhus sixty-three years before at Heraclea.

Hannibal, with his leopard Numidians, rode into the various edges of the battle that was unrolling in front of him. He watched the lines crash together and saw his first demonstration of the stubborn strength of the legions as they impacted mainly the Celts in his center and started to push them back. He had turned the Roman flanks with his horse and light foot and it was here that he put the core of his attention, although the concentrated strength of the Roman center was a fact that never fell far in the hierarchy of the consciousness that would determine the course of that battle.

As the Carthaginian and Numidian horse was crushing the Roman wings, Mago emerged from his ambush and led his troops around the Roman right and into their back. With the exception of about ten thousand legionnaires in the center of the Roman line who had now crushed Hannibal's Celts in his center, the Roman line started to disintegrate under the flank and rear and frontal assaults by his Africans and Iberians who pulled invigoration from the signals of success from the rear and sides of the Roman formation. Romans who stayed on the field, died there. Romans who fled toward and into the Trebbia, died on its banks and in its water. Hannibal moved in and out of the slaughter on the wings and in the rear of the Roman line, and then on the periphery of the general debacle of the whole Roman line as his foot and horse cooperated in moving Romans into bunches and then killing them in bunches from the ground and from horseback.

He had lost about fifteen hundred men, mostly the Celts who were in the center of his line, facing the heart of Sempronius' corps. On the field, on the banks and in the water of the Trebbia, the Romans had left about eighteen thousand dead. Hannibal had taken about five thousand allied and Roman prisoners.

The Roman center that had broken Hannibal's center had formed a circular defensive formation and fought its way to Placentia through a scattering of Hannibal's corps that was largely preoccupied with a slaughter elsewhere. Sempronius, and a few of his staff, managed to use these veterans as a cocoon to survive the Trebbia field. When Sempronius returned to Rome shortly after Trebbia, he babbled to the Senate that he would have won if the weather had been better. Some of the senators, who were close enough to him to look a little deeper than his words, saw a man who still bore remnants of a hell that would soon be named *Hannibal* by most of these purpled men.

A day after this battle, Hannibal, unarmored, sat his horse in front of a rank of his staff officers, looking toward a formation of three thousand allied prisoners which had a non-intimidating bracket of Carthaginian heavy horse. He was fluent in Greek, Iberian, Numidian and Libyan, and several of the Celt-Iberian dialects that passed for communication with the Po Celts. He had acquired Syrian and Sumerian words through a collaboration with a Greek lady of Delphic antecedents that had to be described as close, but irrelevant to his present situation within sight of Trebbia's waters. His Latin was not good. He'd had no opportunity to practice it, and his incentive for it was small. What his Greek and Celt achievements couldn't do for his personal communication in Italy was not of pressing interest. But a new officer in his fold, Dasius the former commander of Clastidium, had fluent Latin. Hannibal addressed the Latin prisoners in Greek. Dasius, mounted, a few paces closer to the listening congregation and to Hannibal's right, put each sentence of the short speech into unambiguous Latin as Hannibal delivered it:

"Hannibal says that he compliments you on your performance in this battle."

"Hannibal says that he has no quarrel with you...with the Latins in Italy."

"Hannibal says that you are free to return to your homes...and that he hopes to have the pleasure of your comradeship against his only enemy in Italy—the Romans."

Some shouts came from the front rank of prisoners and these triggered a rolling cheer that swept the formation. Hannibal saluted them, and then swung around to another post-battle duty of less exhilaration.

His elephants had been decimated by the Alps transit. Their remainder which had borne the winter days up to Trebbia, and then their assignments on Hannibal's battle line, were now all gone. Surus, the Indian elephant, was one that had survived the Rhone and the Alps. Hannibal had kept her out of the Trebbia battle. As he rode up to her now, Suta her Indian mahout standing alongside her at attention, he saw the last of the thirty-seven souvenirs of old Carthage. He had brought them to Italy largely to impress the Celts. Some of the Roman horses still panicked when confronted by the big ears and the trumpeting, but now under battle exigencies the elephants posed as much danger to his own people as they did to veteran legionnaires. Hannibal dismounted in front of Surus and Suta. He walked to Surus and put out his hand toward her trunk. They were old friends. He had ridden her many times, talked to her and Sutu about the eastern lands. Even Alexander had come in a few times, with Sutu suspected of embellishment here.

"You've taken good care of her, Sutu." Surus was rubbing Hannibal's hair with the tip of her trunk.

"*You* have taken good care of her, Lord Hannibal." Sutu had never accepted the informality Hannibal had offered him.

A big Indian like her could have done plenty of damage to the Roman velites and horse at Trebbia. And her broad sides would have been a good target for the heavy-headed pilum of the legionnaire. Hannibal didn't have to remind anyone here that Surus was the last elephant.

"When we move south, I will ask her to let me ride her." Surus had just made an impertinent insinuation of Hannibal's ear with the tip of her trunk.

"We will be honored, Lord Hannibal. When do you think that will be?" Sutu's question had also been raised on the Roman side, even in the senate at Rome when the whispers of Ticinus—soon Trebbia—had matured to strained recapitulations, and shouts.

"When we can cross the Apennines without drowning in the damn snow and ice."

Several hours later, the same question was posed to Hannibal by Silenus, monitored by Sosylos.

"By Ba'al, Silenus, you are touching secret places here outside your purview! I will move *south* when the impressions I get from my scouts, my informants, my engineers and other seers fall into a favorable pattern—and the dispositions of shit from the ravens and hawks fall in propitious patterns across sacred ground."

"*Whose* sacred ground?" Silenus and Sosylos had finally cornered Hannibal near his tent, making a hedge he couldn't push through gracefully.

"*Cathbad's* friends', damn you, Silenus. And you and Sosylos crept too close to the lines yesterday." Hannibal's observation had necessarily come indirectly. During a quick exchange among Hannibal and some officers in an interstice of the surges of battle, one of the officers had spotted Sosylos and Silenus too close to the action.

Silenus had his scroll and lead pencil at the ready. "What are the first impressions that come at you from this battle, Hannibal?" There had been a few questions and answers since the action. The timing of the Numidians wake-up call, some of the subtleties of Hannibal's dispositions of foot, horse and elephants. But Silenus was reaching for the core meat of the interview. Hannibal started to maneuver toward his tent. His friends accommodated him and invited themselves in that direction. He tried an exasperated look at them, but this tactic never made any impression on either the Spartan, or the Iberian Greek who persisted as his close escort.

"The first impression *that comes at me* is that we are damn lucky the Roman center wasn't bigger or it might have chewed a bigger piece of us than it did."

"You put your Celts in front of them...a classic case of discipline confronting posturing barbarians—with a predictable result."

"Those barbarians will make soldiers, Sosylos. We will put armor on them, give them weapons with more scope. Then that posturing can be channeled into fear again for our Roman friends, like at the Allia River—a Celtic-made sore that's festered in their bellies for a hundred and seventy years."

"You will have plenty of raw stock for this work: Celt recruits, foot and horse, are streaming toward you, Hannibal." They had reached the command tent. Hannibal strode inside giving an arm motion that was minimum incentive for the chat to continue inside. He flopped on a couch, and then his host intervened. He motioned toward a wine flask and nearby goblets. Neither Sosylos, nor Silenus, refused. They also bracketed him on camp stools.

"I hope the Romans give us time to use them, Silenus."

Sosylos had filled the goblets; Hannibal tipped his toward his persistent company. His Hellenistic prince would need a good barber to come out, and even then Inanna would have enough material from his face and neck, chest, arms and legs, to put her eyes and her touches on a map of him that she might not want to keep talking about. He was only twenty nine, but the scrolls on him were filling fast and the gods, Hippolyta's God, didn't deny some of the costs a visible access to him.

Silenus' lead and papyrus were still at the ready and Hannibal's terse answer was not the end to his *first impressions* question. Hannibal had replied to Sosylos' point of battle, but Silenus' still dangled, and Hannibal knew it. He took more wine, his eyes on Silenus now.

"The legions like to pile into a tight wedge that is irresistible to most frontally arrayed opposition. Facing equal strength and resolution you have a gridlock here, and the slow diffusion of death into both adversaries. Sosylos can count a hundred Greek battles that ended this way, finally turning on a local accident of terrain, or action, that no commander could claim as his."

"This is a depressing outlook for a man looking to sweep the legions into the southern seas."

"This may be *opportunity* for the same man, Silenus. If he can nudge these legions into their favorite supermen aggregation and then come at them from directions that don't favor their forward momentum, from directions that increase their packing together and hamper their fighting style, the word *slaughter* can be turned back on the Italian Wolves." Hannibal had not broken his eye lock with Silenus, but Silenus felt insignificant in Hannibal's perspective at that moment.

"Then the formations you practiced in Iberia, which didn't like straight lines, are part of this accommodation to the Roman." Silenus had made this more observation than question. This man in front of him, younger then, had already made a habit of grabbing a lot of perspective.

"We are working toward that end—horse and foot together."

"May I interject something that could add to Silenus' scribbling?"

"Don't start playing bashful now, Sosylos."

"You will need the Celt pillar to do this."

"I have said this, already."

"To do this accommodation strategy satisfactorily, you will need to *polish* this pillar the way you've done to the Iberian, Carthaginian and African ones."

"I'll put in your question for you, Sosylos—do I think this can be done? *Yes*. The Celts have stepped in, and out, of the mantle of the finest fighting men in the world for centuries. We will try equipment, training and leadership to make that polish of yours." Hannibal's goblet was empty, Sosylos did his office again. "Who is going to put in the next question that will round out this little speculation of ours?" He hadn't forgotten how to smile. He had, in fact, smiled at junctures of the Ticinus and the Trebbia actions where no other smile could be found within eyesight of him until he started it.

"I think you've already put it, Hannibal; something about *time*, wasn't it?"

Hannibal stood up, and stretched some of the muscles that a cavalryman uses. His company also stood. Hannibal used his right and left hands to nudge Sosylos and Silenus, respectively, toward the exit.

"It was, Sosylos. Time...*time*...*time*. I've kept Heimarmene's ears busy since we started across the Rhone and headed this way, first about survival—now it's about *time*."

"The mercy of time can spread both ways across your line with the Romans, Hannibal. It could sharpen or dull your thunderbolt."

Hannibal pushed both of them out of the tent. "Now that is a nicety I haven't broached with Heimarmene, Silenus. Let's let him try to work *that* out." When he had accomplished solitude for a moment, Silenus' observation still stuck in him. He was a Carthaginian. He was about six hundred miles from Carthage. Other armies had sucked on ligaments from home that were as long, longer. That time, that two-edged *time*, would work for him so long as he had *his* ligaments from home.

13

30 years
June 217 BC—Lake Trasimene

The commander's tent was dark when Sosylos entered. Several hours before, the oil lamps had been dismissed by a curt command to the orderly from the direction of the sleeping area. But there was light enough for Sosylos.

"Lord Hannibal..." A soft voice, probing. He said this again, walking closer to the dark outline of a man sitting on the edge of his bed. He came close enough to a lowered head so that he knew the quality of voice he'd selected could be heard. The head didn't acknowledge the repetition. Sosylos invited himself to a nearby camp chair, a folding design with leather seat and side panels that was a present to the commander for the expedition from a leather artisan of Gades. He didn't speak for several minutes. He knew that Hannibal knew he was there. Hannibal would select the time and quality of the voices, most of the way speech would go. Sosylos had to wait another minute for him.

"A damned one-eyed monster is what's left, Sosylos." Sosylos had been fine-tuned to this voice, its conceivable nuances, for many years. This speech would have eluded him, otherwise. Hannibal would have to expand this a little, give him more guidelines for his tutor's role...now more the confidante's, friend's role, before he jumped in. Another half minute went by. "...I've taken them down near heart of the Romans. Where can I take them now?—a damned, asymmetric Cyclops with half the world lost to him." The voice was more serviceable now, but with a sepulchral cast that Sosylos had never heard before. Hannibal finally looked up at his visitor.

They had left the Po valley in mid-May and come into Etruria through a pass in the Apennines that only the Celts knew, striking the coast south of Genoa and then they moved southeastward along the high ground above the Ligurian sea until they got to the Arnus river. Then they turned northeast and followed the Arnus' right bank, thru Pisae, toward Faesulae. But before they got to the Elysium fields around Faesulae, they had to plow through some hell that was the spring-flood swampland of the Arnus. The Celt and Ligurian scouts had warned about this swamp. But the fact that this maneuver would turn the left flank of the Roman dispositions set to oppose Hannibal's entry into Etruria had overweighed the adverse possibilities of the swamp for an army that was now above forty thousand foot and horse together.

It took four days and three nights to cross the swamp. On the second night, many of his men found some surcease of the muck on top of the bodies of the pack animals who had died by the hundreds in it. Hannibal had put his Africans and Iberians and his most valuable supplies in his van, the Celt foot and horse in the middle, his other horse contingents in the rear to encourage the Celts to resolution in this march. The van crossed the swamp without serious trouble. The Celt foot and horse in the middle suffered most. Hannibal usually rode Surus and was usually somewhere in the van. But when hell started its assertion, he came back frequently to the trouble zones to encourage, to try to bring some order where curses and cries of frustration was the conversation. On the first day, while trying to service continuing local crises on foot, he contracted an infection in his left eye. Syhalus did what he could from his platform of putrid muck, but by the third day, Hannibal's eye was swollen shut, and the infection had started to destroy the optic nerve. When he emerged from the swamp, Surus carried an almost one-eyed man. That night, in the sanctuary of Faesulae, comfortable quarters for Hannibal was the first priority. Synhalus came to him:

"Lord Hannibal., this evil is beyond my power. If I could have had you in the hospital at Nova Carthago we could have done more." Synhalus was also facing a man on a bed, this time lying down, a bandage covering his face. The fever had abated, but an irreversible loss was the topic now. "A Celt captain brought you some lycopodium. He said that its smoke has healed eye diseases for his people. We will try it tonight."

"Thank that man for me, Synhalus now...and I will do it later, myself." Still a commander's voice under the bandage, the implications of what was now almost blackness in his left eye not yet established.

Sosylos had seen him once before after the left eye had become a suppurating anomaly, not yet decided on what permanent mark it would make on him. Like everyone's in his column, Sosylos and Silenus' included, his face had made no concessions to beauty for days. Without a razor for a few more, he would be a bear. The Lady Barca had accused Hamilcar of such abandon just before she used it for a more comprehensive greeting for her husband. But there was no Inanna here to use another bear like this. Sosylos thought of Inanna when Hannibal exposed some of his pain in the latest words. When his world started to shrink, Hannibal, in fact, had thought of Inanna, and then for a second, Kyniska's delight when they played at monsters and mermaids in the pool, flashed at him. Now she would have a *real* monster to glare at her.

"You have suffered a loss, my Lord. But you are Hannibal Barca—this loss will become a new strength."

"You're not obliged to conjure fantasy for me, Sosylos. Tell me how a *commander* makes a *strength* out of a blind side." He swiped at his left eye with a bit of linen.

"You will gain in sensitivity to the world around you to compensate for that eye. You will accept less from your circumstances, be more suspicious of them. The rest of you is *just* the same as before. When you add the new sensitivity to you—I would not like to be a Roman."

"I have lost actual perspective—I am in a two dimensional world now, Sosylos."

"Your friends will compensate for this. If they have been devoted to you before, they will study new ways to improve this honoring. Give the gods a chance, Hannibal! They have tested you before, at the Rhone, the Alps, Ticinus, Trebbia, this miserable hell of the Arnus. They are testing you *now*. And I repeat—I would not like to be a Roman at this time."

"Inanna...she will not know what to make of me." The voice had slipped toward the sepulcher again.

"As a Greek, I resent that slur on our women, and I am amazed that you can deny *any* aspect of her love. I tell you, Hannibal, when the gods have finished counting your graces, I will envy only *one* of them, *Inanna*." Sosylos had stood up and started to pace. Hannibal had made him familiar again. "Have you written her?" Peremptory, and Sosylos had put his face closer to Hannibal's to compound the insolent familiarity. But a crisis of command justified almost anything, and an Inanna connection was the strongest curative Sosylos could think of.

"Four letters." This answer was long in coming, and if Sosylos hadn't left his ears close to Hannibal's mouth he wouldn't have heard it. The voice of it was still a reluctant compromise between friendship and the solace of silence.

Sosylos was about to insinuate another question when Hannibal mercifully preempted him, continuing his answer:

"When we got over the Alps...after Ticinus, after Trebbia." The voice was better, the victories inspiring a slight crescendo which was the best thing the Spartan had taken from that darkness yet.

"You mentioned a fourth letter, my Lord." Sosylos straightened up and then resumed his chair, this conversation still alive.

"During the winter, while we waited to get to this...*paradise* below the Apennines."

"May I suggest that the time is propitious for another letter, General Hannibal?" By Inanna's Heimarmene, the way he loaded that *paradise* with irony was a good sign.

"You will have to do the mechanics of it." This answer was also a slow-comer, but Sosylos had come into the tent for it. He was usually close to a charcoal or lead marker and something to write on, and his pouch this night was no exception. He made conspicuous preparations to receive Hannibal's dictation. Hannibal's sigh was no discouragement.

"What greeting have you settled on, Hannibal?"

"*Inanna* will do."

"You have used *My Inanna* to good purpose, too, my Lord, if memory serves me." Yes, in the exchange shortly before Hannibal enrolled in the Lady Barca's special university, this greeting had figured prominently, although imputing unqualified success to it would be going too far. *Inanna* stayed with the present letter. And then gradually the substance of it was picked out between the two of them. But mainly it was Hannibal and a scribe. The subject of a left eye that had blinked out came up once. Hannibal raised it. He asked Sosylos if he should mention it. Sosylos said that this event would enter Carthage soon enough, to let time handle the communication of it to Inanna, Kyniska and the Lady Barca. They settled on a brief *monster* as a sufficient precursor, for now.

> *Inanna,*
>
> *We have made it across the Apennines and are now sitting below the Romans. I will be facing the consuls Gnaeus Servilius and Gaius Flaminius. All but Sirus of my elephants are gone. She is an impudent rascal, and asks too many questions...but she has been my throne lately as I parade into Etruria. My precious Celts, as you have called them, have been generous with people, horses and supplies. They will be a big part of the army I take toward the Romans.*
>
> *Kiss Kyniska for me. Tell her that I can make a much better monster now, so she had better be a very good girl. I am tending in the direction of Carthage again...my love for you is my strongest beacon.*
>
> *Hannibal.*

When Sosylos stood up to go, Hannibal also stood up, an accomplishment he hadn't made for many hours. Sosylos saluted him in the Spartan style, and then he turned and left. His commander might have been on the verge of words, but a mission had been successful, and further acknowledgement had to be redundant.

Communication between Hannibal and Carthage, and Iberia, had been designed before he crossed the Rhone. The little lembi, specialized to forty oars, single-banked, polished black hulls like eels, rigged to use any wind, were the workhorses. The military shipyard at Carthage built fifty of them to service Hannibal's intelligence network, his gossamers, according to Inanna. The Carthaginians were familiar with Italian ports along the Adriatic side from Brindisi to Ariminum, along the Ligurian and Tyrrhenian sides from Porticello on the tip of the boot to Genoa, along the instep and heel of the boot on the Gulf of Taranto from Locri to Croton to Tarentum to Anxa. The Romans had no match for these messengers, hence virtually no protection against them, and Hannibal was careful to protect his access to them, via horsemen and various agents skilled at blending into their environments. In the few instances of interception, Heimarmene threw loaded dice at Hannibal. This god was, however, careful to protect the gossamers involving Inanna.

In his letter from Faesulae, Hannibal told Inanna that he now faced the consuls Servilius and Flaminius. Actually, Flaminius had subsumed some of Servilius' troops and authority and, with the remnant of Sempronius' legions he'd got by lot at the consular changeover, he now held most of two consular armies under his sway at Arretium, where he proposed to wait for good weather, and then move toward the logical passes where Hannibal might come into Etruria. Servilius was at Ariminum on the Adriatic coast with recruits he had brought from Rome and Scipio's troops who had escaped Hannibal's sword and Flaminius' net. He was positioned to block any move of Hannibal along the Adriatic coast to southern Italy.

But here was Hannibal already in Etruria. And he had flanked both Servilius and Flaminius and was sitting deep in part of the richest bread-basket of Italy. He had told the Druid, Cathbad, that if he could put up a big enough mirror for Flaminius to preen his glory as the Carthaginian column marched along he could probably suck the consul into battle circumstances that would not be Roman propitious.

When word of Hannibal's new presence reached Flaminius, the consul's knee might have jerked, but its effect on his action was minimal thanks to some wise council that had trickled into his camp, along with a horde of scavengers waiting for booty from Hannibal's train after the slaughter. He decided to sit at Arretium and wait for some combination of encouragement: Hannibal's blundering, and reinforcements from Rome and elsewhere which could incite him in the Carthaginian's direction.

"We have a patient Flaminius sitting at Arretium, gentlemen. How do we make him impatient?" Hannibal was standing in the middle of a staff conference in the command tent with Maharbal, Carthalo, Mago, Adherbal...all of his senior officer strengths. They reveled in the resurrection of a commander, silently with looks at him and each other, with the temper of their voices during the play of question and answer. Maharbal was glad to wet his temper in these circumstances:

"You pulled Sempronius out of his warm cocoon at Trebbia with the Numidians—

Flaminius may be susceptible to their charms, too."

"You are a virtuoso with the big black smoke plumes, Maharbal. I think there's plenty of fodder for them in this valley, and in the valley where Flaminius is sitting." He made an involuntary touch of the eye patch—a white silk creation that his engineer Adherbal had designed for him. It was like the head bands Hannibal wore when he had been in a civilian mood in Iberia, an accentuation of the Hellenistic prince that Inanna would not let him deny. But it had an extension that covered his eye, lightly pressed against it by the strain of copper filaments buried in the band and its extension. His aplomb with the patch was improving, however, and his touches of it, and the compensating head movements, were less frequent and more agreeable to his outside world.

"We could play a wonderful tune on these fields and villages, Hannibal. There is plenty here to gorge our train and put smoke enough in the sky to see from Rome."

"If Flaminius sees it I'll be content. And then if we can pull poor old Servilius down from his perch at Ariminum perhaps we can have another picnic with our Roman friends." The way Flaminius had plucked some of Servilius' feathers was among the non-secrets that filled Hannibal's big basket of intelligence. "If we should play with Flaminius a little while and get him excited, where do you think we could find a good picnic place, Adherbal?"

"If you can suck him south, Hannibal, there are some hills and dales near Lake Trasimene that would make a wonderful cavorting ground for your picnic."

"Hills near the lake?"

"Our scouts have mentioned such a treasure, yes...particularly the northern shore."

"What would that lake shore be like in the early morning this time of year?"

"The scouts, and some of the natives we've talked to since the Arnus, have mentioned morning fogs in the valleys around the watercourses. I think fog is likely in the early morning, Hannibal."

Hannibal doubled his patrols, antennae, to detect any Roman movement toward him from the Roman dispositions he knew about, and those that might materialize from the direction of Rome. When he had enough confirmation that Flaminius' feet were temporarily encased in caution at Arretium, he ordered his heavy baggage train to proceed south along the natural contours toward Saena, and he took his battle corps out of Faesulae through another set of contours of the Apennines that led to a broad valley having two distinctions: Flaminius was perched over part of it at his stronghold at Arretium; the seductions of Lake Trasimene formed part of its southern boundary.

Just as Maharbal had promised, this land fed Hannibal's corps very well and it was an intricate canvas where an artist at provocation with fire, and the general tools of mischief, was challenged to do his best work. The black clouds followed the corps along this valley, and Hannibal's chefs and quartermasters took their pick of the meats, wines, cheeses, breads, for their tables and campfires.

At the conclusion of what was a sumptuous meal for an expeditionary force, Hannibal raised his wine goblet to a general audience of his staff. "To Flaminius and Servilius, our splendid hosts." Although Inanna wouldn't have liked the analogy, he was a spider at the center of his web, gorging on fresh conquest, yet sensitive to any vibrations from his filaments—Inanna's gossamers—that could signal new action.

"Flaminius is getting close, Hannibal."

"He is finally moving? This is, unfortunately, news to me."

"By virtue of your inexorable parade toward *him*, we are about ten miles away as we enjoy his wonderful ham, roast beef, pork and chicken." Maharbal's information *wasn't* news. Hannibal had kept good company with his position relative to Flaminius, but it bore repeating.

"I want everyone polished up tomorrow, gentlemen. We are going to make a parade close enough to Flaminius to throw garlands at him."

"Then what, Hannibal?" Mago's question served a lot of mouths.

"Why, we'll just go by, toward the picnic ground. Do we have flutes with us?"

"We have them, Hannibal...for amusement." Mago *would* know this.

"Tell your best flautists to amuse themselves as we pass underneath Arretium. It is unfortunate that Surus is our only elephant. But she will have to make a show for us. Put extra silks—vivid colors—on her and a splash of gold if you can find it."

"You will, of course, do the honors for her, Hannibal." Carthalo's statement was not a question. The Commander's officers had insisted that until he fully regained the reversible parts of his recent indisposition he was to travel via Surus, the Indian.

"We will make this parade in battle order, just in case Flaminius decides to play—and Surus will be my throne." More of that smile was emerging everyday.

"How far do we take this parade, Hannibal?"

"You have gypsy tendencies, Mago—flamboyance, impetuosity. You'll be happy to know that there will be a virtual parade right down to the salubrious waters of Trasimene."

"None of your magic?" Inanna would still recognize Mago. He was a veteran campaigner now, but his gypsy had not been swallowed by this maturity.

"Perhaps a little just at the end. Remember the Numidian conjurer at Hadrumetum? He did some disappearances you liked."

Adherbal's scouts had reported back on the terrain around the northern shore of Trasimene. If they could suck Flaminius out of his stronghold, and pull a provocative Carthaginian tail for bait along this shore, there was a place where Hannibal could play conjurer for Mago, and Flaminius.

The Carthaginian parade marched past Arretium somewhat out of garland range, but the Romans got an unparalleled perspective of a full Carthaginian battle corps, Hannibal style, primped for parade, battle confident, and the flutes *were* in range. His Numidian horse bracketed the column, the leopard skins in the van, lion skins in the rear; his Carthaginian and Iberian heavy horse continued these brackets into the front and rear of the column, respectively. His spearmen and Balearic slingers led the parade for his African and Iberian foot, his Celt foot and horse nestled between them. This column was two and a half miles of provocation, and Hannibal had designed so that the sun's zenith and the parade struck Flaminius at about the same time to justify the polishing he'd ordered. He and Surus walked at the head of his light foot. Surus' mahout, Sutu, always carried a variety of embellishment for Surus, so Hannibal's order of ostentation for Surus had been obeyed with gold glints along her trunk, ankles, and tail, and a draping of oriental silks over her back and sides. To comply further with Hannibal's purpose, Sutu had insisted on a spray of ostrich plumes in the howdah just behind Hannibal, whose armor also picked up part of the sun.

Hannibal's troops were accustomed to oiling and perfuming their hair. Scent was, therefore, put into this column lavishly to complete the decadent— voluptuous—imprint that Hannibal wanted to impress on the frustrated Romans, and their probably enraged commander. The extent to which the air cooperated with him in this part of the impression was unknown, but from Hannibal's position, it worked very well.

To more quickly assimilate the contours between him and Trasimene, when he was out of sight of Arretium, Hannibal ordered the column out of the phalangeal, eight-abreast formation of his parade to his standard four-abreast marching order. About seventeen miles from Arretium, they passed the Etruscan fortress of Cortona on an eastward promontory. A Numidian outrider sweeping past Surus shouted to Hannibal that he could see Trasimene from the height of Cortona. This news prompted a moving staff conference.

Maharbal, then Mago and Carthalo rode up to Surus.

"Trasimene just ahead, Hannibal. Where do you want your picnic ground?"

"Let's wander down the north shore a little while, Maharbal. Adherbal's scouts saw some land abutments that squeezed the access to the lake into some interesting shapes. I would like to be in position tonight, on the good side of these shapes."

"Do you think Flaminius will take our bait—so soon?" Carthalo had reined up close enough to Surus' head that she brought her trunk up to sniff at a great cavalryman.

"You people made a fine, degenerate, parade today under his nose. As a conscientious advocate of Roman probity, I don't see *how* Flaminius can refuse a prompt rejoinder that could start his name ringing in the Comitia—as soon as possible!"

Moonlight was the natural light when they reached the northern shore of Trasimene. The hills gradually took away the scope of the level ground until the defile Adherbal had promised loomed in front of them, constraining the ancient road to a few meters adjoining the lake. Past this constriction, a narrow shrub and tree covered half valley wrapped the southeastward tending shoreline before the hills walked down to the lake again, and the road climbed eastward toward Perusia.

The Numidian horse van, and part of the Carthaginian heavy horse had passed the defile when another Numidian outrider rode up to Hannibal.

"The Roman has left Arretium, Lord Hannibal, in full force."

"Where is he now?"

The Numidian was one of the leopard skins, from whom Maharbal and Carthalo had selected Hannibal's battle field escort. His parade polish was still evident. Among his accoutrements, a white silk headband holding a white ostrich feather accentuated the toothy smile in the ebony frame that came with his answer. "I think he should be close to the Cortona fortress, Lord Hannibal." The opportunity of a chase was one of very few prospects that could put such a smile on a Numidian. Also his leopard skin had a special affinity with a commander who seemed to have similar anticipation tendencies.

A three-quartered moon was good enough to put Hannibal in place that night in the land past the defile: Numidian and Celt horse and Celt foot were in ambush on the hills near the defile entrance to the valley. Light foot, slingers, Carthaginian and Iberian heavy horse were placed on the hillside along the lakeside road. African and Iberian heavy foot were hidden in the terrain at the end of the valley, below the site of his camp, and his personal command post. He had ordered the campsite to be conspicuous, contemptuous of a Roman follow-up...plenty of metal-ware and tents to catch an eye that might be looking toward that hill from the defile end of the trap. To discourage stragglers rounding the lake toward the hills on his left flank, he'd placed the remainder of his light foot in that area, including the few archers he was testing as a battle arm.

From the time he knew that Flaminius *had* taken his bait, he had been apprised of the Roman advance, mile by mile. The final report came at dawn... Flaminius' van had stopped a quarter mile from the defile.

By this time, a shallow fog had formed in the valley, thickest at lakeshore, its gradient toward the hills enough to compound an ambush that held nearly forty thousand men, but not enough to hide the fresh bait of his camp given propitious holes in the fog. To minimize confusion from the fog, he had ordered a trumpet relay to signal when the rear of Flaminius' column had passed the defile.

Flaminius had put out a scant outrider screen, and several hundred yards through the defile it had detected Hannibal's hillside display of contented military husbandry through the hole in the fog layer that *had* come when Hannibal needed it.

"The Carthaginian has put himself on the hillside at the end of the valley ahead of us." The centurion was at rigid attention in front of Flaminius.

"How far beyond this...throat?" The consul motioned toward the defile. Filaments of fog swept the rocky prominence that he had just truly characterized, and all the prompts needed by Aeschylus or Sophocles for their craft were on this stage, or imminent, ready for Flaminius' actors.

"About four miles, Consul."

Gaius Flaminius was serving a second consulship, and was not a novice of battle. He had organized and prosecuted campaigns against the Celts of the Po in a massive colonization strategy that had put many Celts in the camp of his enemies. The Via Flaminia and buildings in Rome in service of the plebeians were inscribed with his name. The word *recalcitrant* might have been invented for him, having pricked the status quo of the formalities of politics, authority, and religion. He was restless, dissatisfied with his past and present scopes. The tail feathers of the impudent Carthaginian degenerate would put him on the right path again. A man like this had to feel uncomfortable near this defile...a report of Hannibal Barca's near presence burning his ears. But *he* had ordered the advance from Arretium to Cortona, to Trasimene, and *he* had no place to turn back to now.

"We will wake him up, Centurion, and then we'll spread his peacock feathers around his hillside." Indeed, peacock feathers had been in the parade in Flaminius' honor at Arretium. In addition to the plume behind Hannibal on Surus' howdah, there had been flamboyant clusters of them carried close to Tanit's disks and crescents leading the foot formations. No Carthaginian major battle column traveled without material for some panoply of mystery and voluptuousness in case the commander, or his men, decided to make one.

It took almost an hour for Flaminius' column to pass the defile. Before the trumpet sounded at the defile and was repeated at 200 pace intervals up to Hannibal, its van was already close to the bottom of his hill. He had detected it himself before Maharbal's whisper:

"He's here...he's here."

"No need for whispers, now, my friend. Flaminius is about to get a salute and another parade."

Through the fortuitous, irregular fog layer, Hannibal could see specks of metal and color in the vanguard legion, precursors of the reverberations of Flaminius' column were no longer his imagination

The orders had been placed for all his men. The officer closest to the defile who decided that the rear of the Roman column had passed, and ordered the signal, was Hannibal's surrogate for beginning this battle.

Flaminius was with his bodyguard of auxiliary cavalry and foot, behind the officer's baggage train. Ahead of the baggage were the camp surveyors, and then the legion chosen for vanguard that day. His scouts had come back to the column as soon as Hannibal's camp was detected. Behind Flaminius were his principal horse, his senior officers, the remaining legions, auxiliaries, and the rearguard of light and heavy horse. Each unit was accompanied by its own baggage. This was a fighting column enmeshed in a traveling column and its precedence was probably engraved in bronze in Rome. No ambush could have asked for a better target.

When his trumpets shattered the rhythms of the marching column, Hannibal made a massive strike at Flaminius' left flank, its apex directed to the center of gravity of the Roman column which happened to be behind the vanguard legion, into the bulk of the legions' foot and horse behind Flaminius' gilded armor. The Celt war cries that cascaded on the Romans was the first pinnacle of a sound that gorged on itself—human and then animal parts that had human catalysis. This quickly matured into a swirling maelstrom of sound beyond human intervention, serving both sides of instants of opportunity— chase, maiming, death that came with the storm of pellets from the slingers, spears from spearmen, the falcatas of the heavy foot, the sabered, lanced, hoofed assault of the echelons of light and heavy horse that rolled against a column that was disintegrating before it had a chance to display Roman invincibility.

The flight to the lake started near the defile, where the Numidian horse had collaborated with Celt horse and foot to make an avalanche of death in the ranks of the auxiliaries in the rear of the column. Hell was away from the lake, so Elysium must be toward the lake, but the foot and horse who reasoned this way were pushed into another hell of reeds and water and if they didn't drown by the weight of their armor, or horses, or comrades, the Numidian lances and Celt long swords did the service of death for them.

This diffusion to the lake propagated all along the line of attack, and reached a maximum terror where Hannibal's African and Iberian heavy foot were driving into the legions behind Flaminius' body guard. This guard had done its best service for him under an unraveling of Roman discipline and posture with no precedence since the debacle against the Celts at Allia River. Flaminius was a particular target of the Celts. He had humiliated them repeatedly in the Po valley. And when his body guard had declined to a few swords and spears, there was a moment of opportunity for a horseman of the Insubres named Decurius. He charged the gilded armor, spear steadied against the fleshed interstice between the red-plumed helmet and the cuirass. The shout was put into good Latin:

"A present for you—from your Insubre admirers, Flaminius!"

It was a solid hit in the throat, and the plebians lost one of their champions. The nightmare had closed for this consul, and its burgeoning up to this moment of his eternity had been like a dream, but it had started *before* Trasimene when ostrich plumes had come under his nose at Arretium, and one of his officers said that he could hear flutes—and smell perfume!

About five thousand of the vanguard had punched its way through Hannibal's light foot on the left of his camp and gone to a stand on a hill toward Perusia, several miles from the half-valley that was now a disorderly sepulcher for twenty thousand of their comrades.

Hannibal had come down from his hill on Surus as his juggernaut gorged on death, closely watched by his leopard Numidians and both Maharbal and Carthalo had also stayed close to him. The grinding of the Roman column into the sand and mud and reeds and water was a process that didn't need their close attention. Their commander's sometime impetuosity, handicapped by a two dimensional world that he had not yet entirely accommodated, did.

But a Cretan archer, one of 500 sent by King Hiero of Syracuse to the Romans, had gotten close enough to Surus to try a shot. The mobile tapestry and distractions of the battle, possibly his yet unaccommodated two dimensional world, didn't warn Hannibal of the Cretan shaft until he heard death's whisper just before it marked his cheek and careened away. He was experimenting with his own archers, and not fully committed to this arm. But one had nearly got him, an event that put a plus mark on *his* archers' prospects, and a shout in his mouth:

"By Hercules' balls, that was a near miss! A good shot! I didn't see him, didn't expect him!" Sutu scrambled to his charge with a bit of linen, and both

Maharbal and Carthalo converged on Surus when the too-near miss had been evident.

"We must thank Hiero for that, Hannibal." This jibe didn't uncover Maharbal's emotion at that moment, but it did uncover one of Hannibal's inimitable gossamers about his opposition.

"How bad is the wound, Hannibal?" Carthalo had come as close as Surus would let his horse.

"A trifle, but I'll have to have a good story for Kyniska and Inanna."

"By Zeus, Hannibal, you've *got* a story already." Carthalo swept the carnage within their vantage with his right arm. "You're destroying their last field army—now you can knock on the doors of Rome!"

This was the first time one of his officers reminded of the ultimate plum coming within his grasp. His father's face, Hamilcar's, fused with his limited panorama for a moment.

By noon, it was over. About five thousand Roman and Allied prisoners, and the vanguard remnant crouching on their sanctuary hill, were all that was left of the army that had entered the defile with thirty thousand. Hannibal ordered his dead and wounded collected and then he asked to see Flaminius' body. After an hour of searching a hellish panorama, a young lieutenant reported back:

"We can't find Flaminius, Lord Hannibal. There were pieces of his armor, but no body...I could ask the Celts..."

"They probably wouldn't help you. Thanks for your effort, my lad." Flaminius' skull was probably on its way to a gold-rimmed Celt ritual bowl. Other Roman commanders had gone this way. But Hannibal had made the effort for an adversary's honorable burial.

He ordered the Roman bodies stripped of armor and weapons, and then he had cremation pits prepared for the men of both sides who had died at Trasimene. His losses were again mostly Celts, about 1500. They paid the price for reckless exuberance, unarmored, in some cases outweaponed. The Roman armor and weapons that came into the Carthaginian coffers that day would help him make his Celt deaths a harder work for the Romans. And he would train them according to his style—as time, and Heimarmene allowed.

His walk around the battlefield was a lesson in the ways men could die, kill, suffer without dying. He stopped many times to talk with men of his army who were waiting for help from Synhalus' corps, or were standing without wounds staring through a quietness that had come down on the place where no demon of sound or substantial force had failed to make an entrance. The short iron lances of the Numidian horse were displayed in every conceivable way of their death message. He could see that the long swords carved big arcs of destruction before their Celt masters fell under piles of Romans. If he could put more discipline and protection into these people, he could promote what he and Cathbad had seen for the Celt pillar of his temple. Dead horses were a bad sight for him, the wounded ones worse. He had ordered them cared for as quickly as possible, and he touched many heads and noses, and closed eyes, of both his and Roman horses, before he finally turned back to some surcease above the principal battle line.

"We have a little unfinished business, Hannibal." Maharbal had ridden up to his commander when he thought that the various reveries of the walk into the battle site were nearly over.

"The piece of the vanguard that climbed out of here toward Perusia, I presume." Reveries, or not, Hannibal never stepped far from his realities.

"By now, I should know better than to try to upstage you."

"You were just thinking of leaving with some heavy horse, Iberian foot, to pay your respects to these gentlemen."

"Precisely. I'll try to find some who haven't had enough exercise today."

"Take our archers with you, Maharbal. I've got new respect for them." Synhalus had stopped the bleeding of his cheek wound, and put an adhesive bandage over the spot that Hannibal had just touched.

Maharbal returned to camp in the early evening. He had about twenty five hundred prisoners, all Romans, which meant that he'd left about that number in various attitudes of defiance and then death on their hilltop near Perusia.

Hannibal moved the camp to a broader expanse of level ground that Maharbal had noticed during his foray against the vanguard remnant. The wine vats, and all the devices of their baggage that could heal, console, mend, were put into action. Wine was used for the inside of men, and the outside of horses, and the foragers took some of the best vintages from the country for their purposes.

Two days into the rest, an Iberian outrider reported that a large party of Roman horse was coming their way from the direction of Ariminum, under the pro-praetor, Gnaeus Centenius.

"What kind of number can you put into *large*?" The direct reporting of scouts to Hannibal was now a habit that no one had any incentive to challenge.

"I had some of your Celts with me, Lord Hannibal. They met some of their people who identified Centenius, and they put a number of four thousand into his column." There, that wasn't so hard. The scout was a young one, and he was learning fast in Hannibal's university.

Maharbal conferred with the scout to get a vector toward Centenius. Then one of Hannibal's right arms went off again with more horse, and light foot, to greet the new Roman.

It was two days before Maharbal returned from this trip into the Umbrian hinterland. This time he had two thousand more Roman prisoners, which left about two thousand more Roman dead on another field. And Hannibal's cupboard for horses had been increased by three thousand.

Trasimene, and the peripheral actions, had yielded about sixty-five hundred Roman prisoners, three thousand Allied. Dasius and Hannibal collaborated on another speech to the Allied ones: *Hannibal had no enmity toward the Allies. His mission is to free Italy from the Roman vice that threatens to strangle her.* Then he released them with supplies to find their way back to their villages. The Roman prisoners here, like the ones after Ticinus and Trebbia, were released to the Celts of the Po valley for ransoming, or slavery which could start with the Celts, or after the Greek and Eastern slave merchants had done their offices.

Every speech that Hannibal made to Allied prisoners, before, here, and hereafter, was designed to be within earshot of their Roman counterparts. Certain subjects were proscribed as reading, or listening material for the legions. The ones in *his* grasp would hear his words—like it, or not.

Mago had commanded some of the heavy horse at Trasimene. There had been official and family connection between him and his brother during, and since that day. In an afterglow that derived from a sumptuous camp meal courtesy the Umbrian cornucopia, and their circumstances of a beautiful sunset and a vantage to appreciate it, Mago had trapped Hannibal in a contemplative moment that seemed to have room for two.

"We're pointing toward Carthage again, big Brother."

"You just plagiarized a bit of my last letter to Inanna."

The subject of Hannibal's left eye had been in Mago's letter to Hasdrubal in Iberia. But no further. Mago placed himself on Hannibal's right side when convenient, but he was careful to keep the eye patch an unprivileged part of his brother's face. He had never broached the eye subject in conversation, except for moments in the commander's tent at Faesulae when he had to enter a pain, the beginning of shocking realization, as a brother...a brother-in-law. Mago, Sosylos, and Silenus, at different times, in different ways, had been major parties to a resurrection.

"Have you told her about your eye?" Mago and Hasdrubal could ask that question. Sosylos had already asked it.

"No. I've been advised that this momentous event will penetrate the sanctums of Carthage soon enough, to let time handle it for a while. This strategy presumes that my friends haven't preceded me."

"I am your friend, Hannibal...I told Hasdrubal. I would not precede you with Inanna. But I need to hurry to another letter to our Iberian brother."

"Your description of a one-eyed idiot perched atop an Indian elephant *should* speed to Hasdrubal. I hear that Gnaeus Scipio has been crowding him. He could probably use a laugh." Profiles only, so far. Hannibal had just realized that a two-dimensional sunset was worth looking at.

"Now you're trying to precede *me*, big brother." Mago gave up his profile paralleling Hannibal's and looked at Hannibal's right side, and then he adjusted his position so he could look face-to-face at his brother. "Actually, my next letter in Hasdrubal's direction will be about a commander who has made every man of his corps strive to be worthy of him."

Mago saw another man approach, and then stop a few paces away. It was Silenus. Mago's slight reaction made Hannibal turn toward the other man. Silenus had talked with Hannibal at Faesulae, mostly he had talked *to* Hannibal when his attention was unknown, or fugitive at best. The Arnus swamp had given nightmare material to his chronicle project. The sequels—the planning and execution of the trap for Flaminius, the annihilation of the last Roman field army—put down the heroic tracks again for the chronicle, but he hadn't resolved the Arnus effect. It was not a subject he knew how to raise *with* his subject; therefore, the official interviews had stalled on this. His personal approach to Hannibal was also affected. A whole man had contended with the Iberian conquests, the other hell of the Alps, Ticinus, Trebbia. He could prod, joke with, even curse with this kind of man. But Silenus had stalled after the Arnus for reasons that Hannibal would have to elucidate himself.

"You and coyness never came together before, Silenus. Come closer and be recognized." Hannibal stood his ground, the sunset making his eye patch a privileged part of his face despite Mago's resolve.

"I've been less coy than you might believe, Hannibal...but you probably didn't hear me."

"I remember Sosylos, Mago, and another one at Faesulae—it was *you*! I should have known."

"I...I don't mean to intrude...you and Mago. I just wanted to see you without a battle between us. When you're ready...we can pick up the chronicle material again." Silenus saluted, and turned to go."

"By your Zeus, Silenus! I expected you'd have Trasimene all packaged up by now, without me." Hannibal stepped closer to his friend.

"Quite a few points, Hannibal, require your inimitable rigor and scope." He hadn't thought he'd need writing materials, so he was bare as a scribe, but he would remember everything under *this* sunset. By his subject's Melkart, that smile had damned near pushed that patch aside!

"The last time we talked—officially—it was about *time*, and crowding the legions into a more susceptible mass."

"Indeed, Hannibal. How do you feel about *time*, now?" Silenus' look picked up Mago, and another smile along the way.

"The armor and weapons the Romans gave us at Trasimene will mostly go into the Celt foot and horse who have joined us. This will help that factor of *time*, it won't eliminate it. As you reminded us in our last *official* talk, time can spread its mercies both ways across our line with the Romans—it's a race of our resources against theirs."

"When you use *our*, you include the future ones from the Celts, Iberia, Carthage...wherever."

"That's a succinct putting of our prospects, Silenus. I wonder why you placed Carthage at the end of them." It was more a muse than a question from Hannibal Barca.

"Perhaps he meant to put the anchor of our strength at the bottom, where it belongs."

"Perhaps he meant Carthage as an afterthought, Mago. This would tend to the seditious, I think."

"May I intrude this introspection centering *me*? I might have been thinking about what you said Cathbad told you: *your ultimate strength will not come from Carthage.*"

"You are excused on this basis, Silenus."

"What can you say, post Trasimene, about that business of *crowding* the legions?" Silenus had watched an example of it that made a slaughterhouse of that lake's shoreline.

"We applied a one-sided strategy to that effect with the results you saw. The real trick will be to do this on good cavalry ground that can hold a hundred thousand Romans." Both Silenus and Mago found Hannibal's face target enough even against the competition of a matured, blood-red, sunset.

"You have conceded the race of numbers to them already?"

"I am conceding only a confrontation that will likely have *unique* numbers involved—nothing more, Mago."

"May I congratulate you on your great victory, Lord Hannibal, and your perspective that continues to justify a chronicle." Silenus gave Hannibal another salute, Greek style, as he resolved to make a second try at exit. There was *nothing* here to handicap the smiles, now.

"You may, Silenus—and next time don't be so damn long about it, and bring your scroll."

"A beautiful day, Gaius.. A pleasure to get away from the Senate house for a moment."

"Your *moment* is reassuring, Fabius. I don't think your colleagues can hold together for much longer—without you."

It was the toga here, two of them, purpled. And two pairs of calceus boots, red. Both men were of a height which was good because it minimized the path between their eyes, a busy one since they'd left the Senate chambers and started their walk toward the Tiber, underneath Capitoline Hill and Capitoline Jupiter, toward Hercules' precincts.

They crossed the forum, and only Fabius commented on a particular of it, looking toward the Temple of Vesta at the end opposite them.

"I hope the vestal ladies are practicing their virtue now. We may need *all* of their example soon."

They passed the forum and now Jupiter's precincts on Capitoline Hill sucked their eyes toward the crest and the ground consecrated to the sacred triad of Rome: Jupiter, Minerva and Juno. The temple was crowned by a terracotta figure of Jupiter, made by the Estruscan, Vulca. It presented the god driving a four horse chariot, holding a scepter and a thunderbolt.

"By *his* name, Fabius, that damned thunderbolt won't go away, will it?"

"I see Jupiter's, Gaius, which one do *you* see?"

"The one assimilated with the name, Barca. The gods of that family are Melkart and Hercules, among several others...all of these have been connected to thunder and lightning."

"You've had the privilege of looking at two of them—up close, I understand."

"Those particular gods?"

"The Barcas."

The walk continued for a few paces around Capitoline's basis perimeter, before Gaius Publius answered.

"I interviewed Hamilcar at his palace in Akra Leuke. Later, he gave me an excellent tour of some of his treasure in Iberia."

"The other one—Hannibal?" Fabius didn't practice his subtlety when he looked at Gaius, the brightness in his eyes an involuntary souvenir of hours in the Senate listening to various recitations of escalating contemporary terror—Ticinus, Trebbia, Trasimene, the destruction of the relief cavalry after Trasimene, and frantic swarms of plans and objections.

Gaius Publius walked some more before he answered the continuation of Quintus Fabius Maximus Verrucosus' question.

"It was at a point of Hamilcar's itinerary for me, a mining and smelting center near Castulo, in Iberia. There was a beautiful girl there, a boy who seemed to appreciate her. Hamilcar introduced the boy to me as his son, Hannibal."

"The girl?"

"Her father did the service for her, Inanna is her name. I understand she has Delphic precedents...she is also now Hannibal's wife."

"Inanna, it doesn't sound Iberian, or Greek."

"She is, as I recall, a fascinating synthesis of Eastern and Greek exotics."

"One more thunderbolt for his quiver, Gaius—a wife who can commune with the Pythian Apollo."

"She is a very good match for him, I think. She was not intimidated by my imperial presence a whit. She carved her words for me like one who is quite conscious of a heritage we are just discovering...trying to emulate."

"And the boy, what about *his* intimidation?" By the sacred trinity that loomed above them! Here was a chat about young lovers, when the thunder and lightning of the mature male of them was rolling toward the forum at that moment.

"There was *none* that I could see. I congratulated the girl on her oracular heritage, suggesting that she might be helpful some day in interpreting the Sibylline Books for us." These books were a tenet of Fabius' stature, one of his fundamentals towards sensible management of Rome. Gaius Publius had just skipped around Hannibal, but his aside about Inanna stopped Fabius' walking, hence Gaius Publius' also. They were face to face again.

"What did she say about your—compliment?"

"She confessed that the Books were too far away for her, and she deferred any predictions of that moment to her companion, Hannibal."

"What did *he* say about this reflection, of your compliment?"

"He said that he thought that he and I would meet again...perhaps in Rome."

Fabius picked up the walk, Gaius alongside, no words as the circularly columned porch of Hercules' temple became an obvious focus for both of them. The low podium of this temple made easy access to the shade under the conical roof, in the annulus between the columns and the sanctuary building.

"How old was Hannibal at this time?" They had stopped in Hercules' shade.

"I think about eighteen years, but under Hamilcar's tutelage a boy could leap beyond his calendar—*that* boy particularly."

Fabius walked toward the bronze door of the sanctuary, touched it, but made no farther physical approach to this god.

"Hercules is a favorite of our businessmen, our international capitalists."

"You've dismissed the Carthaginians quickly, Fabius. I *am* impressed considering our moment in time."

"Your compliment may be overblown, Gaius. Actually, Hercules has inspired me to recall the very profitable trading and business connection between Rome and Carthage that has adorned the banks and private treasuries of both places for centuries. I would prefer to keep these connections with Carthage, rather than cut them with a sword, with unknown consequences at both ends."

"You value this economic synergism between Rome and Carthage over our potentials from war with Carthage?"

"Certainly. There is ground for empire to the north and east of us. Others, the Cornelii Scipiones and the Arpii Claudii, for example, are looking elsewhere: Sardinia, Sicily...Iberia, maybe Carthage. In that direction, I see only irreversible enmity with Carthage, obliteration of a mutual cornucopia—*they* see imperial opportunity."

"But some of this has already been turned into *what might have been,* Fabius. I didn't put my full answer to you about meeting Hannibal. The last time was at his palace at Carthago Nova. He was now Lord General Hannibal, and my intimidation meant less to him then than it did at Castulo—ten years before. At the end of our conference, during which he virtually defied us to stop him moving on Saguntum, I told him that I still credited his prescience—that we would meet in, or near Rome. I asked him which end of his sword he might be presenting at such a time. He replied that he hoped it would be the *pommel* end, saluting my appreciation of fine craftsmanship." Gaius Publius made his own inspection of a detail of the bronze door of the sanctuary, then he turned back to Fabius.

"You know about Hamilcar's effects in their first war with us better than I. But I must tell you, Fabius, that *this* Hannibal has no counterpart in the Carthaginian pantheon of leaders. He is a synthesis of diplomat, warrior, scholar...a cooperatively multi-graced gentleman that I have never seen in Rome, or in my books—and I *know* about Alexander of Macedon."

"Indeed, Gaius Publius, I was wallowing in *what might have been.* My name has popped up for dictator in this crisis that is swarming with your young friend from Castulo and Nova Carthago."

"They say he has moved from Trasimene toward the Adriatic, cutting off Servilius from Rome. Servilius is the surviving consul, and the appointment of a dictator now rests with him. Will Hannibal's maneuver complicate this responsibility?"

"I think so. I have proposed putting the choice of dictator to popular election on the basis of this complication."

"Congratulations, Dictator Fabius Maximus!" Gaius Publius was premature. But the enmity between Servilius and Fabius was well known. Fabius' control of the people's Comitia was also well known, therefore, Gaius Publius was only slightly premature.

As they stepped off Hercules' porch into an enveloping garden area, Fabius noticed a cluster of crocus.

"Ah, a perfect complement of that blue sky, Gaius and perhaps an omen of a Roman propitious summer."

Gaius Publius stepped in front of Fabius and saluted him.

"I pray for your dictatorship, Fabius." Then Gaius Publius cupped his right hand over the back of his right ear, as he studied the bright blue sky of Fabius' reverie.

"What are you listening for, Gaius?"

"Thunder, Fabius—the aftermath and usually the precursor of lightning."

They started back toward the Senate house.

"Italy is a large, complicated, country, Gaius Publius. A stranger here, casting thunderbolts, might get tired out before he could strike a mortal blow."

"That strategy would require a Roman *paragon* of patience and discipline, Fabius Maximus."

"Precisely, Gaius Publius—also generous nods toward us from the god of fate named, *Tyche*, by some Greeks."

Gaius tried to intersect Fabius' eyes, but they were elusive. He had to settle for the edge of what looked like a small smile.

"I think some other Greeks use the name, *Heimarmene*, for this god, or his aura, Fabius."

"Do you have a particular for me here?"

"We have just talked about a young lady of this inclination."

14

30 years
September 217 BC—Carthage

I t was a giggle, hidden behind the cluster of palms at one end of the big pool at the palace on Byrsa Hill. It was also a kind of surrender because it came only when the pursuers—the Lady Barca on left flank, Medina on right flank, and Inanna in center—had narrowed the hiding places down to these palms, had come close enough to detect the giggle that gave away the game that had lasted too long in everyone's opinion except Kyniska's. Inanna's flanks graciously conceded the capture to her. When she emerged from the palms, carrying a laughing bundle of dedication to all of the devilish precedents a mother, grandmother, and father had put into it, two more heads joined Inanna's in close-coupled censure of the bundle:

"You were very naughty running away from Tiba and Maga. They were going to make you more beautiful for our dinner tonight."

"I am beautiful enough, Grandmother."

"There are too many hiding places in this palace, Kyniska. What if we couldn't find you, and you couldn't find your way back?"

"I keep my eyes open, Medina. Daddy says this is good for a lot of things, like hiding."

Inanna tossed the bundle a little way into the air, and it came down bottom side up in her arms again. Kyniska was able to see her mother prepare a big bottom slap.

"This is something else your daddy is good at, young lady." Punishment was gentler than Inanna intended, and provoked an answer:

"He said that a horseperson shouldn't mind a spanking, it toughens the butt."

"Do you know what a *butt* is, Kyniska?"

"It's your seat on a horse, Mother."

Somewhere between the palm end of the pool and the end closest to Inanna's apartments, Kyniska assumed her own legs. Inanna told her to find Tiba and Mago, apologize to them for running away, and to let them make her more beautiful for dinner. As Kyniska obeyed, she waved at her pursuers.

"I think she won again." The Lady Barca's sigh was a summary of other Kyniska victories over supervision at the palace, the plantation at Thurburbo

Majus, and the estates at Hadrumetum and Cap Bon, all places where a preco-cious four year old with natural affinities for horses, peacocks, pigeons, mon-keys, and the curiosities of the people and places of these wonderful panoramas of the Barca empire, could find her challenges.

But this sort of thing could never be a stable annoyance to someone who had been called Hippolyta by a master of recalcitrance like Hamilcar. All the ladies wore light cotton sheaths, quickly adaptable to naked bathing in the pool. Probably Hamilcar's lady *was* the first to add a naked nymph to it, but this honor was a close one over Inanna and Medina, who made it three such nymphs embellishing mobile crystal over tiled dolphins and a mermaid tantalizing a compliant Neptune.

The patterns of combative splashes and laughter, and the flashes of the various symmetries in a woman's physical inventory, arsenal, didn't identify the 20 year discrepancy between the ages of the more mature lady and her companions. There were two raven tresses here, and one that played with antique gold and silver colors. But the voices, their projections into laughter and little screams, the ingenuity and aggression of the water play, and those symmetries involved with it, didn't tell on the ages here.

The Lady Barca moved out of the playful violence and rested against the apron, where more tiled artistry let smaller dolphins and seabirds cavort around the perimeter. The white silk band Tiba had put in her hair had surrendered to the water long before, and now she moved her hands to bring a little order to a cascade of gold and silver that was still long enough to challenge a handmaiden's ingenuity and perseverance. She brushed a vestige of the pool away from her lips, while she watched Inanna and Medina's conclusion of the nymphs' pageant.

She was also watching her continuity. She had used that word with Hannibal close to this pool, more insistently at the Hadrumetum estate when he complimented her stewardship of Hamilcar's legacy. But his history in Iberia after he had left her seven years ago and the chronicle of the Roman crusade he had assumed for Hamilcar—at least what the damned letters and the fragments of the official dispatches she had be able to see had told her—had destroyed that *continuity* word as it applied to Hannibal, and probably Hasdrubal and Mago's use of it, too.

The thunder Gaius Publius had anticipated beneath Capitoline Jupiter was being heard in Carthage. Hannibal had hurled himself at the core of the Romans and even the cynical Carthaginian aristocrats who cherished Roman commercial advantages couldn't mute the crescendo that was building in the forum, the Council. Every place of Carthage, whispers amplified to unabashed speech and increasing surges of Carthaginian pride that hadn't been heard within most of the extant life spans of the men and women of Carthage. Hannibal was the engine for this. She knew she had lost her continuity to a whirlwind that would press against every part of the Roman arrogance before it quieted.

She couldn't deny pride in him—in this extension of Hamilcar that out-reached Hamilcar himself. But her connection to him was memory now, and she had prepared herself to accept nothing more than memory...perhaps nothing more of him than she had taken from the marbled Hercules in Melkart's precincts at Gades. She would be able to touch *various* marbles of him if Inanna's Heimarmene persisted in pointing the glory road for him. They would be wondrous smooth, nearly lifelike, and a proper sculptor could make tricks for the eyes, the tips of fingers...and under propitious air, whispers could be pulled from her to it—not *him*, but *it*. This would be all she would probably get from future Hannibal Barca.

Inanna and Medina had quieted the pool and were wading toward the contemplative lady who had missed none of them while she also contended with continuity, and marbled men at Gades and probably Carthage. Inanna had a slight advantage of approach to the lady, in physical distance and hierarchy. When she started some reconstruction of her own hair with both her hands, she was close enough to the lady to let an almost whisper serve her:

"You are a formidable paradigm of continuity...all of the beauty and elegance I first met at Gades *still* challenges me." Inanna made a light touch of lips with her husband's mother's, and then she moved enough to give Medina some room for *her* smile. Inanna had just used a word in her compliment that now had a sharp edge for her object. But she couldn't know this, and Hamilcar's Hippolyta didn't tell on her.

"My facade evidently still withstands you, but you feed it, both you and Medina—I couldn't want better inspiration." She could serve laughter to a plantation work crew, or to any of the subtleties of intercourse accessible to her. She chose a version that wrapped Inanna and Medina in a perfect sequel to the pool play.

"You must let us follow you sometimes to your secret bower, milady."

"You two have ferreted out all of my secrets already...almost all of them. What could you have possibly missed, Medina?"

"I just heard Inanna praise your...continuity. Surely there is a bower where special waters, herbs, unmentionable exotics, are at the service of your natural aptitudes." Somehow, Medina found the lady's hand in another mélange of womanhood that had just been made at the edge of the pool. She kissed a finger of that hand, before she let a dark-eyed smile of Iberia conclude *her* compliment. And she also had used Inanna's word.

Medina had taken Amalkre's place in Hasdrubal's bed at Carthago Nova.

Moments after the assassin had left her husband splayed in a terrible surprise of death across that bed, she had found Inanna's surcease and a prelude to companionship that had come to Carthage when Hannibal left Iberia for Italy. And she was part of Amalkre for the Lady Barca because Medina had known her and she had, therefore, precious stuff for the lady's ears and eyes when bits of her daughter flashed in Medina's voice and face and hands during some display of memory from this Iberian lady.

"I can't promise you that bower. You and Inanna have seen all of me—literally." She took back the hand that had surrendered to Medina, letting it make a futile sweep for modesty over the air-exposed part of her. "Some horses, some gymnastics, running, archery, swimming...there you have it, Medina." That hand had gone to her lips again, and it couldn't hide some of a smile that still challenged her young companions to probe a little deeper into her composite of Carthaginian aristocrat, near-priestess of Melkart, student of the Etruscan Zortibas and the high priest Acherbas.

Medina's native Iberian intellect, curiosity, her ingenuity and humor, were also indispensable condiments to keep the feast of the Lady Barca and Inanna from wallowing overlong in the prescience that was now a formidable province when both of these ladies worked in it. Delphic competence, woven by a thousand years of Greeks from every part of their recognized universe, had now come together with the Lady Barca's scope of prophecy and fantasy that tapped more venerable Eastern and African sources the Greeks had missed. Medina had been qualified for the shadows these ladies could summon. But she was also sensitive to the sunlight demands on the hearts and minds of Inanna and the senior Lady Barca, and she played her part in the triad of companionship accordingly. The smiles that finally concluded the wet addendum of Kyniska's chase had a solid connection.

The palace steward, Artras, had enjoyed degrees of the Lady Barca's smile, suiting various degrees of her relaxation—never mind *his*. Today, the lady who looked at him from the desk of her palace office seemed to give him as much license for relaxation as he wanted. Inanna, Kyniska and Medina had descended on them over sixteen months ago. These ladies were now indispensable to the palace routine and, he suspected, to the smiles that the Lady Barca had husbanded much less since their advent.

"I haven't heard the waterfront hum like this since Lord Hamilcar's days in Sicily and his homecoming during the mercenary troubles." Artras shifted his stance, and looked toward a window that afforded a closer person a fine view of the cothon, the military and commercial harbors at Carthage. "...Perhaps never!"

"To what do you attribute this excitement?" She was the Carthaginian and Greek aristocrat again, none of the pool nymph who could tantalize Poseidon, or Neptune. The question was redundant, but hearing answers to it, never.

"Hannibal...*Hannibal*, my lady. His lembi from the waters that suck on most of Italy bring in reams of the official news, some of it's filtered down to us. But it's the traders from these same waters, surrounding his Italian playground, and from Greece, Egypt and the Asia Minor parts, that are the big point of the excitement. I hear talk of a new Alexander from these places."

"As a Carthaginian, Artras, this is not a compliment to our family— certainly not to its taproot, Tyre, which that over gilded Macedonian destroyed."

"It's the whirlwind part of him that has brought this comparison, my lady. You know about Ticinus, Trebbia and now Trasimene. The details of these places—that swarm around the unofficial cothon messengers—talk about rivers of Roman blood flowing toward Rome. I think Lord Hannibal has already overcrowded Hamilcar's aspirations for revenge."

"Your word, *whirlwind*, is too apt, Artras. It gives a target that no thought, or prayer, can embrace for long, nor eyes, or ears. It is subject to too many vagaries of its environment to take a comfortable thought from it...whatever the sheen of glory it reflects." She looked toward the same window Artras had used moments before, then his words made her walk to it, words that almost made that gossip from the busy cothon palpable for her. He had accompanied her part way to the window, stopping short of her vantage which gave a superior perspective of Carthage's great ear to the outside world.

"Beyond my objection to him personally, I don't like that Alexander connection. The price for his glory was nothing I would covet for my son." It was a soft ligament of voice between her and Artras. But she had just established an axis between price and glory—so now he had an obligation of further news, officially as her steward, personally as her friend.

"My Lady...there was something else." His voice's timbre made her turn toward him, her face permission enough to continue. "I heard that the Romans now curse a...a *one-eyed devil*. I...I don't know what this..." He *had* heard something about a terrible passage through swamps of the Arnus on the way to the Romans, about a young commander who had lost part of his world and cursed the Heimarmene who had sometimes favored him. What miracles of intimacy could you deny the devices of communication? They had penetrated privileged bowers of Xerxes, Alexander and Darius, Alcibiades, the Pharaohs. Artras saw the look on the lady's face that degraded his role as messenger.

The glory that had been streaming in from Italy had an unambiguous focus. The words that Artras had just relayed from the cothon, *one eyed-devil*, had to have the same focus. She had kept her hand from her mouth by a powerful discipline. She had kept her head high, even raised her chin, by the same strength. And the words from a letter Inanna had shared with her...*Kiss Kyniska for me. Tell her that I can make much better monsters now, so she had better be a very good girl*—came at her now with full realization, almost overriding the strength.

"Nothing more, Artras?" She needed a *personal* connection. She touched his hand. He gave her absolute stillness for her touch.

He told her what little he knew about the Arnus. He added a bit about Surus the great Indian elephant and a commander who used her as his chair for a while while he tried to find accommodation to a life of fewer dimensions.

"Ah, Surus...she is a beauty...I saw her when Hamilcar left for Iberia. I must thank her when I can." The lady removed her touch, and acknowledged Artras' retreating bow. Now she had the massive problem of mixing together Inanna, maybe Kyniska, and a lord commander, a son, who had lost part of his world.

She had tricked Inanna into a little privacy near a fountain in the atrium by asking her advice about a dinner party that was looming, concerning some points of menu.

"I've already bedeviled your cooks into some Greek recipes...they should know how to present themselves, Greek wise, to a sufet, Bomilcar in particular. I understand he has a taste for Greek touches, such as squid, and honey pastries."

The younger lady had never surrendered to Carthaginian dress, but she had been making some Greek concessions to it that were being copied in the Lady Barca's circles in Carthage...long and short chitons, and sheaths, which upheld the simple elegance of Greece but with subtle embellishments of hems, sleeves, necklines that complemented Carthaginian artistry in embroidery. And Inanna kept a close rein on her jewelry, applying the Greek principle of *less is more* to this aspect of her person, as well. The Carthaginian jewelers drew on every significant precedent of east and west for their creations in gold, silver and gems and made no apologies for their virtuosity that challenged, sometimes slightly successfully, Inanna's constructions of the Greco-Carthaginian woman. Lady Barca had anticipated Inanna's Greek tendencies by several decades, so the couch near the fountain was privileged by two ladies who could fit into Athens, or Pergamum, or Ephesus, perfectly.

"You've made a conquest of a sufet, I think, Inanna. His son, Hanno, is one of Hannibal's lieutenants. I've seen him mentioned in dispatches." Hamilcar's lady had moved closer to Inanna, as if to tighten the specifications for the menu that would affect that very sufet.

"I'll try to remember him in my prayers, milady...but they're getting so crowded, lately." Inanna turned toward a passageway of the atrium that gave some view of the fluid crystal playground that had had no room for somberness for three ladies only hours before. "His...his last letter came after this Italian battle at...*Trasimene.*"

"A great victory. Bomilcar told me that Hannibal has destroyed the last Roman field army. He has made the names Ticinus River, Trebbia River—now Trasimene—into screams that are flowing up and down the Tiber in Rome." A brag would be hard to make from the voice the Lady Barca had just used. It was almost a whisper, like a voice that could be used in the hearing of a suspicious, and changeable, god. "Did he say...anything about *himself?*" This voice was better, for a reply. She touched Inanna's hand, while Inanna still used the pool perspective for the background of her thoughts. Inanna returned to her:

"He said he has an interesting scar for my collection on his left cheek, something about a Cretan arrow that had whispered too closely, nothing else..." A small smile filled out a little more of that letter. "He said he is pointing toward Carthage again, using *me* as a beacon. Ah, that was in *another* letter, just after he rounded the Roman flanks in Etruria." That letter was the one Sosylos had goaded out of him. Inanna had just given Lady Barca the cue she hadn't managed to make on her own.

"That letter was the one where he told Kyniska to behave herself, or beware of his monster..." Lady Barca's statement had enough question to prompt Inanna.

"I threatened Kyniska with it. She started to laugh at her memory of her Daddy's monsters."

Lady Barca touched Inanna's hand again...then she took more possession of the conversation and the hand:

"My darling, Artras told me about his latest travel along the docks, our senior ear to the outside world." Inanna was about to say that she had also discovered this facet of Artras' jewel—but Lady Barca's face stopped her. The prescience that had turned Inanna toward the pool could now be tasted in the airspace between the lips of these ladies who had discovered much of the mystery of working conversation into silence.

"He said that the Romans are now cursing a *one-eyed devil.* He said...the eye had been lost to a sickness during a terrible passage through the swamps of the Arnus. A dispatch fragment I saw said that Hannibal had rested at Faesulae, after the Arnus crossing. I think that...your letter was written there...I think it is a monument to three people..." Inanna's hand was on her mouth, but without the hand, her eyes said her mouth would have trouble with words at that moment. "...Sosylos, Hannibal, and you, Inanna. Sosylos has tried to be invisible, but his hand has touched Hannibal in Carthage, Iberia, and in the hells and glories he's shared with Hannibal since they moved toward Italy."

"That letter had part of...of Sosylos?" Inanna had been partially restored by a soft embrace of touch and voice.

"After you read it to me, when you let me look at it, I could feel a collaboration that I *knew* had Sosylos and Hannibal and you in it. It had the feel of a desperation *just* turned away by a present friend and a distant *you*, Inanna. It fits with what Artras told me about the Arnus...and the eye." Her blue eyes had invited extra moisture into them some moments before, and now there was a collaboration with dark eyes that asked for two disciplines to combat tears.

"And then this great battle at Trasimene—so soon after this, and that Cretan arrow. He told me he's heading toward Carthage again. If he has only half a world now, some god *must* have him hitched to his chariot." The Lady Barca's arms became a shelter for her daughter-in-law, almost cheek to cheek, as Inanna took more steps with her words, one of the disciplines against tears not enough. "He told me that *now, he is Hamilcar.* Hamilcar could never have expected *this* of him—I will *never* see him again." The last part was buried in Lady Barca's cheek, but she heard it.

"If a *man* can see you again, Inanna—after what has happened and will happen to him—it will be Hannibal Barca." She separated Inanna from her cheek and kissed her lips, and then insisted steps toward the pool.

"I have tried prayers with Asclepius, .and the Carthaginian Eshmoun...do you have any stronger ones?" Inanna had turned toward her walking companion, her dark eyes picking up a little sparkle from the pool.

"My focus has drifted, Inanna. I tend toward a god I don't know...but I *feel* a central presence. Whether I call the name Melkart, or Tanit, or Ba'al-Hammon...Demeter, I think it doesn't matter. Don't tell Asherbal about this, but I think it doesn't matter, so long as I am focused on a center that really has no name for me...a single presence, but no name."

"Do you think you can make stronger prayers then mine?" It was part of a repeated question, more supplication than challenge.

The senior lady didn't waste time defending herself this time. The kiss was a mutual affair, and then she said, "Of course not," as she insisted them closer to the brightness of the pool.

A Barca dinner party gave the various flavors of Greece priority, although Cosmopolitan Carthage shared the Mediterranean perimeter with many people and their words were another of her tapestries which worked for her prosperity. After over a year of challenges from the world the Lady Barca kept expanding for them, Inanna and Medina could take, and give, something to most of the conversations around them.

Peripherally, this lady was watching Inanna and Medina trace various paths among her guests. In privacies of these ladies from Iberia, there had been a few more tears over a one-eyed man who was putting his thunder into the Roman forum. But the public Inanna had surmounted the Faesulae revelation, and she was now assimilating the congratulations, the implications of conquest that were extravagant, but not unreasonable, by the measure of the faces and voices that presented them to her, and were a general current in the congregation of Lady Barca's dinner party at the twilighted palace on Byrsa Hill.

A gentleman, a merchant prince from Tyre, had just proposed the hostess as the coming queen of Mediterranean prosperity. Two other gentlemen of similar bent and authority, an Alexandrian and a Carthaginian, were also in close attendance to the Lady Barca and they supported the compliment from Tyre. All of them were the first recipients of soft laughter, and accessories of beauty and sophistication that made her protest unconvincing.

"But I tell you, I have students now who are threatening my authority, undermining this *queenhood* you would thrust on me."

"More the acolytes for your temple, Lady Barca." The Carthaginian could see flicks of Inanna and Medina: one an innovating and breathtaking synthesis of Greece and Carthage, the other a frank Iberian statement of scarcely less intrigue. He knew his word *acolyte* would be hard-pressed to contain them, and the lady shortly confirmed this.

She motioned in the direction where she had last noticed Inanna, her smile following: "Formidable acolytes, sir. I am dealing with classic Greece— classic Iberia here. The resolve for perfection, picking what they can from my dotage, is formidable, certainly a shaky basis for this queen of yours..." She used the Carthaginian's given name. Greek was a natural facet of this conversation, and the laughter.

Inanna had intercepted some of her lady's beam and was walking toward this cluster of slightly one-sided optimism.

"My respects, Lady Inanna." The Alexandrian had said it, but his bow was coincident with the Carthaginian and the Tyrian's. Her personal statement this night had been enhanced by touches of gold at the ears and throat that complimented the Egyptian aura, including its commercial cornucopia that these men all shared to some extent.

The Alexandrian eyed the pendant on Inanna's necklace which suggested attributes of a mother goddess: "Isis and Greece and Carthage. The Lady Barca has warned us about your burgeoning scope, Lady Inanna."

"She is my staunchest critic and advocate, sir. Sometimes it gets confusing—but I will take your compliment and study it, later." Inanna's smile, which matured to a pulse of laughter that suggested other precedents of

Hippolyta were at issue here, showed no reflection of the Arnus business that had struck her heart only hours before.

Then Hannibal was honored and Inanna fended the congratulation and prophecy, a persistent pattern of this dinner party, with a balance of grace and enthusiasm which had to bolster the more aggressive claims that had just been made about her. Once, in the middle of a reply to the Tyrian about the new champion who was putting the Italian Wolf into his pen, she and her lady made an inadvertent touch of the backs of hands, and then fingers, which she made clutched during her reply, and helped her finish it.

The touches of Greek cuisine had had the desired effect on the sufet, Bomilcar. He was not a greatly social man. He took his parties and banquets at *his* discretion, and he was usually careful to keep his unofficial man on a short leash at these affairs, which meant he tended to lead the parade to the door at the conclusions. But tonight, when most of her party was a memory, he had contrived to place himself in the sparse tail of the goodnights and compliments so that he could work some private amenities, and conference, with the Lady Barca...and be as uninhibited about it as she pleased.

He was a determined bachelor, but Hamilcar's widow was a pinnacle of womanhood that challenged in a broad arena, and tempted him to run his suitor out for her inspection from time to time. He was about the age Hamilcar would have been, not as well equipped for fantasy and factual passion as Hamilcar had been. But his classic Semitic face had definite possibilities in these directions, especially when he was careful to keep the bear on his lower face in check, and even suffer his barber's encouragement of the curly tendencies of his general hair, which had gone from jet black to mostly gray. He had been a friend of Hamilcar and his Hippolyta. He was one of Hannibal's bulwarks in the Carthaginian aristocracy, and the government. His son, Hanno, was a lieutenant in the heavy cavalry of Hannibal's expeditionary force. His connections to the mother city, Tyre, were as solid as the Lady Barca's. His perspective, therefore, tended to a more worldly panorama than those of some other aristocrats at Carthage who still held their Roman ligaments as tightly as their Carthaginian.

He'd succeeded in nudging his hostess, physically and emotionally, toward a veranda conclusion of her party which brought an appropriate scope of stars and a full moon into it. Bomilcar wore a three-quarter cloak over a white, knee-length tunic. The cloak was Tyrian purple, with gold and silver embroidery of geometrical designs on the facing hems. Glistening black boots, which borrowed from the calceus of the Roman senators, and a gold-mounted ruby ring, finished him out. Most of the other males of that evening had carried a heavier jewelry load.

"You must congratulate the Lady Inanna—she has pricked to life almost all of my good memories of Corinth and Athens."

The Lady Barca had gone almost purely Greek this night—the coiffure, the silk constraints to it, the long chiton, undergarment, and short cloak...all white silk, with thin purple facing hems on the cloak. A woven gold throat band and pendant earrings, both involving emeralds, were her concession to Carthage. She had been looking into a night that showed some outlines of the cothon by lamps along the quays of the military and commercial harbors—the *hum* Artras had told about, palpable. The party's distraction hadn't been enough to silence a specific of it that had struck her as hard as it had Inanna. She turned toward Bomilcar, who was as much a promotion of Carthage as she was of Greece:

"You can do that yourself, Bomilcar. She said something about the *quintessential* aristocrat when she was looking in your direction."

"Was she smiling?"

"Unambiguously."

"Then there is hope for another friendship in your household?"

"I predict it. She has become a fierce student of us—me. She will find her way to you, and your secrets, relentlessly, I also predict." The lady stepped close enough to touch Bomilcar's hand on the balustrade of their terrace. "I'm glad you didn't rush away from me, tonight...Artras told me about the Arnus nightmare, yesterday."

"Hannibal hadn't told you, or Inanna?"

"I think I detected some of it in a letter Inanna let me see. I think Sosylos was in that letter, and it was the closest he would let Hannibal get to that eye." She turned to the night again. "Acherbas and Zortibas have complimented my prescience, but it's a damn curse I can't exorcise! It even comes at me from a letter—that gives his love to Kyniska."

Bomilcar heard all of the softness of that last part. He took a little initiative in the hand business and made her turn toward him.

"Trasimene came after he lost the eye. I am told that his name has crept into the most secret sanctuaries of the Romans. This is not a man devastated by fortune. I am told that that eye has forged another link between him and his men—I would not like to be a Roman at this time." Bomilcar had just exactly repeated Sosylos, near the edge of an abyss at Faesulae...near the edge of a letter.

Then it was *his* turn toward the night. The hum of the cothon, and some other hums that the lady close to him was not privy to, had told him more than she knew about Hannibal.

"You and the Lady Inanna have made a strong Greek statement, tonight and other times. But Carthage is not Greece, milady."

"You and I certainly make some of *your* statement tonight, Carthaginian personified in you, synthetic Greek in me." His Tyrian purple against her Greek whiteness played with their eyes for a moment, but her almost frivolity didn't draw a smile from him.

"We've turned toward much of the Greekness...art, literature, theatre, their gods—but we are a strange mixture of the Africa and Asia that is not Greece. We have crucified more generals than we have glorified. Our talk with them has ended more often in the torture cells than in the forums and councils. This is not the Greeks—not for a *thousand years*."

"What is it to be Greek, Bomilcar?—I seem to have missed the point of all of it."

"It is *people* making and striving to complete dreams...making consensus." It was his crux—it was terribly pertinent to her sons in Italy, but he *couldn't* round it out for her.

"You are degrading yourself. You are almost the capstone of Carthaginian consensus."

"I, the other sufet, Imilco, the Council, the Assembly of the People, the whole packet of us playing at government, are a farce. The Greeks put the people into the *center* of their consensus and then the striving business: Marathon, Salamis, even the debacle of the Spartan wars, are monuments to this commitment. It also has non-military implications—but I've abused your hospitality by putting this stuff into your wonderful evening." He drew back.

"Not true. I put in *Arnus*, and *nightmare*, just after you put in *Inanna*, and *friendship*—this bad responsibility must be shared." For a moment, the east-west synthesis of beauty that had entranced Hamilcar, now compounded by moonlight, came close to him. "But please *stay* with the military, Bomilcar—I have a son who happens to be a general, you have a son who happens to be his lieutenant."

Bomilcar took the lady's hand and touched it to his lips, no interruption of his look to her. "In my devotions to Ba'al, to Tanit, to Demeter, Eshmoun, to any recommended god who will listen to me, I will pray that the *Greek like* part of Carthage is brought to bear on the greatest general who ever carried Tanit's standard into the horizon."

It was easy for her to reciprocate the compliment of Bomilcar's attention. But the urge to return to the balustrade—to the whispers and shouts of the cothon just beyond which would engine the prayers he had promised her—was irresistible.

15

30 years
Summer 217 BC—Umbria

The Roman debacle of Trasimene was hemorrhaging on the ground and marshes below them, when Carthalo told him that now he could knock on the doors of Rome. Having just destroyed the last significant field army of Roman Italy, it had been a reasonable proposal. He could have had his cavalry's lances decorating any of the gates of Rome in two days. He could have made the name Hannibal walk around the forum, echo from Capitoline Jupiter's precincts, bring more than a whisper of degenerate Carthage into the Senate chamber where there was already debate about how much fear should be allowed to swarm into the people. These things were happening—but he could have made them stronger, a stickier part of the nightmares that flourished in thick Roman nights, with a little courtesy visit to those walls.

There were Romans extant who knew that Barca, through Hamilcar, was assimilated with *lightning*, and obviously *thunder*. But the sight and sound of this man had been put mostly into Sicily and the Roman Tyrrhenian coast. When Gaius Publius cupped a hand over an ear in front of Fabius Maximus, invoking a new thunder and lightning from another Barca, it had been partly prescience driven by memory of a boy, and then a young general, whose smiles were hard to intimidate. But Ticinus, Trebbia, and Trasimene had driven hard facts into that moment, and Gaius Publius' gesture was only moments away from a reality that hadn't faced Rome since the Senonian Celts had sacked it 173 years before.

A single battle had preceded that particular debacle. Another Barca was now taking a more methodical and convincing course toward Rome. He had lavished the bodies of the best Roman soldiers over the Po and Etrurian grounds on three successive encounters. And if his horses had wings, the bastion of Rome's walls would be a nonsense now. The two legions within the city were a token against him. But the walls were not. This Hannibal had sworn in front of Saguntum that he would never waste his men on a major siege again. Maharbal and Carthalo had heard him. This pledge had also trickled into Roman ears, and now it was part of the basis for what bluster could be found inside those walls. It was also why Hannibal was turning his army toward the Adriatic after Trasimene.

During some travel respite while his foragers were picking at all the vaults and crevices of the Umbrian storehouse around Perusia, his advisors and his officers had opportunities to consider logic that would determine their next path—separate conferences, nudged toward the commander by Barmocar and Maharbal, respectively. Barmocar was the senior Senate representative for the expedition, Maharbal the ranking officer of its cavalry arm that had put thunder into Hannibal's travel where Gaius Publius, and now Fabius Maximus, could hear it without leaving the forum.

"They've paid you the compliment of a dictator, Hannibal." Barmocar had just entered the tent used for conference by the advisors that Hannibal generally suffered gladly for their ligaments to Carthage, their own intelligence and the various whispers they brought to him from sources that occasionally outdistanced his own.

"I think we are about to pay our respects to Fabius Maximus Verrucosos, gentlemen." Hannibal turned toward the men who had been more prompt to service the meeting Barmocar had called than Barmocar himself.

"What do we know about him?" Myrcan, the strategist, asked. He'd put a general question, but it had tended toward Hannibal, who would carry the burden of accommodating what they decided they *did* know about Fabius.

Hannibal was wearing one of Adherbal's eye patches—a white linen variation. The patch was a prop, no longer a cosmetic. And he used it to temper his personality for his audience. The bare left eye—Synhalus' ministrations had made it a sleepy and nearly agreeable compatriot of his right one, although what one could see of the incomplete iris had upset some of his Hellenistic symmetry—was favored by him and his men for military conversation and the satellites of it that could spin off into laughter and the other vocals of comradeship. Barmocar's suggestion of a meeting with Lord Hannibal, was a patch time. Hannibal waited for the advisors' summary on Fabius, looking at Barmocar:

"The Fabians poked into the first war with Rome. I think *this* man knew Hamilcar, or came damn close to the whispers of his sword and sails." Barmocar picked up Hannibal's look.

"He has some reputation for conservatism." Sulan's was an understatement.

"That would put him at odds with the imperialists: the Claudii, and the Scipiones." Myrcan flashed a look at Barmocar. The Scipios were raising hell in Iberia, and they had popped into this meeting sooner than Hannibal expected.

"If he can drain off some of the Scipios' mischief in Iberia, maybe I can love him."

"That would put more Romans against you, Hannibal."

"Hasdrubal is not having fun with them where he is. They landed at Emporiae, and are now rallying Catalan tribes that I thought we had tucked into our pocket. I would rather play with them myself, on their own ground. We should have pulled Publius Cornelius Scipio's teeth at Ticinus and Trebbia." Hannibal drew out the name to match the error of leaving some teeth in this Scipio, who was now romping with his brother Gnaeus Cornelius in Iberia.

"There was another of that name at Trebbia. I think we can thank him for getting away with some of his father's teeth." Amarcar, the advisor who had the closest ear to the politics of Rome and Carthage, had another tidbit of the same hue. "I think this young image of Publius Cornelius will bear watching—he is said to be something of a student, Hannibal."

"I wonder which university he will enter, his father's...or mine?" No one answered, but Hannibal's smile gave them enough to make an answer.

"Fabius is a religious man." Barmocar was continuing his citation of the dictator.

"All of us can run to the gods on occasion." Sulan was a generalist, religion only a sometime subject.

"He is a *map* to the gods, Sulan, the Sibylline Books are his bible. And if their prescriptions are not heady enough for him, he will run to the digestion of their damn chickens in gold cages, or what revelations his Etruscan haruspices can pull out of their livers and entrails for him...or from watching ravens and hawks shit in the sky."

"You last charge is apt, I think, Barmocar. I've heard Fabius doesn't take a shit without consultation." Myrcan turned to Hannibal. "That might make a good target for you, Hannibal—a man who contemplates his basics overlong."

"It might, if we can catch him with his toga up—but that word *basics* could also involve the word, *survival.* If he hangs on tight to *that* word, catching him with his toga in the right position might be an exercise in frustration." Everyone had been standing. And now Hannibal did some circulation among his listeners. "We have pulled impetuous Romans toward us so far. Our style depends on this. The Druid, Cathbad, warned about the Hydra-headed tendency of the Romans. We may have to borrow some of Fabius' patience to degenerate that Hydra—but not too much, I hope."

"We have heard whispers in the wind that the prime head, Rome, is not in our next direction, Hannibal."

"That wind can be fickle, Myrcan...sometimes it sounds like Rome, sometimes not. We have not yet made a conclusion that wind can get its teeth into."

"*We,* Lord Hannibal?"

"I, and the others who will carry what I decide is my responsibility." He started to walk again, the damned two-dimensional world of him couldn't bring in conference like he wanted. Instead of the deep, comprehensive, target he liked, he had to take it almost man to man. Finally, he worked himself to the front of all of them:

"I am not the Macedonian, Demetrius Poliorcetes—the city besieger. Rome would be a good target for him. He could put his Helepolis towers around the city and piss down on the Romans from all directions. When they were drowning in his piss, he could tip-toe over the walls into the city."

"You are invoking a talent that's about seventy years dead, Hannibal. You are denying progress beyond Demetrius?"

"You are impatient, Barmocar. Rome will still be there when we are ready for her. And as for your *progress* against a bastion like that, it's still the same business: You throw men into cracks and holes until someone decides that the bloodbath, the general death, on one side, or the other, is enough, and then there is an end to it, that *may* be favorable to you. Demetrius put the greatest engines the world has seen into that play, but it always comes down to what I said—. there has been no *progress* in that for three thousand years."

"Another whisper on that fickle wind says that the name Hannibal is being assimilated with the name Alexander. I think he set some enviable standards for the business we are talking about."

"As Carthaginians, Barmocar, you are talking about Tyre to me. It took that Macedonian over seven months, using all the resources of the Greek world, to destroy Tyre. He was not threatened from behind, so he could lavish undivided attention on our ancestors, essentially civilians, pushed to unreasonable heroics by a fanatic imperialist. By the way, Alexander's towers at Tyre were 50 paces high. Demetrius' tower, his Helepolis, was a little shorter, but probably more manageable." Hannibal stepped closer to Barmocar:

"Give me time, and resources, to build towers like these, then give me a hundred thousand men to mount the siege and another hundred thousand to watch my back while we play at siege—I'll take Rome for you."

"Your numbers are intimidating to a Carthaginian, Hannibal, and your appraisal of Rome is depressing."

"Only when you look at her walls and towers." Another step closer to Barmocar made it almost a private conversation.

"I am looking south of Rome, toward the country that is her vitality: Campania, Apulia, Lucania, Brutium. I would like to cut the succoring vines that run from those places to Rome. I would like to bring bridges to Carthage into those places to push Rome back into the sweet nostalgia of agrarian backwater that was her original fame."

"You have specific targets in mind to the *south*, Lord Hannibal?"

"Capua, and Neapolis, leap to my aid for your question, Barmocar."

"We have had agents in Capua for years."

"I think I have supplemented some of yours, Barmocar. Whispers from *that* place, tell me that the Capuan, Pacuvius Calavius, has made progress toward a People's Party in that city, that he is close to throwing off the Roman yoke given some support. Capua is a more seductive plum than Rome. I think the first significant vine cutting could start there. It is the center of economic sophistication and scope in Italy, an Etruscan memory that the Romans have not killed yet. I think it could be the nucleus for our ambitions on the Roman doorstep."

"Then my whisper about Rome, the one preceding yours about Capua, is true, Hannibal."

Hannibal resumed his circulation, meeting most of the eyes on an uneven basis. When he stopped, he was standing next to Myrcan, the strategist who had started the whispers, but he was looking at Barmocar again.

"You have stimulated my juices, my friend. This tends to reduce the subterfuge tendencies I might have been harboring when you walked in. I am, therefore, forced to admit that we will probably be spending a little time near the Adriatic's salubrious shores."

Barmocar had ordered wine for this occasion. When everyone held a silver goblet, furnished with the best wine that Umbria could offer at that moment, Barmocar's slight bow to Hannibal assigned the toast.

Hannibal pulled his dagger from the silk band that girded his waist. They were all familiar with this souvenir of Hamilcar, but when Hannibal moved it upward, and then sideways, to make a satisfying fusion of the oil light with its steel and some of its details of gem and silver, that dagger seemed appropriate to this time and place.

"I am here because of my father. I am using some of his officers, his men, his strategy and I have heard his voice and felt his hand many times since I turned his army toward Italy." The flashing dagger remained the focus of his toast, but he sought as many of their eyes as he could:

"Gentlemen—to the glory of Carthage! May our attributes henceforth draw the aid and comfort that we will need from Tanit and Ba'al and from all the gods—and all the people—who will have reason to admire us!"

Hannibal's generality here included Inanna's Heimarmene silently, but most particularly. The Italian cornucopias that could spew out sustenance for him could also be lifeblood for the legions. He had publicized part of Cathbad's prophecies in various conferences. Privately, the full perspective of them was filling out the deeper he got into Hamilcar's dream.

Synhalus had told him to get up on a horse again after Trasimene. Surus, the Indian elephant, with Suta his mahout, had been a moveable throne since the Arnus, but it was time for the man Inanna persisted in calling Hannibal Barca, even in their private moments, to resume another moveable seat that would put him into the thick of his lioned and leoparded Numidians, into the Carthaginian and Iberian and now his Celt heavy horse, that was the thunder of his army.

"This Umbrian countryside gets more seductive with every mile, Hannibal." Maharbal was riding to the right of his commander, the natural vision side. They rode black Iberians. Maharbal's words were partly for observation, partly to compliment an exuberance that was being rapidly remembered by a man who was born for the back of a horse. But there wasn't much privacy here. An escort of matched Cyrenian grays had formed up close to Hannibal and Maharbal when a little morning ride was seen to be shaping up. All of the Mushrooms were still alive, lieutenants and captains in various horse commands, and they had closely watched Hannibal's progress toward a horse since the dark nights in Faesulae...that only Sosylos really knew about.

Hannibal's laugh reflected off Maharbal and went back to the rest of his escort, and then he said, "I'm counting on that seduction, my friend. I'm looking forward to your virtuosity in taking some of it into our supply train." This was a no patch day, no helmet or body armor. His scouting screen, and informants, had put the nearest significant Romans with Fabius in Rome, and Servilius northwest of him a comfortable distance. That laugh also had some duality—it was appreciation for Maharbal's enthusiasm. It was confirmation to more than Maharbal that a two dimensional world was being accommodated, and that this was not a good time to be a Roman.

"Why are we are going away from the Romans, Hannibal?" The pace, under Maharbal's prompting, had turned more sedate, so the question came from behind him in an almost natural voice. The Mushroom hats were not battle-approved. But they were allowed to come out for outings like this, and several of them *had*.

"I think we will play the reluctant bride for a while...inviting, but reluctant." Hannibal identified the voice and used its name. "I think that combination makes *tantalizing*."

"By whatever gods you're using today, Hannibal, this doesn't look like a good prospect—*brides* to be played by a crew you wetted to a sharp edge *yourself*?"

"You are all actors, as well as troops. I've seen all of you strut this talent around Carthage, and I'm counting on that, also." He would've liked to put his

Iberian into full speed at that moment, but his horse equilibrium was not fully remembered yet, and all of his escort, Maharbal included, watched him closely, if not always directly. Severe decorum in formation continued to prevail.

"I'll take the burden of the fool off the backs of your young friends here. How does a reluctant, precocious bride get us close to the Romans, Hannibal?" Maharbal had essentially called another meeting to order.

"Fabius has taken the center stage against us, as dictator. The Romans have also elected Marcus Minucius Rufus as his Master of Horse. These antique offices are supposed to calm the Romans and scare us." They had come to a small grove of oak, which Maharbal designated as a mounted rest stop, it would make the commander's focus easier to get.

"Rufus was a consul, I think." A Mushroom.

"He has that distinction. He also has the friendship of the Scipios, for another. This puts an interesting complexion on this dictatorship that has been resurrected in our honor, gentlemen."

Hannibal let his Iberian take some steps, but the annulus of men on horses they had put around him was flexible.

"Fabius will not move against us until his auspices, and realities of situation, are all in his favor. Minucius is not so inclined. He has already bragged about bringing us to bay and then, with chains, into Rome. He may be competing with the Scipios for that honor."

"This is no place for a reluctant bride." Another Mushroom.

"If we make her tantalizing enough, I think we can play Fabius' coyness against Minucius' bravado so that we can suck a lot of Romans into a prenuptial celebration."

"You have just used a verb again that can be very naughty, Hannibal, but I think this bride of yours is forming up for me—she's an illusion of ultimate satisfaction for a ravening brute.".

"I think we heard that verb just before Trebbia and Trasimene." The last Mushroom had another question. "What would make this special kind of bride, Hannibal?"

"She would spend a lot of time ravishing the country for her adornment, and to make herself an athletic partner for her wedding night, and she would resist premature coupling. Enough now for your definitions—remember my dependence on your acting. How you bring my horses on and off the stages we make for the Romans will probably determine how zealously they clean the bird shit from my ultimate statue in the forum at Carthage."

"I think you gentlemen will be a very busy, and a very naughty, bride." Maharbal had watched these Mushrooms from vantages in Iberia, Ticinus, Trebbia and Trasimene. They were Carthage in Italy. They were now also part of a left eye.

When the rehabilitation column turned back toward the camp at Maharbal's insistence, the Mushroom component settled back as a respectable escort, with a discreet, mostly silent, separation. This outing had been invigoration for Maharbal, too. At the staff meeting, after Barmocar's, Hannibal had been succinct, less playful, in justifying the turning away from the Roman center of gravity for a little while: The men and horses needed rest and rehabilitation. The country on the east side of the Appenines was another cornucopia for their train, where the threat of his cavalry on the great eastward sloping gradients of that country would keep any Roman adventures manageable. The southern part of Picenum would be a good location for all of this, and also for keeping an ear toward what Fabius, and his chicken guts and livers, had decided. It had been a good meeting. But it had not been vintage Hannibal in one of the respects that distinguished him from Alexander: unforced communion with every rank of his men. Maharbal, therefore, was taking more material for a smile from this ride than he could from the meeting that hadn't used horses. Between these time points, three days, both Barmocar and Hannibal's gossamers had brought in a little more about Fabius:

"Fabius called a meeting of the Senate as soon as his dictator's mantle had settled on him. We hear that he ordered the Board of Ten to consult the Sibylline Books."

"And what did *that* accomplish?" With his question, Maharbal let the commander pick up their pace a little.

"He ordered a new offering to Mars, public prayers, a banquet to the gods attended by their images, a dedication of next spring's produce to them, games vowed to Jupiter, and shrines to Venus and Mens." All this in his honor. He would have to put part of his smile in his next letter to Inanna.

"*Mens?*"

"A devotion to the attributes of man that put him closer to a god."

"That one could be troublesome if they have any luck. Did Fabius dwell on anything with a *military* flavor?" Hannibal's horse equilibrium looked fine even from the corner of questioner Maharbal's eye.

"He's ordered the raising of two new legions, all people in unfortified towns to leave for safer havens and to burn what they don't take. They're going to stuff as much as they can of this year's harvest and the next into the fortified towns."

"That last part might complicate our fun, Hannibal. But I think we can still give Fabius a headache." Some of the big, black plumes from the foraging and sacking operations that Maharbal had been supervising in Umbria were visible evidence that Fabius would work overlong on headache remedies.

The port of Ancona on the Adriatic in Picenum was a natural focus for communication with Carthage during operations in the eastern part of the Po valley, and then the southward penetration that had gone through Trasimene and was now angling eastward for the reasons Hannibal had posed before the advisors, his staff, and his playful Mushrooms. His lembi, a frustration of the Roman navy, had used Ancona for some of his official deliveries, and most of his material personals with Inanna since he had come into the Po country.

Ancona was also a vestige of the Senones, the Celt tribe that had sacked Rome. When Hannibal's corps appeared on the eastern Apennine slopes he started to pick up entourages of Senones, who followed him at least long enough to praise his coming as a liberator against the Romans. The Boii and Insubre foot and horse put extra froth on the exuberance that peaked outside Ancona, near his camp, where the Senones chief, Rhetogenes, had insisted a welcoming party. Celt dialects, the common Greek, some Latin, enabled the talk which usually flicked among all of these with no particular bias, enhanced by a depth of facial signals, gestures using most of the body that was almost unique to the Celts. But Hannibal was relieved that Rhetogenes had good Greek.

"By Taranis, Lord Hannibal, you are the incarnation of Brennus." Underneath the gold goblet that Rhetogenes had raised over his head, he had just compared Hannibal with probably the greatest Celt general; a man also addicted to horses who had paraded down the Greek peninsula like Hannibal was now doing in Italy. He had also just brought the Celt god of thunder and lightning to the service of Hannibal's aura, and the Barca name.

Hannibal managed to touch goblets with his host. He hadn't seen this much gold at a banquet since Hamilcar's victory celebration at Carthage after he had ended the Mercenary nightmare.

"I will strive to be worthy of this comparison, Rhetogenes. Brennus brought innovation into cavalry which I am glad our Roman friends haven't studied." He looked at the round log structure, roofed with log beams and reed overlays. Some details were like he had seen during Cathbad's hospitality, but this room was much larger, and the forty or so guests arrayed on reed mats near low tables straining under Rhetogenes' bountiful repast, didn't crowd the room. The mix of his officers—Carthaginian, Iberian, African, Celt—with Rhetogenes' people, in complete surrender to the frank hospitality, was also a treat for him. This was their first real relaxation in weeks of campaigning when they had upheld a disabled commander, and made him greater by their devotions.

"I wish I could put more of Brennus' precedent into your army, Hannibal, but we are only a backwater now. The Insubres and Boii will have to carry the Senones' sword this time with you."

Rhetogenes was about the age Hamilcar would have been. His hair, mustache, and eyebrows were exuberant in the Celtic style, gray to white. Blue eyes which seemed to strain against the constraints of age, and the typical Celt fastidious assembling of the man for his guest—checkered trousers tucked into black walking hose, white silk blouse underneath a dark blue cloak fastened with a clasp where a peaceful sylvan scene in red enamel was polished into a gold lattice—made it easy to look at him, listen to him. He caught several views of Hamilcar's dagger in Hannibal's sash underneath his tunic. Arms were no insult to a Celt on any occasion. It bespoke a man frank in his devotion to honor and its defense. On the last occasion that Hannibal noticed this flick of interest, he withdrew the weapon, and presented the pommel to Rhetogenes. Natural light coming through roof panels, and oil light from lamps hung on chains from the ceiling, enhanced the presentation. The Celt angled the dagger to several facets of this lighting, and the talk stopped at adjoining tables while he did this.

"I have heard that this is Hamilcar's weapon."

"I have that honor, Rhetogenes."

"I would give what span the gods have left for me to be with you when you take your father's memory—and your own glory—into the Roman face." He inspected the hilt and steel once again, and then handed the dagger back to Hannibal.

"Your kinsmen have already been your surrogate for this. I have been criticized for using them as my shock point against the legions, with high losses. I have talked to the Boii and the Insubres about this. They have told me that a position of honor has a price, and it is their responsibility to worry about this, not mine."

"I have heard that Cathbad has seen you."

"By Ba'al!—is there *no* privacy left?" Hannibal's laugh cut through similar sounds in the room, and Rhetogenes held up his end of it.

Rhetogenes leaned closer to Hannibal, making an unsubtle overture for privacy that quickly drew in all the ears within several spans of a Celt long sword. "Is there any of that chat with Cathbad that could be trickled my way?" Hannibal destroyed any vestige of privacy with another laugh. Maharbal, Mago, Carthalo, Synhalus, Sosylos, and Silenus heard it. This laughter was the best sound they had got from Hannibal Barca in the long weeks since Faesulae.

"He told me that the Celts would be the basis for the last pillar in my Italian temple."

"That particular Druid has a reputation for prescience that puts shine into the auras of all his kind. Could you favor me with a specific of Cathbad's prophecy?" Rhetogenes' privacy was a shambles now, so his leaning toward Hannibal was absolutely unneeded.

Hannibal sipped his wine, and looked around the assembly that, to a man, used him and Rhetogenes as a focus. Uncovering some of Cathbad for this chieftain, on the eve of testing Fabius and Minucius, wouldn't do any harm. He had lost over 3,000 Celt foot in the fighting since Ticinus. He would need this replacement, and more, to play the game properly with Fabius.

"He talked about the Hydra-headed tendency of the Roman. He said that I would need to draw on the strength residing in the northern European Celts: the Belgae, and the Germani, for example—to cope with legions that keep living as fast as you kill them." Rhetogenes' wine was better than his Umbrian stock. He wondered if those blue eyes would have suffered the peaceful aura of that enameled clasp a few years ago. Boar baiting, and dragon fighting were famous in Celt design, and he was sure a younger Rhetogenes would have gone that way in his jewelry.

"Until you reach these people, my emissaries to my kinsmen on *this* side of the Alps are at your disposal, Hannibal—to help against that Hydra head."

Hannibal had anticipated this offer with his own emissaries to the Boii, the Cenomani, the Anares, and the Insubres. But Rhetogenes could strengthen this recruitment. The Celt gossamers of intelligence seemed to be as intricate as his own. He would need favorable breaths from Cathbad, and all who knew about him and Hannibal, to make a proper army for Fabius' inspection...and beyond Fabius.

Rhetogenes had spread his hospitality to include Hannibal's foot and horse. Rehabilitation was still a priority for them, and the food, wine, even some harp and flute music that had gone into the camp from Rhetogenes, was manna. Synhalus had expressed some concern over the scarcity of his medicines to one of his host seat-mates at the banquet. Before Hannibal moved south from Ancona, Synhalus' medicine chests had been bolstered by remedies—mistletoe, selago, verbena, samolus—for everything from wound poultices to snake-bite and cattle disease. The lycopodium, whose smoke had been used to treat Hannibal's eye at Faesulae, had come from the Celts.

Hannibal accepted several more days of Rhetogenes' largesse and then decided that the imposition was enough. On the night before he left, a messenger delivered some more bounty from the sleek black belly of a lembos, anchored in the harbor at Ancona:

> Hannibal Barca,
> Your letter to me beat the official dispatches about your great victory—at some place called Trasimene—by several days. Perhaps I should hire myself out as an official courier. That wouldn't press on your precious prerogatives as commander—would it?

Kyniska is becoming a young lady very fast. She has tricked your mother into taking her everywhere on a horse. Now she wants her own. If I ever saw a butt that needs the attention of a daddy's hand, she has it!!

Medina and I are studying to be great ladies under the watchful eye of you know who. When you come home, we'll have it so that you'll never have to leave your pool to run the estates.

Medina and your mother told me not to mention your eye, the left I think. It is common knowledge around Carthage that the Romans call you the 'one-eyed devil'. Among some of the great armies of Asia Minor, such a general was held to be good luck, his acuities sharpened by what he might have thought was a handicap. This is the opinion held by everyone around <u>this</u> house...and I know that Kyniska can't wait to see what new monsters you can make for her...and me.

You said that your beacon toward Carthage is strong. I tell you that my beacon is just as strong and it points toward you...wherever you are.

Inanna Barca

When Hannibal turned his army south from Ancona, Rhetogenes rode a little way with him. This time he carried a Celt long sword, just for old time's sake, he said.

"Believe me, Rhetogenes, I would value you right here beside me."

But it was time for Rhetogenes to remember reality. When the horses stopped, he pulled his long sword and let it flash in the morning sun. Hannibal pulled his falcata and they rang steel without words. Then Rhetogenes whirled his horse, the long sword still in salute, and galloped back to his memories.

Picenum was a better cornucopia than Umbria. The Carthaginian corps took a wave of pillage and destruction south that specialized in the Roman farms and estates, another bonus for the trail Hannibal had designed for a tantalizing bride for a bashful dictator. The rehabilitation of his foot and horse started to be a moving exercise when they left Ancona. Old wine for the skin of his horses, and some of the best victuals they had had in Italy for his men, streamed into his supply train. Hannibal kept them going south, but Synhalus' orders for the restoration of men and horses were given priority over pace of travel. When the Numidian outriders reported that Arpi and Luceria were within two days march, Hannibal called a general staff meeting.

"We are getting close to the senior breadbasket of Rome, gentlemen—Apulia. I propose to settle down here for a little while. Synhalus has complained about my moving hospital, and wants a steadier ground for his ministrations." He turned toward Synhalus who was not a bashful Chief of Medicine. "You've damn near made drunks out of my horses, but the mange is disappearing and I see more shining coats every day."

"If we sit down for a while, they'll be ready to dance for you in a couple weeks, Commander."

"By Bacchus—who must be smiling on you, Synhalus—dancing horses didn't help the Sybarites. The Crotoni played music for them just before the ultimate battle and the Sybarites couldn't do a thing with their damn horses except throw garlands at them. Unfortunately the Crotoni used some sharper things."

"We are pointing toward where Sybaris used to be, Hannibal. Your story is apt, even if a little insulting." Synhalus had patted ointment on Hannibal's butt when he was nine years old, so he had some leeway in addressing his commander.

"Ah, *used to be*, a sad phrase, Synhalus. I would like to use it on the Romans, some day. Toward that end, gentlemen, when Synhalus gives us permission to travel, I propose usurping the vantage the Romans have made around Luceria. We will lose nothing in victuals and foraging. We will be close to communication points with Carthage on the Adriatic. We will also be able to put our fingers close enough to the Romans to feel any pulses of excitement that Fabius and Minucius can drag from their chicken guts and raven shit."

"Fabius may be stirring already, Hannibal. We hear that he has gone along the Tiber valley to meet your old friend Servilius."

"I never got the pleasure of Servilius in person, Barmocar. Maharbal catered a party for his horse after Trasimene that tended to discourage Servilius' further greetings." This was too modest. Maharbal's defeat of Servilius' horse after Trasimene had promoted the panic that swept through the gates of Rome right into the Senate chamber. Fabius' dictatorship, Minucius' Master of Horse, were partly beneficiaries of Maharbal's party with Servilius' horse.

"You will probably have to defer that pleasure for yet a while. Fabius has ordered him to take charge of the fleet at Sicily. It seems Carthage is not yet dead at sea—we've had a little success with Roman supply vessels."

"Admiral Bomilcar has my fervent good wishes. One contact with his supply line was frustrated near Pisae; I pray for better luck hereafter. There are resources in our arsenals at Carthage that I will be able to use."

"This is an inspirational meeting, Hannibal...what particular resources can you talk about?"

"The Celts will be bulwarks of our line. Their long swords put on a brave show, but the legions have become used to them, learned to counter them. The

Celt swordsmen can be trained to use a modification of the falcata that still gives them good sweep, but with cut and thrust potential for the close quarters that the Romans now dominate with them. I know men in the armories at Carthage who could put the Celt terror back in Roman eyes—given the advantage in height and strength. I will need Bomilcar's ships to bring it to us, so we can take it to the Romans."

"I hear that some Celt foot and horse have caught up with the leisurely pace our doctor has set for us." Barmocar turned to Carthalo, who happened to be the nearest officer.

"About fifteen hundred foot and two hundred horse...Rhetogenes' hospitality has a long arm."

"What size do you set for your corps, Hannibal...given the realities of our Carthage-Italy axis?" Myrcan had just put Hannibal on a spot. The balance between optimism and reality is a nice exercise for a commander, and he has to adjust it for his audience. He had to keep a close rein on the optimism for his present surround of listeners:

"I will take all the Africans, Carthaginians, and Iberians I can get—foot and horse. I will take all the Celts I can get, foot and horse. This attitude doesn't set a limit, Myrcan—my ability to feed them, does."

"There are realities tied to each of these wellsprings, Hannibal, do you have a favorite reality?"

"The Celts. So long as we have corridors to the Po, and the trans-Alpine Celts, I like the Celt reality best." He had just confessed a pessimism against the prayer that the sufet Bomilcar had promised Lady Barca—that the *Greek like* part of Carthage could be mustered on her son's behalf.

"Hence your good wishes for the connection between the armories at Carthage and Admiral Bomilcar."

"Precisely, Myrcan."

While Synhalus worked another of his marvels of rehabilitation of men and horses, Hannibal put his own senses into the reports that his scouts were bringing back from the edges of Apulia. Mago usually rode with him, often Carthalo and Maharbal, and always discreetly present, the leopard-skinned Numidian bodyguard that Maharbal had ordered for him at Ticinus.

The further south they rode, the more the land showed infinities of plain and gently curved ground in the panorama to the east, south-east. The Meseta of Iberia looked something like this, and he had bred cavalry there. But this land on the edge of Apulia stretched an imagination to greater possibilities for the fusion of horse and foot that he had dreamed and planned and partially made. He could gather Romans at propitious points in this country. The schedule was unknown. It would be made by him and the Romans. It would be inadvertent, a succession of accidents of action and inaction which paid the prepared better than the unprepared. From what his scouts and spies had told him about the country of Arpi and Luceria, ahead of him, he couldn't find a better place for preparation.

But it was an evening like some he and Mago had shared, looking toward Carthage from Hamilcar's ramparts at Nova Carthago, when Mago suddenly disabused his reverie of leisurely preparation in the superb parks of Luceria. They had finally broken the rest stop and were camped within five miles of Luceria. Hannibal was watching the sunset beyond the Appenines pull its colors from the sky over the eastern slopes and plains of Apulia. Mago approached the reverie that had been private for nearly an hour. He had come directly from a staff tent where an interview of scouts had just occurred.

"Fabius is on our right, at Accae, Hannibal."

"The old devil *has* moved—and close to us." Hannibal hadn't turned away from his perspective which had now gone to various precursors of a dark night. Accae had, in fact, been a place on his map he had touched with a finger two hours before. Mago's message put Fabius about fifteen miles away.

He turned to his brother. Mago still sneaked unofficial bits of the gypsy into his uniform and his unarmored splendor away from his horses. But this man would put a seasoned campaigner in front of Inanna, and she would see a few scars, and older eyes. He had been with Hannibal at the crucial parts of Ticinus and Trebbia. And at Trasimene, where Hannibal had to be a general atop Surus, Mago had commanded part of the cavalry assaults that had finally obliterated the legions' resolve.

"What force has he brought?" He had had good intelligence about Fabius' trek up the Tiber valley to meet Servilius' remnant army. And the subsequent reports about his travel along the Via Latina away from Rome indicated a leisurely pace dedicated to sniffing Hannibal from a safe distance. But the old boy had angled through Samnium, across the Appenines, and broken into Apulia, increasing his pace somewhere beyond Rome where Hannibal's surveillance evidently had become more permeable. Furthermore, his vectoring toward Arpi put him on an intersection path with Hannibal that had to make another compliment for Fabius' intelligence while Synhalus was making his stationary miracles—by Ba'al, there would be some review of the scouting disciplines!

"He has joined Servilius' corps with his own. We judge him at about Flaminius' strength at Trasimene, about thirty thousand foot, maybe up to two thousand horse."

"We will cut out a lot of that *about* and *maybe* very soon, Mago. Fabius has come right at us—and he sat down damn near where he can see us, watching our scouts running in circles."

"We are not as bad as that, brother. But we *have* done better—we *will* do better." When Hannibal punched Mago's shoulder, Mago's grimace was bad acting, but the grin afterwards was not.

For a week after Fabius had slipped up on him, Hannibal tested the Roman mettle with his Numidians, letting them dart close enough to the Roman outposts to decorate them with a few lances and jeers, just a few impertinent leopard and lion-skinned individuals at first. Then he swung echelons of them close enough to let the Romans feel their wind, but far enough to leave frustration in their wake. Fabius stayed put. He had the back of his legions against the hills where cavalry couldn't get at them. And he made no move forward that could change this situation. If he moved, he took the protection of the land contours with him. His only aggression was against Hannibal's foragers, and his counter raiding parties never exposed enough of him to tempt Hannibal to a major battle alignment.

"By their damn Jupiter—I've had enough of this." Hannibal was with Maharbal and Carthalo, staring at the Roman position through a morning whiteness that revealed nothing.

"I heard you tell Barmocar that Fabius might cuddle up to the word, *survival*. I think he's doing it now, Hannibal." Maharbal broke the three horse rank, rode a little way toward Fabius, and came back, facing Hannibal and Carthalo. "He can stick to these damn hills and nip at us until we have to go into winter camp." He swung his horse to face Fabius again. "We will need tastier bait to bring this old goat out."

"I think such bait might be farther south than we are now. The Romans have two places in Italy that they assimilate with paradise. They call them the Falernian Plain, and Compania Felix." He let a small smile drift toward Fabius. "I could be persuaded of this paradise, myself. Neapolis, with one of the best harbors in Italy, and closest to Carthage, is one of its jewels."

"And there is Capua hovering nearby, a facet of Etruscan economics and beauty you've already put into our schedule, Hannibal. I once heard Hamilcar complain that your curiosity was too big. I'm glad to hear that it remains unabated." Carthalo hadn't turned away from his stare at Fabius, nor did he need to. All of them had returned to that direction, a rank of three horsemen, devoted to study of the bashful dictator.

The next night, the fires in Hannibal's camp were bright and conspicuous from Fabius' perspective. They showed a well entrenched Carthaginian, determined to solve the riddle of the dictator who had been designed to scare him. And in the dawn of the morning after, six thousand of Hannibal's horse made a close pass of Fabius' camp before their sweep northward toward Arpi pulled Fabius after them. When Fabius discovered that he had no chance to catch the wakeup cavalry, or even to monitor its course, the rest of Hannibal's corps and train was already better than half a day's march south of Fabius' original position, having slipped out during the night that Fabius had admired Hannibal's resolute campfires.

Hannibal followed much the same course that Fabius had used to get to Accae. He passed the Roman fortified Beneventum, leaving a big souvenir of foraging in the vicinity. Then he went past Calor and captured Telesia, gathering a rich harvest of booty and supplies. He crossed the Vulturnus River near Allifae, and descended by way of Cales into the Falernian Plain. He had touched part of the Roman paradise.

This time a rank of four horsemen, Hannibal, Mago, Maharbal, Carthalo, made an assessment of position:

"The scouts have picked out a good campsite for us, Hannibal—on our side of the Vulturnus, near Casilinum."

"I hope they are not the same ones who were watching Fabius creep toward us between Rome and Apulia." Mago ignored the insult. He had accepted some responsibility for the quality of the intelligence that was supposed to swarm around the commander. He had chewed some asses for the lapse his brother had just remembered, and Hannibal knew it, but keeping some prod on Mago had ancient precedence.

"I believe your Campania Felix part of paradise is close to that camp." Maharbal anticipated Hannibal's next statement, but he was discreet in licking his lips.

"Your fame as a ravager of Roman resources has reached Rome, Maharbal. Now, you're on the verge of immortality with the Falernian Plain and Campania Felix laid out for you."

"I have done some small good in that respect, Hannibal. Do I have a little part of Maharbal's license for fun?"

"I will need you close at hand, Carthalo. Maharbal may finally get his 'old goat' off Mt. Massicus where he has settled down for a while." Fabius had followed them at several days' interval. He had waded through the souvenirs Hannibal had left along the trail. When Hannibal turned toward Casilinum, Fabius settled down on the slopes of Mt. Massicus near Sinuessa. This position gave him the illusion of a bulwark between Rome and conceivable paths Hannibal might take to Rome.

While Hannibal watched Fabius watching him at his new camp, Maharbal took his Numidians and some heavy horse on a sweep of pillage and imaginative destruction of Roman assets that went as far as Sinuessa, deep into the Falernian Plain. They also put their ministrations into the country just below Fabius' camp. Maharbal had bonfires made of marginal booty whose black smoke drifted into Fabius' nostrils. Minucius and his staff, and most of Fabius' staff, used every curse in their repertoire while restlessly watching the taunts that Fabius resisted—not all of this response aimed at Hannibal.

Hannibal proved that he could roam at will in the richest precincts of Roman authority, under the nose of the dictator chosen to destroy him. The allies in Campania were quickly aware of these facts, including Capua, the Campanian facet that had already glittered in Hannibal's councils. He made repeated displays of various combinations of his strength in front of Fabius, but Fabius wouldn't bite. He had brought his attitude of passive harassment down from Apulia.

After a raid, Maharbal had to have a conference. His operations had brought almost 3000 fat cattle into the Carthaginian fold. While improving the menus of his camp, this particular bounty was not pure manna.

"We are getting too fat, Hannibal. Moving this big belly around could be a problem if Fabius finally decides to get playful." Maharbal had been gone for three days. He was not quite current.

"I've heard that he has moved eastward a little, toward us. Also he has sent Minucius to garrison the pass on the Via Appia near Terracina. The bastion of allied loyalty at Teanum already seems to be a roadblock on the Via Latina. I think, my friend, they are trying to tell us not to use the big highways to Rome."

"That's damn inhospitable of them Hannibal—considering all your offers to play."

Maharbal was about to leave, when Mago made it three horsemen again.

"They've put more people into their garrison at Casilinum." Casilinum was the site of the only bridge across the lower Vulturnus. It was a good gateway to the Campania Felix that promised another trove of riches for Maharbal's attention. Also it was a good escape route for a fat belly headed for southern Campania, and Lucania beyond, with Romans nipping at it.

"I think our 'old goat' is smarter than we thought, Mago. He's nudged his corps closer to where we came in. He's daring us to try a direction toward Rome. We've got the ocean in front of us and now he's making obscene gestures at us from the only bridge into the south at Casilinum. I think it may be time to leave—we won't stay where we're not wanted."

"I think Fabius wants a moving target he can nip. He would like to repay your lesson at Trasimene if he can push us into the right ground for it."

"Perhaps we can give him some, Mago, but let me choose where to deliver this present."

Hannibal ordered a withdrawal toward Cales, a direction that could tend him toward Rome and allow several escape routes to the north, including the one he had used to enter Campania through Allifae. Fabius followed him, keeping his back pressed tight to the life-saving contours to the west and north of Hannibal's track. When Hannibal stopped, Fabius stopped, and he happened to be near Teanum, and the Via Appia. To discourage the notion that he was considering leaving over the pass he'd used for coming, Hannibal had his Numidians make provocative demonstrations in front of Fabius' position—perhaps an overture to an African parade along the sacred Via Appia?

This time Fabius took a little bite of the bait. When the Numidians swept back toward Hannibal, Fabius ordered 400 horse under Hostilius Mancinus to reconnoiter Hannibal's intentions. They rode into an ambush set by Carthalo and his heavy horse. The entire Roman detachment was destroyed, and Mancinus killed.

But Fabius followed his hunch about Hannibal. He moved his corps cautiously closer to the pass to Allifae, stopping close enough to be able to attack the Carthaginian when he got his fat belly well fitted into the crease in the mountains. He put 4000 men on the pass to back up his hunch, scattering them around both slopes .He would welcome a master of surprise before he smashed his main corps into the rear of the Carthaginian snake as it tried to wriggle toward Allifae.

When it was obvious that he and the Roman were now looking at the same parade route out of Campania, Hannibal improved his reconnaissance of Fabius and was soon informed that there were Romans sprinkled on both sides of the approaches to the pass. Between Fabius' position and the pass, there was a saddle of bare land leading to a forested top which blended with the land on the left side of the pass. This saddle had prospects for changing some of Fabius' itinerary for the parade.

After he had maneuvered into position below the pass, Hannibal ordered his men to eat and rest. About 3AM he ordered his stockmen to select 2000 of the strongest beefs, tie bundles of dry wood and pine-pitched sticks to their horns, and then start to drive them over the saddle after lighting the bundles. The light and pain-crazed beasts stormed up the saddle, streaming into the wooded area. He sent 1000 spearmen to back up the stockmen on the saddle. The troops Fabius had sent into the pass interpreted the action as a flanking of their position by Hannibal's main force, and they rushed toward the saddle. When this flow was well established, Hannibal ordered his corps to advance into the pass—Africans, then cavalry, the rest of his baggage and booty train, the Iberians and then the Celt foot was the principal form he slipped into the pass under Fabius' nose that was now occupied with a flaming, howling phenomenon closer to him.

The Roman stragglers in the pass were quickly swept away by the slingers and light spearmen Hannibal had put ahead of his African van. When his column had advanced several miles, he sent Iberian foot back to relieve the spearmen on the saddle. About a 1000 Romans were killed in the process of bringing loose ends back to him, including some good Campanian beef on the hoof that Fabius wouldn't get.

He made his first camp at Allifae, and then went up the valley of the Vulturnus to Venafrum. This was tending him in the direction of Rome, which gave Fabius' cautious trailing routine, his usual two days behind, some extra incentive he probably hoped he wouldn't be called on to use. After this one more tweak of Fabius' nose, Hannibal veered away from Rome toward the northern route to Apulia through Aesernia and Bovianum.

His scouts, now in better graces, told him that the town of Geronium, about twenty miles from Luceria was well stocked with booty and supplies. This was a good objective. It was close to country that could brighten a cavalryman's eyes, it was ground where foot and horse could be refreshed and polished. On his first pass through Apulia, he could feel opportunities there for large scale confrontation with the Roman that Campania, however seductive, hadn't shown him. It was the middle of September, time to fix a winter camp.

Geronium was a Roman-allied, Italian town. Hannibal made a personal embassy to it, offering his protection for them to pursue an independence from Roman authority. He had given the allies his usual message—Rome was his target, not them. He had sent his allied prisoners home, usually with something to ease their passage, or help them start another life away from the legions. To say, and do, these things a man had to have a presence on the Roman ground. They knew that he had won the right to go where he wanted in Italy—Ticinus, Trebbia, Trasimene, were no secrets in this part of Italy. He had just come from wallowing in the Campanian treasure chest of the Romans and part of this escapade had already seeped into Geronium. The destruction of the trap the dictator had designed for the culmination of Hannibal in Italy had not. But the Carthaginian's presence on their doorstep worked against the whispers that, in the south, Fabius planned to swallow him.

Geronium rejected him. They refused to open their gates to him, or to cooperate with any part of his wintering in their area. Fabius had ordered a scorched-earth policy, a retreat into fortified enclaves for the people and supplies that might be affected by the Carthaginian. He had also sent his agents into every allied citadel and town with the message that any allied cooperation with Hannibal would be countered by reprisals on the offending people, especially on the appropriate men and boys who were now serving in the Roman army in Italy, and abroad. The Roman intention to destroy their sons and husbands made it easier to look at the swords and lances of the Carthaginian, and say no.

Hannibal attacked the town, captured it, rounded up the surviving inhabitants and killed them. The buildings that could serve for his warehouses and granaries, he saved. The others he destroyed. Then he ordered a fortified camp outside the town.

The evening of the day that he had ordered the execution of the Geronium survivors, two men approached the command tent, and were nodded forward by the guard who tried a Spartan salute on the tallest of the visitors. Hannibal was sitting at a table, staring at a map.

Silenus was carrying two scrolls. Sosylos carried a wicker covered bottle. Hannibal didn't look up, but he was aware of a specific Greek presence in his tent. The Spartan and the Iberian Greek were now standing at attention, although their baggage was civilian, and a man could have pried a nonmilitary face out of either of them, easily.

"By your damn Jupiter, sit down." A map detail held him for a moment, and then he swept a look toward them—Silenus' face and then the scrolls, Sosylos' face and then the wicker bottle. He was still in his field uniform, and his face, despite his orderly's entreaties, had made no transition from the field to the relaxed sybarite he deserved. These two could pull a smile out of him if anyone could. But it looked like a hard time ahead for this after they obeyed the sitting order. They couldn't jump right into his mood, he had to show some of the map of *him* to start them now.

Since Faesulae, they had been careful about the provocations that had been a didactic tool for them in the past to get into Hannibal's head. The left eye business had posed a dilemma for these two who had licenses from Hamilcar and the Lady Barca to help their son become a man, with inevitable Greek bias. Except for the chronicle, he had almost outgrown them...and then he lost half of his physical perspective, and they had been there for him when Inanna, and his senior lady, could not. Now no one challenged their continuity. Then, with little of their intervention, he had shown them what a man, a commander, could do in this case.

"What's in that wicker, Sosylos?"

"Wine, Hannibal."

"I *have* wine."

"Not as good as this. A scout brought it from Capua during one of the publicity sweeps you ordered for that Etruscan citadel of debauchery. I need three glasses." Hannibal waved toward a corner of the tent, the comfort zone near his cot.

Sosylos poured, and there was more silence. Then he poured three rounds again, the tent still swarming with silence. Hannibal had just accomplished a virtuosity of provocation of the Roman, a miracle of escape, and now a triumph at a key point of Apulia. This was basis for more talk, even laughter, than was occurring under Sosylos' colorful prompting.

One of Silenus' scrolls finally slipped away from him during the drinking. When he picked it up, he didn't look at Hannibal, but Hannibal's next words revealed interest.

"What's in *that* scroll?"

"Campania—what I can remember. The flaming oxen bouquet you gave to Fabius needs more work in particular."

"The second scroll?"

"It's ready for Apulia, Lord Hannibal."

"I haven't done anything yet except kill fifty Italians I hoped to count as allies." That took Hannibal back to the map again. He had killed civilians at Saguntum after monumental amelioration tries. But that was an age ago, when seducing Italian allies to degrade the Roman Federation, was part of theoretical strategy—not an arrow stuck in his present face.

"You have offered friendship to these people since you entered Italy. Your plans for their improvement have been conspicuous in the summations of all your battles here—your entreaty to Geronium was reasonable and merciful."

"Fabius' was apparently more forceful, Sosylos. His damn agents have preceded us at every town and citadel." Hannibal was still facing his map. "Independence doesn't weigh as much as a Roman scourge on your son's back. I can see their dilemma—I will kill no more allied civilians unless there is sabotage or violence against my men."

"Fabius veered away from the Roman presence near Venafrum, toward Larinum. Incautious Minucius is also tending toward Larinum. Should I unroll the Apulia scroll, Hannibal?" That turned Silenus' subject toward him, away from an unpleasant summation.

"Fabius should be catching some arrows from the Senate about now. He couldn't deliver my head in Campania, so his banner of a sniffing puppy is unraveling in front of Romans who prefer a braver icon...I think we can help to hurry Fabius into retirement again."

Silenus playfully started to unroll a bit of his Apulia scroll. He posed his writing hand over it, daring Hannibal to start a smile, and something he could write.

"Fabius is a big landowner in Apulia. I would like to protect a few of his more conspicuous estates."

"By Ba'al, Hannibal, you're imputing *conspiracy* to this dictator—with the *detestable* Carthaginian?"

"It should put another fagot on his back, Sosylos, to light the Senate chamber in case the oxen didn't bring enough." A Hannibal smile, grin, was there now. The visitors had accomplished their mission, but Hannibal had left a loose end for Silenus:

"Why does the prospect of a deluge of Romans make you smile, when some actual triumphs couldn't?" A chronicler would ask a question like that.

"Now you have me talking about killing Romans, instead of allies, Silenus. We will need to bring that Hydra head into *our* battleground. Campania is no place for that, but Apulia *is*. The sooner Maharbal's 'old goat' is gone to graceful retirement, the sooner we can get on with this. He has studied Carthage in the school of the First War. We have displayed some resolve for him. But he is looking over our shoulder at Carthage. Time is his asset—I think he feels that it is not one of ours." He was walking around now. The self-incrimination of his recent allies' perspective was not in this voice.

"That you should see a lack of resolve when looking toward Carthage makes me sorry I brought the wine into this tent, Hannibal."

"I would rather anticipate it *now*, Sosylos, than discover it while running into a sea empty of Carthage. We will try to kill as much of the Hydra head as we can—and we will also study how to make *resolve* flow toward us."

"Not necessarily from Carthage?"

"Precisely, Sosylos. You were obviously standing too close to me while I talked to Cathbad."

16

31 years
Winter 217/216 BC—Geronium

"Fabius' embarrassment in the Senate has pushed some resolve into Minucius. He's creeping up on us, Hannibal."

Maharbal and Carthalo were bracketing the commander while they watched the spectacle of the consular army moving away from the protection of the hills onto the braver platform of the plains in front of the Carthaginians. The absent dictator had left orders that should have kept his passive watch of Hannibal in place. But Hannibal's escape from Campania had left Fabius covered in soot from flaming ox shit. Hannibal's exemption of Fabius' estates in Apulia from his foraging sweeps, the still insolent Carthaginian power that roved at will in all the Roman cornucopias, was seething in the Senate despite Fabius' ministrations to Roman enterprise against Hannibal since Trasimene that had earned his *Delayer* title.

Leaving a garrison at Geronium to protect his stores, Hannibal had moved south from Geronium as soon as Minucius started to stir under the inspiring news of Fabius' official embarrassment. He would watch this Roman, while continuing foraging for his winter headquarters at Geronium. Until the spring harvests and grazing grounds opened to him, thirty-five thousand men, eight thousand horse, several thousand beef, needed more to sustain them than he had brought into Geronium from the Roman treasure chests in Campania.

"Put a thousand light foot and a thousand Numidians on that hill between us and Minucius. Tell them to be conspicuous about it and to act like a lot more of them."

"You will make him think you are matching his famous resolve, getting ready to pounce, Commander?"

"I will not interrupt the foraging for Minucius. If a little line on the ground in front of him can delay him for a few days, we will gain another month of supplies."

Hannibal had put almost two thirds of his force on foraging duty. They were now spread over fifty square miles of Apulian husbandry. This had been a gamble on Minucius' precocity. Rumors that Fabius' discomfort before the Senate had matured to the ignominy of his Master of Horse, Minucius, being promoted above him had certainly reached Minucius. But Hannibal had made the big bet that Minucius' ties to Fabius' apron strings were strong enough to override unconfirmed flushes of glory.

The day after the noisy detachment on the hill was in place, Minucius crossed Hannibal's line and attacked this position with light foot and horse, killing, capturing or dispersing it. Seeing that Hannibal had not made a major commitment to him, Minucius sent his cavalry to harass the Carthaginian foragers and herdsmen. Hannibal's at-home corps was not strong enough to come to their aid and several thousand of these men were killed, or captured. Minucius led his foot in an attack on Hannibal's temporary observation camp, and it was a near thing at those barricades before Hasdrubal, a cavalry officer, brought a relief force from Geronium to enable Hannibal to push Minucius back to the plain.

At the end of that day, the summation for Hannibal was the first poor one he'd had in Italy. He had allowed himself to be drawn into a skirmishing situation that favored the Roman. He had lost several thousand foragers and herdsmen, a thousand foot and horse. Minucius had reported a sweet little triumph to Rome and this put another fagot on Fabius' back. Maharbal and the rest of the heart of his army had stuffed more into the Geronium warehouses and granaries in partial compensation. But he had misjudged the capacity of a man to grow under inspiration and had Minucius grown a little more, enough to send his full force against the Carthaginan supply depot at Geronium instead of ringing steel with Hannibal on the slopes of the Carthaginian hill, the winter situation for Hannibal could have been desperate. All of his staring at the maps, his resolutions, had been turned close to farce by the incarnation of a commander in Minucius, and a gamble against this incarnation.

When Fabius returned to Apulia, he had orders to split the command with his Master of Horse, an unprecedented insult to a dictator. He offered Minucius two alternatives: command on alternate days or take half of the army under his full-time command. Minucius chose the independent role, and moved his half of the army several miles away from Fabius, closer to Hannibal.

"My mistake of underestimating Minucius might have just born some costly fruit."

"Your foraging had justifiable priority, Hannibal. And now you've got his blood up—and he's left Fabius' nest." The triad of mounted officers was looking toward an invigorated Minucius, who had just put another hill between himself and Hannibal. Hannibal swung his black Iberian away from Maharbal and Carthalo and rode toward the Roman. After some private conference, he came back, facing his cavalry commanders.

"Minucius has done us the favor of putting another hill between us. We will occupy it in almost full force—noisily as the last time."

"*Almost*, Hannibal?"

"When the time and light are propitious, put five thousand light foot and five hundred Numidians into concealment on his flanks and rear. There are hiding places enough to make a little surprise for our impetuous new leader." He had scrolled the map of this country into his head as they marched toward Geronium from Campania. Ambush and rolling hill topography are close friends.

"May I use Mago for part of this surprise?"

"He would be insulted otherwise, Maharbal. Put a little history into this Roman."

"Trebbia?"

"Precisely, Carthalo."

When Hannibal's ostentatious occupation of the hill was well along, Minucius started to assault the hill with light foot, followed by horse. Hannibal kept throwing enough support into the front lines to thwart the Roman, feed his frustration. Minucius finally drew his full corps into battle array and ordered it to advance on the hill, a screen of light foot, velites, in the van.

Hannibal committed his own heavy troops and soon had the Roman velites fleeing down the slopes toward the legions, then into the legion arrays. This confusion was shortly corrected by the Roman discipline and the legions continued their advance to the hill.

Hannibal's signal horns cut through the sound of beginning battle, and his troops in ambush on Minucius' flanks and rear entered the action. He coordinated this ambush with full scale assault by his front line foot and horse, with the result of panic in the Roman corps.

Minucius' army was being destroyed on four fronts when Fabius finally reached the scene with his own army. He succeeded in restoring some order to Minucius' remnants, and then he drew up his force in line of battle for Hannibal's approval.

A rank of Carthaginian officers inspected Fabius' audacity from the hill that Minucius had been unable to add to his laurels:

"By fair Tanit, gentlemen, didn't I tell you that one day the thunder that has stalked us since Fabius first looked at us would one day roll down the mountains upon us!"

"It's a fine array, Hannibal. What do you want to do about it?" Maharbal's smile was not the reaction Fabius had designed into his aggressive debut. And going down the line of Hannibal's officers, Fabius wouldn't have found enough respect to build half of a single man's Roman salute.

"We are scattered over the country from chasing Minucius' remnants. I think we will refuse Fabius' gracious invitation."

"I am certain he will thank you—if he can find a deep enough privacy, Hannibal."

So, Fabius finally made a bow to aggression. Minucius was back in the single camp as a compliant subordinate. And Hannibal took the initiative of falling back to winter quarters—he at Geronium, Fabius near Larinum.

During the last two months of the year, Celt foot and horse had drifted into the Carthaginian camp from Celt sources and Celt commanders Hannibal had rubbed against while coming to where he now stood in Apulia: Auros of the Volcae, Thyresius of the Insubre, Leukon of the Boii, Rhetogenes of the Senones—all of this comradeship touched by a Druid's aura that had pulled Celt frustration and pride and ambition into the present moment of another commander, who was not a Celt.

"I want a few long swords left in your hands, Caros. The Romans expect them, they have become arrogant against them." Hannibal was in the middle of an aggregation of Celts and Iberians who were testing ways to mix their fighting techniques in a battle line. The Celt captain he had just addressed wasn't smiling.

"My people like the new Carthaginian sword." He held one. He brought the blade toward horizontal and then flexed it in parry modes.

Bomilcar had finally got a supply ship into the Picenium coast with five thousand like the one in Caros' hand. It was longer than the falcata.The blade was heavier, less curved to bring it closer to the domain of the thrust, but the falcata hilt with the recurved guard was there to remind that it hadn't left the slash domain. It was a superb weapon for a big man, a Celt, who would learn thrust and slash, instead of slash and slash—and often death against a smaller thruster who could get under his arc of terror. The blade outranged the legionaire's gladius by about a foot. But it was the surprise of putting Celts who could thrust *and* slash, together with Iberians who had made their falcata a terror of the Romans that Hannibal wanted. And to compound it for the Roman, he had just insisted that he wanted some of the traditional long swords to play alongside the falcatas and the new *Carthaginian* swords.

Hannibal stepped closer to a Celt who was practicing with the new sword against a straw man, one of hundreds set up for the sword exercises that had been unrelenting since Bomilcar's delivery of the goods from the arsenals at Carthage. The iron for them had come from connections through the Aegean with the Celt smelting masters of middle Europe. This iron was the best basis for steel in the western world. And the Carthaginian metallurgists forged, case hardened and tempered it so that, attached to a Celt arm, it would push more surprise into the Romans facing it. Hannibal's sketches had preceded the weapon, and memories of him and Hasdrubal moving their swordplay from history to research and design, their shouts and laughter replicating in the vaults of the armories under Carthage's walls, were fused with these weapons.

"Thrust man! Thrust! You have a weapon for it now." He pulled his own falcata and gave a thrusting demonstration from frontal and side-stepped positions. He stepped back. The Celt swordsman smiled at him and then, just a quick touch of his blade to his forehead, he showed that he had watched the commander. Hannibal slapped the Celt's back and walked on down the practice line with Caros.

"By your Taranis, Caros, you will have swordsmen yet." He watched other officers and sergeants working with mixed groups of Iberians and Celts, trying to coordinate new and old styles of sword handling, accustoming the men to different uniforms and shouts and curses alongside them.

"The Romans like to establish a rhythm. The shield banging, the steady march, the pilum throw and then into the opposition with a killing rhythm demoralizes good men and feeds the Roman purpose. We will never let them into that rhythm. We will make them improvise on a man to man basis. We will give them a varied opposition of thrust and slash that will suck them into *our* purposes."

Mago and Carthalo caught up with Hannibal while he and Caros were watching the maneuvers of a five hundred foot line of four ranks of Iberians and Celts.

"You're going away from straight lines again, brother." At Nova Carthago, Mago had seen Hannibal make curves from straight lines with formations like this. The curve that had just developed from the horn signals was promising. The Celt and Iberian mix was random, but the earlier tries with such a mix had had more chaos and less beauty.

"Myrcan and Barmocar keep putting more Romans against us. We may have to find ways to make forty thousand act like a hundred thousand...curves might be seductive here, little brother." Hannibal turned back toward the total practice field that held about twenty thousand of his men. He had them trying ranks of four, five, even the eight of the Greek hoplite phalanx, to test how the complication of maneuvering and force presentation was affected by the depth of the line. He was tending to the four rank disposition, for the reason of curves he had just given Mago.

"Caros thinks we are putting too much faith in Celt diplomacy using a random mix of his people with our Iberians." Actually, Hannibal had been amazed that his Iberian-Celt cake mix had not exploded, but there were Iberians in his ranks who now called themselves, Celtiberians.

"This dose of intimacy might be a prelude to something more palatable for you, Caros." Carthalo's look at Caros made a short detour to Hannibal. Hannibal had already told him and Maharbal that separation of these reluctant lovers into companies was a probable step after they had become better students of each other's style and personality. He had made a further projection of his strategy by saying that a line of alternate companies of Celts and Iberians, now good friends, would beat a better rhythm against the Roman line than a soup of individual heroes.

They watched Celts and Iberians watching long swords. The arcs of this traditional Celt weapon had to be coordinated with the thrust and slash devices of the falcata and the new Carthaginian sword. The Celt heavy and light foot were being assimilated into *Hannibal's* corps, their strength and courage unfettered, just a little less panache.

"Do you think your long sword men can tolerate the falcata and the new sword alongside them, Caros?

"If they were given new target opportunities—this breaking up the Roman rhythm you talk about, Hannibal—I think so. But although we love the Iberians, I think seeing a Celt's hand on the other weapons would put more comfort into that situation."

"I have killed several thousand of your people on the center of my front line." Hannibal was looking at a particularly vigorous coordination of a long sword's arc with a thrusting *new* sword. "I am obviously not encouraging shyness from your people now. I will continue to offer you this crucial situation on my battlefields."

"I heard that the Boii and the Insubres have told you that every honor has its price—that it is not your responsibility to worry about this particular one—I would like to reply to you in the same way, Lord Hannibal."

"The armor that the Romans have generously donated to us at Trebbia and Trasimene will be shared by your people and the Africans. This, and the techniques we are now practicing, should help you." Over five thousand Celts were striving to assimilate with him on the field in front of him. Another fifteen thousand, foot and horse, were in the same process at other times. His gossamers had picked up more Celts coming his way from the Po and, nudged by some of Cathbad's whispers, from Gaul. "I pray to the gods under our joint roof of the heavens that I will be worthy of the Celt honors, Caros." He had basis for this prayer, and for extending it a little beyond Caros, toward Cathbad.

"Fabius has agreed to the prisoner exchange, Hannibal, three hundred denari per man. This should work a little in our favor."

"Not so much after Minucius played the soldier for us, Maharbal."

"You must have exorcised *that* demon. Minucius has been a quiet mouse since your last lesson."

"He surprised me. He came too close to a great embarrassment for me. I can't afford the luxury of forgetting it. When and where does the dictator want to make the exchange?"

"He has designated a place roughly between us—level ground with no ambush opportunity, according to his analysis. You may see opportunity that has escaped him, I would bet on it, Commander."

"I have tweaked the old boy enough. His term is nearly done."

"The end of December, I think."

"Then I want a quiet exchange."

"If you want it, he will give it. I'm sure he has the same aspiration."

Fabius had come up short by 247 men—Hannibal had returned 247 more Romans than Fabius' return of Carthaginian foot and cavalrymen. Fabius' debt to Hannibal was, therefore, 74,000 denari, about 13 talents.

Fabius applied to the Senate for payment. The Senate's rejection of the claim was colored by accusations of collaboration with Hannibal, and a review of Fabius' passive tactics which had culminated in monumental embarrassment to the Roman eagle. This was unjustified, considering Fabius had played savior to Minucius, a darling of the Roman war horses, whose luster as the manager of the only success over Hannibal since he had crossed the Alps had not diminished, however minuscule the victory over a peripheral and preoccupied Hannibal.

Fabius sold one of his largest estates in Apulia to pay the debt. This happened to be one of the estates Hannibal had designated as holy ground during the apex of his foraging. The pristine state of this property brought more than the arrears for the prisoner exchange.

Fabius was now ready for a meeting with Hannibal to make payment. Maharbal found Hannibal deep in the practice field, as usual.

"Where?"

"The same place, Hannibal. There is a small grove nearby that would give you and Fabius a little shade...in case there is a tendency to conversation."

"When?"

"In two days. High sun."

"Entourage?"

"Fabius made no specification on that. We will watch *his* entourage early enough to make a proper one for you."

In two days, two hours before the meeting, a Numidian captain made his report on entourage:

"Fabius has started toward the meeting place, Commander. He has two legates and two tribunes, twenty-four horse, and a two horse cart probably bearing his arrears. We went behind him for five miles and could see no surprises."

"No lictors?" This captain had some reputation for precocity and Hannibal had to make a smile on the man he'd addressed.

"The Dictator seems to have taken pains to make a low profile here, Commander—no lictors."

"Then my inevitable leopard Numidians will suffice for him. See that they are polished up more than usual." Hannibal had seen the gleaming teeth under an ebony smile before. The captain saluted and wheeled away.

Maharbal had insisted on a bigger escort, so Hannibal's usual shadow of ten leopards had been puffed up by ten more. When he went to meet Fabius, he also took Maharbal, Carthalo, and Mago as part of *his* aura. Except for Hamilcar's dagger, he was unarmed, no helmet, but he wore his steel muscular cuirass under a white cloak. He would project a reasonably cooperative man to the dictator. His grooms had put some extra touches of silver into the harness of his glistening black Iberian. His officers were not quite so cooperatively biased, to the extent of plumed helmets, full body armor and swords. His Numidians carried their usual compliment of weapons: four javelins and the short sword and dagger, extra sparkle here and there.

Fabius was waiting at the designated place when Hannibal's party rounded a small rise about a quarter mile away.

"He is standing in the sun, Hannibal. Apparently he is putting that conversation tendency in your lap."

Hannibal took the lead and rode to within twenty yards of Fabius, who was sitting his horse about ten paces in front of a formation pointed by two legates, then the tribunes, then his horse escort arrayed in a 4-8-12 echelon, separated down the middle to bracket the treasure cart. This cart appeared to be a stout affair used for baggage trains, minimal embellishment. The two grays drawing it seemed to copy the attention stance of the horses around them.

Hannibal saluted Fabius. It was returned. Fabius was entitled to wear a purple mantle over a tunic, or armor of his choice, sitting a richly caparisoned horse. But his horse and most accoutrements were suitable to a cavalry commander, and Hannibal appreciated this possible bow to him. The purple mantle was there over what appeared to be a simple tunic, and red calceus boots. He was bare-headed, like Hannibal. He was about five years older than Hamilcar would have been.

Hannibal rode to within twenty feet of the dictator, close enough to test the conversation tendency.

"I don't deserve this honor, Fabius." Hannibal's Greek was much better than his Latin, and he hoped Fabius would take the hint.

"No you don't." Fabius had taken the hint.

By Ba'al this old man had a luxurious top of hair: white, imperial. But it probably could lend to any official, or unofficial, byway Hannibal wanted to take. Fabius' first remark confirmed part of this. They both knew why Hannibal didn't deserve this personal attention, but they left it a tacit thing, their eye ligaments private to them.

"I apologize for the delay in my arrears. I had some complication."

"I've heard a little about this complication. Once again, I will claim you spoil me with honor." *Had there been precedence for a Roman dictator selling his belongings to pay a mortal enemy, under no more duress than conscience?*

Fabius made a slight signal with his hand and the cart was drawn to the front of the cavalry and then between the tribunes and the legates to stop about 20 feet abreast of Fabius. He nodded toward it.

"There is gold and silver in the amount of the arrears. Again, I apologize for the delay."

"Your apology is absolutely redundant, Fabius."

Gaius Publius had described Hannibal. There was similarity with Hamilcar, another Carthaginian Fabius had met briefly during another prisoner exchange in Sicily an infinity ago...these Barcas at about the same ages. But this one in front of him had trampled *Italian* ground from the Alps to below Rome, and he had teased, challenged, insulted and instructed him and the best that Rome could throw at him. Now he was *here*, without arrogance, giving a considerate appraisal of a dictator's embarrassment and restitution.

Fabius had earned his title of Cunctator—Delayer—and he might have gained some breath for Rome. But he remembered Gaius Publius' hands at his ears taking thunder from the north down into the forum, and unless the gods could put their own delays on this Carthaginian, Dictator Fabius Maximus would have counted for no more than the pebbles now rolling under his horse's feet. *He looks young. Gaius said that he couldn't intimidate him—a younger version of the seasoned commander in front of him. He started the little joke between us in front of the arrears wagon. He is said to be unbashful around laughter. By Jupiter's curse on me, I could like him...I would like to talk longer with him than we will do in the moments in front of us.*

"I invite you to the shade for more comfortable continuation, Fabius."

The oak grove Maharbal had mentioned was about a hundred paces away. Fabius nodded and he and Hannibal turned their mounts toward it at the same time. Hannibal started to give precedence to Fabius, but the Roman insisted on equal positions.

"I'm about to fade into history,—in about three weeks to be precise." They had reached the perimeter of the shade. They made a few more paces penetration of it, then Fabius stopped.

"Your chronicle will be an honorable, complex, one, Fabius. I would give you my Greek shadow, Silenus, to help you write it, but I need him for mine."

They were facing each other now, horses almost nose to nose, a comfortable talking separation.

"I must return that compliment, Lord Hannibal. Carthage has never had more to honor, and my complexities will pale beside yours."

Fabius dabbed a bit of white linen across his chin and forehead. Hannibal took this lead himself. It was hot. It was probably close to another unprecedented situation—they had been trying to kill each other for months.

Hannibal glanced toward the two formations, his and Fabius', which had not moved a hair since the commanders took their leave.

"I wonder if they think we are arguing about *who* will surrender to *whom*?"

"That is a question the Senate has been debating for some time. It has helped to hurry my official decrepitude. They had us down as *collaborators*." The dictator looked away from Hannibal, toward a sector that probably included Rome, not the one that had an unembellished wagon holding silver and gold. "If I had to have a collaborator—if the gods had given us more common purpose—I couldn't have wanted a better one." Then he came back to the younger man. "But this confession will never go beyond this grove, Hannibal Barca."

"That may be the best honor I'll ever get, Fabius Maximus. Unfortunately I also have to bury it here. But I have a long memory—I will caress it from time to time, privately."

"The complexion of the Senate and the commanders who will try to catch you are changing." Fabius reined his horse to a parallel position with Hannibal's. They were as close now as they would ever be. "I have given you a cautious old man to play with."

"The counting of the score between us will go on long after Rome is deprived of your service, Fabius."

"That may be. But you have made yourself the anvil on which a new Rome will be forged—or broken. You have set the beat for this yourself. And the men stirring behind me have started to pick this up." The dictator's purple mantle swirled as he took the initiative to return to what was left of his term. Hannibal's response still left a talking distance between them.

"I think I will also put Carthage on your anvil, Fabius Maximus."

When Fabius turned to him for the last time, he saw Hannibal's salute, and the smile that Gaius Publius had tried to analyze for himself at Carthago Nova, and then for Fabius on the porch of Heracles' precincts at Rome—tens of thousands of Romans ago.

At the end of December, Fabius' purple cloak was no longer authorized, and Minucius followed his leader down the steps from dictatorship to lesser panoramas of glory. Their armies were assumed by Marcus Atilius Regulus and Gnaeus Servilius. Servilius was the survivor of the co-consulship with Flaminius which had bled out at Trasimene. He had managed to avoid Hannibal since that time, hence was still alive and had recently enjoyed some success against Carthaginian ships near Sicily. Regulus was the son of the Regulus who had been defeated by the Spartan mercenary, Xanthippus, near Carthage in the First Punic War. The interim consuls were enjoined by the Senate to take no initiative against Hannibal. Thus, depressing precedents residing in these men were put on a short leash until Rome could construct a larger inspiration against the Carthaginian who seemed to be committed to wintering, and practicing war, around Geronium.

This inspiration started to progress from grumbling about Fabius' passivity to designs for aggression as soon as Fabius had lost his official force. And it was fed by the news from Iberia, where the Scipios, Cornelius and Gnaeus, had restored Saguntum to Roman control, captured the Punic governor of the Catalan provinces, and, near the mouth of the Iberus, destroyed Hasdrubal's fleet which contained reinforcements and supplies for Hannibal.

The transition from dictator, to interim consuls, to regular consuls, stirred constitutional arguments that were resolved by appointing an interrrex, Cornelius Scipio Asina, to preside over the election of a new consul, with the newly elected consul to preside over the election of his co-consul. This dual election for the year 216, held after the current consular year ended on March 14th, brought the facts and fantasies about Roman superiority, and the manifest destiny of Rome to prevail over the Carthaginian, to a crescendo in the chambers of the Senate, and the people's comitias. The noise of the comitias was louder than the Senate's. But it was mostly background music to the aristocratic effusions from the Senate, the substantial government of Rome, the word *democracy* notwithstanding.

Under the interrex, Gaius Terentius Varro was nominated and elected to the first consulship. Under his own aura, Varro was soon able to preside over the nomination and election of Aemilius Paullus as his co-consul:

"Then it is duly fixed, and hereby proclaimed, that Aemilius Paullus and Gaius Terentius Varro are the consuls for the new year." Varro had several devices for putting an official sound on this statement, and he so ordered. And then a second statement: "Marcus Claudius Marcellus and Lucius Postumus Albinus are appointed praetors, and shall share command authority in their jurisdictions with the pro-consuls Regulus and Servilius until such time as the new consuls assume *their* command." Marcellus would be given the Fifth Legion in Sicily. Albinus would be sent to the Po valley to keep the Celts in check. Regulus and Servilius would remain on their absolutely passive Hannibal watch in Apulia.

But this was almost formula pronouncement. Hannibal's shadow over the Senate chamber became more insistent when Fabius Maximus dug into the debate about the new complexion for the war with Hannibal. He had been unable to stop the elections of Paullus and Varro, disciples of the imperialists for who anything but fully committed aggression against Hannibal was anathema. The young Publius Cornelius Scipio had married Paullus' daughter, Aemilia, and Varro was a protégé of the Cornelii, two connections that outweighed Fabius and his discredited caution on the Senate's immediate scales.

The figure of eight legions against Hannibal had been broached by one of the Arpii Claudii. Fabius was not privy to some of these details.

"You will risk all on a single throw of the dice against him?"

"He made a mockery of us with *your* commitment, Fabius—surely we have learned something from this."

The member of the Cornelii Scipiones had thrown a slippery gauntlet at Fabius, and his eyes and face had broadcast antique innuendos around the Senate chamber while he did it.

"Yes, we have learned from him. He has conducted seminars at Ticinus River, Trebbia River, Trasimene, and scattered less formal instruction for us from the Alps to luscious Campania—I count well above fifty thousand of our students dead in his classrooms."

While he was officially enrolled in Hannibal's classes, Fabius had donated relatively little to this score. He had been criticized, insulted, for his passivity, but he had saved some Romans for another day. Hannibal himself had told him that the score between them would not be counted until long after Rome had been deprived of Fabius' services. This information was not meat for this chamber, where he couldn't stop the warp they would put into it. But as Hannibal had said to him, he had a long memory, and he could trot a compliment out for private caress from time to time, himself.

The full weight of the aggressive partisans was now behind the Roman government and both Paullus and Varro were in the Senate chamber at this moment of the post-Fabius debate. Fabius might have been an embarrassing anachronism to some of the content of that chamber, but his credentials of service to Rome reached back to the First Punic War and were presently anchored in the fact that Varro and Paullus' bluster had been allowed free rein in the Roman Senate instead of being nailed to the wall of a Carthaginian prison. These things made it easy for him—the Delayer—to stand in front of the Varro and Paullus faction as opposition.

"These eight legions you will throw at Hannibal, they are the usual strength?" In the usual counting, a legion meant one Roman, one Allied legion.

"It has been proposed to raise both Roman and Allied legions to a strength of five thousand, with three hundred horse for each Roman legion, four hundred fifty horse per allied legion. I believe you will come to a total here, Fabius, of eighty thousand foot, and six thousand horse."

"Why this is a virtual avalanche of power whose prospects will drive Hannibal into the Adriatic—screaming, no taste for battle." Fabius put his own twist into the words for the Arpi Claudii who had fed him the numbers, and he put a hand to his mouth to simulate a scream from a particular Carthaginian that he knew was implausibility no Greek wordsmith would let touch his wildest conceptions of fantasy.

"You have tickled his feet a little, Fabius. I think the prospects of more significant response to this intruder has unsettled you." Varro had tried to stay aloof from the Fabius tweaking, but this derision was unacceptable to a figurehead for the Aemilii and the Scipiones who had helped make the figures Fabius had just received and reflected.

"He has been getting Celt reinforcements. His foot may be above forty thousand—his horse ten thousand." Fabius had private visions of the significance of *these* numbers.

"We will outnumber him by two to one." The Varro and Paullus faction had formed a phalanx near the first row of seats in the chamber. Fabius and the sparse cluster of conservatives around him were closer to the center of the chamber, all of them standing on the floor. The counter-voices were streaming at Fabius now. He didn't bother to personalize his answers:

"You are counting only the foot part of your juggernaught. You have forgotten the basis of his strength—his *horse*. Ask Publius Scipio about his horse, ask the shade of Flaminius about his horse. I can tell you a little, myself. He has brought a weapon into Italy that neither the Celts, nor Pyrrhus, have shown us. " Fabius could still feel the raw places on his ass where he had rubbed against the land contours trying avoiding this *weapon.*

"You insult our capacity to learn—to grow in front of opposition."

"We are nearly a generation away from coping with his conjunction of foot and horse."

"You have stepped very close to treason here, Fabius Maximus. If your past service to Rome was not so much..." Paullus would share the responsibility of building an army to *cope* as Fabius had just mentioned, and caution was not among his tools.

"I applaud your excellent memory, Aemilius Paullus, or I would take serious offense at your comment that has picked up too much heat from this parody of debate. Your credentials have been extolled in this chamber, your Illyrian successes, et cetera. But you have not faced the Carthaginians, in the First War, or now the Hannibal Barca incarnation of Carthage. And let this caution also embrace your colleague, Varro. He's had an estimable tutelage, partly under you—but still no Carthaginian in *his* past."

"We bow to *your* vast experience in these respects, Fabius." Paullus turned toward Varro, who had remained in his seated vantage above the fray of the floor. Fabius was being addressed by an aristocrat who knew protocol and respect and had blundered a moment ago, but he had recovered enough to keep his eyes mostly on Fabius while he tried to pull Varro and himself into a virtual apology to Fabius.

"Your crush of aggression will have a focus of above eighty thousand devoted to Hannibal." Fabius' voice suited muse more than challenge.

"That is the figure you have just been given, Fabius."

"How do you propose to bring this force and Hannibal into a conjunction?"

"We will watch him—track him."

"I have done that."

"And we will surround him. He will be in the position of starvation, surrender, or fighting—we like the option of fighting as his choice."

"I predict he will make you love him on that last count. But let me change your play a little—Hannibal will fight you when he decides the time and the place are propitious by *his* definition."

"We will prevail—let him use his definitions as he pleases."

"He is visualizing a major confrontation with us. He is training for this now." Fabius stepped in front of his partisans and made sure that both Varro and Paullus could see him.

"I tell you, within the span of the ambition you have spilled in front of me on this floor, Hannibal will work a victory over you that will make Trasimene and Trebbia minor skirmishes. I will pray to Capitoline Jupiter that Carthage will be our ally against him—for we will *not* prevail without her." The little group around Fabius had lost all the votes in this chamber, and it followed him out of it. Fabius had just made an astounding prediction. But he had seen visions in the Sibylline books, in the surrogate eyes of the Etruscan haruspices who were virtual staff to him. He owed Rome this report—let them make treason of it if they can.

Spring was asserting itself over the panoramas accessible to him at Geronium. In a few weeks, the first harvest would be gathered into the granaries and silos of the great plains of Apulia to the east-southeast of him. Myrcan found him at an outpost one day, staring into these directions.

"Cathbad and his friends have insisted a strong Celt flavor on you, Lord Hannibal. I've seen their foot and horse working with you...I think you like it."

"We have put a few changes into the Celt line that might surprise the Roman. We didn't kill the bluster, but I think there's some variety and discipline in it now that will make a better marriage with our Iberians and Africans." Hannibal hadn't interrupted his probe into a complex distance, but formalities were redundant between these two.

"Are you up to a reasonable strength for this year's campaign?"

"Reasonable for the time I have to train the recruits. Reasonable for what the Roman will put against us? You've heard the cacophony from Rome: two consuls who have sworn to out swagger Fabius, with, what's the latest gossip—eight, ten legions devoted to us?"

"Eight seems to be a solid number now. I hear that Fabius has pissed a little into Paullus and Varro's brave stew." Myrcan could have virtually recited much of the debate in the Senate that swirled around Fabius. There were two Carthaginian agents, one Roman, one Italian, present, both with excellent credentials, among the non-senators who audited that Senate hearing. "He's invoked the aid of Carthage to stop you. Before that happy occurrence, he has thrown a disaster at Varro and Paullus' feet if they are not properly cautious with you." That turned Hannibal toward Myrcan.

"By Ba'al and Tanit together—he's not forgotten that we are collaborators!"

"I hear that you two nearly kissed under the oaks when the arrears were paid."

"We exchanged compliments...I vowed not to repeat them."

"What did he mean about invoking Carthage for Roman purposes?"

"Fabius' memory has some anchors in the First War. Carthaginian resolve was not famous then. Its vacuum frustrated my father. Fabius apparently is counting on a reincarnation of it in *my* time, a vacuum at Carthage into which Rome can pour its opportunities."

"Can you tell me anything about your plans?" The resolve of Carthage behind Hannibal had been a tacit, and explicit, subject of many conversations which hadn't always included Hannibal. Myrcan, and others of the staff, had mulled and extrapolated some of Cathbad's remarks that Hannibal had never tried to keep secret. These remarks were trying to intrude now, but Myrcan had stepped aside for Hannibal:

"We need to draw the Roman, in his full force, into *our* battlefield—and to do it this year. Time is not our ally. My collaborator, Fabius, will tell you that. We have done nothing to draw the allies away from Rome."

"I argue that, Hannibal. You have done plenty. I think your efforts will accrue to your benefit...you must be patient in dismantling an empire."

"That attribute favors the Roman, Myrcan. Fabius has just given us a seminar on patience. He has apparently preached its virtues to Varro and Paullus. If they choose to ignore him, we will have our battle." Hannibal had gone back to his Apulian panorama.

"Where?"

"The Roman citadel of Cannae, on the Aufidus River, is a central storehouse for the Apulian cornucopia that gives suck to Rome, and her armies. I think it will be the bait we will use for Varro and Paullus."

"How far is Cannae?"

"Three days, perhaps a little less if we are pulled by incentives and goosed by the Roman."

"There is something else about Cannae besides the storehouses..." Myrcan stated this as another fact of Hannibal's revelation, and he stared at the back of Hannibal's head, waiting for his answer:

"Maharbal took a little tour with some of his Numidians which happened to include the suburbs of Cannae. He said it was the finest country for a run with cavalry he had ever seen."

That night, Sosylos shared the commander's tent for his dinner. They were in the concluding fruit and wine stage.

"Silenus has brought you up to date, Hannibal. He has a big scroll waiting for this year."

"I wish he could make *that* scroll talk to me." They occupied separate couches. Hannibal had just taken as much comfort from his as he could, head back, staring at the roof of the tent. His orderlies had tried to make his tent more like Darius' pavilion, or the silken canopies that Alexander had lolled beneath. But he would have nothing more than bare canvas above him, although his people had sneaked in some Carthaginian rugs, and the couches, which he'd accepted.

"I've heard most of the rumors about the Roman juggernaught that's forming against you. By conservative calculation, they will have better than two to one over you—Hamilcar would have liked those odds."

Sosylos moved his wine goblet against the twilight fluxing through the tent's entrance. It was Tyrian glass, a translucence of the whole spectrum, and with a good wine inside, a man had extra incentive to see, feel, some various dreams. The Italian campaign was coming to a point. Fabius had delayed it, he was now praying against it. This Spartan had never been close to a commander like Hannibal. He had taken men from a dozen different worlds and molded an army that would have stopped Alexander. Sosylos had been close when Cathbad gave his prescription for Hannibal's Italian temple, when the Druid had put more of the vision of the columns for his temple in front of Hannibal. That Celt had not complimented Carthage's resolve. Strains of Cathbad had been persistent in this command tent, and Sosylos also knew that Fabius had just echoed some of them on the floor of the Roman Senate—in the faces of Varro and Paullus.

"By Zeus, this *is* a privileged time—no matter how it comes out."

"You are starting to compose my epitaph, old friend?"

"By our mutual gods, Hannibal, you will never see that day! I was thinking about the battles of Titans that have mesmerized the Greeks. I am sitting in the middle of one—on the edge of a culminating one. Xerxes and Darius and Athens and Sparta, never posed more of a stage for Olympus than this."

"My statue of Alexander at Gades is trembling at your omission of *his* stages, Sosylos."

"I make no omission there. Let the Macedonian sycophants try to make them heroic if they can. Darius fled *all* his fields, leaving a disgraceful banner for his men to rally under. The Persian's Greek mercenaries came within a whisker of stopping Alexander. With only a few specks of exception, he never made conjunction with pride and resolve, like the Roman's, in his trip across Asia that has been warped into a paradigm of glory for the ages." Hannibal had furnished some very good Campanian wine. It had lubricated the Spartan's tongue, but its speech was just what he needed now. "I have heard rumors about your next stage, my lord."

"My privacies are like a fishnet in this camp." Hannibal assumed a sitting position and let a smile accompany his answer to Sosylos.

"What is this Cannae, Hannibal?"

"I think it is the bait we will need to bring the Roman onto *our* stage—if I have to continue this damned Thespian slant of yours."

"May I ask if you and the Lady Inanna have made any conjunctions lately?"

"My lembi surrogates sneaked another of her letters past the Roman scows below Ancona. Now that we are over the eye business...she seems to have relaxed some."

"I will say the same for her husband." The man in front of Hannibal now had been a crucial surrogate for Hamilcar's whispers in the darks days surrounding Faesulae.

"Kyniska is accepting all of my mother's overtures to the Amazon: horses, archery, wrestling—the gods know what else. Inanna and Medina are in her school for women's dominance of Carthage. That's about all I can report."

"I would hope for some private stuff...beyond my scope, my lord."

"There was a little of that and yes, it *is* beyond your scope, my perceptive Spartan friend."

By the middle of June, the sirens of Apulia, calling from the Aufidus River near the Roman jewel of Cannae, couldn't be denied any longer. He had about forty thousand foot, above ten thousand horse, and some new complexions of competence below the limed locks of his Celts that put them into his Africans and Iberians in the way of the army he had seen in successive dreams since Carthago Nova.

He moved away from Geronium at night, and got a half day's march away from Servilius and Regulus before the Romans knew he had gone. And he stormed and took Cannae before the Romans knew his target. Servilius and Regulus asked for orders. They were told to wait, the standing order since Fabius had gone into the archives. Paullus and Varro now had some scrambling to do to make their juggernaught.

17

31 years
July 216 BC—Cannae

Varro and Paullus had succeeded in the numbers of the bluster they had thrown in front of Fabius and the rest of the Senate in March. And in July they came along the Appian Way to Beneventum, then across Samnium to join Regulus and Servilius in Apulia, about two days west northwest of Cannae. The congregation of the two consuls, and the two pro-consuls who had been officially nailed to their spot since the Romans had known that Hannibal was at Cannae, brought eighty thousand foot and about six thousand horse to face the arrogant Carthaginian, who seemed to have Fabius Maximus in his pocket. They had complimented Hannibal by bringing an unprecedented eight legions, sixteen with their allies, into one army to face him.

Before proceeding toward Cannae, Varro told his men that they had beaten the Carthaginian in the line at Trebbia. Some of these men were, in fact, listening to Varro now. They outnumbered the Carthaginian by two to one. They were fighting *for* their homeland, *on* their homeland—advantages that were not in the Carthaginian's bag of tricks. The crescendo of agreement that rolled from these men toward Varro, and the nearby Paullus, seemed to put some substance into the framework of bravado that Fabius had ridiculed. No Roman commanders had ever been swarmed by acclaim like this—which pushed lugubrious Fabius far away from the gilded armor on Varro and Paullus.

Varro and Paullus would command on alternate days. And from the time they left the congregation point and moved closer to him across the Foggian plain, Hannibal had Varro and Paullus' respective command days marked on his calendar. On the second day, post-congregation, from about five miles, the Romans spotted Hannibal's camp on a spur north of the Aufidus River. They camped at this point of first contact.

Hannibal had put his camp on a vantage about three and a half miles west of the ruined citadel of Cannae. The eastern slopes in front of him stretching to the Roman position were an avenue for cavalry. His rear was protected by steep gradients, and the valley of the Aufidus on his right flank was a natural outlet in case the specter of retreat should happen to look at him here. He was powerfully situated, except that foraging would have to pull him down the slope from time to time.

Varro and Paullus, comforted by the *two to one* strength that they had brought to the valley of the Aufidus, took their first step away from the Fabian strategy and moved to deny Hannibal the delights of the foraging grounds between him and the sea, on both sides of the river.

The first day of this new Roman presence was Varro's command. He advanced the army toward the north shore of the Aufidus, and when he got within two miles of Hannibal's outer perimeter, Hannibal sent his Numidians and light foot to acknowledge him. In Hannibal's parlance, the adjective *light* was unfair to the Roman. The lead and marble slugs of his Balearic slingers beat a tattoo of death and maiming on the Roman targets from ranges beyond the best archers of the day, and the accuracy and effects improved with every yard the Romans subtracted from the distance between *their* presence and Hannibal's. Echelons of Numidians swept close to the Roman formation—out of range of the pilums, close enough for their iron javelins to whisper their story deep into the Roman ranks. They opened new target panoramas for Hannibal's spearmen and slingers who had played this ballet with the Numidians on other fields.

Hannibal's greeting was degrading the aura of the speech Varro had made only hours before. To counter it, Varro brought heavy foot and horse forward to establish the avenue to the river bank that Hannibal was denying with flicks of himself. By nightfall, the legions had reached the north bank of the Aufidus, and Varro was able to dig in a camp there. But if the Romans had used the word *juggernaught* in songs, or shouts, coming from the northwest to the valley of the Aufidus, and then southwest along it toward the Carthaginian, that word had lost some sheen by the time night fell.

The next day was Paullus' command. He moved one-third of the army across the river and set up a camp about two miles from the main one. The camps—Hannibal's, the main Roman, the new Roman—had settled roughly on a west southwest-east northeast axis, respectively, about a mile north of Hannibal's bait, Cannae.

A quartet of horsemen was admiring the symmetries of this disposition from the prow of the spur that had been home for Hannibal for most of the two months since Geronium.

"Yesterday Varro crushed his way to the river bank practically under our noses. Now Paullus has advanced some eagles to the other side. They have denied us some of paradise." Maharbal was looking along the axis, toward Paullus. When he used the word, *paradise*, it came out softly, like a whisper, as he estimated the gains and losses of cavalry ground that Varro and Paullus had just put into the game. The southeast wind, the Vulturnus, was a fixture of this valley at this season and it's flux now, like Maharbal's last words, was soft, also toward the Roman positions.

"I cling to your word, *some*...it leaves us a little room for joy, I think." Hannibal's look paralleled his Chief of Cavalry's, although it tended to linger a little longer on the main congregation of Romans, where Varro was holding court. He was a cavalryman. So he and Maharbal came close to the same tuning when they confronted resonances of time and topography that affected cavalry. The great slope below him on the north side of the Aufidus, tending to a cavalry exercise ground toward the Adriatic, had been interdicted by Varro. And now Paullus had done nearly the same thing to ground of similar virtue on the south side of the river.

"If you can't go around, brother, I've seen you go *through*—and *then* around."

Hannibal looked at Mago, who had never bowed to formality. Mago had just recited an action of cavalry that had ended, or set up the stage for ending, a thousand battles.

"You are presuming to preach tactics here, *little* brother?" The smiles would never let words like these get out of hand.

"Mago may have just drilled into some of Varro's, or Paullus' skull, Hannibal."

"I think their play for us would like to have an ending somewhere in the middle of their line crush. Mago's audacity is trying to ruffle the pages of that play." There was silence while each of them looked at some particular of the landscape in front of them that held Hannibal's bait, Cannae. The river and the hills which defined the limits of the plain below Cannae, on the other side of the river, were Hannibal's private thinking course for a while. "Varro, more likely Paullus, has set up to try to deny us our advantage, gentlemen." The looks were silent again while the commander's words *try* and *advantage* shook hands in front of them. The Romans in foot could parade that *two for one*. But that beautiful ratio, on the horse side of this game, fell toward Hannibal.

"Tomorrow, I think we will offer the north side to Varro for our conversation, we may have tickled him enough today to make a hero out of him."

"If Paullus doesn't agree?"

"Then let them choose the side. As always, your confidence is my bulwark, Mago...it will serve us whether we go around them on the north side—or go through, and *then* around them, on the south side of the fair Aufidus." The venerable Hannibal-Mago eye axis was strong here. "Give the word to prepare for battle, gentlemen."

At dawn the next day, after he had put a good breakfast into his army, Hannibal drew it up in battle array on the plain a mile from Varro's position. He waited until noon, and detected no sign of Roman acceptance of his gage. His scouts reported considerable traffic between the north and south Roman camps, but no movement of the eagles toward him. Hannibal rode the length of his line with Mago and Maharbal. He told his men that they made a fine show, that they needed the exercise, and to stay alert and prepared while the Romans tried to make a decision of battle. It didn't come. When Hannibal returned to his camp, his army continued to prepare for a juggernaught.

After a late staff meeting, the oil lamps in Hannibal's tent continued their service. This time he was alone.

Inanna Barca,

I like this greeting better than the others I've used. Sosylos has accused me of being tongue-tied, passionless. But I have never taken more pride in my name than when I put you into it. Sosylos can't peek inside my head—so what does he know about my thoughts of you during a letter...or any other time?

Kiss Kyniska for me. I am very impatient to see the Amazon my mother—and you and Medina, too, I suspect—have put into our daughter. There is wonderful horse country where I am sitting now. Kyniska would have fine ground here for showing me what she has learned about horses...and I would like to have you and your white Parthian beside me here. It is close to a place the Romans call, Cannae.

You know that I have been trying to force a confrontation with the Romans. I think we will finally have this here at Cannae...possibly tomorrow. It is a big Roman supply base, and I am sitting on top of it, with my feet in a river they call the Aufidus. If your scholar friends can find some Italian maps for you, perhaps you can find me. I am close to the heel of the foot on that big leg that Italy sticks into the Mediterranean. I took my calipers to a map tonight, and I see that I am only about 470 Roman miles from you. Tell Kyniska that her daddy can reach that far if she isn't a good girl.

You tell me that you and Medina and my mother are making a matriarchy at Carthage, and that the pinnacle of my responsibility will soon become nothing more than what fruit I will let our servants push into my mouth...in the middle of our tiled dolphins. I wish I could have you in that place, now. A good pool, with a wonderful nymph beside me, will be in my dreams tonight.

Also, Inanna, you must know that if our gods should turn their backs on me tomorrow...if they leave me only a husband, and a father—I will praise them. If they leave me no life—then I order you to praise them for what you have given me.

Hannibal Barca

At dawn of the next day, Varro finally decided to move across the Aufidus, to join Paullus on the south side. It was Paullus' command day.

"They definitely like the *south* side, Hannibal." Maharbal had a few minutes advantage when he reported to the command tent. Hannibal's standing order of preparing for battle if Roman movement was detected had been in progress since the camp breakfast under stars.

"This should be Paullus' day all around with the Romans—I think he saw too much cavalry on our side." Hannibal's orderly was just finishing the final touches on the armor that would cause about 145,000 men and horses to come together in the virtual heart of combat.

Hannibal waited for Paullus to put his full corps into battle disposition. The Romans were making a line that almost paralleled the axis of the camps, facing southwest, their right flank on the river, their left on the hills below Cannae. They were leaving Hannibal a restricted field for his horse, constrained by the Aufidus on his left flank, the Cannae hills on his right—Mago's *through* situation, as opposed to the *around* paradise of the north side that Paullus didn't want to share with Maharbal, and Maharbal's friends. Although all his officers watched the same scene, close to him, Carthalo vocalized what they all saw...his voice soft, a companion this day for Hamilcar's son, like Maharbal, who had also once shared days with Hamilcar.

"Paullus is putting his heaviest horse on his right. Varro seems to have gone to their left with the allied horse. They are packing their line, by Tanit! They seem to be putting close to thirty ranks into both the legion and the allied lines. The hastati, principes and triarii lines are all packed, with damned little separation between them."

For his observation of Paullus' culminating maneuvers, Hannibal had taken his staff along a contour that preserved several hundred feet of elevation above Paullus, and he had finally stopped a little less than a mile from where Paullus was establishing his right flank on the Aufidus. The detail Carthalo was pulling out of the panorama in front and below them was not an affectation for a man who had studied battle arrays over a span that included Hamilcar in Sicily and Africa, and Hamilcar's son in Iberia, and Italy.

"This is the juggernaught we've heard about, gentlemen. Paullus will try to overwhelm us in the first rush." Hannibal let his part of the silence come in for a few seconds, as the Roman disposition spread out across the plain below Cannae. His intelligence reports put some numbers into the scene: "We will have to look tall against about seventy five thousand foot and sixty-four hundred horse." It was a good estimate: light by about five thousand foot, heavy by about four hundred horse—looking at the total Roman there, field and camp together.

"What will you keep in the camp, Hannibal?"

"Let's leave about two thousand there."

"We *will* have to look tall."

"They have tried to design a cavalry frustration into this day, gentlemen. We will try to make a cavalry triumph of it, shared with our line which I think holds a few surprises for Paullus."

"Why are you leaving Varro out of it, so soon, Commander?"

"If he is, as you say, enjoying left-side exposure with the allied horse, I think Varro may have already laid plans to leave himself out of it—at his *very* earliest convenience."

Paullus had placed his veterans from Trebbia into the center of his heavy line, bracketing them alternately with Roman legions of less experience and the allied legions. He put fifteen thousand light foot, velites, across the front of his line in three loose ranks. This disposition accounted for seventy-five thousand of his juggernaught. The remainder of it, six thousand horse, had the responsibility of containing Hannibal's horse until his line could smash through the Carthaginian's and start the general melee where his almost two-for-one could drain Hannibal's blood—and his horses be damned then. So Paullus put his two thousand heavy Roman horse into a width of about fourteen hundred feet on his right flank—on the river, and his four thousand allied horse into a width of about three thousand feet on his left flank—on the Cannae hills. Paullus had bunched both wings of his horse unusually close, like his line, to accommodate an adversary who was also unusual.

When he was ready for Hannibal's inspection, Paullus was stretched out for about two miles, flank to flank, across the Cannae plain. It was too early for the sun to vest the legionary eagles, the cohort and maniple standards, the horns and trumpets, the various armor and uniforms, with the majesty of high noon, but it was a sufficient scene for more silence from an opposition side.

It was time to come down from his hill and pick up Paullus' gage. Hannibal called for thirty-two abreast ranks of his foot and horse. Then with his light foot, his Iberian and African spearmen and Balearic slingers in the van, he started to move his corps toward Paullus: Numidian light horse, then his African, Celt and Iberian heavy foot, then his Iberian, Carthaginian and Celt heavy horse. His column was about one and a half miles long, and most of it was on the slope leaving his camp when he gave a stop order. He would never have a better look at his men, they would never have a better look at him than what that moment offered.

He asked Maharbal, Carthalo, Mago, another Hasdrubal, and other staff officers to come with him while he rode to the front of his column. Then he worked his way back up the slope, shouting names, pointing to specifics of comradeship that no man of his rank ever had in his depth and his truth. Partway back through his column, he stopped. He was in his heavy foot, his Africans, now. He looked at them, into them, calling to them in several of their dialects. Then he looked toward the Cannae plain, and Paullus. The other officers who had kept close to him, and had supplemented his troop comradeship from time to time, also looked away from the Africans toward Paullus. It was a sight time now, no sound except a meadowlark which had stumbled into burgeoning hell, and the whispers of air that would soon mature to the Vulturnus wind and be some transport of hell. The tapestry Paullus had spread across the Cannae plain for Hannibal was the undeniable sight now, tensioned by the closing presence of the man who had caused it, justified it. It was Gisgo, a young staff officer, who broke a silence that had spread its aura a big distance from Hannibal by then:

"There are a *lot* of them, Lord Hannibal." Gisgo's eyes had not left Paullus' monumental display. He was still bound to that direction when Hannibal's hand slapped him on the back.

"But you have forgotten one *big* thing, Gisgo..."

"What is that, sir?" Gisgo was now properly turned for his question.

Hannibal moved his hand in front of the Roman host—left to right, Paullus' right flank to his left flank, eighty-one thousand of him.

"In *all* that crowd of Romans—there's not a *single* man named *Gisgo!*"

Gisgo was the first one to turn an open mouth into a laugh—it was impertinently explosive, coming as it did almost in the face of Lord Hannibal, even though it *was* the provocateur's face. And then a phenomenon, that stuck to Maharbal, Carthalo, and Hannibal long after that day at Cannae, came into being: Gisgo's laugh swept through the officers around him where it picked up support including Hannibal's, and the bolstered laugh then struck into the ranks of the Africans, who could make an explosion of inimitable laughter from a smaller nucleus than the one Gisgo had just given them. And the Africans' laughter was a bigger incentive which spread into the ranks above and below them until there was not a single man of Hannibal's column, from the Balearics in his van, to the Celt horsemen in his rear—all of them sensitive to laughter, could put their own mark on it—who did not know that someone very close to Hannibal, probably the Commander himself, had just laughed at the greatest army Rome had ever put in the face of an enemy.

Command assignments were ancient history now: Carthalo's second in command on the left flank was Hasdrubal, a staff officer whose surname was not Barca. Hannibal and Mago would command the line with a cadre of captains and lieutenants. Maharbal had the specific command of the rambunctious

Numidians on the right wing, but his purview, like his commander's, was the whole battle.

When Hannibal crossed the ford, he started to develop his line of battle. He advanced his light troops in a double line which gradually spread out across the plain below Cannae that Paullus had allotted him. To back up their advance, he separated his Africans into two columns, on his left and right flanks, respectively, and promoted them behind the light corps that was closing the distance to the Roman velites. Carthalo's heavy horse was establishing their formation on his left flank—on the river—and Maharbal's Numidians were doing the same on the right flank which rubbed against the Cannae hills.

He and Mago had a last conference with his line officers and then they separated to control the formation and advance of the heavy foot, where Hannibal had placed his Celts and Iberians in alternating phalanxes, under their own officers. But this was a Hannibal-tempered line now, not a congregation of separate egos imprinted with different gods and battle prejudices.

By placing his Africans near his cavalry on the flanks, Hannibal was creating bulwarks which would tend to warp an advancing line toward his center. He had put Roman armor on the Africans, and with various distinguishing colorful marks of tribal affiliation, he had caught the Romans' attention with them. The Africans had overmatched the legions at Trebbia and Trasimene. Their reputation for cruel ferocity driven by disdain for counter-action put the cement into these bulwarks Hannibal was looking for. In setting up his left and right African columns, Hannibal put the file leaders of the phalanxes on the right and left column files, respectively. A simple ninety degree turn of each man in the columns would thus present the normal phalanxes with the file leaders in place facing each other, making a sandwich of what came to the ground between them.

The light troops were getting within range of each other—rather, the Roman velites were coming into range of the slingers' missiles, and some of Hannibal's Balearic exhibitionists were starting to lob lead slugs into the Roman heavy foot two hundred yards in front of them as calling cards. About 129,000 men and 16,000 horses were moving toward a congregation place of less than two square miles. The sound part of it was starting to displace some of its sights, the air a carrier of foot and horse sounds, armor and weapon noise, some pinnacles of voice challenges—all of this subject to a thousand-fold magnification that would soon use the ground to also carry the message of this congregation.

As the antennae of the armies, the light foot, started to intermingle, Hannibal's refusal to delegate only nuisance value to his version of these troops was soon justified, again. The Roman velites were no match for Hannibal's light corps. His spearmen outranged the velites, outfought them when it came to the sword, and these contests were permeable everywhere to the selective destruction designed by his Balearic slingers.

As the velite survivors started to retreat into the spaces of the Roman heavy foot, Hannibal and Mago rode back and forth along the Celt-Iberian line of heavy foot and started to thin out the eight rank phalanxes into a battle line designed for flexibility.

"Start the crescent, Mago, you have all done this a dozen times before." This was a shouted intersection between brothers. Hannibal's red-plumed helmet was a distinction on the Carthaginian side of the field, but the Roman line had plenty of red in the cloaks of the tribunes, the plumes on the principes' helmets, and the cloaks of the Roman equites, their heavy horse. Hannibal's protective squad of leopard Numidians wouldn't let him get away from them, and Mago shouted something about *baby sitters* as he warped his Black Iberian back toward the line. The leopard Numidian bodyguard had a chore in front of it. The Roman battle line stretched for almost two miles, and their heavy foot which was Hannibal's main concern made up almost a mile of this. He had surrogate officers scattered throughout his line, but his presence, his inspiration, couldn't be surrogated and he knew it and his Numidian shadows were also beginning to know it.

Paullus' juggernaught was closing on Hannibal's crescent—bulging toward the Romans, a five ranked center in the bulge, tapering to three ranks close to the bulwarks that the Africans made with the cavalry. The seductive invitation of the bulge and the intimidation of the bulwarks on the flanks were starting to warp the Roman line toward Hannibal's center. The sound was carried by both the air and ground now, largely sounds of both sides of the foot, the horse part still mostly potential thunder. By Ba'al, Mago would swear he heard that meadowlark again—it had to be a form from Olympus coming to report a battle that would soon rouse most of the gods away from their wine couches.

Hannibal put his personal encouragement as close as he could get to the apex of his crescent which was moments away from impact with the juggernaught.

"Remember the staunch fall back lads—you will keep them in front of you! To the glory of Carthage and Tanit!" Gold disk and crescent standards, Tanit's reminders of glory, were flicking in the growing sunlight throughout the Carthaginian line.

When the Roman line had closed to within two hundred yards of Hannibal's apex—the nice linearity of Paullus' center partially degenerated into a bulge toward Hannibal's invitation—the Roman horns wailed for the first time, and the legions started the shield banging and the chanting to the beat of their march toward victory. Hannibal's Celts and Iberians had been slowed to protect the structure of the crescent, but they put up their own intimidation in the Roman faces—shouts, gestures, pantomime which needed no translation, the Celts virtuosos in sailing insults toward the opposition, accompanied by visions of limned hair that put an extra foot of height on their version of superman. And Hannibal had put Roman armor on the Celts who would be working their new Carthaginan swords this day. The long sword Celts, who eschewed the armor, had even worked out some byplay with their armored friends which had strong hints of various Roman deficiencies, local theatres scattered along Hannibal's line which also needed no translation for the closing Roman audience.

At fifty yards the second wail of Roman horns signaled the lance, pilum, throw. When the legionaires had unpacked these weapons and the first rank was in launching stance, the range had closed to twenty yards, and this was the committing range of the first rank. As the iron heads of the lances crashed into the shield bank of the Carthaginian line, the sound started to carry the spectrums of close combat, and it fed on itself as the desperations of winning and losing spread across the crescent.

Mago and Hannibal, all their officers of the line, moved in and out of the surge of first contact shouting warnings, encouragement, reminding of the staunch fall back that had been practiced, and practiced—although no man could pick out all the threads of reality by practicing reality. But his line seemed to be accommodating the juggernaught. Paullus' thirty rank hammer could use only several ranks at a time, and the flexible non-linearity Hannibal had put in the Roman face was starting to make cooperation feel like stifling congestion in the Roman mass.

The lances had taken a toll. But the Romans had not established their death rhythm yet. They knew what to expect of the Iberians, and they died under the falcatas and spears as they had at Ticinus and Trebbia and Trasimene. The Celt battle personality *was* a surprise. The familiar naked torsos wielding the long swords seemed to be easy targets for the gladius thrusts—but other Celts, armored like legionnaires, came into the picture, and their swords could outrange, in thrust and slash, the gladius, and the death balance had shifted from heavy on the Celt side to even, and now it was slipping to the Roman side as the Celts' belief in their new personality picked up the beat of their own swords on Roman shields, armor, bodies. Hannibal and Mago could hear shouts making the names of Celt gods—Teutates, Lugh, Taranis, Lugoves—and the interweave of Iberian rallies around gods that had some of the same root places, if not the names.

The staunch, orderly, fall back was the essence of what was exploding around him. Hannibal tried to be everywhere along the crescent, now orchestrating a flattening and inversion of it where he had ordered expansion before. The contact had spread out from the crescent along the linear connections to his anchors. Paullus had not gotten his breakthrough, he was still coming, but his juggernaught had lost crucial shock momentum.

The watch on Hannibal included more than his leopard Numidians. His signal officers never lost sight of him, and when he gave the order for Carthalo to attack the Roman heavy horse on his left flank, his signal was sent by four relays of hands and arms, and the distinctive Carthaginian signal trumpets, to Carthalo almost a mile away. Paullus commanded his right flank where Carthalo struck two thousand Roman horse with six thousand Iberian, Celt and Carthaginian horse. Hannibal's order to Carthalo was followed closely by one to Maharbal to unleash his four thousand Numidians against about the same number of allied horse on his right flank, against the Cannae hills.

During Carthalo and Hasdrubal's assault on his heavy horse, Paullus was wounded by an Iberian saber and had to retreat to the rear of his horse line, and then to the relative safety of his foot line when his horse flank crumbled. Before he left an expanding debacle he gave an order which reached Hannibal via a Mushroom officer Hannibal had delegated as a personal connection to various exigencies of the battle:

"Paullus has ordered his horse to fight on foot, Hannibal." The two riders were close. They had been this close before on Mushroom patrols that had challenged Hannibal's innovation, and stamina, on the plains of Carthage, a lifetime ago.

"He might as well have delivered them up to us in chains," Hannibal replied.

Paullus had just given up a tenet of this battle that he was bound to more than he had admitted to anyone, a tenet at the basis of Fabius' warning to him and Varro—that any conception of Roman victory had to assume containment of Hannibal's cavalry. The two-for-one foot banner that Fabius and Varro waived in front of Fabius' warning had not made the old man flinch—or retract a word.

The perception of this battle had better rounding now—and more than sixteen thousand horse were putting inimitable thunder into the air and ground of it. There would be no ultimate crescendo at Cannae. There were silences in the beginning which at least a meadowlark had violated. Then the air and ground perceptions told of heavy movements of men and horses, and then of all the spectrums of a cacophony that a death game of men with men, men with horses, can bring. The crescendos were like random volcanic eruptions in a valley that compete for the attending eyes and ears—no climax here, but sporadic views of authentic hell on top of a deepening cacophony interwoven with relative silences that afforded no real surceases for a living man at this place until the blood marked for draining had run out.

Carthalo and Hasdrubal left very few living Roman equites in their wake on Paullus' right flank. In the course of smashing through the mostly dismounted Roman heavy horse, they started to impact the legionnaires on the right side of Paullus' line, another encouragement of the legions toward the center of the field where Hannibal, his officers and his men, had accomplished an inversion of the crescent to a straight line, then a bulge toward the rear which accelerated the warping of the already overburdened Roman line into a more compact mass—whose now vaunted momentum would bring it into the scope of Hannibal's bulwarks on his flanks.

His Celt-Iberian line was executing a *staunch fallback* that was probably saving this day for him. Celt and Iberian dead were piled among the Roman in payment for this, but the death numbers for his men were a small fraction of what they would have been before they had watched, and practiced, the new ways he had brought to them.

Carthalo took his heavy horse to the rear of the Roman line and then to its left flank where Maharbal's Numidians had kept the Allied horse from the action on the line. When he joined the Numidians, the three thousand odd allied horse still in action were quickly killed, dispersed, or captured, except for a remnant of two hundred that contained Varro and managed to flee the field with him. Carthalo and Maharbal then distributed Hannibal's light and heavy horse along the rear of the Roman line where they applied more incentive for a forward crush into Hannibal's trap. When he knew that the Roman horse was destroyed, Hannibal ordered his light foot around the now unprotected left flank of the Romans to assist in the attack on the rear of the legions.

Mago reached Hannibal with the news that started to put the capstone into his Cannae construction:

"The Roman line has passed the leading ranks of the Africans."

Hannibal stared at this brother who had been immersed in the terrible, wonderful, business of the line with him for nearly two hours. Then he gave the arm signal that would turn the columns of his African bulwarks into phalanxes pointing toward the center of the field, toward the crush of legionnaires that couldn't stop moving forward. This simple rotation was completed almost as soon as Hannibal's signal had been relayed to the file leaders of his bulwarks.

Hannibal had delegated the phalanx attack order to his line officer on his left flank who would know when the Roman target had pushed enough of itself between the African phalanxes. Hannibal heard the signal for this—heard the echoing signal on his right flank—and at that time he knew the Roman line was under his assault on the rear by his heavy and light horse and his light foot, on both flanks by his Africans, and on the front by his Celt-Iberian line which had been his crucial instrument for this moment, and had been in continuous fighting since the first impact on the forward crescent.

His Africans were fresh. When they turned toward the Roman target that the Celt-Iberians had drawn into their range, they used every device learned by resolute killers over two thousand years to cut into the Roman foot, including slashing behind the greaves at unprotected hamstrings to bring a legionnaire to his knees and open new avenues for the maximum thrusts and slashes that piled the dead and dying by the hundreds, then the thousands, around the African avalanches.

A description of the Roman situation as a herd of panicked beasts rushing to the expediting funnel of a slaughterhouse would have been only fractionally good. There *was* panic even in the veteran ranks, then there was pride and bravery, and resignation with bravery. These things, and Carthaginian frustration at an enemy who had been elusive, insulting, arrogant, kept the killing going. Hannibal couldn't stop it. The Roman commanders—now excluding the fugitive Varro—who might have stopped it were either among the dead, or close to their province.

Hannibal had penetrated dangerously beyond the perimeters of this climax several times under the drive of command, or observation. On one of these trips, he heard an African call his name. He was riding toward this man, when a shout from one of his Numidian shadows triggered the reflexive action of his head that caused the spear to only graze his cheek. He heard the whisper of the Numidian's lance on its way to the throat of the centurion who had stumbled through an interstice of the action and found himself within range of Hannibal. When one of Synhalus' orderlies got to him, the wound was bleeding profusely. He was off his horse, talking to the dying African who had also found himself within range of Hannibal.

At about two hours past high sun, the killing stopped. Paullus had gone from his wound in the first horse action to his death in the center of his line an hour earlier. Servilius had finally found the death Hannibal had deferred at Ticinus and Trebbia. Minucius had found some of the audacity he had shown to Hannibal at Geronium, before his death in the line. Both consuls' quaestors, twenty nine tribunes, eighty former, or prospective senators, and almost all of the two thousand knights, equites, in the Roman heavy horse had died.

Hannibal had located one of his Mushrooms, dead. And it was close to this man where Maharbal and Mago found him. He was sitting on the ground, helmet off, his leopard Numidians discreetly attentive. The orderlies had slowed the bleeding on his cheek—but there was blood on every part of him...only some of it his.

Mago knelt close to him, his first shock of Hannibal on the ground now calmed by closer inspection. When he had sorted out the blood on his brother, he almost whispered, "It's over—you have a great victory." At Carthage and later, Iberia, Mago had known the Mushroom who lay beside Hannibal, and he put him into the *you* he had just given his brother.

Maharbal resisted the inclination to kneel beside his commander. But he stood close, and Hannibal sensed him and raised his head to look at him.

"We have taken their two camps, Hannibal. Some horse and foot has slipped away from us toward Canusium—we think young Publius Scipio and Fabius' son are with them. Do you want us to chase them?" Maharbal had also been shocked at the sight of a bloody Hannibal on the ground. Mago's face and words had been some balm, but Hannibal's face, marked by a panorama of slaughter few men had ever seen before, kept some of the shock in him. He had to wait long seconds for Hannibal's answer:

"Let them go...they can advertise for us." Mago was closest, the voice soft even for him and Maharbal barely heard it. Hannibal had just granted another gift of continuity, perhaps life, to his student Publius Cornelius Scipio, and hence to Rome. Also, he had just seen old Fabius in the oak grove again... trying to arbitrate between the consul and general of him who was facing an anathema, and the statesman and man, perhaps the father of him, who would have liked to talk more—truly collaborate—with this Carthaginian.

His orderlies had cleaned him up and he wore a fresh tunic, no armor, to the staff meeting that had convened in the command tent on the prow above the Cannae plain. He had worn no patch in the battle, and none now. Synhalus had put a small bandage on his cheek. His cremation fires had been laying their gray to black signatures over the Cannae valley for hours. At his order, they had finally found Paullus. They had also found some gold goblets and good wine in Paullus' personal train at the main Roman camp and Hannibal had presented a toast to a Roman general who had not run away, before they committed him to the flames.

His military staff and advisors had preceded him. Sosylos and Silenus were standing near the entrance when Hannibal walked in. He noticed them in passing, but said nothing on his way to the focal point of the large tent, which would be wherever he decided to stop. His sometime Greek shadows got the same reaction from his face that had hit Maharbal, despite the careful attention of orderlies, and hours away from the death fields of Cannae. Hannibal stopped near the natural focus of the tent, its center, which happened to include Carthalo, his immediate target.

"What is your latest estimate of our losses?" He had been in the middle of heaps of dead, but the grace of whatever god had finally ended it had enveloped him there for a while, and it did now...death statistics were not really relevant to these moments when a meadowlark could have had some province again below Cannae.

"About six thousand dead—horse and foot."

"Our Celt foot?" Hannibal turned toward Caros, a Celt captain who had been close to him during the practice days at Geronium.

"I think about thirty-five hundred dead, Lord Hannibal."

"I will congratulate your men personally, Caros. That loss is heavy for you. It would have been much larger without the cooperation...you, your officers... your men." The soft voice had slipped in again, also some hoarseness. But Caros, and the other Celt officers present, heard every piece of it.

Hannibal turned back to Carthalo. Maharbal happened to be standing close to Carthalo and Sosylos and Silenus had vantage enough.

"The Romans?" The tent was silent—nothing perturbed this part of the summation that would appall any of the Olympians who had pushed their wine away to watch Cannae.

"We think about seventy thousand dead—foot and horse, Hannibal. About thirteen thousand prisoners. Three to four thousand foot and horse leaked through us in various directions." Those Roman numbers would have shocked Hamilcar. His son tried to digest them—but they were part of panorama that was beyond digestion, comprehension.

Sosylos had never heard of numbers like these adhering to Spartan or Greek pennants in their strongest days. Some of his historians had put greater numbers on Alexander against Darius at Arbela—a hundred thousand dead against a loss of three hundred. If true, a conscientious man would have trouble calling Arbela a battle. The Romans had left no doubt about this issue at Cannae. Darius had fled his field, Varro had copied him, but Paullus, Servilius and Minucius had not.

Silenus now had some uniqueness for his chronicle that would require careful balancing of qualifying adjectives. Many of the assertions he had made for his subject had been easy to write, to defend against Hannibal's amused disclaimers. But he would have to be careful with Carthalo's numbers for Cannae. The face that he and Sosylos had seen enter the tent had been worked by other numbers. There was a dead Mushroom at Hannibal's side on the field. Before he left that field, he heard that three other Mushrooms had died helping to make Carthalo's crucial left flank victory against Paullus' heavy horse. All of them had been close friends. And there had been more numbers outside the report Carthalo had just made...African, Iberian, Carthaginian, Celt officers, who were more than entries on a roster for him. And as he had personally identified many of his men of the ranks during their training and campaigning and night watches together, so he had done this over the dead and dying phase of many of them...all of this made numbers for Hannibal that Silenus would have to be careful about.

"I've heard that Minucius and Servilius are with Paullus."

"We found Servilius. We honored him. We fear that Marcus Minucius has found his ultimate anonymity."

"We didn't find Varro?" Hannibal looked at Maharbal.

"The Numidians followed his dust for several miles and then came back to important business."

Maharbal stepped closer to his commander. Hamilcar's son had just taken him through a carnage of victory that Hamilcar had never imagined in his strongest revilements against Rome, some of which had been put directly into Maharbal's ears, in Sicily, Carthage, Iberia.

"I don't need a gold goblet in my hand to tell you that every man in this space is honored to serve the greatest commander that has ever graced Tanit's standard." The rumble of assent started before Maharbal had finished his virtual toast.

"I have at least as much honor from such presence on my staff."

This moment was the closest Hannibal had been to a smile for hours. Sosylos wanted to touch him—his tunic, his hand, but the complications that now worked Hannibal's face needed more time before Sosylos could test any of his prerogatives with him.

"There is nothing between you and Rome now, Hannibal. I could have you eating dinner on their ceremonial porcelain in five days, in whatever place Fabius Maximus would call his *sanctum sanctorum.*"

Hannibal accomplished a real smile. Then he started to walk around, his attendants in that tent finding pathways for him that made a parade of officers and advisor's faces past him. He stopped near Barmocar who had been close to another assertion such as Maharbal had just made after Trasimene had also left a road to Rome open to him. Maharbal was still accessible, so he looked back at him to answer:

"Fifty miles a day wouldn't kill your horses, but it might do something to my appetite for that dinner you promised." He stayed close to Barmocar, his senior advisor from Carthage who qualified for first service of any answer he could give Maharbal. He picked up Sosylos and Silenus' eyes, and Mago's, and Myrcan's, Amarcar's, Sulan's, his officers'—friends, politicians, strategists, surrogates, before he made another word for his friend, Maharbal:

"Roman and allied, we've destroyed sixteen legions here. We've also done good work at Ticinus, Trebbia, Trasimene—but we haven't made a vacuum at

Rome that sucks us there. Our old friend Fabius is doubtless organizing a home guard right now to stand with the two legions already in the city. That would give us a welcoming party of...let's say twenty thousand." They could still find some smile on him, but it was getting to be harder work. Now he was looking at Barmocar, while talking to Maharbal:

"And if the Romans don't welcome us with opened gates, then, while we stare at walls that make our Saguntum memories into playthings, our thoughtful hosts can pull in legions from Campania, Sicily, Sardinia and Iberia to scratch our back. Let's say seven legions for back-scratching. Oh—I forgot Postumus, bathing his feet in the salubrious Po. He can bring two more legions for our party in front of the walls at Rome. I'm sure the mathematicians here can find a reasonable total quicker then I, but I am staring at a Roman number—a *living* Roman number, now, Maharbal—that refuses to stay below double our *present* strength, and those damned walls are still in front of us with Fabius' *sanctum sanctorum*, and a guard of twenty thousand, still behind them."

It had been a toast to a commander, a qualified acceptance, an assertion that further glorified a commander, and now Hannibal's virtual soliloquy that was pulling some of it down. But he knew how to leave Maharbal a little something. Barmocar gave him an opening:

"Then what has this great victory done for us, Hannibal?"

"It has put the proof mark on an army I am proud to lead—on officers I am privileged to call comrades. No one—certainly not my father—ever felt that all the Italian plums would fall into our basket with a few shakes of their trees. I told you before, Barmocar, that the way to Rome is by cutting the things that succor her. I talked about Capua, and the Campanian ports to Carthage. Cannae has made our path to the allied strongholds in southern Italy easier."

When he walked into that tent, Hannibal asked for numbers from Carthalo. Then he put his own numbers into that congregation after Maharbal placed his invitation to dine in Rome in five days—his ringing cap to the Cannae adventure. And some numbers Hannibal had given Barmocar after Trasimene—that he would play at siege for them at Rome if he could have a hundred thousand men to face the walls and another hundred thousand to watch his back—were also in that tent. Maharbal, the other focus of Hannibal's words, remembered these numbers, and he remembered a younger commander swearing in front of a smaller carnage at Saguntum that he would never put his men into that particular hell again. While still in his full flush as Master of Ceremonies at Cannae, Marharbal thought about telling Hannibal that he knew how to win a victory—but not how to use it...wonderful foot-note words for Silenus' chronicle. But now he was having trouble finding enough glue to stick them together.

When Mago passed the guards at Hannibal's tent that night, he was carrying two baskets and deserved the silent questions that diverted usually stoic stares after permission to enter had been asked and given. Hannibal was sitting at his camp table, the oil lamp above the desk the only light in the modest quarters. A writing sheet was in front of him, Mago could see that it was still virginal. At the staff meeting that evening, he could also see changes in his brother. One of these observations had to be approached more carefully than the other.

Hannibal looked up while Mago's baskets were still in his hands—one was nearly full, and the lamp told on gold in it.

"Penance isn't necessary, Mago—if you have sins I don't know about, you washed them away today. I haven't told you how much you meant to me on that field." Hannibal was wearing a night tunic, his shadowed face gave Mago no target for rebuttal.

"You finally showed me what those curved lines were about at Carthago Nova. I will have memories any man will envy, Commander." He had used that word playfully a thousand times, but there was no smile with it now. Hannibal's voice had not relinquished the softness, the hoarseness, that had been a troubling part of him for his friends since Mago and Maharbal had found him kneeling beside the Mushroom. Mago turned to the baskets he had set down on the floor:

"We've picked up some souvenirs at Ticinus, Trebbia, Trasimene and here" Mago bent down, and traced a finger through the top layer of the heavy basket, filled with the gold rings that marked the Roman equites, and partially the senators and some of the other hierarchy below the consuls. Adding the other basket, Mago had brought about thirty-six hundred *souvenirs* into the tent. He held one of the rings up to Hannibal's lamp, and Hannibal's comment:

"Initials, and a date...unless we took a lot of trouble, he's gone into honorable anonymity with Minucius."

"A Roman prisoner told me that they heard the laugh you started on the slope...on your way to the Cannae playground." Mago hadn't tried to plumb the shadow on his brother's face. Personals would require Hannibal's prompting, so he stayed semi-official for the moment.

Hannibal stood up, made a short trip to a locker, returned to the table and his seat after setting a bottle of Paullus' best wine, and two of his gold goblets, on the table. He did the honors and Mago was capable of accepting them.

"Interesting...what was the reaction?"

"He said that the *two-for-one* that Varro had waved over them on their way to meet you had shriveled some with that laugh...apparently you spoiled a masterpiece of consular inspiration."

"That would help to explain Varro's conspicuous lack of resolution."

Hannibal was quiet for a time that was long for Mago, the letter in front of him beyond his reach now. Then he gave Mago his full attention:

"I would like you to go to Carthage and dump your souvenirs in front of the sufets and senators. Tell them what we've done—try to sniff out what help we can get from the *mother tit*."

If the smile had resurrected some, Mago couldn't see it. The last part had come out with an uncharacteristic cynical inflection for a man who had just taken Tanit's standard to unprecedented elevation.

"Why can't *you* go? You have a daughter who is leaping into precocious womanhood. Inanna hasn't seen you in *two* years." When Mago said the name of the woman who he had confessed had spoiled him for other matrimony, he borrowed some of the softness in his brother's voice.

"I am watched by Roman hawks. Cannae would lose all of its significance if I left Italy for a while."

Hannibal had been looking away, but then it was front-on between them:

"I have acquired some steel in my neck the past two years that makes it easier now to look away from Carthage. You will be my surrogate to the Senate, to our family—and take *damn* good notes or I'll send Silenus after you."

Some vagaries of the oil light, and Hannibal's movement of his head, finally sent a face to match the gypsy's.

18

31 years
September 216 BC—Carthage

It had been three and a half days from Locri when Mago stood on the prow of the trireme and watched the captain warp her into Carthage, past the mercantile anchorage, into the entrance channel of the inner harbor, and then into the thousand foot diameter circle of the military sanctum—where two hundred warships could find repose in the sheds and quays, but such accommodation was barely tested now. He was the first officer who had been with Hannibal at Cannae to reach the mother breast. Cannae had come to Carthage before him by various means, but his would be the first eyes, and ears, which could tell about some hours in Apulia that no surrogates were qualified to touch.

"It has been a fine voyage, Captain...I needed this exposure to sun, sea, wind, and a trireme that can run under hands like yours." Mago saluted the captain and his homage was reflected to him by the captain and six of his officers who were standing close to Mago. It was four hours past high sun. When they rounded Cap Bon from the northeast and vectored toward Carthage, the long coats had come out, all black wool, and they all bore the lion and palm insignia of the Barcas in medallions attached high over the left chest zone. Except for Mago's, the medallions were bronze, his was Iberian silver.

"You have honored us, Lord Mago." The captain could have added that he, his ship and men, would be further honored by bringing more of Hannibal's thunder into Italy, but this attitude had been well presented while he had worked the sails and oars with the winds and currents to make it three and a half days to Carthage from Locri, on Italy's toe.

As he stepped on the gangway to the dock, Mago touched the glistening black hull that had been his horse for a while. A ship like this had brought Hasdrubal's messenger to the Lady Barca eight years before. And eight years before that, one like it, white hulled instead of black, had taken him to Iberia with his mother and Amalkre, and his brother Hasdrubal. When Mago stepped on solid Carthage, he had been away sixteen years.

The black ship had sent precursors into the city before she docked, whispers that became shouts that had rapid diffusion throughout the city. When Mago stepped ashore, he already had an escort of horse waiting for him, three young ones who had helped perpetuate Hannibal's Mushroom corps. They wore the hats; they rode matched gray Cyrenians, and were leading a fourth horse. They gave Mago a good salute upon order of the leader designate. Mago responded in kind, the ship's officers and crew putting a grinning background behind him.

"By Ba'al, gentlemen, Hannibal should be here! Your corps has helped to carry Carthage's glory into the Roman heart. Let me give you the salute I know he would allow me." So Mago saluted the three youngsters again, and they stood their ground, no muscle moving, as Mago played Hannibal for them.

"We will have your baggage brought to the palace, Lord Mago." Surrendering to the Mushrooms, the captain waved toward the fourth horse. Mago's black cloak was no handicap and he was aboard the gray and thundering out of the cothon precincts with a very close escort before a miscellany of welcoming officials could get official.

"We will ride together again, gentlemen. Give me a little time with my family...then we'll see what your horses can do." The mutual salutes flashed again, and then a dismounted Mago turned toward the gate of the Barca palace on Byrsa Hill.

Although there was still a decent enough light for a man to make his entrance, Artras had ordered the gate lamps lighted. But he was a stickler for formality, so he kept the gate closed, although his incentive for instant access to the palace, for a man who hadn't used this prerogative for sixteen years, was building by the instant under the palace chatelaine—now divisible by four—who'd heard the whispers, the shouts, and then had made her own sounds about Mago.

Mago had barely used the speaking portal, when the gate opened. He strode into the palace grounds and stopped near the central fountain that was a harbinger of the sculptural and botanical essences that Hamilcar's lady had put into the Barca precincts here and elsewhere. There was no one in the courtyard, the gate power had vanished. The water sounds and their replication off tiles and masonry were his greeting and it was enough to make a smile. He had been in and out of hell for two years. He had almost forgotten this grace of civilization that had been his mother's insistence.

There was a giggle. She would be five years old now. He would have to be damn careful—play the doting uncle and the swain for her in about equal parts and see how it goes. This was where the Commander should be, he was usurping Hannibal's place in this moment. By Tanit, he should have brought Sosylos, or Silenus, to put what was about to happen into a record for him. Mago started to walk closer to the fountain, his prescience of imminence of attack strong enough to taste—unlike the bile that he couldn't deny at Trebbia, or Cannae, but a complex of mostly strange liqueurs that absence, maturation, curiosity and delightful anticipation had concocted for him. He stopped, and stayed provocatively motionless and quiet. The prescience was being compounded now by other sources. Let the ladies all come—Hippolyta, Inanna, Kyniska, Medina. He'd had his resuscitation on the ship, he was ready for them.

There was a materialization near a cluster of giant ferns, about twenty feet from him. Not a sound, but he was turned to its precise location by the same prescience that had already steeled him for it. She wore a chiton fitted and styled to her, white with colored geometricals along the hems. Someone, probably Tiba and Maga, had plaited her hair in the Greek style with yellow silk ribbon. She seemed tall for five. She started walking toward him, like a priestess under the constraints of ceremony, but awake to prospects for her aura that were not necessarily sanctified. Mago stood his ground, he kept his smile under severe repression, but he was famously capable of a neutrality that could leap one way, or the other, according to the incentives.

When Kyniska was within three feet of him, Mago bowed and when she offered her hand, he touched his lips to it, carefully watching her for the deviation that he knew was part of the imminence that now had him in its focus.

"Prince Mago, I believe," she said. She'd used the Greek, and Mago was glad he'd paid attention to Sosylos and Silenus, and Inanna.

"I have that distinction, milady and you are, I believe...Princess Kyniska." She had kept up the game and never a giggle, just a barely lifted chin and eyes that seemed much older than five. And then she ran into him and the carefully constructed lady spilled over him, and he tried to kiss her—hands, arms, the face, whatever she would offer him. He lifted her off the ground and they started to spin around the fountain, her arms around his neck, laughter and giggles from both of them making a shambles of formality, but it was appropriate to the stage the Lady Barca had laid out for them in this entrance courtyard.

Then the moment got more complicated, and Mago started to feel other hands and arms on him and then he saw Inanna's face, and Medina's, in the melee that had engulfed him. He knew these other ladies very well, so he took what advantage of lips and cheeks and eyes and ears they afforded him. His black cloak swirled with white cloaks on the ladies, and first names were called out, and laughter. Then there was an interstice of the action which let him get a larger perspective and he saw the purple of another cloak near where he had first seen Kyniska. They let him relax his hold to address another lady.

It had been only about two years since Inanna and Medina's last sight of him, but it had been sixteen years for the mature goddess who now surveyed the rambunctious cluster which had finally fissioned into four parts. Her hair was now a blond and white amalgam, but the posture and presence of athletic perpetual beauty gave him most of his answer about her. She stayed where she was. Mago started to walk toward her.

He wore a civilian tunic under his cloak, but with every step toward his mother, she saw more of the soldier who had supplanted her boy. He stopped at arm's length. The smile was still Mago...he was still clean shaven and it looked like the weathered face could serve the playful gypsy who had exasperated and tantalized and provoked cheers and laughter from her family even before he had words. But he couldn't camouflage his eyes, the perspective of them that she probably wouldn't want to know. When she raised her arms toward him, he touched her hands and she pulled him toward her. She kissed his cheek and then there was a lip kiss that lingered, and she moved her fingers through his hair while she looked at his face from the closest possible vantage. Finally, she turned toward the others of this greeting, Mago still locked in a mutual embrace:

"Is this a way to greet a famous commander—all laughs and giggles and completely surrounded by females?" If she thought this would keep them at bay she was wrong. Kyniska and Inanna and Medina merely moved to compound Mago's envelopment.

Then there was a moment for Mago:

"He should be here...I *wanted* him to come." But they wouldn't let him apologize.

After he had taken the full privileges of bath and massage, and the civilian male wardrobe of his suite, he joined the ladies at dinner, and some more facets of his mother's civilization were recalled. He couldn't keep up with the questions, Kyniska's, Inanna's, his mother's, Medina's. He had been warned by Hannibal that he was going into a matriarchal stronghold—but be damned, the laughter and beauty surrounding him made him exercise his gypsy and swain more than it did his son and uncle, brother-in-law and friend, so he felt that Hannibal had overplayed the metamorphosis that Inanna and Medina and Hippolyta were working, and Kyniska was studying.

And until Kyniska went to bed, they had stayed away from Hannibal. Kyniska had asked questions about her daddy. He had answered her. But when she was finally safe in Tiba and Maga's jurisdiction, Hannibal came out. Mago had taken his wine to the balustrade of a veranda overlooking the cothon. His prescience had served him well up to now...he wasn't sure how it would come out when the ladies didn't shy away from Hannibal.

Mago was allowed some quiet study of the cothon area...oil lamps defining part of the perimeters of a maritime and naval strength that, except for the gossamers, had not been a good bolster of his brother in Italy and he had heard Hannibal curse that part of Carthage. Then Inanna's real voice penetrated a complexion of thoughts that in some of his Italian versions had included her imagined voice:

"*How* is he, Mago?" It was soft, still using the Greek. Inanna had often teased him for his reluctance to go Greek in their speech, but now it was a good conveyance for her question that carried as much scope as Mago wanted to put into it. He finally turned to her. She was about ten feet away, a quintessential Greek lady for him, no respect of her that Phidias would have found wanting before he touched her to marble. His mother and Medina had conceded first place to her for the post-Kyniska questions. But they were in a subtle approach to him that would soon let his answers for Inanna serve them also.

"He seems to have compensated for the eye. We, his people around him down to the last man in his corps, feel this."

"I think no man ever had better help for this...but did you answer for his general, or his personal man, Mago?"

"The eye was lost when we came to Faesulae. Trasimene and Cannae, and some wonderful tweaking of the Roman nose between, came afterward, so my first answer must be for his general." Inanna had to wait a while for Mago's answer about Hannibal's personal man, he had turned back toward the part of the night that enveloped the cothon. "He has been marked by Roman blood since we came down the Alps into the Po—you know the place names, I think his letters spelled them out for you. More of it came in the Roman wonderland in Campania, before he turned toward Cannae." Mago's mouthing of the last word put a special mark on it that no precursors into Carthage had done. Inanna came to him, touched his shoulder:

"Tell us about Cannae, Mago. I know about the great victory...but his letters and what I've seen and heard of you since you've come back, need more explanation than the words *victory*, and *Cannae*, can give." By their gods, she *was* beauty and grace. He could understand Hannibal's confession of strength from her reaching to every crevice of Italy where he had been.

"At Trasimene we kept him off the field after he planned his action. At Cannae, he was the inspiration flowing into our line that made the victory. To do this he was everywhere along two miles of men and horses. We have a Numidian guard for him that tries to protect him. He led them in and out of that line, within range of the Roman javelins, they couldn't keep up with him—I couldn't keep up with him."

"We've heard that some officer, named Mago, was also part of the miracle of the Carthaginian line at Cannae."

"There was a pinnacle for that miracle called Hannibal and his friends scrambled around that pinnacle as best they could."

Inanna made him face her, with another gentle insistence.

"Now for those special words, Mago..."

Even face to face now, she had to wait for him again...he seemed to have trouble making their eye axis.

"I saw him after the killing had ended...he was sitting on the ground, marked with blood." Inanna and two other ladies accented Mago's words with hands to their mouths. "A Centurion had slipped through our line and gotten close enough to him to try a spear throw. His natural reflexes saved him and he was only grazed before a Numidian lance ended the Roman. I didn't know the wound was slight. I saw blood smeared all over him, his head bent down to a Mushroom officer who was beyond conversation." Mago turned away and then came back to the Greek lady who had ancestral inoculations of Salamis and Thermopylae and Marathon which qualified her for Cannae words from a man who had been in the place and the time they were forged.

"The stink of blood and guts was so strong I saw men puking with it. He is still only 31 years old!—few men have ever been marked like this. When they told him that young Scipio was escaping with a remnant of Roman horse and foot he shook his head and denied pursuit of this continuity of the Roman Wolf. At that moment the late light was in his eyes, tinted like the rest of him...I saw a mixture that only a god's exaltation—and a devil smearing his face and eyes and ears with what was on that field around him—could put on him." He denied Inanna and the others for a moment and then came back to this Greek lady's demand for Cannae:

"I saw his eyes flicking around the carnage...*over seventy-six thousand dead.*" If they hadn't all been close to him they would have missed the quiet path Mago had just taken. Mago looked at his mother, who was now within arm's reach of him, but she had resisted touching him. "Alexander was never tested in a crucible like this—the bronze that Hannibal put up for him at Gades must have had his head skewed toward Cannae by now."

Inanna and Medina still had fingers crossing their mouths, so the senior chatelaine, with various credentials of fortitude, provocation and aggression, pushed Mago along the questions Inanna had ordered:

"What did you say to him?"

"I told him it was over...that he had a great victory."

"He was on the ground by his friend, spattered with various blood. You saw a god's mark on him and you saw a devil's. This doesn't look like a glory of victory, Mago. And this compassion to a deadly enemy, this young Scipio we've heard about. All of this is a complication I don't think Zortibas, or Acherbas, could untangle." She finally touched her son's hand.

"How bad was his wound, Mago?" Somehow Inanna made the question.

"One of Synhalus' orderlies got a bandage on it and stopped the bleeding.

It will mark his cheek a little. It's another souvenir of close death, the left side, where the eye is gone. Later, he told me that you would complain about his unbalanced defects—all of this *left* side business, and he would try to do better next time." Lady Barca's close attendance helped stop another inclination to tears that still needed all the Greek resolve Inanna could find.

"How is he *now*, Mago?" There were no tears with this Inanna question, a more insistent version of an earlier one.

"His strategy has always been to isolate and shrink the Roman's stature on his own ground, giving the rest of Italy a chance for independent progress, with Carthage, or whomever they choose. He has treated the Roman allies with this respect. They are starting to respond to him...but he is also starting to see the limits to the reach of *his* arms. When we came south from the Po, there were *no* limits on his horizon. He sucked the Romans into his power and gave them lessons on how to pile their dead on their own fields—almost within sight of Rome. But the look I saw on him at Cannae has had some persistence. The killing of Romans is like trying to kill the weeds of Italy—they can draw their seeds from *everywhere*. He has plans and hopes...but he is starting to see limits."

"Bomilcar told me that he will pray for all the Greekness that Carthage can put into his enterprise."

"Tell him that we join his supplications, Mother. Hannibal is looking northward toward new strength of the Celts, westward to strength he left in Iberia with Hasdrubal, eastward to some Greeks who have not forgotten their heritage. But Bomilcar has, as usual, a tendency to put his finger on a central pulse. Without Carthage's ligament to him, Hannibal thinks he will be no more than a scratch on the monument to Roman progress, no matter what other strengths he can find. He ordered me here, in fact, to test the quality of the *mother tit*—his words, by the way."

"I would charge him with unseemly cynicism if I hadn't seen convoys leaving for Sardinia, and other places not relevant to him, Mago. How will you test the quality of this *mother tit*?" The Lady Barca could, and would, use any word that was in Mago's, or Hannibal's vocabulary.

"I will speak to the Senate. If I can manage greater privacy, I will speak to your friend, Bomilcar, and hopefully, your friend and his friend, Imilco. I think the Senate, and the sufets, are the best I can do."

"The worst you can do may also be in the Senate, Mago—watch your back when it is turned toward young Hanno."

"He has assumed the Hanno mantle that tried to smother Father?"

"He is the present spokesman for aristocrats who have not cut their umbilicals to Rome as cleanly as they have confessed. He, and his friends, may be the chief impediment to that *tit* you've raised here."

He could have taken a horse, with escort, to the forum below Byrsa Hill. But it was a day for walking. The air, a synthesis of sea and desert qualities unique to Carthage, and the vistas as he came down from Byrsa Hill that pulled him closer to the old city—mercantile, naval, architectural, botanical, the arenas for discussion and government that Plato had complimented...all of it making a day to suck and then savor the breath that this city had put around him.

He had an escort, a young Greek who had been his personal servant lately, and who had made the mistake of telling Mago that he wanted to accompany him to the forum, and then into the Hall of the Council if it were possible. The lad was carrying a woven satchel over his shoulder which held thirty-six hundred Roman gold rings, plucked from Italian fields between Ticinus and Cannae.

"By your Zeus, Stiros, you will curse that satchel before we achieve the Council." Mago laughed at the lad's discreet shifting of the load to another shoulder.

"If you let me do the throwing in front of the Council and the sufets I will be satisfied, Lord Mago." Black curly hair topped a handsome reflection of the northern Peloponnesus, a face and body that had found a way into some of the running and gymnastics that had been part of Mago's further resuscitation.

"What throwing?"

"Surely these Italian souvenirs will shine brighter on the tiles in front of the senators and sufets than in this bag, Lord Mago."

"You attribute sufets to the meeting.—how do you know we will be glorified like this?"

"Whispers from the forum have long legs, Lord Mago. I think it will be pressed tight with bodies on the floor of the Council chamber, and on the benches of the senators and the sufets when you enter."

"But you will wait for my order, Stiros. If there is to be throwing, then it will be at *my* time." He gave Stiros only part of his smile. This lad, somewhat another of Sosylos' protégés, had been warned by Sosylos' letter that one of Hannibal's several right hands might soon become his responsibility for a little while. Mago's aura as a famously precocious commander close to Hannibal, as a connoisseur of the brighter shades of life, made it hard for Mago to keep a proper tension in the master-servant coupling. And under Stiros' natural inquisitiveness about matters well inside Mago's aura, companions were being made here.

Stiros had been right. They started to pick up the shouts and smiles before they got to the bottom of Byrsa Hill...children, men, women. Cannae had put a crown on Hannibal that no Carthaginian had worn within memory. Hamilcar had a glorious stature here, but his sons, particularly the one still in

Italy and the one who was now striding toward the Council, were vindication of Hamilcar's dreams, and beyond.

The crowns of luxuriant botanicals were in full cry on the buildings below Byrsa along the forum way. By Tanit, this was a city! It had antecedents that made Rome look and feel like a preposterous paraphrase of culture that had leaked out of Alexandria's memories of Greece and Mesopotamia. The crowd of shouts and cries and smiles grew heavier as Mago and Stiros approached the columned portico of the Council building. They were a handsome pair. They would have made some of this greeting without Hannibal, or Cannae, but they *had* this wonderful baggage, and Stiros' grin, Mago's gypsy smile, compounded everything, and made it a close business getting into the vestibule and finally the main audience chamber of the Hall of the Council.

Mago worked forward to just below the first tier of benches, Stiros staying close to Mago's bow wave. The auditors in the suppliants' arena, men and women, gave them some space and when Mago stopped, he had a decent stage of clear tiles around him.

All of the senators capable of walking, or being littered and carried, were in the benches above Mago. The sufets, Bomilcar and Imilco, were in the center benches of the front row. Admiral Bomilcar was close to them in the front row. All of the senior officers of the home force were distributed on edges of the senatorial array. The admiral and the officers were in garrison uniforms. Mago was in civilian form. His tunic had some Roman cast that started a few whispers—but that bronzed face molded by Carthage and Iberia and Italy, and Greek-styled black hair that Inanna had insisted on him, via Tiba, for this meeting—put the Mago Barca stamp on him.

He looked at Bomilcar, then Imilco, then swept a few of the senators into his smile. Old Hanno was dead. His son, young Hanno, was not, and Mago found him in a periphery of the privileged benches but didn't acknowledge him except by remembering his mother's warning about the Hanno faction—a persistent thorn for the Barca's.

This was the official focus of the Senate, so a senator made the first speech:

"We are honored by your visit, Commander Mago." The military title carried less political implication than *Lord* Mago, so the senator used it and thereby set a precedent for any who cared to follow it.

"General Hannibal sends his respects and regrets that the Italian situation must be his first priority at this juncture."

"We have heard about some of the wonderful progress he has made in Italy—Ticinus, Trebbia...Trasimene. And now this Cannae! We are eager for details about this great victory for Carthage which must have echoes in every corner of our world." The senator leaned closer to Mago, and he had plenty of competition for Mago's words.

"As you know from his reports, Hannibal has been trying to pull the Romans into a major confrontation. They have used every stratagem in their book—and any other book they could find—to avoid a pitched battle with him after Trebbia and Trasimene."

"Evidently he found his bait at Cannae."

"It was a major supply depot for their army, and Rome itself. He occupied it and they couldn't refuse his gage this time."

"We understand two Consuls were committed there."

"Paullus and Varro—about eighty-six thousand foot and horse."

"Hannibal had at his disposal at this time?..."

"About fifty thousand foot and horse."

"When did this battle start?"

"Dawn, on the second day of July."

"When did it end?"

"About two hours past high sun of the same day."

"We have heard some things about the end of this battle that are almost unbelievable."

Mago had been looking at the senator during this exchange, but his voice tuned for a larger audience. He started to walk slowly along the front of the bench array, the standing auditors giving him a moving stage. Stiros held his position near the center. Mago would come back to him when he was ready.

"You *may* believe that seventy thousand Roman dead were piled on that field, about six thousand of ours." A general gasp had origins from the floor, and the benches. Mago was about thirty feet away from the introductory senator. He turned and started to walk toward him.

"Paullus, the Pro-Consuls Servilius and Minucius, all the quaestors, twenty-nine tribunes, eight of senatorial rank, and thousands of equites were left on the Cannae field, here are some of their souvenirs:" Mago nodded to Stiros, who spilled the contents of his satchel in a graceful arc on the tiles in front of the center benches. The golden cascade—3600 remnants of young Roman blood that had soaked into mostly Cannae earth—made another gasp, structured like the last one from the bench and floor audience of that hall.

The Lady Barca had warned that antagonism to Rome was ambiguous in some of the heads bent to the trophy Stiros had just laid in front of them. It was not so with most of the floor people, their shouts, and movements to see the gold was the *people's* reaction Mago had expected.

The introductory senator spoke to Mago again, after the tumult of the rings had subsided. "Varro, the other consul?"

"He left the field when our heavy horse got to the rear of the legions and started to attack his cocoon of light horse. Our Numidians chased him a little and then came back to help finish the Cannae business."

"Excepting the redoubtable Varro, what can you say about the Romans who survived Cannae?"

"We took about thirteen thousand captured, foot and horse. We think about four thousand, mostly foot, escaped to Canusium. General Hannibal released the Italian captives to their homes. He held the Romans for ransom."

Another senator's voice: "Surely every Roman of note was not left on the field at Cannae, Commander Mago."

"Young Publius Scipio was in the party that got to Canusium, also young Fabius, the Dictator's son. Hannibal was advised of this...he refused chase at that time."

"This young Scipio...we've heard he also escaped the field at Ticinus—this charmed life may yet haunt us, Mago."

"The man who engined the result at Cannae, who was surrounded by the piles of its dead, was wounded himself, and had just found an old friend among the dead, was the one who was advised of the escape. I cannot explain his decision...but I can understand it."

Another senator: "Did Rome ransom Hannibal's prisoners?"

"Carthalo was Hannibal's emissary for this. The Roman Senate rejected the ransom and had lictors dismiss Carthalo before he got to the gates."

"Why did Hannibal not attack Rome at this juncture?"

"He has answered this question for his staff, and now I bring it to this Council: 'Give me a hundred thousand men for the siege, another hundred thousand to watch my back, and I will take Rome.'" This answer left a thick silence in that hall. Sufet Imilco was the first to break it:

"We have heard about some of the Roman response to Cannae: After frantic perusal of their Sibylline Books, and the exercise of every Etruscan soothsayer who could lay hands on beef livers and chicken guts, our old friend Fabius Maximus was sent to consult the oracle at Delphi. A Celtic couple, and a Greek couple, were buried alive in the Forum Bovarium. All public displays of grief have been forbidden. Every Roman asset for continuance of this war is being combed fine—the armories, the spoils of arms, every trove into which their tentacles can probe for men—including debtors, war prisoners, criminals. Rome has been driven to the wall by Hannibal." Imilco's voice was also designed for the general ear of that hall.

"If the crest of Hannibal's victory wave is peaking—why are you here, Mago? Surely as it moves toward Rome he will need every commander." This was young Hanno's voice. It was sitting on a spot of the third tier of benches where the loyal opposition could feel comfortable. He was about thirty feet to Mago's left.

Mago walked toward Hanno. His father had tried to destroy Hamilcar. He had been described, but Mago had never met this clone of prejudice against the Barcas that had persisted for several generations of the Hanno clan.

"Imilco mentioned a wall against the Roman's back. There is another wall in this picture. Since Hannibal came into Italy, he has received no reinforcements from Carthage, Iberia, or Sicily. Only the Celts have given him the foot and horse which have made Trasimene and Cannae possible." Young Hanno was supposed to have support. Mago walked closer to him, stopping at the edge of the first bench tier, sweeping the faces near to Hanno, and then back to the thirtyish man who seemed to have plenty of time for politics—but none for war.

"Rome has committed *everything* she has against Hannibal—he will need similar sustenance from Carthage."

"This then is what you say: I have slain the armies of the enemy, send me soldiers. What would you have asked for if you had not been so fortunate in Italy? Has a single tribe of the Italian allies gone to Hannibal?—or a single city of the Roman Federation? Has there been *any* intimation of a Roman suit for peace?"

"Capua, the crown jewel of the Roman Federation, has made overtures to Hannibal." By Tanit, the throat of this effete twit was tempting, but some of Sosylos' diplomacy came into Mago at the right time.

"I say that we have upon our hands, now, a war as entire as we had on the day Hannibal crossed the Alps. I say that the resources of Carthage might find a better repository than a grave in Italy."

"I say that it is fortunate Carthage has better resources in this hour of *opportunity* than it can find scraping the slop heaps of the Hannos." Mago got as close to Hanno as he dared without committing to the throat that had tempted him almost beyond Sosylos' caution.

Bomilcar asked him about Hannibal's imminent, or potential, resources:

"Hasdrubal in Iberia is a force that, joined with Hannibal at the right juncture, could break the Roman back. Hannibal has had overtures from Phillip V of Macedon. This Greek has a facility for command and resources in Greece that, again at the right juncture with Hannibal, could make the multi-front war that Hannibal believes will kill the Roman power in Italy. And there are the Celts. The ones on this side of the Alps have already been crucial to his strength. He has knowledge of Celt resources in Gaul and Germania that could add the keystone to the arch of his triumph in Italy." Cathbad, the Druid, had used the image of a temple, and a crucial column, when he talked with Hannibal about his Italian enterprise, and the relevance of his Celts to it—but they were equivalent images, Mago's and Cathbad's.

Imilco and some of the senators asked Mago about the size of a reinforcement that would matter to Hannibal. A body of help consisting of four thousand Numidian horse, twenty thousand foot and four thousand horse from Iberia, took shape between the floor and the benches of the Council Hall. Also enough talents of silver and gold from the Treasury to invigorate Hannibal's proselytizing of the Celts and the Greeks Mago had been talking about.

But when Mago left the Council chamber, the inspiration of venerable Carthaginian artistry in the terrazzo pictures in floors and walls, the elegance of the space and form conjunctions of the Council Hall and then of the exterior progressions into the Forum, that Roman copiers hadn't gotten to, were not enough to make a good ending of that day, despite Imilco and Bomilcar's encouragement.

Hanno was an incarnation of the persistent two-faced aristocracy that had denied the people's voice in Carthage and a chance for the consensus of support that Hannibal needed and was now the crucial element in the Roman armory. He had put insults into a conclave that should have had no trace of anything but acclaim, and opportunity, and expedition of opportunity. The focus in the Roman Senate now was different and stronger—*their* Hanno would have been killed on the spot. Carthaginian Hanno would be a slow poison Mago knew he couldn't exorcise when he returned to Hannibal.

"Do the horses like the battles, Mago?" The voice had been tailored by almost an hour of riding behind Mago, on the big gray Cyrenian he had picked from the stables at the Hadrumetum estate. He had started out slowly with her, a decorous walk, occasionally the trot. But as she tightened her grip around his waist, she made little challenges to this decorum he couldn't deny and he had gone to the canter, and sometimes the full gallop with her as they penetrated the orchards, pastures, the pathways that invited a horse with two people on board who seemed to find laughter and shouts indispensable.

"When they are in line of battle, ready for a charge, it is a great moment for them and I know they like it. Afterwards..." He stopped them, and he turned to where he could see Hannibal's daughter. She was equipped with a Mushroom hat in her size, but so far it had dangled on her back, its leather throng around her throat. Her hair was gold in the bright sunshine, no ribbons of constraint. Her mother had put a copy of Lady Barca's Celt cavalry uniform on her—checkered pants, long-sleeved white blouse, soft black leather boots in the Carthaginian style.

"Afterwards?" Kyniska insisted.

"Then it depends on a thousand things: the shape and timing of the battle, the accidents of the coming together that make a battle, and no man can foresee." Kyniska had to move a little closer to pick up all of Mago's words. "It can become like a waking dream, Kyniska, not all of it something you would want for your memory—the men, *or* the horses."

"I have had some times like that, Mago." She put her face next to Mago's back. "Mother and Father are mixed up in them, sometimes in ways like you said...not good for memories."

They were close to the estate house. Mago assisted Kyniska's dismount and then they walked toward the conclusion of that morning's outing. The ladies had collaborated to make a kaleidoscope of homecoming for Mago—rides and walks, singly and in various combinations, the same for water play in the pools with real and bronzed nymphs, alfresco meals where every attribute of the Barca country sides could beguile him...everything that could be pulled into a homecoming for a soldier that everyone knew was token for a transient of a life that had already gone beyond them. But no one gave up the game of pretense. Mago would return as a permanent strength of Carthage—and *that* was that.

"How long will you be staying, Mago?" Kyniska looked up at the tall cavalryman beside her who had gone to a Mushroom uniform for his equestrian exercise with her that day.

"The Senate has voted a significant force to help your daddy in Italy. I will be leaving in a few days to bring it to him."

"When do you think I will see him?"

"Just as soon as he can make it happen. I will tell him to make it *very* soon—or he won't be able to catch a young lady growing into a queen." She squeezed his hand just before her denial:

"There have been no *queens* of Carthage, not since Dido, Mago. How would I fit into your big compliment?" By her mother's Zeus, this one had overleaped her five plus years! She would soon be a bundle for anyone to handle...certainly for a soldier from the Italian fields, unaccustomed to her aura.

"There are many kinds of *queens*, Kyniska. Carthage will need many forms of them and I think I am holding one of her best prospects—now." Mago's gypsy came in then...eyes, soft laughter, smile...he never had a better audience.

The sufet, Bomilcar, was the Lady Barca's guest at Mago's last dinner at Hadrumetum. His locus in the family as Lady Barca's unofficial swain granted him certain privileges in the company, such as helping to usher Kyniska off to bed. She had captured him long before her Mago campaign, and Bomilcar had already attached the word *continuity* to her like Mago had done, but with his own particulars.

"Hanno was one of Carthalo's right hands in the heavy cavalry at Cannae. The execution of Hannibal's order to crush the Roman right wing horse was the key to the unraveling of the Roman discipline—and the battle." Mago and Bomilcar had escaped the ladies' attention for a few moments of privacy on a veranda which gave a perspective of the seaward estate, framed by a twilight that could promote a strong flux of memories, and complexities of anticipation. Mago had just brought Bomilcar's son, Hanno, into the perspective.

"I have a letter from Hannibal, apparently written in the Po valley, before he went into the hell of the Arnus. He mentioned my Hanno, his pride in him, and his other officers. I'm glad Hanno has not disappointed him."

"If quality and devotion were enough to pull down the Roman cloud over Italy, Hannibal would have conjured universal sunlight over there by now."

"I know these things are not enough, Mago...and I have some news that will not bolster my welcome in this house."

"My prescience has been honed to a new edge since I've been home, Bomilcar. Let me test it again: the new troop allotment will not go to Italy—Iberia's silver is speaking louder to the Senate than Hannibal."

"The Roman successes there have posed more urgency for them than Hannibal's in Italy. You have been ordered to Iberia."

They both faced the seaward part of their perspective. To the Lady Barca, Bomilcar had confessed certain prayers pertinent to this moment. More words, more prayers, probably couldn't serve it, and two of Hannibal's best friends, side by side here, were starting to believe this.

The kaleidoscope had nearly drained out. During a running exercise with Mago, Stiros dared a request that would have been impudent under a lesser bond with a master:

"Take me with you when you return to Hannibal, or wherever the gods lead you."

"My road to Hannibal may be longer than I had expected." They had settled into a comfortable jogging pace for the return leg to the Hadrumetum villa. And they were close enough to serve easy conversation.

"I have never trained for war, Lord Mago, but you have made me feel uncomfortable with this paradise. You and Hannibal are trying to protect it, and I am doing nothing."

"You are becoming a right arm for some ladies who are carrying an important part of this paradise that is also one of the bastions that will keep Carthage alive after this Roman business is over. Your word, *protection*, has a broader scope, my friend, and you are already in it." Mago brushed Stiros with a smile, but the lad was unconvinced.

"I am enmeshed with women—it is not a man's world."

"You are enmeshed with some people who are as close to Hannibal as

Hamilcar's dream that pushed him into Italy. To say that their protection is not a man's game would not be a good way to start a chat with Hannibal. If he comes back—*when* he comes back to Carthage, it would be very good to have the ladies' affairs in the best possible order. If you think this task is not meet for a man, then you grossly underestimate the precocity, ingenuity, and only the gods know what else make up my mother, Inanna, Medina and Kyniska!"

"You have put a heavy portion on my plate, Lord Mago. By Zeus, it is some consolation that General Hannibal doesn't know it, yet." Stiros' grin was short-lived.

"I must deny you that consolation. I have already put you down to Hannibal as one of his assets in Carthage." Mago's last letter to Hannibal *had* noted certain local Barca assets which included Artras, and other prominent strengths of his ladies' arsenal. Stiros had gone into this like a footnote, but he was there. Mago had exaggerated, but he had put back a grin.

In the few hours as the shutter of the kaleidoscope was closing, Mago's communion with his mother had been mostly silent. She *had* talked with Zortibas and Acherbas about Hannibal and Italy, and Cannae. If there had been some metamorphosis of a conqueror in the clues Mago and others had brought to Carthage, the complication was too much for a mortal assertion about this man the gods had noticed. He would have to travel farther with them before any assertions, summaries, were justified. She had used the word *if* sparingly with Mago and tried to use *when* and *we* as much as she could. It was like her last time with Hamilcar at Gades. The prescience of permanent goodbye was as strong now as then. But she gave Mago visions of a lady who could draw Heimarmene's smiles into her future if anyone could. She gave him a ligament of love that would be sustenance no matter where he went from Carthage.

His ship to Iberia had been ordered to cast away from the military dock at dawn. He said what he could for his goodbyes to all of the ladies in the gentle hours before midnight. With Kyniska it was mostly several kisses on the cheek to forestall tears. On the periphery of the emotions, he promised Inanna he would try to contact her father at Castulo. He told Medina he would look for some of her kinfolk. They finally conceded a good night's rest to him.

He let Stiros transport his baggage to the cothon. Wrapped in the black cloak that had entered the palace with him, he was about to leave through the same gate with it, when another cloak, also black this time for she didn't want advertisement, moved out of the night background of the courtyard and stopped between Mago and the final portal of the palace.

Inanna put her arms around him. The hood of her cloak slipped off her head and he could see a cascade of her hair, the special blackness of her that had been her first signal to Hannibal at Castulo.

"Inanna...I wish I could bring you to him...he needs you."

Then she kissed him on the cheek, then the lips, and he had to respond. He was no bronze man at Gades, or the other places of only memories. In those moments before she released him, he was Hannibal, he was her father, he was Hamilcar who had put everyone together, and he was Mago, who had confessed a frustration to her and Hannibal that involved *her*. As she backed away from him into the dark secrets of Hippolyta's courtyard, she touched two fingers to her lips and then moved those fingers toward him. Another ligament for Commander Mago Barca.

19

36 years
211 BC—Cumae, Campania

H is escort had let him keep an unusual separation all the way from their morning camp west of Capua to now where each man of it could conjure private pathways between hell and paradise using the sights, sounds and smells of the Phlegrean Fields into which he was pulling them. Avernus, the lake that the Greeks said was the gateway to the Underworld, was now alongside them. A man could turn the mists and vapors out there into demons, or gods, at his pleasure, but they tended to demons.

Hannibal didn't stop at the lake, his course persisting farther west toward Cumae and the precincts of its Sibyl. The Euboean Greeks had dug a house for her there under the rock of their Acropolis, and for five hundred and fifty years she had shared the auspices of Apollo with a sister who presided at Delphi, above the Gulf of Corinth.

He knew they didn't like this country. His Numidian escort could ride with him into hell—and had. But the tinctures of sulfur in the air were giving them too many tools for working the imagination they had made notorious when not focused on battle, or related deviltry. Maharbal and Carthalo were also with him this morning, but they had let him ride point a good distance from their position in front of his leopard Numidians. After the latest debacle at Capua, where another of his cooperative efforts with the lethargic Capuans had been deflected by the Romans, his staff had left plenty of room for his voice and body to play with the frustration that had been a progressively aggressive shadow since he had made a summit on the Apulian plain at Cannae, five years behind them.

Hannibal had gone to Cumae a few days after Cannae, on his way to Naples to make one end of a bridge to Carthage. He had stood in the Sibyl's precincts as a conqueror, savoring Etruscan and Greek heritage around him that he had matched and bettered. He had made civil supplication to her for her favors in the direction of the sea bridge at Neapolis, and for other Italian enterprises of that moment that he didn't doubt, and the Romans feared.

This time he was coming to her under less exhilarating initiative. He was bringing questions to her. He didn't feel diminished from the earlier time, but if he'd had some arrogance then, a surfeit of the *pothos* that had engined

Alexander across Asia, there was less of it now. He had questions for her: What did the gods expect of a man—*him*? What help did *he* have a right to expect? What were the limits they had put on him?

For example, the Capuan plum that had dropped into his lap a few days after Cannae had fed slow poison to him for years. Capua had seemed a logical focus for designing the Roman demise, a lodestone that would encourage refreshment of his power from the pillars he and the Druid had identified. But the treaty with Phillip of Macedon had been ambushed by the Romans through astounding luck that seemed to bend toward them now. The Greek cities of Italy, some of them with potential for bridges to Carthage as great as Neapolis, had used old antagonism against Carthage against him, and no one had welcomed him. The Capuan millstone he had tied to himself had minimized his personal gestures toward the Transalpine Celts. Cathbad's messages had continued to encourage, but he knew that one old man was not enough to light the signal fires for the Belgae and Germani who could bring a new generation of Celtic surprise and power into Italy under *his* command.

He turned his white Cyrenian away from the lake, tracking toward Cumae, and resisted looking back at probably a collective sigh of relief in the cavalry column behind him, particularly his leopard Numidians, most of whom had survived from the Cannae day they had saved his life. They, the regular Numidian horse behind them, his African foot, his Iberians, Carthaginians, and most of his Celts, had piled more Roman dead in Campania, Apulia, Umbria, Bruttium, and Lucania since Cannae. They had continued to make a mockery of Roman aggression and initiative. They had made fear of *him* a sheen on the marble tiles in the Roman Senate chamber that had been bouncing the bluster back into the senators' faces since he had knocked on their door at Ticinus and Trebbia and Trasimene and Cannae.

The particulars of Cumae were entering their panorama: vestiges and active remnants of the Greeks he had solicited, and of the Etruscans who had dug themselves into his heritage under his mother's auspices. By Zeus and Asclepius and Heimarmene, Inanna would love this place! And Amalkre and Hamilcar's Hippolyta could find all they needed for their images and constructions that had been in his wonder and curses and laughter. He was coming close to the entrance to the Sibyl's grotto. His Numidians had dropped farther back. Maharbal and Carthalo were starting to make a decent approach to him. Damn them, they should be used to his tangents by now—but let them keep their distance as they pleased.

Kyniska would have ten years on her wonderful person now. It had been seven years since he had held *his* lady from Delphi, Inanna. His gossamers of land and sea had sustained their letters and Inanna had been a magician in keeping him tied to their secret places in Carthage using words. By her, their, gods, the Greeks *had* put their magic into this portal to the Sibyl! He dismounted and started to walk into the rock. They had carved the entrance into successive massive keyhole-like portals, challenging the visitor to make a key for her favors. As he passed the fourth virtuosic sculpting of the passage, the chambered air warped the sounds of his footfalls, tempting him to try his voice in salutes to frustration, or laughter, or some measured commander's bravado, or whispers to Inanna and Kyniska. He heard Maharbal and Carthalo's footsteps enter the channel to the grotto. They had also followed him into hell, and they wouldn't let him get so far away from them that he could make plans that didn't include them.

He finally entered the Sibyl's sanctuary. Nothing had changed here since he had come from Cannae. The details of this place were built of shadows that a man, or woman, could work for specific purposes. These precincts now had none of the formalities of Delphi, partly due to his depredations in Southern Italy. But the Cumean Sibyl was still a conduit to the significant gods, so one could place obeisance in front of her for favors granted, or asked. A person could also address declarations of faith, purpose, or frustration to her. Questions could be asked which went to the heart of her function, and she needed no surrogates between question and answer. All of these things could be taken to this simple grotto and its silences were as apropos of respectful communion as any pretentious sacraments claiming closer coupling to the gods.

He walked some twenty feet toward the altar cove and this allowed Marharbal and Carthalo to enter the chamber without crowding him. The air had some refreshment by seaside sources the Greeks had allowed into their rock. This was a space for declaration. But he'd forgotten how his voice sounded here, and for the moment just breathing, and the fluxes of Inanna and Kyniska that had suddenly intruded his initiative in coming to Cumae again, satisfied him.

Marharbal and Carthalo had been with him at Faesulae when he'd lost half his world. They had seen him bring most of it back, right to when a few more resources from the lackadaisical mother tit could have smashed the ultimate Roman citadels within weeks after Cannae had defined Roman terror and *Roman* frustration. They left this Sibyl's space, and moment, to him.

"You would make poor assassins—I heard you, felt you, since this rock swallowed me." He still looked toward the Sibyl's focus, but he had just let them into his reverie.

"We tried to give you a graceful respite with the Sibyl, Hannibal." Marharbal was tempted to take a step toward his commander, but *respite* had been his word, and he stayed next to Carthalo in the deep shadows girding the entrance to the lady's sanctuary.

"What do you recommend—obeisance, declarations, or questions?" Hannibal stared toward the altar, trying to take some hints for his question from both his front and back quarters.

"There is basis for obeisance in the killing of the elder Scipios in Iberia by your brothers and Hasdrubal Gisgo. Perhaps you and Hasdrubal and Mago will share some Italian honors soon, my Lord." Carthalo had just mentioned probably the only recent official basis for his commander's thankful obeisance in front of the present lady.

Hannibal made a rare bow toward the Sibyl's focus. "Give me another such basis quickly, Carthalo—while I'm in good posture to acknowledge it." The flux of Inanna and Kyniska intruded him again and it probably had no place in this particular recitation of good and bad in front of the Cumaean Sibyl. But his orientation, and the marginal ambient light, hid a small, intrusive, smile which had absolutely no military inspiration.

"You still have an army on Roman ground that no Roman commander dares to face. You have held it together by your own glue. It will be the cornerstone of the reinforcement that *will* come from Iberia." This aristocrat, Hannibal, had spent many nights on the ground with his patrols and watches, letting them into his thoughts in unpatronizing ways, acknowledging them. This was rare glue he had spread over a motley corps that could have been a military farce instead of a military miracle in other hands.

"And?" Hannibal still preferred to face the lady while he dug into Carthalo's optimism.

"And Greece, the Transalpine Celts, Carthage." Maharbal had rounded out the response for Carthalo.

"King Phillip has seemed to be a shaky resource. I don't count him among our present Greek, or Macedonian, treasures. Perhaps he will mature while we can still use him." He had turned toward them. "I still like your transalpine pillar, Maharbal. If we can get Cathbad and Hasdrubal together before my brother starts toward us we may surprise old Fabius yet."

"You have left Carthage dangling, Hannibal." The shadows were a useful buffer between Carthalo's face and Hannibal's.

The diversion of resources to Sicily, Sardenia, Iberia—even Carthaginian naval patrols into Greek waters that were the barest peripherals to his affairs in Italy—had been the tap root of his frustration since Cannae. From the various privacies he had declared to them, they had heard him turn this neglect around in every possible way trying to justify it. And then, by the same means, they knew he had finally accepted it as a fact of Carthage that he would overcome—or he would be mixed with anonymous dust like a hundred commanders before him with Carthaginian allegiance.

"You have just put me into a supplication, Carthalo." He turned toward the Sibyl's focus, carrying all the equipment he needed for supplication. He could have been silent about it, but he let them hear him:

"I have my father's precedence in this Italian enterprise. Carthage husbanded its enthusiasm with him, just as she is doing to me, now. We have justified ourselves more than Hamilcar was allowed to do. If I am not clever enough to draw my culminating strength from a world that does not necessarily include Carthage—then I have failed Hamilcar and the gentlemen who call me commander." After a long thick silence, he spoke again. "If I have laid some basis for your smiles, I ask my relevant gods' help, and yours, in concluding this enterprise." It was the kernel of his second visit to Cumae. He had anointed it with some declarations spiked with frustration which Maharbal and Carthalo couldn't hear, but Inanna had told him that the Sibyls could be addressed by thoughts, if necessary.

As young officers of Hamilcar, Carthalo and Maharbal had watched a boy of nine discover the soldier's world as they marched across Africa toward the Pillars and Iberia. They had seen him in every posture of play and mock battle for the boy, and then mostly battle for the man—on his knees after more than one action ministering to men and horses, on his knees at Cannae with Mago, when his own blood displayed with a Mushroom's. Now was the first time they had seen him on his knees in pure supplication. But it was the kind that would neither disgrace a Greek, nor embarrass his Sibyl. Maharbal and Carthalo left the silence in the vault to him and the lady and returned to his nervous Numidians.

Tarentum, the crown port on the gulf that washes the arch of Italy's foot, had been the only gateway to Carthage and Greece that he had taken. Dasius, the Greek commander of the Roman depot at Clastidium, who had surrendered that precious resource and his personal services to Hannibal on the eve of Trebbia, was from Brindisi. He had friends in nearby Tarentum, and he had told Hannibal that he was interested in keeping the Roman Wolf away from Magna Graecia. So, Dasius arranged some treachery among the guards at Tarentum, and Hannibal was able to put an occupying force into that city. Its Roman garrison was still walled up in its citadel, defying him, but it *was* a toehold on the coastline of Magna Graecia. When he went west to respond to Capua's latest appeal for relief from the Roman vise that was closing around her—a repeated supplication that had pulled him to Capua across Apulia, Lucania, and Campania since this ambiguous plum had fallen into his lap after Cannae—he left from Tarentum, taking the core of his army, thirty thousand foot and horse, down through the Roman lines and popped up at his old HQ at Mt. Tifata, within sight of Capua's travail.

Capua was an Etruscan derivative. It was the second city of Italy and the focus for the trade and enterprising that fanned out to the world from southern Italy. The Capuans had given him a conqueror's welcome that included an affiliation whose ligaments depended largely on him and didn't impose inconvenience on their lifestyle that had had tutoring by the Sibarites, and was, in its turn, starting to tutor the Romans. Over the five years since Cannae, by various attempts at cooperative military action and city resource planning, he had tried to provoke the Capuans into aggressive independence from the Roman pall that was drifting over Campania. He had nothing to show for this loyalty but a sapping of his own strength and diversion of his attention from other theatres of resources that might now be inaccessible to him. The failure of the latest attempt to draw out the Capuan's strength in their own defense against the siege lines that six legions were laying around them, under command of Claudius, Flaccus and Nero, proved the futility of his Capuan connection.

After his second visit to the Cumaean Sibyl, he told his staff that a march toward Rome might pull enough of the Romans away from Capua to enable a successful breach of the siege. But no one believed him. He had washed his hands of Capua. He was looking into a resource spectrum now that had been warped and attenuated by his Capuan *obsession*—he admitted this word to his staff, he apologized to them for putting their enterprise into a dangerous weakness by his focus on an Etruscan antique—a resource that was only a mirage.

"You had basis for what you call *obsession*, Hannibal," Myrcan, the strategist in his advisors told him. "The right response from Capua could have drawn all of the Italian Federation, and the Greek cities, into your orbit. The gods' intervention at Troy made a mess of it—I suspect some similar meddling here."

"You are, of course, referring to one of the *lesser* luminaries from Olympus."

"Of course, Hannibal. No one will accuse me of jeopardizing the help we will need from Zeus, and the *major* luminaries."

"Gentlemen, we will march on Rome. If we can suck the consuls Galba and Centumalus after us it will be justification enough for the gesture." Capua was now a million leagues from his planning and they all knew it. He had used the word, *gesture*. He probably could have used the same word if he had succumbed to temptation after Cannae when his critics claimed the road to the Forum was open to him. But he had explained the *Rome* situation to Barmocar on the eve of heading toward Cannae, and there was no need to make another explanation of that situation now—at the nadir of his Capuan obsession.

He put his column into standard traveling formation, and struck for the Via Latina, a brazen avenue to Rome that invited the Romans from their shells at a dozen places. None of them dared to move from their entrenchments at Capua to follow him, nor did his scouts detect aggressive fever from any other Roman strongholds pertinent to this tour that he had carefully designed to be leisurely. Along the way, he ordered his Numidians to make a bow wave of pillaging and destruction of the resources of the country useful to the Romans. Cales, Casinum saw and felt him come. The Roman Latin allies destroyed the bridge at Fregellae on the Liris River, and then after this nip at his progress he came through Frusino, Feretinum, Praenetse and Tusculum. None of the towns opened to him.

When he reached the Anio, he was six miles from the Colline Gate of Rome. He marched along the left bank of the Anio and camped within three miles of Rome. He put outposts closer, where he placed men with shields and weapons polished to mirrors. With a propitious sun, they could send his greetings to men on the Colline Tower who happened to be studying current history warped in his direction.

Fabius Maximus and Gaius Publius had just come from the Senate, where the fact of Hannibal's march on Rome had been put down on the tiles. Their major strength in Italy was tied up in the siege of Capua. As a student of Hannibal—who had been consul twice since Cannae, and was the *cunctator*, delayer, whose tactic of not presenting a solid target for his lightning had probably saved Rome from a younger and stronger Hannibal, Fabius had been asked what he would do about this situation:

"He knows he poses no real threat to Rome, now. This is a gesture, and anyone foolish enough to engage him in passage will probably be killed—I warned you before when you were going to *overwhelm* him at Cannae. He is not as strong now—but we have no one who can win on the fields of his choice. I would keep our present dispositions inside Rome, around Capua. If we allow him some bravado, he will go back to Lucania and Bruttium—and we'll resume our study of how to defeat him." Fabius had put some of his actor into his last words, and if the young tigers wanted to take some insult from them, so be it. He had done his part to set a stage for them that not one of them had trod as Conqueror of the Carthaginian. For years now, it had been mostly reacting to Hannibal's cues under light reflected from him.

Gaius and Fabius were heading toward the Forum when a tribune presented himself:

"Hannibal has reached the Anio, Fabius Maximus."

"Being deep inside a fortress that is certainly inaccessible to him now allows me some bravado, Tribune. I can say such things as, 'What would be the best vantage for watching him?' with complete impunity."

"On his present track, the Colline gate would be his logical focus."

"I am sure that your people have everything well in hand, Tribune. My respects to them. Good looking—if not good hunting." The tribune saluted again and he could have been having some trouble with Fabius' benediction as he excused himself.

On *their* present track toward the Forum, the walkers were tending in the opposite direction from the Colline gate.

"We seem to be going away from the imminent thunder, Fabius." Gaius cupped a hand around his left ear, making a channel for thunder to him, like he had done just after Trasimene, with a younger Hannibal coming their way.

"If it comes to the Colline gate, it will be near enough to me no matter where I stand in Rome—frustration working a man who is discovering that he can't win an empire by *himself* is a sight I would not be sorry to miss." Fabius' voice had personalized this philosophy in a way that made Gaius Publius' look to him irresistible.

They had reached the perimeter of the Forum and a Hannibal presence had already diffused to there, fed by rumors of white-mantled Numidian cavalry already in the city. They were a speck of very rare defectors from Hannibal—but they were good props for the cry, *'Hannibal is at the gates'* that was born in Rome that day, and used as a general threat against complacency for centuries afterwards.

"We've both talked to him—you, at Nova Carthago, I, not long before Cannae in Umbria. You mentioned a smile that was hard to diagnose, Gaius. I saw the same smile." Fabius looked upward toward the Capitoline Jupiter. "I tell you, we must do more homage to Jupiter for the fact that Hannibal does not have a Rome behind him. Have you made *your* tribute of plate and jewels to the cause, Gaius?" Valerius Laevinus had urged the senators to set an example by contributing family treasure to a cause that had been draining Rome of blood and wealth for seven years. The Forum was a depository for contributions from aristocrats and Hannibal had now made plenty of inspiration for contribution from every level of the people because his massive Roman death piles had been truly democratic.

"Just as you, Fabius."

"What do you hear about Carthage's response to *her* side of this crisis of Hannibal?"

"Some of my friends in trade and commerce have told me that they still do some business with Carthage....I haven't heard about any treasure flowing *toward* Hannibal."

They were still walking away from the Colline gate, and were now within bow-shot of the precincts of Heracles where Hannibal had once shared another of their conversations.

"Then the imminent thunder—at the Colline gate, and the rest of Italy—will be smaller than we had a right to expect, Gaius. Apparently even an unexampled commander is not able to draw patriotism from the Punic merchants. A man with a spark in him not wholly committed to Rome could find stuff here for Aeschylus, Euripides." Gaius Publius was looking at him again, but Fabius' classic Republican visage leaked nothing here that was treason.

"Carthage, Iberia, Greece, the Celts—his quiver is not empty yet, Fabius." Hannibal's pillars for his Italian Temple was no secret of Cathbad's councils.

"We have pushed Phillip away from him for a while. Valerius has made a treaty with Pergamum and the Aetolian States that should give Phillip enough diversion. I think he will stay away from us until we are ready for him on his own ground."

"Carthage has killed the elder Scipios in Iberia. Hasdrubal and Mago Barca are two commanders there who could add to what you have just called an 'unexampled commander' who happens to be in Italy—just outside our gate, as a matter of fact."

"Great loss, great potential in the same sentence, Gaius—we must keep an eye on that potential."

"But we have a young Scipio, Publius Cornelius, who might bring a better mettle to some fields pertinent to Hannibal."

"That young man's ambition may outrun his talent, Gaius. But he has powerful adherents in the Cornelii Scipiones, and the Arpii Claudii. To the extent I am able, I will also keep an eye on *that* potential. We have sniffed some of Hannibal's strength—Syphax and his Numidians—at his back, Africa. I have heard that Young Scipio has interest in an African front against Hannibal. This is a tendency that must be *very* closely watched. We can't beat him on *our* ground—what could we do to him on *his* ground?"

"The Celts? Hannibal is known to have tentacles probing on the other side of the Alps. He might touch some strains of power and ambition that could shock us again, under a command that you have just admitted to the Senate is 'inimitable' and—if you'll let me add a word—*unparalleled*."

"We have intercepted writing and talk about the Transalpine Celts that suggest a very troublesome connection should Hannibal work *that* particular miracle."

"We have used his name, and the noun, *miracle*, in the same sentence before, Fabius. But it was an *after-the-fact* connection—I don't like you pushing fate like this. The gods have evidently been pleasured by the Hannibal-miracle conjunction."

"Perhaps we'd better turn around and try to find a place on the Colline Tower. In a few hours, I think the gods will show you that *frustration* is the ultimate gate they put between themselves and mortals—however many pleasures have caressed both sides, before it."

The morning after he had made his camp on the Anio, he formed a party of reconnoiter from two thousand light and heavy horse, with his ten leopard Numidians the inevitable van with him and six staff including Maharbal, Sosylos, Silenus, and Barmocar. Although his visit was now well anticipated, no Roman dared interpose himself between Rome and Hannibal. And this vacancy persisted right up to where the Colline Tower and Gate were within a scorpion shot of him. Rome had nothing to match the horse arm he had brought this day to the Roman wall, and he could have made a dozen circuits of it without provoking Roman bravado—which Fabius had called *foolishness* only hours before in the Senate Chamber., and also in that place just before Cannae had almost cut the heart out of Rome.

Saguntum had been a tight little fortress on a collaborating rocky fastness, manned by Greeks who knew how to make every stone of their wall and citadel a bloody prize. Saguntum had impressed him, prejudiced him against wasting his men in sieges. As he closed to within bow shot of the Colline portal, the burgeoning of the stone and brick massive which girded sacred Rome proved his decision after Cannae to not attempt it without the prerequisites he'd given Barmocar. Hannibal reined up. Barmocar joined him at the point of the Carthaginian delegation that now had Roman observers at embrasures of the wall and tower.

"I said a hundred thousand at my back—another like portion for my front, then we could make a significant presence here for Fabius and his friends." Hannibal's old words were now burnished by air that caressed him and his Roman subject simultaneously.

Barmocar had never been this close to the walls of Rome. Left and right, there was nothing in their perspective of this infinity of a fortress that disputed Hannibal's formula for glory at this place.

"You have me as your devout witness to that wisdom, Lord Hannibal—should the occasion arise to defend it." They were close enough to serve the soft voice Barmocar had used. Both men carried shields, full armor, and a squad of heavy horse had come close enough to bolster the shield array should the Romans send greetings with mechanical arms.

Hannibal detected colors and movements in the Roman panorama in front of him, but nothing to discourage a closer look. He carried a javelin. With sudden encouragement to his white Cyrenian he galloped toward the Colline Gate and from a distance of twenty paces he launched his javelin toward the crease in the gate that could become welcome or denial at the Romans' pleasure. His missile struck at about the height of his head within a hand's span of the crease which was fixed in denial. He pulled Hamilcar's dagger and reared his horse. Such a small mirror to send a greeting to the Romans, but the sun found it, and as he wheeled toward his party, some of the dagger's communion with the sun persisted and he felt Hamilcar's presence at this imperfect apex of a dream.

Before he returned to the rank Barmocar and the rest of his staff had made, his leopard Numidians galloped past him and put five javelins on each side of his, in panels of the crease that Hannibal had just acknowledged. When his formation was complete again, Hannibal ordered a salute to the Roman bravado crouched behind the fortress. In about two thousand polished swords the sun found a better mirror—Fabius Maximus and Gaius Publius, and their memories, would have liked it.

He liked riding conferences. He used them as often as the sitting and standing kinds because they flowed into circumstances better, the rhythms of a horse seemed to jog loose his good options better—and the bad ones tended to fall behind quicker. He was using one now as he left Rome and returned to his camp on the Anio.

"I have not considered using an artist for the Chronicle...until now, Lord Hannibal."

"By Ba'al, Silenus, haven't you had enough of that nonsense? I have just made an ending for it—bad, but an ending."

"The pricks you have just left in the Roman hovel does not make a good end, Hannibal. To make an end the Romans would like will require them crawling away from their fortress and acting like conquerors. Those lances sticking into their pretty Colline gate—*that* only makes a good plate for the Chronicle. I hear there are people among your Celts who are clever with pen and paint." Silenus had gone into almost a soliloquy that ignored a protest. But Maharbal picked up the beat of that conference:

"Now that you have a calling card on a gate of Rome, which direction from here do you like, Hannibal?"

All of them knew the general complexion of the forces the Romans had laid around him: counting the troops in Italy, Iberia, Sicily, and Sardenia, and the men in the fleets, 23 legions had been mobilized against him. If this number was doubled to count the Allied contingent, and a legion strength of 5,000 was assumed, this amounted to 230,000 men against the best he could do at this time, probably 50,000 if he ran a fine sieve through his resources in Southern Italy. But against this massive imbalance he had just put his mark on the Colline Gate—close again to the Roman heart. Since he had paved a plain with their dead at Cannae, no Roman war council plotted aggression against him, even though natural attrition and lack of quality reinforcement had degraded his army significantly in both foot and horse.

"I hear Publius Sempronius is still in the Po valley waiting for Hasdrubal and me to shake hands."

"That is true, Hannibal. And Marcus Junius has an army in Etruria in case Sempronius needs backup against that handshake. These gentlemen are supposed to deny you and Hasdrubal the northern approaches to the city you have just left. I think they could greet you with two legions each—about forty thousand people in all."

"That takes care of the north of us, gentlemen. To the south, we have left a number of Roman friends—counting their allies, about sixty thousand hovering near Capua. In Apulia we could gather at least another twenty thousand of them around us. We seem to be squeezed between two lips of a vise—with somewhat greater substance in command and strength in the lower lip." If Euripides had looked for tragic substance on this face, he would have been frustrated and confused by the contrary moldings that had caressed that word, *vise*.

The conference changed composition and shape from time to time in accord with the terrain, but Maharbal and Barmocar seemed to remain inevitably close to Hannibal. This was appropriate to the occasion because Hannibal was about to pose a strategic question that would strike close to his senior cavalry commander and his senior advisor from the Council.

"If I look north, I can visualize Hasdrubal from Iberia and Cathbad's transalpine friends. If I look south, I can visualize sustenance from Macedonia and Carthage. If I place myself at either extreme, I will jeopardize the other potential assistance." His camp on the Anio had just come into view. Outriders were approaching. Hannibal waved his column toward the camp and drew his conference to a small knoll where he could watch his delegation to Rome rejoin his army.

"If you are posing a question to us, Lord Hannibal, I think it will require some appeal to divine guidance." Barmocar would be a traitor if he said he favored a northern situation over a southern one whose only realistic basis was Carthage.

Maharbal was balancing military realities and possibilities without political coercion. Hasdrubal and his Iberian army were facts and a strong reinforcement possibility. Cathbad's Belgae and Germani might be facts, but the *possibility* of them was no more distinct than the occasional letters to Hannibal from the Druid, or the currents of rumors that never died in the camps of their Celt contingent. Carthage was still a great fact. But her *possibility* in the context that Hannibal had just posed could not be fixed by any man on his staff. And the frustration that had dogged their commander, as precious foot and horse and fleet resources were diverted away from him, had diffused into his staff and men so that Carthage was no longer a beacon shining from the southern alternative that the commander had just posed. Phillip V of Macedonia was still a significant fact. But his *possibility*—this other basis of the southern alternative, was more elusive than Carthage's.

"What gods would you invoke for this divine intervention, Barmocar? I see some conflict here among Celt, Greek, Carthaginian deities who might want a hand in this intervention." It was Hannibal's question, and Sosylos and Silenus used whatever prerogatives they thought they had to edge closer to this question and answer between Hannibal and Barmocar. Carthaginian generals had been handed to the torturers on the basis of reports to the Council from field-advisors with less authority than Barmocar's.

"If I stay on good Carthaginian ground: Ba'al, Tanit...Melkart. If I also go to one, or two, of the Greek and Eastern assimilations...Eshmoun, Astarte, Demeter, I might make a useful supplication for guidance, Hannibal."

"I admire your comprehensive religion, my friend. I will need your prayer soon—the decision, north or south for us, will have to be taken by dawn tomorrow."

Maharbal asked Hannibal what he thought about going *north*:

"I think we can kill Sempronius and Junius in clearing the Po valley for some sojourn for us. We would have the best possible communication with Hasdrubal and there are enough Celts south of the Alps to bolster us while waiting for him. We have held the Roman at bay in the south. Certainly we can hold him in the north where there are more unburied ghosts of defeat to worry him. In the north we also have our best access to the Elysian Fields of Celt power that Cathbad has conjured for us—and I have neglected."

"You have just made a powerful case for turning north when we leave camp tomorrow."

"I have just complicated part of the supplication Barmocar has promised me, Maharbal." Complication might not be the right word here. A crucial point of Hannibal Barca of Carthage had just pointed toward Barmocar, the senior voice of Carthage closest to Hannibal. Logic might not be a sufficient bolster for him—standing in front of the Senate—if he nodded toward the *north*, away from Carthage, and this path disappointed.

In the interest of smoothing some edges for Barmocar, Maharbal asked Hannibal what he thought about going *south*:

"We would improve our access to Carthage and to such aid as Phillip would deign to give us. If we have to leave Italy, our embarkation—considering bringing a fleet in and out, and the proximity of a logical destination—would be easier in the south." The men within his scope of that moment deciphered a soft diminuendo whose subject had been thought of, whispered about, but never in his presence—now it had come from *him*.

Neither Maharbal nor Barmocar could put his own estimation of values into this *south* assessment. Phillip had been humiliated by the Romans on his own ground. By pure chance the Romans had intercepted his treaty with Hannibal and were allowed a luxury of time to counter it. Phillip still had prospects as a significant political and military power, but his present *possibility* was close to zero. This put the south alternative solely on the shoulders of the Mother City. Maharbal and Council Advisor Barmocar couldn't look at Hannibal...and this was an answer to a question he had spared them.

When it was dawn of the next day, he turned them south.

The night of that dawn was the most difficult one of his life and his mother and father had bequeathed equipment for it: an imagination that could pose, and superpose, realities and fantasies about the various edges of his possibilities against the Romans. Mago and Hasdrubal had both come in. He would like to have the gypsy close to him during his culminating time, just as they had collaborated at Trebbia and Trasimene and Cannae. And also Hasdrubal, with his Iberian army, and his own parts of a commander that could bolster whatever communion they could make in Italy. But these brothers had been elusive last night—he never could grab their hands however close they brought their faces, postures, tantalizing gestures, to him.

Carthage was the sole basis for his decision, and he had never taken action on such flimsy projection of success. But he was a general of Carthage. He was the son of Hamilcar, who had understood obligation to his country, and by this tenet—faith in his country. And if, as *he* had said, they had to leave Italy, the path between him and Inanna and Kyniska would be shortest in the south... but this was a private fact.

He left Rome by the Valerian Way, his gauntlet to the Romans still not taken. After crushing several sporadic attempts to raid his baggage train by Flaccus, who had finally come away from Capua and sneaked into Rome while he was approaching from the northern side, he went toward his south alternative through the country of the Peligni, into Samnium, then Apulia and toward Tarentum.

On the evening of the last camp before they reached Tarentum, on the Gulf of Taranto, Sosylos was staring into a complicated sunset on a small promontory of rocks near the command and staff tents. His privacy was not as complete as he had thought.

"Interesting portents out there, old friend?"

Hannibal had not been sneaky in his approach, so the Spartan he had addressed didn't waste time with surprise. Tutor, athletic coach and friend, he had helped take this commander from a boy to a man. These things gave Sosylos the privilege of keeping his eyes in the direction of a sunset that was also intriguing Lord Hannibal.

"I can find almost anything I want out there. Your mother's Etruscan friend Zortibas would be helpful with some subtleties that are beyond my powers." Since the *south* decision, they had not spoken beyond servicing civil amenities that bridged some awkward silences. Sosylos' voice now was too soft for any excursion to whatever portents of glory he could find where he was looking.

"I will have some problems explaining Capua to Zortibas." In Campania, that Etruscan remnant was being torn apart under the Roman retribution that followed Hannibal's dismissal of it as an ally just before he made his Rome gesture.

"You bled yourself on their altar for five years. You offered every conceivable opportunity for miserable effetes to play men . This disgusting souvenir of Etruscan glory has put you into a decision of strategy that no one likes—*including* you." Sosylos had just put his prerogatives with Hannibal Barca to a hard test. But neither he, nor his target, seemed to worry about it.

Hannibal turned toward Sosylos, both their faces tinted with the bloody hue that the high priest Asherbas had seen in cumulous clouds when a nine year old boy stood by his side on Byrsa Hill:

"You know the best part of it...a shortened path to Carthage." For the Spartan, Inanna and Kyniska would have been redundant in this sentence.

"What is the *worst* part of it, Hannibal?" These two had come to many facets of life in their communions, but none of them—even the blackness at Faesulae—had promoted more somberness on the Spartan.

"Inanna has praised the 'gossamers' that have kept us talking for seven years. I think my ones to Hasdrubal and Cathbad—and the value of these men to me—will be sorely tested by digging into the south."

"The depression value of that statement seems to swing on only two pillars for your Italian temple, Hannibal—neither of them Carthage."

"I will pretend that that treason came from Roman whispers, Sosylos." Hannibal actually made a cup of his left hand around his left ear, a gesture he had inspired in both Fabius Maximus and Gaius Publius, when they had listened for *him*. Then he turned that ear westward, toward Rome.

By his Zeus, there *was* a smile for Sosylos in that sunset.

20

39 years
208 BC—Bantia, Apulia

T hree years after he had made the *south* decision outside Rome, his tally counted more Roman dead scattered around Apulia, Lucania and Bruttium. Over a span of two years in Apulia alone, near Herdonia, he had destroyed four legions, two under Flaccus, two under Centumalus. Marcus Claudius Marcellus had come back from his costly triumph at Syracuse to try to squeeze him into a tighter corner, but even the man Rome called *the sword of Rome* couldn't corner a ghost whose magic was still strong enough to make now mostly second-rate troops good enough to face down anything Marcellus could muster against him.

The consuls for this year were Marcellus and Titus Crispinus. They had taken their armies into Apulia near Bantia. Hannibal's track had crossed this area frequently in recent months while he explored possible avenues for his contact with Hasdrubal, should this pillar among his sparse inventory of possibilities finally decide to make his move toward him. This preoccupation with Hasdrubal had been suspected by Marcellus and it seemed to present opportunity for cornering and smashing his assigned quarry. He and Crispinus made their camps about three miles apart, while they waited for a ghost.

When Hannibal finally acknowledged them, he made his camp about midway between the consuls, and put it where a wooded hill was between him and them. He had taken no pains to conceal his approach, and he created a strong incentive in Marcellus and Crispinus to inspect his position, using the seductive hill's advantages of cover and perspective. Before the consuls took this bait, he garnished the hill with two detachments of Numidian horse to make a trap of a wooded vale that was a natural approach for the inspection.

The Numidians finally detected a Roman formation approaching the hill. Two purple cloaks over gilded armor and attendant paraphernalia, including lictors, signaled that both consuls were in the inspection party. The consuls were escorted by two hundred horse and 30 velites. Marcellus' son, two tribunes and two praetors attended the consuls.

Following his commander's orders, the Numidian captain of the trap waited until Marcellus had made a deep penetration of the vale before he ordered an attack on the rear and the left flank of the Roman column. The

Numidians swept away the guard around Marcellus and Crispinus, launching their javelins at close quarters at the consuls and the other officers. Marcellus died with a javelin through his throat. Both praetors and one of the tribunes also fell. Crispinus was penetrated by two javelins in his torso, but the remnant of his guard managed to return him, and a severely wounded young Marcellus, to the Roman camps. Fifty Roman horse, most of the velites, and the surviving tribune were captured. Marcellus was left on the field.

Two days after this action, Hannibal stood in full armor in front of a Carthaginian honor guard. The captured tribune, mounted on one of the Roman horses, was in front of him. He had been allowed an honor guard of ten of his velites. The Romans knew how to stand at attention. An adjutant handed Hannibal a silver urn that contained Marcellus' ashes, the focus of an honor Hannibal had just accorded Marcellus, as he had Paullus after Cannae, and tried to give Flaminius after Trasimene.

"I give you the mortal remains of a man I would rather have called friend, than enemy. You will take this to his son, Marcellus—with our wishes for his speedy recovery." The tribune saluted and accepted the urn. Then he led his formation back to the Roman lines.

Sosylos and Silenus had been close observers of this gesture the Romans had never reciprocated on any field pertinent to Hannibal, or Carthage.

"Perhaps that made Archimedes smile, if he can take time from his geometry and contraptions." Sosylos had just bowed to the Greek genius who had kept Marcellus at bay at Syracuse for months with his defensive engines that made a mockery of the Roman siege action from land and water. After the Romans finally broke into the city, Archimedes was, in fact, studying some geometry in the sand when he was killed by one of Marcellus' soldiers. Hannibal acquired Sosylos' remark directly:

"*There's* a Greek I would have met if our worlds had been tipped differently. We could have taken Rome with half my 'two hundred thousand' if he had been with me."

"Ah, there would have been no time for war, what with you and Inanna tangling philosophies with him day and night." Sosylos came closer to Hannibal. "Now that I've brought Inanna in again, how are the gossamers, my Lord?"

"Those from her are more impatient of an absent husband and father. Those about Hasdrubal have said that he has broken out of Scipio's reach. He has crossed the Tagus, turned the headwaters of the Ebro and is probably entering Gaul at the western edge of the Pyrenees. He will winter in Gaul before he comes to see us."

Publius Cornelius Scipio, the younger, who had seen his father defeated at Ticinus, Sempronius defeated at Trebbia, and who barely escaped the hell

Hannibal had made for his people at Cannae—probably three gifts of life Hannibal had given him—had been made commander in Iberia several years before. Among his honors had been the taking of a barely defended Nova Carthago, and then about a year later he had fought a battle with Hasdrubal near Baecula. Technically it had been Scipio's day, but Hasdrubal had extricated most of his army from the affair and started his march toward Hannibal. Penning, or destroying, Hasdrubal had been one of Scipio's prime responsibilities when he was assigned Iberia. He had failed. Later, Fabius Maximus would not let the Senate forget it when Scipio moved toward greater visions of glory against Carthage.

"What are those north-pointing gossamers made of, Hannibal?"

"Pure Celt. They have the connections thru the countries of the Senones, Boii, and Insubres that should be able to listen when my little brother plucks on his harp." The commander looked in the direction of the Adriatic. "The strands they give me are fragile—given to breaking if the local beer and wine are good— but they are part of the bed I have made and I will try to lie in it." Sosylos had had practice intercepting Hannibal's soft excursions, but this one was barely accessible.

When Hasdrubal's location in eastern Gaul had been confirmed, Hannibal exercised his sea and land connections to send a letter to him:

Hasdrubal Barca,

My congratulations to you in taking the steps forward out of Iberia. I hope we will collaborate in giving young Scipio further lessons in humility.

My Druid friend, Cathbad, has promised me that he can provide you with substantial Transalpine Celt reinforcement. I have advised Cathbad of your situation and suggested certain avenues of communication for this help, such as Auros, Chieftain of the Volcae, who has been studying whatever progress I have made in Italy. Keep your eyes and ears sensitive to these Celt signals which I now regard as a major prospect for renewing our initiative against the Roman.

My current strength situation recommends our meeting along the Adriatic coast. I will try to place scouts as far north as Sena Gallica. I am presently favoring a location near Salapia as my nest while waiting for you to give me some eggs to hatch.

Fate has settled a Celt gossamer (Inanna's word for my intelligence network) on me for your entrance into, and movements in, the Po valley. You and I are aware of its limitations. I know a few Celt invocations to their special gods. I strongly suggest you acquire some yourself and together we can mount a formidable supplication for their help in our enterprise. But I will need all your ingenuity in keeping our communication useful in the crucial time ahead when you move into the shadow of the Appenines—another blind spot for me now.

Following the deaths of their consuls Marcellus and later, Crispinus, the Romans have elected Caius Nero and Marcus Salinator as consuls for the new year, which I hope will herald your advent in Italy. I understand that Nero had a brief sojourn in Iberia—that you know some things about him. He will be the tail wagging this two headed dog that will bark in our direction.

It has been almost ten years for us. I have respected your endeavors that honor our father. I will strive to make us, and Mago, the arm that will finally strike down the Roman.

Hannibal

Inanna's letter from the southern direction came within a few breaths of the dispatch to Hasdrubal and did not relieve the tension that the north and south poles of his present moment were putting into him:

Hannibal Barca,

I have been spending some time at our estate at Hadrumetum. Last night I was at our special place overlooking the eastern sea. I have done some talking to you there...privately, putting words into whatever whispers of the night might take them to you. I was adding up the years that Heimarmene has kept us apart...about ten now, I think. You have a daughter who is thirteen years old—but she acts much older and I must start to use whatever guile is in me to cope with a sophisticated woman when she is near to me.

Last night she slipped behind me while I was talking to you. She waited for me to spill out quite a lot of privacy. Then she touched me on my shoulder and asked me if she could add a whisper to mine. I could feel her breath against my cheek as she said that she and Asherbas had been practicing some new prayers for Hannibal, Commander of Italy...and that Zortibas had been tutoring her in transcribing images and dreams into something useful for you.

There are rumors that Hasdrubal has started to walk toward you. I will invoke whatever privileges I have with my gods to bring you and Hasdrubal and Mago together...and then all of us together.

Inanna Barca

Hasdrubal entered Italy much earlier than either Hannibal, or the Romans, had expected. The praetor, Porcius Licinus, had reported Hasdrubal's progress to Rome, including a reinforcement by 8,000 Ligurians. Hannibal acquired this same information about a week before the Roman Senate via an example of good Celt communication that he hoped would be inspirational to the Celts. The only negative pulse in this news was the Ligurian addendum. Where were Cathbad's Transalpine Celts? If Ligurians had truly supplanted the fresh Belgae and Germani strains, then the Cathbad connection had been virtually worthless. He had used Ligurians ten years before. They had been good soldiers, but their quality, like most of his army, had deteriorated since then and they were not material to make the pillar Hasdrubal was supposed to bring with him.

Before Hasdrubal slipped into the shadow behind the Appenines, the Celt gossamer reported that he was besieging Placentia. This news put Hannibal into a walking, pacing, cursing funk that his staff had never seen. The quick entry to Italy had been fine, it had surprised the Roman, and even without Cathbad's dream, if a connection could be made, *now,* they could capitalize on Roman confusion as he had done many times before—but digging in at Placentia!

"What is he thinking, Barmocar?" He had almost gripped his advisor's tunic with his question.

"You took time around Placentia to impress the local Celts; perhaps he is doing the same. If, as you say, Cathbad could not make a useful conjunction with him, then he will need all the Celt strength he can gather on *this* side of the Alps to bring a useful force to you."

Before his Celt whispers withered into useless blather, they told him that Hasdrubal had finally backed away from an unsuccessful Placentia operation and had started to move southeastward toward the Adriatic.

Hannibal started a restless, erratic, maneuvering in eastern Lucania and Apulia that was as much designed for surcease from the worry about Hasdrubal's situation and intention as it was to keep Nero off his back. He finally settled on Canusium as his nest, and Nero camped within a mile of him, between him and Hasdrubal. He could have destroyed Nero, but this action would not have served a maximum effect junction with Hasdrubal. He was nailed to this spot until Hasdrubal signaled otherwise. But he kept his troops on full alert, and he continually swept Nero's perimeters with Iberian and Numidian scouts.

About two weeks after he had settled into this stalemate with Nero, one of his scouts reported an unusual incident: he had heard from a grapevine, with tentacles into Tarentum, that the Romans had captured a Carthaginian patrol near Tarentum, four Celts and two Numidians. The patrol had been taken to Nero for questioning under a heavy guard of Samnite horse. The special Roman attention to a small patrol spiked special importance to this report.

Hannibal doubled his reconnoiter. Three days after the scout's report, he detected unusual activity in Nero's camp. Nero had tried to cover it by leaking information that he was going into Lucania to undermine Hannibal's support in that area. But this ruse only intensified Hannibal's watch on the gadfly consul. This attention was rewarded a few hours later when Hannibal was informed that Nero had left camp with about six thousand foot and a thousand horse, and he was headed to the northwest, toward Picenum, toward the region that Hannibal had designated as the logical place of conjunction with his brother.

"Where is Hasdrubal?" He threw this question at his staff and advisors. After he had paced two passages in front of them, thru the middle of them, he asked the same question.

"Your Celts..." Myrcan tried to get in.

"Have said nothing but silence since Placentia. I feel now that the patrol captured near Tarentum was Hasdrubal's. What was he trying to tell me? Where is he? Where is he going—*now*?"

Any of them could have asked the same questions. The silence in that tent was thick confirmation of no answers. Then they listened to a soliloquy:

"I can't chase Nero. What if he goes to the Picenum coast and Hasdrubal comes down along Umbria. Or if I sneak up thru Umbria—what if Hasdrubal comes to the coast and confronts Nero and Salinator without my help. Cathbad's dream is no help to my brother now. He needs what *I* can bring him. He needs whatever I have learned in ten damned years of chasing and killing Romans, of sucking their egos into places where I can kill them." He had just put a monument in front of the questions—a tribute to precursors of glorious reunion, or a sepulchral ornament if the answers bent the other way.

Nero was away from his camp for almost two weeks. Frustration, hope, apprehension, dejection, resuscitation of hope, had been Hannibal's occupation during that time. Taking advantage of misguidance by his Celt guides and drunken Celts lolling in tents when he needed them on his desperate line—and then trapping and killing Hasdrubal on a miserable defile of the Metaurus river near Fanum Fortunae on the Adriatic—had been Nero and Salinator's principal occupation during that time.

To say they killed Hasdrubal is not quite correct. When he came to the Adriatic near Ariminum, he moved south along the coast as quickly as a second-rate column would allow. The uncoded, plain Greek, message he had placed with the Celt and Numidian patrol, shortly after leaving Placentia, told Hannibal that he would meet him in Umbria. An implied specific of this plan was that the terrain used by the Via Flaminia would be a logical avenue for him to approach Hannibal. They had agreed on a contact along the Adriatic, but the Romans didn't know this. The message had some prospect of sucking Nero and Salinator inland. He chose men for this patrol who would not task their ingenuity in locating Hannibal, who could be depended upon to wander into the Romans between Placentia and Lucania if anyone could. There had been no communication between him and Hannibal since he had left Gaul. The tenuous prospects of the deceptive dispatch were, therefore, enormously important to him.

But when Hasdrubal got near to Sena, he discovered that two consuls were waiting for him—he had not sucked them inland. The route of the message was, therefore, now an opportunity for him and he retreated, trying to reach the natural amenities that the Via Flaminia would use. Southwest through Umbria he could improvise a new meeting ground with his brother. But his inept Celt guides led him into a defile along the Metaurus River that was better suited for the consuls' purposes than his. Trapped in an impossible defensive, offensive, nightmare, he finally took the summation that Hannibal had been killed, or captured. There was nothing now but to show these Italian Wolves how to die. Before he rode into the center of the Roman line in suicide, he made Nero and Salinator work hard for their victory.

Nero had Hasdrubal's head cut from his body, and then he put it in a wine cask for a southern delivery a few days later.

Hannibal was finishing his evening meal. In the last few days, he had tolerated no company while eating, and the feeling of his staff in this respect was mutual. His orderly had just refilled his Celt silver goblet with wine from the last cask of a Campanian treasure. But the wine was no counterpoise for his mood, and he was making bile from nectar with the few drops that were in his mouth when he felt the perturbation of the normal evening routine outside his tent—a competence, a mystery, Asherbas and Zortibas would have admired. As he walked out of the tent, the light of torches bracketed him. He saw most of his command staff standing in a semicircle, his tent door their focus—the torchlight defining, magnifying, a rigid attention on familiar faces that quickened him to receive a shock that would test whatever man Hamilcar and his mother had put into him.

He picked up Maharbal's eyes first. His lips started to make a word, but they stopped, and he waited for Maharbal—anyone. Then he noticed a lumped sack on the ground roughly at the center of the semicircle. It implied the coarsest vehicle for conveying what had to be the nadir of honors, respects, an enemy could devise for him, his family, Carthage—it *had* to be a Roman offering, but with no tincture of Fabius' mark on it.

He walked to the sack, opened it enough to see a head. He reached into the sack and lifted the head into flickering needles of torchlight that gave more of a devilish palette for him. Hasdrubal's eyes were open, staring into the end of his part of Hamilcar's dream. Hannibal brushed the lids closed, set the head on the bare ground away from the sack. He finally broke a silence that even the night birds had respected. His voice was a miracle of softness after he had worked it in challenges to Fate—Greek and Carthaginian sounds—in the previous hours:

"I think this may also be the fate of Carthage, gentlemen...please let my brother's journey to the gods start here."

An orderly took Hasdrubal's remains away for the cremation ceremonial that had defined part of Hannibal's civilized aggression. Part of Nero's had just lain on the ground. Another part of Nero's was brought into the torchlight: he had sent two Celt and two African officers into Hannibal's camp to finish Hasdrubal's story for his brother. They had been roughly handled. None of these men, from the Iberian army, had ever seen Hannibal. They knelt in front of him, not daring his eyes.

"Stand up and look at me." It was a command, but it used the same voice that had just spoken about Hasdrubal. His look swept all of them, and then settled on the Celt captain who was their senior officer.

"Where was this battle?"

"On a defile of the Metaurus River, my Lord, a few miles west of Fanum Fortunae."

"Who were the Romans?"

"Both consuls, Lord Hannibal—Nero and Salinator. As soon as Lord Hasdrubal detected both of them in the same camp near Sena Gallica he ordered a retreat toward the road through the Appenines." The Celt had to use all his discipline to keep the eye contact with Hasdrubal's brother.

"Apparently he never got to this road." Hannibal came away from the Celt for a quick look at the Celt officers on his staff who were now close observers of this dialogue. The fact that Hasdrubal had come as close to him as Sena put another pulse into him that strained his soft voice resolution. His northernmost scouts had been less than *ten miles* from Hasdrubal before the burgeoning Roman presence nudged them southward

"The column was not well guided..." The Celt had to break contact with this and he stared at the ground at Hannibal's' feet. "He was led into a defile of the Metaurus that offered little possibility against Nero who was able to catch and detain him until Salinator came up with the full Roman body."

"Do you know how Hasdrubal died?"

The Celt recovered his contact. "I heard that he rode into the Roman line—without protection."

"This is an *ending* move for a commander—it signals complete collapse of hope...how do you explain this?—my brother was no stranger to the faces of battle."

"Nero found a weakness on our flank and rear and used it to finally overwhelm our line."

"What was this weakness?"

The Celt took too long to answer. One of Hannibal's Celt officers stepped toward him and was about to grab him by the throat. The Celt shook him off and stared at Hannibal. "I...heard that a number of our people had been drunk and were not fit to confront Nero."

"That *poor guiding* you mentioned that brought such advantage to Nero—who were these guides?"

"*Our* people...also." The Celt had straightened to attention as he uncovered a shame that made every Celt in the ranks beyond Nero's prisoners finger his dagger.

"Do you know the name, Cathbad?" Hannibal had stepped closer to the Celt as he came to the crux of his brother's last affairs.

"I have heard that name...he was said to be a powerful Druid of Gaul... and beyond."

"*Was?*"

"I heard that he had died before Lord Hasdrubal left Gaul for Italy."

"Did Hasdrubal know this?"

"Auros, chieftain of the Volcae, was seen in our camp on the day I heard about this Druid...this was shortly before we entered Italy."

Hannibal let a silence envelop them again. He had not moved more than a few paces from where he had received Hasdrubal's head. The Celt had put enough substance into the visions of Hasdrubal approaching the Appenines, and then of the deadly shadow in which Hasdrubal had traveled to within *ten miles* of his scope of action, and died. The Celt had also given a scenario for Hasdrubal's preoccupation with Placentia—confirming Barmocar's surmise that Hasdrubal had been taking desperate measures to attract some of the Celt ligaments that he had lost with Cathbad's death.

The Celt captain broke the silence that contained various storms of thought in that arena. He took his own measures to shorten the distance between himself and Hannibal, then he kneeled again.

"If you will decimate your Celts for what we have done—take me as the token, Lord Hannibal."

Then his same voice again...a touch of his hand on the Celt's shoulder: "I had counted a Celt pillar for my Italian temple—I did not nurture it sufficiently. The one I am responsible for had a few rotten parts—I apologize to every man of my command, of Hasdrubal's command, for my failure. As for your token, Captain...Hasdrubal will be sufficient for me."

Any vestiges of his northern alternative had vanished. He was close to Bruttium. He would pull that country over himself and wait for a miracle. Nero sent only a small sample of his might to follow him. There had been talk, close to Hannibal, that Nero's head spiked to the Colline Gate would make another good souvenir of the Carthaginian visit to the Roman's holy city. There had been a surfeit of volunteers to make this reply to Nero's vulgar gesture. The Commander thanked them...and then he ordered them south, again.

21

42 years
205 BC—Crotona, Bruttium

The sea and sky perspective of the Promontorium Lacinium, its situation as an end-point of Italy as close as any to the last pillars of his Italian temple, made a marvelous amphitheatre for recapitulation, reappraisals, identifying new directions. Sosylos and Silenus watched him place the bronze tablet on the altar of Hera Lacinia, in her temple on this land eminence, just south of Croton in Bruttium. Hannibal was making his first, and only, formal declaration of his history in Italy, and their credentials as close observers were sound for this event.

His agents had found a bronze foundry man in Croton who had finally satisfied him with a simple tablet that bore an honest inscription, in Greek and Punic, of the forces he brought into Italy thirteen years before: twelve thousand Africans; eight thousand Iberians; six thousand horse. It was bare bones accounting. Considering the thunder he had rolled into Italy shortly afterwards, Sosylos suspected it was also another tweak of the Roman nose.

Hannibal bowed toward the altar and acknowledged the goddess' aura in Greek. He was a Carthaginian, on Italian ground, standing before a Greek goddess...a complicated moment for him, and one also for Inanna. She made an appearance in him as he did both rote, and specialized, acknowledgement of the goddess, Zeus' wife. The specialized, Inanna, part was softer and it strained Sosylos' wondrously acute eavesdropping faculties.

A solid representation of his staff crowded the sanctuary, and after he had made the public and private parts of his obeisance, he turned and swept them with a smile and eye action that finally tangled with his close-coupled Greek mentors' as he left, without using the stage of the Promontorium for the other purposes.

But they all knew about young Scipio's depredations in Iberia that had finally collapsed the flimsy structure Carthage had sustained there; his triumph in Rome, where he pledged the bullion of his Iberian victory to the cause against Carthage; his election to consul and the allotment of Sicily as his province—a conventional step-stone to North Africa and now at Hannibal's back.

This young consul had managed a meeting with the Numidian prince, Masinissa, whose Numidian cavalry had been a moveable sore spot for the

Romans in southern Iberia for years, one of the last strengths attached to Carthage in that land. And he had also gone to Africa on a proselytizing venture that had alerted the Numidians to his interest in their cooperation in defeating Carthage, their overbearing master. This gesture to Syphax, the Numidian king, and the one to Masinissa, had more significance for Hannibal than anything the Roman publicists had conjured for Scipio in Iberia.

His Numidian corps was now a shadow of what it had been at Cannae. It had been his slashing left arm in Italy that had opened the Romans to the intrigues of his right arm. If his Numidian source in Africa was cut from him before he could settle accounts with Scipio, this young consul's chain of luck could slip around his throat and Carthage's.

He had made a classroom for this Scipio—at Ticinus, Trebbia, places where an academic career was almost cut short, and then Cannae, where Scipio had been an eye witness to a Hannibal masterwork—where a lake of blood had turned Hannibal away from another pursuit of a remnant that could also have been an academic terminus. Cavalry had been one of the principal courses of his curriculum for the Romans. Scipio and his indispensable lieutenants, Laelius and Silanus, would try to take the podium away from the master however they could—cutting off the cavalry arm that gripped that podium would be a big way to do it.

And Hannibal's audience at the Promontorium also knew about Phillip V. His status as a pillar had virtually vanished when he and the Syrian King Antiochus III had agreed that the death of Ptolemy IV Philopater of Egypt, and the succession of the boy king, Ptolemy V, had put the tantalizing prizes of Egypt's African possessions in their way. To expedite this windfall, to keep his back peaceful, Phillip had executed a treaty of peaceful coexistence with Rome. Another pillar had fallen down.

Kyniska was sixteen now, physically a lady by any measure, precocious by other measures Inanna and the Lady Barca had had to apply to her years earlier. Her father's decision to make a fortress of Bruttium that was still generally unassailable had several advantages. His concourse with his family could be more than a monthly affair now, with the slippery lembi making a comedy of the naval superiority the Romans claimed for the waters between Italy and Carthage. His concourse with the Council was also facilitated, although this traffic still carried his frustration and the Council's astounding ineptitude for playing the international game with Rome. The first advantage made the second barely tolerable.

Kyniska

Your mother tells me that you have assumed too much authority for the Hadrumetum estate and that this tendency has also threatened certain of the operations at the other places where you have been allowed to roam—the plantations at Cap Bon and Thuburbo Maius, for example. Your friendship with Stiros seems to have some good basis, but, as Mago soon learned, this young Greek also has precocious tendencies which must be kept in check if his good parts are to be appreciated. You know what I mean, and I expect a proper humility and deference from you around your elders.

I am so close to you now that I can almost touch you and your mother in better ways than in dreams. The Romans would like to push me into the sea, so they can forget about me. That time is not quite now, but what work I could have done here is almost a finished dream...so one of these days there will be a fierce old daddy closer to you.

Fierce Daddy

Hannibal's prediction of a closer daddy, and one in a letter to Inanna where he had tied *fierce* to husband, was being implemented by young Scipio. Before the next year had dawned, he had trained an expeditionary force to Africa in Sicily. He had chosen as many veterans of Hannibal's campaigns as he could find, including a remnant from Cannae which had been ostracized to Sicily and had pleaded for a chance at redemption against the Carthaginian. In the spring of the new year—over Fabius Maximus' objections that he was taking the war from Italy, where the Romans still couldn't devise a way to destroy a depleted Hannibal, to Hannibal's home ground—Scipio embarked from Lilybaeum in Sicily and landed on Cap Farina, near Utica, about twenty miles from Carthage. It was an auspicious occasion for the Second Punic War, which is to say, the War with Hannibal.

But this year had also started with a deluge of bad omens for the Romans: crop failures, strange behavior of birds and animals, sky and land anomalies, which Fabius and other veterans of the interminable conflict with Hannibal, were quick to associate with their nemesis. The first recourse, the Sibylline Books, were interpreted to mean that a foreign invader would be repulsed if the image of Cybele, Mother of the Gods, were transported from Pessinus, in Phrygia, to Rome. King Attalus of Pergamum was favorably disposed to Rome because they had both been enemies of Phillip V of Macedon. Attalus arranged for an escort to Pessinus and the amenities of placing the Cybele's image in the

Romans' hands. Before the Roman delegation visited Attalus, it paid its respects to the Delphic oracle, who bound them tighter to the Cybele, saying that her image had to be welcomed to Rome by the *best man in the city* if she was to have maximum effect on their cause.

Inanna Barca,

I wonder if one of your prayers you said you have been saying for me has gone astray.

My gossamers have detected a strange warping of our coupling to the Delphic Sibyl. She has told the Romans that they will push me away for good if the image of the Cybele they are bringing from Pessinus— near the place of your damned, eternally fascinating, antecedents—is welcomed to Rome by the <u>best man in the city.</u> We wonder who this 'best man' could be. Your husband has already killed a lot of them, and the ones that are left seem to be trying to catch him—so where will they find time for this nonsense of the Cybele?

I have cautioned our daughter about asserting unwarranted authority. Has it had any effect?

I understand young Scipio has made an appearance close to Carthage. I predict that he will spend a few months acclimatizing and proselytizing. My previous instructions, suggestions, for conducting your affairs in the near presence of the Romans will start to apply now. If Scipio impends—then doesn't that mean that the fierce husband and father also impends? This terrible thought is sent on my wings of tonight to you and Kyniska.

Fierce Husband and Father

Five years before, Scipio had taken Carthago Nova, an action which had put his Roman publicists into ecstasy. He had learned through routine scouting that the Carthaginian commanders in Iberia had been bickering over priorities and authority, and that they were scattered over the Iberian territory, in no posture for defense of the crown city. He brought 25,000 foot and 2,500 horse to the city which had only a token garrison defense of several thousand. His capture of the city within a few days was heralded as a signal military triumph.

At Utica, he faced more determined defense and his land and sea pincers on the city failed to dent it. Scipio abandoned the siege after a few weeks and settled into winter quarters east of the city, but still on the barren headland associated with Cap Farina.

He had put himself in a precarious situation. He was outnumbered by the force Carthage could muster against him, and Carthage's naval strength was still sufficient to cut off his sea approaches for supplies and escape. But there was no Hannibal on the African side of this war, so Scipio was allowed a peaceful winter, and leisurely opportunity to court Syphax, who, with Hasdrubal Gisgo, comprised the resident military genius for Carthage at this culminating time.

In the spring of the following year, Gisgo and Syphax put their respective armies in separate camps, both within easy communication of Scipio's. Scipio commenced a diplomatic intercourse with both commanders, ostensibly for peace negotiations, but he deliberately prolonged the talks to give his spies ample time to reconnoiter the enemy disposition and strength. He salted his peace envoy teams with veteran officers, and their chief intelligence after some weeks of false conference was that both of the enemy camps used reeds for the barracks and supply structures, and discipline was loose under the atmosphere of the Scipio's promotions of negotiation.

Scipio brought the talks to a pinnacle of optimism for both sides. Then, under this relaxation, he ordered a night attack on both camps using torches as his principal weapon. Neither Hasdrubal nor Syphax had suspected treachery, so their men rushed out to fight the fire storm and were easy victims of Scipio's force.

A little more than a month later, Gisgo and Syphax managed to gather another army, bolstered by Celtiberian mercenaries. Knowing that their commanders had had no time to put a professional polish on the new corps, Scipio attacked them at the place called the Great Plains, about 60 miles southwest of Utica, where the Bagradus river is joined by four tributaries. Gisgo and Syphax were defeated again and managed to escape with their remnants.

For the moment, Masinissa was one of Scipio's arms. Scipio sent him and his Numidian horse after Syphax. Syphax was captured and returned to Scipio, who had now broken the last bond between Carthage and the Numidian allies. Gisgo and Syphax and Carthage had squandered the cream of the resident resources for Hannibal—an effect triggered by Scipio's strategy of false diplomacy.

In the two years since Hannibal put his bronze on Hera's alter at Lacinium, the Romans had made token moves against him, and he had slapped the wrists of the consul, Tuditanus, and the proconsul, Crassus, in local actions which confirmed his status as schoolmaster. But it was Scipio who was now wearing the hat of the circus master, the one who designed the action that dictated the reaction, a hat Hannibal had worn for most of the time since he had entered the Po valley fifteen years before.

Scipio's course had not been undiluted glory. After he left Iberia and had played the right cards in Roman politics to sustain his crusade against Carthage, there were incidents in both Sicily and southern Italy which did not improve the luster of his gilded armor. The vicious reprisals of his officer, Pleminius, against the citizens at Locri had nearly given his enemies in the Roman senate enough to untrack him. While he was in Sicily, presumably whipping an expeditionary force to Africa in shape, rumors of lax discipline, and whispers of hedonism that crept as far as Scipio himself, sufficed to send a senate review team to Sicily. Scipio had enough advance warning of this inspection to prepare both land and naval forces under his command for a quick refurbishing of his image.

But he had finally made the big step from Sicily to Africa. He had landed in the Carthaginian sand box, and he was allowed to pile most of the good sand on his side through treachery and resident Carthaginian military talent that was a sad parody of Hannibal's.

"I'm like a monkey in a cage, watching a fire being built around him—and his piss isn't long enough to reach any part of it." Hannibal was pacing again, in front of Carthalo and Maharbal, Hamilcar's old officers who had watched Hannibal's Italian empire shrink to a few square miles of Bruttium.

His lembi had increased their intercourse with the mother tit to where his intelligence of Scipio's ransacking of it was probably better than the Council's at Carthage.

"Gisgo and Syphax have squandered at least thirty thousand people in bolstering the consul's reputation. We will find the mine where I will have to dig for soldiers to be that much lighter—and Ba'al knows that he has left me damn few veins there that glitter for *us*." The entrance to the command tent faced the Ionian Sea. He stared at the horizon where sky and water fused different blues, making a mesmerizing infinity between him and Carthage.

Maharbal and Carthalo had both put Hannibal's Numidian horse into interstices of battle that had been crucial to success. The overtures Scipio had made to sever it from him had also impressed them. Maharbal stepped toward Hannibal who was still lost in an infinity.

"And Masinissa, the Numidian playboy, is wearing Scipio's blessing now." He was the connection to Hannibal's once great light cavalry arm that could give what remained of it the decisive turns toward Scipio.

"I hear he carries an ivory scepter from the consul which imputes some kingship to him." Hannibal hadn't turned away from the Ionian panorama. "I wonder if Masinissa's ecstasy shields him from the Latin word for scepter—*Scipio*."

"It dilutes his kingship, but Gisgo tried to use ecstasy to *our* advantage—so everyone seems to be working with *ecstasy*."

"I wonder if we could get *our* hands on some of it. What happened to

Sophonisba?" Hannibal's ear had been almost as close to the romantic gossip of North Africa as Carthalo and Maharbal's. Gisgo had given his daughter, Sophonisba, in marriage to King Syphax to protect the cement holding the Numidians to Carthage from further decay.

"Evidently her bedroom talents were not enough to make a general of Syphax, and then my lady's attentions strayed toward another with greater prospects—or Masinissa usurped her, depending on your source. After Syphax's defeat, we hear that Scipio raised the issue of her status as a Roman prisoner... and the lady took poison."

"Not flattering to our handsome young consul, Carthalo." When Hannibal turned back toward the Ionian vista, he was still thinking about this consul who had supplanted Fabius Maximus as his gadfly. He could whip raw recruits into battle shape quicker than any commander in history. But the presence of a cavalry, close to the shades of the kind he had taken into the plain at Cannae, was a work that took more time—more smiles from the gods who had not left him. After he had made a long silence, he turned to his old friends again:

"I need both of you nearer to Carthage. We can match the Cannae ghosts who want to kiss me again and the other foot the consul has jammed into the spaces in his line. But I will need cavalry. Bomilcar has already cautioned about the limitations of his bridge to Carthage. I predict it will carry no horses. With Syphax now a trophy for Scipio, and Masinissa tending to cluster some of the remnants of Syphax's and his own horse behind him, we have a problem of recruitment, with our grace of time dictated by the balance between Scipio's audacity and his temerity."

"And *training*, my Lord, is also clinging to our problem."

"Precisely, Carthalo. You have just justified my order for both of you to start beguiling the Carthaginian beauties again at your *very* earliest convenience." Neither Maharbal, nor Carthalo needed him to pick apart his word, *beauties*. They had heard him use that adjective in front of four-legged prospects for his cavalry, so there *was* some ambiguity here.

In the fall of his final Italian year, the Carthaginians sued for peace. The entire Inner Council of thirty senators came to Scipio at his camp at Tunis. They laid the blame for the war at Hannibal's feet. They claimed that the Treaty of Lutatus Catulus, which had closed the First Punic War, would be a fair and reasonable basis for peace negotiations. Envoys were also sent to Rome with the same message, with Hannibal's betrayal of trust specially embellished for the ears in the Roman Senate.

While the Romans took some sincerity from the offers, because there were Carthaginian aristocrats who had held fast to some of the Roman commercial ligaments throughout the war, they also picked out some guile from them because both Hannibal and Mago were still at large in Italy at this time, and there was no commander in Scipio's trophy bag who compared with either of these Barcas.

After Scipio defeated what passed for the last significant Carthaginian army in Iberia at Illipa, Mago had been ordered to recruit a new army in the Balearics and Italy. He reached Genoa in Hannibal's final Italian year. During his second Italian visit, he gained some Ligurian recruits, but only a few Celts. The Celts of the Po valley were now generally afraid to antagonize the Romans, so this last vestige of Cathbad died at Mago's feet. In northern Italy, Mago was also given some sustenance by Carthage—7,000 foot, seven elephants, twenty-five ships and money for recruitment—with the order to *march on Rome and draw nearer to Hannibal*! When Hannibal heard about this reinforcement—and this order—he said that they were also the sound of his last Italian pillars being kicked over by a Carthage that had no connections to the *real* world.

"Gentlemen, this Bruttium wine is barely sufficient to toast an old friend. We hear from a few of our tentacles that still reach into Rome that Fabius Maximus has been awarded a wreath, with the accolade, *The Shield of Rome.* I believe he would have kept Scipio penned up in Italy. I endorse this wisdom—to Fabius!"

And shortly after this toast from the man who had brought him eternal fame, and to the edges of Aeschylus and Euripides and close to treason, Fabius Maximus—The Delayer of Hannibal, hence The Shield of Rome—died.

The reminiscence about Fabius had barely begun when Hannibal's attention was drawn back to Carthage again.

The lembos had slipped into Croton harbor in the dawn. When the Council's envoys got to Hannibal's HQ, the fanfare ahead of them had been minimal...a chain of mostly whispers had passed them from the harbor's esplanade to his sentries, and finally to his adjutant, Hanno, who had sensed a proper moment of announcement.

"I have the honor to present the compliments of the Council, Lord Hannibal, and will it please you to receive their envoys?" Hanno was at rigid attention in front of his focus who was finishing his breakfast.

Hannibal didn't look up from his fruit and eggs. He put Hanno into ease with a slight signal of his left hand.

"They've come," he said, repeating what the whispers had sustained and Hanno had just proved.

Hanno mentioned some names. Hannibal knew the families of two of the four envoys.

"If they want some fruit, let them in. If they want some pomp, let them wait."

Hanno left and returned a few seconds later with four fruit eaters, all in their twenties. He repeated the names again. The envoys, wearing Punic tunics with geometric borders, red sandals, bare headed, made a rank in front of the seated commander, and bowed in unison. Two orderlies scrambled to put camp stools in place for them, then the fruit display grew larger under the same offices. They all stood until Hannibal sent another signal, this time his face sweeping the faces of *his* focus. His invitation obviously included the fruit.

None of them had ever seen him. They knew about the left eye, which was now a closed companion of his right. He had given up the various patches Adherbal had designed long ago. His face was a virtual map of his Italian odyssey if you knew where to look, and he explained it. Although the Romans had tried, there was not a gray hair on either his rather rambunctious top, or the beard which had become more compact and elegant under the recent presses of Sosylos and hence, also, his Greek personal orderly. He usually wore unadorned tunics when not on the verge of action, and this was what they saw. Hamilcar's dagger, held by a black silk hanger, was his only concession to legend. He smiled, but he gave them no lead...this was their play, let them play it.

"The consul Scipio has made intolerable aggressive overtures around Carthage, my lord Hannibal. The Council has empowered us to order you home to command the forces at Carthage."

"When do expect me to take command of these...forces?"

"As soon as Admiral Bomilcar can bring you transport."

"What does my friend, Bomilcar, say about this?"

"He has told the Council that he can probably put military and commercial vessels at your disposal within a month."

"Then this would *probably* make September an auspicious month for both Italy and Africa."

Hannibal let his apple, and then a pomegranate, share in this momentous scheduling. The envoys followed his lead in suppressing formality. Their words were made by various faces, under no evident hierarchy:

"Scipio has been empowered by his senate to offer peace terms."

"Have you seen them?"

"Insulting indemnities; ruinous concessions; deadly restrictions."

"Scipio was just mouthing inevitability—surely the Council was not surprised by this."

"Nevertheless this Roman stance is intolerable to it—hence its reach to you."

"I have been waiting for this invitation for fifteen years, gentlemen. There are two ends to a *reach*, and neither end is *now* favored to conjure an abrupt dismissal of Scipio."

"We argue that you and your brother, Mago, can do this."

"Where is Mago now?" His Po valley gossamers had fallen silent again.

"We hear he has had success in northern Italy, and is now campaigning against the proconsul Cethegus and the praetor Varus in the territory of the Insubres."

"That is an infinity away from us, now."

"The Council would shrink that infinity, Lord Hannibal—it has sent a delegation to Mago, like ours. Mago will be another Barca pillar at Carthage." The young man didn't know that a once monumental, structural, word had just crossed his lips.

"Your prayers in this respect, gentlemen, are no stronger than mine."

The miserable Carthaginian military situation around Carthage was a subject that could gain only misery at this meeting, and he knew more about it than they did. He hadn't pulled any hypocrisy from these young faces which were doing the best they could, so he would try to hold an image for them.

Admiral Bomilcar brought his bridge to Carthage into Croton at near high sun of a day whose blues in the sky and sea were too good for the occasion. The Greeks called the high prowed, broad bellied, Carthaginian freighters *horses* and *tubs*, and he had plenty of them dispersed among his quinqueremes and triremes. He also had plenty of observers who could count.

"I see two hundred hulls."

"Your optimism has become tiresome lately, Silenus. By Zeus, if there are eighty more than one hundred you can have my wine tonight." The Campanian red had run out, so the Bruttium stock was no great hazard for Sosylos.

Actually, cooler heads determined fifty more than one hundred, so Sosylos' wine was safe, and Hannibal's horses and some of his foot would be denied the voyage between Croton and Carthage which would sweep the Pachyrius Promentorium of Southern Sicily, and then the Melitian Islands before it saw the eastern vestiges of Carthage.

"It will mean pushing eighty men, on average, into each hull, Hannibal."

"Then we are looking at twelve thousand for the head of the *hammer* that will drive Scipio into the sea, Maharbal." Maharbal didn't miss the wry smile that had encrusted *hammer*.

He had brought that many Africans into Italy, an elite corps that had no present counterpart on either side, garnished with six thousand horse and eight thousand light foot also in that vanished category. In the now twelve thousand he would put on Bomilcar's bridge, there would be about fifteen hundred African and a thousand Iberian veterans to make the glue for the Bruttians that were now the bulk of his line. His veteran Numidians and heavy cavalrymen now numbered about five hundred. They would bring barely enough glue for what cavalry he could conjure out of the sands between Cyrene and Hadrumetum, and from the leakages from Numidia that got through the Roman net to the west. He still had about four thousand horses. The Romans were always short of them, so killing them, in lieu of transporting them, would be sound military practice. Maharbal didn't need to look at his commander to analyze the nuances of that summation.

He stalked out of his tent, headed for the horse compounds and his cavalrymen. The order he was about to place would come from him. He and Hamilcar's officers had made his cavalry. It had been the principal charge in the lightning that had made Gaius Publius and Fabius listen to its thunder in the Forum. His presence at the end of it was required—he would destroy its vestiges face to face with them.

He touched noses, mumbled compliments about ancestry and performance, rubbed ears, slapped backs and sides, as he worked himself deep into his horses, and their riders who had followed him as soon as he entered the cavalry compounds. He kept up with the shouts:

"By Ba'al, do you remember chasing those Roman rabbits at Trebbia?"

"Ah, that *was* a good one, and then when Mago brought his light horse in behind them and we closed the trap!"

"Trasimene? By the gods I was a helpless bystander—but I remember Marharbal and Mago making some big dents in Flaminius near the lake."

And when they shouted Cannae at him he had to admit that he was too busy swimming in blood—mostly Roman, to see all of the aspects of his heavy and light horse that helped write disaster for Rome that day. And they wouldn't let him stop there: it was Campania, and Herdonia, and Capua—damned Capua that everyone tried to attach to a good face. And more of Apulia, Lucania, Samnium...where they had taught more cavalry lessons to the Romans. And then back to Lucania where his Numidians had finished Marcellus' bravado and he had shown the Romans how to honor a foe, again.

He had worked himself into a great press of cavalrymen—their voices, his voice, mingled into crescendos of memory. He backed toward a cart used for hauling hay, climbed aboard to get some advantage of them. And then he tried to make another summation. Marharbal and Carthalo were in Africa now, but he felt them, and Hamilcar and Mago, as he tried to make his summary:

"You saw what Bomilcar brought us. I can take twelve thousand to Africa. No horses, except my leopards." They probably knew what that meant. He had taught the Romans well, now they were always hungry for horses.

"I..." He had the words ready about the killing, but they stuck in his throat. He could see veteran men and officers who had helped build Hannibal Barca. He picked up dozens of eye axes that denied him the words—the voice he had even practiced was useless now. He finally found another that could be heard when they suddenly made a silence for him.

"I will be leaving some men of Bruttium behind—we can't have every woman in this land flooding it with tears. The Roman arrogance will finally need good husbands for the land, and they will need good horses. We will work out a fair disposition—so we will be leaving plow tracks here instead of horse bones." They gave him a few seconds more silence, and then it was a general cry for Commander Hannibal—*cavalryman!*

Inanna Barca

I am close to making an end of it here. We've packed about twelve thousand into Bomilcar's hulls and we will head toward you at the first favorable tide. We are a rag-tag band held together by a few veterans who peeked down the Alps at Italy with me fifteen years ago. I am taking ten horses—my leopard Numidian guard that has helped me get as far as this letter. I hope that Marharbal and Carthalo have paid their respects to you and to whatever treasure troves of cavalry Scipio has left me.

I will try to land near at Leptis Minor. I suspect that Scipio will leave us alone until he is convinced that he has some advantage of us. This should give me a little time to play husband and father.

My thoughts now are too muddled to make any good sentences for you. If the task of my life was to destroy Rome, I have failed. If this is not all of it...then we will see what your Heimarmene has written for me. I know that his Inanna and Kyniska parts have been constant jewels in my variable heaven.

I will ask Sosylos to deliver this to you. My schedule will be too slippery to tie to any promises here—but if I can make a time for coming to you, Sosylos will tell you.

Hannibal

He stood at the stern of Bomilcar's flagship, alone, wrapped in a cloak of Tyrian purple, his privacy a respect of the officers of his staff and the ship for a man who was watching a world vanish over the horizon with the Promontorium

Lacinium. Except for his crematories at the battle sites where he had honored his men and Romans alike, the little bronze plaque at Hera's sanctuary was all that could prove he was ever in Italy—although he had engraved thoughts of him on every Roman who could see lightning and hear thunder, and his visage could be pulled from the tiles on the floor of the Roman Senate by anyone who had even flirted with eidetic vanities. But these were transients of him that could be denied as reality, insubstantials that were no proof of him, the working stuff of other chroniclers than Silenus—most of them naturally inclined to Latin.

Hamilcar had told him about the special joys and frustrations of the sea fighter. He listened to the suck of the water against the sleek hull, steadied himself against the thrusts of the oar banks and now the addition of wind impulses going from her sail and mast down into her planks. Carthage could have put many ships like this on her ligament to him, guards for reasonable replenishment that could have sustained his initiative and turned the Roman issue toward *him* after the pinnacle of Cannae. There had been plenty of time to put Carthaginian power into the sea and land interstices of the Roman fear and confusion that could have broken the Roman Federation. Many—on both sides—had used the word *miracles* on him, but no man had ever sustained them all by himself.

Inanna wouldn't let him snuggle too far into the warm recesses of that cloak. In *her* lessons for him that touched the Greeks, and some of her reputed Mesopotamian antecedents, she had said that many estimable men—once she called up the Assyrian warrior kings Ashurnasirpal and Tiglathpileser—had let both passion and logic have a place in them, to the exclusion of neither, in making the course of their lives. And they expected the interventions of the gods to have the same sway when they measured the chain of a man's good fortunes. It had been *his* logic he used when he gave Maharbal and Barmocar and the others his reasons for not going to the heart of the Romans after Cannae. The Romans had nothing between him and Rome. His army was at its peak. No man of it would have disputed that move and resolve. A fundamental breach of the wall at Rome would have been a miracle with his equipment—but had he cut his own chain by not conceding more room for the gods' passions to allow another miracle?

BOOK THREE

African Fields

22

45 years
Spring 202 BC—Zama

H e had led his Mushroom column through country like this. Some of them were still with him, trying to make a glue and some inspiration for his now cavalry that was a perfect complement to the rag-tag army he had described for Inanna. When he had landed at Leptis Minor, Maharbal and Carthalo's report on cavalry confirmed his worst pessimism. Carthage had yielded 500 horses from pools of local talent largely filled by dilettante cavalrymen. They had scraped a thousand horses together from the Libyan sands as far east as Cyrene, and there had been some trickles through the Numidian civil war west of Carthage that had added another thousand horses to him. He had gone into Numidia himself and tracked down Syphax's relative, Tychaios, who had finally donated 1,500 horses after his loyalties and recourses had been bent toward Carthage by the man who was still playing Hamilcar Barca.

This column he was leading toward Scipio—none of his staff had heard him use the word *army*, on it—was now made of 4,000 horse, his 12,000 heavy foot who had come from Italy with him, the 10,000 Balearic, Celt and Ligurian remnant of Mago's army which had come from Genoa, 9,000 of Greek, Iberian, Celt mercenaries, and 10,000 survivors from the armies Gisgo and Syphax had squandered on Scipio's altar, largely people from the Carthaginian and Libyan hinterlands who were months, years, away from a disciplined corps.

And Carthage had voted him eighty elephants. He liked them. He had had them as pets, and he had seen them charge into hells of battle and come out like screaming children spreading unbiased destruction. They might scare some of the youngsters in Scipio's line, make some useful dents. But they were mostly baggage encumbering his forage and water problems...a symbol the Council had insisted he show the Romans in lieu of an army.

Mago should be with him now. He had disciplined himself away from Hasdrubal with a few years' help. But Mago had been within a breath of him. This young one, who had been part of his lightning at Cannae and all the earlier times on the Italian fields, had not come with his army. When he went to the cothon to receive Mago's flagship, Mago's adjutant told about his death on board ship a week out of Genoa, gangrene from a thigh wound he had taken against the Romans in the Po valley. Mago had sent him 10,000 men. But his brother had been worth more than this. He would need to play the magician against Scipio, and he could have given some wonderful parts of this magician to the Gypsy.

He moved around the column, from the baggage train to its cavalry van. His leopard Numidians were under no constraints of protection here so sometimes they let him take his shouts and cheers by himself. This was the undiluted glue that held it all together. If his staff gave him an interstice of silence when he came back into the command echelon of the column, he had a tendency to private reminiscence which had nothing to do with Scipio:

When Sosylos returned from his first visit to the Hadrumetum estate, delivering Hannibal's letter to Inanna, he reported that he had intercepted both Inanna and Kyniska on a riding excursion. They had recognized him first, and let him approach close enough to recognize, in turn, a mature Greek lady, and a younger lady who also represented the best Greek exports of beauty and grace.

"What did they say?" He could have charged directly from the dock to them, throwing aside the clutter of official paraphernalia, but he thought Sosylos' surrogate here might lessen the shock on them. Now he was trying to justify this cowardly delegation of shock in front of a Spartan.

"I was surprised that my lady called my name—and after fifteen years!"

"Their look—what was it like?"

"Haughty, even imperial—just what I would expect from a wife and daughter of Lord Hannibal."

"Not *that* look—the *rest* of them!"

"Your Lady Barca was dressed like a Celt cavalryman—your daughter, too. She graced a black Cyrenian—your daughter a white. After her hail, I stood still and waited."

"For what?"

"For the initiative of Inanna which I knew was sharply imminent."

"When it came?..."

"She got off her horse and kissed me."

"By Ba'al—you've taken this letter carrier role too far!"

"I am obliged to admit there were two kisses."

"By her god, this is outrage!"...but this was a long way from the peaks Hannibal could make of his anger...or its various shadings.

"The second grace was from younger lips, but not inexperienced, nor bashful. She said she was glad to have finally met me. But I reminded that I had held her in my arms before she could even walk."

"Did you have time—between the kisses—to mention *me*?"

"The question of *you*, Lord Hannibal, was also sharply imminent, but they are careful aristocrats...and they let me bring you up in good time."

"How did you...bring me up?"

"That you would greet them as soon as you could. There is opportunity here for a classic surprise—like Odysseus' advent to the hall where his wife was bedeviled by suitors."

"That play won't work on *my* stage...perhaps some subtleties...a casual intrusion of their cavalry exercise. Was there any more from these ladies?"

"Your lady Inanna said that it was Heimarmene's little gift that we should have made such a delightful informal conjunction...she said they pass that way on the third and fourth days of the week, but usually nearer to high sun than I had come."

"Tomorrow is the fourth day. If I came to your place, nearer to high sun than you, perhaps I might also have a fortunate—even delightful—conjunction."

"It is very likely, Hannibal."

A captain of his scouts reported that Scipio was moving westward along the Bagradus River.

When Hannibal returned from Italy, a little steel started to creep into the Council's backbone. The peace terms, that had taken shape under its humiliating denouncement of its commander in front of both Scipio and the Roman Senate, started to unravel once their miracle worker had stepped on Carthaginian soil again. When a supply fleet for Scipio floundered in a storm within sight of Carthage, the Council ordered Hasdrubal Gisgo to take as much booty as he could from the Roman. The Carthaginian warships captured considerable supplies for the depleted coffers of Carthage, and came close to destroying Scipio's supply fleet. The envoys Scipio sent from Tunis to Carthage to protest this violation of the putative peace were handled roughly and returned to him without satisfaction. This incident, and probably some movement in Rome toward diluting his prerogatives in Africa, put Scipio into a campaign of destruction of Carthaginian assets in the hinterland. He destroyed villages, enslaved their people, and generally played with vengeance instead of diplomacy while he tried to divine a regular pattern in the threads of his destiny that had not wrapped inevitable glory as tightly to him as he would have liked since he had committed to Africa, and stepped on it.

Hannibal's pitiful military situation was no secret from him. The sooner he could make a battle, the sooner he could capitalize on this good fortune. With Hannibal's cavalry arm finally virtually severed, Masinissa's Numidian horse was all he needed to allay fear of the miracle worker which Scipio had never admitted—but had sunk into him at Ticinus, Trebbia, Cannae and the other places where he had audited Hannibal's classes. His publicists and political faction had done a good job for him. They had carved a heroic image of him into the chronicles. But what Scipio now saw in his *private* mirrors made Masinissa indispensable. Hence, Scipio's present course bent toward Hannibal's, but it was Masinissa who pulled both of them westward. This flamboyant horseman had been in, and out, of Scipio's aura since the Roman had touched Africa. Now he was supposed to be coming east from Numidia with the large detachment of horse he had pledged to Scipio against Carthage.

After the scout's report, Hannibal replied that it seemed likely an auspicious conjunction might be made somewhere between Narragara and Zama. It was still two, three days away. He had plotted his course to embarrass both Scipio's junction with Masinissa and his retreat to his coastal base—in case Heimarmene's smile on this Roman should happen to lapse a little. But an earlier auspicious conjunction suddenly took priority over Scipio:

He had calculated what time a horse would take to bring him to Sosylos' spot on Inanna and Kyniska's equestrian exercise. Then he had ordered a horse, not a prime cavalry mount, but one that had been kept for compassionate old time's sake, and a Carthaginian cavalry uniform, also a souvenir of bloody contention but still respectable enough for a chance meeting involving an old cavalryman. His last order—three gold wine goblets, and a gold flask of what passed for their best wine, and a pack for these things, made some raised eyebrows and whispers among his staff. Sosylos was more explicit:

"By her Asclepius! You will present them with a disreputable old braggart— and a drunken one to boot?" Sosylos' term of tutor, romantic counselor, and general confidante had built a tower of prerogative that no one else presumed to climb in Hannibal's presence. For his present pains, Sosylos got a salute and that smile.

Sosylos' mark was even then mounting his horse and adjusting the pack for travel. Hannibal wore black cavalry boots, a helmet, but no cuirass or leg armor. Hamilcar's dagger in a black leather hanger was his only other concession to the cavalryman. His helmet was uncrested, but dented enough to add some stature to him and his horse. His leopard Numidians got wind of this before he left camp, but he waved them off, also Maharbal's objections to a solo trip..

At a bend in the equestrian trail there was a cluster of three date palms affording a haven of shade. He made a small cairn of stones, enough of a table for his goblets and flask. Here, dismounted, his horse tethered to one of the palms, Lord General Hannibal made his stand.

He was somewhat early to high sun, but this was good because he had some moments to practice an old souvenir of glory before he heard horses approach and then saw the black and white Cyrenians Sosylos had promised. Two ladies wearing Mushroom hats, warped by their personal biases, were aboard. They wore black vests over long sleeved white blouses, white linen trousers instead of the checkered Celtic version, and black riding boots whipped to a high polish. They closed their distance to him quickly with a smart canter, which he had not yet perturbed. Kyniska said something which made her laugh and look to her mother. Inanna was not so distracted and spotted him at about fifty yards, a discovery she shared almost immediately with her daughter. They went to a walk at about thirty yards, and at ten, Inanna stopped them. By her god, it was a sight! He bowed slightly, but carefully kept the shade on his face, the old helmet also putting some camouflage on him. Inanna had stopped. She could have ridden past him and left her dust in his mouth. But she had stopped. It was time for his initiative:

"Pardon me, my lady. Sosylos told me that I might have the privilege of seeing Lord Hannibal's ladies for a second's passing if I came here at about this time." This was his first words to her in fifteen years. He might not have shadowed them enough, but it was too late now. He watched her carefully. If she could pick him out of that voice she didn't show this. She was a perfect balance of amused surprise and smoothly sheathed perquisites. Kyniska was undoubtedly her consort in these respects, but Inanna was his focus.

In the time for his speech, they had missed none of his accoutrements: the old warhorse, the dented helmet, the uniform, and then the audacity of the cairn, with its glints of gold. Inanna held her position, but she found a voice:

"Sosylos has a formidable span of friendship, you are fortunate to be in it." Her voice was just the same as it had been in memory and the dreams. Dark eyes which had once probed every of his secrets were now assessing him. She moved her horse several steps toward him, Kyniska following her lead. What he could see of Inanna's black hair seemed to be unsullied by any intrusion of maturity. He also noticed that Kyniska had let some of the gold she had taken from Hamilcar's Hippolyta trickle from her hat. Their horses were spirited beauties, but he sensed the light touch of perfect control on both of them. If he ever managed to step into the husband and the father, he would have to be modest with his equestrian vanities around these two.

He kept his head down a little and tried to favor his right side for them. Her horse had just taken another step closer.

"You are obviously a veteran of my husband's cavalry."

"I had the honor of being with him on a few auspicious occasions, my lady."

"You speak well." This lady would not have degraded the compliment with any reference to inferior status. Another step forward, and she was now starting to counter his right side favoring with a slight adjustment of her mounted position.

"Sosylos and Silenus have a way of sticking to you, my lady." That was a mistake. He had just uncovered a friendship that no ordinary cavalryman could claim. He also forgot that he was in the presence of a prescience that had earned compliments from a connoisseur of them, his mother.

"I think we would like to avail ourselves of what I presume is refreshment, sir." Inanna started to dismount.

As she watched him, he nodded toward the cairn and its golden crown:

"Sosylos imputed impudence to that, but he said that I might catch a certain Greek lady's famous sense of humor—if Zeus still favors fools."

Kyniska had followed her mother's lead. Now both were walking toward him. He could only stand and try to keep up with them. But his camouflage and favorable positioning were wearing thin, rapidly. Turning to the goblets, filling them, would give him a few seconds grace.

As he turned to these offices, the pommel of his dagger winked at Inanna, spherical sections of bronze and silver, a red garnet set at the focus—Hamilcar's dagger, which her fingers had caressed at Carthago Nova under various imperatives of emotion.

As he offered the goblets, he still tried to favor his right side as a natural posture. Kyniska accepted her goblet, but before Inanna did, she used both hands to remove his helmet. His hair had been mussed by the helmet, but Sosylos' dictums about the beard and eyebrows were still in force, and like her, maturity had not intruded the curly black top of him. Then she accepted the goblet, and waited for more of his initiative.

"To Lord Hannibal...and to what, according to Sosylos, is part of him—his ladies."

Just before his toast, he held his goblet in front of his left eye. He had come to the point of minimum subterfuge.

With her lips on his gold offering, Kyniska serviced his toast, but Inanna hesitated:

"I would let this lord speak for himself, soldier," she said, spiking him with a soft authority that destroyed his camouflage.

Then she sipped her wine, her eyes drilling the center of his forehead. Kyniska's momentary visual preference was unknown to him. Actually, with eyes which held part of a universe, she was also staring at this battered old cavalryman.

Inanna turned to her daughter. "Would your father approve of a kiss for this stranger's compliments, and consideration?"

"If it would put you in some jeopardy with Father, I would be happy to be your surrogate in this, Mother."

"I will take the chance." And then Inanna kissed him, on the lips—too strongly for a salute to history.

Kyniska would not be denied. She made it a pile of three, and Silenus had missed a conjunction that would tax his reportorial capacity for murmurs, comprehensive kissing, and finger touches and entanglements.

This was his envelope. She had been shocked at what fifteen years of almost continuous battle at done to him, but this was the precious envelope of him she held now. The details of him would be for their later privacies. Kyniska had no prior measures to interfere with the handsome, mature man she saw and now also held.

He told them that there were too many loose ends between him and Scipio for him to linger overlong as husband and father. They took him back to the Hadrumetum estate and prepared to pamper him for three days—the pools, the food, the massages where Tiba and Maga, more mature now, and more resolute, would try to fashion a relaxed, supple, aristocrat out of the man who had fared hardly better than his men over the Italian years.

His mother and Medina were at the Hadrumetum villa when he arrived. The Roman presence around Carthage was complicating the Barca empire, and all of the ladies had been urged by the men of their staff to stay closer to the Hadrumetum facet of it. Hannibal himself had sent a suggestion in this respect that sounded like a command, and this had also tended to achieve the desired focus of his ladies.

He didn't look like a commander. And when the servant's grapevine's signals had drawn his mother and Medina to the entrance courtyard, it could have been Inanna and Kyniska helping an old cavalryman to a peaceful shelter instead of the cavalcade of the man who had pressed the back of a desperate Roman Wolf against the walls of Rome.

Inanna and Kyniska observed strict decorum as they escorted him forward, bracketing him. Not a smile, no hint of the foreplay that Silenus had missed to abolish the pretense for the lady who had been a queen of the Mediterranean for a merchant prince of Tyre, and of the Amazons for Hamilcar.

She and Medina stood on the top level of the entrance steps, so the horse people had no elevation advantage. When the newcomers' rank had come within about ten yards of the steps, Inanna gave a command:

"Flanks stop. Center column forward at discretion." She had stolen some of Hippolyta's thunder.

The greatest cavalry general of the age obeyed Inanna. When his flanks came to a smart stop, he continued forward a few steps, thus making a chevron of horses' salute to the ladies of the steps, and bringing them within easy speaking range. He bowed his bare head to them, and then came up, waiting for his mother. Maybe he was closer to Sosylos' Odysseus thing than he should have been, but Kyniska had suggested that it might be fun to see what Lady Barca would make of it.

It had been twenty-two years since his mother had watched him leave Carthage with Sosylos and Hasdrubal. She was now sixty-three. She and Medina were both dressed in short exercise tunics and wore running sandals, signaling only the gods could know what exercise he had interrupted, or they had finished. Her hair was still that amalgam of silver and gold, now more biased toward silver. He calculated her age, and then roved her figure in amazement. From his distance, she and Medina could be sisters. With these ladies in front of him, Inanna and Kyniska behind him and the quick flush of them still warm, all the rumors he had heard about a powerful matriarchy dominating the Barca empire were now perfectly reasonable.

"You are most welcome, soldier. What news have you brought about my sons, Hannibal and Mago?" He wondered about the way a voice could combat age...the persistence of the sound of *her.*

Hers was the senior prescience in this cluster. It had started to work in her when she heard the hubbub about horse people approaching. When she saw the Inanna and Kyniska brackets around what looked like an old cavalryman, she had a quick flux of images that would have excited Zortibas and Acherbas. She knew he had returned from Italy. He was somewhere between here and Leptis Minor. Iberia and Italy had put nineteen years of command on him, of the kind that could possibly warp him almost beyond her memory.

He dismounted and walked toward her. At the first step he knelt, bowed his head:

"I can bring only one of them to you today, Mother." Odysseus had gone.

She came down the steps, grabbed his outstretched hands and pulled him to standing. He noticed the tears just before she kissed him and somehow Medina made up another complicated three person conjunction.

When he and his full escort walked toward the villa, he had left Mago in abeyance. All of them knew that he had been ordered back to Carthage, with Hannibal. The gypsy would really put this family together again!

"Mago won't be coming. He was badly wounded in the Po valley. He died on board ship coming home from Genoa." That news fitted the battered envelope he was presenting as Hannibal—and his army that, fortunately, was out of their sight.

There had been a few tears at the first conjunction, some more at the second. But the end to Mago's story was properly anointed by all of them, his brother included.

On their first night together, Inanna made him explain some of the new map of him on his face and body. But his history was interrupted by him telling her that he must pay homage very soon to the various gods who had granted him her again. She told him that his old soldier ploy had been *very* amusing, and that she had probably used some of the same gods in her prayers for him that Penelope had used for another old soldier: Artemis, Aphrodite, Zeus, Apollo, and some that Penelope probably had not used...Isis, for example, and Tanit, and Asclepius. He said that he admired the international scope of her supplications, but Penelope might also have known, and used, Asclepius for her purposes. Inanna touched his lips with a finger. And then she said that she didn't think he was right about Asclepius—but she would concede another god to Penelope...if he insisted.

His scouts reported that Scipio had started to turn southeast from Narragara, and that near Magaron the dust from his horses had been greater than they had seen before. This course would put him into a conjunction with Hannibal somewhere near the plains called Zama

"I think our old friend, Masinissa, will be playing on Scipio's side of the field when we see him again."

"He may be bringing about four thousand of what is now the best Numidian horse—we have nothing to match this."

"Let's change your *may* to *will*, Maharbal. That dust is his signature. The consul has turned toward us—he wouldn't do this without Masinissa's new bulwark."

He had some advantage of foot on Scipio, counting only numbers about 7,000. In horse, the part of him that had been the principal of the Roman fear of him for fifteen years, he had disadvantage. In numbers again, with his Numidian transfusions Scipio could field 2,000 more horse, but quality warped this number much larger. Carthalo and Maharbal, and the rest of his officers also knew these numbers, the actual, and the virtual, and these two scales of value applied to most of their foot as well.

"I wish Cathbad were beside us."

"Our puny Celt contingent would be no mantle for such a Druid, Hannibal."

They had camped, and were probably within a day of starting some intercourse with Publius Cornelius Scipio, the younger. Hannibal had opened his tent to discourse, approachable formally, or informally. He had left Sosylos at Hadrumetum. For purposes of philosophical bolstering, this Spartan Greek was a good surrogate for him...the ladies' susceptibility to this sort of inspiration being about the same for his and Sosylos'. Silenus, however, was still servicing his chronicle, and he had just made the Druid connection.

"We could use some of his magic—that part about making my army invisible, and then bringing it out under Scipio's nose in a guise that makes it look invincible. Instant appear and reappear, god-like metamorphosis—we could use *all* of this, Silenus, if that damn chronicle is to come out in the right way for my posterity."

"I have never heard you invoke magic like this, Lord Commander Hannibal." Like Sosylos, Silenus had certain prerogatives that gave him some span of titles for his target, depending on the moment.

"I have never needed it as much as now—that god-like metamorphosis of foot and horse, if you need a specific."

"I have heard some of the numbers—the imbalance doesn't frighten *me*."

"Carthalo, here is our man to delay the legions!"

"If Cathbad's shade can spread his magic enough to make Achilles from Silenus—then you have my applause here, Commander."

There was enough laughter, lubricated with wine from the Barca vineyards, to bring Silenus back to comfortable reality. But Hannibal's word, *delay*, had been used in other recent councils where Silenus' numbers had had more presence.

He moved to within four miles of Scipio's camp. They had been on the same ground before, at least at Ticinus, Trebbia, Cannae, and probably Locri, but he knew more about Fabius Maximus than he did about this Scipio: a mystic, Salian priest, sybarite, studious political sycophant, a student of Hannibal. The Iberian part of Scipio's public envelope was the biggest for appraisal of him. His publicists had made it unmitigated spectacular success, but others, including Romans with Fabius among them, had qualified this facet of Scipio's glory. The word, luck, had been leaned against him. And in formal venues such as the Senate there had been bigger clusters of words like, *favorably fortuitous circumstances of resistance*, put against him. But he had moved behind Hannibal's back and talked to the Numidians both in Iberia and Africa. These conversations might have had some precedence from his father, and others, but young Scipio had pressed them, knowing their significance to the man he had attached to himself as his glorious enemy. And he had been very fortunate in his choice of lieutenants: Laelius, for example, who would be commanding part of the advantage of horse that Hannibal did not have.

Hannibal sent a herald to Scipio, requesting a meeting. Their confrontation would not be resolved by conference, but he wanted to see *this* consul, to hear where some words would go before the inevitable took shape. He had killed consuls, talked with Fabius Maximus when Fabius as dictator in the Carthaginian—Hannibal—crisis, was holier than a consul. But this Publius

Cornelius Scipio was almost young enough to be his son. He had come in and out of the direct Hannibal aura several times, with his *outs* products of mercy and good fortune. He had studied the Hannibal thunderbolt as a target of its strokes, and as an academic using surrogate targets.

This meeting might bring two oaths head-to-head: one actually born at Carthage in Ba'al's precincts, Hamilcar alongside; the other possibly born in a Roman camp after Ticinus, the elder Publius Cornelius alongside, close to death from Hannibal's services. These things worked the father and son images, complicated them, so that a personal meeting, within the forms of truce, would be interesting.

Scipio agreed to a meeting on the following day, high sun, on a hill accessible to the views of both armies. His ready cooperation confirmed that Masinissa's Numidians would play on *his* side this time.

Hannibal waved his leopard Numidians off when he saw a level, logical, ground for a conference. He wore no armor. His Carthaginian tunic and sparse accessories, including a white linen turban, were diplomatic, except for Hamilcar's dagger in a black silk hanger. He had put himself on board a sleek black Cyrenian which was not an honest advertisement of the horse squadrons behind him. His adjutant, conforming to Hannibal's diplomatic cast, was there as one of the two official interpreters the consul had requested. There would be Latin to Punic, and Punic to Latin, here, although Greek was a natural connection between Hannibal and Scipio.

Scipio had put on the military. His purple mantle, gilded helmet, cuirass and greaves, were well inside the limits of his perquisites. The red crest of his helmet matched the one Hannibal would wear when he became formal. The consul had dispensed with lictors, and rode toward Hannibal accompanied by his interpreter, a tribune in full regalia of rank. The four men dismounted, then walked toward each other, stopping within easy conversation distance.

No need to favor a side, Hannibal faced the consul, smiled and saluted. Scipio reciprocated the greeting. From his distance, Hannibal thought the other smile was more tentative than his own design. The sun cooperated with the gilding to put a golden aura around Scipio.

"You are rushing the battle on me, Consul," the diplomat said, roving some of the Roman's splendor, letting the translator work Carthaginian into Latin.

That enlarged the Scipio smile, slightly, but didn't provoke any Latin.

"I am sorry that Carthage and Rome ever came to war. Now we should try to construct a peace that could make amends for forty years of foolish impetuosity."

"Carthage started both wars, Lord Hannibal. You must not be so generous with your foolish impetuosity."

Hannibal's Latin was much poorer than his Greek, but he was able to anticipate most of the tribune's service. The eye axis between the principals was not perturbed by the translators.

"My message is short, Consul—I won't keep you overlong from what I anticipate will be a dazzling exercise of Roman might." The smile, before and after this preface, gave Scipio his full face, and the smile overrode the famous asymmetry that had been used in Roman nightmares.

As a beneficiary of nearly a thousand years evolution in Phoenician-Carthaginian pomp and ceremony, Hannibal could have made a good show here himself. Scipio was obviously uncomfortable with the starkly disparate diplomat-soldier poles Hannibal had promoted.

"We propose the following: Rome will retain Iberia, Sicily, Sardenia...and all the other islands between Italy and Africa. My country has invested heavily in these places. This is the majority of our proposal, and a massive concession. You have been fortunate Consul, but this may not be a good basis for too much confidence—I am major evidence of the fickleness of Fate's caress of a man." Hannibal had put acknowledgement of the Council's past and present presence into his statement of terms.

"No one is more aware of those vicissitudes than I, Hannibal—but as to your terms:

They might be acceptable had you left Italy before the Romans invaded Africa. But now that we control most of the land around Carthage they are not sufficient for your concession to us. You have conveniently neglected to mention other matters which were incorporated in the peace terms that had been ratified by both our senates—before your people's recent outrage on my supply ships. Permit me to refresh your memory: Return of all Roman prisoners, deserters, and runaway slaves; victualling of the Roman forces so long as they choose to reside in Africa; surrender of all but twenty of your warships; payment of an indemnity of five thousand talents of silver."

"Putting your addendum on the back of my original terms makes this unconditional surrender."

"It is—you are in no posture to demand more."

"We will let your opinion rest on the fortunes of battle, Consul."

The diplomat saluted Scipio again, and turned abruptly to his horse. Scipio watched Hannibal mount and ride away before he did the same. He had just confronted the miracle maker. He didn't think he'd been intimidated, with the backing he knew Hannibal knew he had. But that smile had faced greater odds before—and it was still pointing at a Roman face.

The plain of Zama was not the situation he would have chosen if he'd had a bigger part of the corps of foot he had taken into another plain at Cannae. Under more *favorably fortuitous circumstances of battle*, he would have maneuvered Scipio into the hill country where his light and heavy foot would be at better than even odds against Scipio's horse advantage. So a magician was needed who could make horses disappear—and the plain of Zama would have to be his stage.

He had twelve thousand heavy foot, largely his Bruttians, as his basis against the consul. His other troops were staging for them, to let them come against Scipio fresh and unencumbered by cavalry attack. This point of battle had started to evolve almost as soon as his miserable cavalry situation had been verified when he landed at Leptis Minor, and its evolution had progressed right up to the time he knew Scipio would have the horse he needed to make a battle against him.

He made his cavalry assignments: Maharbal with his Numidians facing Masinissa's Numidians; Carthalo with his Carthaginian and various African horse facing Laelius with his Roman and Allied horse. He had tried to excuse his old friends from this action. They were almost in their sixties now, but this nearly made another crisis of horse.

"Your subtlety here is elusive, Hannibal. Here we are trying to prop up some excuses for cavalry against Masinissa and the fabled Laelius—and you are talking about making six thousand horse vanish from the field so you can play with your Bruttians undisturbed."

"We have about seven thousand advantage in foot. If they can act like men long enough, you and Carthalo might be able to lead Masinissa and Laelius to a picnic in the delightful hills beyond Zama—so I can have some time to play."

"Where are you, Cathbad—we need you now!"

"I agree, Carthalo, and I have invoked his shade many times in the last hours. I don't know when your opportunity for breakaway will come—I suspect the elephants might give part of it to you. This might be one time we can *use* their panic."

"We are to pretend a normal charge and then veer away from each other... and hope to take Masinissa and Laelius with us." Maharbal had not made a question.

"As always, you have anticipated me, old friend."

The day after the conference, Scipio's invitation to battle had been completed three hours before high sun on the plain of Zama. He disposed his foot in the usual three lines—hastati, principes, and triarii, with normal line separations of about 100 paces. He placed Masinissa's Numidian horse on his right flank, Laelius and the Italian horse on the left flank. His only big concession to the particulars of this battle was anticipating Hannibal's elephants, and for this he ordered clear lanes through his foot formations instead of their usual checkerboard. His velites were scattered in front of his heavy foot in a loose array about 250 feet deep.

Hannibal accepted the invitation and put eighty elephants in a line about a quarter mile in front of Scipio. Behind his elephants he constructed three lines of foot: the first, with a diffuse front of Balearic and Iberian velites, was backed by Mago's Celts and Ligurians, and Moor mercenaries. His second line held his Africans, Carthaginians and Greek mercenaries. His third line held his Bruttians. His separation of the first two lines was the normal 100 paces. *His* big concession to this battle was an unusually large separation between his second line and his Bruttians—a stadium, about two hundred paces This innovation, a true reserve force, was an insult to the legions in front of him, possibly also the prelude to another miracle if his assistant magicians, Maharbal and Carthalo, could cause horses to disappear. Maharbal faced Masinissa, Numidians against Numidians, on his left flank. On his right flank, Carthalo with his Carthaginian and Libyan horse, looked at Laelius. Both of his horse flanks were outnumbered, and undertrained—a novel circumstance for him that unfortunately coincided with a word, *culmination*, that had been monumentally elusive for him in Italy.

Following some contact between the opposing velite buffers, Hannibal ordered his elephants to charge. They were spread across a front of about a mile and as soon as they started to move, the Romans put up a cacophony with horns and trumpets to start the panic that usually joined such a charge not long after they crashed into an experienced opposition. They were headed for Scipio's accommodating avenues, and starting to wreak havoc among his light foot, when distinctive Carthaginian horns signaled a maneuver which Scipio had not anticipated, but Hannibal's assistant magicians had. The mahouts succeeded in turning about equal segments of their line toward Marharbal and Carthalo's horse, respectively.

It was not a pretty exercise—the geometry was rough, and many of the beasts crashed into the Roman line prematurely. But they did it obliquely to Scipio's avenues and when the panic came to them they were surrounded by Romans instead of Carthaginians, which was useful for Hannibal. It was also useful for him that Maharbal and Carthalo used the screen of confusion the mahouts had accomplished to charge both Masinissa and Laelius' horse, wiping the outer edges of the Roman horse with javelins and spears before proceeding into the hinterland beyond the formal battleground. Masinissa and Laelius decided to join that picnic and another Hannibal miracle might have begun.

His first line had to bear the hastasti crash, and before it started to yield ground, it surprised him by the amount of veteran behavior it showed. But it yielded and then the slow retreat gradually deteriorated to some panic. Hannibal, with his Leopards in close attendance, ordered his second line to resist any penetration by his first line, shouting at them to go to their spears if necessary. Some killing on the spears was done, but this barrier to panic gradually put some veteran behavior back into the first line. As Scipio started to feed his principes and triarii into the action, Hannibal's first and second lines, interspersed by his slingers and javelin men, started a cooperation which was partially inspired by his conspicuous order to his reserve line to not tolerate any intrusion by those now committed to the fight—there was to be no retreat. He got close to his men. His shouts and orders, and the sight of him, moved along the battle front that now contained his first and second lines and the remnant of his velites.

Scipio's gilded armor flashed sporadically along the Roman line and his movement became less leisurely by the minute as the legions' march went from inexorable to stalled all along the battle which now contained his full corps— without his horse.

This was another moment of Hannibal's miracle. He ordered his fresh reserve line into action. His assistant magicians had kept the horses off this field for over an hour. If they could manage to work another half hour into his horseless grace period, Masinissa and Laelius' return might be part of Scipio's epitaph.

His Bruttians worked into the Romans' front and flanks and Publius Cornelius Scipio watched them come until the image of Roman panic, unthinkable with his favorable odds of force, crept close enough for him to hear it, smell it, and then taste its bile. In one instant of action, Hannibal rode close enough so that he could make the flash of Hamilcar's dagger an unambiguous ornament for Scipio's personal scene.

Hannibal had just swept the line with his encouragement, when there was a change in the ground and air that only a cavalryman could feel. He heard the warning shouts of his Leopards, but they were late for him. Masinissa and Laelius were coming back. His magicians' work had been virtuosic, but his gods, Inanna's god, had stopped smiling in his direction.

His Bruttians, and reinvigorated others, continued to grind into Scipio. He tried to warn them, sending his officers out to make cavalry defensive posture from what was now a killing orgy that was spilling Roman blood almost over Scipio's feet.

Masinissa and Laelius were not accommodating this time and the classics of heavy horse butchering of foot started to infuse the panorama of this battle. His Leopards finally succeeded in moving him away from the horse and foot vortex that held the battle flags of his reserve, the shouts of some of its captains and men toward him—the drain hole for the blood of his last army.

He would not put everything into this victory for Scipio. Before he left for Zama, Inanna had told him that a good Greek knew when to turn to other horizons...and she reminded him that, for her, he now qualified as a good Greek.

He and a cadre of officers rode nonstop to Hadrumetum. He promised them his company, and talent at commiseration, and then he went to the Barca villa, alone. Sosylos was there. Silenus had survived Zama, and he would be coming soon for the purposes of a chronicler.

He managed to avoid everyone, but Inanna. When he came to her in their apartments the eastern darkness had started its fusion with the sun. He was ripe for Tiba and Maga's ministrations, but this time he gave his wife almost the full face of battle.

And when he said, "I'm not Hamilcar...anymore," she believed him.

23

45 years
202 BC—Carthage

t was a false twilight. Five hundred ships of Carthage had been put into a graveyard at least a quarter mile into the sea beyond the cothon. The torches had been applied two hours before the official sunset, but this requiem had persisted, as the fire fought natural and Carthaginian obstacles to a quick finish...triremes, quinqueremes, and progeny of the transports that had evolved over eight hundred years of the rule of Carthage, the Mediterranean queen, were wrapped in the tentacles of the fire storm. Every eye of Carthage watched in sorrow as a basis of proud empire disappeared.

Scipio had not yet left for his triumph at Rome. From his quarters at Tunis, this derivative of victory was clearly visible. The Romans had used Greek and Carthaginian precedence to make themselves a sea power in a short time. A ravening fire like this—with no respect for *any* precedence—had to make a thinking man like Scipio wonder when it would apply to Rome. He had insinuated himself into the nadir of their greatest general. Even so, his culminating victory had hung perilously on a few minutes of cavalry that had been displaced to the very end of the action by none of his design. Only a whisper of fate had separated Hannibal from another miracle of arms at the expense of another Scipio.

The balcony of the Barca palace at Carthage was silent for this spectacle. Its red flames swept the faces, and tended to suck the breath from words. Stiros had been invited to be a witness with the family. He stood alongside Hannibal on his left. Inanna, Kyniska, Lady Barca and Medina were on his right. Perched in various shadows and levels, the entire palace household was also watching the cremation of their ships. Sosylos and Silenus were present within conversation range of the Barcas.

Stiros sneaked glances at Hannibal whose face, fluxed by this fire and by fires of other times, was inscrutable. The partially closed left eye gave Stiros nothing. Around the mouth, in the structure flowing to the cleft of the chin, there seemed to be a tension, but he was not a qualified Hannibal observer. He had been allowed to linger within conversation range on a few occasions, and he had seen smiles in his direction that seemed to be shedding ambiguity, but he was still unqualified and his glances were sneaky and quick when observing Lord General Hannibal in front of this holocaust the Romans had ordered.

A few days before, Hannibal had been in the Hall of the Council when the Roman terms of unconditional surrender had been discussed. Scipio had recited some of them to him on the hill above an unbloodied Zama. Now, for a defeated Carthage, the indemnity had been doubled to 10,000 Euboeic talents of silver, to be paid at the rate of 200 talents per year for fifty years. The navy would be virtually destroyed, with a modest commercial transport presence allowed. Carthage was to be a friend to Rome, which meant everything that Hamilcar had denied and died for. Carthage was allowed some autonomy in conducting her affairs, but only under Roman advice and permission for military adventures in Africa. Carthage would victual and pay Roman troops in Africa for at least three more months. Reparation would be made for the damage to Roman property done during the violation of Scipio's truce. Masinissa was to be restored to his full rights of power and property in the Numidian kingdom. And as a guarantee of performance, 100 Carthaginian hostages, young men between the ages of fourteen and twenty, were to be chosen by the presiding Roman general and delivered to Rome.

The indemnity of 10,000 talents brought the biggest groan in the hall. Protection of its income sources, some connected to Rome throughout the war, had always shaped the support the Council had given Hannibal, and this cry of anguish—like earlier others—overbore the echoes of his victories in this same hall.

An officer named Gisgo had worked himself close to a low speaker's dais on the floor of the hall. He claimed the dais, raised his fist and denounced the Roman terms, saying that no true Carthaginian should bear this disgusting yoke of the Roman tyrants. He was picking up a good wind of popular support when Hannibal strode to him and jerked him off the dais. This speaker might have been the same man who had been awed at the Roman juggernaut at Cannae and who had inspired the laughter—Hannibal the nucleus—which had rippled down the Carthaginian formation and into the plain of Cannae where golden Paullus and Varro had heard it.

Hannibal apologized to the Council for his rude behavior on the basis of an old soldier who had been too long away from civilization. And then he told them that Carthage had just lost a *war*, not a battle. She was at the mercy of Rome. The Roman terms of surrender were generous, and every citizen of Carthage would be well advised to cooperate in their implementation—if the lightly sheathed proclivities of what had been called *the Italian Wolf* were not to be loosed on them.

The agony of the ships was nearly finished. Some spires of flame flicked over the more resolute hulls, but it was almost a good darkness now. Nothing had been said for a long time, although every eye on that balcony, and most of those farther away from him had sought some clue to Hannibal's reaction to it. Once again, it was Sosylos who offered to pull a word from him out of improving darkness. He had done it at Faesulae, when a blind eye had dragged the commander into a depth that needed Inanna's intervention to save him.

"I need a word from you, Hannibal...and I think Silenus would find it helpful, consoling. He's been trying to squeeze some thoughts from his pen for this crucial scene."

Sosylos stepped out of a heavy shadow, coming closer to his target. He stopped near enough to understand a complicated softness that might be like the one he had entered in a tent at Faesulae fifteen years before.

"I'm thinking about a bird of Arabia," Hannibal said. That didn't take long, and the voice was loud enough for everyone in the Barca group to hear him. Sosylos studied the face for one of the infinite versions of a smile, but Hannibal protected the inscrutability that had challenged Stiros.

"We've ventured there a few times, Hannibal...but I've forgotten this aspect of my profound erudition." This was too massive a confession from a Spartan tutor to a pupil—Sosylos was using it as a prod for words.

Hannibal finally turned away from the seascape that had brought Hamilcar, and Amalkre, and Mago, and Hasdrubal, and Cathbad, swarming around him...and a thousand images of the death he had piled on the Roman side, and his side, of his ambition. He looked at Sosylos: "This bird—you called him Phoenix—climbed on his funeral pyre...and then, after he had made good ashes, he climbed off it, reincarnated—reinvigorated for further ventures needing good wings and sharp eyes."

By Inanna's Asclepius! There was a smile...small, but Sosylos enjoyed it as much as the speck of one he had finally pulled out of him at Faesulae. Inanna had been holding her husband's hand. Now she squeezed that hand and Kyniska watched her father's face perform a famous metamorphosis that used adversity to make opportunity. Hannibal put his arms around his wife and daughter and warped them into a three figure confrontation with the Spartan.

"With supervisors like these, my friend, I like the Carthaginian prospects that Scipio has left behind." He kissed Inanna, and close-coupled Kyniska showed some precociousness with kisses on her father's chin, and then his cheek, that surprised no one, certainly not Stiros.

The elder Lady Barca, now served by soft light from oil lamps, approached her son from Sosylos' direction...which put her on the side for pulling words out of Hannibal. He had barely become a civilian and his itineraries had started to probe the empire she and her ladies had held in the absence of Barca men. She was, therefore, interested in any clue to his metamorphosis beyond Zama.

"I like your choice of supervisors, Hannibal. What other delegations can you tell us about?" He would have to ask her about the touch of amber at her ears which had just trapped a fragment of light—possibly other jewels from the northern cornucopia Cathbad had once dangled in front of him and Hasdrubal.

"You are rushing me, my lady. I am discovering an empire that Father would have complimented. I hope to find some small place in it that you ladies can tolerate." He managed to bring all of the executives of the Barca estates into a restricted glance and an unrestricted smile.

"Your Phoenix is strong inspiration—I wonder what directions its wings will use?"

"I'm surfeited with Iberia, although Hamilcar and Amalkre have made it a perpetual lodestone for my thoughts. You and your ladies have kept and built interesting ligaments that bend eastward...I think this is the best direction for those wings, Mother."

"I haven't heard of any vengeance attached to this Arabian bird." She had turned to her old friend Sosylos, who had built comfort for her on another terrace when Amalkre's death and a loss of sons to Iberia had been part of another twilight. *Vengeance* had robbed her of a husband and two sons. This remainder of Hamilcar standing close to her could be a precious bastion against this expensive word—if he chose to be.

"Nor I, my lady." But Sosylos was watching Hannibal, a man who could give a home to vengeance if anyone in their world could.

They had to wait a little while for the words this time. He had not relinquished his grip on Inanna and Kyniska, but he was staring out to sea again when his answer came:

"Vengeance burned in that fire. Our bird can take no useful energy from its ashes."

About a year after the bonfire of the ships, Hannibal and his mother were watching Inanna, Kyniska and Medina play with the bronze dolphins in the main pool of the villa at Hadrumetum. He had finally escaped the melee in the water that had had no respect for his age, or his honors as husband, father and commander. The lady beside him had not forgone this local exercise, but when he left the pool, she followed. She had heard a rumor that needed some probing. Wrapped in an unusually discreet robe, she suffered an over zealous attendant's ministrations about her hair, while she watched her son's relaxation that appeared to be genuine.

"Bomilcar tipped a morsel my way just yesterday...I think you are denying me again as a confidante." She waved her attendant away.

"I'm glad you're still accepting Bomilcar. He is one of the pillars from Father's age...anything serious with him, yet?"

"He is a good friend, nothing more...serious. He said you and his son, Hanno, might be making an announcement very soon." She had dismissed his personal probe, but not before eyes, like Hippolyta's, had given him more of an answer.

Hanno had been a lieutenant of his cavalry, and was one of his Italian continuities that had survived the retreat to Bruttium and then Zama. This younger man had no political ambition until some of Hannibal's itineraries started to uncover the people's interest in a more democratic Carthage. Hanno's father, Bomilcar, had been one of the sufets of Carthage, and he had tried to keep the anti-Hannibal faction, also affiliated with the name Hanno, under control during the war. While Bomilcar couldn't mobilize proper support of Hannibal's campaign against a Council-based oligarchy who chose business as usual over protection and expansion of Carthage's sovereignty, he had helped to implement the fleet of lembi, the heart of Hannibal's gossamers, that had probed Roman action and intention during most of the Italian years, and sustained an intercourse between this commander and his family that was the strongest ligament he ever got from Carthage.

Hanno, son of Bomilcar, was, therefore, within a family's breath of politics and when he heard about his commander's Phoenix, and the questions that went into the heart of the Carthaginian people, he thought that, in the right climate, he could become a politician.

Hannibal had dismissed his attendant earlier, and was using the fluffy white Egyptian towel on himself, on the face where his mother could see that a relaxed patrician had finally emerged from most of the forms that Iberia, Italy and Zama had put on him. His two dimensional world was still a fascination for her. She had tried to put herself into it, wondering how she looked to him, how the world looked to him. But, since Faesulae, he had shown them how a man can enter such a world and use it...and she had kept her wanderings in it to herself.

"Hanno has told me that he thinks he and I can make two sufets in the people's image."

Bomilcar had told her as much, but her son had to nail it down. His itineraries in the various corners of what was left of an empire had drawn people after him, *people* who had been left out of the substances the Council had worked with for generations except when more labor, more taxes, more soldiers, were called for. There had been democratic effusions before, but no one who could keep them going and make the People's Assembly the zenith of authority and purpose in Carthage that was implicit in the constitution Plato had admired. Bomilcar's Hanno had followed a leader in Iberia and Italy. Now he had been pricked honestly to follow the same man along another unexampled path. He had his own mind and conceptions of the democratic casts he would make over Carthage, and evidently Hannibal had discovered plenty in Hanno that he could use for their sufets who would finally step away from the ambiguous shadows of their Chamber into the daylight of the People's Assembly—and the Council Hall when necessary.

"There has not been a politician in our family for eons, neither my share of it in Tyre, nor your father's side I think—but only the gods know where *his* antecedents have trickled from." Her son, Hannibal, had just tipped a monumental path change in her direction, but she had kept it light, playful.

Between folds in his towel, Hannibal admired barely concealed female forms that were the basis for laughter and shouts in a restless wet environment, only slightly removed from the loungers. "I didn't give your word, *vengeance*, the proper rounding that night of the bonfire. My answer referred to the Romans—but that doesn't finish it."

Before the lady could work with the unpleasant inference her son had just given her, he leavened it:

"There were several points of progress in my Italian odyssey when timely and proper support from the Council could probably have turned it toward a conclusion under our terms. The oligarchy that continues to dominate this body was responsible for diversion of crucial sustenance away from me. I charge it with our present subservience and I would like to *break* it—in the interest of Carthage, making the People's Assembly more significant than the Council Hall."

He turned to the mature beauty who had just sprinkled Bomilcar and Hanno on him and was now getting splashed by her own initiative. "If a politician should intrude our sacred escutcheon, Mother, maybe I can give him a little honor you can live with—and Father could understand."

"Then you and Hanno will stand for sufets?"

"The Council has already approached me about coming into *that* body."

"No wonder, you've picked up a people's tail that could choke them if you dragged it into their holy precincts as an outsider—but you would hold more power as a senator, than a sufet."

"Not the way Hanno and I would play the sufets. They have put a legal mask on them that is mostly ceremonial. The sufet's power has been sucked away, like the people's voice, in Carthage."

"Apparently, you and your protégé think your democratic overtures have weight."

"If we used the Roman Centurion system, a representative for every hundred citizens who would speak and act for them, I think we could pry those bloated asses in the Council off their marble benches tomorrow night."

"Your father and I have put more discretion in you than *that*." But then she remembered that her words had just gone to a man who had taken more discretion, the enervating kind, out of war than any commander in memory...so why would he become bashful as a politician?

"They think I am useful to them. I have advised complete and cheerful compliance with the Roman terms which continues the kissing sounds many of our elite have made in the direction of Rome since before I left Iberia. Rome has given us a certain latitude in our affairs. If they want me, I will come as a sufet, and a people's representative. Amalkre and Medina's Hasdrubal, and Father, put the authority to elect the sufets in the People's Assembly. They have put some stepping stones down for me—I think I'll use them."

"That would be implicit in the unprecedented popular voice that you've dug up here in the damnedest places since you've come home. Will the Council accept these new sufets with the novel consciences?"

Hannibal Barca stood up, shed his towel, showed his mother that he endorsed the Greek precept that a good body was indispensable to a logical mind...then he accepted the invitation of other sirens without further answers.

Sosylos also had touched the subjects of sufets, and novel consciences, with her. The tutoring she had commissioned long ago had surely let this son of hers look at democracy with some Spartan perspective. She knew that the Spartan Euphorate was the overbearing presence to Sparta that the Council was to Carthage. And when Sosylos happened to mention—just the other day—that he remembered his Spartan lessons better than his Arabian ones, and did she know about Cleomenes and Nabis, the revolutionaries who paved the way for the deflation of the euphors?—another suspicion of hers about the Hannibal and Sosylos axis was confirmed.

Hannibal, son of Hamilcar, and Hanno, son of Bomilcar, were declared the sufets for that year's term. The declaration had come from the Hall of the Council, but the impetus had flowed into the building of the People's Assembly from every corner of Carthage's Africa, and this popular mandate easily jumped the distance across the forum to the Council and did a decision in record time. Hannibal and Hanno then made their first declaration: they would place their philosophy of sufets before the people in the Assembly, and this would be done on their first day of office, at high sun.

Sufets had started out with official garb that nudged close to that of Tanit's high priests, with an implication of mystery, hedonism and power. As their authority was taken away, they tended to dark robes with minimal embellishment that blended well with shadows.

Hannibal and Hanno stood on the rostrum of the People's Assembly wearing white tunics, but with edging of colored Carthaginian geometricals which the Council didn't favor. The Roman senator had beguiled too many of them, and overt homage to Carthage in their official costume, a modified toga, was considered redundant affectation. For two sufets who had ridden to the Assembly on the people's back, a conspicuous uniform that attracted public attention was a natural affectation. Inanna and Sosylos had dug into Arabian lore and designed a hat for them, whose band echoed the geometricals of the robe in a finer silken mesh. Cone hats had been used by priests, politicians, and buffoons in Phoenicia for centuries, so Inanna and Sosylos went to flatness in their hat design.

Hatted, side by side, the elder sufet had the honor of the two, but he deferred the introduction to Hanno, whose name had been twisted with the Barca's in various ways that put a lot of irony on that rostrum.

"I had the honor of serving Lord General Hannibal in Iberia and Italy and Africa. I tell you that now I have this honor in serving with Sufet Hannibal Barca in Carthage. *My* name relates to Bomilcar, the sufet, not Hanno, the Great, and I will design my thoughts and action to serve the *people* of Carthage." Hanno had turned toward Hannibal.

"There are two amateur politicians in front of you: Sufet Hanno has more time than I to make a good one."

"Does your definition of *good* stand as close to *people* as Hanno's, Lord Hannibal?"

"It had better. I have a democratic Spartan on my side, and a wife and daughter who have been weaned on Greek democracy—and you know about my mother. She's been trying to make a good Greek out of me since I was born." The natural banter of the Assembly played for a while and then Hannibal's smile became more official:

"Sufet Hanno and I have been thinking about a few things. I have played the soldier too long to be close enough to you—but there are some things you have told us that we can work with for progress. The Romans have left us with enough to start a new Carthage. We have natural and human resources here, and have ligaments, and can build others to places that complement our assets. We will build new sea legs. We will manufacture the goods, make the wine and grow the crops and livestock that have made us famous in the world. And we will reach out to every shore of the Mediterranean where we have old friends and can make new ones. Our ancestors ventured far outside the Gates of Hercules to touch new worlds. We would not honor them if we failed to pick up this quest in our time. I implore the Punic and Greek gods who now pertain to us to help us sustain this resurrection of Carthage! With your help, we will succeed in peace—make insignificant the defeat in war." Hannibal had put his right hand on Hanno's shoulder just before his pledge.

Carthalo and Maharbal had both survived Zama and had worked themselves close to their commander as he addressed the Assembly. They had had a surreptitious peek into his communion with the Cumaean Sybyl, and he let them stay while he finished his business with her. They noticed that the voice he had just used in his supplication to the gods was very like the one he had used in the temple at Cumae, when a victory at war—not peace—was in his mind.

After their declarations, Sufets Hannibal and Hanno left the Assembly Hall and approached the large fountain in the forum between the Hall of the Council and the Assembly. Twenty-three years before, Hannibal had stood here after defending Hasdrubal the Handsome, Amalkre and Medina's Hasdrubal, in the Council. He had been on the verge of Iberia again as Hasdrubal's officer, and would become almost a stranger to Carthage before he returned.

The sufets were fending congratulations and some questions whose tenor continued their celebration in the Assembly, when one of the senators who had been present in the Assembly put himself on an intersection path with Hannibal. Hanno recognized Hasdrubal the Kid, a spokesman of the Hanno the Great party which had persisted in the Council at very low flame. Hanno stepped forward to make his own interception, but Hannibal's hand touched his shoulder again. No introduction was needed for Hannibal, either. His mother knew that this man in front of him helped carry a nucleus whose destruction was part of her son's incentive for becoming a politician.

"Permit me to add *my* congratulations, Sufet Hannibal." The senator had stopped well short of a suspicious Hanno and an amused Hannibal.

"We accept them, Hasdrubal." Use of that name, now, put some gall in Hannibal's throat. He put his look between Hasdrubal's eyes and then he turned slightly to improve his perspective of the bougainvillea crowns that were topping many of the buildings of the forum on the Byrsa side. He had admired them at the earlier time and had wondered what the Roman boot could do to them. They were in the shadow of that boot now, but for the moment the botanicals afforded pleasant surcease from a sea of faces and voices.

"Beautiful," he said, still turned to the crowns. "You people who have held the home bastion are to be congratulated for protecting beauty that has been part of my sustenance." He came back to this Hasdrubal during the very last of a compliment that carried a monument of irony.

Four other senators who had also just come from the Assembly made a background for this Hasdrubal, placing themselves between the Council and Assembly buildings. Hannibal knew all of them, and brushed a smile on them.

One of the new ones glanced at the Assembly building and then made an axis of it with Hannibal Barca, sufet. "So much aristocracy crammed into them, Lord Hannibal—*your* presence, Hanno's…and then your words that had me scratching our history to find any counterparts."

"You're trying to make a stranger of democracy in this forum. It's walked around here many times, with many convictions."

"You've laid a bold plan in front of them."

"Carthage is on the brink of a Roman vassal—there is no better stage for bold plans." At least one of these senators had banking connections with Rome. Hannibal's word *vassal* didn't splash as much on him as the others

"Our system has kept us afloat, Sufet Hannibal. This flood of people you would release into our every nook and cranny has unsettling prospects."

"*What* you have kept afloat, Senator, deserves more study than we can do on this day with beauty in all directions."

The words were coming from various mouths, but Hannibal mostly focused on the botanicals flowing from the Byrsa gardens, with moments into other parts of this forum whose aesthetics could match any of Greece, or her imitators.

"Your broad map for progress flows into the future, Lord Hannibal. This massive indemnity is staring us in the face—with the first payment due this year. Can your *people* cope with this piece of reality?"

"I think so. Monies from their labor and intelligence have been pulled from them into too many private coffers. When some of this stream is diverted to the State responsibilities, I think they will *cope*." He put the senator's word back into him the same time he looked straight into his eyes.

"But to service ten thousand talents will require bigger streams."

"Indeed. You and your friends will have the pleasure of showing us where to find them. And since you've put your finger right on the principal problem for me, you may have the honor of announcing to your friends that the first installment will come from your side of this forum—I could use a man of your prescience and connections on my staff."

"There is no precedence for *any* of this."

"You are familiar with the labors of Hercules, Senator."

"I bow to *your* erudition here. Hercules was, is, a Barca family god, I think."

"I accept another compliment, and its responsibility. The Stygian Stables come to mind. Hercules did monumental shoveling on that pile of excrement. As his acolyte, so to speak, I itch to start shoveling when I encounter similar piles." He turned to Sufet Hanno, "...*Both* of us have this itch, I think."

When the sufets resumed their sojourn into the forum, the senators were brushed aside with two smiles this time.

"Your forbearance will be useful when we try to make politicians, Hanno."

"I don't know what you call putting the Stygian Stables in front of a principal senator, but you had him sputtering...I wonder if he knows we'll have him shoveling some of his own shit."

Sufet Hannibal was ready with another compliment, but he left it to an entirely natural smile.

Synhalus, his Army Chief of Surgeons , was an old man now, but his office near the forum was still a busy sounding box for a voice that deferred to no rank or privilege, and had lost little of its muscle. He had just finished checking his principal patient.

"You should be taking more exercise, Hannibal. This new *political* responsibility could take as much from you as your army did." Synhalus' *political* wove rebuke with fact in a familiar way and his subject had to laugh this time as he had on other occasions when favored by samples from Synhalus' loom. Actually, Synhalus had been favorably impressed by his latest pokes and probing—stamped by his usual responsibility of caution.

"With the regimens my ladies have put on me, I have little time for anything *but* exercise."

They were finished, and just before Hannibal left he had something else for his old friend: "A good doctor likes to know what's wrong with his patient before he prescribes."

"You are living proof of that wisdom."

"I need to know the fiscal condition of Carthage, before I prescribe a cure."

"I will do my best to reassemble your parts after the Council and the Lord Treasurer get through with you, *Sufet* Hannibal." Synhalus' bow was not convincing.

The Lord Treasurer was not cooperative. He dismissed the sufets' request for a review of the fiscal books with the statement that only the Council was privy to that information. Hannibal had invigorated the Office of Pentarchies, giving it police authority under the sufets' direct auspices. Its arm had been bolstered by foot and horse who had once answered to Lord General Hannibal. Hannibal ordered the Lord Treasurer arrested, his books confiscated and delivered to the sufets' offices.

This was also unprecedented, and Hannibal addressed the outcry in the

Council several days later in the Council Hall after he and Hanno had perused the sad financial story this Council had written for Carthage.

"I think I was fighting the wrong enemy in Italy. This evidence of massive fiscal malfeasance against the people of Carthage is a depressing revelation."

He was standing alone on the dais. Sufet Hanno, and many others of his supporters, on near benches. His quick action against the Lord Treasurer had struck the core of the Council, and when it tried to sputter, he encouraged its best effort with a smile that had troubled Scipio, now called Africanus.

"We have ordered the pentarchies to put men into every nerve center of Carthaginian commerce, trade, manufacturing and agribusiness—what the Lord Treasurer's chronicle of shame cannot reveal, our emissaries will dig out of our communal stable."

"What is your authority for this trespass of the Council's territory?"

"Hanno and I were elected by the people. The attribution of this authority should be clear enough to you..." Hannibal used the senator's name to keep the footfalls toward sedition distinct.

"You and Hanno are putting a military posture on your sufets—we hear about patrols, wearing faces very like your famous cavalry, escorting your... emissaries."

"This is all tied up in that *authority* you just raised, Senator. Every person of Carthage affected by it will be encouraged to listen to it because it is designed for the general good under perilous circumstances spelled Rome... Rome...**Rome**." He slapped a railing. "There are people in this hall who hold themselves outside the pall of these circumstances, but I spoke of the *general* good. We, Hanno and I—until we are replaced by the *people*—are traveling in the direction I have stated, and we will strip ourselves of useless, *destructive*, baggage when and where we find it."

He looked around the Hall, sweeping as many of the privileged benches into his right eye as he could.

"There is a place for peaceful intercourse with Rome under our rehabilitation. Our plans will not be prejudiced against her, but they will not countenance arrogant Carthaginian independence that defeats this rehabilitation." He picked up the senator who had raised the specter of cavalry: "Tonight, you should thank your gods for men who were soldiers in your behalf, and now work as hard for the peaceful strength of Carthage. My first, and probably one of my best, accomplishments as sufet was to grant citizenship to some of these men who had been good enough to shed blood for Carthage— but not as her citizens."

"This enfranchisement of mercenaries is a dangerous precedent."

"I think not. I consider Rhodes a jewel of the sea that washes us.

Consideration of *all* the people who serve her has paid handsome dividends to her, and we are also studying her economics as a model for swimming out of a stench that was partly made in *this* hall." Another slap on the railing—sufet Hannibal was close to a wakening rhythm here.

"Taxation innovation is *our* prerogative." There was still an axis between Hannibal and a particular senator.

"Not any more—so long as Hanno and I have the peoples' voice. I expect to see the overburdening bougainvillea creep toward the *fertile* path that will be laid between this Hall and the People's Assembly as you study cooperation together."

The smile Consul Scipio Africanus had finally seen up close was diffusing inevitability and fear into a congregation of arrogance. Gaius Publius and Fabius Maximus, standing near the Roman forum beneath Capitoline Jupiter, had felt that smile on them, with some similar results.

The first year's indemnity had been paid, and the payoff had been doubled for the next two years without Rome's prompting, in fact with some of Rome's misgivings. Carthage had not died of shame and frustration on her sands. Her mercantile fleet, with better ships, was plying familiar waters in the Mediterranean, and there were reports that her hulls had been probing outside the Gates of Hercules to the tin ports of the northern seas that the Romans had yet touched only by the grace of old Carthaginian chronicles, and the memory of the Massillian Greek explorer, Pytheas.

One day, when her schedule as an estate executive and her husband's as sufet gave them some time for a ride, and a long kiss on horseback, Inanna probed this new economy:

"But the people feeding our coffers are still the same, maybe a little fewer. What have you done?"

"My third arm, Hanno, and other good arms, have plugged some holes that were draining those coffers into ducts that flowed mostly away from official Carthage."

"You have shoved Rhodes into the bellies of the Council—why were you and Sosylos laughing about this just last night?"

Sufet Hannibal, in comfortable garb that still paid some respects to his Mushrooms, tried another kiss, but she frustrated him using a facet of fine horsemanship.

"Rhodes has been the cardinal example of success with simplicity and compassion in taxation. You must have crept up on some laughs inspired by *any* simplicity creeping into official Carthage."

"I heard the speech you gave about that in the Council. You also used Egypt, under the Ptolemies and their Greek moneymen, as the antithesis of Rhodes...arrogant imposition of the State into every nook and cranny of life, with the cream mostly flowing to those unofficial ducts you just mentioned." She let him get closer and then she cooperated in another kiss which almost needed completion on the ground...it *was* the incentive to continue their chat, dismounted.

Finally she prompted more of an answer to her economic, Rhodesian, question:

"I decreed a two percent tax on imports and exports as our major medicine for a very sick patient. Rhodes has done everything a country needs to do with that income, and the honest servicing encouraged by it."

"Synhalus would be proud of you." This had been whispered, into his left ear. "But surely this simplicity is not the total of your innovations that have made Rome nervous again."

"Where did you hear *that*?" He knew a foolish question before it left his lips. Inanna's present gossamers were as good as his—in fact better in certain channels.

"You have made adjustments in some private accumulations that have no place in this splendid regimen of Rhodes you have pushed on us." Some Carthaginian aristocrats who had built castles on corruption were watching the sand under them flow toward the sea as Hannibal and Hanno poked at it. A lot of this sand was salted with Roman sparkles.

"Why am I trying to answer your questions?—Silenus should be here scribbling as fast as he can, looking at *you*." Inanna made a small payment for her impudence and she even added some interest.

"I hear that we could pay off the indemnity within two years if we wished. Surely such prosperity doesn't worry you." When her lips had finished the words, she touched them to his left eye, one of the caresses she had insisted during their first night after his return from Italy. Using his remnants of a hardened campaigner brushed by every particular of war, this Greek lady had pulled years off of him and made him think about such things as Polaris entwined with diaphanous silk that contained a wife. "Please put me in touch with your sources. Hanno and I feed on such stuff. And I should say that Hanno—son of Bomilcar—has nearly eclipsed Hanno the Great, and the son of the Great." His eyes slipped past her for a moment. "But what an eclipse can hide, can reappear if it's a fundamental of our universe. Those *adjustments* you brought up...unless we can get more voluntary compliance there..." He left that particular threat to a comfortable shadow unfinished. He had been cooperative and playful...right up to the philosopher who suddenly talked about the slippery shadows of eclipses.

"This wonderful universe of ours—surely it would never tolerate people like the Hannos who once bedeviled you and Hamilcar."

His answer was a kiss that prompted more of *her* cooperation. And they used it to break her last question into silence.

24

52 years
195 BC—Carthage

The lembos slipped into the entrance to the cothon and signaled that she wanted comfort in the inner harbor, once a citadel of the Carthaginian navy. The inner circular harbor had recently been forced open by commerce, favoring ships that bore marks of wealth, authority, or a mystery of provenance strong enough to intrigue the harbormaster. This sleek, black-hulled, ship qualified on all of these bases as she worked through the outer harbor bulging with commercial hulls of every Mediterranean nation able to climb on the invitations Carthage had been sending to the world since Hannibal had changed from general to sufet.

This lembos was like the ones that had been the backbone of his gossamers. The Romans had appropriated those that had been abandoned during the exodus from Bruttium, and occasionally these lembi appeared at Carthage holding one, or more, Romans who had some official connection with the mutually prosperous peace their greatest enemy had accomplished. This particular ship had more snap to its management, and its general condition and appointments bore more of Hannibal's style than its precursors that had carried Roman pennants into this antique Carthaginian sanctuary below Byrsa Hill.

It carried three Romans. Two were obviously prosperous businessmen. The third man was harder to classify. He had been quiet throughout the voyage from Rhegium. His speech had been terse and conclusive. Although his cloak and tunic had no fresh cast of aristocracy, his venerably sheened calceus boots, and several accents of gold, put a quiet exclamation point on him that the officers and crew, and the other passengers, were careful not to test.

After they had secured to a place that had held triremes and quinqueremes, the quiet Roman asked for the harbormaster, and then gave this Carthaginian official a request that was civilian and civil, but with imperium enough to sharpen his ears:

"Please convey my compliments to Sufet Hannibal. Tell him that an old friend from Carthago Nova would value a few moments of his company. I will remain by this ship until I know his pleasure."

This Roman's target had made some new molds for sufets who would follow him. His curiosity about the world outside his official sanctum sometimes eluded his escorts—and the fact of an escort for a sufet was unusual, his itineraries for the escorts were unusual. One of them had taken him as far west as Naraggara. And there had been whispers at that time that a lone horseman, riding a big black Cyrenian, had been seen near, probably on, the battle plain called Zama where a general, a famous horseman, had come to one dream's end. The man and this horse had often been seen closer to various parts of Carthage, sometimes in the twilight, or dawn. But mostly when he rode officially there was no mystery, a frank presence open to question and answer, or reasonable conversation.

The harbormaster's message had come to the Barca palace on Byrsa Hill when the torches were being lighted along the cothon. *An old friend from Carthago Nova* could cover a lot of ground—a Celt, Iberian, African, Carthaginian remnant, Greek...someone from the big spectrum of that time that could defy any memory. By the gods he had left in that place, it could be *anybody*, and the years would have complicated, obscured, the man. But the invitation was intriguing and he would use the declining light to feed the drama a little himself.

The black horse was not seen until it had finished a steep passage from Byrsa Hill, a virtual secret trail for its master from a Byrsa palace to the heartbeat of Carthage that pulsed around the cothon area. It reached the cobbled annulus of the circular harbor and then an interposed gate was quickly opened when the rider was recognized and acknowledged with a military salute that was outside the perquisites of an ordinary sufet.

The soft sounds of that twilight gave precedence to the hoof beats of the black Iberian as it traveled the stone periphery of the great circular arena that had made naval history for centuries. The lembos could be recognized by extra torches the harbormaster had ordered—and by a coupling between the man of the horse and this kind of ship that would have made their contact possible even in better darkness.

Hannibal stopped his black about forty paces from the ship. A man in a Roman cloak stood on the flagstone quay adjoining the ship. The horse's sounds, and some particulars of its rider, had alerted the quay man seconds before, and an axis between the Roman and the rider quickly evolved.

Hannibal was starting to dismount, intending to walk the remainder between this specter from Carthago Nova and himself:

"By our mutual gods, Hannibal—let me study your previous incarnation just a moment longer!" This tangible memory of the greatest cavalry general in history justified Gaius Publius' request.

The Roman was probably in his seventh decade. He had not listed a Roman when he was counting possibilities for *the old friend from Carthago*

Nova. But that voice was familiar. If a body had been protected and respected, its voice could be a wonder of continuation, and he had heard this voice... several times in Iberia, not only at Carthago Nova.

Hannibal stayed in the saddle and advanced the black to within ten paces of the Roman. In this position, one of the two smiles that had blossomed along the axis had some climbing to do.

"You acknowledge mutual gods—by them I declare you to be Gaius Publius!"

"You've got me. But how am I to greet a famous sufet who comes like a ghost that has paraded in front of—and *in* our holy metropolis on the Tiber."

"I never made it *in*—as you say, old friend."

"Ah, Fabius Maximus and hundreds of thousands of others could argue that point. You were *in* in the ways that kept us busy with the Sibylline Books and other foolishness that had to do with chicken guts and the trajectory of pigeon shit in the twilight—and you made us old while we did this!"

Gaius Publius had had his look at a reincarnation. After dismounting, Hannibal finished the distance between them and then there was a clasping of right arms, hands to forearms.

"We are *all* old, Gaius—Scipio convinced me of it."

"He sends his respects to you."

"We've had some correspondence. I think I like him—although the commander in me still argues that concession."

They started to walk, Hannibal's black following them.

"I've heard that he has defended me in your Senate. This is unprecedented for a Roman conqueror. I owe him more than a letter...but improving my gratitude could be complicated."

They reached a vantage that gave a good sweep of the outer harbor, the normal humming of commerce silent at this hour, but the international emanations were still powerful.

"*Pax Hannibalis.*" Gaius left it at that as he looked at the crowd of ships and barges.

"You ascribe too much to me, and compliment my poor Latin." It had been all Greek up to Gaius' acknowledgement, and then Hannibal's modesty quickly brought it back.

"I deny that. You've made Punic speakers of some of us—even in the Senate. Cato's protestations to the contrary, the axis between Rome and Carthage has never been more prosperous for both poles."

"You are tending to Publius Cornelius Scipio again. The peace terms that have made some of this resurrection possible are as much his work as anybody's."

Gaius Publius studied Hannibal at a few paces' range. The boy he had met at Castulo, and the young commander he had met at Carthago Nova on the eve of Hannibal's Saguntum trigger for the Second Punic War, were long gone. This man had put on the mask of the aristocrat after taking off the various ones that had bedeviled Rome for an eternity—almost a complete miracle of self-sufficiency. Gaius wanted to touch the real Hannibal.

"My compliments to your Inanna, and I hear there is a daughter whose beauty and independent competence do no insult to her mother."

"They are my best honors and legacy. You must meet them as my guest at Carthage, or preferably Hadrumetum, where we could serve your sybaritic tendencies a little better."

By Jupiter, that smile suddenly erased a lot of years, it also put a sudden weight into Gaius' feet that hampered his part of this reminiscence. He looked away from Hannibal, and that moment triggered a famous prescience that Hamilcar's Hippolyta had helped to build.

Hannibal stepped closer to the Roman. He had to wait a few moments. Gaius seemed to find a lot of detail in the watery certificate of prosperity in front of him.

"We are back to Publius Cornelius Scipio again. I'm standing in this place that swarms with imperial memories—and *your* qualities—because of him." This particular Roman had a famous facility for pushing a conversation along, but he seemed to be having some difficulty now. "...The consul sent me to convey a warning. Looking at this harbor, feeling the pulse of a *real* Carthago Nova while I was still miles from this cothon, makes me a minion of irony—the most *distasteful* situation I've ever confronted." He completed looking at Hannibal at close range.

"Cato's blustering has reached us—I think we've demonstrated a peace that will mute him."

"You are giving us too much credit for common sense. Our Senate is polluted with petty, vindictive, near-sighted men. Fabius Maximus would have sided with Scipio in scourging these people who see some weird profit in upsetting an axis that has far exceeded reasonable expectations—a paradigm of peaceful coexistence after the madness of two wars."

They started walking again, Hannibal's black was now waiting at a point of their trajectory that might be used again.

"You have jeopardized yourself by coming here...I regret that the scope of my protection for you is limited."

"Scipio and I have been traveling far away from Rome in search of salubrious air. On *this* trip I happened to end up in Rhegium."

"The connection between Rhegium and Carthage is not so accidental.

You have honored me with a tedious, dangerous, voyage." Hannibal stepped in front of Gaius Publius, his hand on the old Roman's shoulder. Part of his mother's legacy insisted a better excuse than salubrious air, or a political tidbit, for their present conjunction.

"An embassy is coming here—ostensibly commercially driven. Actually, it is empowered by the Senate to demand your extradition to Rome."

"That's an old rumor—I've patted it down in our forum a dozen times in the last five years." But Gaius Publius standing in front of him, under Scipio's auspices, had suddenly stuck fact, instead of rumor, in his face.

"The apologists for this outrage have used other rumors for their purpose: You have conspired with Antiochus III against Rome. You have conspired with Philip V of Macedon against Rome. You are secretly building another army and navy to renew your onslaught on hapless Rome—you are a *very* dangerous man, Hannibal Barca. You have made many Romans very wealthy since you became a civilian strategist. This is shocking corruption of Roman morals and modesty. Thinking about all this...I may have to take back that *minion* insult to myself." These two could provoke smiles easily...but Gaius couldn't find one for himself now.

"Let me drain your Roman indignation a little, my friend: You put Philip down for good at Cynoscephalae. Antiochus' empire now includes our mother city, Tyre. Our commercial spheres now overlap significantly with Antiochus' and my only intercourse with this king has been in the direction of trade and commerce. Some of your newly wealthy Romans have been very much intertwined in this *dangerous* axis between Antiochus and me. And if you can find an army and a navy hereabouts on a course of vindictiveness against *hapless* Rome—then there is a military genius hiding in my government who should be proselytized at once to a civilian career and glory in that direction—including making more wealthy Romans."

Hannibal stepped away from Gaius and did his own scan of part of Gaius' irony swarming the harbor in front of them. If his mother, and Amalkre, and Inanna, maybe now Kyniska too, were famous for images, then they would have to study at his feet because the storm of them assailing him now was of Olympic quality. They were all part of it—even Hamilcar was fluxing in it. He didn't trust his voice in front of Gaius, so it was the Roman's turn:

"Can the popular voice you've resurrected here protect you?" This time, Gaius Publius had to use patience to wait for a voice.

"I've been working the clay of a democratic Carthage for less than five years...I don't think the form I've got is ready for the wax and bronze. It couldn't make a voice that could carry to your Senate...it couldn't make an army to surround me." His sound was like an emanation from the Sibyl's grotto at Cumae...Maharbal and Carthalo had heard some of it.

Hannibal walked back to Gaius Publius, his hand finding a shoulder again.

"The lances I stuck in your Colline gate were souvenirs of some of my lessons in war—apparently my curriculum on peace hasn't been good enough either. Tell Publius Cornelius that his friendship and trust have been among my useful treasures...for that last part."

He released the old plenipotentiary and senator and turned back to the crowded harbor, part of the proof of Hannibal Barca he had brought back to Carthage. There was addendum:

"If men like you and Scipio are now finding your salubrious breaths away from Rome, I think the Romans will soon need stronger medicine than the Books and pigeon shit—I'm sorry they'll be wasting precious energy on a phantom enemy."

This garden was accessible from the Barca apartments, and Medina's suite. It was a natural arena for someone crowded with images, affording reflections and sources for various voices such a person might find useful in private recapitulation...challenging. Hannibal found this garden after midnight. Medina had found it a few minutes before him.

Wearing a black robe, he was using a reluctant avenue through the plants to reach a small balustrade with a harbor view when he saw her standing near his target. She was wearing a white silk night chiton, no Iberian subtleties... just a minimum sheath, adequate for the night. He could make no secret of his approach. When he reached the balustrade, she looked at him, and then he saw the tiny silver beads from Castulo at her ears, so she *had* brought some of Iberia with her, some of Inanna, in fact.

She and Amalkre had been close friends, and sometime collaborators in conjuring, receiving , images. This place and time, therefore, drew him into a logical greeting for her:

"I think you and I may be staring at some of the same vapors from Iberia... this should justify my intrusion." Actually, Iberia covered only a small part of the spectrum that had been working him since he had put Gaius Publius on his return ship near Hadrumetum.

"Did the Roman's visit stir yours up...those Iberian visions? Your Gaius Publius refutes the arrogant Roman. I could talk to him...I think our lives would have been very different if there had been more like him. I was sorry to see him leave Hadrumetum." The mature beauty, the Celt-Iberian princess with the veneer of Carthage his other ladies had put on her, looked back at the space in the night that probably still contained a vision he had just interrupted.

"You and Kyniska almost wore him out with your questions, but you were a rare treat for him. His visit didn't bring many smiles...but I think he took some back." His voice trailed away from her, and he had looked away. But she kept him close to her question—he had just made a mistake and she was the one to label it for later use.

"You've laughed at our images, Hannibal. You've obviously brought some of yours here tonight—time to make *me* laugh."

Inanna still used the Greek style for her black mane that he loved to discover and undue and try to reconstruct. Medina used braids, or free cascades of much the same stuff which had put Iberian accents and more frustration than satisfaction into most of the eligible blades of Carthage over the years her presence had favored them. Tonight it was cascades and he thought she had been crying when he surprised her. By her order, humor was now incumbent on him, but like Gaius Publius' recently, a famous capacity had obstacles.

Scudding clouds sweeping in from the Mediterranean blocked the moonlight for a few seconds. It gave him a prop for his true stage, but he tried to serve the lady of the present garden:

"I may have to take an extended business trip to the East, carrying my imperious supervisors' shopping lists, of course."

"Your attempts at humor are cheating me, sir, and after the trove of it we've given to you." He was under close Iberian surveillance now. He was talking about business which she had heard him and the Roman discuss—not the images which had brought him to her side by his own confession and had just made a mistake in front of her. But she would play with him a little.

"Inanna will have the chance to visit some of her fascinating antecedents."

"It will not be a convenient trip for her...perhaps when I've cleared some ground she can come."

The second mistake and both he and Medina knew it. The trip announcement, the trip qualification, should have gone to Inanna first. But part of what had brought him here had been images of a shocked Inanna—losing him again. He could feel Medina's study. She was capable of cooperating with him. If he could diffuse the shock by some kind of spreading rumor, a logical absence, she could be his agent...but Medina was already ahead of him.

She had been crying over a kaleidoscope of memories of a companionable Hasdrubal and her family and an Iberia she would never see again. Inanna had suddenly intruded this little impromptu in this ambiguous night and garden and Medina was well qualified to pull some threads out of the skein that Inanna's Hannibal, this paragon of the New Carthage, was now cradling and to make her own design with them. Why did that last tear on her cheek seem to veer toward Inanna? Hannibal and Inanna were close to the hard won pinnacle of their life and the Roman had used the culminating complement, *pax Hannibalis*, again at Hadrumetum. He and Hannibal seemed to mold the Rome and Carthage business into something palatable, burgeoning...enduring. Until Inanna entered her life, Medina had no background in the Greek playwrights. But she didn't need this competence to recognize actors when suddenly—under Hannibal's prompting—both the likeable Roman and Hannibal walked into her this night.

"You've moved again, Father."

Kyniska had set up a clay board in an arbor near the swimming pool at the Byrsa Palace, and for a week she had managed to trap Hannibal for a few minutes' sitting each day. The bust was starting to reveal a man, shoulders up, but the quality of her realization was still largely dormant in the clay.

"By your mother's Asclepius—I've held to a fraction of my pose!"

His daughter was in silent creation for a few minutes. They were alone, and his thoughts had plenty of scope. It had been almost a week since he had blundered into Medina with that damn long face. He'd had no further talk with the Iberian seer except pleasantries of the moments they'd happened to share. The prospect of a business trip had held its potential as a palliative for Innana and Kyniska, but nothing yet had pulled it out of his mouth in front of his wife and daughter.

Cato's latest effusion, **Carthage must be destroyed**, was becoming a hallmark that he stamped on his every speech in the Roman Senate. He was an enemy of Scipio, dating from some association in Sicily, before Zama, where his star had been frustrated in joining Scipio's in a glorious orbit. Present Carthage, a swiftly reincarnating queen of the Mediterranean, was a testament to Scipio's prescience that a virtually unencumbered Hannibal could make a better restitution for the Second Punic War than waves of the Senate's vengeance splashing against a still formidable bastion. But Carthage—and Scipio—were persistent pricks in Cato. For many Romans, he was only an amusing anachronism of a man cluttering the issues of prosperity and empire that occupied most of the other senators and realistic businessmen.

But Gaius Publius had come to tell him that Cato's inane focus had finally become significant. The remnant of his gossamers that still probed Rome hadn't caught up with Gaius Publius yet, but he couldn't wait for them and ignore Gaius' warning about the *commercial* embassy. Reconstruction had been his present business and he would keep his family in this agenda if the gods would let him. But the Romans were forcing a deadly issue on him again—outside the purview of a reconstruction that still couldn't protect him from Roman vengeance resurrected by a madman.Kyniska was starting to shape his head. The rambunctious beard and top of his campaigner had gone to the sleek aristocrat, so he was a fit subject now for a Carthaginian princess who was favoring him with one of the facets of her competence. Her alternation between him and her clay was busy—but not enough to exclude a comment on agenda that woke him up:

"This business trip toward Antiochus sounds fascinating, Father." Medina *had* done some of her work. Kyniska made a small cut in the clay that was becoming an ear. If she was about to unleash his mistake in front of Medina on him, she was remarkably casual about it, and he made a small prayer to her mother's Asclepius that they could stay in the light vein she had just opened.

"He's the lord of Tyre now...we must acknowledge him." She had posed him so that he couldn't read her face.

"From what I hear, acknowledging Antiochus' empire could take a broad sweep of a trip."

"I will remain flexible in my itinerary."

"You will leave some vacuum here. I like Hanno, but *this* Nova Carthago is engined by you." She was walking around the clay, testing her perspective against him, seemingly preoccupied with sculpture, no voice or motion clues that the pages of the play he and Gaius Publius had done in front of his ladies at Hadrumetum were about to be scattered in front of him.

"I have good lieutenants in my government and in my family...it is a great comfort that I'm not indispensable."

"Some of Mother's antecedents would be hard for you to avoid on this *flexible* trip, Father." He doubted that Medina had prompted her on this. "This question of indispensability will be tested less if she is with you."

He now realized that Kyniska had mixed rumors she'd had from staff, and her various sources in the world outside Barca premises, with what Medina had told her—she was close to putting that sculpting tool next to his heart. He tried a diversion:

"Don't copy that bronze the African did of me at Gades. I think the thing is now at Thymiatherion on the African western coast. He made a Hellenic prince—which I never was."

"She never saw it, but I did, Hannibal. I liked what the African did with you...he put some of my own thoughts into that clay and hence the bronze." Inanna had slipped into the modeling session. He wondered how long she had been there—how much of Kyniska's dialogue had been overlapped by the principal lady of his life.

He was trying to be a good model. This gave him credentials for silence. But he was filing through some of Sosylos' insights on Greek tragedy to find a situation like his at that moment.

"You were going to surprise me—that's why Medina tried to push a little inadvertence back into her mouth." Inanna came around to him—now he had no excuse for not looking at her.

"It's a business of indefinite scope...if it succeeds properly, I'll send for you. I've been reminded of your antecedents, several times. We could serve them well under Antiochus' no doubt gaudy auspices when the time is right."

"Who will decide about this *time*?" Inanna had moved closer to him.

. Kyniska had given up her creativity and was watching her parents start to dig into rumors that could incite the famous Barca images if anything could.

"That is my prerogative—as your husband, to recognize an agreeable situation for you."

"I'm not a hothouse plant to shun the terrors of the real world—you *know* this! I volunteered to be some adjunct of your strength in Italy. I am volunteering again for this new chapter of you. *Indefinite* scope you say, but *much* more peaceful—therefore more susceptible to my touch." He thought he had plumbed all of her eyes over their years—but she had just shown him some of a new world in them.

She had just come from a riding exercise, flushed with it, now with him. He wanted to take her in his arms, to smell the fresh air and taste the Greekness of her that could, as she had just said, be crucial sustenance for him. But he looked away from her, remained seated.

"This *business trip* of yours has a pretension of stress and danger that is becoming tedious and insulting." Inanna looked at Kyniska and then backed away from him to make some space for a summation. But this defense of her position suddenly spilled some of the intimations of *his position* on the tiles between them. His ladies—she, Lady Barca, Medina, Kyniska, had conjured more from the pleasantries he and the Roman paraded in front of them at Hadrumetum than he had intended. And they had had other material to work with, kept largely in whispers, away from him. All of it, from all the sources, was focusing on her now—and *his position* had just come into it—the stage for *her* had suddenly grown smaller.

"Blame Gaius Publius for that. He brought a warning from Scipio that Rome will demand my extradition." Like his semi-Odysseus, just before Zama, a curtain he had tried to put in front of her had just come undone.

"On what basis?" Her hands were on her mouth. Her eyes were like some she had made for various rumors when he had been in Italy—but he had never seen these eyes before.

"Various conspiracies against Rome in violation of the peace."

"Nonsense! They called you a magician of battle—now everyone is calling you a magician of *peace*. Rome has no more prosperous ligament than the one to you—now, and future!"

"Cato the Elder has apparently prevailed against your compliment."

"When?" Inanna reached for him and insisted his standing. He was still committed to maximum softness with her—but he didn't trust himself so he kept his hands off her after she had him standing.

"I will leave in a few days. Antiochus was not a lie. He is master of the new Asia...I might make a refuge with him that I could use to bring us together."

Inanna had been watching him like the Delphic Sibyl might have watched the Greeks explaining Darius to her. He hadn't expected tears and she didn't give him any.

"Take me with you. You have said that your Barca lieutenants have everything well in hand—one less won't matter at all."

"You are me at Carthage while I'm not here. You are my anchor point, my gossamers to detect the changes that will probably erase this latest nightmare." *Gossamers* had been her word. He had used it for years, it had been some of his life's blood...now he gave it back to her.

Inanna hadn't moved. She stared at him. She had probed the night a thousand times with eyes like these trying to find him—was the man in front of her a specter she had finally conjured?

"God damn you to hell, Hannibal Barca!" But this was the shortest curse he'd ever had in his face—she was trying to bury herself in his arms as soon as it left her lips.

Kyniska had moved close to her clay work as her father and mother untangled the rumors. When Inanna breached her husband's careful concern with the curse and then came as close to him in standing as she could, Kyniska held her breath, her eyes her mother's bequest for these moments.

"Take me with you," Inanna said again. But it was whispered, and she knew he was right—his immediate plans, his presence at Carthage in her.

Kyniska struck the clay, knocking her work to the floor—then she ran from the place with some of the tears her mother hadn't allowed.

She had asked him not to tell her when he was leaving. She knew his boat was ready. She had seen him talking with his mother, Sosylos and Silenus, and knew that other parts of him had gone to his officers, Maharbal, Carthalo, Hanno...remnants of the thunderbolt that still replicated off the walls of the Roman Senate. She didn't know about a letter to a daughter that tried to tell of pride and love and explanation.

On this night, they talked about various strategies for coming together again. Tyre would be a good place, Rhodes...Pergamum, or Alexandria...places where they could dive into her Greeks as much as she liked. If there were some tears, he kissed them away with the help of new parts of the strategy game they were playing.

Later, she saw a shadow leave the room, trying to respect her slumber. But then a shadow was all he ever gave the Romans for the time that Heimarmene had smiled on him...and this caused her to remember that this god's actual smile for them, *Hannibal and Inanna,* had lived *much* longer than the one Amalkre had conjured for them at another place called Carthago Nova.

25

64 years
183 BC—Bythnia

"There is talk of Romans in the village, sir."

"*Of* Romans?" The speaker straight tall for his age, tall for *the* age, didn't let these words perturb his look out the window, toward a familiar viewscape that had some of Marmara's water, and more in imagination. The images fluxed to him depending on his mood.

"*About* Romans—some may have been seen near here." The Greek boy stood at another window, but the man was the other end of his present axis of attention, and the angles of this conjunction let him see part of a smile that had come to be precious substance lately.

"Your intelligence is good, Celtus...I may have to reconsider that promotion."

"*What* promotion, sir?" Neither had moved. The man's smile was still not fully committed. Even so, the lad wasn't sure he wanted to see all of it. His smiles seemed to have an infinity of edges and you could slip off them with plenty of places to go where a smile wouldn't be good baggage.

"A front rider of my chief scouts."

"But you don't like my riding. You have said that your chief scouts would drown me in their dust—that your Numidians would have to make up some new jokes just for my case." Still no collision of the eyes, the man's smile still tentative, but the last words *had* burnished some of its edges. The youth had turned enough in the direction of his words to see this—but more words from him needed more courage coming from the man's direction.

"I like your eyes and ears better now, Celtus. I think they will give you better glue to a horse. I have known improved intelligence about the world around him to give a man's ass and his legs and hands a wonderful affinity with his horse." The man turned away from the window and faced the handsome youth who was his last connection to civilization. "Such a man—with a horse to match him—should be good enough for a front rider of my scouts. My Numidians would *trade* jokes with such a man and horse." He had stepped closer to the boy. The left eye he had donated to the sticky swamps of the Arno was not covered with a patch. It wasn't bad to look at—the dark brown to the almost black one on his right side, the lid of his left eye opened only enough to show a paled imitation of an eye. It was asymmetry that he had used to his purposes in jokes and anger—and all the stuff in between—that this man had kept in his stew for the thirty five years of what the Romans, *more* than just the Romans, had called the *one eyed devil*.

The young Greek looked away from the man, out *his* window again. He had seen some of the colors of Prusias' men flicking around the rocks, and then he had seen a flash of a red cloak that could have smelled like a Roman's—all of this in the scattering of big rocks between the man's house and the tentacles of Libyssa's ramshackle waterside clusters that were reaching toward the house.

From another window, the man had seen movement and colors like this, but he wouldn't give away the little game they were playing to the end. When he looked away from the boy, out *his* window again, the flicking colors were closer, and now they had spread to all the decent directions where a good run could be made. The walled enclosure of the house—he had laughed at Prusias' claim of a *villa* for it—was only a tease of escape and now it was coming down to a proper goodbye for the boy...and not much time for that.

They had read and done some acting around with Pindar that morning. The boy had been well stuffed with good Greek words, and he had the face and voice and sometimes the body to service the best of the words. Although the man had been working with the sounds and sights of Greek words for a long time, and his Greek was good, the boy had corrected him several times in the past weeks on nuances which wouldn't serve Roman purposes. They *did* serve the two of them when they confronted a point of drama, a declaration of love, anger, the laugh, the debauchery, the Greek inclinations toward the heavens which had pulled the man away from the cold efficiency of the Punic a long time ago.

He was close enough to the boy for his goodbye. Celtus had just renewed his window intelligence, and he didn't know how long the man wanted to play this game of almost silence about the colors in the rocks. This man's prescience was famous. With Pindar that morning, he had picked up new motions on the man's face to go with some new bendings he put into his words. These things were a fore shine of the colors trying to hide in the rocks. He now knew this, and he waited for the man to make a summary for him. They had made a lot of them since the man had picked him out of Prusias' court and made an honest man's companion out of him. The man had any privilege of him he wanted. But they had touched only their minds—maybe their hands had slapped together when they fell into the same crack of a humor at about the same time.

The gold ring on the man's left hand shot a soft gleam toward him. Its decoration had a miniature of the emboss that had been on the man's shield, a lion in aggressive and inquisitive hunting posture against an Africanscape.

The top of the ring, the home of the lion, was flat, and once when that hand had come close to him while they were testing some point of philosophy, or they were wallowing in one of the corners of this man's mind that seemed like an expanding labyrinth, he thought that the flat part might come up on tiny hinges. But he had never gone beyond the eyes for this point, and he wouldn't now, although somehow he felt that this ring and the burgeoning colored encirclement were part of a summary this man was about to make.

"It is several hours before high sun, Celtus, a good time."

"Why is it better than others, sir?"

"A man is awake by now. He has analyzed his day, his plans, his strategies and the limits to him. He has found the friends near to him, and it is the time for all these heads to turn in the same direction for a little while...I have always liked this time."

"Was it one of these times at Cannae...Trasimene...Trebbia...Zama?" The boy had heard some of the man's own words about these places—truthful overlays of what had been mostly Roman invention and false veneers to cover monumental loss of honor.

The man laughed. "By Ba'al, Celtus, you bring the peaks and valleys *close* together! See now!—I *am* justified in greater faith in you. There *is* a philosopher trying to peek out of you." He wanted to punch the boy's shoulder, but he was close enough for the purposes of a summation. The windows revealed more than he needed to see now. He ignored a noise in the rocks at the rear of the house. A little piece of his cavalry would have smeared those clumsy ass holes over those rocks hours ago.

The boy watched the concert of light and shadow on the man's face as he looked at places in the room where they had done the poetry and drama and philosophy and history. There were some of the man's souvenirs in this room: mostly carvings, some small vases and plates, a few tributes to Punic carvers in gold and silver, parchments with his writing and that of others. The only souvenir of a soldier was a dagger of the size a cavalryman could hide in his boot. The blade was Phoenician steel, polished like a mirror, with two guards of this steel flowing into two short arches that could have been a devotion to Tanit. The handle was circles of leather interspersed with silver and ivory rings. The pommel was spherical sections of bronze and silver, with a red garnet inserted at its focus. It was not much of an ornament even by the standards of the strutting insults to manhood in Prusias' court, certainly not by the measures of the peacock ostentation that crowded what was left of the Syrian courts of Antiochus—but it had been said that the redness on *this* particular dagger had colored years of Italian skies and the Romans had reason to call it the *Carthaginian stone.*

The man's silent recapitulation of memories seemed to be compressing into seconds now. He started to walk toward his bedroom, and his looks at the souvenirs, memories, included Celtus and there was a better smile on him now for Celtus to use as his paradigm. Just at the door to his bedroom, he stopped and turned to the young Greek.

"Another good thing about this time of the day is that the light will give you about as much help as it can for looking inside and outside of you." A motion of his left hand brought the soft pulse of ring reflection again, but before the lad could tell how the lion was looking that morning, the man had gone into his room without closing the door. Usually this meant that some tentacle of talk was still permitted to walk in, or out that door.

The dark premonition of a summation hadn't left the boy. He knew that the window work was done. He knew that their horses, their legs, would be useless affectations now so late in the game. He was only qualified for silence and waiting for the summation. When the pounding finally came to the front door of the house, he ran toward the silence in the man's bedroom. The man was on his knees, beside his bed, his head almost to the floor. His right hand was on the bed. His left, ring hand, on the floor. The lion's place on the ring was opened, and there was a little white powder still left in the space that he had suspected the lion had sat on. A glass lay on the floor, and what wine the man hadn't taken was soaking into the Armenian carpet.

"Lord Hannibal." He was close to the man's ear, on the side of the blind eye. His whisper brushed a sweated face close to its infinite dream. There was a small motion of the man's lips, enough to release some spittle, but not enough, or the right kind, to help a summation. He moved the hand that was on the bed so that the body could come to a comfortable position on the rug. He closed the eyes, and used his hand cloth to wipe the face and mouth. The hair was still very strong against the gray for a man so old. The scars he had made him tell about: the one below his left ear where the Centurion's spear had grazed him at Cannae; the one on his left cheek where the Cretan arrow at Trasimene had given him an inch's grace of life; the one at the V of his throat from when he shared the final maelstrom of Zama with his veterans before he accepted the commander's responsibility of continuity—these were part of the summation. His compliments, his promotion, his graceful company when they played the colors game only moments before—these were also part of it.

He had mentioned a parchment on his desk, something about friends in Africa and Spain who had been told about a young Greek adjunct of an old man, some strategy for getting to these friends that might interest a young Greek who had shared touches of the philosophers' stone with a relic of thunder and helped pull out a few more smiles, even laughs, from him...from the two of them.

They didn't break down the door. They waited for him to open it. And then they stood there—three of Prusias' men and a Roman Centurion who had orchestrated the last moments outside the house.

"Lord Hannibal is dead." Then Celtus moved his hand toward the bedroom. The soldiers didn't move, and the Roman face was the one that gave the best reflection of a summation. He gave the Roman soldier's salute, and then he turned and walked away from the house. Prusias' men stared into the dark space of the house, like visitors to a museum of treasure. They had no precedence for here, except betrayal, and that was mostly innocent bragging about a legendary protagonist who was still stirring a little fire under the Roman ass in Prusias' behalf.

After they left, Celtus went back to the man's bedroom and arranged him on the bed in fresh linen, hair combed more than the man would have liked, although the mouth, nose, forehead, the ensemble of his face, were still good enough to put passionate wiggles on women's tongues when he had occasionally gone afield for exercise or exploration, or consultation with the vacuum that was Prusias' little piece of the universe. He put the dagger inside the man's tunic, but away from his hands. This man had tried to use weapons like a plow to prepare a field for planting. He had fertilized it with rivers of Roman blood, but there was too much of this blood for the amount of his field, the amount of his workers. The parchments, the souvenirs of manual artistry driven by other dreams, were better companions for his hands, but they were inconvenient just now.

He found the parchment the man had spoken about concerning *him*. He would read it later, after they had taken the man from the house, if Prusias would give him some time alone in the house. The man had said that this was a good time of the day. It was a good time for tears—but he wouldn't cry in front of this man and he had heard that many others had felt the same constraint in front of him.

A breath from Marmara moved through the silk draperies of the room, traveling the man's face before it reached his. He'd had second service from air like this down in the Peloponnesus, and in Athens, when he stood close to marbled gods—their faces, and then his, for the air that had insinuated his inspection. He liked what the Greeks had put into their marble. He liked what the Greeks had put into their expectations of most of their gods. This man's last words, the effusions of a *private* summation that were possible for him, would have been interesting. He had come close to godlike perturbation of the currents of things. Maybe he had failed to show enough imperfection to the Olympians for them to grant him more complete enterprise. He had laughed a lot—he could put many different coats on words to suit their aggregations of his moments. Surely he could have kissed his imperfections better for his benefit—but the face that Marmara's breath was giving priority in these moments had now composed enough of a smile to challenge *this* conclusion.

During his last look at the man he had formally acknowledged at the last breath of life, Celtus touched the dagger and then part of the smile the man had made for eternity. He saw a glint of silver on the floor, near the bed. It was a fine chain, and when he pulled it to better view he saw the pendant, a silver bas-relief set in an oval frame of woven gold wire. The image was of a lady, suggesting an elaborate headdress that must have been for one of the Iberian goddesses the man had talked about—surely the face of her was for such a person. This must have slipped away from the hand that didn't have the lion ring. Celtus put the pendant back in that hand before he left the house.

Epilogue

The unassailable facts of Hannibal's life, including the various chronologies used to track him, are sparse. No one, to my knowledge, has mentioned his mother. In my story, she is a positive force of his life. I hope my inventions for her conform to some estimates of Carthaginian women of the age, even nudging close to the powerful influence Spartan aristocrats of her gender had achieved at this time. I have placed another imaginary woman into this story: his wife, Inanna. There are indications that Hannibal married a woman from the Iberian mining center, Castulo, and that they had a child...so I took it from there.

Hannibal might have been born at Carthage. Some of his early years might have been spent in Sicily while his father, Hamilcar, continued to prosecute the First Punic War from bases in northwestern Sicily. He went to Iberia with his father when he was about nine years old. He had Greek tutors for mostly the non-military parts of his development. His father, his father's officers, were his military tutors, in addition to a rare perception of the violent world around him which added to the later, possibly unparalleled, military man. When his father was killed, Hannibal probably was sent back to Carthage for further development under more propitious environments. His brother-in-law, Hasdrubal, assumed Hamilcar's reins in Iberia. Hannibal assumed Hasdrubal's authority in Iberia after Hasdrubals' assassination. At this time, under the chronology I've cemented to this story, Hannibal was 27 years old; 30 years old when he took his army to Italy; 44 years old when he left Italy for Carthage; 45 years old when the remnant of his army was defeated at Zama in Africa. He left Carthage forever when he was 52 years old. He had about 12 years left, which is where the heavy fog settles in.

He probably spent some time at the court of Antiochus III ('The Great'), where his military credentials were largely ignored to Antiochus' detriment. After Antiochus had been humbled by the Romans, there are rumors that Hannibal showed up in Armenia where he was influential in siting and planning the capital city of Artashat for King Artashes. Following Armenia, he was reported in Crete, and then Bithynia, where Bithynian bragging about a slippery old general—and an old admiral who invented snake missiles—triggered a long memory and

Roman vindictiveness for the greatest humiliations in their history.

Until someone discovers Silenus' reputed chronicle of Hannibal's life in Iberia and Italy, most of any story of him is challengeable. His Alps crossing may be the most popularly famous memory of him. Unfortunately, it's also the least documented of his adventures. Within the scope of my story, I've touched on its aftermath, and will say that, otherwise, it should be another, largely fictional, story. In Flaubert's *Salammbo*, he calls Hamilcar's daughter by that name. I've called her Amalkre, and my intuition, in this instance, may be as good as Flaubert's.

His deadly enemies, the Romans, gave him the ultimate compliment. The emperor Septimus Severus is said to have erected a monument to him near Libyssa, the little town near Marmara's waters where the Lady Barca's oldest boy decided to make his last summation.

The question of how Hannibal might have changed world history had his fortunes not been tangled with the greatest enigma of the age, Carthage, is a powerfully seductive one. He showed greater overall capacity than Alexander—probably as a soldier, certainly as a civilian leader. There were Celt allies within his potential scope who could have made him irresistible against any military power of the Europe of his day—putting new complexions into the evolution of his part of the world under a leader like him.

Sources

'm indebted to the following sources for most of what I know about Hannibal Barca and his times...what I've done with it is on my own head.

Bath, Tony, *Hannibal's Campaigns*, Barnes & Noble, 1981

Boardman, John, Jasper Griffin and Oswyn Murray, Editors, *The Oxford History of Greece and the Hellenistic World*, Oxford University Press, 1991

Boardman, J., J. Griffin and O. Murray, *The Roman World*, Oxford University Press, 1989

Bradford, Ernle, *Hannibal*, Dorset Press, 1981

Casson, Lionel, *The Ancient Mariners*, 2nd Ed., Princeton University Press, 1991

Casson, Lionel, *Ships and Seamanship in the Ancient World*, Princeton University Press, 1971

Caven, Brian, *The Punic Wars*, Barnes & Nobel, 1980

Chahin, M., *The Kingdom of Armenia*, Dorset Press, 1987

Charles-Picard, Gilbert, and Colette Picard, *The Life and Death of Carthage*, Taplinger Publishing Co., 1969

Christ, Karl, *The Romans*, University of California Press, 1984

Clagett, Marshall, *Greek Science in Antiquity*, The Scholar's Bookshelf, 1988

Connolly, Peter, *Greece and Rome at War*, Macdonald & Co., 1988

Cottrell, Leonard, *Enemy of Rome*, Evans Brothers, Ltd, 1960

De Beer, Gavin, *Hannibal, Challenging Rome's Supremacy*, The Viking Press, 1969

De Camp, L. S., *The Ancient Engineers*, Dorset Press, 1990

Dodge, T. A., *Hannibal*, Greenhill Books, 1994

Dorey, T. A., and D. R. Dudley, *Rome Against Carthage*, Doubleday & Co., 1972

Fitzhardinge, L. F., *The Spartans*, Thames & Hudson, 1980

Frazer, J. G., *The Golden Bough*, Collier Books, 1963

Gabriel, R. A., and K. S. Metz, *From Sumer to Rome, Military Capabilities of Ancient Armies*, Greenwood Press, 1991

Garnsey, P., and Richard Saller, *The Roman Empire*, University of California Press, 1987

Garnsey, P., Keith Hopkins and C. R. Whittaker, Editors, *Trade in the Ancient Economy*, University of California Press, 1983

Grant, M., *From Alexander to Cleopatra, The Hellenistic World,* Collier Books, 1990

Grant, M., *The Ancient Mediterranean,* New American Library, Meridian, 1988

Griess, T. E., Editor, *Ancient and Medieval Warfare,* Avery Pub. Group, 1984

Hackett, J. H., Editor, *Warfare in the Ancient World,* Facts on File, 1989

Hamilton, E., *The Greek Way,* Book of the Month Club, 1991

Harden, D., *The Phoenicians,* Frederick A. Prager, 1962

Healy, M., *Cannae 216 BC,* Osprey, 1994

Hubert, H., *History of the Celtic People,* Bracken Books, 1993

Jones, A. H. M., *Sparta,* Barnes & Noble, 1993

Kincaid, C. A., *Successors of Alexander the Great,* Ares Pub., 1985

Koester, H., *Introduction to the New Testament, Vol. 1,* Fortress Press, 1984

Lazenby, J. F., *Hannibals's War,* Aris & Phillips Ltd, 1978

Livy, *The War with Hannibal,* Penguin, 1972

Müller, C., *The Costume Time Line, 5000 Years of Fashion History,* Thames & Hudson, 1993

Oakeshott, E., *The Archaeology of Weapons,* Barnes & Noble, 1994

Polybius, *The Rise of the Roman Empire,* Penguin, 1979

Potter, T. W., *Roman Italy,* University of California Press, 1990

Pritchard, J. B., Editor, *The Ancient Near East, Vols. I & II,* Princeton University Press, 1973, 1975

Rawlinson, G., *Ancient History,* Barnes & Noble, 1993

Roux, G., *Ancient Iraq,* Penguin, 1992

Scullard, H. H., *Scipio Africanus: Soldier and Politician,* Cornell University Press, 1970

Settis, S., Editor, *The Land of the Etruscans ,* Scala, 1985

Soren, D., B. Khader and H. Slim, *Carthage, Uncovering the Mysteries and Splendors of Ancient Tunisia,* Simon & Schuster, 1990

Thiel, J. H., *A History of Roman Sea Power Before the Second Punic War,* North Holland Pub., 1954

Toynbee, A. J., *Hannibal's Legacy, Vols I, II,* Oxford University Press, 1965

Warmington, B. H., *Carthage,* Frederick A. Prager, 1969

Wise, T., and R. Hook, *Armies of the Carthaginian Wars 265–146 BC,* Osprey, Pub., 1991

www.ingramcontent.com/pod-product-compliance
Lightning Source LLC
Chambersburg PA
CBHW031031030726
47497CB00004B/1091